Warner Arundell,
The Adventures of a Creole

Warner Arundell,
The Adventures of a Creole

By E. L. Joseph, *of Trinidad.*

First Published
Saunders and Otley, Conduit Street, London
M.DCCC.XXXVIII

Edited by Lise Winer

With annotations and an introduction by

Bridget Brereton, Rhonda Cobham,
Mary Rimmer and Lise Winer

University of the West Indies Press
Barbados ● Jamaica ● Trinidad and Tobago

University of the West Indies Press
1A Aqueduct Flats   Mona
Kingston 7   Jamaica

© 2001 by The University of the West Indies Press
All rights reserved. Published 2001

05 04 03 02 01   5 4 3 2 1

CATALOGUING IN PUBLICATION DATA

Joseph, Edward Lanzer.
  Warner Arundell, the adventures of a creole / by E.L. Joseph;
  edited by Lise Winer with annotations and introduction by
  Bridget Brereton . . . [et al.]
  p. cm.
  Originally published: London: Saunders and Otley, 1838.
  Includes bibliographical references.
  ISBN: 976-640-109-8
  1. Arundell, Warner. 2. West Indies, British – Description and
  travel. I. Winer, Lise. II. Brereton, Bridget, 1946–. III. Title.

F2121.A7J67 2001   972.983

Cover design by Robert Harris. Book design by
ProDesign Ltd, Red Gal Ring, Kingston, Jamaica.
*Cover illustration: The North Coast from a Fort at Maqueripe
Bay,*† Jean Michel Cazabon,† *c.*1870. Private collection.

Printed in Canada

Contents

Contents

Volume III

Acknowledgements

We acknowledge with pleasure the patience, generosity, scholarship and acumen of many people who assisted in the search for identification of everything from sailing terminology to medical history. Any errors of commission or omission are, of course, the editor's responsibility.

Anna Barber

Hans E.A. Boos

Robert Cockburn (University of New Brunswick)

Elizabeth Craig (University of New Brunswick)

Margaret de Castro

Rafael de Castro

William Derby

Franz Eppert (University of New Brunswick)

Douglas M. Haynes (University of California, Irvine)

Sylvia Heredia (Amherst College)

Eugene D. Hill (Mount Holyoke College)

Russell Hunt (St Thomas University)

Trevor Jackson (University of the West Indies, Mona)

Christoph Lorey (University of New Brunswick)

Randall Martin (University of New Brunswick)

Marc Milner (University of New Brunswick)

Edward Mullaly (University of New Brunswick)

John H. O'Neill (Hamilton College)

Jacques Rebuffot (McGill University)

Louise Robertson (Nahum Gelber Law Library, McGill University)

James Shaw (Shakespeare Institute Library, University of Birmingham)

John V. Singler (New York University)

Stephen Sloan (Harriet Irving Library, University of New Brunswick)

Adrian Tronson (Memorial University of Newfoundland)

Steven Turner (University of New Brunswick)

Marie-Louise Thomas

Jesús Vázquez Abad (Université de Montréal)

Kathleen Wilker

Michael Worboys (Sheffield Hallam University)

The editor is grateful to the National Endowment for the Humanities (United States) for a Summer Stipend grant in 1994 to work on this project.

We would like to express our appreciation to Pansy Benn (Arawak Press, Jamaica), who shepherded this series through the acceptance process at the University of the West Indies Press.

Contributors

Lise Winer is Associate Professor in the Department of Second Language Education, McGill University, Canada. She is the author of *Trinidad and Tobago: Varieties of English Around the World* 6, *Dictionary of the English/Creole of Trinidad and Tobago,* and articles on Caribbean language, literature, and culture.

Bridget Brereton is Deputy Principal and Professor of History at the University of the West Indies, St Augustine, Trinidad. Her major books include *A History of Modern Trinidad; Race Relations in Colonial Trinidad;* and *Law, Justice and Empire.*

Rhonda Cobham is Professor of English and Black Studies at Amherst College, United States. She has edited special issues of *Research in African Literatures* and the *Massachusetts Review,* as well as *Watchers and Seekers: An Anthology of Writing by Black Women in Britain.* Her essays on Caribbean and African authors and postcolonial theory have appeared in *Callaloo, Transition, RAL,* and a number of critical anthologies.

Mary Rimmer is Professor of English at the University of New Brunswick–Fredericton, Canada. Her publications include an edition of Thomas Hardy's *Desperate Remedies* and articles on Thomas Hardy, Margaret Laurence, and Nino Ricci.

Introduction

The Historical Corpus of "Trinidad Roots"

In his pioneering study of the West Indian novel,[1] Kenneth Ramchand accepts George Lamming's definition: "the novel written by the West Indian about the West Indian reality" (1983, 3). That is, he considers for inclusion all literary works that "have a West Indian setting and contain fictional characters and situations whose social correlates are immediately recognizable as West Indian. The books have all been written in the twentieth century; and their native West Indian authors include descendants of Europeans, descendants of African slaves, descendants of indentured labourers from India, and various mixtures from these" (Ramchand 1983, 3). However, stipulating that the books "have all been written in the twentieth century", by "native West Indian authors" arbitrarily cuts off novels that fulfil the other requirements, and which can provide data crucial to understanding the development of later works.

The present series of historic republications of "Trinidad Roots" comprises four Trinidadian novels published between 1838 and 1907. These virtually unknown works constitute roots of a much longer and deeper local literary tradition and foundation in Trinidad – and the anglophone Caribbean – than hitherto realized.

- E.L. Joseph's *Warner Arundell, The Adventures of a Creole* (London: Saunders and Otley, 1838) is the first novel set at least partly in Trinidad and is a good candidate for the first Caribbean novel in

---

1. "West Indies" and "West Indian" are the terms most often used to refer to both the anglophone Caribbean – that is, former British colonies whose official (and therefore literary) language is English – and to the entire region – that is, both the islands of the Caribbean Sea and many of the countries on the bordering mainland, such as Guyana. Recently, the term "Caribbean" has been used more frequently in this manner. Both terms are used in these senses throughout the introduction and notes to this series.

English. Joseph came to Trinidad from England as a young man; he is well known for his *History of Trinidad*, which appeared the same year as the novel, and which demonstrates an intimate knowledge of the island. The novel takes place in a number of Caribbean settings, primarily Grenada, Trinidad, Antigua and St Kitts, as well as the Spanish Main (Venezuela and Colombia). As many of the characters in the novel were based on real figures, openly or thinly disguised, the book caused a sensation on its publication (Pocock 1993, 166–67). In the story, Warner Arundell, a white creole of British descent, is born in Grenada and brought up in Antigua and Trinidad. He is defrauded by lawyers, studies law in Venezuela and medicine in England, then goes to seek his fortune. After many adventures, he is reunited with the coloured branch of his family, and with his Spanish lady love.

• *Adolphus, A Tale* (Anonymous) was serialized in the *Trinidadian* newspaper, from 1 January to 20 April 1853. Given its viewpoints, it was probably written by a Trinidadian of mixed race, thus making it the first Trinidadian – and possibly Caribbean – novel by a presumably non-white writer born and raised in Trinidad, and the first novel set almost totally in Trinidad. In the story, Adolphus, the son of an enslaved black woman raped by a white man, is raised by a kind Spanish-Trinidadian padre. Adolphus grows into a handsome, well-educated, noble character. He falls in love with Antonia Romelia, a beautiful mixed-race woman. She is kidnapped by the villain DeGuerinon, a cruel slave owner who appears to be white. Helped by Cudjoe, one of DeGuerinon's slaves, Adolphus and his friend Ernest rescue Antonia, wounding her captor. As Antonia is restored to her family, her mother dies in her arms. Adolphus and Ernest flee to Venezuela until it is safe to return, and Adolphus and Antonia are free to marry.

• Mrs William Noy [Marcella Fanny] Wilkins, author of *The Slave Son* (London: Chapman and Hall, 1854), was born in Ireland in 1816 but lived in Trinidad for some years, thus making this one of the earliest Caribbean novels by a woman. Explicitly inspired by Harriet Beecher Stowe's *Uncle Tom's Cabin*, which was published first in newspaper serial, then in book form in 1852, *The Slave Son* was written to support the abolitionist movement in the United States. The heroine of the novel, Laurine, is a mixed-race freed slave who is working to earn enough money to buy the freedom of her mother, an enslaved black woman owned by St Hilaire Cardon. Laurine loves Belfond, a mixed-race slave who has escaped from (his father) Cardon's estate, but she refuses to run away with him or to use stolen money to buy her mother's freedom. Belfond becomes involved in a conspiracy with his uncle, the African obeahman Daddy Fanty, to poison Cardon and his family. There are extensive scenes of brutal estate life under slavery; Mr Dorset, a white owner of a neighbouring estate, tries to treat his slaves more humanely. Belfond is recaptured by Cardon; Mrs Dorset and Laurine plead for him. A slave uprising leaves Cardon dead. Belfond and Laurine escape to freedom in Venezuela.

- In Stephen N. Cobham's, *Rupert Gray: A Study in Black and White* (Port of Spain: Mirror Printing, 1907), the character of Rupert Gray was probably based on that of Henry Sylvester Williams (Hooker 1975, 24–25). Williams was a lawyer educated in England and was the founder of the Pan-African Association, a black man who in 1898 married Agnes Powell, a white woman he met in the course of their mutual work in the temperance movement. Cobham was black, a friend and colleague of Williams (Hooker 1975, 39, 51). In the novel, the hero Rupert Gray is a highly educated black accountant, of noble character, who works for Mr Serle, a white businessman who thinks highly of him. When Serle's daughter Gwendolyn returns from England, she and Rupert fall in love. Gwendolyn's friend Florence Badenock, a Scottish doctor, comes to visit. An ungrateful jealous black co-worker, Jacob Clarke, starts a poison-pen campaign against Rupert and alerts Serle to the affair. When Serle finds out, he attacks Rupert and refuses to forgive his daughter. Rupert goes to England under the patronage of a white English lady. Gwendolyn falls into a decline, her father drinks himself to and Gwendolyn finally dies as well. When Rupert returns, as a ldeath, awyer, to Trinidad, he is contacted by Florence, and a court trial over the Serle estate ensues. In a dramatic courtroom scene, it is revealed that Gwendolyn is, in fact, still alive. Helped by her faithful maid, Edith, she had fled to recuperate in Scotland with Florence. Rupert and Gwendolyn are married, have children, and live happily – though shunned by "society" – ever after.

Several additional works were "rediscovered" but excluded from this series. Michel Maxwell Philip's *Emmanuel Appadocca: Or, Blighted Life, a Tale of the Boucaneers* (1854) was reissued in 1997, edited and with an introduction by Selwyn Cudjoe. Written by a prominent lawyer of mixed race, the novel has some local setting, although it is almost entirely in Standard English. Other works not reprinted include the following. Mrs Graham Branscombe's *Edith Vavasour* (1876) has only a few chapters set in Trinidad, and it appears the author relied heavily on other sources. *Who Did It?* (1891) was written by James H. Collens, an Englishman who came to Trinidad as a young man about 1877, and who stayed as a teacher and civil servant the rest of his life; nonetheless, the book shows no real local knowledge or orientation. Neither does George Masson's *Her Nurse's Vengeance* (1898), though set partly in Trinidad. Finally, J. Douglas Cameron's *Richard Malmort, or Trinidad and Trinidadians* (1905) is an abominably written, thinly fictionalized political tract on Crown Colony government, worth analysis only as a curiosity.

Of particular interest is what might well be considered a Jamaican novel set in Trinidad: Grant Allen's *In All Shades* (1888). Allen, a popular Canadian author of the day, spent considerable time in Jamaica, and apparently lived in Trinidad for a brief time. His local knowledge is very weak, and the language is Jamaican influenced (though not totally inconsistent with other Trinidadian records of the same era). Moreover, the whole premise of the plot is that "blood will out", that is, that any part of "blackness" will eventually overcome – in a bestial fashion – the goodness represented by that portion which is "white". The story is based almost wholly on the 1865 Morant Bay Rebellion of Jamaica. Allen simply transplants attitudes typically associated with Jamaican (also British and American) sources of the time. (See reference to other literary representations of this event in the section *"Warner Arundell* and the Caribbean Literary Tradition" below.) As Ramchand has pointed out, "there is a long and still active tradition of liberal and exotic writing in English about the Negro and about the West Indies" (1983, 3);[2] Grant Allen's *In All Shades* certainly falls into this category. However, the four novels in the present series were all written by people who were known – or who can reasonably be presumed – to have been born in Trinidad or to have lived

---

2. For two excellent – and egregiously inaccurate – modern examples of this genre for Trinidad, see Belva Plain's *Eden Burning* (New York: Delacorte Press, 1982) and Shirley Lord's *Golden Hill* (London: Frederick Muller, 1983).

there for a significant part of their lives. The themes, settings and language are accurate – in fact or folk belief – and intimately local; they cannot be dismissed in any way as "foreign".

Social context is a particularly important aspect of Caribbean literature (McWatt 1985). The novels in this series have a strong political and social impetus. Several speak out against slavery at a time when it was already abolished in Trinidad but still legal in the United States; Mrs Wilkins cites this explicitly as a reason for writing *The Slave Son* in 1854. In later works, stakes are upped from slave emancipation to more freedom under – not from – colonial rule. All of the novels support more rights for the disenfranchised mixed-race and, sometimes, for the black segments of the population.

The novels also share an underlying thematic continuity with the non-class-based "social consciousness" of later Caribbean literature. As Ramchand explains:

> West Indian novelists apply themselves with unusual urgency and unanimity to an analysis and interpretation of their society's ills, including the social and economic deprivation of the majority; the pervasive consciousness of race and colour . . . the lack of a history to be proud of; and the absence of traditional or settled values . . . this social consciousness is not class-consciousness. This is one point at which the West Indian writer naturally departs from the nineteenth-century English novel with which he is most familiar . . . Most West Indian novelists write about the whole society . . . the chaos . . . the open possibilities of their society . . . along with an interest in the previously neglected person. (1983, 4)

The Slave Son's debt to *Uncle Tom's Cabin* is explicit, and the series novels work to some extent within the nineteenth-century Anglo-American tradition of protest literature or the "social problem" novel. The connection is especially evident in the way the novels mobilize sentimentality to approach such delicate issues as interracial marriage. Elizabeth Gaskell's *Ruth* (1853), for instance, the first British novel to use a "fallen woman" and unmarried mother as a heroine, and to keep the focus of the plot on her long after her sexual "fall", uses a sentimental treatment to try to prevent readers from rejecting Ruth in automatic horror. Similarly, several of the Trinidadian novels handle such controversial issues as interracial marriage by deploying a sentimentality that enables the authors to bend or break social conventions without completely alienating readers.

Trinidad's Literary Roots

When did a literary tradition "begin" in Trinidad? Ramchand does not mention Trinidadian literature earlier than the 1934 publication of Alfred Mendes's *Pitch Lake*. In a more recent work exploring the origins of the "literary awakening" that occurred in Trinidad during the 1930s, Reinhard Sander (1988, 7) states that "Until the late 1920s the literary scene in Trinidad, by contrast [to Jamaica], seems to have produced nothing very remarkable." He quotes Anson Gonzalez (1972), that there was "the occasional work of fiction"; however, Gonzalez himself had seen almost none of these (Gonzalez, personal communication, 1990). Similarly, J.R. Hooker notes that

> Until the 1950s, when Trinidad's literary talent began to astonish the English public, the island produced very little literature. Between Cobham and Naipaul there is only C.L.R. James. There was a small body of fiction preceding the 1907 appearance of *Rupert Gray*. All had grave weaknesses, mostly involving the melodramatic use of two-dimensional characters, but generally they used local settings and hung their plots on actual issues: in Cobham's case, inter-racial sex. (1975, 127–28)[3]

The "Trinidad Awakening" is considered to have begun in 1927, with the publication of C.L.R. James's short story "La Divina Pastora". This was followed in 1929 by the launching of the short-lived *Trinidad* magazine, and its successor the *Beacon* (1930–33). Writers such as C.L.R. James, Alfred Mendes, C.A. Thomasos, Percival Maynard, and Katherine Archibald published short fiction in these magazines. They experimented with various language registers in their narratives and dialogue, and the *Beacon*'s editorials campaigned for the use of more realistic themes, settings and language in local stories. In his introduction to *From Trinidad*, an anthology of writing culled from these journals, Sander points out that "what distinguishes the writers and intellectuals who were involved in the publication of *Trinidad* and *The Beacon* from [other earlier West Indian writers] is primarily their appearance as a group, which fostered the exchange of views and theoretical discussions and prevented creative loneliness and frustration" (1978, 2). However, it would be a mistake to read

---

3. Hooker goes on to mention one of the novels in the current series – *Warner Arundell* – as well as *Emmanuel Appadocca; Dolly, Only a Country Lass; Who Did It?* and *Richard Malmort.*

this absence of a record of earlier group activity as a sign of complete literary stagnation. It now appears that literature in Trinidad was not totally asleep throughout the nineteenth and early twentieth centuries. The earliest novel in the present series predates James's story by eighty-nine years and Mendes's *Pitch Lake* by ninety-six years; the last of the novels was published only twenty years before the former and twenty-seven years before the latter. That the novels were published over a span of time – 1838, 1853, 1854, 1907 – rather than during only one short time period (though with an intriguing "cluster" in mid-century) supports a picture of a much longer and deeper literary tradition than has been posited previously.

There is at present no way of knowing how much direct influence these novels had on writers at the time or later. Certainly *Warner Arundell* was publicly reviewed at the time of its first appearance (see discussion in the biographical note on Joseph below), and *Adolphus* was serialized in a well-known newspaper. Though it is likely that some copies of the published books were available, there were probably never very many around, given the scarcity (and incomplete condition) of known surviving copies today. Nevertheless, these novels show "Trinidad Roots" as a manifestation of the same social, cultural, and literary impulses, orientations, and concerns that have been considered archetypally West Indian, both historically and currently, and are an integral part of Trinidadian and Caribbean literary tradition. Recognition of the deeper literary roots of this tradition should strengthen, rather than weaken, this view of thematic and stylistic continuity. The awakening did not occur without warning; the same impetus that drove the first works of literature lay "sleeping" until conditions arose in the 1930s to *re*awaken it.

The Social Context of Trinidad

Trinidad has had the most varied ethnocultural and linguistic history of any island in the Caribbean (Winer 1993, 8–11). The original Amerindian inhabitants were conquered by the Spanish in the sixteenth century and rapidly disappeared due to death, forced migration, and assimilation. The island's population remained very small until 1783, when settlement was opened to Roman Catholics from countries other than Spain, encouraging massive immigration from the French Caribbean. When the British conquered Trinidad in 1797, the island's population was predominantly French- and French Creole–speaking, including whites, blacks – often also speaking African languages – and mixed-race "mulattos" or "coloureds". After this date, incoming population came mostly from the United Kingdom and from other British Caribbean colonies. The abolition of slavery in 1834–38 led to increased labour demands, resulting in immigration from Africa and the smaller Caribbean islands, and, in smaller numbers, from Venezuela ("peons" of mixed Spanish-Amerindian, and sometimes African, descent), China, Madeira and elsewhere (see Brereton 1979, 1989).[4] The overwhelmingly dominant language of Trinidad was still French Creole, locally called "Patois", but there was, nonetheless, a considerable use of English Creole, called "Negro English" and "broken English". English Creole became widespread by the end of the nineteenth century, and it eventually became the dominant vernacular language of the island.

In light of this context, which the four novels in the present series certainly inhabit, it is particularly interesting to note that the "open possibilities" of Trinidadian society seem to have allowed for a wider range of literary responses than is found in any other contemporaneous writing. The reasons for this contextual difference may lie in the social conditions and history of the colony. Trinidad was late to enter into plantation development; thus the African population was always fairly small and the ratio of slaves to free people in the society was low in comparison to that in the mature slave colonies. Moreover, the experience of plantation slavery was brief – about fifty years – perhaps the shortest of any significant ex-slave society in the New World; thus, its legacy was probably less overwhelming than for many other West Indian societies. Furthermore, Trinidad entered the post-abolition era with "an unusually large 'middle tier' of free coloureds and free blacks . . . It included estate owners and former slave-holders who . . . formed part of the economic elite (the top tier) by virtue of their status as landowners and employers. Yet they often encountered discrimination and prejudice based on their race from resident whites" (Brereton 1993, 34).

The population of colonial Trinidad was also more racially mixed than that of many other Caribbean colonies. This stemmed both from racial mixing of people within Trinidad, and from the variety of immigrants who

---

4. By the 1850s, importation of indentured labourers from India had begun, but this population remained relatively isolated on rural estates and is absent from all four novels under consideration.

entered. In the Trinidad context, race and class membership alone were not considered sole determinants of either character or ultimate fate; individual character is good or bad in any combination of race and class. In *Warner Arundell*, for example, though the main character is white, he has a large number of mixed-race half-siblings, through his father. They are portrayed as sympathetic people who help him and welcome him, and who end up happily.[5]

A Biographical Note on E.L. Joseph

Edward Lanza Joseph was born in 1792 or 1793 in London, an Anglo-Jew. According to the editor of a Trinidadian newspaper,[6] he came to the island in 1817, intending to join Simon Bolívar's forces fighting for independence in South America. Joseph's fascination with the story of the Wars of Independence in "Columbia" – that is, modern Venezuela, Colombia and Ecuador – is vividly demonstrated in *Warner Arundell*. However, Joseph remained in Trinidad for the rest of his life; he died in Port of Spain in July 1838, at the age of forty-five, during an outbreak of yellow fever.

We have no information on his early life or his education, but the same Trinidadian editor stated, at the time of his death, that he was "totally without the advantages of education" but "evinced, from early life, an ardent love of literature". In Trinidad, he seems to have earned his living in several ways: he was probably a teacher; he stated in one of his newspaper editorials that he had been "a planter" for a time (meaning, probably, a salaried manager rather than the owner of an estate); he worked as a journalist and a newspaper editor; he wrote poems and plays; he organized and acted in amateur theatricals in Port of Spain; he wrote the first published history of Trinidad; and he was the author of *Warner Arundell*. In short, he was a leading light in the very small literary world of

---

5. In the present series, the hero and heroine of *Adolphus* (1853), both mixed-race, do suffer outrageous slings and arrows, but Adolphus rescues his beloved, and though he has to flee temporarily to Venezuela, he presumably returns to marry her and live happily ever after. In *Rupert Gray* (1907), though the hero is black and the heroine white, at the end of the book clear reference is made to their legal marriage and resulting offspring, perhaps the first literary instance of mixed-race origin not from non-legitimized or coerced unions. These narrative strategies are discussed in greater detail in the critical discussions of the novels that follow in each of their introductions. However, they clearly share a viewpoint, quite progressive for the times, that individuals' worth is a result of their personal character, not their race or class.

6. Biographical details are based on: *Trinidad Standard*, 10 July 1838; *Port of Spain Gazette*, 13 April 1838; and A. de Verteuil, ed., *The Urich Diary: Trinidad 1830–31*, trans. Irene Urich (Port of Spain: A. de Verteuil, 1995), 114–15, entry for 11 March 1832.

Port of Spain in the 1820s and 1830s. Though he was at the centre of several of the literary and political controversies fought out in the island's newspapers, when he died, one of his opponents paid tribute to him in these terms: "In private life, Mr Joseph exhibited the strictest integrity, and possessed a truly English feeling of independence." Friedrich Urich, a young German who ran a store in Port of Spain, testified in a diary entry for 1832 that "the Jew" (as he described Joseph) was always good company: "He amused us very much with his odd ways and witty stories which are really clever."

Joseph tried his hand at several kinds of literary production. He wrote several skits and at least one full-length play, *Martial Law*, which was apparently published locally, described as a farce on local themes. This play was staged at least once in Port of Spain under Joseph's direction. He organized and led the Brunswick Amateurs, an amateur theatre company which put on plays in Port of Spain in the late 1820s. In August 1829, they staged a farce, *Amateurs and Actors*; Joseph certainly wrote the prologue to this play (appealing to the public not to judge too harshly the efforts of the amateur players), and perhaps the whole work. In the following year, the Brunswick Amateurs put on Shakespeare's *Richard III*, with Joseph in the title role, exhibiting "his great theatrical talents" to their "full extent". Joseph deserves to be remembered as a pioneer of Trinidad's theatrical tradition. Joseph also wrote poems which were published in the Port of Spain newspapers, usually over the initials "E.L.J.". In 1829, for instance, the *Trinidad Guardian* published his "Lines Written at the North Signal Post, forming part of a Poem on Trinidad Scenery" and "Original Stanzas for Music", a "drinking song". Joseph frequently contributed articles to the local newspapers, usually "sketches of West Indian society and manners", many of which were apparently published in the *Trinidad Guardian*. According to the editor of another Port of Spain newspaper, some of these sketches were sent by Joseph to England for publication there; they fell into the hands of the editor of the British *Monthly Magazine*, who put out "abridged, or rather mutilated, extracts" as his own work under the title "Leaves from my Log".[7]

---

7. *Trinidad Guardian*, 25 August 1829, 21 September 1830; *Trinidad Standard*, 10 July 1838; *Trinidad Guardian*, 31 March 1829, 7 July 1829; *Trinidad Standard*, 23 March 1838. We have not yet located issues of any *Trinidad Guardian* containing Joseph's "sketches", and only one "West Indian Sketch", that is, "The Maroon Party", in the *Monthly Magazine*; it is included in this volume as the appendix.

The book for which Joseph is best known is his *History of Trinidad*.[8] It is the first book-length historical account of Trinidad, as well as the first sustained attempt to portray the island's natural resources and geography. Joseph provides a brief, sketchy account of the period of Spanish settlement; only for the years 1783 to 1803 does he attempt a fuller narrative. After 1803, he gives only a brief outline of events, explaining that a more detailed account would be "not to treat of history, but to discant on that ungrateful subject, the politics of a small community" – a rather ironic disclaimer, given the many controversies in which he was engaged as a result of his writings on Trinidad. Joseph's historical account is neither scholarly nor objective, but he was able to use manuscript sources (such as the minutes of the Cabildo) which disappeared later in the nineteenth century, giving his work real value for his successors. As an Englishman with no real ties to the local landowning elite, which was mainly of French or Spanish descent, Joseph showed little sympathy for either the French or the Spanish settlers of Trinidad. The former he described as unscrupulous debtors fleeing their creditors and as disorderly adventurers, and the latter as indolent and ignorant; he therefore considered the British conquest of 1797 an unqualified blessing for the island. Similarly, as a person with (it seems) no significant stake in the planter/slave-holding economy and society, Joseph took a detached line on slavery and emancipation (he died just one month before the end of slavery in August 1838). He fully acknowledged the horrors of slavery and showed no particular sympathy for the slave owners' cause; in this, his work was very different from that of the other two nineteenth-century historians of Trinidad, P.G.L. Borde and L.M. Fraser (Brereton 1995). This cool, rational approach to the slavery issue is apparent in *Warner Arundell*.

---

8. The original hard-bound *History of Trinidad* was published, according to the title page, in Trinidad, by Henry James Mills, in London by A.K. Newman and Co., and in Glasgow by F. Orr and Sons. A 1934 *Trinidad Guardian* article (28 January, 1; reprinted 26 May 1993, and 16 August 1993, 13, pictures only) states that Mills published an *Almanac* in which was included the *History of Trinidad* by E.L. Joseph. However, the cover page of the *Almanac* reads: *"Mills Trinidad Almanac & Pocket Register for the year of our Lord 1840 . . .* Printed and published by Henry James Mills, Booksellers, Binder, and Stationer, Gazette Office, No 6, Frederick Street", and there is no reference to the *History* on the contents page. It is possible that Mills printed the original *History* in London, and that poor sales led him to bring either the plates or the printed sheets to Trinidad, where he included them in his *Almanac,* which consisted of three parts: an almanac and year book; an account of the island's geography, flora and fauna; and a history. A facsimile edition of the second and third sections was reissued in 1970, under the title *History of Trinidad,* by Frank Cass and Co.

In the small world of the Port of Spain intelligentsia (if such a thing existed at all) of the 1820s and 1830s, Joseph was a controversial figure, frequently embroiled in newspaper "wars" of one kind or another. He was, of course, an outsider – probably doubly so because of his Jewish ethnicity and his presumably humble class origins in England. He seems also to have been touchy and difficult, and perhaps foolish in not anticipating the fury he would arouse through his unflattering descriptions of local notables in his "sketches", his plays and, above all, in *Warner Arundell*. Or it may be that he deliberately sought such a reaction. One of his opponents, the editor of the *Trinidad Standard*, described him in 1838 as "that most perfect specimen extant of the 'genus irritabile' " and as a man who had "invariably forced himself on their [the public's] notice in every possible shape and . . . has so singularly contrived to disgust them with his insufferable egotism and . . . besetting sin of notoriety"; in short Joseph's "greatest enemy is – HIMSELF". Though this is certainly not an impartial judgement on the man, there is evidence to suggest that it had some validity.[9]

For instance, Joseph was on at least two occasions publicly chastised in the local newspapers for plagiarizing the work of others or repeating his own lines in what purported to be a new piece. (Thus, perhaps, the disclaimer of the "Editor" that "I am the less scrupulous in embodying the following sketch in these memoirs, because I originally wrote it" [p. 115].) In 1829 "Quintillian" attacked his poem "Lines Written at the North Signal Post" as simply a rehash of a production published some years earlier under the title "A Farewell Address". A rather foolish correspondence in the *Trinidad Guardian* followed (Joseph described it as "this very silly affair"), ended only by the re-publication of "A Farewell Address"; the two poems are, in fact, quite similar in general style, language and sentiments. In 1834 "Thomas Floghim" sent the *Port of Spain Gazette* a poem which included the following couplet: "And what with plunder'd plots, and language too, / Dressing old farces till they look'd quite new." This referred, apparently, to Joseph's farce *Martial Law*, which was his only published play. Joseph replied, refuting the accusation of plagiarism: the play had originated in a "sketch" written earlier and was later turned into a farce; its chief characters were drawn from life and its plot was based on actual, well-known incidents in Trinidad's recent past; the praise it had won from "hundreds" who saw the play performed was due to the many

---

9. *Trinidad Standard*, 27 April 1838.

local persons and episodes it faithfully portrayed. "Floghim" shot back with a letter to the editor, phrased with extraordinary vehemence, dismissing Joseph as a "paltry rhymster" and a deliberate plagiarizer; Joseph replied in a similar vein, calling his adversary a "hoary buffoon who for years has been going about picking up every little witticism and passing it off as his own". Though Joseph got the better of this ill-tempered exchange – pointing out quite reasonably that "Floghim" had not quoted a single line from *Martial Law* which he could show was plagiarized – the attack clearly stung. Four years later he described it as "one of the most disgraceful libels against me that ever polluted a public journal: the gentlemanly authors of that production should have recollected that 'I too could write' ".[10]

This phrase referred to *Warner Arundell*. The last months of Joseph's life were consumed with controversies caused by the local reaction to his novel, especially the fury at his "libels" against well-known Trinidad notables who, it seems, appear in it only lightly disguised. In April 1838, he resigned as editor of the *Port of Spain Gazette,* a position he had held for only eight months. He did so because (as he stated in a letter to the paper's subscribers and readers) he could not allow its proprietor, H.J. Mills, to suffer from his own unpopularity caused by the publication of his novel. In this letter he stated that Mills had not seen the novel before publication and bore no responsibility for anything in it. In published correspondence with F.C. Bowen, the proprietor of the *Trinidad Standard,* Joseph similarly exonerated Bowen from any knowledge of the passages in volume three which are "supposed to reflect on the private character of certain residents of this Colony". "I am alone responsible," Joseph wrote, "for all the scandals, libels on public or private character, illiberality, immorality, sedition, and treason, contained in 'The Adventures of a Creole'; no man but myself wrote or corrected a single line, or even word of it." He ended with a defiant refusal to alter anything in his novel. The editor of the *Trinidad Standard* commented:

> As regards the causes which induced this resignation, we could not have expected the community to have acted differently. Mr

---

10. *Trinidad Guardian,* 31 March 1829, 10 April 1829, 14 April 1829, 21 April 1829, 24 April 1829; *Port of Spain Gazette,* 1 April 1834, 11 April 1834, 15 April 1834, 22 April 1834; *Trinidad Standard,* 27 April 1838. We have not been able to identify "Quintillian" or "Thomas Floghim"; they may well be the same person.

Joseph has been guilty of grossly libelling several most respectable residents of this colony . . . Mr Mills' subscribers have consequently expressed their determination not to recognise any longer, as an organ of public opinion, a man who could so far degrade his pen as to descend to the most gross and disgusting personal abuse and detraction; and Mr J's "voluntary resignation" has been the result.

Personally, the editor concluded, he regretted Joseph's resignation from the rival paper, for "we never could have hoped to have met with an antagonist more unfitted to cope with us, by want of temper, of judgement, and of every other quality that could render an adversary formidable", a comment that nicely captures the nature of the relationship between Trinidad's two small newspapers in 1837–38.[11]

Despite these strictures, the *Trinidad Standard* as well as the *Port of Spain Gazette* (still edited at that time by Joseph) reproduced a generous review of *Warner Arundell* published in the British *Metropolitan Magazine* for February 1838. The anonymous reviewer wrote:

This is a very original work, and its originality is of a varied and good kind. We seldom see such copious evidence of a direct copying from nature, both animate and inanimate. We scarcely know whether we most admire the author's description of gorgeous and romantic scenery, his delineations of human character, his pathos, or his drollery – for throughout there is a fine undercurrent of quiet and rich humour. The general style and language of the work are admirable . . . In the way of humour, many of his sober hits are wonderfully effective.

The reviewer commented that Joseph's accounts of incidents always rang true, suggesting that he was informed by actual participants or witnesses, and that he paid a "nice attention to localities. He seems to be perfectly at home in every part of the West Indies, and in some respects a better notion of that country [*sic*] is given in his three amusing volumes than is to be obtained from many heavy books of voyages and travels." This glowing review concluded: "We can honestly recommend these 'Adventures of a Creole' as being alike instructive and amusing. The multitude of well

---

11. *Port of Spain Gazette,* 24 April 1838; *Trinidad Standard,* 27 April 1838; cf. *Port of Spain Gazette,* 6 April 1838, 13 April 1838.

drawn characters it contains is really surprising. Negroes, planters, pirates, privateers, West Indian doctors, magistrates, merchants, Spanish dons, South American Indians, monks, and missionaries, are all painted to the life." Commenting on Joseph's career just after his death, the editor of the *Trinidad Standard* noted that his novel had "met with a fair portion of success", and regretted that the "ill advised personal attacks" which it contained had deprived him of full credit for his "general literary success".[12]

It is quite possible that Joseph deliberately included unflattering and lightly disguised portraits of some of his enemies in his novel in order to take revenge for what he regarded as libels against him – and for who knows what other, privately administered slights and snubs. Or he may have had a more elevated agenda. In a *Port of Spain Gazette* editorial written just days before he resigned from the paper, he wrote: "Our main wish is to procure for this our adopted country a radical change of men and measures and to obtain this the 'Port of Spain Gazette' is only one of the means. Our labours for attainment of this desire are not confined to columns of this paper – that the enemies of the Colony either know, or if not, they shall soon know."[13] Was he referring to *Warner Arundell*, published and reviewed in Britain but not yet, when he wrote that editorial, available in Trinidad, or to his forthcoming *Trinidad Almanack*, which included his *History*? Or did he have other plans and projects? His life was cut short a few months later, and Joseph remains, in many ways, an enigma.

Warner Arundell and the British Literary Tradition

Locating a literary work within a historical period always poses some difficulties, especially when, as is the case with *Warner Arundell*, it falls near the boundary line between two eras. Published a year after Victoria ascended the throne in 1837, *Warner Arundell* might be classified as a Victorian novel, all the more readily if we date the beginning of the Victorian era in literature before 1837. Other dates sometimes used are 1824 (the death of Lord Byron), 1832 (the deaths of Sir Walter Scott and Johann Wolfgang

---

12. *Trinidad Standard,* 23 March 1838, from *Metropolitan Magazine,* February 1838; also in *Port of Spain Gazette,* 23 March 1838; *Trinidad Standard,* 10 July 1838.

13. *Port of Spain Gazette,* 13 April 1838.

von Goethe), and 1830 – a round-figure compromise. Yet, in its literary affiliations, *Warner Arundell* seems closer to the Romantic period and the eighteenth century than to the early Victorian age.[14]

Warner Arundell is almost certainly too early to have been influenced by Victorian novels; it seems to reach farther back for at least some of its models, especially to the Gothic novel. In British literature (as opposed to architecture) Gothic is a late-eighteenth-century genre, not a Victorian one. There is late-Victorian neo-Gothic – for example, Bram Stoker's *Dracula* (1897) – and the mid-century sensation novels – for example, Wilkie Collins's *The Woman in White* (1860) – substantially influenced by the Gothic, but Gothic proper had run its course by the time the Victorian era began.

Late-eighteenth- and early-nineteenth-century Gothic novels such as Ann Radcliffe's *Mysteries of Udolpho* (1794) are a major influence: though Caribbean settings do not lend themselves to the Gothic machinery of hoary castles, dungeons and prison-like convents, the "two-dimensional characters" in early West Indian novels that Hooker refers to (1975, 127–28, see above) are often a feature of the Gothic, which characteristically pits the beautiful and innocent against the villainous and corrupt. Some quasi-villains in the present series of novels, such as the tortured Julien Fédon in *Warner Arundell*, echo the related Byronic tradition. Byron and other nineteenth-century writers were fascinated with the Gothic villain: since the narrative function of the Gothic heroine and often-absent hero is largely to be passively terrorized as they are persecuted, imprisoned or pursued, the active villain tends to usurp narrative interest. In some examples of the Gothic this interest intensifies because the villain, like Radcliffe's Schedoni in *The Italian* (1797), is tortured by remorse, by mixed feelings or by an evil/unfortunate past. Latent in the Gothic villain, this tendency becomes an important feature of the Byronic hero, who typically combines ruthlessness with a kind of honour, and whose mysterious, often sinful, past enhances his attractiveness even as it suggests that he is dangerous.

Considering *Warner Arundell* in a Romantic context, it must be

---

14. This is particularly understandable when we consider that in 1838 many Victorian writers (for example, the Brontës, George Eliot, and Robert Browning) had as yet published nothing. Dickens had only *Sketches by Boz* (1836), *The Pickwick Papers* (1837) and *Oliver Twist* (1838) to his credit; Tennyson had brought out only two collections of poetry (1830 and 1832), to indifferent reviews; he was to revise many of the poems in them for the 1842 *Poems* with which he began to establish himself.

remembered that to contemporaries the literary landscape in the first two or three decades of the nineteenth century did not look quite as it does in retrospect. When E.L. Joseph left England in 1817, shortly after the end of the Napoleonic Wars, the leading writer was Byron, followed by Sir Walter Scott (best known as a poet, but beginning to write historical novels by this time); figures we now think of as "minor" poets (for example, Thomas Moore, Thomas Campbell) were popular. To the extent that he was known at all, Shelley had a higher profile as an atheist than as a poet, and Keats was a recognizable name only to a handful of writers such as Shelley and Leigh Hunt. What little audience William Blake had in his own lifetime thought of him primarily as a painter. Wordsworth was known, but had nothing like the profile of Byron, Campbell, Moore and Scott. After Byron, Coleridge was probably the best known of those now usually labelled the "major" Romantic poets. Moreover, though the twentieth-century conception of the Romantic age emphasized its "rebellion" against eighteenth-century literature, eighteenth-century writers such as Henry Fielding, Thomas Gray, William Cowper, Oliver Goldsmith, Alexander Pope and Laurence Sterne were still widely read in the nineteenth century, as *Warner Arundell* attests. Of writers from earlier eras, Shakespeare and Milton were especially influential.

Romantic literature, especially as created by Byron and Scott, characteristically celebrates individualism (and sometimes even lawlessness), and takes an elegiac attitude towards the personal and historical past; the Byronic hero, who embodies the Romantic mood in himself, frequently turns up in one form or another. By 1838 that hero – brooding, melancholy, restless, dashing, plagued by a remembered past sorrow or crime – was a familiar, almost conventional figure. Though pre-eminently an individualist, he could also have a political dimension. "Liberty" was a central value for many writers in this period, and if that sometimes meant the private freedom of the imagination, the concept could be and was applied to political contexts, both within and beyond literature. Byron, for example, devoted considerable money and energy to the cause of the Greek struggle for independence from the Ottoman Empire. His fiercely independent heroes, his references to Greece's captivity in his poetry, and his public adherence to the Greek cause all did much to inspire support for that cause in Britain, and by extension for other independence movements, such as the South American one, under Bolívar, in which Warner Arundell participates.

Joseph clearly kept up with literary developments in England, as one would expect a man of letters to do; his quotations include Byron's *Don Juan* (1819–24) and Scott's *Ivanhoe*, both published after his departure for Trinidad. Yet on the evidence of his quotations in *Warner Arundell*, it seems that his "ardent love of literature" (see the biographical note in the preceding section) was shaped before he left England, by the literature of the day and still more by that of previous generations. Shakespeare is quoted far more often than any other writer (twenty-three quotations, not to mention the allusions); the seventeenth- and eighteenth-century poets Milton, Cowper, Goldsmith and Pope are quoted four to six times each, while apart from Byron (ten quotations), nineteenth-century poets (for example, Wordsworth, Scott, Campbell and Coleridge) are represented by one or two quotations apiece.

In the genres he draws upon, Joseph seems primarily affiliated with eighteenth-century writers. Although in the introduction the "Editor" identifies the "personal narrative" as the best part of Warner Arundell's "mixed manuscript", the novel as it emerges remains a mixture of genres, embracing the travel book, the historical memoir and the Gothic as well as the picaresque novel. An episodic and satirical mode originally centred on the *picaro*, or rogue who lives by his wits, the picaresque was adapted in England by eighteenth-century writers such as Henry Fielding. In Fielding's *Tom Jones* (1749) the titular hero is more rash than roguish: the imprudent Tom has difficulty restraining his sexual urges, yet is also more generous and honest than many of the people he encounters in his adventures. Similarly, Warner's penchant for duelling is something he must learn to curb, yet because his willingness to fight stems from his sense of honour, it wins him friends as well as enemies. Like Tom, he is warm-hearted and somewhat quick-tempered, and has been done out of his inheritance by greedy villains. He shares with the heroes of the picaresque the habit and necessity of frequent travel, and his narrative is consequently episodic, shifting its characters and scenes frequently.

We are told at the outset that Warner, assisted by his "most powerful memory" (Introduction, p. 4), has recorded many more things about the places and events of his life, and the stories he has heard from others, than the editor can fit into the book; the "abridgement" that he advises and that Warner licenses presumably reflects, on a smaller scale, the "mixed" nature of the "voluminous" original, with its "truly alarming bulk and weight" (p. 4). Here, another of the novel's eighteenth-century connections is likely relevant. The title of this original manuscript – *The Life, Adventures and Opinions of Warner Arundell, Esquire* – echoes that of Laurence Sterne's rambling novel, *The Life and Opinions of Tristram Shandy, Gentleman* (1759–67), and though Joseph's book by no means approaches the degree of digression and delay which makes Tristram devote some four volumes to his conception, birth and baptism, Warner's manuscript does seem to have a Shandean inclusiveness and delight in digression. Novelists such as Sterne – even his more orderly contemporary Fielding – treat digression almost as opera composers do aria, that is, not as interruption, but as the focus of the performance. Warner's inclusion of "a history of the Bucaniers, and an immense number of anecdotes of all the old families of the West Indies . . ." (p. 4) echoes the eighteenth-century delight in the book as diversion, conversation, and education rather than as single-voiced, spell-binding story.

The "Editor of the present memoirs" (chap. 28, p. 191) functions as a kind of check on Warner's literary impulses, a mediator between the bulky, weighty manuscript with its roots in an earlier century, and the "present age of light reading" (Introduction, p. 5). The editor figure would have been a familiar one to most readers in 1838, who could have encountered the device in texts as diverse as Daniel Defoe's criminal biography *Moll Flanders* (1722), many of Scott's *Waverley Novels* (1814–32), and Thomas Carlyle's mock-biography *Sartor Resartus* (1833–34). This editorial fiction allows the author to maintain some distance from his material (distance Joseph might well have needed in light of his references to characters with living "originals"). It allows him to confuse the trail by introducing layers of authorial and editorial responsibility: as Warner's "papers" pass through the editor's hands they are abridged, selected and shifted from one genre to another, and names are changed. The first "I" we encounter is the editor's, telling the story of his meeting with Warner Arundell and their subsequent acquaintance – events that will be retold from a different perspective in chapter 28. At that point, when it would be feasible to name "Mr. Joseph", the editor instead sidesteps by using a dash: "Mr. ——, a person attached to the *belles-lettres*" (chap. 28, p. 191). The convention of replacing names with dashes to add verisimilitude, and supposedly to avoid identifying real people, was even then such a time-worn fictional device that it undermines a sense of the editor as a real person, making it still more difficult to locate the "authentic" authorial voice within the layers of narration.

Warner Arundell and the Caribbean Literary Tradition

Because its picaresque style can accommodate a plethora of plots and subplots, *Warner Arundell* manages to touch upon practically all the themes and literary strategies that have since become commonplace in anglophone Caribbean literature. These include a concern with issues of race and social justice, the development of a comic sensibility, as well as an interest in what, in recent years, has come to be termed the "Atlantic world" (see Gilroy's *The Black Atlantic* [1993] and Edmondson's *Making Men* [1999]). In addition, the novel tackles many of the technical problems associated with the integration of Creole words and expressions into Standard English texts (see D'Costa 1983, 1984). Several of its strategies in this regard anticipate techniques used by later Caribbean writers.

The novel's digressive story line provides us with a running commentary on the ways in which the peripatetic culture of the Caribbean basin continually repositions its inhabitants within a broader Atlantic tradition. Warner is born in Grenada and educated in Antigua, Trinidad and Caracas before he first visits England. In Grenada and Antigua he enjoys the lifestyle of a favoured scion of a well-connected, if somewhat down at heel, slave-owning family. Even without family connections or properties in Trinidad and Caracas, Warner can still rely on an automatic network of support available to him as a white creole, although matters of language and religion become more important. In England, however, his creole status is a liability rather than a source of privilege. Like Lamming's characters in *The Emigrants* (1954) or Jean Rhys's stranded heroines in *Voyage in the Dark* (1934) and *Wide Sargasso Sea* (1966), Warner experiences the mother country as a place of displacement, loss of privilege and an absence of nurturing. Anticipating such novels of return as Lamming's *Of Age and Innocence* (1958), V.S. Naipaul's *The Mimic Men* (1967), and Erna Brodber's *Jane and Louisa Will Soon Come Home* (1980), Warner comes back to the West Indies with an altered understanding of his place in the world. Although he still identifies with British values, his loyalties now are to the New World rather than to the Old, whether these take the form of fighting with Bolívar's rebels in South America for independence from Spain, or refusing, despite his abolitionist sentiments, to spy on local planters on behalf of the anti-slavery society in England.

Encompassing all these movements is the pervasive presence of the sea. Like the language in the poetry of Derek Walcott and Kamau Brathwaite,

Joseph's narrative is always restless, mirroring the predictable volatility of the sea. Time and again, he pauses to describe the movement across the water of canoes, sailing ships, and, in one memorable sequence, a steamboat. Like Walcott's Shabine in "The Schooner *Flight*" (1977, 3–20), Joseph's narrator points out the contrast between the boorish, often cruel, aspects of shipboard life and the courage and energy with which the sailors spring into action when pitted against the elements. The camaraderie of the sea, the way in which it makes equals of all men, is demonstrated vividly when a Muslim slave navigates a ship on which Warner is travelling through a dangerous passage. The African's piety and his solidarity with his leprous master, despite his clear understanding of the injustices of slavery, are made all the more poignant on account of his skilled seamanship. For him, as for Walcott's Achille in *Omeros* (1990), the sea becomes an ennobling medium, a location beyond the constraints of an oppressive social order in which a man's true worth can be measured.

Contemporary Trinidadian and Jamaican authors tend to write less about the sea or about ocean travel than do their small island counterparts. The distinction may be a consequence of the smaller island communities' acute vulnerability to the sea's moods, and their greater dependence on the sea for their livelihoods and for communication. Among twentieth-century Trinidadian writers there is also a tendency to concentrate on culture rather than nature: to see the island's cosmopolitan society as a microcosm of the outside world, and to dwell within that microcosm as their narratives explore the range of human frailty. The tone of Trinidadian prose writing, as a consequence, often is suffused with the kind of irony we associate with comedies of manners or with the calypso tent – a knowing tone, that can take aim at minutely observed human foibles, sarcastically or with gentle humour, and that depends for its effect on local audiences recognizing familiar characters and situations. *Warner Arundell* makes liberal use of such resources, as the history of the novel's contentious reception in Trinidad makes clear. Although the exact targets at whom Joseph's satire takes aim are no longer self-evident, several of the satiric techniques developed by later Trinidadian novelists can be divined in his writing. Stories, like the one about the beached whale that escapes with the tide because the local villagers are too intent on hacking off parts of its living body to secure it to the shore, have the same semi-apocryphal ring as do the stories Naipaul ascribes to Mr Biswas's newspaper columns, which all begin *"Amazing scenes were witnessed when"* (Naipaul 1961, 228).

Similarly familiar urban legends, involving flamboyant local characters or unusual dilemmas, also figure in the novels of Earl Lovelace, Samuel Selvon, and Robert Antoni. They underline the connections between the writer's craft and that of the journalist and the calypsonian, in a society notorious over centuries for its bizarrely imaginative crimes and its idiosyncratic public figures.

Where *Warner Arundell* differs from later Caribbean writing, its differences are also instructive. Joseph's views on the possibility of racial reconciliation are comic rather than tragic – closer to the optimism of Wilson Harris or Lovelace than to the pessimism of the later Lamming or of Rhys. Whenever the protagonist encounters a new location or community, he pauses to revel in its racial and cultural hybridity. Thus, Warner's first impression of Trinidad as his ship docks in Port of Spain is of a chaotically vibrant city in which one can hear as many languages as there are complexions and dresses to be seen:

> Chinese, corrupt Arabic, spoken by Mandingo negroes, a hundred different vernaculars from Guinea; English, with its proper accent, and then with its creole drawl; Spanish, with its true Castillian pronunciation, as well as with the slight corruption with which South Americans speak it; creole French, European French, Corsican, various kinds of patois, German and Italian were all spoken in this town. (P. 85)

The narrator's description and categorization of racial types and styles bear quoting in full:

> Here strutted the gaudy officer of the militia . . . There lounged, but in less pomp, an officer of the line; here and there rolled along a naval officer; the gaily dressed Spaniard shewed his laced frill and gold buttons; and the plainly dressed Englishman, with his nankeen jacket and jean trousers, stood beside the smart Frenchman, with his powdered hair, cue, short inexpressibles, silk stockings and buckled shoes. Sometimes a Chinese or two would appear; and ever and anon an athletic and ferocious-looking sambo* [*The mixed race between the Indian and negro.] would pass; together with groups of the mixed race between Indians, negroes and Europeans called *Péons*, – all wearing the dangerous *cuchillo* (knife or poniard). Crowds of negroes walked to and fro,

chattering, jesting, and laughing, as merrily as though slavery and degradation were blessings, while here and there were numbers of tastily-dressed women, of the classes called mulattoes, mestees and quadroons, who were the most beautiful of those classes which I, at that time had ever seen. (Pp. 84–85)

Similarly, Bolívar's ragtag army is apostrophized on account of the amazing array of people, cultures and weapons it brings together – from indigenous peoples armed with blow darts and poisoned arrows, to machete-wielding Péons, and Europeans with swords and guns. Significantly, the white creole protagonist Warner embraces the sinister line in his family. He is grateful for the help and affection of his "mulatto" half-siblings when his circumstances are most straitened, and he records without comment that the white daughter of his disgraced estate manager is able to rehabilitate her fortunes by marrying a brown Arundell.

In this regard, Joseph's novel differs from those of most later white creole writers, who, while pointing the reader toward the evils of racial prejudice, rarely allow their white characters to overcome their obsession with racial purity. The white protagonist's childhood friendship with his East Indian playmates in Ian McDonald's *The Humming-Bird Tree* (1969) does not survive the strains of adolescence, and Joe, the main character in Mendes's *Pitch Lake* (1934), resorts to murder in order to prevent his East Indian mistress Stella from giving birth. Rhys's Antoinette, in *Wide Sargasso Sea,* chooses incarceration and insanity over the protection offered by her mixed-race cousin, Sandy. It is worth noting, however, that the plot of *Warner Arundell* goes to great lengths to ensure that the protagonist's estates are entailed in such a way that there is no legal or ethical imperative for him to share his father's wealth with his half-siblings. Nevertheless, the brown Arundells seem a handsome, prosperous bunch, less interested in money than they are in ebullient family reunions. One must wait more than a hundred and fifty years, for the byzantine repeating tales of Antoni's *Divina Trace* (1992), to find a novel by a white West Indian writer that approaches the racial optimism of *Warner Arundell.*

Joseph's novel is particularly sanguine in its rejection of the trope of the "tragic mulatto". This figure became a staple of black and white American writing about race in the 1930s and gained some currency among West Indian and American authors writing about the West Indies in the mid-twentieth century. Such works make use of stock types, like the victimized mulatto woman, too fragile to rough it out with her black sisters, but too racially compromised to have dependable access to white privilege. Tom Redcam's *One Brown Girl And——* (1909) is an example of this type, as is Edgar Mittelholzer's tragic heroine in *The Life and Death of Sylvia* (1953). Lucille, the ill-fated mulatto beauty in V.S. Reid's *New Day* (1934), starts off as a paramour of the white custos (magistrate), von Aldenburg. She runs off with the mulatto rebel Davy, but eventually is killed when the Great Kingston Fire of 1907 sweeps through the black brothel where she lies in a drunken stupor. Another variation on this theme is the "untrustworthy mulatto" – the brown man who betrays the former slaves or their former masters, depending on the ideological bent of the author. Lamming's character Slime, in *In the Castle of My Skin* (1953), though not described explicitly as being of mixed race, is a negative proto-type for this figure, while his protagonist, Fola, in *Season of Adventure* (1970), represents its positive antithesis. Slime organizes the first coopera-tive bank for the Barbadian villagers, but then uses its proceeds to divest them of their rights to land. Fola never discovers whether her absent father was white or black, but by throwing her lot in with the celebrants at the Ceremony of the Souls, she chooses to identify herself with the folk rather than with their oppressors. Walcott takes the figure of the mulatto to another level in *Dream on Monkey Mountain* (1970), with its vivid por-trayal of Corporal Lestrade, whose very name has him straddling the fences between the races. For Walcott, the figure of the mulatto becomes a site of refusal, marking the possibility of transcendence in a culture con-sumed by the shibboleths of race.

The mixed-race characters in *Warner Arundell* are different again. They range in characteristics from the brooding Julien Fédon, wracked with guilt by the memory of the excesses of his revolt, and sick with nostalgia for his beloved Grenada; to the boisterous Arundell clan, who seem com-fortable and well established in the nineteenth-century Leeward Island business community. Along the way we meet mulattos who are committed royalist soldiers, mixed-race entrepreneurs who own slaves, brown house-keepers who control the estates and beds of their white employers, and mulatto slaves whose planter fathers have omitted to manumit them. But ultimately, their mixed-race origins do not define the actions of these char-acters. Nor is the range of positions they take on such matters as slavery and independence represented in terms of "treason" or "loyalty" to other racial groups. This may be because for Joseph, as for many of his contemporaries, West Indians of mixed race constituted a group (or groups) in their own right, with distinct political aspirations. To represent such characters uniformly as defined through "lack" – that is, through their inability to identify fully with either blacks or whites – would have made very little sense to his readers or to himself. Moreover, racial categories per se are rarely salient in this novel. It is more important for the purposes of the plot to know if a character is a creole or a royalist, a Jew or a Catholic, a coward or a man of honour, a free man or a slave. Among the slaves, Warner distinguishes further between Muslim slaves and slaves who practise vodoun, between slaves born in Africa and those bred in the New World; between slaves who hire themselves out and pay part of their wages to their masters, and slaves who have no freedom or recourse and are brutalized by their masters. There are slaves who will fight to the death for their freedom and in the next breath put their lives at risk to support or defend their former masters. In short, a character's race in this novel tells us very little about that person's intrinsic qualities, or even about what the tensions in the development of his or her role in the plot are likely to be.

It would be misguided, however, to read this "colour blindness" in *Warner Arundell* as an indication of unusual prescience or liberality on the author's part – although Joseph's politics, by all accounts, were indeed progressive for his time. Rather, the difference in tone between this early West Indian novel and later writing about race highlights the degree to which the category of race, defined as the privileged dyad black versus white, only became codified in the way we understand it at the end of the nineteenth century. Joseph died in 1838, shortly after the publication of his novel and on the threshold of emancipation in the British slave-holding colonies. At that time, slaves in the West Indies, whether they were black or brown, were defined by their labour and their legal relationship to their owners, who may have been white or brown, or, in some cases, even black. After emancipation, the demise of the category "slave" necessitated the production of a new dyad for the articulation of difference. Under the influence of new cultural theories associated with the expansion of the British Empire and the burgeoning rhetoric of social Darwinism, racial distinctions became metonyms for evolutionary hierarchies of fitness. By the end of the nineteenth century, blacks were defined by biology, which was seen as offering a scientific basis for their inferiority to whites (Brantlinger 1986; Stepan 1982). "Brownness" destabilized this dyad: it was seen as an unstable category – a problem to be eliminated in the course of a romance; a rich source of narrative tension within the development of a plot; a controversial site of contradiction or transcendence in poetry and drama.

One sees the extent to which, by the late nineteenth century, this new orientation had become the norm in the literary and journalistic responses to the 1865 Morant Bay Rebellion in Jamaica. Less than a century earlier, debates about the Haitian Revolution, though replete with racist assumptions, had been able to entertain such ideas as the inherent equality of all races and had led to the advancement of blacks, whites and mulattos on all sides of the conflict (James 1963). The rhetoric around Morant Bay, by contrast, was firmly constrained by the language of racial supremacy. In novels like Grant Allen's *In All Shades* and in later fictional treatments of the rebellion by H.G. De Lisser in *Revenge* (1919) and by Reid in *New Day,* the central issue becomes the extent to which the black masses had been misled by, or had escaped the control of, their leadership, which was assumed to be either mulatto or white (Cobham 2000). Thirty years after Joseph's death, black "blood" had become synonymous with absence of courage, vision or aptitude, and black resistance was automatically attributed to the lust for revenge. Even at its most positive, black motivation was represented merely as a monolithic reaction to oppression. *Warner Arundell* fascinates because it offers the reader an opportunity to view such twentieth-century literary commonplaces from a perspective that denaturalizes them. Every time the modern reader translates a recognizable detail about a character's race into an assumption about what that character's role in the plot is likely to be, the novel "fails to deliver", and we are forced to reflect on how entrenched racial stereotypes have become in our symbolic order, determining the way in which we interpret all racialized signs, in literature as well as life.

Linguistic Aspects of *Warner Arundell*

Like the Caribbean writers who have followed him, Joseph had to grapple with the extent to which he could integrate non-standard language registers into his narrative. On the one hand, such language had to be present in the environment if the novel was to ring true. On the other, too heavy a reliance on non-Standard English could distance his English readers from his story and affect its success within the literary marketplace. Characteristically, Joseph utilizes the full range of techniques employed by later Caribbean writers to accommodate his multiple language registers in *Warner Arundell*. He annotates non-Standard words and phrases; he offers us parenthetical explanations of some of their meanings within the text; he uses Creole in dialogue and Standard English in the text. He even risks losing the reader occasionally by offering no translation, when he judges that stopping to explain a word would ruin the flow of his story.

The linguistic characteristics of Joseph's novel are described in detail below, but from a literary perspective, the stratagem that most distinguishes this novel within the West Indian literary tradition is Joseph's use of a framing device to introduce Warner Arundell's story. As noted earlier, such framing devices were not uncommon in eighteenth-century novels; Fielding uses something similar to great effect at the beginning of *Joseph Andrews* in order to lay out a complex defence of the new genre of the prose epic.[15] The tone of such prefaces is often ambiguous: on the one hand self-deprecating, on the other, subtly undermining of the readers' social prejudices and literary assumptions. In *Warner Arundell*, the anonymous editor goes to great lengths to apologize for inflicting "Creole barbarisms" on his cultured readers, and yet it is obvious that the text revels in its linguistic hybridity. By inserting the self-deprecating editor between the reader and the text, Joseph is able to eat his cake and have it too: he pays lip service to his readers' sensibilities, while establishing himself as their equal in terms of his mastery of language and his erudition. At the same time, the frame allows him to define a space within which he can experiment with language registers that challenge the boundaries of what in his age would have been considered cultivated speech.

Later West Indian writers do much the same thing when they draw exaggerated distinctions between the creole speech of their characters' dialogue and the elevated language of their omniscient narrators. But in their work such distinctions are implicit rather than explicit, and they rarely stop to discuss their use of language in the way that Joseph's editor does. The closest approximation to Joseph's strategy probably is the use of Standard English introductions written by actual editors, in works such as

---

15. Fielding writes the preface to *Joseph Andrews* in his "own" voice, but its alarms for the "comic-epic" have some of the tongue-in-cheek quality noted here. For a discussion of this preface, see Judith Frank's *Common Ground: Eighteenth-Century English Satiric Fiction and the Poor* (Stanford: Stanford University Press, 1997), 31–46.

Sistren's *Lionheart Gal* (1986), edited and introduced by Honor Ford Smith, or in the prefaces by notable personages that introduce poems written in Caribbean creole languages by authors such as Claude McKay, Louise Bennett or Paul Keens-Douglas. Such introductions are considered useful because of the widely held assumption that creole-language texts cannot stand on their own in the literary marketplace without the support of a sponsor whose credentials within the world of letters carry more weight than the language of a subaltern group. The tone of such editorials may patronize, champion or defend, but inevitably they speak *for* the creole speaker, whose agency is thus deferred. Yet this approach is seldom as pernicious as the strategy of editors and amanuenses who do not identify themselves as such, thus failing to distinguish between their own agendas and the agendas of the creole speakers on whose behalf they mediate or translate. Inevitably such editors end up putting their own issues into the mouths of those for whom they speak (Spivak 1994). By using a literary device to call attention to the fiction of the patronizing editor, Joseph engages a literary dilemma that continues to exercise authors and editors within Caribbean literary circles to the present day.

There has been considerable study of the language represented in modern Caribbean literature (for example, Bernhardt 1983; D'Costa 1983, 1984; O'Callaghan 1984; Warner-Lewis 1982; Wyke 1991). In the corpus novels, these earliest known works of Trinidadian literature, the authors manage to convey a great sense of the complexity of the social context, to a large degree by employing an array of linguistic varieties that were all part of the Trinidadian speech repertoire of the time. The language varieties and styles of the characters' speech reflect historical, social, racial and personality factors.[16] And in *Warner Arundell*, the hero is often explicitly helped by his multilingual fluency in English, English Creole, French Creole, Spanish and Latin.

Standard British Literary English comprises both formal and idiomatic (for example, conversational), correct Standard English, with no grammatical irregularities or dialect forms, such that most readers in England would readily understand this language as more or less normal for novels. This would include the acceptable use of local creole vocabulary within the passage as long as it is contextually explained and there is not a good Standard English equivalent – in fact Joseph (or "The Editor" of *Warner*

---

16. For an extensive discussion of linguistic aspects of these works, see Winer and Rimmer 1994.

Arundell) explicitly apologizes for "creolisms" not expunged from the text (but see above for the possible disingenuousness of such an admission). In *Warner Arundell*, this English is used for the main body of the prose, both the somewhat more formal narrator's prose, and dialogue spoken by educated characters – white, mixed race and black.

Up to the nineteenth century, British Dialect English was used almost exclusively for comic effect in British novels, and marked a character as uneducated or lower class. Many nineteenth-century novelists, however, beginning with Sir Walter Scott, used dialect for characters whom they expected readers to take seriously, and even for protagonists.[17] The outstanding examples in *Warner Arundell* are the Cockney speaker who complains that people are not *"hacting according to Oil!"*, and Holywell, whose use of slang is remarkable, though not without precedent.[18]

Trinidadian English Creole (Winer 1993) is spoken by some blacks and all slaves in the earlier books, but is readily understood by local mixed-race and white characters. Although *Warner Arundell* has few examples of Trinidadian English Creole, it does have extensive examples of Grenadian English Creole, mixed with French Creole, both completely plausible for Trinidadian English Creole as well, for example:

> *"Apropos* – comrade, I think I have seen that respectable figure of yours before?"
>
> "Oui, Monsieur Louis," replied the bearer of the flag of truce: "you bin a see me at Massa La Roche's habitation."
>
> "As I live, it is my old friend Quashy! I always knew you to be a coward, and how came you in Fédon's army?"
>
> *"C'est la faute* de Monsieur Victor Hugues; he bin make me a volunteer against my will."
>
> "How did he manage that, *compère?* (P. 22)

---

17. Novelists such as Sir Walter Scott, Charles Dickens, Elizabeth Gaskell, Emily Brontë and Thomas Hardy had varying degrees of familiarity with the dialects they represented in their books (Lowland Scots, Cockney, Lancashire, Yorkshire and Dorset, respectively), but even those like Scott and Hardy, who had grown up with the dialects they assigned to their characters, often used conventional literary representations of dialect in writing for a metropolitan audience (Page 1988, 55–96).

18. Over-the-top and half-invented treatments of slang were not unknown in nineteenth-century literature, especially in books that parodied authors such as Harrison Ainsworth, who laid it on with a trowel; his first novel, *Rookwood,* came out in 1834, and *Jack Sheppard*, the most extravagant in its use of slang, in 1839. The idea of using slang for comic effect in novels was clearly current in the 1830s.

"Yankee English" is a stylized version of some generalized speech habits of uneducated Americans, not including any distinctly Southern United States English features. It is characterized mainly by lexical items such as *guess* and by descriptions such as "nasal twang". A "tall, slender Kentuckian, called Ezekiel Coffin" uses the Americanisms *guess, calculate,* and *old Kentuck,* in *Warner Arundell* (chap. 39). Such speech is rare in British novels of the period. Its presence in the Trinidad novels, used by helpful or at least sympathetic characters, all white, thus implies both greater familiarity with and greater acceptance of this speech variety.[19]

French Creole – referred to as "creole French", "Negro French", "colonial patois" and "broken French" – was widespread in the Caribbean and was the lingua franca of Trinidad until well into the twentieth century. (English Creole was also widespread, and obviously more comprehensible in an English-medium novel.) In *Warner Arundell,* the hero on occasion finds his knowledge of this language explicitly helpful, as when he can understand the conversation of the treasure-seeking villains. French Creole can be found in the novels with or without translation. Sometimes it can also be understood as represented by an equivalent level of English Creole or even English.

> My father opened the letter. While he read this, Louis La Grenade ordered some food and drink to be given to the poor devil, Quashy. The letter alluded to now lies before me. It is written in French; but, having a number of creolisms in it, I prefer translating it rather than giving the reader a mere transcript. (P. 23)

Spanish was locally common in Trinidad until quite recently, as a result of long-standing trade, migration and social relations between Trinidad and nearby Venezuela. This is well represented in the first three novels of the corpus. There is a considerable amount of attention to Spanish domains in *Warner Arundell,* as the hero fights in the wars for independence along the Spanish Main, and there are long critical discussions of

---

19. Page suggests that Dickens's representations of American speech "made considerable humorous and satiric capital out of eccentricities of this kind . . . the dialogue makes an important contribution to the impressions of rawness and oddity that Dickens wished to create in his picture of frontier society" (1988, 159). While the Trinidadian novels may poke a certain amount of fun at Americans' speech, they appear fundamentally respectful. Certainly the professed American ideals of action, brains, democracy, and practicality would appeal more to liberal West Indian than traditional British sentiments, despite the much longer period of slavery in the United States.

Spanish law. Several Spanish phrases are included, and again, his knowledge of Spanish is very helpful to Warner in several situations.

Latin is used in apt quotations and proverbial mottos by the narrator and by educated characters, particularly those with legal training.

> Fight they did, but not like men; they fought like enraged bulls.
> "Ac velut ingenti Silâ, summove Taburno,
> Cum duo conversis inimica inpraelia tauri
> Frontibus incurrant." – Virgil. (P. 52)

Quotation and Allusion in *Warner Arundell*

Quotation and allusion, familiar features of eighteenth- and nineteenth-century novels, abound in *Warner Arundell*. These devices function in a variety of ways. By setting up a complex web of intertextual reference, they index the book's literary affiliations, as noted above. They also emphasize its inclusiveness: as a "mixed" novel from a "mixed" source, *Warner Arundell* invokes many other forms, from popular song and poetry (songs by Thomas and Charles Dibdin, Charles Wolfe's "Burial of Sir John Moore") to Byronic epic (*Childe Harold*), and mock-epic (*Don Juan*), to plays (Shakespeare, Goldsmith), to Latin verse. Further, the quotations point to the book's literariness per se, that is, they are part of a display of wit and learning, features which an audience of the period might enjoy for their own sake, much as they might enjoy digressions. The quotations can be satirical, as when the magistrate Pennyfeather is likened to Shakespeare's inept Dogberry and Verges (chap. 42, p. 327), or humorous, as when quotations from Milton, Shakespeare, Ovid and Byron (most of them serious in their original contexts) are playfully marshalled to punctuate the story of the beached whale. Or they can be part of a performance within a performance, as in the case of Dickson, the poetic tailor in chapter 11, who seems to be something of an alter ego for Joseph. Though he is given the derogatory label of "poetaster", Dickson's exuberant use of rhyme, quotation and "judicious alteration", his bravery, and his underdog courtroom victory over Carr, all make him an attractive as well as a comic character. Moreover, Joseph's own use of quotations, like Dickson's, tends to be brash and provocative rather than elegantly understated, as in the boyish pun on "Greece/grease" (chap. 20, p. 118), which applies Byron's famous philohellenic comment on captive Greece to whale blubber.

The quotations themselves are frequently not quite accurate, or are misattributed; like most men of letters in his time, Joseph probably quoted from memory rather than checking sources. Where the variations are substantial, or may be intentional, the quotations are left in the text as they are, and alterations pointed out in the notes. In any case, we can only guess which editions Joseph may have been using: some "inaccuracies" may have been textual variants, especially if he was using pirated American versions of, for instance, Byron.[20]

Joseph's quotations sometimes have a sombre effect, as in his epigraph to the last chapter, Samuel Johnson's (1760) poignant reflection on the ending of his *Idler* essay series: "It is very happily and kindly provided, that in every life there are certain pauses and interruptions, which force consideration on the careless . . ." In that last number of *The Idler*, Johnson modestly hopes that his readers may be "unwilling to part" with him (p. 314), if only because they have grown used to him, and because "the termination of any period of life reminds us that life itself has likewise its termination" (p. 315). Johnson sees dying, bringing the series to an end, and parting as cognate acts, each a form of dissolution, and although this reflection may seem heavy-handed as the ending to a novel of episodic adventures such as *Warner Arundell*, it is as apt there as it is at the end of *The Idler*. An end, as Johnson notes, comes at last "to every thing great as to every thing little" (p. 316), and there is a long-standing tradition of using literary endings and death as metaphors for each other.

Ending the episodic picaresque novel poses special problems: the restless narrative energies it sets going, like life itself, resist containment and closure, making the eventual stasis of the end all the more of a death-like contrast. For Joseph, and for Warner, it is the return of good fortune that brings narrative and protagonist to a halt. Having re-established his reputation, regained his fortune and been reunited with Maria Josefa, Warner finds his stopping point: "Since that [wedding] day, the current of my life has been too smooth, and my happiness has been too uniform, for a description of it to be interesting. Hence the creole, Warner Arundell, has

---

20. Until 1891 American law did not provide copyright protection for anyone but American citizens and residents. Many American publishers even reprinted the popular works of living authors without seeking permission; errors easily crept into such pirated editions.

no more adventures to recount" (p. 436). Adventures, misfortune and villainy make for narrative interest: happiness brings all that, and the book itself, to a close.

Law and Medicine in *Warner Arundell*

The novel *Warner Arundell* has a great deal to say about two professions in particular: the legal and the medical. While it does not seem that Joseph was either a lawyer or a doctor, he does appear very familiar with the professional preparation and practice of the time. Although Trinidad became a British colony in 1797, much of Spanish civil and criminal law, and judicial practice, was continued (with some modifications) until the 1840s.

> There was . . . a general agreement among all sections of the leading classes that something had to be done about the criminal and civil law. In 1840 it was, as it had been since a Proclamation of 19 June 1813, a cumbersome and illogical mixture of the Spanish, Roman, and English systems, and great areas of legal uncertainty existed for lawyers. It was based on the archaic corpus of the Laws of the Indies, aided by the Roman law where this was defective, but the English law applied in certain fields of which the most important were trade, navigation, and mutiny. Also binding were English laws made since the Cession in which Trinidad was specially mentioned, and Orders in Council. For many years there had been complaints about so unsatisfactory a system which took years of study to master fully, and there had even been a Commission from England in 1827 to examine it. But the Commissioners had been largely concerned with the law pertaining to slavery, far more liberal in spirit if not in letter than in the old English colonies, and apart from recommending a few changes in other fields, they recoiled from a radical and sweeping reformation and held that the time was not ripe for the introduction of trial by jury which the English in the island had been loudly demanding. They advised a policy of gradualness by which defects would be remedied as they came up during the work of the courts. Before 1840 a few piecemeal alterations had in fact taken place . . . but the confusion among the lawyers and discontent

among the public who were caught up in the toils of the law still remain[ed] because judgements could be swayed by mere trivialities. (Wood 1968, 182–83)

If the requirements or possibilities of the law were confusing for lawyers, they were even less clear to the ordinary citizen, especially considering that much of the population did not speak English (or English Creole). Indeed, as late as 1841, after forty-four years of British rule, Governor Henry MacLeod expressed dissatisfaction with a situation in which two thirds of the population were still speaking French or Spanish, and could not truly speak or understand the language of the laws by which they were governed, leading him to encourage the establishment and increase of English-medium education (Carmichael 1961, 223–24).

With an intensity of feeling approaching that of Dickens's *Bleak House* (1853) – though leavened with more humour – Joseph portrays lawyers as greedy, incompetent and parasitic, for example: "Messrs. Keen and Leech of St. Kitt's, who had, to use a Cockney's expression, 'done for' my father's St. Christopher and Antigua estates; or who, as we say here, were good hands at 'draining' plantations" (p. 40).

Joseph has, understandably, little respect for judicial proceedings in which ignorance and self-interest reign, and he seems to have a special affection for the "poetic tailor" Dickson, who not only is an expert in extemporaneous versifying, but who uses his sense and linguistic skills to outwit opponents in courts of law. (As discussed in the biographical note above, the author himself was frequently embroiled in wrangles over issues of libel and plagiarism.)

Joseph's portrayal of the medical profession is somewhat more even-handed, though he rightly criticizes those who are greedy or incompetent, or both, and he raises significant moral questions about a doctor's role in battle. He includes descriptions and diagnoses that are very accurate for the time period, and gives an excellent picture of the overall health (or disease) characteristics of the region.

New World indigenous peoples were devastated by diseases that descended on this immunologically defenceless population from Europe and Africa: smallpox, measles, diphtheria, trachoma, whooping cough, chicken pox, bubonic plague, malaria, typhoid fever, typhus, cholera, yellow fever, dengue fever, scarlet fever, influenza. Particularly hard hit were the indigenous people of the Caribbean islands; compared to those on the islands, populations on the South American mainland were exposed to fewer outsiders and diseases, and the environment in higher elevations was less encouraging for mosquitoes.

The intensification of the slave trade in the early sixteenth century "brought African pathogens as well as Africans, both of which had heretofore only trickled into the Caribbean and now began to pour in" (Kiple 1993, 500). In addition to Guinea worm, yaws, leprosy, yellow fever and falciparum malaria came the filarial worm, also carried by mosquitoes, and the "hookworm" *Necator americanus,* which "found the West Indian sugarcane fields an especially favourable habitat" (Kiple 1993, 500).

> The slaves had lived with both of these tropical killers [malaria and yellow fever] for eons and in the process had developed a relative resistance to them. But in addition, they were also accustomed to most of the other Old World illnesses that had proven so devastating to the Indians. The ironic result of this ability to resist disease was that it made blacks even more valuable as slaves. The Indians died of European and African diseases, the whites died of African diseases, but the blacks were able to survive both, and it did not take the Europeans long to conclude that Africans were especially designed for hard work in hot places. (Kiple 1993, 499)

Although yellow fever[21] and malaria were the chief killers of whites in the Caribbean region, the victims were generally newcomers. "Most of the slaves reaching the Americas originated from deep within the endemic zone, and consequently would have acquired immunity to yellow fever

---

21. Yellow fever can appear with symptoms ranging from extremely mild to malignant; in classic cases it is characterized by fever, headache and muscular pains, jaundice, high protein content in the urine, and haemorrhage into the stomach and intestinal tract. Caused by a virus that enters the human blood stream in the blood meal of the female *Aedes aegypti* mosquito, the mingling of infected with uninfected recent or established residents provided the context for repeated epidemics. Although high mortality rates were frequently recorded during epidemics, we know today that yellow fever mortality is actually relatively low, suggesting that most cases were mild and went undiagnosed (Cooper and Kiple 1993, 1100). "Yellow fever flourished in the Caribbean wherever the virus discovered a sufficient number of non-immune persons to host it, for the [*Anopheles*] *aegypti* is a domesticated mosquito that lives close to and feeds on humans . . . Anopheline mosquitoes that carry malaria, however, are not so tied to humankind and consequently are not spread evenly across the Caribbean" (Kiple 1993, 500). At the end of the nineteenth century, Guadeloupe, Dominica, St Lucia, Grenada, Trinidad and Tobago were among the places in the Caribbean where malaria was most prevalent, whereas it was rare in Antigua, St Vincent and Barbados (Kiple 1993, 500).

before they ever stepped aboard a slaving ship" (Cooper and Kiple 1993, 1102). Old residents had usually suffered from yellow fever while quite young, at an age when the malady is relatively gentle with its victims, and in the process earned a lifetime of immunity against another visitation. Similarly, resistance to malaria was gained by repeated bouts with the disease although this was not so perfect an immunity as that acquired against yellow fever (Kiple 1993, 500). One political consequence of the European battle over New World territory was the deaths of "tens of thousands of non-immune soldiers and sailors sent to do that fighting who died, not from battle, but from yellow fever and malaria . . . Blacks, on the other hand, although remarkably resistant to these diseases, suffered greatly from other illnesses that generally bypassed whites" (Kiple 1993, 500). These included tetanus infections, and poor nutrition, which left slaves less able to combat other ailments, and which may have led directly to nutritional diseases such as beriberi (related to thiamine deficiency), pellagra (niacin deficiency), marasmus and kwashiorkor (from protein malnutrition). The exact identification and cause of the slave illness called *mal d'estomac* are not determined, but it is most likely "dry" beriberi. "Dropsy", listed as a common cause of slave deaths, can probably be attributed to kwashiorkor, "wet" beriberi and hypertensive heart disease.

Though Warner, as the narrator, often comments on relatively harmless versus harmful treatments, many of the remedies described in the novel strike the reader today as dangerous if not murderous, such as the use of arsenic and mercury. In some cases, however, not only were these the best remedies available at the time, but a few are still used today, though in very modified form. The real causes of many diseases and disorders mentioned in the text – from ciguatera and mal d'estomac to yellow fever – were unknown at the time, and the control of disease vectors by public health measures was still a long way in the future. Joseph himself, despite his obvious awareness of the dangers of fevers and poor medical treatments, probably died of yellow fever. It was not until the end of the nineteenth century that it was learned that yellow fever was transmitted by the *Anopheles aegypti* mosquito, and not until the first decade of the twentieth century that the disease was controlled by mosquito eradication (Cooper and Kiple 1993, 1105).

British Medicine in the Early Nineteenth Century
(*by Douglas M. Haynes*)

It is no surprise that Warner Arundell, the namesake of the novel, decides on a career as a general practitioner. For the gentleborn with uncertain prospects, or for someone from a modest social background, medicine was one of the most accessible vocations. Ostensibly, the practice of medicine was divided into three legal orders, whereby physicians treated illness, surgeons excised disease and apothecaries compounded the prescriptions of physicians. Sixteen self-governing corporations in the British Isles awarded diplomas, certificates and licences to practise medicine of one sort or another.[22] However, rapid urbanization and a rising standard of living during the eighteenth century blurred these neat divisions as the demand for medicine ballooned. It was in this context that the general practitioner emerged (Loudon 1986, 129–151).

Until 1815 there was no formal qualification for the general practitioner. Much to the disgust of physicians, both surgeons and apothecaries prescribed and dispensed drugs while engaged in general practice. The passage of the Apothecaries Act changed this state of affairs. Thenceforth, all medical men, including surgeons, who wished to engage in general practice had to secure a licence from the Society of Apothecaries. Candidates for the apothecary's licence had to be twenty years of age, complete a mandatory five-year apprenticeship with an apothecary or surgeon-apothecary, and provide proof of appropriate medical education. Neither the Society of Apothecaries nor the College of Surgeons of England provided instruction; the formal requirements of the act would have been inconceivable without a pre-existing informal system of private medical education (Loudon 1986, 167–70).

Warner's training would have been familiar to many a practitioner. Dr Grey, whom he befriends on the return voyage to Britain, encourages Warner to apprentice with his former pupil, Dr Molesworth, a surgeon-apothecary, as a worthy practitioner to learn from. Until its abolition in 1858, the apprenticeship system was the cornerstone of medical training.

---

22. Five were in England: the universities of Oxford and Cambridge, the College of Physicians of London, the Company of Surgeons, and the Society of Apothecaries. Scotland boasted seven: the universities of Edinburgh, Glasgow, St Andrews, and Aberdeen (originally two); the Royal College of Surgeons of Edinburgh; and the Faculty of Physicians and Surgeons of Glasgow. Ireland had four: the University of Dublin, the College of Physicians of Ireland, the Royal College of Surgeons, Ireland, and the Apothecaries Hall of Ireland.

In exchange for a fee that ranged anywhere from £150 to £300, an established practitioner lodged and directed the training of a teenaged youth from the lower middle classes or an older apprentice. Ideally, this system provided a measure of supervision for youths before they entered their formal studies as adults in London. It could also serve as a gateway for entering into a practice or launching one in the future after securing a formal qualification. As a master-servant relationship, however, the reality of the system could be rather grim. The apprentice had no control of his labour; the educational value of attending to the fire, looking after the horse, and serving as a messenger was non-existent. Apprentices, to be fair, learned while doing – for example, compounding drugs and filling prescriptions and being exposed to different clinical conditions. However, for most practitioners, it was grinding commercial imperative rather than the advancement of knowledge that dictated the nature of the education obtained (Loudon 1986, 176–80).

Apart from consulting books on *materia medica* in Molesworth's library and observing the occasional clinical case, Warner does not learn much from his tutor. Instead, he obtains the bulk of his knowledge of medicine and surgery from attending the course of lectures at the various London teaching hospitals. His lecturers include Sir Charles Bell, a surgeon, anatomist and physiologist at Middlesex Hospital in 1812 and co-founder of the medical school in 1828 (Sebastian 1999, 113–14).

Here, too, knowledge came at a price. Admission to these lectures, like other aspects of medical training, required a fee. At Middlesex Hospital, Warner "walks the wards", which involved accompanying a hospital physician on his rounds. Ideal for gaining clinical experience, this also required a fee for the privilege. Warner caps his training by becoming a dresser to the hospital surgeon at Middlesex. Under the supervision of the surgeon, the dresser provided rudimentary care. Although nominally remunerated, the position was important to the organization of labour in the hospital, by freeing up the time of the hospital surgeon and physician. This post – and similar ones – offered the student exposure to actual clinical conditions and patient care, while also providing the opportunity to cultivate contacts with prominent members of the hospital staff, which could be of some use when seeking a future hospital appointment or patient referrals. Later, Warner is befriended by Matthew Baillie. Baillie, who specialized in diseases of the respiratory system, was a consulting physician to St George's Hospital and attended King George III (Sebastian 1999, 97).

To the extent that his hospital experience provides tangible benefits, Warner accepts the exchange of his labour for the acquisition of knowledge. But he cannot mask his contempt for Molesworth. The tension between the parochial Molesworth and the urbane Warner reflects the wider status anxieties of general practitioners. Nothing stirred the resentment of status-conscious practitioners more than the provision in the Apothecaries Act that mandated apprenticeship for all applicants for the apothecaries certificate. This provision reinforced the elite status of the College of Physicians of London, which drew its members from among the graduates of Oxford and Cambridge. It also associated the training of general practitioners with a field of medicine that was associated with retail trade and that recruited from among the humbler social orders. Little knowledge could be gained, much less produced, from an apothecary's shop; Warner's refusal to work behind the counter of a druggist would resonate with other practitioners. But the vast majority had little choice (Loudon 1986, 189–207).

As drawn by Joseph, Warner fits the classic profile of the outsider as social critic. His genteel birth sets him apart from most practitioners while framing his criticism of the commercial ethos of medicine. So, too, does Warner's Caribbean connection. It both stamps him as a marginal figure in Britain and provides an alternative space for remaking medicine. He rationalizes his decision to return to the West Indies without securing a qualification from the College of Surgeons as a protest against the social exclusiveness of the College and the artificial distinctions between medicine and surgery: "However, I cared little about this, because I intended to practise in the West Indies, where the obsolete distinction between physician and surgeon is little attended to: both branches there, as they ought to be every where else, are practised by the same person" (p. 165).

Warner's decision to return to the West Indies reflects the dense circulation of people between the British metropole and its Caribbean periphery. Before and after the Revolutionary and Napoleonic Wars (1793–1815) Britain was already a destination for health restoration for the planter class as well as other beneficiaries of the slave-based economy. The image of the tropics as an alien disease environment for the European "constitution" further popularized the therapeutic value of spas and springs in England: in the novel, Dr Grey, a thirty-year resident of the tropics, was one believer (p. 152).

As a centre for medical training, London attracted students from the white settler colonies who had hopes of making a medical living on their return. Warner's tutor Molesworth even seems to specialize in training medical students from the West Indies (pp. 151, 175). Edinburgh was also a popular destination for medical education for white West Indians (Sheridan 1985, 55–63). Furthermore, the maintenance of Britain's territorial empire in West Africa, the Caribbean, and India proved to be a major source of demand for practitioners. The surgeon colleges in England and Scotland harnessed this demand as an opportunity to enrich their coffers with examination fees and to enhance their corporate influence in the empire. Their licences established eligibility for appointments in the army, the navy, and the East Indian Company (Watson 1970, 3). Additionally, in response to humanitarian campaigns, Parliament mandated surgeons on convict and slave vessels (Watson 1973). Warner himself returns to the West Indies by signing on as a ship surgeon on the *Saucy Jack*, a passenger vessel sponsored by the anti-French aristocrat Don Mendez (pp. 178–80).

For all of Warner's criticism of the rigid organization of medicine in Britain, the periphery was not a wild "frontier". In Crown territories, British-qualified practitioners were entitled to practise locally without examination. But the registration of practitioners varied from colony to colony. In 1814, Sir Ralph Woodford, the governor of Trinidad, mandated that all prospective practitioners submit their credentials to a local medical board for approval. This requirement, which was the first of its kind in the West Indies, regulated the practice of medicine locally by formalizing the imperial jurisdiction of British qualifications; a licensing law was not established in Jamaica until 1833 (Sheridan 1985, 48–52).

In the novel, the governor of Trinidad, Sir Ralph Woodford, doubts Warner's explanation of why he has no licence by insinuating that he might be merely from the counter of an apothecary (p. 231). His comment underscores the association of general practitioners with the low-status trade in drugs. It also reflects the fact that while many of the practitioners who travelled to the colonies as military or contract surgeons possessed the certificate from the Society of Apothecaries or a licence from the College of Surgeons, or both, others simply absconded to the colonies with little or no training. However much Warner resents Woodford's snobbishness, Warner himself has had his own experience with dubious practitioners such as Dr D'Alentour (pp. 35–37).

In the West Indies, as in Britain, the understanding of health and illness revolved around balance or imbalance in the physical presentation of the body – that is, the state of the humours of blood, phlegm, yellow bile and black bile. It is for this reason that practitioners treated the symptoms of disease. They prescribed a range of drugs such as opium (to relieve pain), quinine (for fevers), and mercury and antimony (for cutaneous eruptions, gout, apoplexy), or in combinations to restore "balance". However, these therapies were generally not effective, in large part because knowledge about the causes – much less the biochemistry – of illness and disease simply was not available. (See discussion in the preceding section.) It is for this reason that practitioners – and not infrequently at the patient's insistence – secured a second opinion to confirm a diagnosis and recommended treatment. Some, such as Dr D'Alentour, refused to consult with a mere surgeon, even one who had had some success in treating patients in Grenada (p. 36). By contrast, Baillie concurs with Warner's treatment strategy for Rivers's tertian fever – probably caused by a mild case of malaria or yellow fever (p. 171).

Epidemic visitations of yellow fever exposed the limitations of British medicine. In the West Indies, especially in the wake of wars, yellow fever struck nearly every year. Warner observes:

> Nothing could look more gloomy than the capital of Trinidad, during the prevalence of this malady. Business seemed to stagnate: many fled into the country, vainly hoping to escape the disease: nothing was heard but the tolling of funeral-bells, and little seen but the long processions of the slowly arrayed Catholic priests, and their red-habited choristers, acolytes, and crucifers, going to administer extreme unction, or singing funeral dirges, and carrying the scarcely cold, yet already putrid, victim of the epidemic to the house appointed for all. (P. 227)

The epidemiological response to the disease reflected the divided opinion about its cause. "Anti-contagionists", who linked the cause to generalized environmental conditions or miasmas, and "contagionists", who attributed the disease to a specific agent such as the black vomit of terminal cases, recommended flight or quarantine respectively (Curtin 1989, 68–70). Although little understood, quinine or "cinchona bark" proved to be the treatment of choice, especially for patients with febrile conditions whether in the "tropics" or in Britain, but even quinine did not prove to be the miracle drug that it was purported to be without an understanding of its active ingredients or proper dosage. Its absence, however, provided a serviceable excuse for the inadequacy of medical intervention and public health.

Notes on Editorial Procedures

In a very few instances, obvious typographical errors have been corrected, for example, *Cheltentam* to *Cheltenham*. Variant author spellings – for example, Shakespeare/Shakspeare, villan/villain – have been made consistent with the most common modern spelling. Consistent author's spellings – though now considered incorrect, variant or obsolete – such as "bufoonery" (buffoonery) and "makeral" (mackerel), have been left as in the original, with any comments in the endnotes. Following the author's, rather than modern, convention, names of ships are not italicized.

The chapter numbers of the original text have been modified so that they are continuous throughout the entire work rather than beginning again with Chapter One in the second and third volumes; however, the three original volume divisions are maintained. For the convenience of the reader, the first few words of each chapter text have been added to the table of contents.

Joseph's original footnotes are included on the relevant pages; the author's original symbols have, however, been replaced by continuous numbers. All items in the text that have been annotated by the editorial team in the endnotes are identified by the symbol †; endnotes are arranged consecutively, according to text page number, at the end of the novel text.

Joseph's 1835 "The Maroon Party: A West-Indian Sketch" is the appendix to this volume. It was included to provide access to a piece which contains a number of references to events – and, to some extent, characters – that appear in modified form in the novel. It is more or less in "memoir" form, rather than "history" or "fiction", and has not been annotated.

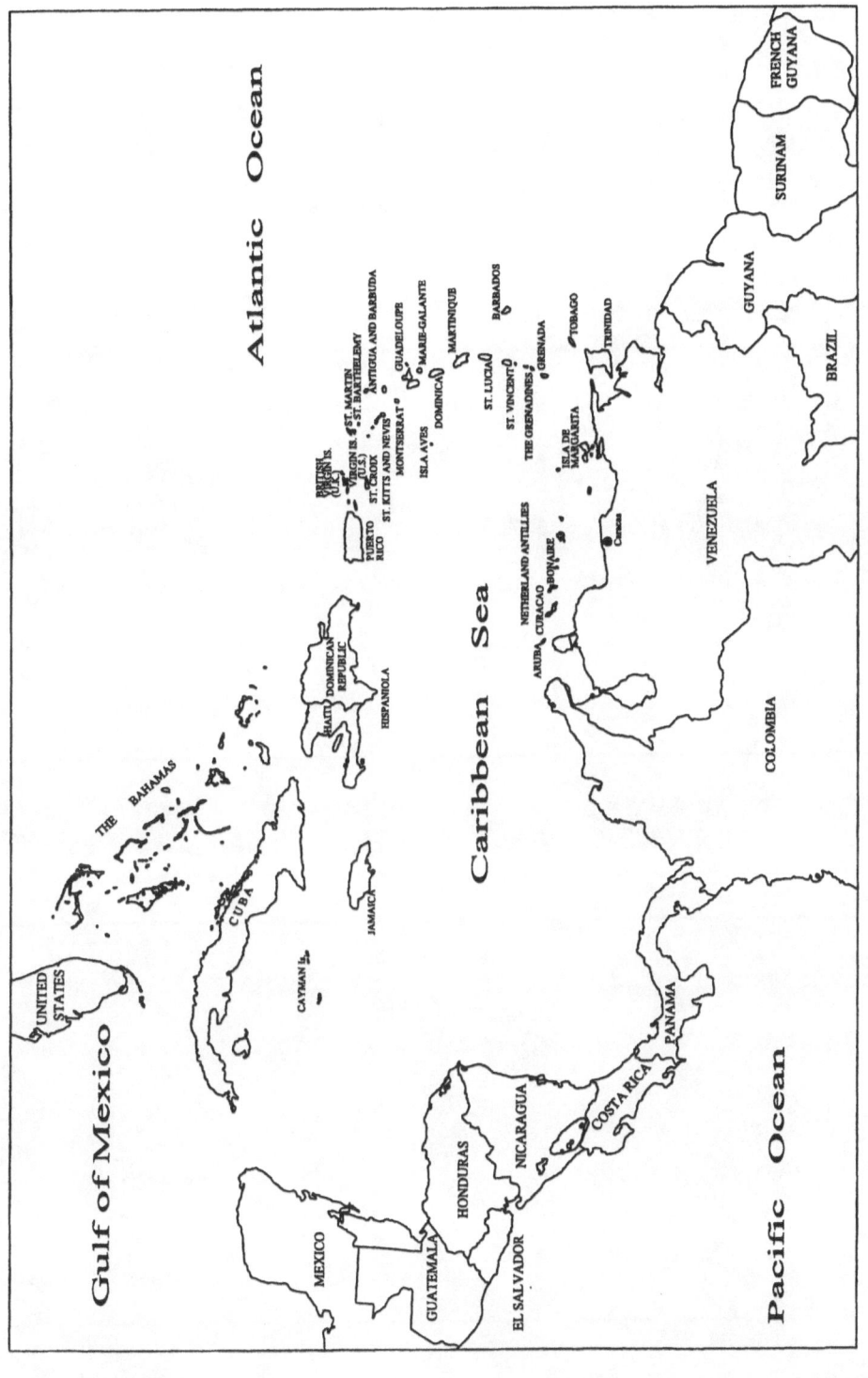

TO
THE RIGHT HONORABLE
LORD BARON GLENELG,
HER MAJESTY'S PRINCIPAL SECRETARY
OF STATE FOR THE COLONIES.

MY LORD,

SHOULD your Lordship condescend to honor these
Volumes with a perusal, their Author flatters himself they will direct your attention to many abuses
in our West Indian Colonial System, which call
loudly for correction. The hope of bringing some of
them under your notice, has induced me to take
the liberty of inscribing this Work to your Lordship.

I have the honor to be,

MY LORD,

Your Lordship's humble Servant,

EDWARD L. JOSEPH.

PORT OF SPAIN, TRINIDAD,
Aug. 20, 1837.

INTRODUCTION.

Previously to submitting the following narrative to the reader, it is
necessary to inform him that it is taken from a very voluminous
manuscript, which partakes of the mixed nature of memoirs, a journal,
an autobiography, and a collection of letters and essays. These bore, in
their title-page, the following inscription: "The Life, Adventures, and
Opinions, of Warner Arundell, Esquire."†

The Editor of these volumes thinks it his duty to inform the Public
under what circumstances he came into possession of these papers of Mr.
Arundell. In giving this information, he prefers speaking of himself in the
first person singular, rather than assuming the right of Editors and Kings,
— viz. to talk of themselves in the plural number.

Amongst a thousand and one literary projects which I had formed, one
was to write a history of the war of the independence of Columbia,
Mexico, Peru, Chili, and Buenos Ayres.† When I designed this Work, I
considered more what ought to be done than what I was able to accomplish. The paucity of materials for compiling a good account of this most
momentous occurrence, renders it necessary for him who would undertake to become the historian of this important revolution, to visit all the
principal cities on the great South American continent; in order to
inspect such few scattered records as were preserved during this most
sanguinary civil war, and to consult with all the surviving chiefs who
figured in the contest, whether living in the New World or in Europe. To
do this required leisure and a fortune, neither of which I possessed.
Hence, I was obliged to abandon my project — certainly for the present,
probably for ever.

During my various and generally fruitless attempts to obtain materials
for my projected history, a friend suggested that, as Mr. Warner Arundell
had spent some years on the Main,† during a most interesting period of the
wars of Columbia, he might be able to give me some information on the

subject; especially as it was known that Mr. Arundell had of late commenced journalising.

My acquaintance with the Gentleman who is the hero of these volumes,
commenced twenty years since. I first met him in London, in the house of
Don Louis Mendez. After this, I became his companion during a remarkable voyage across the Atlantic, recorded in the second volume of this
Work. We separated on our arrival in Trinidad, and did not meet again for
some years: subsequently we both were residents of this colony; but, living
far from each other, we seldom met.

During this residence of Mr. Arundell in Trinidad, he was the subject
of a most disgraceful persecution. He left the island, but returned in a few
months, possessed of a very large fortune, and here married a most
amiable and lovely Spanish creole.[†]

But, notwithstanding our old acquaintance, I applied to him for the
information I required with some reluctance; for, although I was one of
those who refused to join in the frantic and disgraceful hue-and-cry
against him, yet fortune had placed us in very different situations. He was
in the possession of great wealth; I, after many years' residence here, was
in an humble situation. But I still took the resolution of waiting on him. I
sent my name to him: he came to me. The instant I beheld him, I perceived I had wronged him by my diffidence. He did not receive me as
some rich men meet an old acquaintance, who has been subject to harsh
treatment from fortune. No; he took my hand as that of an old friend, who
had dared to defend him when he was assailed by calumny.

In Mr. Warner Arundell I perceived a man who had been proud in
adversity, unbending when suffering under persecution, but affable and
amiable in prosperity; one who endeavoured to forget injuries, and sin-
cerely forgave insults, although he possessed "the memory of the heart," as
gratitude has been beautifully denominated.

On making him acquainted with the cause of my visit, he immediately
offered to put me in possession of that part of his journal which related to
his adventures in the patriot camp: and he informed me, that, by looking
through his papers, amongst a load of dross I might find some ore, from
which useful metal might be extracted. He, however, added, —

"I fear you will not have the phlegm[†] to inspect all my papers."

"Never doubt that," was my reply; "I have had the perseverance to read
through the whole of Abbé Raynal's historical romance."[†]

"That," said my friend, "was rather a trial on your credulity than on your patience: my voluminous manuscripts will put your application to a much severer test."

On my persisting to request that he would allow me to read his manuscripts, he took from a chest a mass of papers of truly alarming bulk and weight. They consisted of *thirteen hundred and seventy-eight sheets of foolscap,*[†] closely written; to compile which, he had employed the leisure time of some years.

Lest the reader should wonder what there was in the life of this worthy Gentleman that required so much time and paper to record its incidents and reflections, I must explain, that he possessed a most powerful memory. Every thing he had heard, seen, read, or thought, he seemed to recollect, when compiling his voluminous manuscripts. For example, he opens his journal with an account of the first settlement of his family in the West Indies. This induces him to give a history of the Bucaniers,[†] and an immense number of anecdotes of all the old families in the West Indies; with a vast variety of traditional stories, which relate to the Arundells, and the descendants of Sir Thomas Warner,[†] the first English governor of St. Christopher's, who was his maternal ancestor. In short, the part of the narrative which I have abridged into the first short chapter of the first volume, takes up so much space in his manuscripts, that, if it were printed *verbatim*, it would be equal in length to the whole of that volume.

In the progress of his Work he gives the whole history of the two Maroon wars in Jamaica;[†] an account of the rise, progress, and termination of the wars in the West Indies consequent on the French revolution: he carefully transcribes every letter that he ever received or wrote, and all remarkable conversations that he ever heard: he gives his thoughts on a vast variety of subjects, and relieves the narrative with all kinds of essays on various matters which came within the scope of his observation; such as, on the mode of education in Caraccas; on militia training; on naval and military affairs; on medical education in London; on the practice of physic in the West Indies, &c. In short, his voluminous journal embraces a number of treatises, which, however unfit they may be to publish in an autobiography, I may one day print, under the title of the 'Arundell Papers;' as this Gentleman has given up his Work to me for my own advantage.

But I anticipate. I kept the papers of Mr. Arundell until I abandoned all idea of writing my projected history. I then returned them. At the same time I informed the worthy autobiographer, that, if he would take the trouble of extracting from his MSS. that which might not be improperly denominated the personal narrative, it would form a moral, and, I believed, a not uninteresting production.

"Have you," said he, "any inclination to make the abridgement yourself? it will be an easier task than to write history, and, during the present age of light reading, a more direct road to fame."

I at first declined this proposition, saying that he might get others to do more justice to his papers. To this he replied, that I was the only person he had met with in the colonies who shewed a disposition to pursue literature as a profession; and that, if he sent his manuscript to England, its bulk would frighten any Publisher or Editor. Perhaps a few scattered essays might find their way into the periodicals of the day, or a few stories would be trimmed and dressed up by literary caterers for the monthly appetites of readers of magazine; these same purveyors being so utterly ignorant of West India manners, feeling, and even climate, that the most egregious blunders would be introduced into every paragraph. In short, Mr. Arundell prevailed on me to undertake the task which I had suggested to him.

I really believe that his motive for urging me to become the Editor of his production was, that he hoped its publication would be productive of profit to me. This, with a delicacy of feeling which has always characterised him, he never mentioned. One condition alone he attached to the leave he gave me to publish a part of his journal: it was, that whenever I wrote of living persons, or of those recently dead, I should, instead of real, use fictitious names or initials.

The above statement will account, if not apologise, for many defects in this production. When the reader observes some parts of these volumes too much abridged, and others too much extended, he will please to take into consideration the difficulty one has to encounter who attempts to condense into three small volumes the substance of a manuscript closely written on more than three reams of foolscap.

Amongst the many errors in this Work, I throw myself on the mercy of the reader for one class in particular. Mr. Arundell's papers are full of those peculiarities of language which may not improperly be called 'creolisms.'† My wish has been to expunge these, and substitute English words; or, if the story required the creole words to be retained, I have endeavoured to explain them, either in the text or by notes. But, having myself resided for nearly twenty years in the colonies, it is very probable that I have unwittingly copied into these volumes many expressions which will be scarcely understood on the other side of the Atlantic, without having given the necessary information. For this I entreat the indulgence of the liberal. It is difficult to live many years in a country without contracting some of the peculiarities of its dialect or idiom.

I have not a few words to address, not to the English Public in general, but to my fellow Colonists in particular. Not having used the real name of a single person now alive in these islands, should any one on this side of the Atlantic perceive, amongst the numerous pen-and-ink sketches contained in this Work, any delineation which should strike him as having an ugly resemblance to himself, let him not make me accountable for caricaturing him. All I have done has been to select a few out of many of Mr. Arundell's sketches, reduce them to a moderate size, erase the names they bore, substitute other appellations, and fit them for their frames.

After this declaration, I hope no one will give himself the unnecessary trouble of calling on me for *satisfaction* for any remarks contained in the following pages: for, although I was once silly enough to make a voyage to Lospatos,[1][†] to give a young Gentleman, as the term goes, *satisfaction*, — that is to say, to stand up while he twice fired at me, — I have, thank Heaven, lived to see the folly and wickedness of fighting duels to satisfy the caprice of any one. I have now reached the age of forty; a time of life when a man's fighting days, as well as his dancing days, ought to be over — unless he be a soldier or a dancing-master.

---

1. A small island, situated in the Gulf of Paria, between Trinidad and the Main, where duels used frequently to take place. See the 7th chapter of the second volume of this work. [Chapter 31 of this edition.]

VOLUME I

CHAPTER 1.

"Days o' lang syne."
BURNS.[†]

I AM DESCENDED from one of the most ancient English families known in the West Indies. The "Arundells" came to the New World when it was possessed by the Spaniards exclusively. The aboriginal Indians were nearly exterminated; the few of them that remained were powerless; and all Europeans were prohibited by the subjects of the crown of Spain from settling either in these islands or on the neighbouring continent: nor were they even permitted freely to navigate these seas.

When the Arundells first made their precarious lodgment in this part of the globe, they came with a few hardy adventurers, their own countrymen. These met and joined with some Normans and Dutch; and all together essayed to establish a settlement in the island of St. Christopher.[†]

The plantations of these people having been destroyed by the tyrannical Spaniards, the oppressed planters revenged themselves by slaughtering the cattle of the St. Domingo colonists, and by manning small vessels, and retaliating, as freebooters,[1] the cruelties of the Iberians, who gave to those wild bands the names of "Picaroons," and "Bucaniers."

One of the earliest, and not the least valiant, of the freebooters — Christopher Arundell by name — was the progenitor of the author of these memoirs. This rover, under the assumed name of Hurrican, or Harrigan, carried terror amongst the Spaniards, not only in the Atlantic, but also in the Pacific Ocean, until the appellation of the latter became a misnomer.

At length, having amassed an immense fortune, under what may properly be called his *nom de guerre*,[†] he settled in Antigua, married, and had his real name introduced into his marriage contract. This was in accordance

---

1. Freebooter; hence the French Creole term of *flibustier*.

with the custom of bucaniers; hence, formerly, in the West Indies, the following sentence was proverbial, "A man's name is never known until he marries." The vestiges of this custom may still be traced amongst the French creoles,[†] who, in ordinary affairs, are called by, and even sign, one name, and yet, on solemn occasions, subscribe another.

When, in 1713, the inhabitants of Antigua killed the tyrannical and infamous Governor Park,[†] a descendant of this Arundell, who was my great grandfather, was foremost in executing this decree of summary justice.

My father's name was Henry Bearwell Arundell. He, like his ancestors, was what in the West India islands is called an *Antigonian;* and lest the mere English reader should not comprehend this Greek-toned word, I must explain it to mean a native of Antigua, in which island my father possessed considerable property, titles, and honours. For example, he was in the commission both of the peace and of war; being an assistant judge, a brigadier-general of militia, a coroner, and a member of the House of Assembly. Many anecdotes I have heard of him in all those capacities: two or three I will relate, as they serve to illustrate the manners of the colonists in those days.

When his majesty, at that time Prince William Henry,[†] visited Antigua, preparations were made by the militia in order that his royal highness might see with how few blunders it could go through Dundas's eighteen manoeuvres.[2†] The troops mustered in the morning in their *drill* pantaloons,[†] and fiery red and hot jackets (whose very appearance in this torrid climate might cause a scarlet fever), all armed and accoutred, in order to be exercised for the review that was to take place in the evening, to gratify the royal visitor, who was at this time a midshipman in the navy, and, consequently, an excellent judge of military matters.

As the line was forming, my father heard the sergeant-major of the black regiment give, what, time out of mind, was a standing order in all West India militias,[†] which he did in these words: "A you wa no *hab* no shoe no 'tocking, tan in a rear" (*Anglice,* "All you who have neither shoes nor stockings, stand in the rear)." My respected parent conceiving it improper for royalty to review shoeless troops, determined to supply the *extreme* wants of the sable warriors; so, marching them down to his store (warehouse) in St. John's, he caused the whole regiment to screw their splay feet into shoes with which he gratuitously supplied them. Most of

---

2. At that time called the Prussian manoeuvres.

these people having *Guinea feet* (i.e. great toes which stood out at right angles from the foot), felt pain at having them cramped with the work of the cordwainer; but they, notwithstanding, gave three cheers to the generous Brigadier Arundell, because they knew that shoes would give them corns, which might prove useful vouchers that they were of free condition.

This requires explanation. During former wars, when any merchant vessels were captured in those seas, there were often found on board many black and coloured persons. If amongst them any appeared who had corns on their feet, they were deemed free, and treated as prisoners of war: such as unfortunately were destitute of corns, were naturally supposed never to have worn shoes, as shoes were not allowed to be worn in those islands by slaves. *Ergo,* said the salt-water logicians, those who are without corns can't be free; and, accordingly, those who had no corn were sold in the first friendly or neutral islands as slaves, for the benefit of the captors. I have explained this, because I conceived that no European reader ever before heard of the advantages of having corns.

On another occasion, two militia officers, one a Major Morgan, and the other a Captain Hazell, had a dispute. The major told the captain "that he had a dash of the tar-brush on his skin;" that is, his race was tainted by having a slight admixture of African blood in it. This was at that time considered a more infamous reproach than to have said that the father of the captain was hanged; for a man to have in his escutcheon a bend sinister[†] in the form of a gibbet, was a trifle compared to his having on his skin the stain of the "tar-brush." A challenge was the consequence of this affront. The parties went out; and the captain vindicated the purity of his blood by shedding the heart's blood of his opponent. The parties met at Green's Bay, and fired at six paces, before crowds of witnesses; and the major fell, to rise no more.

My father, in his office of coroner, summoned a jury to "sit on the body" of the deceased; and, after hearing all the evidence of the case, charged the jury, whom he enlightened with many a quotation from Coke, Holt, Forster, and Blackstone;[†] for, like most other unprofessional West India gentlemen of the old school,[†] he had what is a most dangerous thing, namely, a little legal learning. These citations were intended to set forth the difference between justifiable homicide, manslaughter, and murder. My worthy parent argued, that if two persons go out and fire at each other, at the "gentlemanly distance" of ten or twelve paces, should one be killed, the survivor could not be considered guilty of murder; because, he said, both parties aiming at each other's life, each one acted *se defendendo,* and that, *ergo,* neither the dead man nor the living one committed a crime. "Nay," argued the learned coroner, "as there are great chances of a man escaping unhurt when fired at with a pistol at twelve paces, when, unfortunately, any one is slain at that distance, the law ought to consider it nothing more than chance-medley,† which Judge Forster derives from *chaud mêlé;* which means a hot mixture. And we all too well know how many duels take place in these islands in consequence of taking too much of hot mixtures. "But, gentlemen," added my father, "the case is very different when two persons stand so near each other as five or six paces, and fire — he who stands at that distance to receive a shot, is morally sure of being killed, so that he commits *felo-de-se;*† while he who shoots him does not kill him fairly, but butchers him. Now, to butcher a man is to slaughter a man; and I need not add, he who slaughters a man is guilty of manslaughter."

Thus argued my father; but the jury took a different view of the case: and, after consuming a great deal of time, and twelve bowls of *sangaree*† in debating the question, whether they should pronounce a verdict of "accidental death," or "died by the Visitation of God," wisely returned the latter verdict, doubtless conceiving, that to be shot in a duel is to receive a divine visitation. The coroner, who, like most men that puzzle themselves into error, was outrageously intolerant of the errors of other people, felt quite indignant at this unreasonable decision, and said he hoped shortly to see the time when he who sent, or carried, or received a challenge, would be considered all equally guilty of murder. On hearing this, Captain Hazell threatened to horsewhip my father. Whatever might be the feelings of the coroner, the creole blood of the Arundells revolted at this insult. My father, despite his own tirade against duelling, that day sent a message to the captain, met him in the evening, and gave him a dangerous wound in the neck, from which Hazell with great difficulty recovered.

But it was as a member of the Antigua House of Assembly† that my worthy father shewed to the greatest advantage. That respectable body, like most other West Indian duodecimo editions of Parliament, from time immemorial claimed a right always to keep up a standing quarrel or two either with the governor or the chief judge, or with both. Whosoever "his excellency," or "his honour," for the time being might be, they were ever with one or both at open warfare; or,

"Nursing their wrath to keep it warm."†

In those disputes, my father was always the colonial

"Hampden, who, with dauntless pride,
The little tyrant of his *isle* withstood."†

Many are the protests kept in the records of the House of Assembly against the ruinous and unprecedented encroachments on the liberty of the subject of some nowforgotten governor, in which my father's name stands at the head of the protesters; and many a ream of paper he consumed in writing home memorials to the secretary of state for the colonies against judges and attorney-generals, no longer remembered.

So great was my father's fame as a senator, that his friends persuaded him to get into parliament. In an evil hour he followed their counsel: he mortgaged an estate he held in St. Kitt's, and another in Antigua, to raise what may be called the sinews of politics as well as of war; and, in 1782, crossed the Atlantic, bought a borough,† and took his seat on the opposition side of the house: this was during Lord Shelburne's† administration.

His first essay in parliamentary debate was rather inauspicious; he made a speech of some length, but without that applause he was wont to command at St. John's, and was replied to by a young member, who made some witty, but rather unjustifiable allusions, about the house being enlightened by a wise man from the west. He further threw out some hints about my parent being a negro-driver,† and the descendant of a bucanier, and then sat down. After this, two or three members rose to rejoin; and, amongst the rest, my father. The speaker considering, perhaps, that as his character had been attacked, he ought to have precedence in reply, therefore pointed to him and wished to call his name, but this the noble speaker could not recollect; so, instead of calling out Mr. Bearwell Arundell, he said Mr. Bear, — and made a sudden pause; which awkward affair convulsed the house with laughter, and gagged my parent.

The following year, Lord Shelburne having been ousted, the coalition administration came in, upon which my father, for a valuable consideration, accepted the Chiltern Hundreds,† and ever after disclaimed against the corruptions of parliament.

Some twelve years after this, a hurricane having injured my father's St. Kitt's and Antigua estates, he was obliged to give them in trust to the mortgagees, Messrs. Keen and Leech, of St. Christopher, and retire to live on a fine plantation he had in Grenada. Here, at an advanced period in life, he married a young lady of the old creole house of Warner; and, notwithstanding the great disparity of age between the parties, they enjoyed, during some months, much domestic happiness.

CHAPTER 2.

"Oh, bloody times!
Whilst lions war and battle for their dens,
Poor harmless lambs abide their enmity."
SHAKESPEARE.[†]

M y father's marriage took place in 1794, and the following year the West Indian colonies were convulsed in an awful manner, from one end to another.

St. Domingo[†] was suffering from the united curses of a servile and a civil war, which terminated, after years of misery, in the extermination of the white colonists, the liberation of the black bondsmen, and the establishment of the worst form of government known — a military tyranny.

Jamaica was ravaged by the maroon war; Martinique, Guadeloupe, and St. Lucia, having been inoculated with the French revolutionary eruption by that barbarous agent of the convention, Victor Hugues,[†] took the infection; the people of these islands acted, on small stages, the bloody tragedies which were performing in Paris. The nominally free blacks were more cruelly beaten than while they were called slaves; but this was done with staves, on which were written *"Liberté et égalité!"*[3] and the scanty population of Trinidad, which, both in manners and language, were more French than Spanish,[†] were ripe for rebellion.

At the same time Victor Hugues sent his agents to St. Vincent and Grenada, these men, in the former island, excited the black Caraibes[4][†] to revolt, who, for many months, desolated that beautiful island; while in Grenada, so well did the emissaries of Hugues succeed, that most of the white French, and by far the greater part of the slaves, free black and coloured population, unfurled the standard of rebellion, and commenced hostilities by treacherously capturing the governor, and fifty of the

---

3. A fact.
4. Black Caraibes, a mixed race from the Caraibes, and a cargo of African slaves said to be wrecked off Bequea.

principal English inhabitants, whom, with the exception of three, they slaughtered in cold blood: a war of the most cruel character was then continued in this island, which threatened to end in the extermination of one of the belligerent parties.

The emissaries of Victor Hugues committed a capital error in intrusting the chief command of the rebellion to a rich coloured proprietor, named Julian Fedon,[†] instead of confiding its conduct to the more energetic Lavallée[†] or the more sagacious Louis La Grenade;[†] both of whom, in common with the former, were mulattoes. Fedon was not destitute of courage and ordinary abilities, but in the former he was inferior to Lavallée; and as to talent, he could not compete with La Grenade.

The French agents chose Fedon, on account of his estates forming a good *point d'appui*.[†] The latter offered to make La Grenade second in command, which offer Louis indignantly refused, and then threw the weight of his power into the scale of the British. Lavallée was then appointed second to Fedon, but was fortunately killed in a broil in his own camp, early in the war. These events were propitious to the English, whose troops, joined by the island militia from the commencement of the rebellion up to the arrival of the immortal Abercrombie,[†] displayed nothing but ineffectual valour, repeatedly suffering themselves to be surprised by their more vigilant enemy. I am obliged to make the above historical sketch of the state of Grenada in 1795, or what follows would be somewhat unintelligible to the reader.

At the beginning of the war my father's estate was desolated, and his young wife and himself narrowly escaped through the fidelity of his slaves, who defended a mountain tract, over which they passed. My parent had long since resigned his rank as brigadier-general, in consequence of some dispute with Governor Home.[†] During this war he acted as a volunteer, in which capacity he took charge of a post on the north side of the island, where a quantity of military stores were deposited: he preferred his comparatively defensive station, as it allowed his being near his beloved wife, who was far advanced in what ladies call an interesting state. No doubt some of my fair readers will exclaim, why not have sent her to a more secure and tranquil place? To which exclamation I may reply, that security and tranquillity were scarcely to be found at that period in the West Indies.

The sun had declined beyond the hills when one of the assistants of the commissary entered my father's apartment; and, with trembling hands, gave him some despatches.

"What is the matter, Conway, you look alarmed?" said my father.

"No wonder," responded Conway; "the negro that brought this said he was five times fired at in passing the guava-bush, within a mile of this post. Gracious me! who would imagine the rebels would dare to approach so near us? But I always said, one day or the other, we should be dislodged, and then who would be able to retreat?"

"You would, at all events; at that part of a soldier's duty you are very active! — but let me peruse this letter. Ah! ah! 'tis from Louis La Grenade. So! so he tells me that, from the movements of Yoyo's[5] partisans, he judges the sansculottes† will make an attempt on this post. Send hither Sergeant Bluit; we shall have warm work this night!"

"God, in his mercy, forbid!"

"Call the sergeant; and, if you can help it, don't let the artillerymen see the miserable state of fear you are in: but I forget, it is your nature, which you cannot help: remain here. Sentry, pass the word there for Sergeant Bluit!"

My father paced the room in agitation.

"Where," said he, "shall I bestow my dear Louisa?"

"I will remain with you, and partake of your danger!" said his wife, who had entered his room unperceived. She added, "you have assured me, love, that the post is impregnable; and, as to the mere report, smoke, and smell of powder — although the first is not music, the second incense, nor the last perfume — yet, woman as I am, I have enough of the blood of the Warners to tolerate them!"

She said this in a calm tone, which strongly contrasted with the cowardice of Conway.

"And do you really anticipate an attack?" said the latter.

"Yes, Conway; we shall have warm work of it, you may swear!"

"*We* have warm work — not *me*! You remember General Lyndsay† placed me in this situation, to assist the commissariat, with my pen, and — "

"Not with your sword! I remember you used to fall in fits at the commencement of every action, until your behaviour caused so much scandal to the militia, that no one would stand next you. Strange that an Irishman, and a gentleman of good family, should have so poor a set of nerves!"

Sergeant Bluit now entered the apartment; my father gave the necessary orders to prepare against surprise; he also consulted with the sergeant as to

---

5. Yoyo, a creole alteration of Joseph.

the safest part of the irregular fort in which to place his wife. At this part of the conference Conway interfered, and reminded my father of an armed schooner,[†] called the Hostess Quickly,[†] which was hired by the government for the service of the commissariat, and which was anchored off the fort.

"Better allow me," said Conway, "to conduct the lady on board, and I will take the greatest care of her."

"And of yourself too, doubtless; it is certainly a safer and more commodious place during the expected attack, than in this imperfect garrison," observed my father.

The lady dissented from the proposition of being sent on board the Hostess Quickly, whose captain was a complete sot; but, after some little persuasion she consented to embark, which she did in a canoe, accompanied by the timid Conway.

The watch was well kept during the night in the fort. About two in the morning, the dark outlines of a body of insurgents were discovered issuing from the neighbouring hills, and stealing along different tracks towards the station. Each little group was followed by negro women,[6] carrying knapsacks — *gyars*,[7†] and ammunition; for, during this war, these members of the *fair* sex were indispensable auxiliaries: no body of rebels moved without this kind of baggage.

"They advance!" whispered Sergeant Bluit; "I'm blowed if it isn't wonderful how quietly they move, considering their rear-guard is composed of women."

The insurgents had now formed themselves into a compact body; they paused, and one of them advanced to reconnoitre; the tall form of this man bespoke him to be the leader, Joseph Cateau, *alias* Yoyo.

"Down with your rifle, Cadjo,"[†] said my father, addressing a Coromantee[†] negro, who, a day before, had deserted from the enemy's camp, and joined the little garrison; "down with your rifle, or you are a dead man! I suspect you. Do you wish to fire, to give your old friends notice that we are awake?"

But the suspicion was ill-founded, — thirst of vengeance, and not treachery, caused the African thus prematurely to level his piece. "Damn

---

6. The negresses of Grenada, during this rebellion, used cheerfully to perform the parts of horses in dragging artillery.

7. *Gyars*, a sort of rude basket, attached to the shoulders, back, and forehead, to carry loads. The name and invention are Indian.

Yoyo," muttered the negro, lowering his arm; "me want for pay him, because he curse my mama in Guinea, and call me black nigger-dog; Goromighty make black man first, white man after; but debil put it in a buckra man and nigger woman head to make (beget) mulatta bastard."[†]

Yoyo now was seen to approach the fort; it was so contrived that no sentinel appeared on his post: the mulatto leader beckoned his party, who approached the garrison, gliding through the darkness as noiselessly as ghosts; they had come within pistol-shot of the walls.

"Steady, boys; musketry and carronades[†] together — fire!" At this order thirty muskets and rifles were discharged; and, at the same moment, a masked battery of three pieces of ordnance vomited their deadly charge of grape and canister[†] amongst the enemy, who, being taken themselves by surprise at the moment they expected to surprise the fort, were thrown into confusion: the fire was, however, returned, with little effect, by a small body of white French soldiers, who shouted *Vive la république!* Some advanced even to the walls, but those could not be surmounted, for the party that carried the scaling-ladders had fled. A few English gunners, under the command of Bluit, served the cannon, which again poured their mortal charge amongst the besiegers, who were obliged to desist from their ill-fated enterprise, and retreat, leaving more than forty of their number dead on the field, and carrying away many wounded.

Cadjo, the deserter from their camp, did not fire with the rest of the besieged, but rose to the top of the ramparts in order to make sure of his aim, whereby he exposed his person, and received three wounds, which did not make him change his position, nor alter the stern glance of his protruded eyes. At each wound his muscles slightly quivered, and he drew his breath sharply: through his clenched teeth, so as to produce a kind of hissing sound, which were the only indications he gave of feeling the balls, although each wound was mortal, so intently was his vengeful search directed to light upon the man who had committed the unpardonable offence of cursing the mother of a Coromantee. At length he discovered Yoyo trying to rally his flying partisans; the African aimed at, and shot him through the head; and then fell himself; having just time to say, "Ah, ah! Yoyo, no go curse me mother again; me go." Here a slight tremor shook his frame, and he expired.

"Well done militia and artillery," said my father, when this brief affair was over; "it will be long ere they will pay us another night visit. Ah! what can that drunken brute, Keating, be doing with the Hostess Quickly? See, he is carrying the sloop round the point. What made him hoist anchor at this hour? perhaps Conway has infected him with his cowardice."

My father's attention was suddenly called off from the schooner by hearing a volley of fire-arms in the neighbouring hills, over which the discomfited rebels had retreated. "Bravo!" he exclaimed; "that fine fellow, La Grenade, is, according to promise, intercepting the retreat of the insurgents."

"May I never see the trunk-maker at the corner of St. Paul's again," cried Bluit, "if the *darkies*[†] and *Johnny Crapaus*[†] an't catching it this here blessed night!"

As conjectured, the intrepid Louis La Grenade had intercepted the retreat of the rebels, amongst whom dreadful havoc was made. Despite his order, his people gave no quarter, not even to the women; such is the nature of a mixed civil and servile war!

Morning broke, and La Grenade arrived to congratulate his brother victors of the garrison; he was, however, concerned for the mysterious disappearance of the schooner.

"Perhaps," said Louis, "Captain Keating is gone round to the carenage;[†] yet, what can be his motive? He is a steady seaman when sober, and sober he must have been last night, for yesterday he sent to me for a little *taffia*,[8] protesting he had not a drop on board; but this I took care to forget to send."

Sergeant Bluit now said that he recollected the last evening, when Conway went on board the Hostess Quickly, he carried a case of curaçoa.[†] On hearing which, my father turned deadly pale.

Several militiamen, who, in disobedience of orders, left the fort to pick up conchs[†] and chip-chips[9†] for their breakfast, now returned with alarm, and stated they had discovered on the beach a part of the body of Conway, dreadfully mutilated by the sharks, the back part of the skull being perforated with a ball. Subsequently the bodies of the captain and several of the crew of the schooner were found, all bearing deep wounds, and all more or less torn by those ravenous fish; and several canoes were seen adrift, which, on being brought ashore, La Grenade identified as belonging to the rebels.

The mysterious disappearance of the Hostess Quickly was now too well explained. During the attack on the post, which was so signally defeated,

---

8. New rum.
9. A sort of shell-fish.

another party of the enemy had boarded the schooner and captured her, doubtless slaying every one on board, save a young man of the name of Smithson, who saved his life by swimming.

Often have I heard La Grenade attempt in vain to describe the agony of my parent for the loss of the wife of his bosom, — the lovely, young, and affectionate wife of his old age: this was so dreadful, that the mulatto wished death, or even insanity, would come to the relief of his friend.

La Grenade at length, partly by force hurried him from the fort, in order to make him go to the capital, St. George's; but shortly after they commenced their journey, accompanied by some partisans, they were attacked by a party of the enemy. A man standing by my father was shot, and fell: this event aroused him to action, he seized the arms of the wounded man, rushed amongst the enemy, and performed such desperate acts of valour, that he seemed possessed with a demon: indeed he was so, possessed by the demon of revenge.

The mulatto leader, though himself as brave as most men, was utterly astonished at the terrible acts of his friend, who, from that time to the end of the war, associated with him in all his enterprises. Grief had paralysed my father, but vengeance aroused him. In so much fear was he held by the insurgents, that they called him *le beque tigre*[†] (the white tiger)

During one of La Grenade's expeditions, the advance-guard, marching amongst the mountains, suddenly came on a party in an *ajupa* (a temporary hut).[†] It was suspected that Fedon was there, which made the advance-guard pour a murderous volley into the ajupa, and all within it fell, either killed or wounded.

On examining the ajupa, it was found (shocking to relate!) that the killed and wounded were all women, who had been employed in a pious purpose; they had been singing a kind of creole requiem over the corpse of a white lady, decently decked in grave gear, and laid out, according to the custom of French creoles, with a crucifix, and a plate containing a fowl's foot with some salt in its breast. The body was supported by a temporary bier, composed of palm-branches (or rather *fronds*), while two resinous brands, in lieu of candles, were blazing at its head and feet.

La Grenade and my father now came up; and the latter, with indescribable emotion, discovered that the corpse was the earthly remains of his beloved wife. He embraced it, and, for the first time since his misfortune, shed a flood of sorrow. He had conjectured that his wife, like most women taken by the enemy, after suffering unutterable cruelty and indignity, had been murdered. The spectacle before him seemed to contradict these fore-bodings, for the corpse bore not the slightest mark of wound or mutilation. On the contrary, it had those gentle, and even beautiful, although pallid traits of countenance, which Shakespeare,[10]† with anatomical truth, describes as shewing the difference between the body of one who died naturally and one who had been murdered — "a timely parted ghost."† Besides, the care bestowed in laying out and attending the body, indicated that the lady's deathbed had not been surrounded by monsters of iniquity. My father felt what Ossian, or Macpherson, called "the joy of grief."†

What a strange composition is man! The very black troops who, in error, fired on defenceless women, employed in a pious purpose, and who, when they discovered their mistake, thought more about the loss of the ammunition expended than of the people slain and wounded, now shed tears at seeing my father recognise the body of his wife.

In silence the troops carried the bier and the corpse through the rugged pass, preceded by a few drums and fifes playing a dead march. This artless procession had a solemn effect as it moved amid the mountains.

---

10. Henry the Sixth, Part II., Act iii., Scene 2.

CHAPTER 3.

"Rest thee, my darling, the time it shall come,
When thy sleep shall be broken by trumpet and drum."†

The protracted and ruinous war of Grenada at length drew towards a close. The great Sir Ralph Abercrombie arrived in the island; and, after complimenting the troops of the line and militia for their bravery, he lamented that, through the procrastination and indecision of their commanders, their valour had not been productive of better results. He reconnoitred the enemy's position, and declared that in twenty-four hours the whole of the strong posts would be in his possession: and he kept his word. By a series of prompt, simultaneous, and masterly manoeuvres, he surrounded the enemy, dislodged, and dispersed them. The blow was most effectual; the rebellion was crushed. After this no effectual stand was made or attempted. Many were killed in pursuit; many were made prisoners; many availed themselves of the pardon offered, on condition of their surrendering within a limited time; while some, who were conscious that they ought to expect no mercy, still concealed themselves in the mountains. The deceived slaves had joined the insurrection, because the mulatto leaders promised to establish in the island liberty and equality; by which they meant, that they, the mulattoes, should be free and equal to the whites, not that the poor negroes should be equal to them. These misguided men returned to their work, singing in creole French,† with melancholy voice,

"*C'est mulatte qui manier nous ça.*"

('Tis the mulattoes who brought us to this.)

How different from the tone they used when, hauling cannon up the hills, they chanted, "Fire in a mountain!"[11]†

---

11. A rebellious negro song.

At this period of affairs, my father one day was sitting in the tent of La Grenade, beside a beautiful lake called the Grand Etang,[†] when an orderly announced the arrival of a flag of truce. "Admit him!" was the order, which was readily obeyed. A negro belonging to the insurgent party was admitted blindfold. He held a long sugar-cane in his hand, to one end of which was appended a fragment of a white shirt, to shew that he came as the bearer of a flag of truce; the other end of the cane the negro was gnawing. The fold was removed from his eyes; and he stood in all the dignity of an African ambassador. His woolly hair had been plentifully dusted with powdered lime, by way of apology for hair-powder. He wore over his cocoa-nut formed head a French cocked-hat, to use a naval phrase, "athwart ships." On this hat was a staring tricolor cockade, on which some literary character of Fedon's camp had written, *"Liberté et égalité."* On a negropennistoun[†] jacket he had a large pair of worsted epauletes. A cartouch-box[†] he wore in front, as a Highlander carries his purse. Under this he had a canvass apron, which reached down to his knees. This was necessary, as, in the most literal sense of the term, he was a *sansculotte.* He also had a bayonet without a scabbard at his side, the point of which, to prevent accidents, was stuck into an Indian corncobb.[†] He was round-shouldered, and so miserably "knock-kneed," that it was wonderful his lower limbs supported his body.

"I say, *compère,*[†] has General Fedon many more such fine troops as you?" asked La Grenade. *Apropos* — comrade, I think I have seen that respectable figure of yours before?"

"Oui, Monsieur Louis," replied the bearer of the flag of truce: "you bin a see me at Massa La Roche's habitation."

"As I live, it is my old friend Quashy![†] I always knew you to be a coward, and how came you in Fedon's army?"

"C'est la faute de Monsieur Victor Hugues; he bin make me a volunteer against my will."

"How did he manage that, *compère?*"

"Ma foi, Monsieur Louis, he take me from massa plantation, and tell me to fight for liberty and 'quality. Me been a tell him me no good for soldier, 'cause me so lame dat me no sabby (cannot) run away. When he heare (hear) me say dis, he call out, 'Ah! bah!' like one man-sheep[12] dat choke wid him fat; 'ha! bah! citoyen!' he say, "'spose you no sabby run

---

12. Man-sheep, in the negro lingo, signifies a ram, as woman-sheep means a ewe. Men and women are often used by negroes as synonymous with male and female. Thus, the Chinese call a male infant a "bull child."

away, you go make the most best soldier in a world. Me want soldier for fight, no for run away; so me no take you *lame* excuse. So him send me to Monsieur Fedon, who make me brave man, 'cause he go shoot me if me coward. But me no like Victor Hugues, 'cause he make Sunday come only once in ten days: that the way French buckra[†] cheat nigger."[13]

"But who sent you with this flag of truce?"

"General Fedon, him send me; but tell me after I bring letter, give Monsieur Arundell no 'casion for come back."

My father opened the letter. While he read this, Louis La Grenade ordered some food and drink to be given to the poor devil, Quashy. The letter alluded to now lies before me. It is written in French; but, having a number of creolisms in it, I prefer translating it rather than giving the reader a mere transcript. It runs thus:—

"The White Tiger doubtless regards Fedon, the mulatto chief, as a monster; but you will say, long after my ignominious death, or banishment from this fair island, that I was not uniformly cruel.

"You remember a brute named Smithson,[†] who, but two years since, came out to Grenada, and was sold on a puncheon to pay his passage. This man, on the public parade, reviled because my skin was brown, reproached me with the vice of my father, and taunted me because my mother was a slave. He would have struck me, but that you interfered, and told him you would resent a blow given to me as though it were aimed at yourself. You called him a contemptible scoundrel for daring to abuse a man of colour who was scarcely allowed to defend himself, although that mulatto was every way his superior. I saw the effects your interference produced on Smithson. He trembled with fear: he was as cowardly as he was tyrannical. I then vowed vengeance against him, and gratitude towards you. My first vow is unfulfilled — my insulter has hitherto escaped me; but I have requited my vow of gratitude towards you. On the night Yoyo attacked your post, I surprised the intoxicated Keating and his sleeping crew. They shared the fate of those who suffer themselves in war to be surprised. Amid the carnage, I heard the voice of a female calling on your name. It was the voice of your wife. A ruffian French sailor had raised his hand against her: a

---

13. Alluding to the total changes in the calendar, and the institution of the decades instead of weeks. The French negroes thought this change was made merely to cheat them out of one day of rest per month.

blow of my cutlass slew him. Your beautiful spouse fell on her knees and embraced mine. I thought on the hour when you vindicated the cause of the poor despised mulatto and I saved her.

"This unhappy war led me such a wandering life, that I never could find a time to restore her in her delicate state of health. But she had every necessary care bestowed on her until she died, while giving birth to her child. I would have caused her to be decently interred, but that the troops of La Grenade butchered the women who were employed in the pious office. However, the infant lives, and draws the milk from the breast of Julie, the nurse of one of my children. I will place your boy in your hands, if you will meet me tomorrow evening, as the sun descends, near the large rock beside the three cocoa-trees, at the nearest bay of St. David's. But be sure to draw off all the troops stationed about there, or never shall you behold the beautiful infant of your age. I fear no treachery from Arundell; but, should any injudicious friend of yours attempt to betray me, the life of your boy shall be sacrificed. Remember the hour is sunset."

"JULIEN FEDON."

On reading the above extraordinary letter, my father remained some minutes absorbed in mental devotion. He then asked La Grenade's opinion as to his mode of proceeding.

"Meet him by all means," said the partisan captain. "I will take care that all the troops be withdrawn from the bay. I do not think he intends treachery. At all events I will be concealed with a party behind the rock, so as to give you succour should the worst happen."

"But you may sacrifice the life of my child?"

"No; I will not appear unless you call my name. I do not wish to entrap poor Fedon. It is not the part of a skilful captain to slay an opposite leader, if the latter happen to be a man of common-place abilities, because his successor may be a superior man. What a choice Victor Hugues made when he appointed Fedon to head the insurrection!"

Had my father been at leisure for reflection, he might have observed a trait of old rivalry in La Grenade's remark. But he was too much absorbed with the thoughts of obtaining his child to pay attention to Louis's jealousy. He agreed to La Grenade's arrangement, and the friends separated for the night.

24

CHAPTER 4.

"What have I gained by this adventure?
A child."

BEAUMONT.†

The sun was sinking in that glorious tabernacle which generally receives him near the equator, when my father stood beside the surfy shore of the little bay, indicated by Fedon as the place of rendezvous. My parent had lulled the suspicion of La Grenade, who was persuaded not to conceal a body of his partisans, as proposed, behind the rock, as it might endanger the life of the child; for Fedon was a proscribed man: Abercrombie had set a price upon his head. If any ambuscade was set near the place of meeting, some one of those who composed it might fire on him for the sake of the reward; and, exposing the mulatto chief to this risk would have been an act of treachery.

The scene where my father stood was solitary and gloomy, for the demon of war had lately traversed the spot, and desolation followed his foot-prints. My father beheld the now set sun, and cast his eyes most anxiously toward the mountainous interior of the island, whence he expected the arrival of the brigand; but he came not. Suddenly a faint dash was heard from the calm sea; my father instantly wheeled round, and beheld Fedon and eight or nine other insurgents at the shore, beside a canoe, which bore marks of being newly made, and very roughly finished: it had, in fact, been constructed by the party who now sat in it, in order to make an attempt at escape. But four days since this frail vessel was the trunk of a tree which vegetated in the neighbouring mountain; and it had only been brought down the previous night, and concealed behind the very rock where Louis La Grenade proposed to place an ambuscade. Had this been the case, the hours of Fedon's life had been brief; but my parent's foresight saved the insurgent leader.

The faint sound which aroused my father's attention was caused by the brigands launching their canoe. Their chief looked cautiously about to see if there were any enemies in view; but my parent and La Grenade had drawn off all the troops from the neighbourhood of the bay, otherwise the situation of Fedon would have been desperate.

The brigand general approached my father, followed by an old negress belonging to the latter, called Phoebe, who had fallen into the hands of the insurgents the night of the capture of the Hostess Quickly. She carried an infant, which Fedon took from her and placed in the arms of my father, who regarded the child with inexpressible feelings of pleasure, and noted, or thought he noted, a resemblance between the features of his child and those of his departed wife: he pressed the child to his bosom, until Phoebe, almost by force, took the babe from him, and enveloped it in a shawl to keep it from the night air.

"Fedon! may God, in his infinite mercy, bless you for this act of humanity!" sobbed my father, grasping the mulatto's dark hand.

"Arundell, I thought not that a man lived who could draw a tear from mine eyes; little thought I that I should weep for a white man; and least of all, that that white man should be a Briton."

"What unhappy event caused you to be the tool of the monster Victor Hugues?"

"You were witness of that event, Arundell. Nay, start not: do you not remember when Smithson, on parade at St. George's, spit on me, and called me a mulatto dog? You must remember it, for you nobly vindicated the cause of the degraded man of colour. That day I retired to the Belvidere plantation, weeping with rage, and cursing my dead parent for having brought me into this world, to be taunted, spurned, and despised by the basest of white men; until a sudden design of vengeance occurred to me, which I immediately prepared to put in execution. And to do this, I loaded two pistols: with one I intended to shoot Smithson, and with the other to blow out my brains: this would have afforded a noble example to my despised brethren. While I was in the act of loading my pistols, there arrived on my estate two agents of Victor Hugues, who at once offered me the means of vindicating my own insult, the insult of my race, and of satisfying my vengeance."

"And your ambition," added my father; "and so, to revenge the disgrace of being affronted by a contemptible wretch, you placed yourself at the head of an insurrection which has deluged this lovely island with blood."

"No; not merely for revenge, and certainly not for ambition, did I consent to become the leader of this war: my object was more noble. I fought for liberty and equality — not as these words are, I find, understood by the hollow-hearted French, but I aimed at emancipating the slaves, although I myself possessed a valuable gang. I wished to make the negro respected despite his inky skin, to induce the mulatto to consider himself a man, although his brown complexion told him he was the son of the tyrannical white man. Yes, Arundell, when I reflect on the myriads brought from Africa, and sacrificed in these islands to European greediness, I sigh when I recollect that I have not in my veins the pure blood of the naked and savage African. Look on these lovely islands: did the Supreme Creator bid them raise their verdant heads from the Atlantic that they should be made altars whereon that insatiate devil, European avarice, should sacrifice millions of the dark children of Guinea, after having immolated the whole race of Indians?

"This archipelago," continued Fedon, "once possessed a numerous and happy progeny; the white man came, and the red children of the Antilles were exterminated. Millions after millions of the dark tribes of Guinea have been brought hither by white men: where are they? They have perished, except a miserable few, who live to give birth to offspring whose inheritance is bondage, whose complexion is reproach." Fedon paused; then added, "Farewell, Grenada! land of my birth, adieu! No more shall I behold your fertile valleys and breezy mountains, unless I get from afar such glimpses of you as the damned get of Paradise."

Saying this, the brigand chief grasped my father's hand, then rushed into his frail canoe, which, in an instant, was propelled out of sight by eight paddles. Scarcely had it disappeared, ere the face of the sea assumed a frowning aspect, its waves blackened and foamed, and the winds moaned over its surface, indicative of the coming storm. At the same instant, from the mountainous centre of the island a loud and long-echoed peal of thunder roared and rebellowed, as though the demon of war gave a parting salute to the chief who had kept the island in a state of commotion for fifteen months.

Phoebe hurried my father and the infant under shelter from the coming tempest; my parent put up a sincere prayer for the safety of the preserver of his child, amid the storm, which raged with awful violence, and to which the desperate insurgents were exposed, in a miserable and scarcely finished canoe, on the bosom of a turbulent ocean.

Nothing further was heard of Fedon by the inhabitants of Grenada; but a few days after, the canoe, upside down, with a compass nailed to its bows, was picked up at sea, which seemed to indicate the fate of the party.

The infant, preserved by the humanity or gratitude of Fedon, is the writer of these pages.

CHAPTER 5.

"Oh! that I were once more a careless child."
COLERIDGE.[†]

I was christened by parson May, a clergyman who was, in the most literal sense of the word, a good defender of his church; for when, during the Grenadian war, the rebels attacked the parish church of St. David's, which was converted into a temporary fort, the worthy minister fought like a hero, while a major of the St. George's militia was on his knees in prayer.

My father had me called by my mother's maiden name: I bore the designation of Warner Arundell.

Such havoc had been made among the women of Grenada by the war, that it was with extreme difficulty my parent procured a nurse for me: this at length was found, in the person of Mrs. M'Shain, the wife of an Irish soldier. During the latter part of the war my father had become very active, for he was spurred by vengeance. After the expulsion of the enemy he lost that stimulus, and naturally fell into his former habits. During his youth and middle age he was of a procrastinating disposition, and, like most creole gentlemen, indolent, save when extraordinary occurrences excited him, on which occasions few men could be more active and indefatigable than he. He had now fallen into "the sere and yellow leaf:"[†] his Grenada estate had been destroyed at the beginning of the insurrection, and he failed to exert his interest to obtain compensation for his losses from the British government. His St. Christopher and Antigua plantations were put out to dry nurse, under the care of Messrs. Keen and Leech of St. Kitts; which gentlemen managed his estates very well for their own interest — for they were honourable men, who never committed an act of injustice towards themselves.

During the war, all my father's papers relative to his Leeward Island plantations were either destroyed or carried off. He might easily have replaced them, by going to St. Kitts and Antigua; but he deferred this from time to time, until he appeared to have forgotten the loss, and at length he could not bring his mind to think of business. His favourite amusement seemed to be ramier[14][†] shooting, which required little activity; as, by sitting all day under the berry-tree on which those splendid birds fed, enough game might be shot to satisfy a good fowler. Yet, indolent as this kind of sport was, his failing energies gradually became insufficient to prosecute it. He then practised a system of shooting which, I believe, has now become obsolete. He used to seat himself in an arm-chair in the pasture along the sea-shore, with one negro holding a large parasol over him, while two or three others drove flocks of sand-larks near him. "Out of the way, boys!" he would say, and then scatter his small-shot amongst the feathered tribe. The earliest recollection I have of my father, is seeing him seated in his easy-chair, with his powdered hair, straight and well-bound tail, a large panama straw hat, green spectacles, white jean pantaloons, and nankeen spenser.[†] His gun, when not levelled, nested against the arms of his chair. On one side of him, on the ground, was placed the now dis-carded punch-bowl, and (by way of sangaree cup) a most ingenious vessel, which, although merely basket-work, was so well wrought that it held any liquid without leaking. It was the fabrication of the celebrated black Caraibe chief, Chatoyer,[†] who presented it to my father during a visit that the latter made to St. Vincent in 1792, accompanied by Sir William Young.[†]

My father's revenue daily decreased. This was derived from a number of negroes belonging to him, who either hired themselves in the capital or on estates, or turned fishermen, chip-chip finders, or land-crab catchers. These people gave my father what they pleased out of their earnings; he scarcely took any account of what his slaves paid him, — sufficient for him was it, that one part of them supplied him with enough to satisfy his immediate wants. The rest waited on him, or waited on each other, or, most properly speaking, waited for each other to work. Thirteen adult slaves and three boys lived in his house: their united labour might have been performed by two or three English domestics. Their time was chiefly spent in eating *wangoo* (boiled Indian corn-flour), fish, land-crabs, and yams;[†] sleeping; beating the African drum, composed of a barrel, covered with a goat's skin; dancing, quarrelling, and making love after their own

---

14. The ramier of Grenada, and that of Trinidad, are two most beautiful species of wild pigeon.

peculiar mode, their notions of the tender passion being very similar to that of Tom Pipes in "Peregrine Pickle."[†]

When any work was to be done, mutual accusations were bandied from one to another for a long time ere the job was set about, if it ever was commenced. If a gentleman arrived on a visit to my father, ere one could be persuaded to take his mule or horse into the stable, the female part of the establishment were obliged to call their male fellows in bondage, lazy black *raskels*, which the latter resented by ungallantly designating the ladies black female dogs; and these criminations and recriminations generally lasted half-an-hour, ere the *buckra's* beast was taken out of the sun.

Yet, with all the faults of these poor people, I should be unjust did I fail to acknowledge that, to my father and myself, they were most affectionately attached. My parent, like most creole gentlemen of the old school, had high notions with regard to the absolute authority of an owner over his slaves; yet, like most creoles, was an indulgent master and more under the influence of his bond-servants than he himself was aware of, or than the mere European would believe. When in comparative prosperity, he was kind to his domestics, which they gratefully recollected when age weighed down his energies, and adversity clouded his approach to the grave.

In our house, there was not the slightest appearance of what the people of England (rich in terms of domestic economy) call tidiness; yet, nothing touching the comfort of my father or myself was neglected. Scipio was our *valet du corps* at table; he used to watch my father's appetite with as much anxiety as a young physician observes the appearance of his first patient. If my parent shewed less than ordinary relish for his food, he (Scipio) used to become (to use his own expression) *blue bex*; although, how a negro could become blue vexed, is in vain to inquire: but wo[t] betide cook Cæsar if my father disapproved of the fish-soup, or if the green turtle was over or under dressed; he would, if that happened, leave the hall in which we dined, dart into the cook-room (kitchen), and, if he did not break Cæsar's head with the kitchen-ladle, he would fracture the latter with Cæsar's tough and wool-defended cranium. Should Mass Warner (myself) appear puny, this circumstance would cause a choral anathema to be poured from the throats of the whole female part of the establishment, in every key from C minor, to F alto, which discordant notes were intended for the ears of old Phoebe, whom they would accuse of negligence towards me, and whose black mother in Guinea they would execrate. Strange to say, the first reproach one negro generally makes to another is respecting the sableness of their skin; thus verifying the adage of the kettle calling the pot smutty names.

Sometimes it was imagined by this dark coterie, that my nurse, Mrs. M'Shain, obliged me to apply too studiously to the lessons in reading and writing which she gave me: when those suspicions were awoke, the whole black train, men, women, and children, would give tongue to the worthy Irishwoman, calling her a white cockroach,[15†] and flat-footed buckra,[16] and telling her she would kill poor Mass Warner with "read," and make him "learn book till he grow double." Of these there was little cause of fear: poor Mrs. M'Shain was tenderly attached to her foster-child; and as to my growing double, considering my age, I was as tall and as upright as an Indian corn-stem.

I was most fortunate in having so kind a nurse. Through the doating affection of my father, he would never suffer me to be sent to school; so that, but for this worthy woman, I should have passed my infancy without necessary instruction.

She was the wife of a soldier, but had received a tolerable education; her husband had kept a small shop in Sligo,† until he commenced clandestinely to deal in whisky made by people of short memory; that is, who always forget, if not their own duty, at least the duty of his majesty. From selling illicit spirits, he took to drinking them, which caused him to neglect his shop, until his landlord seized his stock in trade to pay his rent. Whisky, the cause of his misfortune, became his consolation, until, at the Sligo fair, a recruiting serjeant, whose tongue had come in contact with the stone of Blarney, drew such a picture of the salubrity, riches, and beauty of the West Indies, and the joys of the life of a soldier in those colonies, that he induced M'Shain to enter into one of the regiments going out with Sir Christopher Grey's expedition. His worthy wife followed his fortunes. She had a child born about the same time that I first saw the light, who died the day after my father received me from Fedon: hence she supplied the place of a wet-nurse. She was, therefore, taken from the degraded situation of a camp-follower, and placed by my father in his own house, where her husband occasionally used to visit her. He, partly through good conduct and partly through bloody wars and sickly seasons, obtained promotion to the rank of a lance-corporal; and, no doubt, he would have obtained further preferment, but for an unfortunate discovery he made;

---

15. A name of reproach for a white person.
16. A European of low origin.

namely, he found out that rum had a strong resemblance to whisky: hence he was too often seen in the canteen, where new rum, improved by having tobacco infused into it, consigned him to the hospital; and, in those days, from the military hospital to a soldier's grave, was the brief and general route. Poor M'Shain died by that poison commonly sold in West Indian canteens, and which, during the last war, killed more British soldiers than did balls, bayonets, or yellow fever.[†]

After the death of her husband, my nurse became more attached to me than ever.

But, to return to my father's slaves:— those who worked out, although they seldom paid above a tithe of what they gained, never failed to bring to their master some little present for himself or young massa. If a fine chicken-turtle,[†] a large grouper,[†] or delicious rock-hynd,[†] was caught by any of our fishermen, no price would tempt them to sell it; no price would tempt them to sell it; no, it must be sent or brought as a present to massa. The finest pine-apples, sappotillas,[†] or shaddocks,[†] that could be gathered, or even pilfered, by our people, were continually sent to Massa Warner; in short, if my father received little money from his slaves, he wanted little, and fared sumptuously in consequence of the presents he received, and these were always given with pride.

Two of our people had acted so bravely in saving my parents' lives at the beginning of the war, that my father emancipated them; another, named Cuffy, had performed such signal service as a guide and partisan, that the local government purchased his liberty. Yet, these three free men treated us, if possible, with more respect and affection than even our slaves. I verily believe those men would have fasted a whole day, ere they would allow us to be without any luxury they could procure. Cuffy was a creole of Herculean stature and strength; and, withal, as brave as he was powerful. Wo betide the black or coloured man in Grenada who would refuse assent to Cuffy's continual assertion, — namely, that the extinction of the rebellion was owing to the skill and bravery of his late master.

None of our slaves would ever hear us talked slightingly of while they had the power of firing a lick (making a blow), or hitting a butt,[17] at the calumniator. He who dared say aught against Massa Arundell in the presence of any of his negroes, generally suffered assault and battery.

---

17. Negroes and creoles generally fight more with their heads than hands.

CHAPTER 6.

"Last scene of all,
That ends this strange eventful history,
Is second childishness, and mere oblivion."
SHAKESPEARE.†

M y father gradually sunk into a state of lethargy; his fowling-piece was laid aside, and he used to spend hours gazing affectionately at me; now and then a mournful observation would escape him, which seemed to be predicative of my future destination. His once large fortune had now melted down into a small competence; and, as he foresaw I should have a long minority, he judged that what little property he could bequeath me, would be wasted ere I became of age; for, in the West Indies, the property of minors was wont to be managed so well by the administrators as to have given rise to a proverb; viz. "Appoint me to be your executor, and I care not whom you constitute your heir."

Sometimes, after gazing at me so perseveringly and doatingly, he would break his long and melancholy silence with brief, but mournful observations, such as these: "Late marriages make early orphans." "Poor Warner! you came into this world amid troubles, woes, and dangers, and your life will correspond with your birth." I was but seven years old when I heard him frequently make those observations: at that time I knew not their import, but I have often since then thought of them, when misfortune laid her leaden hand on me: how far they were prophetic, the reader will be able to judge.

At length, age and sorrow confined my father to his bed, on which he was visited by a French emigrant, who, during the late troubles in Grenada, was fortunate enough to choose the right party, that is to say, the party which ultimately was successful, and by this choice he saved his estate.

He advised my father to send for *le médecin* D'Alentour, who had lately arrived in the colony. I must say a word or two of this learned Theban.[†]

D'Alentour was a Frenchman, who, for some political offence or jealousy, was sent to perish amid the pestilential swamps of Cayenne,[†] whence he escaped to this island. Having a prepossessing appearance, and that sort of tact for imitating their superiors with which most Frenchmen of the humble orders of society are endowed, the pretensions to noble blood, which he did not fail to advance, were admitted by most persons whom he met in Grenada. He who possessed a good stock of impudence could bring that commodity to no better market than the West Indies, and this D'Alentour soon discovered. He pompously asked several colonists, in which of the learned professions a gentleman was most likely to succeed, as he could easily qualify himself for the pulpit, the bar, or the practice of medicine: that is to say, he proposed turning a priest, without knowing a word of Latin; becoming a lawyer, without understanding a syllable of the language in which the laws of the land were written; or, finally, getting a license to kill, without knowing a bone in the human body. This last profession he fixed on.

Dr. D'Alentour came to my father's bed-side, took snuff with the grace of one who had a Warwick Lane[†] dispensation to break the sixth commandment, felt the patient's pulse with the adroitness of an Edinburgh professor of physic, and

"Having three times shook his head,

To stir his wit up, thus he said:"[†]

"Ma foi! I wish I had been called in sooner," (which, doubtless, he did, as he would have made his bill longer). "Monsieur Arundell," he continued, "has got a severe *coup d'air*," — which term is a generic name amongst the French of the West Indies for all that numerous class of diseases which attack men, women, and children, on those parts of their bodies situated between the crowns of their head and the soles of their feet.

The doctor ordered my father[†] to wash his legs with eau de Cologne, tie round his temples the leaves of the *Palma Christi*,[†] and take every hour a spoonful of what he called magnesia-water, which he thus prepared:— He mixed an ounce of calcined magnesia in a pint of water, and, on the mixture settling, drew off the clear liquid. Now, as the water could not, in nature, contain much of the medicine, the patient might as well have taken the former ere it was mixed. But, it may be said in favour of

Dr. D'Alentour, that if his prescriptions did no good, they did no harm;[†] and I wish all medical practitioners could claim equal negative merit. Nay, as watching the hour by the chamber-clock, to direct him in taking the "magnesia-water," afforded some amusement to my worthy parent, I verily believe that the doctor's visits might have been of some service to him, but that he suffered, at one and the same time, from the effects of two disorders, to neither of which it was in the power of science or quackery to minister; I mean, old age, and a mind diseased.[†]

The next remedy administered by this professor of the art of killing, was a dose of what he called "tincture of cream-of-tartar," which he prepared by mixing a gill[†] of brandy with an ounce of cream-of-tartar, and then straining off the spirit. Now, as cream-of-tartar is no more soluble in spirit than powdered granite, the medicine did as much good as did the flint in the soup, as recorded by Joe Miller,[†] or some such classic. The patient drank the cognac neat as imported; and, being little accustomed to drink raw spirits, the "tincture" increased his lethargy. An English friend of my father advised him to call in the aid of Mr. Martin, the assistant-surgeon[†] of the neighbouring garrison, who had of late been successful in treating the officers who had the *sangaree*, and the men who had the rum fever. But Dr. D'Alentour dissented from this, alleging that "he could not consult with Martin, because the latter was only a surgeon, whilst he (Dr. D'Alentour) was a physician;[†] and that the patient's case was not a surgical one." Urging, further, that he had no means of consulting with Martin, because he (Martin) was so ignorant that he could not speak French," — this modest man not recollecting that surgeon Martin might, with equal right, have upbraided him with ignorance in not being able to converse in the English language.

"I would propose," added D'Alentour, "to hold our conference in Latin; but the English pronounce Latin so barbarously, that no civilised nation can understand them. Mais," added the doctor, "nous autres Français prononçons la langue Latine avec le veritable accent du pays Latin!"[†] Be it known that Dr. D'Alentour knew as much of Latin as of Chinese.

While riding home, the doctor met with a former patient, by name Coteau, whom he had attended while attacked with bilious fever,[†] but whom he left when he supposed he was dying, and who, nevertheless, on Martin being called in, recovered. Dr. D'Alentour expressed surprise at seeing the late sick man well, after he had pronounced his sentence of death. Coteau explained, that after he was given over by D'Alentour, he called in Martin, who gave him other medicine than *eau de magnésie*,[†] and *teinture de créme-de-tartre.*[†]

"What did he give you?" asked the sapient doctor.

"Ma foi, replied Coteau, "he poured calomel[†] into me until he drove away the fever. I am now nearly well; but I have so much mercury in my bones, that I am a living barometer. In short, I can't touch a dollar or a joe[†] without their turning as black as a silver spoon boiled in poisonous fish.[18][†] *Bon jour, monsieur le médecin;"* and, saying this, his former patient left him, and turned up to his small coffee plantation.

Left to himself, D'Alentour resolved to follow Martin's plan, and administer calomel. Without considering, according to the creole parable, that "What cures a ratcatcher kills an overseer," he prepared a large box of calomel pills, and sent them to my father, with directions to take one each hour throughout the day. Ere half the contents of the box was taken, salivation ensued, which so debilitated the poor patient that he died. His skilful physician arrived while he was expiring; shook his head; said that the case was desperate; but sagely observed, that had my father been a younger man, and possessed of a stronger constitution, he might have recovered.

---

18. In most of the West India islands certain fish, such as the dolphin, grouper, cavally, &c., are sometimes poisonous, owing, as some say, to the copper-banks, or, as others affirm, to the mamanilla-apples[†] on which they feed; and hence there is a custom of boiling a silver spoon, or other piece of plate, with fish. If the silver turns black, the fish is thrown away, as unfit for food.

CHAPTER 7.

"Do all we can,
Death is a man
Who never spareth none."

P.P. THE PARISH CLERK.[†]

A West Indian funeral has fewer of the trappings of wo than a European interment. In Europe, the custom of keeping the corpse unburied for a week or two after death, allows the ceremonious mourners time to rehearse their parts, while the first paroxysms of wo of those who sincerely grieve for the deceased have somewhat abated; but this ardent clime prevents our keeping the mortal remains of the departed above ground for more than a few brief hours, or, at the furthest, for more than a day. Little preparation can be, therefore, made for the mournful occasion. Here, we hear of the sickness of a friend in the morning, and receive an invitation to his funeral that very evening. The relatives of the deceased appear overwhelmed with the first and full flood of sorrow; and those mockeries of wo, hired mourners and mutes, are here unknown. The acquaintances of the deceased often appear at the funeral in coloured garments, the time sufficing not to allow them to furnish themselves with black habiliments. But, although they have not the livery, they have, in general, the looks of wo. In the West Indies, the progress of the angel of death is terrifically rapid; and ghastly corruption closely pursues his gloomy flight. Hence, in these islands, those who follow the remains of a late friend to the "house appointed for all," look, in general, more under the influence of awe than do European attendants on a funeral.

My father's mortal remains were followed by many friends, and by all his slaves, whose grief, though brief, was yet violent and sincere. He, having been a brigadier-general of militia, was buried with what are called military honours; that is to say, the solemnity of the burial-ground was disturbed with three vollies of musketry and artillery, instruments mounted by man, for the Christian purpose of destroying his fellow-creatures. The day after the funeral, the Hawk, sloop of war,[†] anchored in the carenage. The vessel brought my uncle, George Arundell, from Trinidad. He was my father's younger brother, who inherited some property in St. Christopher; but, being of a roving disposition, he obtained a commission in a regiment which had originally been raised in St. Domingo during the time the British made their ineffectual descent on that noble island. This regiment was composed principally of those colonists who wished to favour the English ascendancy in Hayti; and who, when the fortunes of war made the British abandon their enterprise, followed the standard of St. George,[†] as much from necessity as from choice.

My uncle having been with his regiment at the reduction of Trinidad,[†] he found that magnificent island so fertile, that when, in consequence of the diminution of French influence in the Caribbean Seas, the profession of arms became here less exciting and promotion went on less rapidly, he sold his commission, as well as his St. Kitt's estates, and became a Trinidad planter. He had heard of my father's mortal indisposition, and, sailing hither, he arrived a day after his brother's interment.

Our meeting was affectionate; he was a good-humoured, kind-hearted man, although somewhat eccentric. He seemed to think the great object of a gentleman's existence was to acquire dexterity in the use of arms; and hence, he never went even the shortest distance from home without foils, masques, gloves, pistols, &c. &c. I would not have the reader imagine by this that he was one of those pests of society called duellists; no, he had too much benevolence in his disposition to admit of his becoming one of that fraternity: he merely practised with the foil or pistol through such motives as induce peaceable people in England to fee a great, strong, vulgar-looking fellow, with crooked fingers and broken nose, to box them soundly, because it is possible that the tyro may, at some period of his life, find it necessary to box some one else. The fact was, the officers of my uncle's regiment were men of desperate prospects and ruined fortunes; and hence duels among them were so common, that they became shunned as dangerous men amongst societies whose humblest members, down to the very tailors and carpenters, settled their disputes according to the laws of honour.[19]

---

19. In the Island of Trinidad, I knew an instance of a tailor and carpenter going out: the affair terminated by the former being mortally, and the latter dangerously, wounded.

My uncle George had too often acted bravely in the field to leave a doubt of his courage on the minds of his brother officers. He was too good-humoured to be quarrelsome, and was a complete adept in the use of arms, which reasons combined to render him the only gentleman in his regiment who had never either sent or received a challenge.

After shedding a few tears over the grave of his elder brother, my uncle placed the remains of my father's shattered Grenada fortune in the hands of Messrs. Flint and Sharp, merchants of St. George's, gentlemen very like Messrs. Keen and Leech of St. Kitt's, who had, to use a Cockney's expression, "done for" my father's St. Christopher and Antigua estates; or who, as we say here, were good hands at "draining" plantations. The former firm so managed matters, that, although my slaves were much harder worked after than during my father's lifetime, yet I seldom got a sixpence through their exertion. They were all employed about the house, store, and plantation, and on board of the shipping of Messrs. Flint and Sharp; yet, so heavy were the doctor's and nurse's bills for them when sick, and so trifling were their earnings to me when in health, that the "succession of Bearwell Arundell" always appeared on the debtor side of the books of Messrs. Flint and Sharp; and the debts so augmented in the course of years, that those respectable gentlemen were obliged to bring my slaves to the hammer to pay off the debts incurred by them, their head clerk buying them in, and the next day transferring them to the house: and it is remarkable, that when they became the property of Flint and Sharp, they were considered the most valuable slaves in Grenada. I relate this matter for the information of the European reader, for those of the West Indies well know, that minors' property in these islands has this peculiarity — it never prospers until it becomes that of the executors.

My father's Grenada estates being, as my worthy uncle aptly said, settled (as a man is said to be settled after having his brains knocked out), he commenced examining into the state of my education, which, thanks to Mrs. M'Shain, was respectable for a boy of my age. I could read fluently, write a fine hand, and knew the four first rules of arithmetic; besides which acquirements, I could swim, ride a donkey, and talk creole French, which was as much my mother tongue as English.

"Can you stand fire, Warner?" asked my uncle George.

I replied, that I had never tried.

"What!" said my uncle, with astonishment, "never taught to stand fire! My poor, dear child, how your education has been neglected! who ever before heard of a boy of eight years of age, brought up in a Christian country, without being able to stand fire? Why, my dear Warner, your cousin Amelia, when she was a year younger than you are, would, without winking, suffer me to shoot a sappotilla from off her flaxen head; and she could handle her pistol dextrously before she finished her first sampler."

Having expressed my willingness to learn, my uncle placed a wine-glass in my hand, which he bid me hold by the foot, with the tips of my finger, with my arm extended in an horizontal direction: he then retired about twelve paces from me, and cocked a loaded duelling-pistol.

"Now, dear Warner," said he, "steady! look at me, not at the glass; don't allow your hand to shake — the pistol is only loaded with powder; look straight at me, not at the glass: so —" bang went the pistol, which, as he said, was only loaded with powder. "Bravo!" he exclaimed; "you are steady under fire; and now, hold it once more, for the other pistol. Steady, again; open your eyes and shut your mouth and see what the pistol will send you."

Again the pistol went off; but this time there was a ball in it; for I, at one and the same moment, saw the flash, heard the report, and felt the glass break in my hand, my uncle having struck it on the rim.

"Bravo! my dearest child; you are a true Arundell," said my relative, embracing me with as much ardour as though I had learned the most difficult and useful lesson.

In order further "to teach the young idea how to shoot,"[†] he brought from his trunk a pair of pistols of about seven inches in length of barrel, and shewed me how to charge and discharge them; at first with corks, and then with bullets. In the course of that day and the next, I became so dexterous in the use of the "marking irons," that my uncle and myself contrived to break every glass in the house, and were, consequently, reduced to drink out of calabashes and cocoa-nut shells,[†] until a fresh supply could be procured from town.

My uncle next taught me fencing, together with a little negro, whom he instructed purposely, in order that I might contend with one of my own size. Owing to those lessons, and to subsequent practice, I have seldom met with one who could compete with me in fencing, and certainly never with any one who surpassed me in the dexterous use of fire-arms.

This necessary part of my West Indian education being completed, my uncle proposed to send me from the land of my birth to the land of my father's — namely, to Antigua; for, at this period, there was scarcely a good school in Grenada. To get me to the latter island, however, was no easy undertaking; for, at this period, the Caribbean seas were infested with privateers.[†] But Lieutenant Rotherham, of his majesty's ship Hawk, coming round to Guave,[†] near which bay was my father's house situated, he offered my uncle, to give me a passage to Antigua: he had orders to cruise amongst the islands for some weeks, and then sail for English Harbour, at that time the general rendezvous of men-of-war.

No objections were started to my making a voyage amongst the Antilles, as it was judged good for my health. True it is I was free from all kinds of disease; but I shot up so tall for my age, that, as my worthy nurse and preceptress, Mrs. M'Shain, expressed it, "she was afraid I might outgrow my strength." This kind-hearted woman entreated, and was permitted, to accompany me; she seemed to have for me all the affection that a widowed mother has for her only son.

CHAPTER 8.

"O'er the glad waters of the dark blue sea,
Our thoughts as boundless and our souls as free."
BYRON.[†]

I took leave of my uncle, and of the slaves, with such tears as a child
sheds; and, accompanied by my nurse, embarked on board his
majesty's ship Hawk. She weighed anchor, and stood out for sea, making a
serpentine course among the Grenadines, an immense number of little
islands lying about and between Grenada and St. Vincent.

I experienced little seasickness, and had, therefore, leisure to look about
me. I remember what struck me the most was the extraordinary difference
between men-of-war sailors on board, and the same men on shore. I had
often noted them when they were rambling up the country on "liberty"
(leave of absence), running about as frolicksome and thoughtless as boys
just let loose from school; capering, as though the island was scarcely big
enough for their "land-cruise," and calling the negroes "darkies," "snow-
balls," and "tea-pots;" while the latter would in return denominate them:
"Jack tâ," and mimick their expressions; such as, "I say, darkie, gi us a
junk[†] of sugar-stick," as, they call the sugar-cane. Yet, the negro and the
man-of-war's-man are uniformly good friends, because the latter are the
only white men who, in these colonies, will drink with slaves: both, too, in
common, love a good-humoured laugh; and each looks on the other with
kindness and pity, unalloyed with contempt.

But how different are sailors on board ship! The fact is, the business of
a seaman is far from being of that light nature which we, "who live at
home at ease,"[†] are too proud to suppose. So much is there to be learned
ere one can become an able seaman, that, to be master of the profession
of a sailor it is absolutely necessary to be a man of good sense. I am
aware that much of the steadiness of the British sailor is owing to the rigid

43

discipline kept up in the navy; yet, whoever has observed the countenance of the English sailor during a storm, a chase, or a battle, and noted the quickness of his eye, the lines of deep thought his visage displays, and his calm, grave, yet intrepid demeanour, must allow him to be a very different sort of man from the frolicksome being his gambols on shore would seem to indicate.

We quickly passed the Island of Cariacou,[†] with its sugar estates. The oval-formed Union Island[†] displayed its undulating and verdant land, looking like consolidated waves of the ocean. Mayaro[†] and Canaan,[†] with their cotton plantations, disappeared before us, and at night we lay becalmed off St. Vincent.

A shore-boat came off to us with despatches from Governor Bentinck,[†] which informed our captain that a French privateer lugger,[†] called the Sansculotte, carrying only three guns, but full of men, had lately been doing much mischief amongst the small craft navigating amid three Grenadines.

Lieutenant Rotherham could not avail himself of this information until the morning, on account of the calm; but with the sun arose a fair breeze, and away darted the Hawk in quest of her quarry, taking her flight round the islands and rocks between St. Vincent and Canaan, but without success; and at length we put into the bay of the latter island. Here came on board a Scotch gentleman named Allardice, the owner of a cotton plantation in the island, who informed Rotherham that, from an elevation of his estate, he had seen the privateer off the point to leeward, and bearing towards Mayaro; at the same time introducing to the captain a good-looking Mahomedan negro, named Sayebe, a fisherman, well able to act as a pilot amongst the Grenadines.

"I," said Mr. Allardice, "will pledge myself for his fidelity; he served under me as a ranger during the Caraibe war,[†] and has no reason to favour the French. But, away with you — you have not a moment to lose."

The ship was put about, and in a few minutes we were clear of Canaan harbour. Scarcely was this the case, ere the Sansculotte appeared in sight, right to leeward, and bearing towards Mayaro. A moderate breeze was blowing, every stitch of canvass was hoisted by the Hawk, as well as by the chase; but it soon became apparent that the Sansculotte would be captured if she continued running before the wind, for we were gaining on her, as the sailors express it, hand over hand: she, therefore, hauled her wind, and stood towards Union Island. The Hawk immediately did the same, occasionally firing her long Tom[†] at the lugger with some effect; although, standing on a wind, she was rather gaining on the sloop-of-war.

Off the end of Union Island there is an islet, or rather rock, called Prune. Between this and the island there is a hazardous passage, so narrow that it would seem impracticable to any thing larger than a good-sized boat; but this passage the privateer, in its desperate situation, resolved to try, to the astonishment of Rotherham, who now proposed running down to the leeward of Union Island, and cutting her off as she came out of Prune Passage, as it is called. The pilot opposed this, assuring the commander that he would arrive at the other side of the passage too late to cut off the lugger. The negro cast his eyes upwards to consult the appearance of the weather, and then said, —

"In a few moments it will be nearly calm: this, I well know. It is flood-tide — there is room enough — if you wish to take the lugger, you must follow her through that passage: there is space and water enough; and by the time we are in, the wind will have died away, and we can then warp[†] her through."

"What!" said Rotherham, "carry the Hawk into that narrow creek! Impossible!"

"Shorten your sail, and get a kedge[†] over your stern; and, if I do not bring the ship safely through the passage, blow out my brains."

There was an earnestness in the black pilot's manner that convinced Rotherham of his good faith. In an instant he acceded to his proposal; the sails were shortened; Rotherham himself took the helm; and in a few minutes the Hawk was in the Prune Passage, standing after her chase, to the manifest dismay of the latter. "It appeared to me, that, had the Hawk been one foot wider across the beam, she would actually have struck and been jammed between the rocks of Union and Prune. Here and there the passage widened; when it did, the breakers were seen to fling their white foam against the sides of the Hawk, as though the waters of the creek were displeased at her intrusion.

The long Tom was now discharged at the lugger with such fearful precision, that a loud crash, accompanied with piercing shrieks, followed the thunder of the cannon; producing frightful echoes among the rocks, to which the startled galdings[†] and fishhawks responded. At this instant, the crew of the Sansculotte became desperate. Her anchor was cast; she had no room to swing round; and her stern lodged on the rocks: by which manoeuvre the captain of the privateer endangered both his own and his enemy's vessel, whose destruction he contemplated by it. But it had been foreseen and provided against by the commander of the Hawk; and, accordingly, in an instant every stitch of canvass, save her flying-gib,[†] was let go, streaming in the light air, which, as the pilot had foretold, had nearly died away. She ran down the passage with a gentle course; her kedge, or stream-anchor, being thrown over her stern, just brought her up as her bowsprit came within a few feet of the lugger, whose crew had abandoned her and sought refuge on Prune Rock; while the steady seamen of the Hawk, with sweeps and spars, kept their ship off the rocks on both sides of the creek.

In less than a minute, a part of the Hawk's crew were on board the privateer. These active fellows soon cut her cables and warped her off the rocks. One of her boats was lowered over her bows, by which she was safely towed into the open sea, followed by the Hawk.

Fortune favoured the enterprise. Had the wind, contrary to Sayeb's calculation, not languished into a calm, the injury, if not the destruction, of both vessels would have been inevitable; but the knowledge of the weather which the fishermen amongst the Grenadines possess, is astonishing. The parties who now go shooting amongst the islets, view with wonder this passage, rendered memorable by the capture of the Sansculotte.

The Mahomedan slave having assured Rotherham that the crew of the lugger could not escape from the rock, on which there was not a drop of water to be found to sustain life, the latter gave himself no trouble at all about them; but, in the evening, they appeared, hailing the Hawk, and hosting a shirt on a stick, and then lowering it by way of signal of surrender. They were soon brought off, guarded by a few marines.

On the arrival of the prisoners on board, our captain wished to speak to them; but not one of them understood English.

"Pass the word," said Rotherham, "for any one on board who can *parley vouze Français.*"

No one answered, until I stepped up and said, I could speak French. The fact is, I spoke the jargon called in these islands, "creole French," a lingo principally made up of corrupt French, but mixed with African, Spanish, and English words. However, this *patois*[†] is the mother tongue of about a million and a half of people in this part of the world. Fortunately for my credit as a linguist, most of the privateer's men had been long enough amongst the islands to learn the lingo alluded to, so that I did duty as a good interpreter. I pleased the commander, and the crew, and myself, by shewing I was of use on board. To use a creole expression, "I looked on myself as somebody." I became such a favourite with the officers and men, that it was said of me, and a great Newfoundland dog on board, that "we were in everybody's mess, but in nobody's watch."

CHAPTER 9.

"Near fair St. Vincent, quite unknown to fame,
An island stands, and Bequia is its name."
LINES IN THE *ST. VINCENT GAZETTE*.†

I n the course of the afternoon, I overheard a conversation between
Lieutenant Rotherham, and the black pilot, which made a strong
impression on my mind. The lieutenant was so pleased with the man's
conduct, that he proposed to him to buy his manumission, provided the
pilot would volunteer to serve in the Hawk; to which the negro objected.
He frankly, but respectfully, told Rotherham, that he did not wish to
change one kind of slavery for another, — for in such light the negro
regarded the discipline of a man-of-war. Any service he might be considered to have rendered as a pilot, he would thankfully receive payment for
on his arrival at St. Vincent; "But as to my freedom," added the pilot,
"that I shall obtain when it pleases Allah to take my young master from a
troublesome world." The tone of deep devotion with which the negro said
this, interested the commander and other officers, who proceeded gradually to draw from him his history; of which I shall give, as concisely as possible, the particulars.

Sayeb was a Mandingo of the tribe called *Foulahs*;† he had been captured in war, and hurried down to the mouth of the Senegal, and there
embarked on board of a slaver. He resolved, rather than remain in the
hands of *Caffres* (heathens),† to commit suicide; but, conceiving it would
be sinful to mutilate one of Allah's chosen creatures, he resolved to kill
himself by abstaining from food, and actually remained without taking any
sustenance for three days; nor could persuasion, threats, nor force, cause
him to change his resolution, until the surgeon of the vessel, who spoke
the corrupt Arabic of his race, dissuaded him from it, by convincing him of
the sinfulness of self-destruction. The medical man promised him his
friendship: this promise he kept. During the voyage he distinguished him

from the rest of the slaves on board; and never obliged the Mahomedan to eat or drink aught forbidden by the Koran.

On the arrival of the cargo of *human cattle* at St. Vincent, the doctor settled in the island, and bought Sayeb, whom he made his confidential domestic. This confidence was well merited by the grateful African. Sayeb took unto himself a wife of his nation, by whom he had several children.

On the breaking out of the Caraibe war, the savages, and their scarcely more humane comrades, the French brigands, murdered Sayeb's wife and children, together with the family of his kind master, save one child, who concealed himself in a cane-piece. Having one common cause of enmity, Sayeb and his master fought bravely, side by side. On one occasion the slave was desperately wounded, and the master stood over the disabled negro, and bravely kept him from falling into the hands of the barbarous foe; on whose retreat, the surgeon carried him off in his arms. Sayeb recovered from his wounds; but his master, during the progress of the war, received a ball in his body, which decided his fate. Ere he died, the Mahomedan swore to protect his only child: this vow he faithfully performed. He worked for the child as though it had been his own son. So successful were his labours as a pilot and fisherman, that he gave his young master a good education. Poor Sayeb could himself read a little Arabic, and was, therefore, not unacquainted with the advantage of letters.

"It had pleased Allah," he said, "to visit his young master with a dreadful affliction." In fact, the poor boy had that most loathsome and incurable malady — the leprosy, and was obliged to go and live remote from man; on the little islet called "Petty Nevis;"† but his faithful Mahomedan never forsook him, nor ever allowed him to want for anything which the negro could procure, or the diseased youth required.

The story of poor Sayeb affected the commander and officers of the Hawk so much, that, in addition to a handsome gratuity for his services, a liberal subscription was made for his benefit, in which most of the seamen joined, when informed of the affection the poor slave had evinced for his afflicted master.

"What a pity," said the surgeon of the vessel, who was a Scotchman, "so good and sensible a man should be doomed to perdition on account of his being a Mahomedan!"

I was at that time little of a theologian — I am not now a profound one; but I then thought, and have since continued to think, that the man who conscientiously follows the religion of his fathers, and fulfils his duties to his God and to his fellow-men to the best of his abilities and limited know-ledge, will never be doomed by his merciful Creator to eternal perdition.

★   ★   ★   ★   ★

Night came on, the winds were light, and the Hawk, with her prize in tow, glided on amongst the Grenadines. The silver moon threw her trembling reflection on the deep blue surface of the Caribbean Sea, and made the salt-crowned rocks and islets appear covered with a robe of whiteness. When I first beheld in Europe a winter landscape, with its clothing of snow, it reminded me of this scene.

After kissing my nurse, and begging her blessing, I retired to my berth. I heard the long-drawn "Allahoo" of the Mandingo negro, as he, with mellow voice, chanted his evening prayer to the God of Mahomet. The tones of his devotion had a solemn effect even on those who knew not one word of that most magnificent language, Arabic.

At length the copious prayers of the Mahomedan set me asleep; and that, too, so soundly, that it was not till I awoke the next morning, that I became aware of a severe tempest that had overtaken the Hawk in the night, and considerably damaged her sails and rigging, as well as those of her prize.

The little island called Bequia[†] being under our lee, our commander ran into its fine harbour, called Admiralty Bay, to refit. In this island there lived, and I hope still lives, a family bearing my paternal name; one of whom invited my nurse and myself to pass our time on shore at his house, whilst the Hawk refitted.

Bequia owns the completest specimen of white creoles that I have ever met with in the West Indies. These live at the west end of the island. They are a slender race, with flaxen hair, keen grey eyes, deeply sunk in their orbits, with skins as white as chalk, save where the sun has freckled them; and the freckles in their faces and hands bear as great a proportion to the white parts as the holes in a crumpet bear to the even part of the cake. These freckles give them a kind of pepper and salt coloured complexion. They have just as much muscle as prevents the sharp edges of their bones from cutting through their skins, but this muscle is as tough and dry as whipcord. They are a hardy, active, hospitable, and thoughtless race, who indulge in intemperance without a headache, enjoy indolence without *ennui*, and are pugnacious without being malicious.

Each family of them has one or two slaves, who live on terms of equality with it. They cultivate a little cotton and provisions; or, as they call it, "bread-koind;" but their principal dependance is on their fishing, the finny tribe that swim around their island plentifully supplying their tables. Their best friend, however, is the hawk's-bill turtle, the shell of which is hoarded up by them; and once a-year, or oftener, the head of the family procures a passage on board a drogher[†] to St. Vincent, where he disposes of it. It then finds its way to England, where it is called (I know not for what reason) "tortoise-shell." With the proceeds of this shell, the Bequian buys a quantity of lines and cords, sufficient to keep his nets in order, and as much dry goods as his family requires; and with the residue of his cash he purchases a puncheon of liquid fire, commonly called rum, with which to give a "jollification." This only finishes with the contents of the cask, after which he spends two or three days in allowing a few wounds on his cranium to heal, and then soberly recommences his cotton cultivation, his fishing, and his turtle-catching. The destructive and irreclaimable vice of solitary intoxication is foreign to his habits.

Their dance is peculiar to them: they use two or three negro drums, beaten with their hands; and these produce monotonous notes, to which they dance with more agility than grace, though not entirely without the latter. The male dancers carry what they call a beau-stick, which is a heavy piece of cinnamon-wood, not thicker than that which the humane law of England allows a man to beat his wife withal, and about thirty inches in length; and with this beau-stick, they, at irregular intervals, strike at each other, still keeping time to their rude music. The person struck at generally is active enough to ward off the blow; otherwise, the only check the stick receives is on its encounter with the head, limbs, or body of the party aimed at, who takes the matter in excellent part retaliating on the striker, or "firing a lick" at some other person near him. The dexterity displayed in warding off blows, and the good-humour shewed when they receive them, are astonishing.

As the *taffia* (new rum) circulates, the mirth and fun grow fast and furious; the combat darkens, the blows thicken, sticks and heads rattle; until, amid laughter, the lights are extinguished, and thwack! thwack! thwack! resounds, each laying about him without seeing, knowing, or caring whom he strikes. Those whose heads are made of penetrable stuff now make a rush towards the door, or bolt through the sides of the fragile, wattled house. All this is done in the best possible temper. Such are the humours of a west-end Bequia "jollification."

The cotton-planters of Bequia have a high notion of honour; and this I shall best exemplify, by relating the particulars of an encounter I witnessed.

A Bequian, named Derrick, was caulking his boat, aided by his negro. They had been quarrelling, as it appeared; for, as I came up, the African said, "You take 'vantage ob me, 'cause me *is* one poor slave; 'spose me been free, you no go tell me so."

"What!" said the master, throwing down his caulking-mallet, "do you *rââly* think I'd tell a slave what I'd be afraid to say to a free man? I'll put myself on a footing with you, as I would not own a man I am afraid of. Come on," said the cotton-planter, putting himself in a boxing attitude; "if you behave like a coward, I'll flog you like a dog; but, if you licks me like a man, I'll give you a joe."[20]

"I call on you, little buckra," said the slave, addressing me, — "I call on you to be my *wickedness* (witness) that massa wants me for fight him. Remember this, if it come before justice."

At hearing this, the cotton planter looked a sublime picture of Grenadine rage and offended dignity.

"You infernal blood of a ———! when did you ever know me, Jack Derrick, to be fond of justice? (he meant law). Put down your mallet, and fight like a man!"

Fight they did, but not like men; they fought like enraged bulls.

> "Ac velut ingenti Silâ, summove Taburno,
> Cum duo conversis inimica inpraelia tauri
> Frontibus incurrant." — VIRGIL.[†]

Each looked scowlingly at the other, and then walked back several paces, with their chins resting on their breasts; and then, at one and the same instant, both rushed forward, their organs of combativeness (situated opposite to where Gall places them),[†] encountering with a most violent shock. Some years after this, I heard an officer recount that, at the siege of Badajos,[†] two shells, fired from opposing batteries, met mid-way in their flight, burst, and spread destruction around them; on hearing which, I thought of the encounter of the heads of Jack Derrick and his slave. The simile, however, was incomplete; the shells burst, but the *crania* were of a less fragile material.

---

20. A johonnes, eight dollars.

Dire and long was the conflict; the heads, knees, and unshod feet of the combatants, were much used, but their hands very little; save when each tried to get hold of his opponent's ears; in order, as he expressed it, to *"butt his brains out!"*

During a pause in the fight, a brother planter, named Simmonds, brought Derrick a large glass of grog, who drank half of it, and then, with a chivalric air, handed the remainder to his slave, saying, "Here, drink half with me. I'll take no advantage of you; I'll beat you fairly, or you shall me." The grog finished, the ram-like encounter recommenced.

The African had the more strength, but the creole the more activity, of the two: the black possessed better wind, but the white more bottom. At length the Bequia Mollineux[†] fell, and declined further combat; on which his master, after kneeling down and inspecting his bleeding head, bid him go to his mistress and get his wounds and mouth washed with rum; cautioning him not to swallow more than a mustard-phial of it, and further advised him to *pay his skull with glue.*

The negro went; on which Derrick threw off his light cotton dress, took a bath in the sea, dressed, and went to his work, as if nothing had happened to him; but, by this time, his spouse had appeared on the late scene of action.

"Is this the way you treats your poor slave?" said the enraged virago. "You only has one neger to fetch your children a pail of *wââter,* and you beats his head till it's as soft as a boiled pumpkin!"

"No such thing," replied the husband; "I fought him fairly; he is made of good stuff; I would not take a hundred joes for him."

But, not wishing to hear any more of this affair, I now passed on.

CHAPTER 10.

"Ihn sagt es sey nichts als glluck,
Zu siegen ohne die taktik;
Dotch besser ohne taktik siegen,
Als mit derselben unterliegen."[21†]
TYROLESE SONG.

The Hawk having been refitted, we embarked, and stood out of Admiralty Bay to cross the channel to St. Vincent; but, the wind proving contrary, we had a long passage across that rough channel.

Mr. Allardice of Canaan was on board, and entered into conversation with the commander on the subject of the late Caraibe war in St. Vincent, as both had been actively employed in that affair. The lieutenant severely criticised both the conduct of those who commanded the militia and the regulars during that war, in marching with their drums beating, and their colours flying, to fight a savage enemy who crouched like foxes, and glided like serpents, from their foes; yet, at unexpected times, darted like rattlesnakes upon their less vigilant, but better disciplined enemy.

"Whenever," said Rotherham, "the lobster-backs† beat, it was owing to their courage; but whenever the darkies and brownies† got the better, it was caused by the soldiers fighting with tactics against a cunning enemy who defied all tactics, and against whom tactics could be of no avail."

From talking of the war generally, they spoke of many events and anecdotes that each, and sometimes both, had been concerned in. One of those occurrences was the taking and retaking of Dorsetshire Hill, a

---

21. This may be done into English thus:
"You say 'tis nought but luck alone
Makes those beat whom no tactic sown;
Better, without, the foe to beat,
Than with those tactics to retreat."

fortress on a mountain which commands Kingston,[†] the capital of St. Vincent, in which affair the commander of the Hawk had borne a conspicuous part. I will relate it, as nearly as I can recollect, in Rotherham's own words:—

"It was midnight — the Hawk was anchored off Fort Charlotte,[†] and I was waiting on the governor for orders; when his son, Colonel Seton, rushed into the room panting for want of breath (like a grampus[†] coming up to blow), with his face begrimed with powder, as sooty as Jack in the dust, and with three musket-ball holes through his hat.

" 'What are you doing here?' said the governor.

" 'Dorsetshire Hill is taken!' said the colonel.

" 'What! Dorsetshire Hill taken by a set of undisciplined savages; while a son of mine, with a regular force, had the charge of it!'

" 'We fought,' said young Seton, 'while our ammunition lasted; we killed twice our own number, and then charged our way out of the fort with our bayonets.'

" 'Dorsetshire Hill taken!' again cried the old man. 'The wretches must never remain in possession of it until daybreak, or the island will be lost. You shall have plenty of ammunition; Foster's Regulars, Whytell's Militia, and Seath's Rangers, shall assist you. Return, sir, and ere day allows the savages to look down on Kingston, exposed to their mercy, retake the fort. Do this, or never more return.'

" 'My men,' said the colonel, 'are disheartened and exhausted.'

" 'Dare a son of mine,' said the old man sternly, rising from his seat, — 'dare a son of mine stand there, when I bid him begone to retrieve his lost honour; and start obstacles, when it is his duty to devise expedients? Have I begot a coward to disgrace my old age?'

" 'Coward!' proudly echoed the son, casting a look of offended pride, at the old man, and leaving the room.

"The governor looked after his son, then, clenched his hands, and strode across the room several times: at length he paused suddenly, and exclaimed, 'He *will* fall! my boy *will* perish! My son, the prop of my age, I have sent on a murderous expedition, whence he will return no more. But it is no fault of mine: my honour — his own honour requires the sacrifice: yet, would to God we had not parted in anger!'

"At this juncture I ventured to speak to him; but scarcely could I say, 'Your excellency,' when the old man turned round, and looked surprised and displeased at my having been in the room to notice his agitation.

" 'Well, sir,' said he, sternly, 'what do *you* want?'

" 'Merely,' said I, 'to ask your excellency's permission to allow me to join Colonel Seton with the seamen of the Hawk; we may be of some use to him.'

" 'You have my permission,' said the old man; 'it is an excellent idea; perhaps you may save my son — I mean, take the fort.'

"He then grasped my hand; and I hastened from his presence, and in a crack collected my lads. With the permission of young Seton, I led the way, we having a negro guide before us. At each step of the steep track leading from Kingston to Dorsetshire Hill, we expected to meet a sentry on the look-out, but the devil a man did we meet. The fact is, the Caraibes and brigands, after the capture of the post, found a large cargo of spirits stowed away, with which they spliced the main brace; and were as merry and groggy as tars at Portsmouth Point[†] after taking a Spanish galleon.[†] We could hear their songs and laughter a mile off. They had entirely forgotten to set the watch on deck; so up we went until we reached the ramparts, where we perceived a black Caraibe three sheets in the wind,[†] who steered from a sentry-box, carrying a gun athwart his shoulder as a milk-maid carries her yoke. As agreed, we all fell flat on our faces; while Bill Weighton, our boatswain, advanced, with the intention of getting the weathergage of the sentry, and clapping a stopper on his muzzle before he could give the alarm. Bill was a humorous fellow: he was such a mimic that he could imitate any voice or sound. He had blackened his face and his hands; and as it was that part of the West India day which is darkest — I mean, just afore twilight appears — he might have passed off well enough for a black nigger. So he advanced on the Caraibe.

" 'Wha come da?' cried the half-drunk savage. 'Stop da! 'spose you stand, me chuck (stab) you; 'spose you run away, me shot a you! Let me see wha you go do.'

"Now, to threaten to bayonet a man if he stand, and to shoot him if he run, is to place a man in a quandary, or, as our schoolmaster used to call it, a 'dilemma;' and so Bill answered the darky in his own jargon, coolly crying out:

" 'Me no da stand, me no da run, but me da come for bring you a lille (little) taffia.'[†]

" 'Ah!' answered the savage, 'him bin de right tuff (stuff).'

" 'Dat you go know when you taste um,' said Bill, handing the savage a large flask of strong rum, without which the boatswain seldom left the

Hawk. The Caraibe grounded his musket, took the flask, put it to his thick lips, and was taking a long pull; but, while the liquor was glucking down his throat, Bill seized his neck with the force of a screwjack.[†] I heard a kind of a gurgling noise, as the strong rum, and stronger grip of the boatswain, choked the Indian; and a blow from my cutlass settled the fellow, who fell without a groan.

"We passed without noise into the fort, and surprised the enemy in the midst of their carousal. It was no fight — it was a mere regular slaughter; and in a few moments the fort was cleared of the enemy. As day appeared, we hoisted the colours of Old England on the flagstaff; and, as the morning-breeze fanned the ensign of St. George, we hailed it with three cheers, which were replied to from below by the inhabitants of Kingston, who were overjoyed to see the fortress again in the possession of their countrymen. Twice, during that night, had Dorsetshire Hill changed masters. Never shall I forget the meeting of the old and young Seton. The colonel looked proudly, yet affectionately, at his father; and the old man so far forgot the soldier, that he wept like a father on seeing in safety his wronged but victorious son."

CHAPTER 11.

"Thou, too, would crowd the lovely scene,
  Delightful garden of the West,
  Clear are thy streams, thy valleys green,
  Majestic is thy woody crest."
  STANZAS ON THE GRENADINES.†

T he wind at length favoured us; we passed the frowning rocks and batteries of Fort Charlotte, and entered Kingston Harbour, a beautiful
and deep bay, well protected by that fort, and one on the opposite side,
bearing the poetical denomination of "Fort Old Woman." Dorsetshire Hill
guards the town to landward.

The first view of St. Vincent's is magnificent: its noble mountains rise
in masses, each higher than the one before it; until the mountains of the
centre, crowned with mists, seem to look down with majesty upon the
subject hills around, which gradually decrease in height, until they
approach the Caribbean Sea, whose deep blue waves fling their snowy
foam, conch-shells, sponges, marine eggs,† and white coral, at their feet.
The fertile plains and vales are hidden by these mountains, which have
perpetual verdure: yet, owing to the cultivation of their bases, sides, and
even summits, and the ever-varying kaleidoscope of light and shade caused
by the shifting clouds, the surface of this island has a singularly party-
coloured appearance; and, when the traveller looks from its elevations, his
eye is gratified with the sight of the Grenadines, which, although no longer
fertile, are so beautifully placed and so fantastically formed, that they
heighten in an eminent degree the beauty of the sea-view; while a hundred
vessels, sailing among those countless islets and rocks, appear like gigantic
bees hovering about their hives.

Lieutenant Rotherham having borrowed a pony for me, we rode in
company over several parts of the island: we visited the botanical garden,

established at a vast expense, by government, but abandoned subsequently, to the reproach of the *generous* inhabitants of St. Vincent. We made an expedition to those fertile plains in that part of the island called the Caraibe country, and then newly brought into sugar cultivation: we inspected the awfully grand and tremendous crater called the Soufriere,[22†] which, a few years after this, opened its terrific jaws, and blew from its infernal throat a burning flood, which spread ruin over the island, and affright amongst the windward Caribbean islands.

We also climbed to the summit of the mountain called the Bonhomme, preceded by a negro guide, who called our attention to a brief but very pleasing song of some invisible bird; our cicerone informing us, that, although this song was ever heard on the Bon-homme, and no where else, yet, so shy was the songster that it never was seen by human eye: indeed, our guide expressed some doubts of its being a bird at all.

I asked him if he thought it was a *jumby* (spirit).

"May be," responded the negro; "although some think it a little snake, and others say it is a lizard: but, whatever it is, its song is ever heard here, and no one ever saw the singer."

Whether this tradition, which is pretty generally believed, be, or be not founded in fact, I cannot determine. To use the proverb of the negro, "I sell the story for the same price I bought it."[†] The invisible songster would form an excellent subject for a poem, to any one capable of writing it.

Mentioning poetry reminds me of an eccentric character whom we met while riding from Caliagua to Kingston. He was a middle-aged man, of rather corpulent form, short, with little fat hands, short feet, and high insteps, as though balls of flesh had been added to them; and, on the whole, his person had more of the appearance of a globe than of any thing human I ever beheld. His dress was singular, and most inappropriate for a West Indian climate; it consisting of a green round jacket,[†] buckskin inexpressibles,[†] top-boots, and a little round wig: his fat cheeks, and soldier's allowance of mouth, appeared to have been often moved by mirth; and his little gray eyes seemed to correspond with his risible features. Altogether, his visage declared that he was no child of wo; but, on the contrary, that he looked on the world as pleasantly as rhymsters generally do. Real poets appear to be a care-worn race; but, in general, poetasters live on excellent

---

22. A general name for a volcanic mountain in the West Indies.

terms with themselves. The former think profoundly, to please others; while the latter think, superficially, to please themselves.

Rotherham asked this original the road to Kingston, who immediately answered, —

"To Kingston, the road
Is easily *shewed*;
Mark but this track, the way it goes,
Open your eyes, and follow your nose.

"Excuse me, sir; but, having the gift of versification, I sometimes use it too frequently. I, sir, 'look through nature up to nature's God,'[†] not through the green spectacles of prose, but through the telescope of divine poesy."

The lieutenant complimented him on his ready rhymes, as well as on his apt quotation.

"True, sir," said the poetaster, "I have read a little; and, as for rhymes, I can make one off hand for any word in the English language."

"Can you make a rhyme for *silver*?" asked Rotherham.

The man of verse now checked the mule he rode, paused for about fifteen seconds, and then delivered the following stanza:—

"Winter clothes Albion with *silver*,
　　Unlike the hot clime of this isle;
Fleecy looks the land *until ver-*
　　Dure of spring makes nature smile."[†]

"You see, sir," said the poetic tailor (for such was),

"'The poet's eye, in a fine frenzy rolling,'
often glances at a lucky thought."[†]

We were now joined by a gentleman whom the lieutenant recognised as a physician, and who saluted us, and then said to the man of rhymes, —

"Well, Dickson, you are, I suppose, entertaining the lieutenant, and delighting this young gentleman, with your verses?"

"Yes, doctor," was the reply; "I left no calling for this idle trade, for I stick to the shop.

"But who, to dumb forgetfulness a prey,
　　This pleasing anxious being ere resigned,

Left the warm precincts of the cheerful day,
    Nor left one poem, verse, or rhyme behind?"[†]

"I know not," said the doctor, "whether to admire most your extemporary rhymes, apt quotations, or judicious alterations: but what, Dickson,
makes you wear that hot dress and, above all, in this sultry weather?"

"Habit, sir, habit — all dress is habit (ha! ha! a good one that); but I've
worn a wig ever since I left home: I believe there is more in a wig than you
suppose. Why, sir, I believe our colonial judges would be wiser, and our
lawyers more learned, if they wore wigs: how grave and lion-like the lord-
chancellor looks in his wig! and, captain, even your profession might be
rendered more noble in appearance by wearing peri-wigs,[†] as every one
knows who has seen that beautiful specimen of art, the monument of Sir
Cloudesley Shovel.[†] What can look more graceful than the figure of the
admiral, thrown on shore from the wreck, with his immense periwig on his
head? I wrote a poem on the degeneracy of the navy, since seamen left off
wearing wigs, and substituted little pigtails. It begins thus:—

"Sir Cloudesley Shovel looks so big,
    In his full flowing periwig;
Not such rats'-tails as they wear now,
    Sticking out at their ears like the bristles of a sow."

The doctor now spurred his horse into a trot, evidently to get rid of the
rhymes of the tailor, for he seemed to be inclined to proceed to a great
length with his poem. The lieutenant spurred his horse into a canter; my
little pony got into a gallop; while the tailor whipped his mule to keep up
with us, at the same time continuing to recite his beautiful verses — but at
length ceased, either through lack of breath or verses; on which the doctor
pulled up his horse, and we followed his example.

The tailor now turned up a little road to leave us; but, before he did so,
said, "Good bye, gentlemen: if you should visit Kingston to-morrow, be at
the court-house; my action against Rose comes on. I plead my own cause;
and that impudent little fellow, Carr, is opposed to me: he threatens to cut
me up; 'for, e'en though vanquished, he can argue still.'[†] I've not forgotten
his conduct during the Caraibe war.

"Full measure for measure I'll give to this knave,
    If he makes me a *butt*, why, I'll give him a *stave!*"

The little tailor now left us.

"A singular character this," said Rotherham.

"He is as singular as he seems," replied the doctor: "I served with him during the Caraibe war, and must say, in spite of the proverb which makes tailors ninth-parts of humanity,[†] that he is a good man; a braver little fellow never drew trigger. He kept our detachment alive, with his doggrel verses and mis-applied quotations. The lawyer he talks of as about to oppose him is a scurrilous dog, and, withal, a coward. On the night of the famous affair of Dorsetshire Hill, he was; as the marshal says, *'non est inventus.'*[†] We might have concluded he had been killed, but that we knew him to be too great a poltroon to expose himself. What had become of him no one could conjecture, until the poetical tailor dragged him out from under a newly-tarred canoe, amid peals of laughter. This, Carr has never forgiven; and, no doubt, to-morrow will give the man of rhymes a severe handling, for old enmity's sake; but he'll get what the tailor calls 'measure for measure.' If you have time, I'd advise your being at the trial."

We took the doctor's advice, and next day went to the courthouse.

As I do not write these memoirs merely for the West Indian reader, I shall often be obliged to pause in my narrative, to give to those who have never visited these islands, explanations which such as have resided here will find unnecessary. The latter have my full permission to pass over any such explanatory passages, the generosity of which permission, to skip whole paragraphs, can only be appreciated by the learned; that is to say, all who write that they may see themselves in print.

But now to my explanations. From time immemorial, it has been the custom to allow to the lawyers of these islands a latitude in abusing their learned brethren to whom they are opposed, as well as the suitors and witnesses, which the gentlemen of the long robe in Westminster Hall[†] seldom indulge in. I know a contemptible little wretch here, who has not sufficient talent to make a respectable parish-clerk; who has too little honesty for an exciseman; who has repeatedly been detected in the most nefarious transactions; and who lives in the open violation of all the decencies of life, — I say, I have heard this miserable creature utter the most revolting falsehoods against the character of as honourable a soldier as ever bore his majesty's commission. I also knew an old gentleman of the bar, so remarkable for the fluency, violence, and bitterness of his invectives, that, as a last threat, it was common for an enraged dun to tell his close-fisted debtor, "If you do not settle your account, I will fee old ——— to *blackguard* you."

Such being the practice of the West India bar, it is not surprising that the parties abused often have recourse to what, in most places, is called 'club-law;' but what, in St. Vincent, is called 'cinnamon-law.'[23] Thus are lawyers often exposed to serious quarrels; and hence, to be a good advocate here, requires a man of some personal bravery; and it is not more necessary for him to study 'Tidd's Practice of Pleading,' than to practise at a mark is. 'Coke on Littleton,' and 'Wood's Institutes,' are scarcely as essential to him as are Mortimer's hairtriggers.[†] These circumstances, and the diminutive size of legal libraries in the West Indies, gave rise to a proverb which runs thus:— "A lawyer's tools are, — 'Blackstone's Commentaries,'[†] and a brace of pistols!"

John Felix Carr, the lawyer who was opposed to the rhyming tailor, possessed little personal courage, as the story of his being dragged from under the fresh-tarred canoe testified; but, whatever he wanted in that bravery which is here essential for the practice of law, he lacked not scurrility.

The action in which the man of rhyme was plaintiff, was to recover a sum of money for clothes made to order. An attempt was to set up a defence on the plea of overcharge, but it failed: however, it afforded the defendant's counsel an opportunity of speaking, which the latter shamefully abused: indeed, seldom have I heard such a flood of invective as was poured out by Carr against the knight of the thimble. His dress, personal appearance, misapplied quotations, and, above all, his doggrel verses, were ridiculed most unmercifully; when, at length, the lawyer sat down, having exhausted his copious vocabulary of scurrility.

All eyes were now fixed on the tailor, who pleaded his own cause. He rose to make his reply, and, fixing a stern glance on the lawyer, said, —

"John Felix Carr,
You run me very hard at the bar;
but when I smelt *powder*, you smelt *tar*."

In an instant the tables were turned on the gentleman of the long robe: peals after peals of immoderate and uncontrollable laughter burst from every part of the court-house at this grotesque allusion to the well-known and luckless canoe adventure of Carr. Spectators, lawyers, and even judges, joined in the general chorus of cachinnation: all save the tailor, and

---

23. A stick of cinnamon, or cassia-tree, is the weapon generally used to convince lawyers that they are in the wrong.

the person whose exploit the triplet celebrated; the former eying the latter with looks of defiance and triumph, while John Felix Carr indicated by his appearance that he wished for a trap-door by which he might sink down to the antipodes. The poet's victory was complete — he gained his cause.

Just as the next trial commenced, the court was interrupted by a singular event. It was the last of the week, and, as usual at this time of the war, beef was scarce and dear: several days before, an advertisement informed the good people of Kingston, that on the Saturday, here would be slaughtered a cattle.[24] This unfortunate cattle happened to be a superannuated bull, who, on the Island of Canaan, was the patriarch of many a horned quadruped; and the poor animal, having served his master long, perhaps conceived it was not altogether correct to be dragged to the shambles[†] in his old age. The court of law stood very conveniently on the ground-floor of a house in the same square with the slaughter-house: the bull, doubtless, thought he had a right to appeal to the hall of justice; and so he broke his halter, crossed the square at a gallop, and forthwith burst into the court-house, amid astonished judges, jurymen, lawyers, witnesses, suitors, and the whole host of woolly-headed auditory which generally attend a West Indian tribunal.

Here was a scene "easier imagined than described;" here was a novel and unexpected plaintiff, that would not be *browbeaten*. The tables were turned in a literal sense, and with them their loads of papers and ink-stands in one chaotic mass; whilst lawyers, judges, and spectators, rushed out of the doors, and sprang through the windows. The court was cleared as quickly as though Beelzebub, *in propriâ personâ*,[†] had appeared to claim his own.

This event was what Scotch lawyers would call *charge of horning*.[†] Most fortunately, however, it happened that the bull was neither guilty of assault nor battery; he merely contented himself with appearing in court and protesting against his ill treatment, which he did by standing on the floor, lowering his head, extending his tail, and lowing both loud and deep: perhaps he was *cowed* by the novelty of his situation. Several butchers soon followed him into the court, and tried to turn him out. He would not allow them to enforce their writ of *habeas corpus*; he stood there lowing and stamping, as immovable as a chancery suit.

---

24. In the West Indies the word cattle is not applied to all tame animals of pasture, but only to the neat kind.[†] The word is here used in the singular number: a cattle, although not good English, is good creole.

This ridiculous scene was at length terminated. Above the court-house was kept a quantity of militia arms and ammunition. Lieutenant Rotherham and the poetic tailor, having loaded two muskets, descended into the court-house, fired at, and killed the bull, whose foaming blood copiously stained the hall of justice. I need scarcely add that, after the decision of this extraordinary case, no other trial came on that day.

CHAPTER 12.

"With haste
To their known station cheerfully they go;
And, all at once disdaining to be last,
Solicit every gale to meet the foe."
DRYDEN.[†]

I again embarked on board the Hawk, who was ordered to cruise amongst the singular crescent formed by the Caribbean Islands, for a week or two previous to her going to Antigua. On the eighth day of our cruise, while we lay off the insalubrious island of St. Lucia,[†] we received information that a fine French brig of war,[†] called Le Premier Consul, was amongst the islands, upon which we ran down to "the Saints,"[†] where we discovered a brig to leeward of us, which, as it afterwards appeared, mistook us for a merchantman,[†] and immediately beat up to windward as if in chase of us. Rotherham manoeuvred so as to keep the weather-gage[†] of the enemy, and yet seem endeavouring to escape, which was done to deceive the Frenchman, our commander judging that the brig of war could outsail us. Suddenly, when the vessels were near enough, the Hawk altered her course and ran down to Le Premier Consul to engage her; upon which the latter, discovering her error, shewed a disposition to escape; but, finding flight impracticable, she began the engagement by pouring a broadside into the Hawk, as the latter came within range of her guns.

Prior to this, my nurse and myself were ordered into the cockpit: the order Mrs. M'Shain obeyed, but I evaded. There was a lad on board of the name of Jack Thompson, a midshipman, and son of the purser, who, although several years older than myself, was scarcely my height. Between us there naturally arose such a friendship as boys are capable of feeling. Just before I was ordered below we had the following conversation:—

"Now," said he; "Warner, we shall see glorious fun; *we* shall take the *mounseers*, see if we don't. I am stationed here to see that the boys are smart with the ammunition: it will be such a *lark!*"

"But," said I, "are you not afraid?"

"Afraid!" he ejaculated; "no; the *mounseers* are afraid of *us!*"

When I heard a lad not my size declare that the enemy was afraid of us, by which pronoun he included himself, I felt an inclination to see what he called the *glorious fun*. I asked my friend if I could remain on deck.

"To be sure you can; the skipper won't notice you; and if the *Johnny Crapeau* should board, I'll protect you!"

Saying which, he touched his little square-dirk,[†] and looked an inch taller. On deck I remained with Jack Thompson, to see what he called the larks: but the enemy's broadside convinced me there was no *fun* in the matter; it drove three of our ports into one, and killed and wounded several men and one officer.

"Don't mind it, Warner," whispered the undaunted little Jack, on his observing me turn pale; "you'll see such a *go* just now."

"Don't return their fire," said the commander; "let them go on, we'll pay them off just now. Ready about; raise tacks and sheets; mainsail haul; let go, and haul."[†]

All these orders were given with coolness; and obeyed with alacrity, while the enemy was blazing at us. Round went the Hawk; and, while she lay with her waist-guns almost touching the stern of the enemy; she backed her main-topsail,[†] and poured into Le Premier Consul a destructive broadside, the effect of which was murderous. The enemy replied with two stern-chasers,[†] but their effect was insignificant compared with that of the guns of the Hawk, whose position was such that the artillery of her whole broadside swept the length of her opponent's deck; upon which the Frenchman strove hard to get from his disadvantageous situation, but this he did not effect until he was most severely cut up.

Although a mere child at the time, yet I well recollect the sensation I felt on this occasion, when I first saw the men strip themselves of every article of their clothes save their trousers, and gird their loins as tight as they could with their handkerchiefs, and heard them cheer, and the valiant Jack Thompson say, "Now we shall *see a lark*." I shared in the general excitement during the silence that immediately preceded the enemy's broadside; felt a sensation of awe and restlessness not easily described. I had no inclination to go below deck, but a kind of nervous wish to move about; not merely to get out of danger, for of that I scarcely had a clear idea. When the sudden flash, smoke, and burst of thunder, poured from the side of the French brig, my respiration was checked; and, as I noted several of our men fall, and the moment after the lee scuppers† running with blood, I felt a dizziness of head and sickness of stomach; but no sooner did the Hawk return her fire with a murderous raking broadside over the enemy's stern, than I partook of the undaunted Jack's enthusiasm, and thought it "glorious fun." If courage consisted in mere insensibility to danger, boys would be more valiant than men.

Thrice the enemy attempted, in vain, to board: twice, when the yard-arms† of the hostile ships crossed each other's decks; and once, when they had injudiciously run their bowsprit† into our midships. On this last occasion, they were not only repulsed with great loss, but raked again, with such murderous effect, that, after an ineffectual attempt to sheer off, and a brave, but useless resistance, Le Premier Consul hauled down her tricolor, having three-fourths of her crew either killed or wounded.

During the engagement, I stood by my little friend, the purser's son. On one occasion I caught the eye of the commander, who called out to me, "What do you do here, you little creole imp of darkness? get below!" when something occurred which called off his attention from me, and I remained near the midshipman, resolved, as Jack said, to see the *fun* out.

But poor Mrs. M'Shain suddenly missed me, and, amid the din of arms, inquired in a distracted manner for me, of all who were below deck. These consisted of the surgeon, his mate, the wounded who required to be dressed, and such as were employed conveying them into the cockpit. She received no answer to her anxious inquiries, until the steward, having to support a wounded officer down to the surgeon, told her that I was with Jack Thompson, on deck.

The love for the child she had suckled now overcame all her womanly fears: she sprang on deck, caught me in her arms, and rushed towards the companion;† but, ere she reached this, a random musket-shot from the enemy's vessel prostrated her on the deck, a warm and bleeding corpse. Stunned by the fall, I lay some moments in her arms, covered with her blood; and, when I was enabled to disengage myself, I stood up, and called upon my affectionate nurse not to mind the loss of a little blood, as the doctor would make her better — promising, if she would go below with me, that I never would leave her again: but she stirred not. I knelt down to kiss her; to do which, raised her head, when her fixed and glazed eyes told me too well that she was dead. I had seen the corpse of my poor father, and, child as I was, could recognise the ghastly visage of death. I knew she had died in the attempt to save my life, and felt that I was the cause of the mortal wound which deprived my orphan childhood of an affectionate nurse, whose friendship I needed, whose love for me equalled the love of a mother for an only infant, and whom I loved as much as child could love mother. I clasped her warm, yet inanimate hand to my lips, held it there, and cried as though my little heart were breaking: the tears I at that time shed were the bitterest that ever moistened my cheeks, for they were the tears of grief, despair, and remorse.

As this transaction took place at an important part of the engagement, it escaped general observation. A few minutes, however, after the enemy struck, Lieutenant Rotherham discovered me weeping beside the body of the poor Irishwoman; which scene moved him to more sorrow than he expressed for the slaughter of a considerable part of the crew of the vessel he commanded. All the Hawk's hardy men sympathised in this melancholy event; and even many of the brave prisoners who were brought on board, when informed of the circumstances attending the death of my poor nurse, shed tears.

After the engagement we were becalmed, and the body of my best friend, together with those of such as had fallen in the engagement, were committed to the deep; to be torn to pieces by those ghouls of the ocean, the sharks; who, allured by the taste of the blood which had poured from the scuppers of the hostile vessels, absolutely swarmed about them. War's parade is magnificent; while in action he is exciting; but when, from exhaustion, he reposes from his murderous efforts, his countenance becomes more hideous than that of any other demon that quits hell to afflict the earth.

A breeze sprang up in the night; and the next evening the Hawk, with her prize, accomplished the dangerous navigation into English Harbour; and the commander, after paying his respects to, and receiving the thanks of the admiral of the station, took me to St. John's, and presented me to my aunt, a very old lady, who had a large family of children and grandchildren. I was kindly received by my relative.

CHAPTER 13.

"A man severe he was, and stern to view;
I knew him well, and every truant knew . . .
Full well they laughed, with counterfeited glee,
At all his jokes — for many a joke had he."

GOLDSMITH.[†]

Antigua, although on the whole a beautiful and healthy island, did not charm my youthful eye as did the lovely land of my birth. The flat lands, rising here and there into hillocks, and salt springs[25] of the former, compensated not for the noble mountains, fertile valleys, beautiful lakes, murmuring cascades, and diamond streams, of Grenada; yet was Antigua well chosen for my education, for it had several schools while Grenada, at that time, had scarcely one.

The first evening I spent in St. John's, I was surprised at the cries of the negroes vending their wares; some, who sold candles, calling out, with a creole drawl, "Fine mould câânles! hard like a tone! (stone) burn like a wax! (then, in *sotto voce*) half a bit and four dog[26†] a-piece!" and ever and anon another itinerant merchant would call out — "You want any prat?" meaning by the last word, sprats. Negroes have an utter aversion to the sibilation of our language, and hence they generally cut out all the S's while speaking English.

A few days after my arrival, I was sent to a school kept by the well-known Tom Harris. The mention of this worthy's name will create in Antigua many a pleasing, and many a painful recollection. Many an assistant judge, member of the house of assembly, and colonel of militia, will

---

25. The aborigines called this island *Jamaica*, which means, "Land of Springs." This designation is applicable to the fine island which still bears the Indian name, but not to Antigua, unless the Caraibes named it with reference to its salt-springs.

26. Dog is a small copper coin.

recollect his *lengthy* form, deep voice, and creole jokes; nor will they easily forget the terrible quantity of tamarind-rods,[†] kept in pickle in a Bristol tripe-jar, wherewith to coerce the obstreperous young West Indians to learn their lessons.

Harris was, to use a trite proverb, which he himself was fond of quoting, "neither crab nor creole, but a true-born Barbadian."[†] Why a Barbadian considers himself not a creole, it is in vain to inquire, for they have all the peculiarities which distinguish natives of the West Indies in a more eminent degree than any inhabitants of the Antilles.

It has been observed of brother Jonathan,[†] that, from some peculiar anatomical conformation, he has an aversion to let that part of his body rest on a chair, which the chair-maker intended should occupy his handi-work. If this aversion results from the physical conformation of the Yankees, then creoles in general partake of this peculiarity; for brother Jonathan is not fonder of cocking up his heels than is the genuine home-bred West Indian. Indeed, so indispensable to the West Indian's comfort is this posture, that an Antigonian having, late in life, for the first time visited London, where he was lodged in elegantly furnished apartments which had door-windows, the creole, not finding his accustomed window-ledges whereon "to rest the *heels* of his feet," after in vain trying various positions and expedients in order to get into his old easy attitude, he at last exclaimed, "What an uncomfortable room; there is not in it even a place to cock up one's legs!"

I never saw a man who was fonder of elevating his heels above his head than was the respectable pedagogue, Harris. The moment the school was dismissed, he would stretch himself on a sofa, raise his legs over its arms, so as to be at least eighteen inches above the level of his head, and then call out, "Molly! come here, and scratch my head; and you, Tom, rub my legs." On which, a bee's-wax-skinned damsel, and an ebony-coloured youth, whose nails were pared for the purpose, would commence applying friction to his lower limbs and upper story, the titilation of which seemed to be to him a source of calm gratification, for he would lay for hours enjoying this process of dry-rubbing without changing a glance of his eye, or a muscle of his features, which all the while expressed tranquil delight.

Tom Harris was extremely fond of news; not general political news, but the gossiping intelligence of Antigua and the neighbouring islands, to obtain which he had the custom, on entering the school-room in the morning, of asking the boys, "What news?" when each scholar who had aught to communicate, in his turn stood forth to relate what he knew or had heard, or even sometimes invented.

"What news, boys?" inquired he, the first morning I went to school; on which a coloured lad, named Dyer, said, —

"Bruce's schooner, loaded with mol-bonies,[27] and consigned to Lightfoot and Hill, was yesterday wrecked off the Five Islands."[†]

"Any other news?" asked the pedagogue.

"Yes, sir," said a tall youth, named Langton; "last Thursday, in the court-house at Montserrat, Lawyer Daniels said something disrespectful of Tom Piper; and so, sir, he waited until the court broke up, and then broke the lawyer's head as he was going down the steps of the courthouse; and they were to go out when the Flying Fish came away."

"Any more news?" said our master.

"Yes, sir," said a little black pupil, named Semper; "Sam Matthews,[†] the poet, has made a new song about young Mr. Jepson, who is to be married to Miss Lightfoot, which he sung last night at his lecture on heads."

"An excellent subject," said Harris; "both the lovers stutter; should they marry, they'll *hesitate* before they have matrimonial differences, as neither of the parties use the *parts of speech* readily — ha, ha, ha!"

And here our preceptor laughed at his own joke; and we, as in duty bound, laughed at his sally.

"Any other news?" asked our dominie.

"Yes, sir," said a young man, named Morgan, who was the oldest scholar Harris had; "my father arrived this morning from St. Kitt's, and told me that, as one of the clerks of the house of Sommersall and Sons bottled a pipe of old madeira. He was surprised to find it only run twenty-seven dozen; and, on rolling over the cask, something heavy was heard inside, upon which they opened the cask, and found in it a cooper!"

"A cooper!" ejaculated the pedagogue.

"Yes," rejoined Morgan, "a madeira Portuguese[†] cooper. The body was well soaked in wine; but the doctors found out that the man had been killed by having his skull fractured, and his brain *confused* with a stave. How he got into the pipe, nobody can tell, sir; but they all suppose that he was killed in the cellar where the wine was kept that the murderer, to get the body out of the way, headed him up in the wine-pipe, and had him

---

27. A kind of mackeral.

shipped to St. Kitt's, where he was found with his leathern apron, adze, and all!"

"And what did they do with the body?" asked Harris.

"The coroner sat on it with his jury, sir, and they brought in a verdict, 'that the deceased, whom nobody knew any thing about, came by his death, God knows how!' and so, sir, they buried him."

"I dare say," said our master, "that he was killed in a quarrel occasioned by drinking; at all events was found in *liquor*. I shall be cautious how I drink any of Sommersall and Sons' madeira, lest I should take a dose of Portuguese tincture of *cooper*. Any other news, boys?"

A little boy now stood forward, and informed the pedagogue that Parson Audain, having heard, that Mr. O'Halloran had spoken slightingly of one of the *parson's* privateers, that respectable clerical character came down from Dominique[†] and horsewhipped O'Halloran, and that they were on the point of going out, when a Moravian brother, being shocked at the idea of a minister fighting, got the parties bound over to keep the peace.

"Is there any more news?" asked the dominie.

"Yes, sir," said a lad in a sailor's jacket and trousers; "Captain Morris has run away from the French prison in Guadaloupe."

"Captain Morris run away? impossible!" exclaimed Harris; "it was only the other day that he lost his leg. How could a man, with only one leg, run away?"

"He hopped away, sir: I saw him myself as I was coming to school; and see, sir, if he isn't coming this way!"

Sure enough a middlesized man, rather slender, but remarkably well made, with a lively countenance and but one leg, entered the schoolroom with a short, but hearty laugh, having neither crutch nor wooden leg, and holding a stick in his hand, which he used more to flourish than for support. On entering he gave a loud cheer, in which our master and all the scholars joined. Morris had been the pupil of Harris; and the former was so delighted at meeting his old master, that, with incredible agility, he hopped over all the forms and desks, and, in a moment, was in the arms of his old preceptor, who was so delighted at seeing his pupil safe, that he gave the boys a holiday, although the greater part of us preferred stopping to hear Captain Morris give an account of his escape from the French prison, which he did pretty nearly in the following words:—

"You must have heard of my taking a hooker[†] bound from Bordeaux to Guadaloupe, quite close to that island: I looked at her cargo, and found it made up of hams that hadn't as much fat as would grease a marlingspike; vermicelli that looked quite wormy; sausages as black and as hard as lignum vitae;[†] olive-oil, and belly-vengeance claret. The old skipper as owned her cried so hard, that I was moved; and so, said I to the old *moun-seer*, take your hooker and rot; get cargo into Point-Petre;[†] but remember, don't let the governor know I am beating on and off here for at least twelve hours after you get in, which he promised to do, and then talked a great deal about *reconnaissance* and *honneur*; but no sooner did the old French beggar get in than he 'peached[†] me. Well, on the information of the vermicelli captain, a large sloop-of-war was sent out after me; the breeze lasted long enough to bring her up, and then died away: there was no sheering off, so at it we went, hammer and tongs. The *mounseers* had three times my weight of metal, and four men for my one; but I arn't the boy as calls for *quarters*,[†] when, as Jonathan says, I can 'go the whole hog.' I nail my colours to my mast;[†] sink I may, but never while he has the command, will Morris strike.[†]

"We worked round the *mounseer* like a cooper round a cask, and I am sure I should have licked him, but as luck would have it, a chain-shot[†] carried away my starboard pin,[†] and I lay on the deck bleeding and stunned; on which my lads got disheartened, and allowed the *mounseers* to fight us at long shot, when, of course, their heavier metal told so well, that we got dismasted, and my lads surrendered. I told them before we began the action, never to haul down their colours; but, both our masts being carried away, they said they had not gone against orders in calling for *quarters*, because there were no colours to strike; they having come down when the masts fell.

"They took me into Basseterre,[†] where a French doctor cut away and trimmed my limb. They treated us like dogs, which was a shame. I defy the *mounseers* to say that ever I ill-treated a prisoner; and Victor Hugues can tell that boatload after boatload of French that I captured, have I sent to Guadaloupe, without ever asking a *sous* of ransom; and as to humanity, I blew out the brains of Jacob Swainson, the Swede, because he dared take liberties with a French mamsel. But what did they do with me and my crew? they sent us up into the belfry of an old church, where they fed, or rather starved, us on black bread and *soupe à l'onion*, made with two buckets of water to an onion.

"When I got well, they said I might go about the island, if I'd give them my parole not to slip my cable; but I politely told 'em, I'd see them dammed first; for that, though I had but one pin left, yet I would give them *leg*-bail† — that I owed them a grudge, and would pay them off in *hops*! Upon which they asked the interpreter what I meant; but, *Lard*! the beggar couldn't tell; for they have such a poor language, that they can't translate a good English joke into French.

"But to make short of my story, they cooped me up with the rest of the crew in the belfry, the door of which they kept barricaded. Once a-day they sent up a man in a basket, with our miserable rations: they hoisted him up outside the church, with a tackle and fall. One day, as the fellow stepped out of his basket, I *fired a lick* at his head which stunned him, and I then emptied his basket and got into it. The man below took me for the man as went up, and lowered me down; however, he soon found his mistake, when he tried to seize me; but I gave him a *box* with my *head* in his *victualling*-office that upset him, tied and gagged him with his own rope, and then, hop, pop, hop, away I went, like a locust, at the rate of eight knots an hour. But the alarm was soon given, upon which I crept into a copse and hid until night, eating guavas to keep the devil out of my stomach.

"After it got dark, I partly crept and partly hopped towards the sea, where I found several canoes; but the *Johnny Crapeaus*, to prevent my getting off, I suppose, had hauled them up on shore; besides which, they had set sentinels all along the coast. Howsomever, I crept under one of these canoes; and, from time to time, I raised my back and *coaxed* it towards the shore, some'at like a snail carries his shell. At length I got it to high-water mark; but a sentry, who walked fore and aft, kept such a sharp look-out, that I could not venture to turn it over so as to right it.

"I was much annoyed by a number of Guadaloupe hogs as came rooting under the canoe when they smelt me: those beasts are as lank as greyhounds. The negroes say our hogs are gentlemen, because they do not work; but that the French pigs are blackguards as are obliged to work hard for their own living.

"When the serjeant came to relieve the guard I took advantage of it; and, while they changed sentries, I capsized the canoe without being heard, got in, and shoved her off with my stick, and then broke out one of the thwarts, of which I made a paddle, using it first on one side, then on the other, Indian fashion. But the soldier heard this, and called out, *Qui va là?*† which was a hint for me to say nothing, but get as far off as I could; then bang went his gun, the ball whizzing over my head: away I worked for life or death. I now heard and saw a crowd of soldiers, with flambeaux,[†] bellowing and *sacréing*[†] on the shore, and in a minute five or six canoes were after me, but their flambeaux enabled me to see them, although they could not see me; so, instead of pulling out to sea, I worked round a point, on which stood a small battery,[†] while they, on a wrong scent, went out into the offing, but at length returned in despair, upon which I ventured with my canoe to sea. I wondered I was not discovered from the fort; but, as Cudjoe[28†] says, 'night has no eyes.'

"Guided by a star, I now paddled away for life, until with fatigue I fainted away. I must have been insensible for several hours, for when I awoke, I found the morning was breaking; howsomever, the tide, as the Lârd would have it, had carried me out to sea. I saw an English frigate[†] cruising within a mile of me, but I also saw about a dozen canoes leaving the shore in pursuit of me. What was to be done? I had lost my *jury* paddle[†] when I fainted; but with pleasure I found what I did not expect, that is, a pair of broad-bladed sculls,[†] chained to the inside of the canoe beside the rowlocks, which night hindered me from seeing before. No time was to be lost; with a strong pull I broke the padlock which held the chain, and out went the sculls. In a moment I made my canoe leap from wave to wave, like a flying-fish; but some of the French canoes, having eight paddles, were gaining on me, until one of them fired at me; the ball, however, missed my *head*, and glanced off one of my *sculls*. This attracted the attention of the frigate; the first-lieutenant, who had the watch, at once guessed what was going forward, and, in a quarter-less-no-time, stood towards me. My eyes! how the canoes did take French leave of me when they saw the frigate stand towards the shore! I got on board of her safe and sound, but almost exhausted, just as the French batteries kindly told the captain that we were very nearly within the range of their guns."

Such was the account given by Captain Morris, of an escape which, considering that but eight weeks before he had lost his limb, was a surprising achievement. As this man was the most extraordinary privateersman known in those seas since the days of the bucaniers, I will pause in my narrative to give some account of him.

He was a singular amalgamation of good and bad qualities; brave to recklessness, generous to prodigality, and, withal, a religious enthusiast.

On one occasion, being off the French port of the island of St. Martin,[†]

---

28. A general name for a negro, as Paddy is for an Irishman.

the enemy from a fort fired pieces of iron at his vessel, and carried away his main-topmast.† These, he said, were unchristian shot, and for that reason swore he would, that night, carry away their flag-staff to replace his mast. And he kept his word; for that night he landed, stormed their battery, killed and wounded twenty men, brought off their flag-staff, and absolutely made a top-mast of it.

Repeatedly has he been known to restore a prize because it had been bravely defended.

When on shore, he was a constant attendant at church, where his piety, although somewhat *outré*, was, to all appearance, sincere. Often have I seen him in his pew, with his weather-beaten countenance screwed up to three sharps, in order that he might seem devout; his boatswain-like voice giving the responses to the litany louder than the clergyman's. During the sermon, he would rivet his eyes on the preacher, and, at every period, utter a groan loud enough to distract the parson, and attract and disturb the attention of the whole congregation.

On one occasion, a French refugee from St. Domingo having uttered some senseless observation against Divine revelation, Morris called him out, and, to prove himself a good Christian, shot the French free-thinker; on which occasion the unhappy Lord Camelford was his second.

But Morris's death, which happened many years after this, was inglorious. At the end of the war his fits of devotion became more frequent; he seldom went abroad without a Bible, seeking persons to dispute with him about the meaning of particular passages. His favourite part of Scripture which he loved to descant on, was the shipwreck of Paul:† he used to designate the sailors of the ship of Adramyttium as lubbers, for throwing out four anchors from the stern.

At length, for want of employment, his time began to hang heavy on his hands, to remedy which he entered into the smuggling trade: this he did for the mere love of the excitement it afforded, for he was at this time wealthy, and he was never avaricious. A brig-of-war gave chase to the vessel he commanded, suspecting her of being laden with contraband articles, and fired at her with blank cartridge, in order to make her lie-to; but this signal he did not obey, although several times repeated. At length the man-of-war sent a ball at his lugger, which, unfortunately,

"Laid him low on the deck, and he never spoke more."†

Such was the end of a man who was for years the terror of the French in the Caribbean seas.

But, to return to Harris. He was not a brilliant genius; he possessed, however, sufficient talent and application to fulfil the duties of a West India schoolmaster. Creole children in general make remarkably apt scholars; and I was not an exception to this rule. While I remained in Antigua I was the favourite pupil of Harris; that is to say, for more than two years.

CHAPTER 14.

"Nothing like your real Trinidada."
BEN JONSON.[†]

An event took place which called me from Antigua: my uncle George had lost his only daughter. This young lady was on the point of marriage with an officer of a regiment stationed at Trinidad. The lovers, while imprudently attempting in a gig[†] to cross a stream, — which at that time, was swollen by one of those floods so frequent in that island, — were swept away, and not until the next morning were their bodies found, a mile below the ford, locked in each other's arms.

This was a terrible blow to my uncle. He had a partner in his plantation, named Señor Thomaso, a worthy creole Spaniard,[†] who wrote to my Antigua friends the account of this melancholy event; and his letter advised my being sent immediately to Trinidad, as my uncle, who was a widower, had residing with him what is here called a housekeeper, a French creole female, of mixed blood, although of a very fair complexion, called Fanchinette. This young woman, Señor Thomaso more than hinted, had obtained an improper ascendency over my uncle since the death of his only daughter; which ascendency she was likely to abuse. Thomaso, therefore, recommended my being sent to Trinidad, in order to remind my uncle that I was his natural heir.

I must explain that the term housekeeper, in these islands, is not applied to those steady, political, female stewardesses, who so demurely manage the domestic affairs of a family in England; far from it. Many persons here, who keep no houses, keep housekeepers.

My aunt took three weeks to consider the good advice of Señor Thomaso, and then sent me to Trinidad. I was shipped on board a kind of yacht,[†] called the "Game Cock," belonging to a Mr. Warner, of Bequia; which vessel its worthy owner had caused to be built and maintained for the purpose of taking him and his matchless, yet often matched, breed of cocks from colony to colony, in order that they night fight the chanticleers of every island in the Caribbean sea.

Mr. Warner, a very distant relation of my mother, was going to Trinidad, because he was told that some one there possessed the finest breed of cocks in the West Indies. He promised to take great care of me, and kept his word; his attention to me was almost as unremitting as that which he bestowed on "Iron-Beak," his favourite cock, which, he said, had won for him more than four thousand dollars. Our voyage was very long, in some measure owing to calms, light and contrary winds, but the principal cause of its length was this, — whenever the winds became baffling, or died away, Mr. Warner landed on the nearest island, taking with him a coop of birds, and anxiously inquiring, "if any person, of untainted blood, would sport a main?"† as he would not degrade his cocks, by allowing them to contend against those of people of colour, much less with those of persons of pure African blood. Altogether, we were no less than sixteen days beating-up from Antigua to Trinidad, including the time lost in beating-up for matches at cocking.

At length, before day-break, on the seventeenth morning of our protracted voyage, we made the northern shores of Trinidad. As the brief twilight illumined the horizon, I viewed this fine island, which appeared to me totally different from any other in the West Indies. The other islands have, from the sea, a light verdant hue, while the northern mountains of Trinidad have a sombre appearance, on account of their being clad from their bases to their very summits with gigantic timber of super-luxuriant growth, whose colossal columns support endless varieties of mosses, wild pines,† vines, tendrils, and parasites; some depending from the venerable branches of trees of centuries, like immense beards streaming on the morning-breeze; others, parasite plants, decking the sons of the mountains like party-coloured robes; some graceful vines were entwined round a hundred trees, like magnificent fringes. Here and there the fantastic limbs of the giant *Bombex cieba*† shook its leaves above the surrounding ocean of foliage; while the fig-tree,† with its hundred trunks, twisted its *ungrateful* leaves,[29] like the convolutions of immense serpents, round its neighbouring trees, which soon must fall beneath its insidious embraces. The extraordinary means which this last wonderful tree uses to aggrandise itself, by destroying its

---

29. The Spaniards call these leaves, which at first get support from surrounding trees, and then destroy them, *los ingratos*. The English negroes give them the less poetical, but more humorous name of *Kotchman* (hugging creole).

neighbours, seem more to belong to animal instinct, than to mere vegetation. While the mists of morning hang on these mountains, they have a sombre appearance, but it is the sombreness of uncultivated fertility.

We made several ineffectual attempts to pass through the *bocas*,† — passages formed by several small but beautiful islands, which rise abruptly from the flood, and stand, like bold sentinels, between Trinidad and the opposing point of South America, breaking the turbulent force of the ocean, and guarding the tranquillity of the noble gulf of Paria: without these isles roll the billows of a roaring sea; but within them, seem to ripple the waters of a lake of Paradise.

At length we succeeded in getting through the boca, called Apes' Passage, into this magnificent gulf, in which the united navies of the world might safely ride at anchor. The sun had risen over the silvery waters of Paria; the mists gradually formed on the mountain-tops, many rolling themselves into one, like extended lines of an army concentrating into columns. Slowly they ascended above the mountains' heads, assuming red and purple hues, and leaving the outlines of the extraordinary range to stand in bold relief to a sky of cerulean loveliness. The mountains of Trinidad differ in their form, as well as hue, from all others in the West Indies. The latter rise, range close above range, to the centre of the island, where one mountain stands superior to the rest, which look as though they had risen, and were rising from the ocean. Trinidad is a square island, apparently an amputation from the great South American continent, and rent therefrom by some unrecorded convulsion of nature. If this conjecture be correct, the range of mountains which extend across the northern side of Trinidad, in a direction from east to west, must have joined a similar and corresponding range, which appears on the opposite coast of Paria, and which traversed the whole continent of South America; being, in fact, the termination of the Andes.

The centre of the island is nearly flat, save that two hills gradually rise there, — one called Tamana, the other Montserrat.† Towards the south, the land becomes undulating; and, at the southern extremity, hilly, but by no means mountainous, although these hills are marked in the maps as "inaccessible mountains." The explanation of which is, that the English have never made a survey of the interior of this island;[30] but have con-

---

30. Captain Columbine has made a good survey† of the north coast of this colony, the interior of which is, to this day, unsurveyed.

tented themselves with merely copying the Spanish maps. The surveyors who made these, although they gave tolerably correct outlines of the coasts, and such few parts of the island as were inhabited; yet, when they came to the uninhabited portions, with the characteristic indolence of their nation, they put down every hill that was fatiguing to climb, as "inaccessible;" and Mallet's map,[†] from which all the rest are copied, although it impudently pretended to be taken from actual survey, was a mere blundering transcript and translation of the Spanish map;[†] I say a blundering transcript; for the following most ludicrous mistakes appear in it:— In about one hundred places in the Gulf of Paria, of that correct specimen of hydrography, we see such notices as these, "14 breakers, 13 breakers, 12 breakers," &c. Now, as any one, who has ever been in the gulf, knows you may as well look for icebergs there as breakers, they are puzzled to understand it: the fact is, the Spanish hydrographers put down all over the gulf 14, 13, 12, not breakers, but *brazos*[31] — *Anglice*, fathoms. "For this mistake," says a late visitor of this island (Coleridge),[†] "he ought to have his head broke."

The foregoing ridiculous error reminds me of one in 'Zuñiga's History of the Philippines,'[†] wherein the Sandwich Islands are called, *Los Islos de San Duisk* — the islands of Saint Duisk! Who would have imagined that Lord Sandwich would have been canonised as a saint?

As the sun arose, I saw a flight of more than ten thousand flamingoes[†] winging their way from Trinidad to the Spanish main, having the appearance of a triangular body of fire, as they majestically flew over our vessel.

To this succeeded flights of millions of the parrot tribe, varying in size, from the seven-coloured parroquet,[†] about the dimensions of a lark, to the large and gaudy macaw.[†]

The breeze freshening, we were enabled to keep closer in shore. Our ears were now astounded by one of the most discordant cries I ever heard. This *hurrah* proceeded from the throats of about one hundred red, or Alouto monkeys,[†] the most wild and untameable of the Simian tribe. The sound that approached it nearer than any other that I ever heard, was produced by the hooting, howling, and groaning, of a drunken, yet thirsty English mob, at an election, when they wished to shew their disapprobation of the party which did not give them beer.

---

31. Sometimes written *broços*, but pronounced *brathos*. The z, or ç, in spanish, is pronounced very like our th.

By means of a telescope, I was enabled to see thousands of brilliant humming-birds, the appearance of whose waving, ruby, topaz, and golden plumage, and graceful forms, delighted my youthful eye. Here, the humming-birds are so numerous, and so beautiful, as to justify the original name which the aborigines gave to this island; and by which it is still known, by their few descendants, who yet inhabit the isle of their fathers; I mean "Iëre;" that is to say, island of humming-birds.

The Game Cock now passed between an islet, called Gaspar-Grandé,[†] and Trinidad; on the first of which, fortifications were being then erected, which have long since been abandoned. There it was that the brave Spanish admiral, Apodaca,[†] saved his fleet, consisting of four sail of the line, from falling into the hands of the English, by setting fire to them, and then rowing away to Port of Spain. The flames of one of the ships were extinguished by Admiral Harvey, who captured her; the remains of the other three may still be seen under water.

We now approached town; and the apertures between the mountains, which form the beautiful valleys of Cuesa, and Diego Martin,[†] relieved the sameness of the hills, which bounded the view from the gulf. The sombreness of the virgin forest was here and there contrasted by the cultivation of man; and the dense woods themselves assumed a smiling aspect; for, amid the waving expanse of dark foliage, here and there blossomed the pouij,[†] a tree as tall as any which Europe produces, and the flowers of which are of the most brilliant golden hue; while below, rows of majestic "bois-immortels,"[†] with their deep rose-coloured foliage, glowed like fire, as the sun shone on them: these gave a grateful shade to the pleasant alleys of cacoa.[32] The scene was diversified with a hundred different kinds of palm, including the palmiste,[†] or palmetto, which here rises at least fifty feet higher than do any I had seen in the other islands. Here and there I observed cane plantations, but these appeared to lack that neatness which the sugar estates have in Antigua; yet the canes of the latter place bear as great a resemblance, in point of size, to those of Trinidad, as a porpoise bears to a whale. Altogether, the prospect of the coast, sailing from the Bocas to Port of Spain, is the finest I ever beheld, or ever hope to view.

---

32. The tree which produces the chocolate-nut (*Cacoa theobroma*), is erroneously written cocoa; which latter produces the cocoanut, its botanical name being *Cocos nucifera*.[†]

CHAPTER 15.

"Oh! villainy, villainy, villainy!
I think upon't; I think I smell it; oh, villainy!"
SHAKESPEARE.[†]

We landed at Port of Spain, the principal town of the island of Trinidad, and which was, at that time, most unlike what it is at present. It was then a straggling town, composed of wooden houses; yet its stores were crowded with rich merchandise, for commerce shed her golden smiles upon the island. We landed on a Sunday; but there was not the slightest appearance of that respect for the Sabbath which I observed in Antigua, although the Sunday market was, at that time, common to every town in this part of the world.

The bustle of this place astonished me; as did also the mixed hue and costume of the population, and Babylonish variety of tongues. Here strutted the gaudy officer of militia; for there had been a parade that morning, and almost every man in the island is in the militia, — there being a colonel, and a more than proportionate number of majors, captains, and subalterns, to every fifty men. There lounged, but in less pomp, an officer of the line;[†] here and there rolled along a naval officer; the gaily dressed Spaniard shewed his laced frill and gold buttons; and the plainly dressed Englishman, with his nankeen jacket and jean trousers, stood beside the smart Frenchman, with his powdered hair, cue,[†] short inexpressibles, silk stockings, and buckled shoes. Sometimes a Chinese[†] or two would appear; and ever and anon an athletic and ferocious-looking sambo[33][†] would pass; together with groups of the mixed race between Indians, negroes, and Europeans, called *Péons*,[†] — all wearing the dangerous *cuchillo* (knife, or poniard).[†] Crowds of negroes walked to and fro, clattering, jesting, and laughing, as merrily as though slavery and degradation were blessings;

---

33. The mixed race between the Indian and negro.

while here and there were numbers of tastily-dressed women, of the classes called mulattoes, mestees, and quadroons,[†] who were the most beautiful of those classes which I, at that time, had ever seen.

The dialects of the people of Port of Spain were as mixed as their complexions and dresses. Chinese, corrupt Arabic, spoken by the Mandingo negroes; a hundred different vernaculars from Guinea;[†] English, with its proper accent, and then with its creole drawl;[†] Spanish, with its true Castilian pronunciation, as well as with the slight corruption with which the South Americans speak it; creole French, European French, Corsican, various kinds of *patois*, German, and Italian, were all spoken in this town.

But I have a more melancholy task to perform than that of describing the party-coloured inhabitants of Port of Spain. On Mr. Warner presenting me to Señor Thomaso, as the nephew of his late partner, that worthy man informed us that my uncle had died twelve days since, having neglected to make his will, as he believed; but the worthy Spaniard informed us, that he suspected an infamous conspiracy to have been entered into between Fanchinette, an *escribano*, or notary,[†] named Gregorio Nunez, and four others, to deprive me of my uncle's property. As these suspicions afterwards proved to have been too well founded, I will at once relate the particulars of the conspiracy.

Fanchinette and Nunez got up a *post mortem* will in the following ingenious, but by no means original method. After my uncle died, they placed his corpse in a chair, where it was supported by two of the conspirators, whilst a third held the head from behind by the hair; Nunez then read a will, which purported to bequeath the whole of my uncle's property to Fanchinette, at the end of every clause of which, the corpse was made to nod, as assenting; and, when the whole had been read, a pen was placed in its cold hand, and its name signed to the paper.

The Spanish law, in force in the island,[†] required seven witnesses to a will; but as Febrero (the Blackstone of Spain) says, that an escribano represents the Trinity, he therefore counts for three ordinary witnesses: thus, the oath of Nunez, and the affidavits of four other scoundrels, were sufficient to render the pretended will valid.

But the parties, to make assurance doubly sure, had caused a drunken Spanish priest, called Puablo Valdez, who had been chaplain to Apodaca's ship, to marry Fanchinette to the said inanimate body. This marriage was managed in the following manner. Valdez they knew to be a priest incapable of doing a villainous act when in his sober senses, which, unhappily, was seldom the case; and, indeed, never after he had taken his dinner. He never drank before mass, in the morning; but what he took at night was sufficient to muddle him during the forenoon. Late in the afternoon, this priest was sent for, by which time he had taken his twenty-seventh glass of old rum and water. On his arrival, they informed him that my uncle George, on his deathbed, wished to make reparation to Fanchinette for having cohabited with her without leave of Mother Church, by marrying her, and requested, that he (Valdez) would perform the marriage-service. Now, occurrences of this nature often did take place in Old Spain; and hence the priest naturally believed what he had been told: and, moreover, Fanchinette and Nunez plied the unhappy man so plentifully with noyeau[†] before the performance of the ceremony, that he might, perhaps, have seen an elephant were it within a few feet of him, but as for human beings, they were objects far too minute for his clouded vision. He was supported into the room where lay the corpse: he mumbled through the matrimonial service by rote, as reading it, from his state, was out of the question; and the next day he absolutely imagined that he had united, in the holy bands of marriage, George Arundell and Fanchinette La Roche.

To fill up the measure of her iniquity, two months after this event, Fanchinette declared herself with child by her late husband; and, nine months and two weeks after the death of my uncle, she gave birth to an infant. Thus it became a common saying in Trinidad, "that a dead man made a will, married a wife, and begot a child." I have seen the infant of Fanchinette, which is as like the squinting, villainous-looking escribano, as one logger-headed shark is like another.

Señor Thomaso took a liking to me, and persuaded Mr. Warner to leave me with him: this the latter consented to do, provided my aunt at Antigua made no objections; and to this the old lady agreed. Señor Thomaso, from some threatening expressions dropped by one of the witnesses of Nunez during a quarrel, threw the matter of the will and marriage into court; but, alas! it was a Spanish court of law. Enough evidence was obtained to throw a doubt on the authenticity of the will, and the validity of the marriage, but not enough to set them aside; at least so the lawyers said. These gentlemen made their pleadings so voluminous, that, long ere the cause was decided, the estate of my uncle was swallowed up by law-expenses. To give the reader some idea of the administration of justice in Spanish courts, I will relate the following fact. A barber who had, previously to its interment, shaved my uncle's corpse, charged four dollars for the operation, and, like every debt owing by or to the succession of George Arundell, this demand was thrown into court, where the charges on it alone amounted to eight hundred dollars; which were paid out of my uncle's estates, the judge, escribanos, and advocates, pocketing it all, and the poor barber getting nothing but the satisfaction of feeing his own lawyer. We have all heard of two cats, who found two pieces of cheese, and, disputing about their respective shares, applied to a monkey, who, in order to equalise them, piece by piece ate up the claims of both parties. If any human, or rather inhuman, tribunal resemble Jacko in the fable, it is a Spanish court of law.

In the meantime, Señor Thomaso sent me to a school in Port of Spain, where the English, French, and Spanish languages are taught *indifferently*, in both senses of the word. I had, naturally, great facility in acquiring languages; my knowledge of creole French made the study of good French easy, and, living with a Spanish family, I soon acquired a respectable knowledge of the Castilian tongue.

I must now pause in my personal narrative to relate a public event, which, however, was fated to have an influence on my own fortunes. About this time, the island was kept in a state of alarm by frequent rumours, and official accounts, of a strong French and Spanish fleet being in the West Indies. Here they effected no conquest, for this they had no time to attempt; but they levied contributions on different islands, some of which they had not time to receive, ere they heard that the hero of the Nile was in pursuit of them: they started away without pocketing the booty they were on the point of receiving at Barbadoes. The very name of Nelson made them fly, although they had twenty-one sail of the line, and he but ten.

At length, however, the fleet of Nelson did appear off the northern coast of Trinidad.[†] There was an old Spanish fort on an eminence, at the place called Las Cuevas,[†] garrisoned by a few black troops, and commanded by a French emigrant in the English service. Nelson attempted to communicate with this little fort, but the Frenchman could not understand his signals; on which the admiral despatched two or three boats for shore, when the Frenchman, well knowing the fort could not be defended, spiked his two guns,[†] pitched them into the sea, blew up his little fortress, and set off to town,[34] there spreading a report that the enemy's fleet were in sight. On

---

34. This trifling circumstance has, I believe, not been noticed by any of the biographers of Nelson.

Nelson's part the mistake was mutual: seeing the fort destroyed, he naturally concluded the enemy were in possession of the island. He had long
been in search of the combined fleets, and he hoped he had now, at length,
caught them. He accordingly sailed into the Gulf of Paria, with the hope of
making the mouths of the Oronoke[†] as famous in history as he had rendered those of the Nile. Certainly, no part of the world possesses a sheet of
water better adapted for the collision of hostile navies than the Gulf of
Paria. Two fleets encountering in this gulf must fight, without hopes of the
defeated party escaping: it affords a fair *sea* and no favour.

On Nelson discovering his mistake, he scarcely waited to explain — he
merely sent on shore a commissary, named Whitmore, a passenger from
Barbadoes to Trinidad, with a hasty letter to the governor, to which he
awaited no reply, but sailed away in pursuit of the enemy. Such was the
decisive promptitude of him who, a few months after, fell gloriously in the
arms of victory at Trafalgar.

On the false alarm of the French fleet being in sight taking place, three
guns were fired, and a red flag hoisted upon every fort in the island — a
signal that the colony is placed under martial law. Immediately all was
bustle and confusion in every street of Port of Spain; drums rolled, fifes
squeaked, and bugles brayed; in every house was heard the ringing of iron
ramrods in the barrels of their muskets; the clattering of sabres in their
steel cases; the clicking of pistols; the reports of every kind of fire-arm; and
the clanking of the horses of the cavalry, mounted infantry, officers, and
aides-de-camp, as they galloped to and fro.

In a few minutes the whole of the militia turned out to a man, and
assembled on the parade-ground, there awaiting the orders of General
Heslop,[†] who was at this time governor and commander-in-chief. The
general rightly judged the capital to be indefensible, and therefore ordered
all the merchant-shipping to anchor under Fort George,[†] an unfinished
fortress, situated on a high and steep hill, near the sea, about four miles
from Port of Spain. He recommended the inhabitants to send their most
valuable effects up to the fort, whither he despatched the greater part of
the militia and troops of the line. This was the best thing that could have
been done, had the alarm been true, for the town was indefensible; but the
fortress, garrisoned by all the disposable force of the island, and well provisioned, could not easily be reduced. It commanded all the roads to town;
so that the capture of the latter, while Fort George held out, would be
little acquisition to the enemy, in a military point of view.

All were in haste to send their valuable property up to the fort: carts, mules, &c. were employed to transport money to it; merchants' books, and public records, were sent up on the heads of negroes. Scarcely was the steep road cleared of those passengers, ere the militia began their march, commanded by officers who shewed more zeal than discretion; hurrying their men up the steep path, or permitting them to hurry themselves up, in double-quick time, although the thermometer was at ninety in the shade — but no part of the winding and precipitous road *was* shaded. The men were clothed and accoutred in heavy marching order, although only citizen-soldiers, and consequently unused to military fatigues. To complete the whole of these absurdities, they were marched in subdivisions, instead of ranks of four, so that the road was unnecessarily crowded. This ridiculous march caused the death of many men.

My worthy friend, Señor Thomaso, went out with his company — he being a captain in the militia; and I, as well as I could, ran by his side. Like most Spaniards in this part of the world, he possessed a broad leathern belt, for the purpose of secreting specie about his person in times of public danger, which belt l saw him fill with doubloons ere he set out, and brace round his body over his shirt. He was aged, and rather corpulent: the road up to the fort being steep, long, and intolerably hot, ere he got more than two-thirds of the way he turned pale, complained of fatigue, and a few minutes after fell. The event created a little confusion: some privates removed him off the road, and placed him under the shade of one of that species of palm called *cocorite*,[†] one man belonging to his company volunteering to keep guard over him. When, in a few moments, the whole of the militia had ascended above the spot where Señor Thomaso lay, in his fainting fit, the sentinel loosed his coat, waistcoat, and stock; knelt down to observe his captain, and then said to me, —

"My good lad, is this your father?"

I informed him he was not, but "my kind friend."

"Then, for Heaven's sake, my boy, run up to the fort, and get a little vinegar[†] — it's the only thing that will save Captain Thomaso's life! Run, for the love of God!"

In an instant I rushed up the steep hill to the fort. I did not take the winding road, but, with the agility of a kid, scrambled through the bushes in a direct line.

Out of breath, I arrived at the garrison, where all was tumult; many of the men, from causes before stated; had fainted, and some were attacked with *coups de soleil*.[†] In vain I implored for a little vinegar; no one could or would grant my request. At length I saw a surgeon, who was in attendance on the sick, and him I entreated to grant me that which I was told would save the life of my friend. He asked me what I wanted with vinegar? I told him the accident that had befallen Señor Thomaso. It appeared he knew the worthy Spaniard; and promised go with me himself and see him, the moment he could give relief to those who were dangerously ill.

Two or three militia-men were attacked with apoplexy, from wearing the stock with which the British soldier is absolutely tortured in an intertropical climate, and the surgeon had to open their temporal arteries,[†] which operations took up more time than I wished; but at length the doctor, hastily tying up his small case of instruments, and taking in his pockets a phial or two, bade me lead on, and followed me down to where lay Señor Thomaso. In a few minutes we arrived there; but, alas! he was beyond all human aid. There lay his corpse, with his little bag of Catholic relics suspended round his neck; but his gold cross and heavy belt of doubloons, had disappeared — nor was the sentry to be found.

I thought not of the doubloons, nor of the sentinel, for grief overpowered my young mind. It appeared to me that all those who attempted to befriend me were doomed to death. I felt myself an orphan boy in a land where all things were strange, and all men were strangers to me. I wept until I thought my heart would break.

The next day, when the false alarm subsided, the relations of Señor Thomaso made inquiries as to who was the honest sentinel who had so kindly volunteered to guard their deceased relative. This was easily ascertained, nor was it difficult to conjecture what became of the doubloon-belt; but not one shadow of proof could be obtained to criminate the suspected thief, even before a court-martial. He said that he *voluntarily* watched his captain until he died; but that he neither *volunteered*, nor was ordered, to keep sentry over a corpse. And he further alleged, that the moment he found the captain was dead, he went up to his duties at Fort George. This statement he could not prove; but such was the confusion in the fort at the time of this occurrence, that the friends of Thomaso could not disprove it. On the whole, nobody believed this man innocent of stealing the belt, and yet no one could blame the court-martial, which unanimously acquitted him.

The same man, three years after this event, was very busy, during the conflagration[†] of Port of Spain, in saving his neighbours' goods, while his own house was burning, by which disinterested conduct he lost all he had in the world — at least he often said so: and yet, "such is the envy of this wicked world" (as the old women say), that there were not wanting those who asserted that he had plundered to the amount of many thousand dollars during this calamity. One thing is certain, — namely, that, a very little while after the fire, he rose like a phoenix from its ashes, and became a *respectable* merchant; respectable in the sense of the word as used by the witness in Thurtell's trial — "because he drove his gig."† This man is still alive, but his name I will not mention to those who are not and have not been inhabitants of Trinidad, as to them it would be useless; and to those who are, or have been in the colony, it would be needless.

CHAPTER 16.

"With stern, resolved, despairing eye,
   I see each aimed dart;
For one has cut my dearest tie,
   And quivers in my heart."

                BURNS.[†]

I lamented the death of the good Thomaso with a grief more deep and lasting than is felt, in general, by youth; for I felt that, by his decease, I was left a friendless and plundered orphan, in a land far from my own.

Friendless altogether I was not: the surgeon of whom I have spoken took me to his house and treated me kindly; and, two days after the alarm had subsided, brought me to Dr. Manuel Lopez[†] — not a doctor of medicine, but, like most Spanish advocates, a doctor of laws. This gentleman enjoyed the situation of guardian-general of orphans, the name of which office sufficiently indicates its nature. I have but one observation to make against this office, which is this:— the more the guardian-general of orphans involves in litigation the property of those whom the laws commit to his protection, the greater are his emoluments. This remark is intended to apply to the office, not to him who filled it; it were ungrateful in me to complain of the honour of Dr. Lopez. There are some persons possessed of such natural probity, that they will act with rectitude despite of the severest temptations of the enemy of mankind; hence we sometimes meet with even honest Spanish lawyers; one of these *rarae aves in terris*[†] being Manuel Lopez, doctor of laws of the University of Caraccas, and guardian-general of orphans of Trinidad.

The doctor was a little thin man, with features which, at first view, seemed rather mean; but, on looking well at his finely formed forehead, arched eyebrows, and penetrating eyes, any one would form a different opinion of him from that which a first glance might give. His eyes were the most lively I ever saw, their brilliancy seeming to illuminate his dark and deeply pock-marked visage. Taken altogether, his countenance, when well considered, indicated shrewdness and integrity; at least I thought so when I knew him. Most of us think ourselves physiognomists; and, after we are well acquainted with a person, are apt to persuade ourselves that his conduct corresponds with the impression which his features made on us from our first acquaintance with him.

On the surgeon's introducing me to Dr. Lopez, the latter received me with a kindness that seemed really parental; and, on his being informed that I was the nephew and probable heir of the late George Arundell, he immediately despatched one of his clerks for the Padré Valdez; for something had occurred which fully convinced the priest that he had been imposed upon, when in a state of intoxication, to marry an intriguing woman, not to a dying penitent, but to a corpse! and for which act, horror and remorse had seized the old man, and were weighing him down to the grave.

With tottering step the padré entered the room; his eyes were dim with age, and a long course of inebriety had distorted and bloated his once fine set of features, now rendered haggard by the anguish of remorse. On being told who I was, the old man was much affected; his pale aspect assumed an ashy hue, and he trembled in every limb; but, recovering himself, he made the sign of the cross on my forehead, saying, *"Benedico te in nomine Patris, et Filii, et Spiritûs Sancti! Amen."*†

He then fell on his knees, placed me before him; and, taking my closed hands between his own, which he held up in a supplicating posture, he poured forth a prayer in his noble mother tongue, with a deep voice rendered absolutely awful by strong emotion.

"Holy Mother of Heaven," said he, "pardon me for the odious offence which I have committed in profaning the ordinances of thy Son, while in a state disgraceful to a brute beast, doubly disgraceful to a man, and unpardonable, save through thy intercession, in an anointed but unworthy son of the altar. Forgive, Holy Virgin, the injuries which I have been instrumental in inflicting on this defenceless and plundered orphan boy; shower thy blessing on his youth, his manhood, and his old age; protect this fatherless child in his pilgrimage through this valley of the shadow of death; and sanctify his deathbed; so that, when he awakes from this mortal dream, he may open his eyes to the view of the glory of thy Son; but let him not wake to the immortality of torture to which we wretched sojourners on earth would be condemned, but for the sacrifice of thy offspring."

The priest now repeated in Latin the first of the seven penitential Psalms,[†] during the progress of his recital of which, his sobs became frequent, and the tears flowed down his aged cheeks in a copious stream: at length his emotions got so far the better of him, that the surgeon and Dr. Lopez raised him from his knees, and conveyed him to a sofa in the next room; where he fainted. I must relate the cause of this scene. One Antonio Cardoza, a wretch with one eye, like a Scotchman's herring,[35] an accomplice of the escribano, Valdez, having taken an inflammatory fever during the late marching and counter-marching, sent for the man-of-war priest, and made to him a confession of the whole infamous proceeding with regard to the false will and pretended marriage. Scarcely had the penitent finished his guilty confession, ere, terrified with the exclamations of the astounded and horrified priest, he fell into a fainting-fit, from which he only partially recovered, when, gasping for breath, an awful rattling in his throat told that he was summoned to answer for his crimes before a tribunal which required no witnesses. Padré Valdez now, on bended knees, and with tears, besought Cardoza to permit him to publish his confession, his vow not allowing him to do so without the consent of the penitent; the priest telling him, at the same time, he could not give him absolution without this consent: upon which the dying man muttered something, which Valdez believed to be consent, and yet was not assured of it; and Cardoza then died, without making any other sign.

The unhappy, but conscientious priest knew not what to do under these circumstances; he wished to make reparation for the crime he had been unwillingly led to commit, and yet he felt not assured that he ought to make use of the confession of Cardoza. He immediately wrote to the bishop, who lived at Angostura,[†] up the Oronoke, an account of this extraordinary affair, without mentioning names, in order that the bishop might get a dispensation from Rome, to allow him (Valdez) to publish the disclosures of Cardoza. In the time of war, when letters have to cross seas between countries engaged in hostilities against each other, their conveyance is tardy and uncertain; and hence the dispensation did not arrive until grief, remorse, and the severe penance he underwent, had brought Padré Valdez to his deathbed: but, ere he quitted this life, he had time to make, before competent witnesses, sufficient disclosures to expose the

---

35. The negroes say, that "Kotchman ge herring wa hab one eye;" namely, a herring split down in the back. In fact, half a fish given instead of a whole one.

whole conspiracy of Nunez and Fanchinette. The priest (Valdez) was incapable of committing a crime when in his sober senses; but he was addicted, as already mentioned, to one vice, which is the most profligate parent of many crimes.

The police were sent in pursuit of the escribano, Fanchinette, and the three surviving witnesses to the will; but the latter had long since left the island, being of the lower class of Péons, who pass to and fro between Trinidad and the Spanish main, and which class is stationary nowhere; and as to my uncle's late housekeeper, and her paramour, they were far too nimble for the tardy *alguacils*[†] of Port of Spain: they escaped to Cumana.[†]

After this, I was declared the undisputed heir of my uncle's estate: but, alas! there was no inheritance to dispute about; the whole of his property having been torn and devoured piecemeal by a set of legal sharks, who bore the names of oydores, assessors, escribanos, depositaries, sequestrators, advocates, alguacils, alguacil-mayors, &c. &c.[†]

Why the Spanish laws continue to be, in part, in force in Trinidad, against the wish of every honest man in that island, the various colonial secretaries of state for the last thirty years can tell — or, perhaps, cannot tell.

During the many months the above events took place, I resided with Dr. Lopez, who kindly wrote to my friends in Antigua, and proposed taking charge of my education. This proposal he made when he had hopes of recovering some part of my uncle's estate; yet, when those hopes proved fallacious, he, notwithstanding, continued his kindness towards me. The doctor occasionally employed me in translating law-papers from Spanish into English. He had commenced studying our language late in life; so that, when he met aught, in reading English, which he did not understand, he applied to me for explanation, which I easily gave.

One day I so pleased the doctor, by giving an extemporary translation of a passage in 'Coke's Institutes,'[†] that he said I would make a good lawyer. I expressed hopes of becoming one, when he immediately proposed to send me to the University of Caraccas. To this I readily assented, and the doctor wrote to Antigua, requesting my aunt's acquiescence, proposing himself to defray all charges consequent on the measure. To this the old lady acceded immediately. In truth, I think she would have started no objection, had he proposed making me a cobbler, a priest, or a duly qualified Italian opera-singer; for, although she had been kind to me during my infancy, yet she verified the old proverb, "out of sight, out of mind:" besides, she was the mother and grandmother of a numerous, indolent, and spendthrift family. Dr. Lopez gave me a little money, many books, much good advice, a letter of credit, and several letters of introduction. He then shipped me on board the schooner Baracouta, a vessel employed in the clandestine trade carried on, even during the war, between this island and the Main. I was consigned to Professor O'Keilly, of the University of Caraccas, and a Spaniard of Irish extraction.

CHAPTER 17.

"O'er the wild mountains, and luxuriant plains,
Nature, in all the pomp of beauty, reigns."
MONTGOMERY.[†]

——— "March the heavy mules securely slow,
O'er hills, o'er dales, o'er crags, o'er rocks they go."
POPE's *Iliad*[†]

Captain Jones, of the schooner Baracouta, after a passage of five days, anchored his vessel off La Guayra,[†] took me ashore, and, as directed, delivered me to Don Pedro Jenkinson, an English merchant, who, having married a Cadiz lady, put a Spanish handle to his name, to the scandal of all the "Old Christians"[36] of the vice-royalty.

Don Pedro Jenkinson, as he loved to be called, received me politely. After reading Dr. Lopez's note of introduction, he despatched a letter by a muleteer over the mountains to Caraccas, to Professor O'Keilly; and the following day the professor sent his own mule for me, by his servant, José Garcia, mounted on another mule, to act as my guide, and a third mule, led by a negro-boy, for my luggage.

We set out together, about two o'clock; to traverse the mountain which lies between La Guayra and Caraccas, ascended the zig-zag road, and, in about half-an-hour, I found myself in the coldest region I ever entered, for I had never before been on such an elevation. The view from this mountain track was magnificent: below us lay the city of La Guayra, with its old fortifications, its streets and spires; around us were three ridges of uncultivated, unsurveyed, and boundless mountains, with rich valleys between

---

36. European Spaniards called themselves Old Christians; natives of South America, they denominated Creoles; and Protestants, who conformed to the rites of the Roman Catholic church, New Christians.

them, over the bottoms of which cultivation spread her light green carpet: this strongly contrasted with the sombre verdure of virgin forests, that shaded the whole of the mountains around us.

José now called a halt, we dismounted, and unloaded the sumpter mule.

"Let us," said Garcia, "*milk a tree.*" I stared at this proposition; and José climbed an ordinary looking tree, which had thick dry leaves, and roots above ground. When he got to one of its lower branches, he made a cut with his *matcheti*[37] into this branch, and instantly issued a stream of liquid, resembling milk in colour and consistency; José caught this in a large calabash, and gave it me to drink, assuring me that it was both sweet and wholesome. I tasted it, and found it deserving of Garcia's praise; it had a fine aromatic odour and flavour: altogether, it is one of the most grateful and least cloying assuasives of thirst I ever drank. The *palo de vaca*, or cow-tree, is the best friend the traveller amongst the mountains about Caraccas can encounter. The Indian tradition says it sprang from the grave of the general mother of mankind.[38]

We now came to what the Caraqueños[39] call the saddle, that is, the highest ridge of the mountain between La Guayra and Caraccas, which is about six thousand feet above the level of the sea. The mule road up which we passed had been cut with great labour, but, ever and anon, it looked awful to one unaccustomed to mountain tracks. But from my infancy I had been a mountaineer, and therefore heeded not the giddy path up which our animals dragged themselves, nor the ugly-looking log bridges; thrown over chasms, mountain streams, cataracts, and dried gullies. The latter, during the rainy season, carry tremendous torrents down their red and pebbly canals. The sagacious mules, ere they place their sure hoofs on a doubtful log of those precarious bridges, would stoop their heads and smell them; when, being urged from behind by the voice of José calling out, "*Mula! mula! caramba!*" they would tread on, or leap over, the said log, as best satisfied their judgment. I assure the reader, that, notwithstanding their near consanguinity to the animal which has ever been emblematical of stupidity, the mules of South America possess judgment.

---

37. *Matcheti* is a kind of cutlass.[†]

38. Its botanical name is *Galactadendron utile*. I am told it is mentioned by Humboldt,[†] whose works I have never seen. Mr. Lockhart of Trinidad,[†] attempted to naturalise this tree in the latter island, but, owing to accident, he failed.

39. Natives of Caraccas.

At length we obtained a view of the city of the valley, the noble Caraccas: it lay spread out beneath us with its many cross-surmounted spires, its countless roofs, and hundred thousand inhabitants. A part of the city was built on the rising of the circumjacent mountain, a part on the banks of a beautiful stream; but it principally stood on the plain part of the valley, whose real beauties far exceed the imaginary ones of the happy valley of Rasselas.†

Caraccas being about two thousand feet above the level of the sea, its air is delightfully cool. The gardens round it nourish all the delicious fruits which an inter-tropical climate can boast of; while on the towering elevations by which it is surrounded flourish all the fruits and vegetables of Europe.

José Garcia delivered myself and baggage to Professor O'Keilly; who received me in a friendly manner. Like most dignitaries of the University of Caraccas, Dr. O'Keilly was in holy orders: his clerical duties, however, took up little of his time, and less of his attention. He filled the moral, philosophical chair; but, although a very learned and laborious man, he was yet a very eccentric one. He read much, as it appeared to me, for the mere purpose of picking out all that was odd and whimsical in books; as some collectors of objects of natural or unnatural history set the greatest value on monsters. The more improbable any theory appeared, the warmer was it espoused by the professor. He broached few of these theories in his lectures, because some of them were scarcely deemed orthodox; but I, being an inmate of his house, and his favourite pupil, was enlightened with all his private opinions. Like Lord Monboddor he conceived that man originally had a tail.† Some philosophers think that man is, by nature, a quadruped; but Professor O'Keilly, on the contrary, held that man is, by nature, a quadrumanous animal, like the monkey. He conceived that man's *lower hands* had grown into feet by their being cramped into shoes; nor would he admit the appearance of the Indians as offering proofs against his theory. Those people, he said, had, for some thousand years, worn no shoes; yet they all descended from the common parents of mankind, who, shortly after the flood, had cramped, by means of shoes, their lower hands into their present forms. He contended that an ape, and not a serpent, tempted Eve. He believed that the land of his fathers (Ireland) was the land of promise held out in the Scripture; that comets were hells for the damned; that the Iliad was the production of King Solomon; and that all the rest of the works which men take in general to be the genuine works of Greece and Rome, are forgeries of the middle ages. Further, he held that the modern pantomime was the remain of ancient paganism, handed down by tradition; and that our old friends, Harlequin, Columbine, Pantaloon, and Clown, were no others than Mercury, Psyche, Charon, and Momus. He believed Europe to have been populated by an Egyptian colony, who, after the lapse of ages, nearly exterminated an aboriginal race they found there; and that the modern gipsies are actually the descendants of this aboriginal people. He contended that they were neither Egyptians nor East Indians, but nothing more nor less than the vestiges of the aborigines of Europe.

I said I was the favourite pupil of Dr. O'Keilly: this was owing partly to my being a *protegé* of Dr. Lopez, and partly to my being a good listener; but principally because I was looked upon as a prodigy of the university, on account of my possessing an extraordinary memory, and a surprising aptitude in mastering both living and dead languages. I, with great facility, made Latin verses; and, although the sense of these somewhat halted, yet they marched on regular Roman feet. True it is, that one-third of each verse was made up of phrases taken from Horace or Virgil; another third of expressions plundered from Ovid, or other authors of the Augustan period; while the remainder was original nonsense; and yet they passed muster for collegiate poetry. My themes, too, used to be much lauded; and, although they wanted depth, yet they had the requisite length and breadth, and were all, Cerberus-like, three-headed. True it is that the style of these productions was loose and careless; yet they were *closely and elegantly written*, as far as related to penmanship. Their logic was flimsy; but they were composed in better Latin than at that time was used in the university, and hence they were universally admired.

But here I must pause in the list of my collegiate acquirements. In the mathematical sciences I made no progress: no mule on the road to Porto Cabello, when being flogged because he would not cross a log bridge which he conceives unsound, ever displayed more obstinacy than I shewed in crossing the *Pons Asinorum*.[†]

CHAPTER 18.

"I plunged beneath the ocean wave,
And viewed the monsters of the deep."
OLD SONG.†

During the times of vacation, and other hours not set apart for the study of mathematics and humanity, I used to practise what may not be improperly called inhuman acquirements. I renewed the lessons in fencing, and firing at marks, which, some years since, my uncle George had given me; besides which, I learned to handle the spear, and throw the poniard, as practised in South America, with great dexterity. José Garcia taught me to play some Castilian airs on the guitar; and I acquired the art of rattling the castanets, and dancing fandangos and boleros, without any teaching. Hence I became rather a favourite amongst the piebald members of the fair sex of the city of Caraccas, than which few parts of the earth possess a lovelier collection of women, and no place a greater variety of complexion. The purest white that ever left Europe, the most glossy black ever stolen from Africa, with all the endless grades and shades caused by the intermixture of Spanish, Moorish, Jewish, Indian, and negro races, might here be met.

Sometimes, during the vacation, I made excursions amongst the mountains and savannas,† where I acquired that which availed me more than the art of "making up" Latin verses — I became an extraordinarily fearless and safe horseman. I was remarkable for my equestrian acquirements, even in this land where beggars ask for *"un medio real,"*† in the name of the Virgin, while they are on horseback; and where it is common for a lad to spring on the back of the wildest horse that ever flew across the plains, and break him in, or break his own neck.

I also learned to throw the lasso with great dexterity: I could noose any given limb or horn of the wildest bull that ever made the savanna rebellow

101

with his roar. At La Guayra I learned to swim to such perfection that I became a perfect creole Leander.† I could swim further, dive deeper, and keep longer under water, than most pearl-seekers of the island of Margarita;† which last acquirement had one day nearly cost me dear, as the following fact will testify.

Being in La Guayra during the month of June, I was tempted by the heat of the lowlands to bathe in the sea: I swam out to some rocks, which lay a quarter of a mile from shore, and then dived to pick up some beauti-ful shells. As I got near to the bottom I balanced myself in mid-water, to observe a most beautiful phenomenon. It being noon, and the sun crossing the equator, near which stands La Guayra, his beams were reflected with surpassing splendour on the surface of the water, which was agitated into rippling waves by the mid-day breeze: these little waves were reflected on the sandy bed of the sea, which reflection shewed like a waving and shift-ing net of burnished silver. I saw this net, with pleasure, spread as far as my eye could reach, save where my own shadow, as it were, intercepted it. Suddenly this was overshadowed by a most terrific object. I instantly cast my eyes upwards, and, gracious Heaven! I beheld, right above me, one of the most terrible monsters in nature, known, the English in these seas under the appellation the shovel-nosed shark (*Squalus tigrinus* of Linnaeus). The extreme hideousness of this fish can neither be described by the pen, nor delineated by the pencil. Its body, although much thicker than mine, and thrice its length, was nothing compared to its laidly† head; the latter formed, as it were, the upper line of the letter T, while its com-paratively slender body was like the vertical stroke of that letter: a pair of enormous azure eyes protruded from either end of this T-formed head. Below this — but, alas! above me — opened a semi- circular mouth, big enough to swallow me entire. This, I perceived, was furnished with several rows of saw-like teeth. The appearance of this monster gained nothing from the light in which I saw it; it being, as I before said, right above me. I cast a few glances aloft, and observed his glaring eyes, that looked at once stupidly dull, and frightfully malignant. Their savage ken was directed down upon me; its greedy mouth was opening and shutting, as if in antici-pation of swallowing me.

I cast a glance at my limbs, and over my body, and mentally asked my Creator (may he forgive the involuntary thought) if he intended that his image, into whose nostrils he had breathed the breath of life, should become the prey of such a marine demon as floated above? This singular idea flashed through my mind with the speed of lightning: there was little time for reflection.

I swam, still under water, to another place; but I could observe, by the shadow of the monster, that he still followed me. Upwards I dared not look; in vain I tried to dodge my tormentor: where I stopped, he stopped; and, go where I would, still his shadow fell upon me.

What was to be done? My strength and breath were fast going; to remain much longer under water was impossible, and to rise was to make for the jaws of perdition. I sank to the bed of the bay, to arm myself with some conch shells: these might have been of some use, could I have gained the surface of the water unharmed, in which case I might have hurled them at his enormous head. But no, — the shark seemed aware that I could not long remain below, and he appeared determined to catch me as I rose.

Suddenly a ray of blessed hope shot across my benighted mind. I was beside a rock that had a small cleft through its centre, which, near the bed of the bay, had a horizontal passage: down this cleft I had often gone out of mere boyish desire of adventure; and to this chasm I swam, and in an instant darted into the horizontal part of it. Ere I did this, the hideous fish became, too late, aware of my manoeuvre; and, from the pressure of the water, I became sensible that he sunk down towards me: but the love of life made me too quick for him, even in his own element. I passed through the horizontal passage, and in an instant I was buoyed up through the vertical cavity of the rock, and rose to the surface of the water, all but suffocated, to inhale the blessed air. Still the persevering sea-devil followed; it had also forced itself through the aperture of the rock, but whether this was too small easily to admit its enormous head, I know not — certain I am, that the shark did not pass the cleft for some seconds after me. By this time I stood upright on the top of the rock, on which there were two or three feet of water, and a few rapid steps brought me out of immediate danger.

I had gained a part of the rock which was out of the water, although it afforded but bad footing, it being as sharp as the blade of a boat oar. On this I, however, got as the monster emerged from the passage, still pursuing me: it made a rush towards where I stood, but I was out of its element; it raised its huge head as if to ascertain here I was, and, at this instant, I hurled one of the conch-shells, which I still held in my hands, at his head with such effect as to stun the fish. It now lay motionless for some seconds; while I, to prevent the sharp edges of the rocks from cutting my feet, was obliged to kneel, and partly support myself with my hands. I now perceived the fish lashing the waters upon the rocks until they were in a foam; the fact was, it was high tide when we both came up, and, as the water was fast receding, it could not get off for want of depth. Some minutes had elapsed ere I perceived its predicament, for my attention was directed towards the shore, to which place I called for succour, using every exclamation of distress that I recollected: at length the fish became completely high and dry, and I perceived the danger of my late mortal foe, but felt no generous pity for him. I now fearlessly changed my uneasy position, and stood upright on the flat part of the rock. I was too much exhausted by my late adventure to essay swimming ashore, and saw with joy a canoe approaching me: one of the three men in her proved to be my old friend, José Garcia; who, being informed of my late escape, called out, "Santa Maria! it is *el capitan del puerto* (the harbour-master) that is on the rock!"

I must inform the reader, that I had often heard of a large and well-known shovel-nosed shark, called *el capitan del puerto*; who, in the Bay of La Guayra, was as well known as Port Royal Tom was in Jamaica. Whether my late foe was the identical *capitan del puerto*, I cannot take upon myself to say; but José, and the two men of the canoe, treated him with little ceremony: they beat the helpless shark's head with their paddles until he was again stunned, and finished him by cutting off his tail, and running a matcheti through his brain.

"You seem well acquainted," said I to José, "with *el capitan del puerto?*"

"I have reason so to be," replied Garcia, "Señor *Juana*" (Warner, he wished to say).

He shook his head, as though he knew more than he wished to communicate before strangers: I, therefore, asked him nothing further about it at that time; but the next morning, while on the mountainous road to Caraccas, after exacting from me a promise that I would not betray his confidence, he told the following story. The poor man has been now many years dead; and, therefore, I neither betray nor injure him by giving an account of his adventures with *el capitan del puerto*.

"You must know, Señor Juana, I was not always the steady servant of a Christian professor; but, some years since, I was as wild as a Savanna colt. I used to purloin little articles from the cargoes of your countrymen at La Guayra; but, by the blessing of San Antonio, I always kept from pilfering any but heretics. I was one concerned in robbing a bale of India goods with a French sailor, named François: he was not altogether a heretic, but almost as bad, for he was an Atheist; that is, he did not believe in God."

Here José crossed himself.

"Well, señor, I one day met this François in Caraccas: he beckoned me to follow him; I did so. When we got out of the city, François said, —

"'José, may I trust you?'

"'To be sure,' said I; 'especially while it is my interest to keep good faith with you; for you know, without good faith, we never can rob together.'

"'Do you see this key?' said the Frenchman; 'I made it myself; I am a bit of a blacksmith, and lately worked at Thomaso del Fuego's forge.'

"'What of that?' said I.

"'It fits,' replied François, 'the back-door of the great cathedral; I got the impression of it in soap while I was talking to the purblind sacristan. This blacksmith's child is a passport to the cathedral: let us, this night, carry off the *chapel*[40] and strip the Virgin of her pearls and diamond crown; it will make our fortunes.'

"I was shocked at this sacrilegious proposal, and threatened to 'peach him; but the Frenchman pretended it was all a joke, and we parted: but, four nights after this, to the horror of Christians of the viceroyalty, the whole communion-plate, golden candlesticks, and jewels of the Virgin, had disappeared.

"The bishop and all the priests anathematised the unknown robber, and all concerned with him. Wherever I turned, I heard people talk of the robbery; they said the plunder was worth fourteen thousand doubloons. Now, although I would not assist, nor be in any way concerned with François in the robbery, yet I thought it but fair that he should give me some part of the immense booty to make me hold my tongue. Where to find him I knew not, but guessed he was at La Guayra; so I hired a mule to go thither; but, coming along this same road, while passing the cross which was erected over the grave of Felipe St. Jago, who was murdered the year before, the beast absolutely took fright at seeing the cross, and threw me on the rock beside the road, and I broke my arm in the fall. I was taken back to Caraccas, and a terrible fever fell on me: I looked on all this as a judgment from heaven — for why? because I was thrown near a cross. I immediately sent for Padré Buen Intento, and told him of all I knew of

---

40. So the entire communion-plate is called.

François: he would not give me absolution until I made a secret declaration of this to the alcalde. After I did this, the police sent its alguacils in pursuit of the French sailor, and he was taken; but, save my secret evidence, nothing appeared against him.

"The priests wanted the civil authorities to put François to the torture;[†] but the oydor,[41†] who was half a heretic, and belonging to Miranda's party, declared that, by the *Partidas*,[42†] torture could only be used to extort confessions where there existed what the Spanish law called half-proofs; but with regard to the French sailor, nothing appeared against him but suspicion. This decision by no means satisfied the bishop, and so, as usual, the clergy and the lawyers went to logger-heads; and all this while François was imprisoned at La Guayra, and I was in the hospital, recovering from my fall.

"At length Padré Buen Intento, who was a wily Italian priest, proposed to me to get further intelligence from François; and I followed his direction. As soon as he recovered, the padré got me arrested, and, with the understanding of the police, I was lodged in prison, in the same room with the French sailor, under pretended suspicion of being concerned with him in the robbery.

"François at first was shy, because he suspected that his arrest was caused by my information; but, on being told that I was imprisoned on the same charge as himself, he opened his breast to me. I found he had, somehow or other, got files, and had nearly made his escape, by cutting through the window-stancheons: he told me, if I would go off with him, he would shew me where the concealed plate and jewels were. To this I consented; and that very night we made our escape. We got a canoe just as day dawned, and paddled out to the very rock on which I found you and the shark.

"He asked me if I could dive? I told him that, since my arm was broken, I was even afraid to swim, until the bone became better set. Out of the canoe went he — dived — and, in a moment, brought up the jewelled coronet of our Lady of Caraccas, shining with its pearls, and glistening with its brilliants.

"'There!' said François, holding up the crown; 'this is worth one hundred thousand dollars: with this, and what is below, we will steal off to

---

41. Judge; literally, a hearer.
42. Spanish code of laws.

Trinidad; there is enough to make men of both of us. One who is poor is a dog; he who is rich is a man.'

"Although I had acted under the direction of Padré Buen Intento, who, I suspect, even caused François to be supplied with files; yet, I confess to you (may all the saints forgive me!), that when I saw the rich crown of our lady, I was tempted to join the godless French sailor in his flight to Trinidad, although, doubtless, he would have corrupted me with his impious conversation: but I made up my mind, as soon as I came to Trinidad with the plunder, to become a pious Christian.

"Again he dived, and brought up the heavy gold candlesticks of the cathedral; then brought up the chalice: in short, he completely freighted the canoe with the objects of his sacrilege.

"He called on me to balance the canoe while he jumped in.

" 'Now,' said he, laughing, 'we'll start along shore for the Gulf of Paria; we'll bid defiance to the bald-head priests, and all their curses, bells, books, and candles.'†

"And, as he said this, he made an effort to leap into the canoe, when his thigh was seized by the shark well known in the Bay of La Guayra by the name of *el Capitan del Puerto*. The shrieking Frenchman was dragged under water, and with horror I beheld the sea-demon cut him in two; and devour him piecemeal. In less than a minute nothing was seen of him but his blood, which dyed the surface of the water."

"And what," said I, "became of the church-plate and jewels?"

"What should become of them?" replied José, shocked at the terrible punishment which revenging Heaven had inflicted on the sacrilegious wretch: "I immediately paddled to the shore, sent for Padré Buen Intento, related what had taken place, restored the property, made my peace with Mother Church, and became a reformed man."

"And what reward did the Italian priest bestow upon you?" said I.

"He gave me absolution, and his blessing," replied José.

CHAPTER 19.

"Earth felt the wound, and nature from her seat,
  Sighing through all her works, gave signs of wo."
  MILTON.[†]

I had now spent seven happy years in and about Caraccas; I was seventeen years of age, and nearly as tall as ever I became: I was little short of six feet in height. True, my frame was slender, and better calculated for acts of agility than of strength; although by no means deficient in the latter quality. I passed as much of my time in open air as my studies would admit of. Often have I slept in a "chinchora," (that is, a net-work hammock, suspended from the branches of a tree), with no other covering than the foliage afforded.

The fact is, I had a keen relish for sports and athletic exercises. They were generally solitary. I was but little disposed to be associated with those about me, who consisted of my fellow-students, most of whom were devoted to gaming and rioting, to neither of which I was ever inclined; and, as to the bigoted professors, few young men would think of forming friendships with them. I occasionally made acquaintance with a few English and French residents of La Guayra and Caraccas; but these acquaintances never ripened into friendship, for they were mere money-making animals.

Sometimes my old intimate, José Garcia, used to chat with me; but, having an opportunity of observing him closely, I found him one fourth knave, and three fourths bigot. His superstition, though strong, was only enough to keep his roguery in check. José's education was just sufficient to enable him to read certain parts of the missal which are in daily use; but, had his obtuse mind been sharpened by certain productions from Voltaire[†] and Tom Paine,[†] he might have been what the French, during their first revolution, called a philosopher: in which case he never would have gone to church, but I am not sure that he would not have gone to the gallows.

I was a great favourite with Professor O'Keilly, so that I obtained all the benefit of hearing his fanciful theories. He could not explain these to many about him; for, some of them being heterodox, by making them public he might have incurred ecclesiastical censure: the fact is, I believe, the professor, although in holy orders, was scarcely in all respects a good Catholic.

He, however, counselled me, if it did not militate against my conscience, to be a pretty regular attendant at mass. This prudent advice I followed; although I still continued a member of the Church of England. The calls which the regulations of the university made to attend mass, during Passion-week[†] of 1812, became tedious to me: hence I often used to steal from church, and go shooting in the neighbouring mountains; which was the case on Holy Thursday[†] (March 26th, 1812). On the afternoon of that day, I was reposing under a wild fig-tree, on a mountain to the northward of the city. I was enjoying the beautiful prospect. Two thousand feet beneath me lay Caraccas; above and below me wound the mountain track, on which were many passengers hurrying into the city to attend to their religious duties. The weather had been extremely sultry, and at that moment not a breath of air was stirring: all was life on the road, but all stillness in the valley below; not a sound arose from it, save, now and then, that the church-bells called the pious to devotion.

Suddenly I heard a low, dismal, booming, rumbling noise, which I am unable to describe, because it was unlike any sound I ever heard. Could the reader imagine two grand armies engaging each other with musketry and artillery, in an immense mine ten thousand feet beneath him, he might form some faint idea of the sound I heard. This portentous noise was uttered from the mass of mountains and valleys that lay above, around, and beneath me. No wind stirred; and yet, in the distance, I saw the gigantic trees more agitated than if they had been lashed by a tempest. This agitation of the woods gradually approached me: it was visible to the sight some moments ere my bewildered mind divined the cause (for I at first conceived it to be a visionary delusion); but soon I perceived, with terror, that the world of stupendous mountains amongst which I stood was distracted by an earthquake, of such awful might that they seemed ready to fall on each other and the valleys beneath, and mingle their earth, rock, and forests, in one chaotic mass.

The agitation of the earth increasing, until the surface of the whole panorama was in undulating motion, the subterraneous noise became louder. I cast my eyes on the city below me: the earth on which it stood waved like the vexed bosom of the ocean when a tropical hurricane careers over it. Her countless roofs and tall spires rose with this motion; and, as the agitated earth sank, with the deafening roar of a thousand thunder-clouds, her long streets and grand edifices were prostrated on the shudder-ing earth, burying ten thousand of her shrieking inhabitants in the ruins: the subterraneous noise was now overpowered by the frightful groans which rose from the fallen city.

An immense thick cloud of dust arose from the ruins below me, and mounted like a column of smoke: this, to the survivors of the valley, dark-ened the sun for some minutes; while to those who, like me, stood above the city, it gave to the orb of day a deep red dye. Gradually this cleared away; pure light shone again on the valley of Caraccas, to exhibit to the survivors of the late calamity their noble city a heap of ruins, and their kindred and friends either slain, mutilated or buried alive under tons of overthrown building materials. Here and there the earth shewed dreadful chasms, newly opened; and from the mountains were hurled immense rocks, or rather quarries, which rushed down the woody sides of the hills on the devoted city. One stupendous rock, weighing many hundreds of tons, was detached from the earth above me: it plunged past me, crushing whole trees; and, after five times crossing the winding road, on which it destroyed four mules, and seven human beings, it alighted in the suburbs of the city, having fallen three thousand feet.

The earthquake ceased.[43] I breathed again, and hastily prayed: it was "terror" which had taken "devotion's mien;"† but, after a few moments, my mind became more calm and, consequently, more fit for devotion: I knelt and addressed my Maker in mingled supplication and thanksgiving. Long and fervently I prayed, until I felt myself called upon to use exertion to succour my fellow worms — for so proud man appeared to me.

Immediately after this awful demonstration of the weakness of human-ity and the power of the Creator, I made my way down to the grand scene of desolation; a journey not unattended with danger and labour. The detached rocks frequently blocked up the mountain track, and obliged me

---

43. The hands of several clocks, that were overturned without being entirely destroyed pointed to seven minutes past four: this afforded something like data, as to the time when the first shock occurred. How long each shock lasted, many pretend to tell with great minute-ness; but no two agree; nor does any one state that he held a stop-watch in his hand during this event. Perons who believe these *earthquake meters* have little idea of the state of bewilder-ment such a visitation occasions.

to climb around and over them; most of the bridges over torrents and gaps were destroyed or injured, and large rents appeared in the winding path; most of which impediments I surmounted by climbing from tree to tree, on each side of these chasms, by means of their branches.

I was young and active; yet so laborious was the journey into the ruins of the city, that it took me three hours to arrive at the scene of devastation.

The moon had risen in surpassing beauty, shedding her placid light over the prostrated city and her woful children, whose distress beggared description. Dying moans, and groans of distress, mingled with cries of anguish and sympathy: here a group of sons and daughters of a family were flinging aside rafters, tiles, and bricks, to discover, and, if not too late, relieve their buried parents: there, wildly shrieked a mother, bearing in her arms the mangled corpse of her infant: here strode a resident of the mountains over ruins, to discover, and, if possible, to assist his friends. All was distress, exertion, and confusion: every one who escaped unhurt from this terrible visitation, exerted himself to relieve his fellows; but there was no one to direct his labour.

I at length entered a church, which had not been thrown down by the convulsion of nature, although the roof and walls were cracked in all directions. Here were a number of priests and old people, supplicating aid from their wood and stone saints, who were, I thought, scarcely in a condition to afford assistance — every image of them had been overthrown. Suddenly, a tremour of earthquake was felt, when instantly arose the cry of "Santa! Santa Maria!" but the damaged temple withstood the slight shock. Considering, however, that if any other violent trembling of the earth were to occur, the dilapidated church would be the very worst place to be in, I quitted it.

A keen north-east wind gave me a sensation of cold, as I scrambled over masses of ruins, — now and then lending a helping hand to extricate some sufferer, or to drag out some one whose sufferings were passed, — until I arrived at the spot on which, a few hours since, stood the house of Professor O'Keilly. It had fallen, and killed my friend the professor, José Garcia, and all the servants of the establishment, save one gray-headed negro, who was sitting on an overturned pillar, weeping the fate of his master and his fellow slaves, — amongst whom were his wife and three children, — all of whose bodies had been taken out.

Weary with my exertions and emotions, I again scrambled over prostrated streets to find a shelter for the night, until I came to a house that was uninjured. Here I heard several persons talk English: I solicited, and obtained an entrance. The house belonged to a Mr. W——, an English merchant. I found several Englishmen here assembled, who, like myself, had been exerting themselves to aid the distressed. Strange to say, although there were many English in La Guayra and Caraccas, not one of them was injured by the late awful occurrence. Some refreshments were offered me, of which I thankfully partook, and then slept under a kind of portico. I record one fact, which does honour to the Caraqueños: not one robbery was known to follow the visitation of Heaven, although property of immense value lay exposed to any one who would disgrace human nature by turning thief on such an occasion.

The earthquake of Caraccas prolonged the domination of Spain over Columbia.† Some years before this, Miranda, secretly instigated by the British government, sailed from Trinidad with an expedition, composed principally of adventurers who were, like himself, natives of South America. Their object was to gain the independence of their native land; and their project would have succeeded, but they were opposed by the clergy, who, at that time, were a potent body. They availed themselves of the occurrence of the earthquake: this, they persuaded the people, was a judgment from Heaven, on account of the rebellion; hence the liberation of Columbia was deferred. She *is* now independent, I hope she will be happy.

The two following days, my humble exertions to aid the distressed were renewed, amid scenes too painful, and too much alike, for description.

In the suburbs of the city I found a mule quietly grazing: this animal, the worthy but eccentric Professor O'Keilly had presented to me but one week previous: I also recovered some part of my wearing apparel, and my fowling-piece. I crossed the mountains to La Guayra; the bridges and gaps in the road had been roughly repaired, so that I gained the seaport without accident.

I found La Guayra had shared the fate of Caraccas; it was a heap of ruins. I sold my mule to Jenkinson, and took my passage on board of a launch bound for Trinidad.

CHAPTER 20.

"Pistol. — Si fortuna me tormenta,
Sperato me contenta."
  HENRY IV.[†]

A South American launch is a strong, ugly-looking vessel, of most inar-
tificial build, about sixty feet in length, and eight in width. When
loaded, its gunwale is only a few inches from the water; but it has a kind
of bulwark around it, composed of tarpaulin; a deck, made of canes, or
reeds, which is covered with undressed bull-hides; it has two large and ill-
formed latine sails,[†] and a jib-sail. The launch I sailed in was manned
with five naked Indians, and two péons, including the patron. Its cargo
was of the true Noah's ark description: it was made up of tasso,[44†] wild
hog's flesh, smoked goat's flesh; several kinds of dried fish; ropes made of
various kinds of palm-fibres; cassada bread, flour, starch;[†] inferior kinds
of sugar-loaves, called papilones;[†] plantains, pompions,[†] Indian corn,
turkeys, fowls, monkeys, macaws, parrots, parroquets, dogs: a full-grown
ant-bear, or sloth,[†] and a young tiger,[†] in a wooden cage, completed this
collection.

The passage was long, yet by no means unpleasant. The mode of our
navigation was as primitive as the construction of our vessel; we had not,
nor did we need a compass, because we hugged the land the whole voyage,
which was made during the nights: when the wind was favourable we
sailed; when otherwise, or calm, the Indians rowed with broad-bladed
oars, standing up while they pulled. During the day the patron sent out a
kind of wooden mud-hook, composed of several pieces of forked guava-

---

44. Smoked beef.

branches, lashed together, which did duty for an anchor. During the heat of the day the crew slept; their nap lasted about eleven hours. When the sun was setting they awoke, and took an enormous meal, which served them for twenty-four hours. When the sun set, up went the wooden anchor, the sails were set, or the oars put out, and away went the launch from headland to headland.

During the day, while the crew of the launch slept, I went ashore, and amused myself with shooting. At night I slept soundly; the creaking of the bulwarks, as the seamen pulled the launch, and their singing a kind of monotonous extempore song, acted as good soporifics. The continual change of scene, and my favourite diversion of shooting, served to alleviate my grief I felt for the loss of my Caraccas friend; but I was of an age when hope is too vivid to let sorrow take a deep root in the mind: hitherto I had been used to lose, but never to be destitute of friends. At length, on the eleventh day of our voyage, the launch anchored off the King's Wharf, in Port of Spain.

The capital of Trinidad had been totally destroyed by fire since I left it; but, in place of the straggling wooden streets which existed during my sojourn there, the foundation of the finest town in the West Indies was laid, which was finished a few years after, under the government of Sir Ralph Woodford.[†]

My meeting with my worthy patron, Dr. Lopez, was affectionate; he had heard of the awful catastrophe at Caraccas; the evil news travelled faster than a South American launch. The doctor's fears for my safety were at an end, by my appearance; but I brought him news of the death of his friend O'Keilly, which much affected him.

The next day the doctor commenced inquiring into the state of my education; during which inquiry my vanity received a severe check. I thought to surprise him with my proficiency in the dead as well as living languages; but he treated my accomplishments rather coolly, and begged to look at some of my theses, which he examined with different eyes from those employed by the head of the University of Caraccas: for the latter had looked for beauty of style, and purity of Latin; the doctor, on the contrary, scrutinised their reasoning. They would better stand the review of the Senatus Academicus than the criticism of Dr. Lopez. The university admired their flowers of rhetoric; but the doctor searched, in vain, for the fruits of logic. The fact is, Lopez was himself a poor linguist, and, like most other men, he thought lightly of such acquirements as he himself could not master: but he piqued himself on being a good logician; and hence he candidly told me he conceived my memory was cultivated at the expense of my understanding, — saying, "he wished, instead of my having been taught to read, write, and speak several languages, that I had been taught to think deeply in one."

My worthy patron himself displayed no great depth of thought by the remark, as profundity of thought cannot be acquired by precept.

The doctor counselled me not to prosecute my studies of the Spanish law, because he believed that, in a short time, it would cease to be the law of Trinidad. To use an expression of Junius, "he was a good lawyer, but no prophet."[†] In 1836 the colony is still hag-ridden by a legal monster, more hideous than that of Frankenstein, having a body very like the *corpus juris civilis*.[†] The laws of the Indies[45†] form its legs; one arm is made up of orders in council, the other of English common-law; and, although it is gifted with an English tongue, its head and features are Spanish.

On my going to see if there were any letters for me at the post office, I found one from my aunt, who had grown very frail: she expressed a desire to see me ere she died. This letter had remained in the post-office for more than three months, although at the arrival of every packet, Dr. Lopez sent to ask if there were any communication for me, and was answered in the negative. This shameful kind of neglect is too common throughout the West Indies. The great man of letters, Sir Francis Freeling,[†] should be informed of this circumstance.

By Dr. Lopez's direction, I immediately prepared for a voyage to Antigua; but, no opportunity offering, I was kept two or three weeks, in Trinidad waiting for a vessel.

During my short sojourn in Port of Spain, an event took place as alarming and as ludicrous as that which, some years since, broke up the court at St. Vincent. In the latter island a bull came into court; but in Trinidad a much greater body, viz. a whale, tried to go to church. Instead of describing this event from my memory, I will make an extract from an old newspaper, 'The Trinidad Observer,' in which it is recorded.

I am the less scrupulous in embodying the following sketch into these memoirs, because I originally wrote it; therefore there is no plagiarism in the case; for, according to Tony Lumpkin, "a man may rob himself at any time."[†]

---

45. So the Spanish colonial code is called.

"A Tale of A Whale.

'Who ever heary a tale afore
Of big fish left in a lurch?
No somebody sabby a whale afore
Take path for go in a church.'
Negro Song.

"The busy hum of man had ceased"[†] — nothing was heard but the buz of insects, which, as Bryan Edwards[†] says, 'produces a pleasing sound,' notwithstanding the reflection that the notes of some of them (the mosquito, for example,) are preceded, accompanied, or followed by a sting: besides these sounds, the stillness occasionally was broken by a thousand cocks, which, in this island, crow through the night; and the barking of a thousand dogs, which keep up a continual chorus. As the incessant yells of these curs preclude their being of any use as watch-dogs; as nobody here keeps hunting-dogs in town; and as the heat of the climate puts lap-dogs out of the question, I have yet to learn why these canine enemies of Somnus are permitted to 'murder sleep'[†] in this town. However, with the exception of those weak sounds, all was tranquil in Port of Spain.

"Suddenly was heard a lowing, moaning — in short, an indescribable noise, such as imagination might give to an enormous ox the size of Tamana Mountain.

"'What could it be?' asked all who heard it, — that is to say, all the inhabitants of the town: no one could tell. Some conjectured it was the sound of artillery, caused by a sea-fight: this it could not be — it was not so distant: others took it for the rumbling which preceded an earthquake; but then, again, it was not a subterraneous noise. Whatever was the cause, the mysterious notes, like the ominous voice which the Scotch usurper heard, bid the denizens of Port of Spain 'sleep no more.' The sounds grew louder and louder: mingled prayers were heard in English, French, and Spanish; and I regret being obliged to record, that 'curses, not *deep* but *loud*,'[†] were uttered in the three languages: these were, no doubt, used as mere interjections, expressive of astonishment. Many were the mosquito doses[†] swallowed to allay alarm; and many were the vows of repentance: these were so sincere, that some of them were remembered six hours after.

"Darkness, which increases fear, at length began to disappear; yet the indescribable sound continued — until, for a moment, it was lost in a louder noise, for the morning gun was discharged from the sea-fort; and, as its echo died away amongst the mountains, and on the placid Gulf of Paria, it was answered by the cracked bell of the old Catholic church, which announced the time for celebrating early mass. In all the streets leading to the church might be seen crowds of decently dressed females, followed by little 'niggars,' carrying chairs and prayerbooks; and even a few men were observed walking towards the time-worn edifice. As these approached the church, the noise that had rendered the preceding night sleepless became louder, and, on their arrival, it was explained; for on the shore, near the church, was seen a *rudis indigestaque moles*,[†] which, as Polonius has it, was 'very like a whale;'[†] (two novel quotations, by the by). The leviathan had been pursued by a thrasher[†] and a sword-fish, until it ran ashore, and the receding tide had left it 'high and dry.' I suppose this, as there is no authentic instance of a whale going to church — as the old negro song from which I take my motto wisely observes.

"Any whale that is found on the shores of Britain becomes the property of their majesties, — the head falling to the share of the king, and the tail to the queen, in order, as our lawyers say, to supply their wardrobes with whalebone: this being rather a whimsical reason, considering that useful whalebone is found in the head alone. But here, the royal claim is either unknown or disregarded; so that the fish was considered the property of all those who chose to cut blubber off it; and all who, having Russian appetites, took slices of its red flesh for their breakfasts.

"Many of those who, the preceding night, were terrified by the bellowing of the stranded fish, now laughed at their fear, and seized on axes, adzes, and cutlasses, to revenge themselves on the unfortunate cause of their alarm, and to secure a part of the prize. All was bustle:

'The fishermen forsook the strand,
The swarthy smith took dirk in hand,'[†]

to hack and hew the poor whale, who protested most loudly against the inhospitable treatment. It is true that the fish could use but one of the nine parts of speech — that is to say, the interjection; but this he employed, *ore rotundo*,[†] most lustily: insomuch that it disturbed the devotion of the few in the church, — as Padré Arestimone that day said mass to a thin congregation.

"The cutting and slashing of the whale proceeded rapidly; but it never once occurred to any one of those on or around it to secure the fish. This was everybody's business to do; but, as usual with everybody's business, nobody did it. The whale's bellowings had become fainter, and at length had ceased. His butchers, therefore, conceived,

'''T was *grease*, but living *grease* no more.'[†]

The fish was thought *dead stock*: few supposed he would become *floating capital*.

" 'I say, you lubbers!'[†] said the mate of a London vessel, formerly in the Greenland trade,[†] 'you are not *hacting* according to *Oil*!' (he was a cockney.)[†] — why don't you run a harpoon into him, and belay it to that ere *house* with a line?'

"The only one who took notice of this good advice was a negro boatman, who, like the whale, was half seas over (the tide had risen); and he replied in an old proverb, giving it a new reading, — 'Ebbery body for myself.'

"The dissection proceeded; when suddenly
'Rose from sea to sky the wild farewell —
Then shrunk the timid, and stood still the brave.'[†]

"In short, the whale, by a desperate effort, dashed from the strand into the middle of the gulf, carrying about twenty involuntary passengers on his lacerated back; while the unfeeling spectators on shore gave them three cheers as they went off.

"Here was a scene which may be imagined more easily than described: it could be well depicted by Cruikshank. Johnny Gilpin flying by the Bell at Edmonton,[†] on the back of a restive horse, is a subject 'flat, stale, and unprofitable,'[†] compared to the view of the dingy inhabitants of Port of Spain going to sea on what they erroneously supposed was the back of a dead whale. Away they went, shrieking, yelling, *blubbering*, and *wailing*, until the fish, by sinking, washed them off his back.

"I am happy to be enabled to say, that all the crew which performed this unprecedented voyage were safely landed: this was owing to their being all good swimmers, and to the prompt assistance obtained from fishing canoes. They escaped the jaws of sharks and barocoutas (creole cod-fish),[†] who were employed more profitably in pursuing the whale than in attacking his late tormentors.

"What became of leviathan has never been ascertained; it is supposed that, wishing to indict the inhabitants of Port of Spain for cutting and maiming, under the *black* act,[†] he caused a meeting of all the sea-lawyers in the gulf of Paria."[46]

---

46. Sailors call sharks *sea-lawyers*, and denominate lawyers *land-sharks*. I know not for what reason, as no two things can be more dissimilar than lawyers and sharks.

CHAPTER 21.

"A conflagration labouring in her womb . . .
Dark and voluminous the vapours rise,
And hang their horrors in the neighbouring skies;
While though the Stygian gloom that blots the day,
In dazzling streaks the vivid lightnings play."
                    COWPER.[†]

A few days after this event I embarked for Antigua, on board of a
cutter[†] called the Sea Fairy, — a beautiful vessel, built at the
Bermudas, of the fragrant cedar of those islands. The captain of this
passage-boat was a negro, called Joe Rogers, a Bermudian, and, like most
of his countrymen, or rather fellow-islanders, a marine Jack-of-all-trades;
viz. a ship-builder, rigger, sail-maker, caulker, sea-cook, wrecker, smuggler, fisher, whale-fisher, pilot, and privateer's-man. Joe had seen the
world. He had, as he informed me, been captured by a French frigate, and
sold as a slave in Martinique, whence he attempted to escape in a boat
with three others; when they were picked up by a Dutch privateer, and Joe
was obliged to act as cook, until, on the arrival of the Dutchman in the
Channel, he planned another escape, which, from its nature, could only
have originated in the brain of a semi-amphibious native of Bermuda. He
secretly got a quantity of corks, which he sewed up in various parts of his
dress, especially his pockets; and, with his habiliments thus rendered
buoyant, he determined to jump overboard in the Channel and swim
ashore, as soon as he was informed which was the English coast. In this
attempt fortune favoured him. In coming home, the Dutchman ran a-head
of his reckoning, and, on a foggy morning, found himself nearer the
Cornish coast than he either wished to be or calculated on being; when all
hands were hastily piped to put the ship about. During the bustle occasioned by this event, Joe jumped overboard.

"We were," said the negro, "hardly eight miles from the shore, which, you know, sir, an't nothing of a swim for a Porgie,[47] even if I hadn't the corks."

After half an hour's swimming, he was picked up by an English brig-of-war. He gave information of the Dutch privateer: the latter was pursued and captured; and the captain of the brig, to reward Rogers, impressed him. The poor fellow served, as he expressed it, *the* majesty, for ten years, during which time he got four wounds and lost three of his fingers, and then obtained his discharge, a small pension, and a good deal of prize-money, with which he returned to the "still vexed Bermuthes;" for it is a well-known fact, that the Bermuda negro fears exile more than slavery — at least, the mitigated slavery of Bermuda.† This circumstance confers honour both on the bondsman and the master. However, Joe, for a very little sum, obtained his "free paper,"† and his old master employed him, giving him the charge of the Sea Fairy.

We set sail at noon, cleared the Bocas ere evening, and the next morning were off Cariacou, running with the wind three points free† — when astern we discovered a suspicious-looking schooner, which immediately gave chase to us.

Joe, being confident of outsailing the schooner, hoisted British colours: the strange vessel informed us she was an enemy, in as plain language as her bow-chasers† could speak; but the shot, although well intended, fell short of the mark. Joe took the helm, and kept the enemy's two masts in one, as he called it; that is, he kept right ahead of her, so that the bow-guns she from time to time fired, retarded the schooner. The cutter suddenly went about,† and ran close under one of the numerous Grenadines.

"Good-by, *monsieur soupe-maigre!*"† cried the Bermudian; "you'll not catch me this time: Joe Rogers won't be sold again to dig cane-holes† after having served *the* majesty ten years."

The chase was interesting. Had we been in the open sea, and the breeze a little stronger, the schooner might have captured us, but the light wind suited our beautiful cutter to a crack; she drew less water than did our pursuers — consequently, could run into creeks, and so near the land that the schooner dared not follow us. Joe evidently knew the Grenadines better than did those on board the schooner; which causes all combined to

---

47. A favourite fish of the Bermudians, and hence natives of the Bermudas are called Porgie.

favour the escape of the Sea Fairy. In a short time the enemy's hull was below the horizon, then her lower sails disappeared; and, on running round Mustique,[†] we completely lost sight of her.

Joe having heard from a fisherman off Mustique that an English brig-of-war was cruising to windward of St. Vincent, he beat up to the northward of that island, where he fell in with her, ran his cutter under her counter,[†] and gave information of the privateer being amongst the Grenadines.

"Can I depend on your information?" said the captain.

"To be sure you can: do you think I'd deceive you after I've served *the* majesty for ten years?"

Immediately the man-of-war was put about in pursuit of the schooner; and, as she left us, we heard her drums beat to quarters.[†] She, however, did not succeed in capturing the privateer. Several months after this she was taken near Barbadoes, but not until she had done great damage to our colonial trade.

A light wind now carried us opposite the Bay of Chateau Belair. We were completely becalmed all night. About midnight I heard what I took to be a peal of artillery from the interior of the island. I went on deck to ascertain the cause of this alarm. Scarcely had I got up the companion ladder, ere I supposed one of the crew was throwing sand on me from above. I called out for such as were playing their practical jokes to desist: no one replied, and this unaccountable pelting continued: the skipper told me it had been falling all night, but he was ignorant of the cause. I looked above, and found the sky the darkest I ever beheld; the sand-storm and singular report continued. I remained awake the whole night, which seemed interminable.

Morning at length arrived, but she arose not with those blushes with which she generally greets the Caribbean Sea. Slowly and sullenly the gloom of night retreated and was succeeded by a dismal twilight: hours passed, but the face of heaven did not brighten, although the sun was many degrees above the horizon. The fall of sand, mingled with ashes, continued until the surface of the sea seemed discoloured; the bold outlines of St. Vincent were the same as I before beheld them, but its beautiful hues were gone; her tree-crowned mountains, cultivated valleys, galba-fenced[†] plantations, picturesque villages, and gushing cascades, bore but one ash-like hue; the very air was so mingled with the sand-shower that it appeared of a gray die.

My attention was now called to the Souffriere,[†] or volcanic mountain.

This is the last of a chain called *Morne*[48] *à Garou*: it poured out volumes of thin black smoke, together with the showers of sand, which fell in every direction for the distance of thirty leagues.

Not a breath of air stirred; we were, therefore, constrained to lie off the Bay of Chateau Belair all day.

Noon came, but the sky assumed the hue of midnight; for the rush of smoke from the volcano had completely overclouded the whole atmosphere. Gradually, the volumes which burst from the crater assumed a red hue, expanded, and rose with awful rapidity, and with a roar so deafening as to spread alarm through every island lying within two hundred miles of St. Vincent. Birds were beat to the ground, the starving cattle ran, bellowing, about the sand-covered pastures, and the shrieking Indians and negroes urged their flight to the capital.

The air became hot and sulphurous, and the island was shook by repeated earthquakes; not, indeed, such visible undulations as I lately beheld overturn the city of Caraccas: the surface of St. Vincent trembled with a horizontal motion.

The gloomy evening was succeeded by a night palpably obscure; the dome of heaven was completely overclouded by the volcanic canopy, and seemed as starless as a subterranean vault: the gigantic torch of the Souffriere rendered the darkness visible. A conflagration now rose from its summits in the form of a reversed pyramid, apparently as huge as the whole island. The extent of this fire may be guessed when the reader is informed that it burst from a new crater one mile in extent; and the terrible outlet of the lava formed but the apex of this fiery triangle, over which hung masses of clouds of truly Stygian hue and density. These clouds were continually rent in all directions by what appeared to be electric flashes; while large globes of igneous matter were hurled in every direction over the island, setting fire to it in a hundred places.

The Sea Fairy lay to the north-east of the Souffriere. The lava poured out from the new crater, and rushed down towards us: opposed by a high point of land, the liquid flame accumulated until it assumed the appearance of an infernal lake; augmented by fresh streams of lava, it arose above its mountain barrier and precipitated itself towards the sea, carrying down with it an immense wreck of rock and burning wood. Before midnight this cataract of fire reached the sea, while another burning torrent rolled down the eastern side of the mountain.

---

48. *Morne*, in creole French, signifies a hill: I believe this word is a provincialism.

An earthquake now shook the island; this was succeeded by a fall of cinders; a more alarming shower of stones, mixed with fire, followed: the latter lasted until near daylight.

It fortunately happened that the stones sent from the volcano were very light; hence, few were hurt, and fewer slain. From the immense quantity of ashes which covered the island and the Grenadines, famine was apprehended: this was obviated by the prompt humanity of the neighbouring colonies.

One plantation (that belonging to Thesega) was so completely covered with volcanic matter that it was obliged to be abandoned. The negroes and Indians accounted for this by saying, that the black Caraibs, who formerly held the lands of this estate, had put a malediction on it previous to their going into exile.

Geologists, who have been compared to an insect on the back of an elephant, speculating on its intestines, declared that this extraordinary eruption was connected with the earthquake of Caraccas, which that day five weeks I had witnessed. About this time the valleys of the Mississippi and Ohio were convulsed by some subterranean action. What connexion these events had with each other, is not for me to say.

A breeze sprang up early next morning; the Sea Fairy took advantage of it; and the following day we anchored off St. John's, Antigua.

CHAPTER 22.

"What strange event, what aggravated sin?
They stand convicted of a darker sin."
HANNAH MORE.[†]

M y aunt appeared to be in a dying state; but her physician had supposed she would die every day for the last four months, and she
lingered on for fourteen months more. Through life she was of a dilatory
disposition, and she absolutely seemed to procrastinate her death. On my
arrival she again sent for the doctor, and asked him to tell her, candidly, if
she had any chance of recovery: he answered her in the negative. On
hearing this, she ordered every one out of the room except myself; she
then rose, and bade me open a part of the mattrass on which she lay: she
told me to take out a fragment of an old silk gown, in which was sewed up
a quantity of gold Spanish and Portuguese coins, to the amount of about
two hundred joes.

"Here, Warner," said the old lady; "your father lent me, just after I
married, twice the sum which is here. I might have noted this in my will,
or bequeathed you the sum; but I have no faith in wills — I always thought
them unlucky: nobody ever gets any thing from wills in the West Indies
but executors. I am sure, if I left you two hundred joes, you would never
get it; so I give it you, or rather pay you half what I owed your father. But
if I should recover (and I am only eighty-two — and there is old Mrs.
French, who is hearty, and lives on chocolate, although she is one hundred
and seven) — but what was I saying? ah, yes! if I should recover, then,
Warner, I trust in your honour, as the son of a gentleman, to give me back
the two hundred joes; because, you know, you could never force me to pay
you, for your father made me sign no paper when he lent me three thousand dollars. However, I give you all the money I have by me, in case I
should die, as an act of justice; but don't let any of your cousins know a

word about it. Perhaps the doctor is right, and I am on my deathbed; therefore, promise me, Warner Arundell, always to act as a gentleman, in never suffering any one to insult you with impunity."

The little traits of selfishness which my aunt's speech betrayed did not much impress me with reverence for her: however, I promised to fulfil her requests.

The day after this interview with my aunt, I visited my father's Antigua estate, now put out to dry-nurse[†] under the superintendence of Messrs. Keen and Leech, of St. Christopher's, merchants who kept their books with great regularity — especially the debit sides.

When the slaves learned that I was the son of their old master, their reception of me was painfully affecting. All the old people, who remembered the kind treatment which they experienced from my father, kissed me, and wept like children. The whole gang[†] blessed me, and prayed that I might inherit my rights, and become their master. One and all complained of the most inhuman treatment which they experienced from the manager of the estate, an Englishman, of the name of Lowery. It is a remarkable fact, that, with the exception of emancipated slaves, Europeans, in general, make far more oppressive slave-owners than creoles.

I inquired into their complaints, and discovered that they were too well founded: I therefore immediately laid them before the attorney-general, whose duty it was to attend to such charges. This officer, with both zeal and abilities, redressed the grievances of the poor people. He instantly caused Lowery to be arrested, and a strict investigation to be made into his alleged offences: the result was, he was fined and imprisoned.

For the credit of Antigua, I must record, that, after his imprisonment, Lowery was so universally scouted,[†] that he was obliged to leave the island. He went to the southern states of America, where he continually abuses his country; which, he says, is completely enslaved, — without recollecting his own tyranny, and that his adopted land of freedom contains three millions of the least protected and most degraded slaves in existence.

I was so pleased with the conduct of the attorney-general, that I called to congratulate him: he observed, that he had only done his duty.

"Good God!" added Mr. Attorney, "had I not prosecuted this Lowery, what would they have said in England?"

I suggested, that it was our duty, in the colonies, to mitigate the evils of slavery by punishing its abuses, without regard to what might be said or thought elsewhere.

"Right, young gentleman," said the attorney-general, "your sentiments do you honour: it becomes us all to love justice for the sake of her intrinsic beauty. I am most happy in being the instrument of exposing and punishing the inhumanity of this scoundrel; it will let them know, in Downing Street, that we crown-officers of the colonies are not unmindful of our duty. The prosecution and conviction of this Lowery will make quite a sensation in the Colonial Office:[†] I should not be astonished if I were to be appointed to the first vacant judgeship that occurs in the West Indies."

Young as I was, I had sufficient penetration to perceive that, while the attorney-general talked of loving justice for the sake of her intrinsic beauty, he had an eye to the first vacant judgeship. Poor human nature! he who would think well of you, should endeavour to find apologies for all the backslidings of mankind; but, when he beholds any one perform a laudable action, he should not too curiously pry into the motives which instigated it.

Messrs. Keen and Leech gave orders to Lowery's successor not to admit me on the estate: these orders I set at defiance. I sent word to the manager to recollect that I violated no law in visiting my rightful property, and, therefore, would defend myself, if he dared attempt to turn me off: of this I had little fear. I always went on the plantation during the day, when I was surrounded by my father's faithful slaves, who would have risked being flayed alive rather than have allowed me to be insulted. This fact the manager knew, and, being of a pacific disposition, affected not to see me.

I soon became wearied with the sameness of Antigua scenery, and its Lundy-foot coloured soil.[†] This caused me to visit St. Christopher's. This island bears the same verdant and mountainous aspect as Grenada and St. Vincent. It is a beautiful colony; but I would advise its inhabitants to look out for a commodity of good names: why this fine country should be called St. Kitt's, its inhabitants be designated Kittiforrians, and two of its noblest prospects be called Brimstone Hill and Mount Misery, cannot be easily explained.

On visiting my father's St. Christopher's estate, a similar scene took place between the negroes and myself, as that which was acted at Antigua; but with this difference, — the manager was an old man of exemplary humanity, and all the negroes were loud in his praise. It appeared that, during my father's life, he had been an overseer on the same plantation. On my arrival on the estate, with true West Indian frankness and hospitality, this worthy old gentleman, whose name was Codrington, came to me and begged me to spend *a year or two with him:* he called all the negroes before the house, told them I was the son of their old master, gave them the rest of the day for a holiday, sent them five gallons of rum belonging to the estate, and a fat sheep and two dozen of madeira from his own store, to make merry withal.

A negro ball was the consequence of this munificence. Invitations were sent to Codrington and myself, which were accepted. The orchestra consisted of a cracked fiddle, *minus* the first string, three African drums, two tambourines, and a triangle. This music, although it mocked all tune, did not mar the dancers' skill, for most creoles dance remarkably well. The hearty manager "frisked beneath the burden of threescore,"[†] to the tune of "Go to the devil and shake yourself."[†] I danced with his grand-daughter, a very pretty girl of fifteen, three or four shades darker than her grandfather.

These proceedings were by no means approved of by Messrs. Keen and Leech, who sent word to Codrington to order me off the estate. To this message the latter refused compliance, declaring that, while he had charge of the estate, he would admit whom he chose on it. He further threatened to leave the plantation instantly. This the worthy partners by no means relished, for reasons which I may explain at some future period. They wanted to keep on good terms with Codrington; hence I was allowed to visit the property as I chose.

Messrs. Keen and Leech began to look on me with alarm, and it became evident they wished that I had been swallowed up by the earthquake at Caraccas. After a few days, they sent Mr. Arnold, their head clerk, to me, to propose purchasing a commission for me in a West Indian regiment,[†] and charging the same to my father's encumbered estates. In order to induce me to accept of this offer, Mr. Arnold said, "that such was the mortality amongst the officers in the West India station, that I might calculate on rapid promotion." This observation had the contrary effect it was intended to have. I had as little fear of death as most young men, but I did not like to expose myself to "bloody wars and sickly seasons,"[†] in order to gratify the amiable wish of Messrs. Keen and Leech.

I proposed that they should allow me three hundred pounds per annum until I came of age, in order to enable me to prosecute my legal studies. To this they would by no means agree: they said the bar in England was overstocked, and as to colonial legal practice, they declared it most unprofitable. The fact is, they feared, if I became a lawyer, I should too soon discover their most profitable colonial illegal practice.

After two days spent in negociating, they finally agreed to allow me two hundred and fifty pounds sterling per annum, on condition that I instantly went to England to study medicine. I left St. Christopher's for Antigua, to take leave of my bed-ridden aunt and thoughtless cousins, previous to my embarking on board the Tickler, a ship lying at St. John's, and partly belonging to Messrs. Keen and Leech.

I must here relate a circumstance connected with my visit to St. Christopher's, which will shew the effect of old West India prejudice.

In coming away from Basseterre,[49] just as I was getting into a boat, a negro, apparently inebriated, put a letter into my hand, and said that he had been looking for me half the day. I was belated, for the small sloop which was to carry me to Antigua was under weigh, and had a favourable slant of wind. I took the letter, jumped into the boat, and, fearing to miss my passage, caught hold of an oar, and pulled until I got alongside. As soon as I was on board, the vessel made all sail for Antigua, running, with the wind off her beam, at the rate of eight knots an hour. We were half over before I recollected that I had not read the letter. I broke the seal, and found it to be from one of my brothers; for it appears I had five, and two sisters, of whose existence, up to that moment, I never heard. The fact was, that previous to my father's marriage he had a large family of coloured children: these, although neglected and looked down upon in consequence of having committed the sin of bearing a brown complexion, were, in every sense of the word, respectable. The letter ran thus:—

"SIR,   Basseterre, July 23, 1822.

"I HOPE you will not be offended at your coloured brothers taking the liberty of writing to you; but, having heard of your bold and humane conduct, in vindicating the cause of our late father's oppressed slaves in Antigua, we (that is, our brothers, William, Henry, Clarence, George, our sisters, Jane and Anne, and myself) judged you to have too good a heart to look with scorn on your poor coloured brothers and sisters. Jane, who saw you at Government House, said you resembled our lamented father, and had such a kind-hearted look, that she was sure you did not know she was your sister, or you never would have passed her so coolly, although the tears were in the poor girl's eyes.

49. The capital of St. Christopher's.

"I hope, Mr. Warner, we shall not offend you in what we propose. We are all, thank God, well to do in the world, and know that, although you are our youngest brother, you are the head of the family, because you are a white man. We therefore beg that you will come and live with us: we will maintain you as a gentleman; and, when you are of age, between us we will find money enough to make Keen and Leech give you back your rightful property. We advise you not to enter into any arrangement with these scoundrels.

"Do, good Mr. Warner, remain with us at St. Kitt's; we all love you, and dear sisters Jane and Anne, although both married, will take much care of you, and be as kind to you as sisters should be to a younger brother.

"Hoping these lines will give you no offence, I remain, dear Warner,

"Your dutiful Brother,
"RODNEY ARUNDELL."
"TO WARNER ARUNDELL, ESQ."

While reading this affecting and affectionate letter, I was obliged to pause repeatedly, in order to wipe away the first warm tears I had shed for many years. My kind brothers and sisters were offering to act as my parents, and yet addressing me in the humble style of slaves, fearing to give offence while they were inspiring me with gratitude. I, in a moment, recalled the features of my poor sister Jane, as she regarded me, with tears in her eyes, at Government House; and, while her warm heart overflowed with affection, she feared to accost me, lest, influenced by the abominable prejudice of the West Indies, I should repulse her sisterly love, and treat her with scorn. Such was the accursed distinction which existed between members of the same family, whose complexion differed.

I begged the skipper of the passage-boat to put back, in order that I might visit my worthy brothers and sisters; but neither entreaties nor proffers of bribes could induce him to do this. He said he had letters from the house of Keen and Leech to the captain of the Tickler, which must be immediately delivered: in fact, the skipper was the agent of these people.

On my arrival in Antigua I hired the swiftest boat I could find, which I despatched with a letter to my affectionate family. In my epistle I expressed such sentiments as any one not dead to all emotions which do honour to human nature should feel. I regretted that the intoxicated messenger of my brother did not give me his letter till the moment I was getting into the boat, and that I did not read it until I was half way to Antigua. I further informed them, that I could not return to St. Christopher's at present, because the vessel on board which I pledged myself to take my departure was expected to sail in a day or two; if I missed my passage in the Tickler, I could not go until next year, for she was the only ship that was to sail before the hurricane season, so that I should have to wait for the next convoy, which would not sail, perhaps, for six months. I implored my brothers, or one of them, to come over to Antigua by the return of the boat, and bid me farewell ere I crossed the Atlantic.

Away went the boat, as swift as six oars could propel her, the coxwain promising me to be back in sixteen hours. The next morning I anxiously looked for the return of the boat — but she came not; noon arrived, but no boat appeared; the sun was declining, and I looked in vain at the harbour for the boat I had despatched for my brothers. My anxiety now became intolerable, for the captain of the Tickler sent me word that he would sail the next morning at eleven. I accused myself with having treated with neglect my affectionate brother, and even meditated breaking my engagement to sail with the ship, rather than leave the West Indies without an interview with my family. Walking up and down the wharf to look out for the boat, I overheard one merchant ask another, who was using a spyglass, what vessel that was which was beating up to get into the harbour?

"I can't make her out yet," said he of the telescope.

Soon the vessel, which was a ballahoo schooner,[†] made another tack; and he said, "I see it's Rodney Arundell's ballahoo: what, I wonder, brings him to St. John's? I suppose it is passengers, for his deck seems crowded with men, women, and children."

This was sufficient information for me; I at once comprehended that my brothers, sisters, and their families, were coming to visit me. The ballahoo soon worked through the harbour, and ran within fifty feet of the shore ere she came to an anchor. I called for a boat to go on board: none coming readily, in a moment I threw off my jacket, waistcoat, and shoes; and, regardless of sharks, plunged into the water, swam alongside, and, while the vessel was swinging round to the anchor, I caught a rope, jumped into the main chains, thence on deck, and rushed, dripping as I was, into the arms of my brothers and sisters.

The scene which now ensued was one of such intense pleasure that it operated on the feelings like pain: had not the fountains of my heart overflowed, it would have burst, as my affectionate and long-neglected sisters and brothers embraced me. I will not dwell longer on this interview, which, even now, I cannot think of without strong emotion. If the complexion of my relatives indicated they were natural children, their conduct demonstrated they were natural brothers and sisters.

My family was larger than I calculated: until the last two days I knew not of the existence of either a brother or sister. I had no less than seven of them: all these had families of children, which they brought to see me; so that I was introduced to an extensive and fine collection of nephews and nieces. The Arundells were ever a prolific generation.

I slept not that night, but spent it, on board of the ballahoo, in recounting all I had heard and seen, and asking and answering questions: the replies bore about the same proportion to the interrogatories as one bears to ten.

The next morning I took leave of my Antigua friends, and went again on board of my brothers' vessel, where I took breakfast. The captain of the Tickler made a signal for the passengers to embark, on which my brothers' ballahoo ran alongside the ship, and placed on board, by way of sea stores, such a collection of sheep, goats, turtle, poultry, plantains, yams, sweet potatoes, edoes, arrowroot,[†] Guinea and Indian corn,[†] cayenne pepper, fiery pickles, guava-jelly, pine-apples, tamarinds,[†] and so many kinds of fruits, both fresh and preserved, that I was well provisioned to go round the world on a voyage of discovery.

The hour of parting arrived: my brothers embraced me, and wished me good luck; my poor sisters kissed me, and prayed God to bless me. I experienced that heaviness of heart which none can conceive who have not bid farewell to dear friends, when they know they will not meet again for years.

As the ship achieved the dangerous navigation amongst the reefs which surrounded Antigua, my brothers' vessel, with all the family on board, accompanied us. When we got into the open sea, the vessels separated; my brothers gave three cheers, by way of exhilarating me after our mournful leave-taking, and my dear sisters waved their handkerchiefs to me while we continued in sight of each other.

CHAPTER 23.

"And now I'm in the world alone,
Upon the wide, wide sea."
BYRON.[†]

When the mournful thoughts which always attend the separation of friends had somewhat abated, I was presented by the captain to my fellow-passengers.

It has often been observed, that nothing brings people so well acquainted, and in so short a time, as being confined in the same cabin during a voyage. The vicissitudes of the weather, the tedium of unemployed time, and the want of a hundred little comforts to which landsmen are accustomed, and which are not to be found on board the best provided ships, are severe tests of the tempers of passengers; and the small space in which the little community of the cabin are necessitated to move, brings them in such continual contact, that he who has sailed four thousand miles as fellow passenger with another, generally knows more of him than he could learn by living together in the same house for twenty years: hence, in a short time, I soon became well acquainted with all the inmates of the cabin of the Tickler, whom I shall proceed to describe, beginning with the officers of the ship.

First, let me speak of the "sailing captain," as he was called by the crew. Captain Medway was a native of Surrey; a rough-spun seaman, who was always swearing at the crew, but was civil and obliging to the passengers. He used to excuse his language to his men by reminding us that they were not Englishmen, but men of all nations. This was common in the merchant service during the war.

"If," said Medway, "I spoke polite English to these Frenchmen and Dutchmen, they would not understand me; but when I swear at them, they know well enough what I mean — because why? — an English d—mme, like an English guinea, is well understood, and passes current all over the world."

Medway classified European foreigners into two divisions: all born to the northward of Great Britain he denominated Dutchmen, and all to the southward he called Frenchmen.

Medway was a good practical sailor — few men could better manage a ship when under canvass; but his ignorance of the theoretical part of navigation was astonishing. The latitude he could contrive to discover by means of his quadrant[†] and 'John Hamilton's Moon Tables.'[†] He did this, however, merely by rote, without shewing the slightest knowledge of the principles on which those tables were constructed. Having no chronometer[†] on board, he was obliged to depend on his "dead reckoning"[50†] for his knowledge of the longitude; for of lunar observations, to make use of one of the "fighting captain's" expressions, "he knew as much about them as a dog knows of his father."

My readers must be rather puzzled at the expressions, "sailing captain" and "fighting captain," on board a merchantman. I will explain. During the voyage out, the ship was under the command of Captain Trevallion, and Medway was his mate. The former was a native of Cornwall, and as brave and skilful a seaman as ever fought or sailed; but, having been an old privateer's man, he was little calculated for the merchant service, being much too fond of fighting. He had orders from the owners of the Tickler to run out to Antigua as quick as he could, without the convoy, and, should he meet with an enemy, to avoid an engagement, if possible; if not, to make a running fight of it, and, at all events, to aim only at beating off his opponent. Trevallion, however, little regarded these orders. In the middle of the Atlantic he met with and relieved the crew of a sinking vessel, just as she was going down. Hence the Tickler became well manned. A few days after this event, a French corvette[†] gave chase to her. Trevallion took the helm, and, by false steering, allowed the enemy to gain on him. Suddenly he put about, ran across the bows of the corvette, and raked her. The Frenchman found he had "caught a Tartar."[†] Nevertheless, he fought bravely, as Frenchmen usually do, but shewed little skill in the engagement. After considerable loss of men, he contrived to bring his corvette yard-arm and yard-arm[†] with the Tickler; and the fight was maintained on more equal terms. The corvette was more numerously manned, and had more guns; but the decks of the Tickler were much

---

50. "Dead reckoning" means the situation of the ship, calculated according to the distance run, without regard to observations made by quadrant or sextant.

higher. The Frenchman mustered his crew in the waist,[†] preparatory to his boarding the ship. Trevallion had foreseen and prepared against this event. He had broken away a part of his quarter bulwark; wheeled round one of his quarter-deck guns, until its muzzle became almost pointed forward — it was charged with musket-balls. He depressed the piece, levelled it himself, and fired it amongst the intended boarders. The gun went overboard; but its discharge was murderous to the enemy. After this, they again attempted on board, but, weakened in numbers, they were repulsed with ease. The third attempt to board the Tickler so far succeeded that they gained the deck of the ship; but, after a smart hand-in-hand engagement, they were driven partly into the sea, and partly back to their own vessel. The corvette then attempted to sheer off, but could not effect her escape. The wadding of one of the Tickler's guns had lodged between the stern-post and the rudder of the corvette; this prevented her going about. Trevallion availed himself of this accident, and got his vessel in such a position as to rake her over the stern; this he did so effectually that the corvette was obliged to strike, having three-fourths of her crew killed or wounded.

The account of this action I had from the supercargo.[†] It tended to raise Trevallion more in the estimation of the Patriot Committee than in that of his owners. True, he had made a prize, but he had *disobeyed orders:* hence he was divested of his command, but allowed his pay. The charge of the vessel was given to the *ci-devant* mate,[†] with orders that if, during the voyage home, the Tickler was obliged to defend herself, Trevallion was to have the command during the engagement.

The supercargo was a Mr. Holywell, a native of London, and a man of Herculean stature; with that fresh and ruddy appearance which, in England, is said to be "the picture of health," but which, in the Antilles, indicates that the firm of "yellow fever, apoplexy, and company," have a mortgage on the person, foreclosable at a moment's warning. He had a constitution well calculated for home *consumption*, but not for exportation to the West Indies. He was an excellent-humoured, good-hearted, but somewhat vulgar man — not vulgar in his acts, but in his words. He had an inimitable twang of cockneyism in his discourse, and was ever using such terms as "bang-up," "how are you with your eye out?" and other phrases equally Attic[†] and expressive. His great delight was to talk of the ring, not of Hyde Park,[†] but at Molsey Hurst;[†] and "the court," by which he did not mean the court at St. James's,[†] but the "fives-court."[†] He boasted of being "the best amateur boxer in England — a regular right-and-left-handed hitter, and an ugly customer for any scientific man." By *science*, Holywell meant the knowledge of boxing.[†] The fact is, his discourse was so mixed up with the cant of the boxing-ring (which, I am told, is precisely the same with that spoken in the felon side of Newgate),[†] that I was often puzzled to know what he was saying.

On the occasion of the enemy boarding the Tickler on her voyage out, this regular right-and-left-handed hitter behaved with extraordinary bravery. He caught up a sword with his right hand, whilst with his left he grasped a double-headed shot.[†] Thus singularly armed, he rushed amongst the boarders, and dealt destruction around him. The sword he only used to ward off the blows of his antagonists, while he struck, with his left hand, with the double-headed shot, and always with good aim and deadly effect. This *scientific* mode of fighting was at once so novel and tremendous, that he knocked down — I beg pardon, "floored" — eight of the enemy, and created a complete panic. During the whole of the time he was engaged in this extraordinary conflict, he was (as Trevallion told me), purely for his own satisfaction, invoking "inverted blessings"[†] on the bodies, souls, eyes, and limbs of the enemy.

Of the passengers, properly so called, the oldest was Doctor Grey, a physician, who, for thirty years, had taken care of the health of the good people of Montserrat, until his own health had decayed. He retired from the West Indies, with an entire fortune, and a broken constitution.

The next of my fellow-passengers I proceed to notice was Mr. Moses Fernandez, a native of Curaçoa. He was of the Jewish tribe; a rather small, compact-made man, with handsome features, strongly indicative of the race from which he sprang. He did not mess[†] with us — this his religious scruples forbade; all he ate of fresh animal food was poultry, which he killed himself, dressed by his own slave, and in his own utensils. It was wonderful how rigidly this man adhered to the laws of the Pentateuch[†] and the traditions of the rabinim.[51][†] During the most stormy weather he never neglected, in the morning, to bind his phylacteries[†] on his forehead and left arm; and then, with his face turned to the east, he repeated the long Hebrew prayers of his forefathers.

Although he took his meals apart, he usually joined us after dinner; causing, at the same time, his servant to place on the table a bottle or two

---

51. Commonly written rabbins,—as the plural of seraph is commonly written seraphs.

of exquisite wine, or of a curious cordial: a large stock of both of which he possessed, and liberally supplied us with. His conversation was entertaining, if not instructive. Like a pocket encyclopædia, his mind was stored with a little of every thing, whilst yet he knew no subject profoundly, save music. His skill in playing on the guitar surpassed that of any one I ever heard of or met with. He could imitate in a surprising manner, with this simple instrument, the sounds produced by a military band — using his fingers on the board to produce the tones of a drum. His knowledge of vocal music was great; his voice was a fine, deep-toned tenor, inclining to bass. During the silence of a mild moonlight night, while the ship stole over the silvery waves, it was truly delightful to hear this son of Israel sing a Hebrew psalm to one of the beautiful traditional airs which are, perhaps, as ancient as the words which he sang, accompanying them with his dulcet guitar.

Thirdly, there was a Monsieur Blanchard — a refugee from St. Domingo, who, during the revolution there, escaped to Jamaica, and finally settled in St. Christopher's. Although this gentleman had been seventeen years amongst Englishmen, he could not speak one word of our language. Frenchmen, in general, have such a high opinion of their own tongue, that they seldom learn any other; hence they are, commonly, the worst general linguists in the world. However, although M. Blanchard did not speak English, he understood it pretty well.

I will next enumerate Ensign Rivers and family; the latter consisting of his wife (a very beautiful young creole), an infant of about two months old, and Lucy, a mulattess,[†] who attended the lady and child.

Lastly, although not the least diverting of the passengers, there was, belonging to the ensign, a large African baboon, called Jumbee;[52†] not inappropriately named, as I thought, for this brute had more of the devil in him than any animal of his species.

We were three days running down to the Virgin Islands. We passed Anguilla passage,[†] and got into the Atlantic; but on the fourth night of our voyage a hurricane came on, which blew with greater violence than any storm I ever witnessed. The Tickler with difficulty escaped wreck; but, having sprung her mainmast,[†] and being otherwise damaged, we were obliged to put into St. Thomas's — a Danish island, at that time in our possession.[†] In an agricultural point of view this colony is unimportant, its

52. An African word, denoting an evil spirit.

soil being rather sterile; but it is invaluable on account of its situation for commerce. In no part of the world I have ever visited could so many of the good things of this life be procured, at so cheap a rate, as at St. Thomas's. Since its restoration to the Danes it has become a free port; and, I am sorry to be obliged to add, it is now a complete receptacle for slave ships. I believe the Danish government do not encourage this infamous traffic in slaves; for — to their honour be it spoken — Denmark was the first nation who abolished the slave-trade: they ought, however, to look to what is going on at St. Thomas's.

CHAPTER 24.

"For England when with favouring gales."
DIBDIN.[†]

We remained eight days at St. Thomas's, whilst the ship was being refitted, and then embarked, with a fair but moderate breeze. My time was passed as pleasantly as time is generally spent by landsmen on shipboard. During fine weather I used to fence with Blanchard, or practise pistol-shooting with the ensign: when the wind did not admit of these pastimes I amused myself as well as I could, chatting with Mrs. Rivers; talking to Doctor Grey about my intended profession; listening to Holywell's historical accounts of pugilistic encounters; teaching several parrots we had on board their accidence;[†] playing with the baboon; learning the use of the quadrant; climbing the rigging; feeding my poultry; reading and re-reading several letters of introduction, which were given me in St. Christopher's and Antigua, for various persons in London; building castles in the air; and practising other rational and irrational amusements. Amongst the latter, I may comprise eating and drinking when I had neither thirst nor appetite, and going to bed when I was not sleepy. If it were not for the many hours spent in eating, drinking, and sleeping, the life of a passenger across the Atlantic would be intolerable.

The first day after we left St. Thomas, being placed at table opposite to M. Blanchard, I pledged him in a glass of Madeira, saying, — *"A votre santé, monsieur."* Holywell, who knew not a word of French, must needs follow my example, but blundered most unfortunately. He filled his glass, looked at the Frenchman, and said, *"Vous sentez, monsieur."* Blanchard perceived the ridiculous mistake, but knew no offence was intended; he therefore bowed to the intended compliment, and replied, with the deepest gravity, — *"Vous mentez, monsieur."*[†] This was mistaken by Holywell for a return of compliments. Every day during our voyage this ridiculous scene was repeated. Generally about the third glass, after the cloth was removed, Holywell bowed formally to Blanchard, and, ere he sipped his wine, said, — *"Vous sentez, monsieur."* *"Vous mentez, monsieur,"* constantly answered the Frenchman, with the apparent solemn politeness of one who replied to the commendation of a monarch; while all at the table who understood French, — that is, Doctor Grey, Fernandez, the ensign, his lady, and myself, — were in danger of being choked from suppressed laughter.

After we had passed the Tropic of Cancer the weather became unfavourable for the prosecution of our voyage. From day to day occurred "a succession of light airs, languishing to calms," as midshipmen's log-books have it.[†] Sometimes the vessel had barely sufficient wind to make her feel her helm; and sometimes, for a whole day, she lay on the blue, glassy surface of the water, with her useless wheel lashed to its standard, and her sails flapping against her masts and yards, helpless as a dying giant. The passengers lounging listlessly under the awning; the captain looking out for a breeze, and marking those distant rufflings on the face of the ocean called "cat's-paws," occasioned by light airs which die away ere they reach the vessel; the mate whistling in vain for a wind; the seamen lazily and unwillingly employed making spun-yarn, or painting the boats. Even the finny tribes of the deep seemed to participate in the indolence which the calm inspired. Sometimes a solitary grampus shewed its uncouth form above the waters, and, after blowing with the force of a high-pressure steam-engine letting off its vapour, it leisurely dived from sight; whilst, ever and anon, we discovered those wolves of the ocean, the sharks, slowly prowling about the vessel, as if waiting for some one imprudent enough to bathe — or some wretch whom accident or death should consign to the deep.

During one of these calms, the baboon, Jumbee, went aft, and deliberately took up his mistress's gold watch, which had been incautiously left on the capstern. He held it up to his ear, as if to ascertain how it went; he then tried to open it — in this he did not succeed. He next began to knock the watch on the capstern: his master, on seeing this, rushed aft to rescue the watch from his clutches. Jumbee perceived his intentions, and, as quick as thought, sprang into the mizen-chains.[†] Up he flew; and, in less than six seconds, was snugly seated on the mizen royal yard,[†] holding up the watch as if in triumph; chattering and grinning, as though he enjoyed his master's vexation. What was to be done? From experience we knew that it would take all the men in the ship a full half hour to catch this active rascal; and it was conjectured that, during the chase, he would throw the watch overboard. The steward, who was a favourite with Jumbee, went below and brought him up a plate of sweetmeats, an article on which the baboon doated. The steward called him by his name, and held up the plate. On seeing and smelling this, Jumbee "grinned horribly a ghastly smile"[†] of approval, pitched the watch overboard, and, seizing the royal halyards,[†]

> "The cords slipt lightly through his glowing hands,
> And, quick as lightning, on the deck he stands;"[†]

not, however, like William in the song, to receive kisses sweet[†] — but, in lieu thereof, a shower of curses, kicks, and cuffs, which his master bestowed upon him. The ensign at last walked away, fairly weary with the exercise. The poor lady wept at the loss of the watch, which happened to be a family-piece; and we suspected the circumstances of the ensign were too straitened not to render the loss important, even in in a pecuniary point of view.

I hinted this to Captain Trevallion, the supercargo, and the rest of my fellow-passengers, and proposed a little subscription to purchase another watch on our arrival. This was instantly agreed to: and it was further proposed, that I as the originator of the subscription, should present Mrs. Rivers with the toy; when the conference was laid aside on the boatswain's calling out, "A shark hooked!" All hands ran aft as the mate began to haul in the line. When under the counter, he proved to be an immense fish, insomuch that it was found impracticable to take him out of his element with the line. "Drown him!" cried the captain. To drown a shark seems paradoxical; it means, however, to keep his head above the water, with his mouth full of that element, until he is almost stifled. A Norwegian sailor darted at the fish his graives (a harpoon, with a number of barbs): this prevented his escape, as he, by plunging, soon afterwards broke the hook: however, the stern-boat was lowered, cords were run about him, and he was safely brought on deck. The throbs of the captured fish now became so violent, that I feared he would beat in the deck. At last, the black cook, with his kitchen-cleaver, by a well-directed blow, severed his tail from the rest of his body; and the Norwegian gave him a finishing stroke, by running a harpoon into his brain.

The liver was taken out for the sake of its oil, and two Russian seamen took a large allowance of his flesh. The rest of the crew not "liking shark," the carcass was ordered to be thrown overboard. Dr. Grey requested to be allowed to dissect the maw, in order to shew me a peculiarity of the stomach of the shark, and to demonstrate the surprising power of the fish's gastric juice. By means of a large knife, he cut into the maw; and, behold! amid a quantity of beef and pork bones, which had that day been thrown overboard, to our joy and surprise we found the very watch which had been, but half-an-hour before, thrown into the deep by Jumbee. What is not the least extraordinary part of the event is the fact, that, although the works were deranged by the fall, the glass remained unbroken. The fish, doubtless, caught it in its fall, and mistook it for food. We bore it in triumph to its fair owner. I thought this one of the lucky discoveries made by comparative anatomy.

I forgot to relate that Jumbee was, immediately after the theft of the watch, condemned most unanimously to be chained for the rest of the voyage in the long-boat: this sentence the steward and carpenter executed, whilst Jumbee protested loudly and forcibly against this encroachment on the liberties of the simian subject. The tones of his protest were, however, too discordant to be eloquent.

After this adventure, a number of stories were related about sharks; amongst the rest, that of Port Royal Tom, and the shark which brought to light the concealed papers of the American ship, and caused its condemnation. I, also, related my adventures with *el capitan del puerto;* of La Guayra's, and José Garcia's encounter with the same fish. A light breeze sprang up, and the ship proceeded at the rate of three miles an hour. It continued during the whole day and the following night, but the next morning it died away. The Tickler lay

> "As lifeless as a painted ship
> Upon a painted ocean;"[†]

or, rather, like a dead whale on the water. The captain now talked of putting us on a short allowance of water. All the passengers became listless and dispirited, when an event occurred which strongly agitated the feelings of every one on board the vessel.

The mulatto servant of Mrs. Rivers was walking on the quarter-deck[†] with the child; she became weary, and sat down upon a hen-coop, placing the infant beside her. Something attracted her to the side of the vessel; and, for a moment, she left her little charge alone. The baboon, who had, unperceived by any one, disengaged himself of his chains in the long-boat,[†] flew on the quarter-deck. Before any one could interpose, he caught up the child; and, with as much rapidity as he had mounted the rigging on the preceding occasion with the watch, did he scale aloft with the child to the mizen-royal-yard, keeping the infant in his paws, and chattering as though he enjoyed our alarm.

I cannot describe the feelings of the wretched parents, as they beheld the pledge of their mutual loves, one hundred feet above, and *over* the surface of the ocean, into which they momentarily expected it to be plunged by this hideous caricature of humanity, then to be devoured by some monstrous fish. The shrieks of poor Lucy were distressing; the lady fell into a fainting fit; whilst the silent sufferings of the father convulsed every muscle of his body.

Captain Trevallion now took upon himself to order both the wretched parents, and their scarcely less suffering attendant, to be forced into the cabin. He further ordered all on deck to go below, or hide themselves. This could be safely done, as not a breath of air required the attention of the crew, even to the wheel.

I concealed myself under a tarpaulin, near the taffrail;[†] Captain Trevallion was beside me. A few moments before this unfortunate event I had loaded my pistol to fire at a mark. I took the weapon (still loaded) with me, conceiving that circumstances might require my using it.

The baboon, finding we had all disappeared, ceased his savage grimaces; and, sitting on the royal-yard-arm, commenced, in that frightful situation, to dandle the child, much in the way he had seen the nurse do on deck. He flung it up, and caught it, until it made us shudder to look at him: but he displayed no malice towards the poor babe — quite the contrary; had it been its own cub, he could not have guarded it with greater care. In fact, the males of the simian tribes have much of what phrenologists call philoprogenitiveness; the infant, too, had always appeared a favourite with him: at the same time, he shewed no disposition to descend from his perilous situation.

Captain Trevallion looked around, sighed, and whispered to me that, in a few moments, the fate of the poor babe would be decided; as, by the appearance of the clouds, a brisk gale, if not a storm, would arise from the southward, and that it would be necessary to call up all hands to take in sail for our general safety. Scarcely had he spoken ere the brute shewed that he, also, anticipated the coming gale. He commenced looking towards, and apparently smelling to, the southward; and we began to breathe, as he descended to the main-top-gallant-mast,[†] holding the child, of which he took the most extraordinary care, by its clothes with his teeth. He made his way by the shrouds[†] into the main-top:[†] here the infant began to cry, and the brute absolutely sat down and dandled the child, to quiet it. The cries of the infant increasing, he grasped its arms with his hind paws, caught the mizen-stay[†] with his fore ones, and warped himself into the mizen-top,[†] carrying the child suspended, as it were, to his hind paws. Here he took the child again with his teeth, and descended by the mizen-shrouds,[†] until with pleasure we beheld him bring the babe to the very spot from which he took it. But the adventure was not yet finished. Lucy had left a saucepan of pap[†] on the hencoop, and the baboon brought the crying child there for no other purpose but to still its wailings with food. He commenced, after a fashion, to feed it. This he did so awkwardly, that he endangered choking the babe by cramming too much food into its mouth. The cries of the babe became distressing; at the same moment the steward raised his head above the companion ladder. The baboon seemed to comprehend the intention of the steward, and shewed no disposition to relinquish his hold of the infant. He caught it up; and, with chattering noise and diabolical grimaces, was rushing again towards the mizen-chains, when a sudden project occurred to me, and which I executed almost as quickly as the thought flashed across my memory. My unerring pistol was in my hand, cocked and loaded: ere he could leave the quarter-deck I levelled and fired at him, with so true an aim that the ball passed through the head of the beast without injuring the child: it glanced by the steward, and lodged in one of the spokes of the wheel.

A simultaneous huzza from the crew cheered this perilous and successful shot. I caught up the infant, and consigned it to the arms of its late frantic, but now happy, parents; and, as I received their blessings, thought myself the happiest of human beings. The reader will believe this the more readily, when I state that I entertained for this creole lady the warmest emotions of affection short of love. Poor Mrs. Rivers was so beautiful, that it seemed to me impossible to look on her without affection; yet, innocence was so sweetly blended with her youthful, but matronly loveliness, that he must have been a heartless libertine who could have entertained a dishonourable thought respecting her. The poor young lady scarcely recovered the shock her nerves sustained by this event during the remainder of the voyage.

The carcass of Jumbee was consigned to the sharks. Meanwhile the clouds had blackened on high, and the ocean beneath us had changed its azure hue to an inky dye. To the southward the billows raised their foaming heads as if to inform us that the wind had awoke from its slumber, and was advancing on us with the might of a giant refreshed by his long sleep. All hands were called. The flying kites, as seamen call the upper sails, were taken in, after a good deal of swearing from the captain, and skipping about of the crew. The lower sails of the Tickler were next reduced — but not a single moment before their reduction was necessary. One deep and long-continued peal of thunder roared and re-echoed around the horizon. The foreign seamen anticipated a hurricane, which they imagined must follow the slaying of the baboon. To attempt to argue such men out of a superstitious notion were useless labour. They believed that bad weather would follow the death of the brute as much as they believed in their own being; but could no more account for their belief than they could explain the cause of their existence.

At length the breeze caught us, and with such force that the Tickler could not shew a stitch of canvass, save her jib, storm-staysail, and fore-topsail closely reefed:[†] by means of these we scudded at a tremendous rate. However, the wind was steady, and as fair as it could blow; so that we made progress to the northward and eastward, for six days, at the rate of twelve or thirteen knots an hour. The seamen thereupon changed their opinions: they said the baboon had no hand in the good breeze, but alleged that the hurricane we had met with before we put into St. Thomas's, and the long succession of calms after we left that island, were caused by Jumbee being on board.

"It is quite clear," argued these profound sea-logicians, "that this must be the case; because since he was thrown overboard we have had the finest breeze ever remembered."

Running rapidly to the northward obliged me, for the first time in my life, to cover myself with a blanket at night when I went to bed; for in the West Indies, and South America, I used only a sheet.

As we drew towards the banks of Newfoundland, the weather became hazy, damp, and foggy. This is more intolerable to the native of an intertropical clime than the severest cold.

Our steward was a Barbadian, who had never been out of the Caribbean sea until the present voyage: his predecessor had died at Antigua, of the "new-rum fever." One morning, after we got into cold weather, as I was talking to Doctor Grey, he came to us, looking very pale, with his eyes protruding from their sockets, like a harpooned dolphin, and altogether appearing as much alarmed as though he had been visited by the ghost of his friend, Jumbee.

"Oh, doctor!" said he; and he stopped short, as though his utterance were choked.

"What is the matter with you, man?" inquired the doctor, hastily catching his wrist, and feeling his pulse, as it were mechanically.

"I is a dead man," said the steward, mournfully and syllabically.

"You have the strongest pulse for a dead man I ever felt. In the name of God, what ails you?" said the physician.

"Don't you see?" rejoined the steward.

"See what?" asked Grey.

"Why," replied the steward, "the smoke is coming out of my mouth!"

The fact was, the Barbadian never having been in a cold climate, he was utterly astonished on perceiving, when he came on deck, as he expressed it, that the smoke came out of his mouth — in other words, that the rarity of the atmosphere made his breath visible.

After explaining to the poor Barbadian the cause of his needless alarm, we enjoyed a hearty laugh at his expense. It was, however, no laughing matter to the steward; for fear had so got the better of him, that he was sick for four days after this — yet was he any thing but a coward. He was twice wounded at the taking of Martinique, in which affair he acted as a volunteer. He belonged to the division called the "Barbadoes flute-players."

The last phrase I must explain. During the late war, an expedition for the purpose of capturing one of the French islands sailed from Barbadoes. A number of Barbadians joined the expedition as volunteers. On debarking on the hostile shore to take the capital of the island, the Bains[53] separated themselves from their comrades, ran into a cane-field, where each cut as large and straight a sugar-cane as he could find, which he commenced gnawing, holding it in his hands and bending his head to it, rejoining, at the same time, his division. Now, these cane-eaters at a distance looked, for all the world like men playing on flutes. When the enemy, therefore, beheld on their shores an army which possessed a body of flute-players comprising several hundred men, they came at once to the

---

53. A cant phrase for Barbadians.

conclusion that the expedition must be far too strong for them to cope with; and, under this persuasion, immediately surrendered the capital at discretion.

Such is the story of the "Barbadoes flute-players;" and, whenever it is told, a hearty laugh at "little England" is generally created. Of course, I do not pledge myself for the authenticity of the story.

During our voyage we often met with suspicious-looking vessels, but we generally outsailed them. Sometimes, too, we observed privateer-looking schooners; but they always kept at a respectful distance, being, doubtless, awed by the high decks and eighteen guns of the Tickler. I did not regret this, having little confidence in the motley crew which navigated her.

As we approached "the chops of the Channel,"† an immense number of vessels, of all sizes, bearing English colours, passed us; indicating that we were fast approaching the Mistress of Colonies, the Queen of the Ocean, the Empress of Commerce — Great Britain!

At length, on the forty-second day after we left St. Thomas's, "land a-head" was discovered at day-break. I did not rise for three hours afterwards; so that, when I came on deck, we were well up with the Cornish coast.

I felt a degree of emotion at beholding the land of my ancestors — the land which I even had been taught to look on as "home."

"This is," said I, "the country whose sons conquered at Agincourt, Poictiers, Blenheim, and Trafalgar; the land which produced Shakespeare, Milton, Bacon, Newton, and Locke!"

"What! that land?" said Captain Medway, pointing to the gloomy coast of Cornwall; "it never produced nothing but tin-lead and parsley-pie!"

A fishing-boat came alongside the Tickler, and, for a few bottles of rum, supplied us with mackerel and new potatoes, which we ate with surprising relish. We had left a country in which turtle is the food of the poor, and pine-apples are often given to swine; and yet we considered new potatoes and fresh mackerel as absolute delicacies. So true it is, that the scarcity of almost any eatable article will cause it to be considered as a luxury.

A pilot-boat, belonging to the Island of Scilly, came alongside, and asked us if we had any passengers going ashore. We asked them what they would take to land us at Falmouth?

"Three guineas a passenger," was the reply.

We offered them one-half.

"I suppose you take us Scilly folks for fools," said the person in charge of the boat.

This specimen of Cornish wit, I suppose, is traditional; as the man who uttered it had a countenance far too expressive of solid honesty to indicate that he was guilty of perpetrating a new pun: however, finding we were eight who wished to go ashore, he agreed to land us for twelve pounds. We went into the boat with our light baggage, leaving the rest of our luggage to be brought up the Thames by the Tickler. Two hours after we left the ship, we landed at Falmouth.

★　　★　　★　　★　　★

END OF THE FIRST VOLUME.

Volume II

CHAPTER 25.

"England, with all thy faults, I love thee still."
COWPER.†

The whole of the passengers of the Tickler remained two days in Falmouth, to recruit after our voyage, as well as to see the few lions of the place, and to visit the surrounding country. The greatest sights of Cornwall lie below its surface; but, being neither a geologist nor mineralogist, the tin and lead mines were *beneath* my notice.

We hired two post-chaises,† in which we went to London. I found myself, during my journey, in a new world: the climate; the lofty houses, with glass windows, and chimneys; the immense population; the total absence of black, coloured, and Indian people; the rosy looks of the women, so different from the languid and lily complexions of my fair country-women; the ruddy appearance of the children; the masculine, and often corpulent, figures of the gentlemen; the clownish aspect of the country people, with their smock-frocks, worsted stockings, and ponderous lace-boots; the immense size and fatness of the horned cattle; the noble figures of the horses; the sheep, clad in thick woolly coats, so different from the light hairy jackets in which Nature has arrayed the sheep of the Caribbean Islands;† the endless variety of the costume of all the people I met, so different from the eternal white jackets and trousers of the Antilles; the dissimilarity of the feathered tribe; the absence of the palms of a tropical climate, and the total difference of all vegetable nature — for not a tree, shrub, fruit, legume, leaf, flower, nor even blade of grass, was exactly like aught I ever before beheld, — all, all I saw made me feel as though I was transported into another planet. True, I had seen most objects I looked on, delineated in wretched pictures; but these gave me about as good an idea of what I was a spectator of, as the miserable images we see on China cups give us of the Celestial Empire: for, excepting a few portraits, I scarcely saw a good painting in the West Indies. The only pictures popular in the Antilles, are those of the King of Spain in profile, delineated on an ounce of gold or silver, commonly called doubloons and dollars.

The first part of our journey lay through the sterile-looking hills and plains of Cornwall; afterwards, the appearance of the country ameliorated. Towns, villages, farms, and cottages, sprang up before my eyes in endless variety. True it is, that, in England, I looked in vain for the noble mountains and deep valleys of the West Indies, or the more stupendous scenery of South America; but, instead, I viewed a country rendered pre-eminently beautiful by cultivation, where every hut and rustic gate seemed to me to be placed to increase the picturesque effect of the landscape. Cowper has said, that

"God made the country, but man made the town."†

After my long residence in Caraccas, I did not think the poet's opinion was correct with regard to England; for, wherever I looked at the country through which I passed, I beheld the natural beauty altered by the art of man. He who is wishful of beholding the works of the Creator in all their solemn magnificence, should visit the mountains and savannahs of Columbia.

When we stopped at an inn to refresh, or lodge for the night, the extreme neatness and comfort of all that could render our stay agreeable, were, to me, remarkable. The civility of the host and hostess, the activity and intelligence of the servants, delighted me: this at once, shewed that I was in a land of freedom, where the exciting hope of gain stimulates men and women to exertion ten times more arduous than the fear of the scourge of slavery. In the West Indies there are not many inns and taverns, and fewer good ones: there, as well as in private houses, the black and brown domestics move about as little as they can help. Every trifling office you want a West Indian servant to perform, must be repeatedly, and often peremptorily ordered, before it is done — if it ever be done: here, the waiters, and well-called servants of all-work, seemed to anticipate your wants, and, before you can ask for a thing, it is at your command. In the West Indies, a servant drawls about the house as though locomotion is painful to him; while the English domestic talks, acts, and runs, as though he were doing it for a wager against time. The free servant of Great Britain works five times as hard as the slave of the West Indies; for the energies of the latter are weighed down by bondage. I am aware some will say that the indolence of the slave is caused by the climate; yet, how is the following fact to be accounted for — viz. at a negro ball, the sable dancers use thrice as much exertion, and continue thrice as long, as any set of dancers in England? Notwithstanding the oppressive heat of the climate, a negro sportsman, when engaged in a pedestrian hunt in Trinidad, uses violent efforts from which an English fox-hunter would shrink. The fact is, our bondsman, unless it is for himself, works like a slave — that is to say, most indolently: when he diverts himself, he feels, for the moment, that he is free. By looking at the very slave's walk, one acquainted with them knows if they are walking on their master's business, or their own.

As the post-chaise drew near the capital, I was confused at meeting an immense crowd of vehicles of all descriptions, — from the light tandem, with its slender bloods, to the ponderous waggon, with its long train of burly cattle; from the splendid carriage of the nobleman, to the high-piled cart of the farmer. As we entered the town, I was absolutely rendered giddy by the opulence and grandeur of the shops, the thronging of the population, and the deafening noise; while the smoky atmosphere, unlike aught I ever before beheld, weighed down my spirits.

On entering London, I took leave of all my fellow-passengers with mutual good wishes, save Dr. Grey. He invited me to remain with him a few days at the Tavistock Hotel, Covent Garden,[†] until, by the advice of himself, and such friends as my letters of introduction could procure me, I should resolve where to fix my residence during the time I was obtaining my medical education.

The doctor had not been in London two days before he met with an old fellow-student and correspondent, named Molesworth, who was in extensive practice as a physician in the west end of the town. He had been the preceptor[†] to several medical students from the West Indies, and, many years since, knew my father. After introducing me to him, Dr. Grey proposed to place me under the tutelage of his old fellow-student; to which Dr. Molesworth made no objection. We agreed that I should become a resident in the doctor's house during the prosecution of my studies; and I arranged to pay him 150*l.* per annum for my board and lodging. He promised to assist me in my studies, to take me with him occasionally when he visited his patients, and allow me the use of his valuable medical library.

The next day I removed from the Tavistock Hotel to the doctor's house in Bedford Square:[†] I sent to the West India Docks[†] and obtained my luggage, and found myself comfortably located with Dr. Molesworth, an excellent physician, but an avaricious man.

After this, Dr. Grey set out to all the medical springs and baths in England,[†] to clear his inward and outward man from the accumulated maladies obtained during thirty years' residence between the tropics, — a usual practice with old retired West Indians. At Cheltenham, the doctor fell in love with, and married, one of the water-nymphs of the place:[†] she had long been looking for a suitable match. The lady verified the old proverb about the "gray mare," &c.[†] This was not to be wondered at: at the time when the doctor wanted an old nurse he married a young wife. A year after his marriage he died, and she inherited his hard-accumulated property: three months after, the lady married Ensign O'Donnehoo, of some marching regiment.[†]

As few or no West Indians have ever given an account of England, I will, for the information of such of my fellow-colonists as have never crossed the Atlantic, subjoin my recollection of the impressions which England in general, and London in particular, made on me. I wish not to alarm my creole readers by heading the following desultory paragraphs, 'The Domestic Manners of the English;'[†] I would rather they should consider it as

A CREOLE'S NOTIONS OF 'HOME.'

Amongst the first things which struck me in England, was the brief speech and rapid pronunciation of all orders of people, save those who are, or affect to be, taught the *haut-ton*.[†] It would not please the Bond Street[†] loungers, or the dancers at Almack's,[†] to be told that, when they lengthen their words, and speak in that drawling tone which is, or at least was, fashionable when I was in London, they merely imitate the lower orders of people in the Caribbean Islands; yet such is the fact.

Let two creoles, of the humbler classes of society, meet in the West Indies, and something like the following dialogue ensues. Each word is lengthened as though the parties spoke by musical notes, and each syllable were a breve.[†]

"How you do, my body?"

"Pretty, well, thank you, old fellow; how yourself?"

"Well, thank you; how your family do?"

"All quite well — only Samuel, Daniel, Jonathan, and Jacob, have the fever every night; but their health is good, for all that."

"Thank you; but how is your negro boy, that have *mal' d'estomac?*"[†]

"He is dead, thank you, body."

And so they continue the conversation for about twenty minutes. But in London, two persons of the lower order of society meet: each nods to the other when they are about eight yards off; one says, "How do?" the other does not reply, but says, "How do *you* do?" By this time a few rapid steps brings them together (for all in London walk as though they did it for a wager): one says, "Fine weather;" the other replies, "Yes; only a little foggy, rainy, and cold." By this time the parties have passed each other, and each turns his head round, so that his chin rests on his shoulder, to continue the peripatetic discourse; yet disdaining to lose time by stopping — like two vessels passing each other on opposite tacks, and asking their respective longitudes, without heaving to. "Any news?" says one; "Nothing strange," says the other; "Good-bye," calls one; "Good-day," replies the other. Both nod like Chinese mandarins; at the same time, they look one way and walk the other, until each runs against another passenger in the crowded street.

Should a West Indian ask his way to Cornhill[†] of a passenger in London, he gets for answer, "Turn to your right, and then take the second to your left; take the third to the left, and follow your nose along Fleet Street, and any fool will shew you the way."

This is said so quickly that the informant leaves the stranger to doubt if he ought to turn at first to the right or to the left. But let an Englishman ask his way in the West Indies, and the following dialogue is likely to ensue.

"Can you tell me the way to Mr. Muscovadoe's[†] estate?"

"What, sir! don't you know the way to Mr. Muscovadoe's?"

"No; or I would not ask it."

"You must really be a stranger."

"I am a stranger; but will you please to direct me?"

"Why, let me see — do you know the Dry River?"[†]

"Yes; I do."

"Well, it's not there." After a pause, your guide adds, "But you'll cross it, hearee (do you hear)? and when you get to Cane Garden, you'll strike across the pasture, till you come chock against the fence; then keep up to windward,[54] till you meet up with the bottom of the valley; you'll then

---

54. Eastward and westward is called windward and leeward, on account of the trade-winds. Creoles are remarkably fond of maritime phrases.

cross the gully, and, when you get to the cock-pit, any nigger will shew you Mr. Muscovadoe's estate."

The fact is, he first ascertains that you are a stranger, and then gives you such directions as none but a native can comprehend.

In the West Indies, most persons shew a desire to know how their neighbours get on; in England, people are too much occupied with their own business to think about that of another. This may be attributed to the small communities in the colonies, and the vast population of the mother country: yet, with all allowance for these, the coldness of Englishmen respecting the concerns of their neighbours struck me as a remarkably general trait. A friend of mine, a retired West Indian, who lived some years at the Hummums,[†] Covent Garden, told me an anecdote, which strongly coincided with my conclusion. It ran thus:—

Two gentlemen were in the habit, for some years, of dining in adjoining boxes at that tavern. After three years, by dint of rubbing their elbows against each other, they became so intimate as to nod, as they passed to go into their respective boxes. At the end of five years, they used to exchange brief "how d'ye do's?" but, although they, every day for seven years, dined at the same hour next to each other, they were never known to dine together, nor were ever seen to shake hands. How different is this from the continual shaking of hands in the West Indies!

The following fact I can speak of from my own knowledge. I once, in company with Dr. Molesworth, visited an old gentleman who lived in Bloomsbury Square:[†] he sent for the doctor to consult him, he being slightly indisposed. The doctor, among other questions, asked how he slept the preceding night. "Very badly," was the reply. "I was kept awake by a racket in the next house. I don't know the cause of this merry-making of my neighbour; I never knew the family to have any noisy party at their house before."

Now, the fact was this: the old gentleman had lived for thirty years beside his neighbour without being intimate with him or his family; and the merry-making which kept him awake was caused by the marriage of his next-door neighbour's only daughter.

In the West Indies, I often read of Old English hospitality: I suppose this term meant the hospitality of England in days of old, for the English of the present time do not seem to understand the meaning of the word. I certainly did meet with some hospitality in London, but it was in the apartments of retired West Indians. These were generally located in and about Sloane Street;[†] they generally live in pairs, unless the parties have families. I always knew where to find them by these signs:— They generally have a pair of green parrots hanging out of the parlour window, and a monkey chained down the area; have the doors and windows carefully lined with list,[†] and a black porter or lackey to open the door. When introduced to them, I found in the room of audience a sideboard, laid out in the West Indian style, — with much glass, and little plate; large glass candle-shades, a huge sangaree-bowl, with an open bottle or two of madeira — for, in general, West Indians do not decant their wine. One or both of the hosts lay swinging in a cotton hammock, from which they scarcely rose to receive their visitors, who were desired to help themselves, or to call for what they wanted.

If two persons in the West Indies live on terms of intimacy, the parties never think of giving each other an invitation to dinner, unless the inviter entertains a party, as an invitation would be thought too formal. A friend is expected to drop in at meal-times, and partake of what is going on; to announce his intention of taking coffee or soup with his friend, — that is to say, coming to breakfast or dinner with him: this he does with as little ceremony as he asks for a pinch of snuff. All this is necessarily different in England: none there thinks of inviting himself to take coffee or soup with any one; and, as to an invitation, he who visits a friend in England on the strength of one of them, will find the party too formal to be hospitable.

One practice at dinner in England I must protest against: an invited guest is not allowed to do as he pleases. I felt this as a great annoyance, after being used to the free-and-easy tables of the Caribbean Islands. At every formal party I was at in London, I was pestered beyond my patience to partake of things which were my aversion, after having satisfied my appetite with viands that I liked. The worst of all this was, that, while the host and his family were persecuting me, in order to make me cram as much into my stomach as though it were a cotton-pack, the parties absolutely conceived they were exercising politeness and hospitality.

Nothing astonished me in England more than the frequency of the repasts. In the West Indies two meals in twenty-four hours is all we think of; in England they consume four solid repasts per day, and a good supper at night.

Notwithstanding our abundance of turtle; the endless variety and delicacy of fish; the venison-like taste of our lean, but delicious mutton; the abundance and good quality of poultry in the colonies, — yet the *matériel* of the kitchen in England is infinitely superior to that of a West Indian "cook-room:"† but I think the cookery of the West Indies much superior to that of England. I have dined in houses that sported first-rate French artists, but thought their compounds beyond comparison inferior to those of the black and brown cooks of the West, whose culinary system is a kind of composite order between the solid Doric dishes of the British, and the Corinthian cookery of their Gallic neighbours.

The few words employed in business in England is astonishing. In London, two merchants will negociate the sale of a West Indiaman, with her whole cargo, in less time and with fewer words than a storekeeper on our side of the Atlantic would take to sell a demijean of rum. This brevity is so remarkable, that mercantile business is more rapidly transacted in England than in any other country on earth. A merchant in one of the Antilles wrote a most elaborate and "lengthy" epistle to a London house, and received for answer a letter running thus:—

> "Sir,
> "Write shorter letters, and draw for your money.
> "Your obedient," &c.

When a West Indian wishes to express that any business is set about, he says it is on the carpet; an Englishman says it is on the anvil. The latter certainly uses all his energies to strike while the iron is hot.

This brevity in transacting business is carried into English courts of law. When a wigless colonial lawyer is retained, it is expected, whether the cause in which he is engaged will admit of a speech or not, that he will make one, to shew that he merits his fee, to gratify his client, and to amuse the party-coloured auditors who always loiter about a West Indian court of law, who are as fond of hearing suits determined as were the Athenians of old. With the periwig-pated fellows of Westminster Hall the case is different: when nothing need be said, or nothing can be said, the English lawyer wisely holds his tongue. Eloquence in Westminster Hall may be used to support argument, but the judges there would frown most awfully on any one who should presume to use oratory for the mere purpose of earning his fee, or of amusing the bystanders.

The apparent want of charity in the people of England often shocked me. In the West Indies, it rarely happens that any one complains of hunger; when it does, the wants of the unfortunate are promptly supplied. If application be made to the house of the opulent for succour, the distressed man is sent into the kitchen, or a small table is laid out for him in an out-house; if the party appealed to be of the humble order of society, he is generally asked into the hall,[55] and such provision as the house affords is given to him.

Often have I witnessed acts of benevolence from persons in the colonies, who have a multitude of sins for their charity to cover. Many a wretched white man, when attacked at one and the same time by poverty and the yellow fever, has been succoured by poor mulatto women of the most unfortunate and degraded description; many a houseless white has been nursed into health by those women, or decently buried by them, although the names even of the parties in whose behalf their humanity has been exerted were unknown to them. It is remarkable that this has been the common practice of poor mulatto women since the earliest days of colonisation in this part of the world, as we learn from the oldest Spanish historians of these islands. In the Antilles, even the poor slave allows no child of want to solicit in vain, while he has the power of relieving him. Often have I seen sailors who had lost their way up a West India colony, or who had been turned adrift for misconduct — often have I seen such feeding out of the calabash of the poor negroes.

When white men become incorrigibly bad, and are deserted by all, they skulk about the negro village of a plantation, and are maintained by the slaves.

Having witnessed the above general benevolence of the Caribbean Islands, I was frequently shocked in England at beholding the indigent solicit in vain the cold hand of charity. Much of this apparent hardness of heart is, doubtless, owing to the poor-laws, and to the number of impostors which a dense population always possesses, who are ready to abuse and deceive benevolence; yet, amongst the many fortunes that were wrecked during my too brief sojourn in England, I never heard of one that was ruined by charity. I know that political economy condemns the giving of alms and relieving of wants, as injurious to society; but, thank God! I am not a political economist.

I more than once witnessed a greasy well-fed magistrate bully and abuse a parcel of houseless wretches, who had violated the vagrant-law; in other words, had committed the sin of being miserably poor. I felt as pleased

---

55. In the West Indies, the hall is the main room of the house; or, what is called in England, the parlour. In London, the word is generally applied to the vestibule.

with the well-fed reprover of poverty as I suppose an Englishman would feel, on his first arrival in the colonies, at beholding a negro-driver, with his cartwhip, persuading a slave to work faster by means of the *argumentum a posteriori.*[†]

That the English are not wanting in public charity appears by the fact of the existence of an immense number of noble public institutions, in which all kinds of calamities are relieved, and to where the unfortunate of all descriptions can retire. The hospitals of London bear glorious testimony of national benevolence, and, I hope, call down blessings on that "province covered with houses."[†]

Often, when viewing those magnificent receptacles for the maimed and worn-out defenders of their country at Greenwich and Chelsea,[†] I felt the justness of the observation of a foreigner, who, alluding to the wretched-looking palace at St. James's,[†] and the splendour of the hospitals for decayed seamen and soldiers, said, that the English lodge their kings in a hospital, and their beggars in palaces.

The women in England are, in general, beautiful. The great advantages they possess over the fair of the Antilles is in having countenances more expressive and animated, and complexions more beautifully variegated. Nothing can exceed the transparent skin of the women of England; and the mingled white and red shewing through it, like the delicate tints of well-painted porcelain appearing through the glaze which art gives it, while the blue veins being visible, render the whole so lovely, that it can be compared to nothing so aptly as the fleecy pods of new-opened cotton, wet with the sparkling dews of morning.

The complexions of creole ladies, of unmixed European descent, are fair as lilies; but the rose is seldom reflected on their countenances. Their lips are well formed, but want the ruby die of fair Englishwomen. Their lack of expression and animation is owing, doubtless, to their sedentary habits and retired manners: that the climate alone cannot account for. This is proved by the fact, that no women on earth have more animated and expressive visages than women of colour.

The women of the Caribbean Isles do not, in general, carry the folly of tight-lacing[†] to the pitch that it is enforced in England; hence, their *tournure*[†] is often better, and consumptions[†] less common among them. I know, a waist pinched in like an hour-glass is, in England, thought a beauty; so is a crippled foot in China, a flattened forehead amongst the Caraibs,[†] and a tattooed face amongst most savages.

The Creator made women of the most lovely form: what a mixture of folly and presumption it is to attempt to alter that which came perfect from His hands!

The eyes of the fair creoles are fully as beautiful as those of English-women: the former are languishing and indicative of benevolence; the latter, animated, lively, and expressive of every emotion of their active minds.

The women of England — and, from what I have seen, those of France — may learn one thing of creoles: that is, to walk. The French ladies trip as though they walked on sharp pebbles; the English fair marches with the long pace of a light-infantry man; the creoles walk gracefully.

From the pictures I had seen of John Bull, I was led to believe that all Englishmen had that deformity of the abdomen called a corporation: this is not the case in general; although I think, if Englishmen were less stout, they would look less clumsy.

One of the first things that struck me in viewing the people "at home," was their extraordinary cleanliness. This, in the houses of the great, did not astonish me; although the extreme neatness of every article of furni-ture, every domestic utensil, and all the servants, both in and out of livery, enhanced considerably the luxury by which I was surrounded, during a few visits I paid to the great. The very stable of an English gentleman, and the cow-house of an English farmer, shew the peculiar neatness of the people. But what most surprised and gratified me, was the scrupulous regard to cleanliness which the poor evinced. During my medical studies, I visited the indigent sick; and yet I could have eat off the well-scoured floor, on which lay a flock† bed supporting the patient. Often have I observed, with pleasure, a poor woman with four children taking the air, on a Sunday, in the Park: the dresses of the whole were not worth half so much as a single massive gold button, two pair of which a negress com-monly wears in her sleeve; and yet the patched and repatched habiliments were as clean as wedding garments.

I was much edified by attending public worship in various churches of the metropolis. The unostentatious devotion of the congregations, and the eloquence of the preachers, gratified me; but I felt as a drawback the wretched screeching and hissing of

"Sternhold's creeping lays;"†

or the Psalms done into English by Tait and Brady,† which the parish-clerks call — "singing to the praise and glory of God."† I would advise some of the churches to send to Antigua for negro Methodists,[†] who would form a much better choir than those they possess.

Being a stranger, I, of course, went to see all the stone lions of the town. I am no judge of architecture; but most of the buildings in London appeared to denote that their erectors bestowed more labour than taste on their works. From this censure I, of course, except Westminster Abbey, Somerset House;[†] the noble piles of Wren, Inigo Jones, Gibbs;[†] and the glorious bridges which span the noble Thames. The English display more genius in constructing bridges, docks, arsenals, hospitals, and ships-of-war, than in raising palaces, public offices, and churches.

I shall not attempt to describe my emotion the first time I saw a play in London. True it is, I had witnessed a dramatic representation, or misrepresentation, in the West Indies; but these were amateur performances. Some of the amateurs possessed abilities; but ridicule was thrown on the whole attempt by the ladies' characters being acted by young men. Let the reader, if he can, conceive a tall youth of twenty, playing Lady Randolph[†] ('Douglas,' by the by, is a favourite amongst amateurs)! The young man will not consent to lose his whiskers; he therefore endeavours to conceal them under the lappets of his cap; and, ever and anon, as he turns his head, his "favourites" peep out. Conceive a person so situated acting the part of Lady Randolph, and, with a full tenor voice, address Anna (represented by a tall, dunning clerk), and saying to the said Anna, —

——— "I found myself
As women wish to be who love their lords."[†]

or let the reader suppose he witnesses the exhibition of Otway's 'Orphan,'[†] the part of the tender Monimia enacted by a short, squat lad, with a woolly head, a mask of paint over his dark face, and a pair of large ear-rings suspended by thread from his unbored ears; suppose such a youth, wishing to be pathetic, exclaiming, with the voice of a bull-calf, —

"Why was I born with all my sex's softness?"[†]

Let the gentle or simple reader suppose all this, and he will form a faint conception of a West India dramatic exhibition, and have a fainter idea what my feelings were at beholding the supernatural or preternatural 'Macbeth' of Shakespeare, while Kemble and his still more illustrious sister,[†] played the principal characters.

Unused as I was to theatrical display, the accuracy of the scenery, the shadowy way in which the witches performed their incantations, and the picturesque appearance of the plaided warriors, delighted me. But when I heard Macbeth deliver the immortal air-drawn dagger soliloquy; when I saw his daring lady tempting him to blood, like an incarnate fiend; when I witnessed the confusion of the guilty pair after the murder of their sovereign; and, above all, when I beheld the conscience-haunted sleep-walker, endeavouring to wash from her hands the "damned spot," — I quailed with horror, and yet, at the same time, felt intense delight. This is a paradox which I shall not attempt to solve: the pleasure resulting from beholding a sublime tragedy, well acted, has often been attempted to be explained, but without success.

I must add, that the after-piece appeared to please "the million,"[†] better than the masterpiece of Shakespeare, supported by the talent of Siddons[†] and Kemble; for the latter was sustained by greater performers, viz. a stud of horses.

I had read, both in the West Indies and in England, of the open immorality practised in the colonies. The censures, although a little over-drawn, were true in the main; but, after perusing them, in the simplicity of my heart I conceived that the morals of England were pure as the unsunned snow of the climate. This error was removed on my entering the saloon of a London theatre. I will venture to say, that the profligacy I there beheld shocked me more than any Englishman was ever shocked by contemplating any scene of libertinism in our part of the world.

Creoles in general are well pleased with themselves, and consequently pleased with all around them. If a calamity happen to him, he persuades himself that it was caused by no fault of his, and that another year will amend the misfortune. The next year, in the West Indies, has become proverbial; the next year is to redress all grievances, and to compensate for all losses: but the "next year" of the creole, like the "tomorrow" of the debtor, never arrives. The fact is, hope is the consolation of mankind in general, but it is often the evil genius of the creole. He passively hopes for the best at the time he should actively prepare for the worst. Such being the failing of my compatriots, I could not but be forcibly struck with the countless number of croakers[†] I met with in England. The creole air-castle builder is less prudent than the English grumbler, but not a whit less wise. During every war for the last two hundred years, our West India colonies suffered cruelly. Provisions were, at times, so dear in the colonies, that wheaten loaves were often too expensive to be seen on the tables of the most opulent; and the mass of the people were obliged to live on the crude vegetables of the islands. But the creoles who suffered such privations consoled each other by saying, the times would change, and that flour would be at two dollars a-barrel "next year;" while, at the same time, if an English operative was deprived of the slightest article of consumption, which we in the colonies consider as luxuries, he would be ready to rise in rebellion at the call of the first "man of the people" who should propose to attack the Tower[†] or plunder the Bank.

The disposition to grumbling is not confined to the lower orders; but the pleasure of the well-educated croakers in England consists in pretending to be miserable, and in the amiable endeavour to make others as unhappy as they wish to appear. When I first came to England, the long wars[†] afforded sufficient themes for croaking: when I left it, the well-informed croakers were predicting all sorts of misfortunes, because many persons were using their best endeavours to educate the lower classes of society. They prophesied that national schools[†] would become national evils; that, as the humble ranks of society became well-informed, they would become discontented; that all people would cease to obey the laws when all could read them, and a revolution would be the consequence. I regretted to hear this; because I came from places where the labouring classes are illiterate, and I have beheld the evils resulting from the want of letters among the cultivators of the soil, the hewers of wood and drawers of water.[†]

Those who fear that education will cause a revolution, know nothing of history, or treat it as an old almanack. Were the furious outbreakings, during the middle ages in France, which were called *Jacqueries*,[†] caused by the diffusion of useful knowledge? Were the riots of Wat Tyler[†] and Jack Cade[†] brought about by national schools, or the want of them? To come nearer our own times — was the frenzy of the Parisian mobs, during the Reign of Terror,[†] caused by its members being too well instructed? No, no; the rising of "the great unwashed"[†] has often been occasioned by want and oppression — more often by their ignorance, being misled by artful demagogues: but never did men rise, never will men rise in revolt because the schoolmaster is abroad: rebellion, generally, is the child of ignorance. The insidious harangue of the factious orator is never more dangerous than when addressed to an illiterate mob.

That venerable monarch, George III,[†] wished that every one of his subjects had a Bible, and were able to read it: a more benevolent wish was never expressed by any prince; a wiser saying was never recorded of any king since the days of Solomon.

One of the many things which astonished me in England, was the want of geographical information that pervaded all ranks of society. Great Britain rules one-fourth of the globe in all parts of the world; she possesses colonies; her merchandise and manufactories supply every mart; her ships crowd every sea; her travellers penetrate every inhabited and uninhabited country: and yet the English, in general, know as much of geography as a mole knows of longitude. The ignorance I complain of was often taken advantage of by the writers on both sides of the controversy, during the long agitation of the question of colonial slavery.

Some years since, a book was published, purporting to be a description of the West Indies,† which placed Trinidad in the Gulf of Mexico. This geographical blunder, and twenty others equally gross, passed unobserved, although the book was reviewed by most of the principal periodicals of the day. Repeatedly, in the House of Commons, the most finished orators have talked of "the Island of Demerara;"† and I myself heard a senator of some celebrity say, "he hoped to see the day when the negroes in the West Indies would peaceably *enjoy their own firesides!*" Talk of a people enjoying their firesides in a climate where, in the month of January, the mercury stands at 92° in the shade! there is fever in the very thought. I could, if I chose, write a whole volume on the subject of the ridiculous geographical blunders which I heard people in England make.

Such are the impressions made on me by English society: I describe them with some diffidence, because I know from experience how easily a stranger is led to make erroneous conclusions. I have often laughed at the ridiculous mistakes that tourists have made in the West Indies.

CHAPTER 26.

"Oh! woman, in our hours of ease,
Uncertain, coy, and hard to please . . .
When pain and anguish wring the brow,
A ministering angel thou."
SCOTT.[†]

"I at last their miseries viewed
In that vile garret, which I cannot paint."
CRABBE.[†]

Having taken up much time to relate what I thought in London, it is now time to tell what I did.

On the sailing of the first West Indian packet[†] after my arrival, I wrote to my brother Rodney, but received no answer by the return of the packet. Months elapsed, and no reply arrived. I wrote again and again, but no answer came. At length I thought the family slighted me, and I wrote no more. My letters were intercepted: the reader shall be informed, in due time, how this occurred.

Every quarter I received a brief letter from Messrs. Keen and Leech, enclosing a bill of exchange for 62*l*. 10*s*. on Messrs. Sucker and Sons, Fenchurch Street, at ninety days' sight, which was duly honoured.

I became a pupil[†] of Dr. Molesworth, attending with him whenever he had an extraordinary case, and I could find time. Occasionally I took instructions from his apothecary in the *materia medica*.[†] I lost no time, but attended Brooks's, Carpue's, and Bell's lectures:[†] I walked the Middlesex Hospital,[†] and became dresser[†] to one of the principal surgeons; studied chemistry and botany; read every book on medicine which Dr. Molesworth recommended. My knowledge of Latin and French served me much in this respect. In short, I displayed assiduity to gain a knowledge of my profession as a surgeon; for the gentlemen of Warwick Lane refuse to grant a diploma to any one who has not washed his hands in the Cam or Isis.[†] However, I cared little about this, because I intended to practise in the West Indies, where the obsolete distinction between physician and surgeon is little attended to:[†] both branches there, as they ought to be every where else, are practised by the same person.

As the progress I made in my medical studies can have little interest to the general reader, I will pass over them, and merely state, that my application was noticed and praised by all whose lectures I attended.

Nothing worth relating occurred until January 1815; when, during one miserable foggy and snowy day, which is peculiarly unpleasant to a native of the torrid zone, I went into a hairdresser's shop in Warwick Street, Golden Square,[†] to get my hair trimmed. The operator and his assistant were both employed; I was, therefore, obliged to wait until one of them was disengaged. The barber observing, by my blowing my fingers, that I was disagreeably affected by the cold, asked me to go into his back room, where there was a fire. I agreed to this proposition, and went in, took a seat before the grate, and warmed myself, until the hairdresser despatched his customers. On looking round me, I saw on a side-table a body of the most beautiful hair I ever beheld. It was of a light-brown colour, most elegantly curled, more than six feet in length, and of the most silky texture I ever touched.

The man of the shop, having finished with his other customers, came to me. He was a short dapper man, with a deep pock-marked countenance, which looked as though it had been sculptured with a rough chisel out of a cask of tallow: and yet his pale crumpet-looking features[†] had the traits of good-nature and intelligence so plainly written on them, that, ungainly as they were, they seemed any thing but disagreeable. Real good-humour can throw a pleasant expression into an ugly visage.

"You seem, sir, to enjoy the fire; you don't like cold," said he.

I replied, that a clear frosty day was tolerable, because I could brace myself with exercise; but that I hated the foggy weather of his climate.

"Perceive, sir, you are a foreigner?"

"Not exactly: I am a West Indian."

"Bless me, sir! you are a West Indian, and yet you are as fair as any Englishman! I thought you natives of the West Indies were *molotoes* (mulattoes)."

I smiled at the man's mistake; which, however, is common in England, where most persons conceive mulattoes the pure descendants of whites, rendered dark by being born in a torrid climate.

"You would prefer, perhaps, that I should cut your hair here, to sitting in the cold shop?"

I consented to this suggestion; and, with that despatch remarkable to the tradesman of London, he tied a napkin round my neck, and commenced reducing my superfluous hair.

"You don't have your hair cut too close; I would advise you against that, for one who possesses so fine a head of flaxen locks."

I told him to operate as he chose.

"There, sir, you shew your good sense: leave the matter to me, and I'll set off your head to the best advantage. A young man's prospects are often influenced by his hairdresser: nothing conduces so much to improve the appearance of a youth, as having his locks skilfully trimmed; it gives him a prepossessing appearance, which often does him good service. A handsome look, sir, is often more valuable to a young gentleman than half a fortune. Having the head well trimmed on the outside, does a youth sometimes more service than having it well lined with brains. I see, sir, you wince as the cold scissors touch your neck: always know a man from a warm country by that, sir. There, sir, I think that will do. You look admirably, although I say it that should not say it, inasmuch as I contributed to your good looks with my own hands and scissors."

I peeped into a small mirror, and expressed myself satisfied, for the man had really performed his operation well and quickly. I gave him a shilling.

"Here, sir, is your change," said the man of the scissors; and he tendered me sixpence.

"Never mind the change," said I.

"Bless me! I would not mind it were you a few years older; but, sir, sixpence is my price, and I could not think of taking more of a youth than I charge a man."

Perceiving I still neglected the change, he added, —

"Well, sir, as you choose; but I'll give you a piece of advice which will, perhaps, be worth more than sixpence. Never offer a tradesman double what he asks, because he pays a compliment to your appearance. Excuse me sir, — ha, ha, ha!"

I thanked the man for his advice, which was not bad, considering I paid for it. The loquacious barber perceived I fixed my eyes on the hair I have spoken of: he said, —

"Fine hair, sir: I have been in the trade, man and boy, thirty years, and never saw any article so beautiful. It is the colour of your hair, only half-a-dozen shades darker. It is lovely, and it belonged to as lovely a young woman as ever I saw. She is, like yourself, from foreign parts, because she has a blackamoor woman[†] as her servant. Poor young lady! I gave her, last week, twice as much as it was worth in trade, because she appeared in distress: she took the money with a tear in her eye, which she tried to conceal. I got anxious to find out who she was, and sent my boy, Bill, — a 'cute lad, sir, — to follow her: she went to a butcher and a baker, where she bought some provision, which her tawny servant carried. Bill then followed them to a back alley in Swallow Street, where she lives. Bill asked all about her, and found she is the wife of a poor sick officer, and mother of three children. The good creature sold her beautiful hair to satisfy the hunger of her sick husband, and famishing babes — God bless her! Why, love you, sir, you have a tear in your eye! You need not hide it: you should be ashamed of selfish tears, because they are unmanly; but the tears that are shed for the distress of another do us honour."

"Will you allow your boy," asked I, "to shew me where this lady lives?"

"That I will," replied the worthy trimmer of hair; "and the more willingly because I believe your visit will be one of benevolence."

He called his boy, and bid him shew me where the distressed family resided. He took him aside ere we left the shop, and I heard him say to the boy in a whisper, —

"Now, Bill, if he offers you any thing, don't accept it, and I'll give you what he wants you to take."

I took leave of the kind barber, and followed his lad about four hundred yards: he took me up a dark alley.

"This is the house," said the boy; "you will find the family in the garret."

Up I went; but, before I got to the first landing-place, I paused to recollect what I was about. Affected by the story told by the barber, I resolved, in the first impulse of my feelings, to relieve the distress of the family. I possessed the means of doing this, having just returned from the city with my quarter's allowance in my pocket. But, would my visit be well taken? The husband of the lady was an officer in the army, and might resent that as an insult which I meant as an act of kindness. I recollected that the husband was sick, and I resolved to introduce myself as a medical student, and to beg permission to prescribe for the gentleman. Approving of this thought, I ascended, and knocked at the door of the garret.

"Come in," said a faint voice.

I lifted the latch, and a sight struck my eyes which astonished me.

The garret had no covering but the tiles of the house; the light was admitted through a single window, a leaden lattice, which held green and knotted panes of glass, some broken, and mended with paper. Through this window was seen a vast mass of roofs of houses, thickly covered with the discoloured snow of London; in a small grate lingered the embers of a nearly extinct fire: an ancient table, with two old-fashioned chairs, were the only articles of furniture in the room. Against one of the rafters hung a tarnished and worn uniform of a lieutenant of infantry; and beside the wall was a letter-holder, full of those vouchers of poverty, pawnbrokers' duplicates.[†] In one corner of the room crouched a mulattoe, with a blanket over her: she seemed to try in vain to keep herself warm. As I entered, she rose, and I at once recognised her to be my old friend, Lucy. On a flock-bed in a corner reposed my fellow-passenger, Rivers, with two children by his side; the three were covered by a military great coat. The father was so worn by misery, that, had I not known Lucy, I should not have recognised him; beside his bed sat his beautiful wife — for beautiful she was, despite her wretchedness. Although famine had thrown his pallid hue over her cheek, she supported an infant in her arms; her dress bore marks of faded gentility. Grim poverty seemed to pervade the cold room.

"Massa Warner!" screamed Lucy; and, after a second, the distressed couple both exclaimed, "Mr. Arundell!"

I knelt to embrace my old friend; after which I exclaimed, looking round me, "Good God! Captain Rivers —" and checked myself.

"I understand you, Mr. Arundell — you are shocked at our wretchedness: and, truly, these are not splendid apartments for the lieutenant in his majesty's army — the heir-presumptive of a large estate; nor is this furniture suitable to the rank of the daughter of a colonel. But what brought you here: I thought indigence concealed me from all my acquaintance."

I stammered out something, not very coherent, about my coming to visit a person I heard was sick, in order to improve my medical studies.

"Arundell," said he, grasping my hand, "you are a worthy young man; but be advised by me — never attempt a falsehood. Nay, I meant no offence. Never attempt dissimulation; for, practise it as you will, your countenance is too honest for you to become an adept in it. So, Amelia, our young friend, who saved our eldest boy, has paid us a visit to try his hand at doctoring on me: like P.P. the parish clerk, to bleed adventures he not, except on the poor.† But, whatever brought you here, I am happy — most happy — to see you."

"Mr. Warner could have no other motives in visiting us but those of kindness; he is, therefore, welcome," said the lady, extending her hand; which I took. "Here, Robert; here is your old acquaintance, who shot Jumbee. Nay; don't cry so; the gentleman is a friend."

But the poor child wept on; and the other two joined him, despite their mother's attempt to quiet them. Their's was not the mere weeping of infancy; it was the wailing of famine. Each cry reverberated in the hearts of the father and mother. Most agonising to the ears of the parents are the cries of the children for food, when the latter cannot satisfy the cravings of their offspring!

"How are you, Lucy ?" said I.

"Pretty miserable, Massa Warner; hope you are the same."

"You seem weak, Lucy. I hope you are not sick?"

"No, massa; only a little weak and cold. This country cold for true; and every body heart cold like the country. I have no other sick (sickness) but hunger."

"That is a disease I can easily remedy. Rise, if you are able, and get something to eat for yourself and order some coals up instantly — I am perishing with cold."

I put a guinea into her hand. She understood my meaning, which was to send her for something to satisfy the cravings of the starving family, without offending the lieutenant or his wife.

"Blessings on your good heart, Massa Warner! I just tell missis, God Almighty go send him angel to help us; and him send what is more better than angel — him send a kind young man to relieve us, and feed the starving children," said poor Lucy, bursting into tears.

I hurried her out of the room, and, on the landing, gave her directions what she should procure for the immediate use of the hapless family.

"Arundell, this is most kind," said Rivers, grasping my hand with all the strength that sickness left him — his felt deadly cold; "but I shall never be able to pay you. The poor half-pay of a lieutenant scarcely supports us when I am in health; and now disease has reduced us to this state of misery. For the last week I have been subsisting on my poor Amelia's hair; and, just before you came in, she talked of selling her teeth to a dentist."†

I endeavoured to divert the melancholy conversation by inquiring after his malady. This I found to be an inveterate tertian fever.† Under pretence of getting some medicine, I stepped out and purchased a bottle of port wine. On my return, I found that Lucy had been most expeditious: she had procured ready-dressed provisions and fuel. In no place can all these be obtained so readily as in London — for money; but without it, a man stands a greater chance of famishing in Fleet Market[†] than on the rock of Sombrero,[†] or in the wilds of South America.

The children and Lucy ate so ravenously that I was obliged to interpose. The lieutenant and his lady ate more sparingly. I, however, caused them to partake of a little wine; and Rivers explained the cause of his present misfortune.

Previously to my acquaintance with him, he had been captured by the French, and sent to Cayenne.[†] In the same prison with him was a colonel and his daughter, his present wife, whom he married; a chaplain of an English regiment, also a prisoner, performing the ceremony. Shortly after this, Cayenne was taken by the British. His father-in-law was sent home, and, subsequently, to Ceylon.[†] Rivers remained in the West Indies, until ordered to England in 1812. On his arrival, his father was mortally offended at his marriage, because he maintained an old grudge against the father of his wife: he would not speak to him.

Rivers, having nothing to depend upon but his sword and his ensign's commission, joined his regiment in Spain; his affectionate wife following him; and her old slave Lucy took service in a West India family. Three years' hard fighting, and two wounds, got him promoted to the rank of a lieutenant. At the peace, in 1814, he was put on half pay. His father now sent for him, and made the following shameful proposal: viz., as he was married in a French prison by a clergyman now dead, without the necessary formalities being observed, the father told him, if he would take advantage of those circumstances, and deny the validity of his marriage, he would give the lieutenant 10,000*l.*, and settle an annuity on the lady. Rivers would not listen for one moment to a proposition so infamous, and upbraided his father in no measured terms. The old man's wrath knew no bounds: he bought up all his son's debts, and caused him to be arrested and thrown into prison. His wife sold all her little trinkets to free her husband; and even Lucy (who had rejoined them) added her savings. He got out of gaol, but was attacked by a tedious malady. The expenses occasioned by this reduced them to their present misery.

I remained with Rivers long after night set in, and then trod my way through the snow, to my apartments at Dr. Molesworth's. The next day, as I left my residence to visit Rivers, I met the celebrated Dr. Baillie.[†] He had repeatedly seen me with Dr. Molesworth, and was condescending enough to pay me some attention.

"Have you," said he, "ever seen a case of *Chorea Sancti Viti?*"[†]

I replied in the negative.

"If you have nothing better to do, step into my carriage, and I'll shew you a most extraordinary case."

I told the doctor I had a patient of my own to visit.

"You a patient!" said the doctor, good humouredly. "What, not being duly qualified, you are going to kill without a license! This is downright poaching upon our manor."

"I am," replied I, "acting under peculiar circumstances."

"I have little time," rejoined the doctor, "to listen to peculiar circumstances, in this cold weather, at the door of my carriage. I am going towards St. James's Square; if your patient lives in that direction, take a ride with me."

I entered the carriage, and begged him to take Swallow Street in his way. This he ordered the coachman to do. Seated in the coach, he asked me about my patient. I, as briefly as I could, related how I became acquainted with Rivers, and in what state I found him and his family yesterday. The doctor seemed interested in the story, and asked me how I intended to treat the sick man. I said that I had ordered him to take a dose of antimony,[†] combined with the submuriate of mercury;[†] and that, if the medicine operated well, I intended to administer alternate doses of solution of arsenic[†] and Peruvian bark.[†]

"Not a bad method of treating a tertian," said the doctor; "but will you suffer me to act as your consulting doctor?"

To this humane and condescending proposition of the physician of royalty, I, of course, consented; and, in a few minutes, we were at the entrance of the alley in which lived the lieutenant: the doctor readily mounted to the garret with me.

Rivers was surprised, and seemed rather chagrined, at receiving a visit from Dr. Baillie, whom, however, he did not know; but the doctor's kind inquiries soon dispelled the cloud from his brow. His displeasure, doubtless, arose from being seen under such indigent circumstances. After inquiring into the patient's symptoms, he gave me directions, in Latin, how I was to treat him; begged that I would visit him at his house in the afternoon, and left me with Rivers.

After the doctor went, I could not but observe what an air of cheerfulness the trifling sum I had given Lucy had diffused around the miserable garret. Rivers inquired who the kind physician was whom I had brought to see him? I told him, and then went to a neighbouring apothecary, where I got the medicines recommended by the doctor. The lieutenant's disease, which had never been well treated, soon gave way to the remedies recommended by the great Baillie.

On visiting the doctor in the evening, he, after inquiring how the lieutenant got on, addressed me thus: "Look you, Mr. Arundell, just before I saw you this morning, I visited a hypochondriacal peer — one of those who, for ever,

——— 'The doctor tease
To name the nameless, ever new disease.'†

"Vexed at being sent for to treat an imaginary complaint, when I had more patients really sick than I could attend, his lordship perceived my impatience, and was offended. I left him: he sent his valet after me with a note, which informed me that he would dispense with my future visits; but it enclosed a check on his banker for fifty pounds. As I dislike pocketing fees from people who are not sick, I resolved to give the money to some charity. Now, Mr. Arundell, I will thank you to give or send to your poor friend the fifty pounds, without letting him know from whom it comes."

I consented to aid the doctor's act of benevolence, and sent the money by a man belonging to Middlesex Infirmary. I enclosed it in a letter, and made a fellow-student write the address, lest Rivers should know my hand-writing.

The next day I visited my patient: he challenged me with having sent the money to him. I pledged my honour that the money had never been mine. He asked me if I would declare that I did not know who sent it. I declined answering. He rightly guessed whence it came. He said he would not accept it; but that he felt himself so much better, that he would receive it as a loan, being convinced that he should be able to repay it in a short time.

In a week or two he was so far advanced in convalescence, that he was enabled to employ himself copying drawings for a picture-shop in Rathbone Place. The emoluments he received for his labour were but trifling; but they helped him to eke out the slender income of a half-pay lieutenant. He removed to a more decent lodging, whence poverty was banished: he had learnt frugality from misfortune — that stern teacher of the use of money.

In a few weeks after this, the wholesale human butcher, Buonaparte, having escaped from Elba, set Europe once more in a ferment.[†] Rivers readily joined his regiment, and behaved so well at Waterloo that he was promoted to a company. The last time I heard from him in Europe, he was with the army of occupation in France, where he lived comfortably with his family on the full pay of a captain.

CHAPTER 27.

"Ah! I am but a ball for Fortune's foot
To spurn where'er she lists."
THE TWO CITIZENS.[†]

In 1816 I studied hard, in order to pass examination as a surgeon; and calculated that my next quarter's allowance would pay all the fees of my license, as well as purchase a small case of instruments. One afternoon, I heard the postman's peculiar knock at the door. This was opened by the porter, and I heard the man of letters announce, "Mr. Warner Arundell, — two shillings and two-pence." I sent the money; and, on looking at the address, I recognised the well-known writing of the head clerk of Keen and Leech. The address was ominous; having a Mr. before my name, instead of an Esquire after it. It was a single instead of a double letter; consequently contained no bill of exchange. The contents ran thus:—

"Basseterre, St. Christopher's,

"SIR,   April 1st, 1816.

"Referring you to London prices current for low quotations of muscovadoes,[†] and at the same time to accounts current, hereto annexed, exhibiting increased expenses and decreasing crops of your late father's estates (Arundell and Clarence) in this island and Antigua, we beg leave to advise the foreclosure of our mortgages on the same, so as to save any further loss to our house.

"Under these circumstances, it will not be in our power to continue the remittance (per your order) of 250*l.* sterling per annum. We regret that the kind feeling of our senior towards your late respected father's memory should have induced him to advance (per your order) the several sums we have remitted since your departure for England with which your account now stands debited in our books, and which, together with the old balance, we trust you will speedily liquidate.

"Hoping to hear satisfactory accounts of you (post-paid or franked), we beg leave to assure you of our readiness to forward your views, whenever you may be pleased to place us in funds.

"We are, Sir,

"Your obedient faithful Servants,

"KEEN *and* LEECH."

"*To MR. WARNER ARUNDELL, LONDON.*

(*"Per Packet."*)

The news contained in this rascally letter came upon me unexpectedly, and threw a damp upon my spirits. I was not much in debt; but, on the other side, I had little money. At no period of my life was I a good manager in pecuniary matters; and all the money my aunt gave, or rather paid me, together with my last quarter's allowance, were nearly expended. While I was reperusing the epistle of Keen and Leech, Dr. Molesworth came in. He asked me what news I had received from the West Indies. I put the letter into his hand. He read it, and said, —

"Sad news this, Mr. Arundell; more especially at the present, when you most want money. But, at the same time, I cannot help observing how admirably this letter is written, What a business-like style!"

"D——n their style!" said I.

"Hush!" said the doctor; "don't swear: it is highly immoral. Learn to take matters philosophically. Young men are apt to be violent. Take pattern by me; see how cool I am."

"Truly, doctor, you are as cool as Cooper,[†] amputating a limb, and upbraiding the patient for groaning. But can you please to advise me what I had better do in my present difficulty?"

"Why, in the first place, you are stopping with me at much expense, when you might live at very trifling cost, at those cheap lodgings kept by persons who, in the phraseology of the bills they stick in their windows, 'take in young men, and do for them.' "

"I will follow your advice to-morrow morning, as soon as I find any one who will *take me in* and *do* for me, if you have no objection."

"None in the least; because I expect two pupils from the West Indies, and your chamber will be wanted for the accommodation of one of them. And then let us see what you had better do. Were you licensed as a surgeon, I could get you into an apothecary's shop. Your pay would not be great at first; but, after a time, it would be augmented; and, if you behave yourself, you might become a partner in the shop."

"A partner in an apothecary's shop!" said I, with some disdain; for I had the ridiculous prejudices of creoles against shopkeepers.†

"What!" said the doctor; "you think it degrading to turn shopkeeper? We have in scorn, been called a nation of shopkeepers;† yet he who so denominated us found us too powerful for the nation of cooks and dancing-masters, that for a dozen years had cringed and fawned to his tyranny, and a dozen years before that talked of liberating the world. But, as you object going into an apothecary's establishment, would you like to go as surgeon on board a South Sea whaler?† I could, I think, get you that appointment."

"That would be more acceptable, doctor."

"Or how would you like to go as surgeon on board a vessel bound to Sidney with convicts?"†

"Or to go," added I, "as passenger on board the same vessel at the charge of government, with a letter of recommendation from the Recorder of London,† written in a business-style at the Old Bailey.† But, on the whole, I prefer going in a whaler."

"I'll see about it to-morrow. You can remain with me to-morrow, at all events, and I'll make no charge for the day's expenses. Let me see; how does our account stand? You owe me a month's board this day. True it is you are not quite of age; therefore, in one respect, incapable of contracting debts; but then, you know, I can demand by law from a minor any reasonable expenses for his maintenance."

"Dr. Molesworth," said I, with a little warmth, "I often heard you say that you knew my father to be a gentleman in every sense of that noble word: I have lived four years in your house, and trust you have not found me degenerate."

"By no means," replied the doctor.

"Then why talk to me of a legal demand? I fairly owe you some twelve or thirteen pounds. Gentlemen pay their just debts because they are just, and wait not for the law to oblige them to do an act of common honesty."

"Heyday! young man; I never before observed you were proud."

"Because you never before knew me poor."

I was getting angry: I had received bad tidings enough to ruffle the temper of most men, and I thought the doctor's selfish remark was ill-timed. Fortunately, the discussion was cut short by the arrival of company. Wine was introduced, of which I partook freely; but it failed to elevate my spirits. At an earlier hour than usual I retired, taking leave of the doctor with cool politeness.

Arrived in my chamber, I looked over the state of my finances, which I found rather above twenty pounds. I went to bed, but not to sleep. After tossing and tumbling for three hours, I fell into a doubtful slumber: but unpleasant dreams tormented me. I thought I was in Antigua, on the Clarence plantation, and my father stood beside me; that Keen, Leech, and their clerk, Arnold, were in conversation with my parent. The old gentleman, methought; upbraided them with cheating me, when Leech threw an immense ledger at my sire: it missed him, and knocked me down. As I fell, I thought the account-book lay on my mouth, so as to prevent my breathing; while, at the same time, Keen, aided by his clerk, rolled a hogshead of muscovadoes upon me. In vain I attempted to roll off the ponderous cask, and remove the heavy ledger from my mouth. I could not respire, while a ton-weight lay on my breast. I tried in vain to shriek; and, at last, did so: until, with a start, I awoke, and the incubus vanished. I found myself lying on my back; the bedclothes had lodged over my mouth and nose so as to impede my respiration.

I could not sleep after this attack of nightmare, but patiently listened to the information attempted to be given by the watchman: he, every half-hour, called past ——— o'clock; what the intermediate word was I could not catch, but he always added, "a cloudy morning:" for the watchmen in London[56] are paid for waking people, to tell them the hour of the night and the state of the weather.

Day at length dawned; and the watchman's cry gave way to the sweep's wailing call, which sounded like "Weep, weep!" To this succeeded the dustman's annoying bell; then followed the milkman's call. A hundred voices formed what is called the "Cries of London," mingled like a Dutch medley, and proclaimed that the busy metropolis was awake.

I arose, made my hasty toilet, sent the doctor what I owed him, and set out to look for a place where, according to cockney phraseology, "young men are taken in and done for." After walking about for half an hour, I found myself in the Haymarket;† when suddenly, passing Panton Street, I encountered my old friend, Captain Trevallion.

---

56. This was in 1816.

We warmly saluted each other; and he asked me to adjourn with him to his lodgings in Jermyn Street. Arrived there, he inquired about my prospects. I briefly explained my situation, and shewed him the "business-like letter" of Keen and Leech.

"Very concise and satisfactory," said Trevallion; "but I wonder; when they advised you to pay postage of any letter to them, they did not pay the postage of their letter to you. Well, Master Arundell, what do you think of doing?"

"I have not made up my mind about that."

"Do you wish to make your fortune? I suppose you do. I will tell how this can be done hand over hand. You know what is going on in South America; the whole continent is in a state of war.[†] An expedition is fitting out to assist the patriots: amongst the rest, I go with a recommendation from Don Mendez for the command of a ship in their service. You ought to know their country; you have been there, and speak their gibberish: that is the country for you. Bolivar[†] is carrying everything before him. In a few months after our arrival, the republicans will be in possession of Peru and Mexico, where gold and silver are more plentiful than tin and lead in Cornwall."

"How am I to get there?" asked I; "I have not the means of paying my passage."

"Take no thought about that. You are a surgeon — not licensed; but no matter, you are able to set a broken limb, or, if necessary, to dock one: that's all that is required.[†] The Saucy Jack sails in a few days from Portsmouth: the agreement with the passengers is that a doctor shall be provided for the voyage. You are the man; you'll get your passage free. Take breakfast with me, and then let us go together to Mr. W——: he will introduce you to old Don Mendez, who will give you a commission as surgeon in the Columbian service; and as to the owners of the Saucy Jack, I warrant they'll give you a passage if you will consent to act as doctor during the voyage."

I took breakfast with Trevallion; during which repast, he seemed so enthusiastic about his future prospects in South America, that I entered into his views ere we swallowed our first cup of tea.

Half an hour's walk brought us to the house of Mr. W——, in a street leading out of Tottenham Court Road. I found him the very merchant at whose house I took refuge during the night after the earthquake at Caraccas. He did not recognise me at first, but I made him recollect me:

he received me with great warmth, heard Trevallion's account of me, and proposed instantly to introduce me to Don Mendez. To this we consented: the don lived close by, and I was ushered into his presence.

He seemed a little elderly man, with a sallow complexion and hawk's-eye, which was lively enough to have belonged to a man thirty years younger; his room was crowded with solicitors for the honour of bearing commissions in the South American service. He gave a brief audience to each candidate in his turn, and always granted his recommendation of the applicant for a commission; which recommendation he addressed to the different insurgent chiefs: none were rejected. I never saw so many heroes in one room — according to their own account. Each had seen the most extraordinary services, and had been in all the battles that had been fought since their birth. One sallow-looking, middle-aged man, who had been in the East, and was dismissed the Company's[†] service because he was too lucky at cards, said that he, with a single company of sepoys,[†] had defeated the grand army of *Raja Roul Jowler Rum Un*.[†] I am not sure that I am correct in the orthography of that potentate's name, never having seen it written; but that was the way it was pronounced by Captain Curri, late of the East India Company's service.

There were several Frenchman in the room, who were not a whit behind the English candidates for commissions in bravery: not a Johnny Crapeau of them but had been in all the scenes of glory which were recorded on the Napoleon column in Paris. They proposed to eat all the Spaniards in South America! Verily, they looked hungry enough.

All, both English and French, had cultivated most warlike whiskers, and some had extensive mustachios. Perhaps, when they modestly pretended to be heroes, they feared that they should look barefaced; and hence encouraged the growth of hair on their countenances: or it might have been done to conceal their blushes.

Many of them said they had been majors — who, perhaps, had been serjeant-majors; and one or two shewed the marks of drunken broils as the scars of honourable wounds. Old Mendez appeared to believe all, and granted every one the commission he required, provided he could pay his passage on board certain vessels. The fact was, this patriot was leagued with a set of scoundrels, who were speculating on the credulity of certain persons, by fitting out ships for the purpose of carrying passengers to South America, making them pay enormously high for villainous accommodation; hence, while the trumpeters of their own exploits thought they were deceiving Mendez, they were his dupes: this I afterwards discovered.

At length my time arrived to be presented to the don. Mr. W—— introduced me as an old friend, a graduate of the University of Caraccas, and a pupil in surgery and medicine to some of the first physicians of London: he added, that I was solicitous to obtain the appointment of surgeon to the South American army, and willing to officiate as medical man on board the Saucy Jack. Finding that, unlike my fellow-candidates for promotion, I did not blow my own trumpet, Mr. W—— kindly consented to give a blast or two of his own in my favour. The don spoke to me in Spanish, and was pleased at finding I replied in pure Castilian: he asked under whom I had studied at Caraccas, and who were my preceptors in London. Being well satisfied with my answers, he said to W——, in a low voice, —

"This young gentleman will do well; he is superior to the flock that apply for commissions, although he does not sound his own praise."

He then wrote out my commission, with an order on the Columbian government for pay, at the rate of 150 dollars per month, to commence from that day. He advised me to join the Saucy Jack the evening of the following day, and he would acquaint the owners that he had found a surgeon; he further told me, that all the passengers were already on board, and they only would wait until I arrived. I promised to obey his instructions, and took my leave.

I went to Dr. Molesworth's, took a cold farewell of him, removed my luggage to Trevallion's lodgings, and commenced taking leave of a few friends. My time was too short to allow my taking out my license as a surgeon: in this, as well as in all I did since I received the letter of Keen and Leech, I acted precipitately, and shewed little knowledge of the world.

In the afternoon, as I was walking along Fleet Street, I received a hearty slap on my back. Turning round to see who gave me this rough salute, I recognised Mr. Holywell, the late supercargo of the Tickler.

"How are you, with your eye out?" said he.

This was his customary salute, for his language was the same he used during our voyage home. Four years' residence in London made him appear more stout and rosy about the gills. During the passage I often saw him naked, taking a shower-bath, and used to admire his fine muscular frame. He appeared to possess all the traits of irresistible strength of the Farnese Hercules,[†] without the heaviness which characterises that celebrated statue; but now, being dressed in what he called his "swell toggery," with his enormous crop of cravats, huge bunch of seals, red waistcoat, frock coat, and ill-cut duffle great coat, he seemed a Hercules covered with the skin of a new-slain bear. The people of London seem to dress for three purposes: for warmth, decency, and, lastly, to disfigure their forms.

"How are you, my trump? You look in prime twig!" said Holywell.

We in vain tried to enter into conversation. We were partly hindered by the number of cant phrases with which Holywell interlined his discourse, but principally by the abominable noise of a thousand vehicles, many of them carts loaded with iron bars: these prevented, with their noise, our hearing each other. My companion seized me by the arm, and led me up one of those retired alleys which lead off from most of the noisy streets of the city. We entered into one of those quiet, cleanly, but dark houses of accommodation, something between a chop-house and a tavern.

"Waiter!" said Holywell.

"*Sar!*" replied a voice; and immediately, out of a dark recess in the room, appeared a smoke-dried-faced waiter.

"A bottle of blackstrap," said my friend.

"*D'ractly, sar,*" replied the waiter, vanishing into darkness, and immediately reappearing, as if by magic, with a bottle, two glasses, and a corkscrew. These he placed in a little box, uncorked the wine, and once more left us. The wine was superior to that Day and Martin-looking composition which, I believe, is a mixture of sloe-juice and gin, but which the inhabitants of London swallow for port, *"neat as imported!"*†

We entered into conversation. Holywell informed me that, from having been the managing clerk, and occasionally the supercargo of Sucker and Sons, he for the last three years had been in business for himself in Wood Street, and that he was doing well. I, on my part, related all that had occurred to me since we parted, up to the hour of my receiving the letter of Keen and Leech. He read it, and said, —

"They are out-and-out coves, and up to the time of day: they got you away until they were able to trump up a Flemish account against your estates, and then bilked you out of them. But you don't intend to put up with all this?"

"What can I do?"

"Get a license to use your lancet; cross the *herring-pond* to St. Kitt's; live by physicking the darkies; in the meantime, appeal against the foreclosure of the mortgage, and bring the matter before the chancery beak."

"I have but one objection against following your advice — I have no money."

"It won't take much blunt to do what I recommend, and for that I give you *tick*, and you may pay me when you are flush of skreens.[57] I'll come down with the dust this moment. Waiter! pen and ink. I'll give you a flimsy (check) on Ransom, Moreland, and Co. What shall it be for? one hundred, or one hundred and fifty? — say the word."

The ready way that Holywell offered his assistance astonished me; I never could have supposed that one who used such vulgar language possessed so munificent a disposition. After thanking him for his generous offer, I told him that I could not accept it, explaining that I was under engagements to Don Mendez.

"Cut the old cove, by all means," said Holywell, "or you'll be *spiflicated*. He's a knowing blade. Lord love your West Indian simplicity! What a cake you are, not to see the rig! He is playing into the hands of a set of cross ship-owners, who are fitting out vessels to carry passengers (spoonies like yourself) across the *Dolphin River*. The accommodations on board these craft are on the cheap-and-nasty plan, and yet the blunt for the passage is shamefully high. A set of coves apply to him for commissions, telling the old one long yarns about their service; he seems to swallow all their crammers, and grants them whatever commissions they ask, — captains, majors, colonels, — all the same to Mendez, and all the same to those who get those humbug commissions. They think that they humbug the old codger, and he well knows that they are his gulls. My Lord! Warner, I did not think you were such a Johnny Raw!"

I tried to combat his disparaging notions of Mendez, and did this with greater warmth because I suspected that they were true, and that I had been duped. I, however, told him that I paid nothing for my passage, because I agreed to act as a surgeon on board the Saucy Jack.

"So far," observed Holywell, "so good: you'll lose nothing, perhaps, except your time, and will gain what I suspect you want, — that is, experience. The patriots and royalists are fighting like game-cocks: should the Spaniards floor the Americans, you're done up; but if the republicans succeed, they'll give you a large tract of ground, which will be like that of Teague,[†] — if you have it for nothing, you can't make your own money of it."

"There you are mistaken," said I; "the land in South America is very rich."

---

57. Bank of England notes, I believe.

"So," replied he, "is the bottom of the sea: but how we are to get the riches out of it, is a question that would puzzle a horse to answer, and he has a longer head than either of us. Arundell, don't go!"

I was, however, obstinate, because I suspected I was wrong. Finding I was resolved on going, he ceased persuading me against it, but asked me if I wanted any thing for the voyage to which he could assist me? I replied in the negative. He inquired if I had a set of surgical instruments: if not, he could recommend me to a friend of his who would supply me, to be paid for when I could. I answered, that I certainly wished for the instruments of my profession, but could not afford to buy them; neither would I take credit for them, because I conceived it dishonourable to run in debt without having any prospect of paying for them.

After discussing a rump-steak, dressed in the unrivalled London fashion, we separated with mutual good wishes, but not until Holywell asked me where my present lodgings were. We parted about four o'clock.

The next morning, after I had breakfasted with Trevallion, the servant of the house brought in a large parcel. On opening it, I found it to contain a complete set of surgical instruments, in three cases, with my name engraved on each case, and a letter, written in a disguised hand, which stated that the instruments were the present of a lady.

It was easy to see through Holywell's generous device: I was intimately acquainted with no lady, and surgical instruments were not presents that women would think of making. If I had the slightest doubt as to who, with such despatch, sent me the cases, it was removed by looking at the seal of the letter. It bore the impression of a negro supporting a cup, designed to represent the cup presented to the boxer Crib, after his defeating an American negro.[†] I had noticed this impression on one of the large seals worn by Holywell, and a lady was not likely to have a *fac-simile* of it.

My first resolution was to return the instruments to my generous friend; but, on reflection, I thought it would be ungrateful. I recollected that I possessed an old-fashioned and valuable gold watch and appendages, which had belonged to my father, and which had been in my possession ever since my childhood: these I proposed to send to Holywell. As I looked at the last vestige of my poor father's property, I shed a tear at the thoughts of parting with it, and kissed the toy; as though it possessed feeling. I consoled myself with the reflection, that, if my sire's spirit hovered about me, he would not be displeased at my sacrificing this relic to satisfy a proud sense of honour.

"Pardon me, dearest parent," apostrophised I; "pardon your orphan son, for parting with this, your last relic: but my motives for so doing are such as you, were you beside me, would approve. Your mournful prophecy, made during my infancy, is being fulfilled; but, though indigent, I will never be despicable: oppression and misfortune may weigh heavy on me, but they shall never bow me down to dishonour or beggary."

I wrote a letter to my friend, in which I took no notice of the instruments, but requested him to keep the watch until I should return; and, if he never should see me more, to retain it for the sake of our old friendship. I packed the watch in a small case, directed it to Holywell, and ordered the landlord of the house to send it the next day: this he promised to do, and kept his word. That evening, with five pounds in my pocket, I took my leave of London, and, accompanied by Trevallion, seated myself on the top of the Portsmouth stage, to join the Saucy Jack. As day dawned, the coach descended Postdown Hill, and, after taking breakfast at the Blue Posts, I went on board the Saucy Jack. The captain said he was glad to see Trevallion and myself, as we were the only passengers he had to wait for. In the afternoon the pilot came on board, and, with a light breeze, we worked out of Portsmouth harbour.

CHAPTER 28.

"While I have time and space,
  Before I further in my tale do pass,
  It seemeth me accordant unto reason,
  To tell unto you all the condition
  Of each of them — so it seemed to me;
  And who they were, and of what degree."
          CHAUCER.[†]

"On, on the vessel flies — the land is gone,
  And winds are rude in Biscay's sleepless bay."
          BYRON.[†]

It was evening before we fairly got into the British Channel. During the night we passed the coast of Devon, with a light but favourable wind; the next morning we were off Cornwall; and the third day of our voyage, the land of Albion had vanished from our view.

It is now high time that I should say something of the vessel I sailed in, and the captain and passengers I sailed with. The first had been advertised as "the celebrated fast-sailing American schooner, Saucy Jack," which had been captured during the late war, and had been fitted up with superior accommodations for passengers to South America: but, instead of being, as pretended, a Baltimore clipper,[†] she was built in the north of England, and was as mere a tub at sailing as ever fell behind a convoy. The accommodations were most incommodious, and the provisions abundant, but execrable. She was about 100 tons burden; had on board a skipper, mate, five seamen, two stewards, and a cook; and carried thirty-seven regular passengers, besides two females, — one the wife of the captain, and the other that of the cook.

I will describe the captain, and some of my fellow-passengers, as I did on a former occasion. Firstly, there was Captain Canter. Never was a man better named; for he was a hypocrite and a knave, with the fear of the Lord for ever in his mouth, and the lowest scoundrelism in his heart: he would have been atrocious, but wanted force of character. He said he had been a master in the navy: I hope, for the honour of the service, that this was not the case.

He had a wife, not altogether deficient in personal attractions; but she had a mouth — such a mouth as used to be painted on a signboard, ere John Bull learned French, when the Boulogne Mouth was represented by a bull, and a human, or rather inhuman, mouth.† As this poor woman was not destitute of modesty, she confined herself to her cabin, where her situation was most pitiable; the other female was the cook's wife, from the lowest order of Gosport.

The passengers were divided into two classes — those who were going to South America to enter the navy, and those who intended to join the army. I shall give the naval gentlemen the precedence.

Firstly, there was Lieutenant Jenkins. He was, as he used to describe himself, "all as one as a piece of the ship." His father was a purser; he had been born on shipboard, and had passed so much of his time afloat, that he was ignorant of the ways of the world to an incredible degree. If ever the expression of a man's having sailed round the world without going to it, was applicable to any one, it was to Lieutenant Jenkins. I never saw a landsman, who had not seen the sea, so completely unacquainted with the names of different parts of the ship, as Jenkins was of the different parts of a house.

Jenkins's personal appearance was remarkable. He was six feet three inches in height, but his limbs were out of all proportion short; hence, when he sat down, from the extraordinary length of his body, he looked as tall as ordinary men standing. He had a most indescribably comic visage: the countenance of Liston,† beside his, would look awfully tragic. He generally smiled, or, to speak more correctly, grinned; but when he tried to look serious, it seemed an effort against nature, for it was evident that his heart was almost bursting with mirth. His laugh was droll; but his attempts at screwing up his features to three sharps, in order to look grave, was enough to convulse with cachinnation a whole Quakers' meeting. I have spoken of his ignorance of the ways of the world: this I will illustrate by an anecdote.

One evening we were talking of the inhabitants of London, when, unexpectedly, Jenkins wedged in his opinion of the people of that capital. He said that the Londoners were the greatest set of cheats alive. Several persons disputing his judgment, Jenkins was called on to explain the cause of his sweeping censure.

"Because," said Jenkins, "they took me in."

"How were they cunning enough to do that?" asked several of us. On which the lieutenant told his story thus.

"You must know, when I was laying at Yâârmouth (he pronounced the last word *ore rotundo*), I heard two or three fellow-middies say as how in a *tragedie* they always spoke the best English. Now, you know, I don't speak the best English, because why? I've been all my life at sea: and so, said I, how can I hear a *tragedie*? And so Jack Phillips, our master's-mate, says, says he, 'You may hear and see a *tragedie* in Lunnun.' Well, I axed liberty to go up to Lunnun to see a *tragedie*. I took a quarter-deck passage on board a stage-coach. We bowled along, at the rate of eight knots an hour, until we got to a large house in Lunnun, with a board before the door, that had a picture of a large pig with a long snout and a fort on its back."

"The Elephant and Castle,"[†] said several voices.

"That's the name of the ship-house, I mean, I axed the way to a play-house. They told me to keep before the wind for half a league, and I'd meet with one, beside a stone bridge over the Lunnun river."

"It was Astley's,"[†] said several voices.

"I dare say it was," replied Jenkins. "Well, I got there. They had lights all round the house, — bow, midships, and stern; and I heard the band sawing away at their fiddles inside. I was going in, when a man, in a little box, called to me, 'Pay here, sir.' 'How much,' said I, 'do you ax to let me in?' 'Four shillings,' said he. 'Won't you take less?' said I. 'We never make any 'batement,' says he. But I axed him, suppose I paid him four shillings, whether he would shew me a *tragedie*? The man in the box looked at me, and, with a purser's grin, said, 'To be sure, we will shew you a *tragedie*, or any thing else you like.' Well, I paid him a crown, and would not take the change; so much did I wish to see a *tragedie*. In I went. Now, instead of a *tragedie*, what do you think they shewed me?"

"What?" asked a dozen persons.

"A *pony-race*!" said Jenkins, striking the table with his fist, so as to make all the glasses on it rattle. "A'nt I right to call the Lunnuners a set of scoundrels? I paid my money to see a *tragedie*, and they shewed me a pony-race!"

He was promoted, at the late peace, from long services as a midshipman, to the rank of lieutenant, and put on half-pay. This was humanely done by the Admiralty to many a friendless midshipman, who otherwise would have been turned loose on the world, without the means of subsistence.

The second was Lieutenant Jack — a handsome, dapper little fellow, who would have been an agreeable companion, but for one monomania. He took it into his head that he could sing with an ear so accurate, that if he heard 'Tally high O the grinder,'[†] played in slow time, he would guess it to be the 'Dead March' in Saul;[†] and a voice as agreeable, though not so flexible, as that of a turkey-cock. Lieutenant Jack imagined he could sing. He had an astonishing memory, insomuch that, I believe, he knew every song in the English language, and sung them all to one tune — if tune it could be called that tune had none. Not contented with torturing regular songs by his manner of gabbling them, every fine piece of poetry that struck him in Wolfe (the 'Death of Moore' was his favourite), Byron, Moore, Scott, Campbell, and Coleridge, he committed to memory to be sung by him. He even used to attempt passages out of Milton's 'L'Allegro,' and 'Il Penseroso,'[†] set to his own music; and, while he had the atrocity to mangle the most beautiful poetry ever composed, he absolutely held our taste in great contempt, because we did not admire his singing.

The third was a Lieutenant Britton — a large, raw-boned, hard featured man; a native of Shields, and what is called in the navy a north-country Jock.[†] Seldom have I seen a better sailor, and, at the same time, never one less calculated to make a good officer. He was repeatedly turned back, as the term goes, when he wished to be passed as a lieutenant; and was at length promoted on account of many acts of personal bravery in boarding and cutting out.

Like Hamilton, Britton was "single-speeched:" he seldom said more than two or three words at a time,[†] unless when any person or thing provoked him. When the former was the case, he clenched his bony hand, which formed a fist that might have done honour to Front du Boeuf,[†] and addressed the offender thus:

"Look you, mate, if you do that again, I won't box you — no, I'll only give you one blow, that shall make you smell hell![†] and it shan't be between the eyes neither."

Britton used to sleep in a hammock, out of choice; and, if any one played him the stale trick of cutting down his suspended bed in the night, his roar would awake all of us. He would exclaim, —

188

"Look you, my hearties, if I lay my grip on the mackerel-faced son of a marine as cut me down, he had better have hold of the moon with his fingers greased! I'll not box him — no, I'll only give him one blow as shall make him smell hell! and I'll not hit him between the eyes, neither."

This threat of avenging himself by means of one blow, which was not to be given between the eyes, was used, with little variation, not only when persons annoyed him, but when things displeased him. If we found any part of the provisions bad (no unusual thing) he'd exclaim, —

"I wish I had the owner of this craft here; I'd not box him — no, I'd give him only one blow," &c.

The same threat was issued against the maker or purchaser of every article that displeased him; he menaced to make them smell the sulphureous regions by means of one blow, which was not to fall between the eyes.

All on board became anxious to know where Britton intended to aim this mysterious blow; but, he being a powerful man, no one wished to ascertain it from personal experience: in fact, the mystery of the threat awed all the turbulent spirits on board the Saucy Jack. I, one day, asked him in what part of the body he intended to strike some one he was using his old threat against.

"Why, doctor," he replied, "being, as I believe, the strongest man on board this craft, it would not be fair for me to attack any one; but I'd advise no one to mislest (molest) me, or, by ———, I'll not box him, because he couldn't stand against me — all I'd do would be to give him one blow — no more; he should smell hell; but I'd not hit between the eyes, neither."

I need not describe Captain Trevallion; but shall only state, that, when he found out the deception practised on the passengers in passing off the Saucy Jack as a Baltimore clipper, and beheld the shameful want of accommodation and badness of the provisions, he saw into the scoundrelly tricks of old Mendez, and augured badly of the expedition. This preyed on his spirits. Hence, he took to the bottle: after the first ten days of the voyage he was seldom sober.

The rest of the naval passengers were midshipmen and masters'-mates, discharged at the peace, and young students who were dismissed the naval college. A wilder set of youths could not be found. Be it recollected they had no one to command them; every one on board was as good a man as another — if he could box as well.

The Saucy Jack was a complete floating republic: the captain had no authority. Twice or thrice Canter told them to behave better, for fear of the Lord. He was laughed at. Once he attempted to enforce order, by threatening to put some riotous young men in irons; but he was frightened from his purpose by being threatened to be cobbed.[†]

Before I speak of the military gentlemen, I must state, that we had a person on board, by the name of Price, a lieutenant of marines, who said he intended to take service in either the Columbian army or navy. In one respect, Lieutenant Price had a stronger constitution than most men I have met with: he could eat more and sleep longer than any one I ever saw. When not engaged at one or other of these diversions, he used to amuse himself by practicing, on a single-keyed flute, an air which he intended for "God save the King" as he kindly informed us.

The first in years and rank of the military gentlemen was Major M'Donald Glenlyon. He had seen much service in various parts of the globe; but his fortune and prospects had been ruined by a love of the bottle. His features, and especially his eyes, gave indications of his unfortunate propensity. Yet they bore marks of having been handsome. His fine brow, covered with curled; but gray locks, and the whole *contour* of his physiognomy, shewed the veteran of twenty campaigns, and the toper of six bottles. If the heathen deities existed, Bacchus would have been propitious to the Saucy Jack.

We had two German gentlemen on board; soldiers of fortune — that is to say, soldiers without fortune. Both had titles in their own country, which they prudently dropped on board the Saucy Jack. When not persecuted by the ruffianly part of the passengers, I used to spend my time teaching these gentlemen Spanish, and taking instructions from them in German.

The next I shall notice was one who called himself Dr. Beadle; a delicate lad, and a warm-hearted simpleton. He had been an apothecary's shopman, in Islington, and solicited and obtained the appointment of assistant-surgeon to the Columbian forces — at least, Mendez told him so.

I will not weary the reader by describing the rest of our motley collection of passengers. Some had been officers in volunteer corps; some went to join the South American army, to avoid going into the Fleet. Several were sent by their friends to Columbia, in the hope of their getting *settled* in that republic; and thus saving their families the disgrace of hearing that they had died of a sore throat, occasioned by their being kept in a state of suspense while cooling their heels, for an hour on the stretch, before the debtors' door in Newgate, by the recommendation of the Recorder. One had run away from a scolding wife; and one because, according to Serjeant Kite, he had disobedient parents. Two or three exceptions must be made to the above censures. Amongst these was Mr. ———, a person attached to the belles-lettres.[58]

Such were the men who, early in the struggle between Spain and her colonies, went out to take service with the latter. Their behaviour, during the protracted passage of the Saucy Jack, made me disgusted with my species.

In the early part of the voyage, the military part of the passengers were mostly sea-sick. In mere joke, they were treated most inhumanely by the naval people. When the sea-sickness passed, the pipeclay aristocracy,[†] as the sailors were called, prepared to retaliate; and a serious *fracas* was about to take place. This happened near the Bay of Biscay; when hostilities were suspended by the occurrence of a most tremendous storm, which blew with awful violence for four days. At the commencement of this "blow," it fortunately happened that Trevallion was sober; and the skipper, knowing the superior skill of the Cornishman, gave him temporary charge of the vessel. The event justified the deference paid to Trevallion: we escaped as violent a storm as ever was remembered, with little or no damage.

When the weather modulated, a peace was effected between the belligerent passengers; and a set of rules were drawn up for the maintenance of good order. We all signed them; but they were broken before the subscriptions were well dry. I have already stated, the captain had no command over the ship, and the sailors refused to interfere with the *gentlemen*: the whole of the passengers used to drop their own disputes to unite against the skipper when he dared to interfere: in fact, we were in a complete state of mutiny.

Practical jokes, of the roughest and most dangerous kind, were continually being played off. These brought on fights — not duels, but boxing encounters — which generally terminated in favour of the naval gentlemen; because the sailors had their sea legs, and the landsmen were less steady on board of a little vessel like the Saucy Jack, while under weigh. But it was not an uncommon event to see a landsman beaten during rough weather; and, afterwards, the vanquished would attack the victor in a calm, and beat him in his turn.

---

58. The Editor of the present Memoirs.

I escaped these blackguard encounters until we got beyond the latitude of Madeira, when I was one day addressed by a youth of the name of Purcell, a ringleader in most of the horse-play on board. He was a stout-made man, with a ruddy complexion; hair the colour of a gravel-pit, and extensive whiskers to match. He asked me to lend him a nameless implement out of the medicine-chest, for the purpose of playing off some abominable practical jokes. This I refused to do. He called me a loblolly-boy:[†] I took no notice of the insult. My forbearance imboldened him: he then said I was a coward: this my creole blood could not brook. As they say in dinner-speeches, "Unaccustomed as I was to public boxing," I rose with considerable reluctance, but with great fury. I had made up my mind to have the first blow at the first one who should force me into an ungentlemanly combat. I did not follow the intention of Britton in not aiming between the eyes; I precisely struck Purcell in that part of the "index of his mind."[†] The blow was given with such force that it made him, to use Britton's elegant phraseology, "smell hell." Down he went, and rose again to come to the scratch. His eyes had two black rims round them, which contrasted strongly with his arnotto-coloured[†] eyebrows. He possessed science, but I had superior strength, and fought with a violence he could not resist in so confined a space as below the decks of the Saucy Jack. I fairly beat down his guard by main force: I then adapted creole tactics; I caught hold of both his flaming whiskers, stooped my head, and beat his visage against it by drawing him towards and pushing him from me alternately, until his features became undistinguishable, being all mixed up together and run into each other, until his "human face divine"[†] was, as the Barbadians say, "mashed up like a sour-sop."[59] I did not let him go until he called for quarter.

Purcell did not recover the beating for three weeks. This event gained me some respect: I had overcome one of the best boxers on board.

As we advanced into warm latitudes, the jokes became more frequent. We had two or three pigs on board; these the jesters would not allow to be killed, as they aided their bestial frolics. They were continually introduced into the berths of the passengers; and if the party in whose dormitory the quadruped members of the swinish multitude were placed complained of the nuisance, a dozen buckets of salt water were flung into his berth, over bed and bedding, to cleanse it. No one at night could venture on deck

---

59. A sour-sop is a soft kind of fruit.

without the certainty of getting a duck for his supper. The mate and crew used to join in these "sky-larkings."

But it was when the naval part of the passengers used to remain up at night to take a lunar observation, that there was, to use their own expressions, "the devil to pay, and no pitch hot." For us to get sleep when a lunar was to be taken, was a *lunatic* hope. On those occasions, the mirth and fury grew fast and furious. Shark-hooks were affixed into the mattrasses of those who attempted to go to sleep, and just as they were dropping into what Jenkins called "the arms of Murphy" (Morpheus),[†] by means of a line and a block or two; the mattrass was dragged from under the dozer, who was thrown out of his berth, and the next morning a dozen mattrasses were found hanging up the masts or rigging.

Little Beadle, who considered me in the light of a brother ship, had a berth right over mine. We contrived to make our respective mattrasses fast to each other's berths, and so to secure them with small tacks that they could not be easily dragged from under us. The next night a "lunar" was to be taken (of the correctness of these lunar observations, I shall have occasion to speak anon), but by this time the word lunar had become synonymous with a mad uproar; insomuch that the two Germans, who knew little of English, believed that the words "to take a lunar," really meant to get intoxicated for the purpose of committing outrages.

On this occasion, a shark-hook was let down into little Beadle's berth; but, in consequence of our precaution, his mattrass could not be dragged on deck. Down went one of the gentlemen lunarians; and, not daring to attack me, slipped a cord over the heel of poor little Beadle, while we were asleep. At a given signal he was inhumanly dragged out of his berth, had his head severely cut during the execution of this shameful plan, and was suspended down the hatchway by the heel, like the infant Achilles being dipped by Thetis into the Styx.[†] I was awoke by the cries of murder. I hastily rose; and, by the light of the full moon, perceived the poor little apothecary hanging by one leg down the hatchway, his other three limbs and his body wriggling in all directions to relieve himself from his torturing state of suspense. Blood was dropping from his forehead; and his shirt, from his reversed situation, thrown over his head.

"Murder! murder!" vociferated Beadle; "I am murdered! you'll all be hanged if you don't cut me down!" I got the poor man relieved from his unpleasant situation, dressed his wounded forehead, and put him to bed.

After this I declared aloud, that, whoever was the scoundrel who prac-tised such an atrocious act against so delicate a young man, he was unwor-thy being called a gentleman; nevertheless; if he possessed the spirit of a man, I hoped he would declare himself, and that I would meet him with pistols as soon as we went ashore. If he did not declare himself, in addition to his being cruel he was cowardly; and if I, at any time, should discover who he was, I would publicly horsewhip him.

This speech produced a buzz of applause from those who were not lunar observers, and much murmuring from those who were: no one, however, seemed inclined to accept my challenge. During the preceding day, the German gentlemen and myself had been practising at a mark with duelling pistols, and my proficiency in the use of those arms astonished all on board; I having hit a penny-piece fourteen times running, at ten yards' distance, although the schooner was in motion at the time I fired, which I did at the word of command.

The apothecary sent for me, and said, "I thank you, doctor: you are a genuine gentleman, without any adulteration or admixture; but, please God, I shall find out who the scoundrel is, and then heart's blood shall pay for this night's frolic."

I thought this the mere ebullition of impotent, but excusable rage. I have subsequently found that Beadle expressed his fixed determination: he was delicate and nervous, but not a coward. I told him, however, to compose himself, and not to think of revenge.

The next morning I found him much better than I expected, although I saw that he would bear to the grave the scar of the wound he had received on his forehead. Several of the naval passengers declared to me at dinner their determination of taking another lunar observation, as their sextants were adjusted, and the moon was within observing distance.

"Look you, gentlemen lunar observers;" said Major Glenlyon, "I give you fair warning that I have arms in my sleeping-place: therefore, if, during your nocturnal rambles, you should pay a visit to my *berth*, you'll meet your *death* — and there's a pun without intending it. But, seriously, twice within this week has my mattrass been dragged from under me; and, if this stale trick be again tried to be played off, he who makes the attempt may expect an ounce of hot lead, or a foot of cold steel, in his breast. I'll drill a hole through the body of the first man who disturbs my rest."

Several of the lunarians got together after this, and said they were deter-mined to get the major's mattrass on the top-gallant-mast-head that night.

I advised them not to attempt it; I bade them recollect the major was a veteran, and not at all likely to make an idle threat. They laughed at what I told them The result proved no laughing matter.

Glenlyon prepared to make good his word. Price, the marine officer, was a kind of parasite of the major; they slept in contiguous berths, in a narrow passage opposite the bread-room. The lieutenant offered that night to keep guard over Glenlyon; the latter took into his berth a loaded pistol, a *skean dhu*,[†] or Highland dirk, and a bottle of whisky. The first part of the night he was undisturbed. Finding his arms to be useless, he applied his mouth to sip the mountain dew. In a few minutes after tasting his darling beverage, the whole of it was transferred to his stomach; and shortly after, his nose gave intimation to the lunar observers that he slept soundly. On this, Britton descended the companion-ladder,[†] and made towards his bed, with a shark-hook in his hand.

"Who comes there?" called the vigilant marine officer.

Britton stood aside; on which, Price rose to seize the man who, with a shark-hook, tried to murder sleep. But, like most persons leaving their beds in the dark, he knew not which way to turn; and, groping about, he unfortunately ran the index finger of his left hand into the mouth of the snoring major. This partially awoke the sleeper, who was dreaming of whisky and shark-hooks. Being but half awakened by the finger's entering his mouth, he was confused: he, however, concluded that it must belong to a hand that intended to bowse up[†] his mattrass, and his jaw closed on the finger with such force as to bite it off at the second joint. The major then struck out with his dirk: it passed through the muscles of the upper arm of the unlucky marine, and was stopped by one of his ribs, or the thrust would have been mortal. This was not all. The blood of the Glenlyons was roused: the half-dreaming, but enraged and whisky-inspired veteran fired his pistol in the dark, with a better aim than he used his skean dhu: the ball passed across the breast of Britton, and inflicted an ugly flesh-wound. All this was done between sleeping and waking, drunkenness and sobriety. So much for taking lunar observations, and bottles of whisky to bed.

A howl and a deep moan from Price were the first sounds we heard of this affair. To these succeeded a flash, and the report of a pistol; and the next moment, we heard an exclamation in the dark, of —

"Oh, I am shot, by ———! If I find the man who fired at me, I'll give him only one blow, that shall make him smell hell; and I'll not hit him between the eyes, neither."

This was enough to tell us that one of the wounded parties was Britton: lights were called for, and brought. Suspecting what had happened, I hurried to the narrow passage near the bread-room. The first object which met my eye was poor Price, seated on the companion-ladder. He was, indeed, an *object*; his left hand was *minus* a finger, and the arm fairly pinned to his rib by the dirk, which was still in his flesh: I hastily drew it out; he moaned most ludicrously. Against the bread-room stood Lieutenant Britton, with a wound in his breast. The ball had passed right across it, carrying the whole of the wadding, and a piece of the waistcoat, into the flesh, for he was only three feet from the muzzle of the pistol at the time of its discharge: his shirt, when I looked at him, was still on fire: he stood swearing to finish the man who wounded him, with one blow, which, as a matter of course, was not aimed at between the eyes.

I caused the lantern to be brought to Glenlyon's berth, whence, I rightly guessed, all the mischief proceeded.

"What the devil have I in my mouth?" said the now fully awake and sober major.

I looked, and beheld it was the missing finger of the poor marine officer, which the major bit off at the commencement of the *tragedie*, as Jenkins called it.

With as much despatch as I could I dressed the wounded men. I was obliged to probe the wound of Britton deeply, in order to get out the wadding and piece of cloth carried into it. I, however, got them to bed; and, just as I was putting up my instruments, a deputation, consisting of Lieutenants Jenkins and Jack, and about ten other naval passengers, came to me to ask my opinion of the state of the wounded men.

I told them I saw no immediate danger from the wounds; but unpleasant consequences might result from locked-jaw:[†] fever might also be occasioned, by the circumstance of the men being wounded during a transition from a cold to a warm climate. This indirect danger might, in some measure, be obviated by their being kept quiet, as any disturbance in the vessel might bring on fatal consequences.

This I said in order to get a little peace on board the Saucy Jack. I might as well have preached peace to a hurricane.

Lieutenant Jack said, that they wished to know if the parties wounded were likely to do well; in which case they would not 'peach the major,[†] but they intended to cob him. I protested against such an indignity being put on a veteran who had served his country honourably for twenty-five years. They said they would cob him, despite of me.

"We will see that," said I, taking out a pair of loaded pistols. The Germans, who only partially understood what was going on, asked me about the matter: I briefly explained it to them. In an instant they drew their sabres, and swore to stand by me in protecting Glenlyon. Poor little Beadle, wounded as he was, left his bed, took a blunderbuss without a lock, and swore to stand by me, whether I was right or wrong. The apothecary did not know the occasion of the quarrel. Others of the military passengers appeared armed: the lunar observers also armed themselves. The captain's wife shrieked in her cabin; and the skipper told us to keep the peace in the name of the Lord. All was instantly confusion and uproar below the deck of the Saucy Jack.

At this juncture the major left his bed, with a pistol in his hand, and called out for a parley in a clear voice, which was heard above the loud affray. There was something so marked and impassioned in his manner, that he instantly commanded attention. He spoke thus:

"Gentlemen, however I lament the accidents of this night, I blame not myself. I warned you against disturbing my rest; you disregarded my caution, and must take the consequence. I deeply regret having, unintentionally, wounded Lieutenant Price, and am ready to make him every reparation in my power, and to offer him every apology an officer should demand or a man of honour give. As for Lieutenant Britton, I am not sorry for wounding him; my only regret is, that when I fired my pistol in the dark, he did not receive the ball in front, instead of in an oblique direction. If he feel himself aggrieved, I will give him satisfaction; but my weapons are those of a soldier and a gentleman. I fight not like a costermonger or a coalporter: I am too old to receive a box, even if it be not aimed 'between the eyes.' I will not submit to what you term *cobbed*. *Look here!*" said he, throwing back his shirt, and exhibiting his almost naked frame. Old as he was, it was evident that nature had modelled him in perfect manly symmetry. His skin was as white as alabaster; but it bore many a deep scar. He pointed to those marks, and said, — "Look here! This wound I got at Alexandria, in the forty-second, when that regiment annihilated the invincibles; this was given with a French musket-ball at Maida;† these two in Spain; and this sabre-cut in France. Think you, gentlemen, with these vouchers for having done my duty, I will tamely suffer insult and degradation? No; rather than that shall take place, I'll send this schooner to the devil! I am not in jest.

Just below me are eighteen barrels of powder, consigned by the owners of this vessel to the patriots: on the first assault on my person, I'll fire amongst the ammunition, and up we'll all go together; thus finishing the voyage with *éclat*, by paying a flying visit to the upper regions."

He cocked his pistol and depressed its muzzle; ready to make good his awful threat that instant. If there was any doubt of his resolution, his appearance set this doubt at rest. His body was projected forward, so as to rest principally on the right foot, while his left toe touched the floor; his right finger was on the trigger, just touching it, without the slightest tremor; the pistol was pointed downwards towards the magazine; his left hand clenched; his nostrils distended; his look directed, like the pistol, downward; and the spirit of the great devil gleaming in his eye. I never saw so complete a picture of calm desperation.

"Major! for God's sake, major, 'twas a joke!" shouted a dozen voices.

"Be it considered a joke," said he, letting down the pistol to half-cock; "but do not carry the jest too far, if you do not wish to visit the upper regions."

"Give up the pistol!" said several naval passengers, advancing on him.

Instantly he recocked the pistol, held out his left hand, and said, "Stand off!" with a voice of thunder.

Again his looks became as stern as those of Satan, and the lunar observers stood back overawed. I now interposed.

"I hope, Major Glenlyon, you do not suppose that these German gentlemen and myself would put an indignity on you, or voluntarily suffer others to do it?"

"No, Dr. Arundell," said he; "you, and those German gentlemen, are men of honour."

"Then why play Guy Fawkes and send us up into the air?[†] We, perhaps, have no wish to go to the next world with the present respectable company. I am sure you must be ware that we have journeyed sufficiently long together on this globe. Come, come, uncock that pistol, and retire to your bed; we will pledge our honours to protect you."

Again he uncocked his pistol, took it in his left hand, placed his right in mine, and said, "Doctor, you are a gentleman: nothing better can be said of the Prince Regent; nothing worse shall ever be said in my hearing of Warner Arundell, while M'Donald Glenlyon can hold a sword, or draw a trigger. Good night. I'll carry this with me to bed, but will only use it defensively."

Saying this, the major went to his berth, and the rest of the passengers moved off, either to rest or to talk over the events of the night.

As Jenkins went to his dormitory, he said, "This looked more like a *tragedie* than a pony-race."

I have related at length the above events, because they were the most serious in their consequences of any of the practical jokes played off on board the Saucy Jack; but, unless during a storm, not a day, and seldom an hour, passed without the occurrence of similar pieces of bufoonery.

CHAPTER 29.

"And then we cotched the trade-winds,
   and over the line we runs;
When Neptune cummed on board,
   to shave his younger sons."
      SAILORS' SONG.

"Fué por luna y volvio trasquilado."
      CERVANTES.[†]

At length we approached the tropic of Cancer. It has been the custom for centuries to shave, as it is termed, those who cross for the first time the tropic, unless the vessel is to pass the equator, in which case the shaving is deferred until the equator be traversed.

This absurd custom originated with the bucaniers. These men pretended that, when they passed the tropics, they were no longer subjects of any European power. Hence their proverb, "No peace beyond the line."[†] But the free-booters called themselves the children of Neptune: they had a ceremony, over which they supposed that deity presided. One of the free-booters came on board, dressed ludicrously as Neptune, and baptised his children. I have seen a manuscript, written in 1609, in possession of the descendant of one of the bucaniers, which describes this ridiculous and somewhat impious ceremony in such a way as to leave no doubt that the modern nautical saturnalia were derived from the old bucaniers. The oath administered by the freebooter, Neptune, not to eat biscuit while the party swearing could get wheaten bread, unless he preferred the biscuit; of never kissing the servant, when he could kiss the mistress, unless he liked the servant better, &c. &c., were, according to this manuscript, just the same as the oath administered by the representers of Neptune of the present day. During the last century, the sailors have kept up this mummery; "Because," say those excellent geographers, "while the ship is crossing the line the captain has no command, it being in neither latitude nor longitude." This idea reminds me of the prayer of the Irish emigrant in Canada: "Lord have mercy on me, a miserable sinner! three thousand miles from my own country, and seventy-five miles from anywhere else!"

On the occasion of the Saucy Jack crossing the tropic, much preparation was made; but these saturnalia were to differ from all others of the sort; insomuch that, as it is usual for the parts of Neptune, Amphitrite[†] (or, as the old sailors call her, Mrs. Neptune), the Tritons, or Neptune's barber and barber's clerk, and other *dramatis personae* of this salt-water mummery, to be played by the foremast men on this occasion, — it was agreed that the *rôles* should be filled by such of the naval passengers as had crossed the line, and that none who had not passed the tropic should be allowed to escape shaving by paying a fine. This displeased the common seamen, as it prevented their getting some little perquisites from the sons of Neptune.

The night before we expected to cross the tropic, Beadle had stowed himself away in a boat amidships, to avoid being pelted with potatoes, which happened to be the gentle diversion of that evening. Under that boat the principal actors of the forthcoming drama consulted how to perform their parts. They agreed that, in addition to the usual rough frolics practised on these occasions, the most revolting additions should made; and that the major, the two Germans, and myself, were to be singled out to be shaved with great severity. Beadle communicated this to me, and I immediately set on foot a counter-plot. The major and the Germans I could depend on to back me; the rest of the military, and such of the naval passengers as had not crossed the tropic, promised to aid me. Trevallion, who in most disputes stood neutral, now took my side, so that I was well supported; while Neptune's party could muster but eleven hands, including Britton, who was too recently wounded to be of any assistance to them.

By my advice, we all secretly sent trifling presents that night to the seamen and stewards, telling them that certain passengers had taken the shaving into their own hands, but that we did not wish to deprive them of their accustomed perquisites. The men were thankful; and I, by this manoeuvre, succeeded in gaining their neutrality, if not their friendship.

The next morning, at breakfast, I called the attention of the whole of the passengers; and said, as it was customary that passengers should be shaved when they first crossed the line, or pay a forfeit, we preferred the latter. I said, for my own part, I was born southward of the tropic — consequently, must have passed it; nevertheless, I was willing to pay the forfeit.

"No forfeits shall be accepted," said Purcell; you shall all be shaved, by G——d!"

"We shall see that," said I. "He who lays hands on me may meet with *keener* usage than he expects. Once more I caution you against molesting us, or you'll get lathered and shaved yourselves."

My caution was laughed at; and the captain advised me to submit, for the sake of the Lord.

"Captain Canter," said Major Glenlyon, "let me advise you, in the forthcoming affray, to stand neutral, unless you wish to be made accountable for the acts of these men. If you interfere in the slightest degree, the moment I get ashore, you must meet me as a man of honour."

"And me, also," added I, "should the major fall."

This threat had the effect of securing the neutrality of Captain Canter. Noon arrived; and several of Neptune's party stuck a hair across their spy-glasses, in order to make the lubbers who looked through them believe that the line was visible on the horizon. We were ordered below. This order it was not our design to oppose. Down we went; and the farce commenced.

"Schooner, ahoy!" said a voice in the main chains.

"Ay, ay!" replied the skipper.

"What are you? whence come you? and whither bound?"

"The Saucy Jack, from Portsmouth, bound to South America, with passengers to liberate Columbia."

"I took you," said Neptune, "for a transport, going to Botany Bay with a cargo of convicts."

This sally of Neptune caused a laugh. It was, however, a calumny on those

"Who left their country, for their country's good."[†]

"Rule Britannia" was now struck up by two flutes; and his godship appeared on deck. The flutes then played one of Dibdin's songs, commencing "Daddy Neptune one day;" and I recognised Lieutenant Jack's turkey-cock gabble, trying to sing "The tight little island."[†] Neptune was rigged out with three sheep-skins, had a swab over his head, by way of a wig, and looked sublimely ridiculous. This part was played by that most ludicrous-looking man, Jenkins. The Tritons were dressed with equal elegance.

"Can you give me something to drink?" said his godship.

Canter gave him a square case bottle, which held three pints of rum. Neptune held it to his lips, and emptied a third of it at the first pull. He drew a long breath, and then renewed his draught. The Tritons now interfered, in order to get their share. Neptune resisted their claim: in about two minutes he drank the whole.

The effects of this were instantly visible: he squinted awfully; looked, as we say, nine ways for Sunday; talked thick, and hiccupped every third word. This act of inebriety afflicted him for five days with *delirium tremens*.

"Have you (hiccup) any of my children on board?" said the staggering Neptune, in a falsetto voice.

"Here is a list of them," said the captain, handing him a paper.

"Let's have a squint at your list," said Neptune. In truth, he did squint at it. After a hiccup or two, he said, in two voices — one bass, the other high falsetto — "I see you have plenty of (hiccup) cockneys on board. I don't like them (hiccup), because they took me in. They made me pay (hiccup) four shillings to see a (hiccup) *tragedie*, and shewed me a pony-race. And who have we here? one Dr. Arundell (hiccup). Why, he's a creole: one of those (hiccup) who live by eating (hiccup) crabs; and when they die, the (hiccup) crabs eat them. Bring up the (hiccup) doctor, to begin with."

Down came three of the Tritons — Purcell was one — and seized me.

"Hands off, gentlemen," said I, "or you'll repent it."

They were hurrying me towards the companion ladder, when, at a signal agreed on, my party rushed on them, overpowered them instantly, forced them into three chairs, gagged, and well bound them. Immediately their hair was cut close, and their heads lathered. We now cautioned the Tritons not to stir, or the razors would cut them. In the course of a few minutes their heads were shaved so clean, that they looked like gigantic billiard balls. All this time the hatchway was closed by our own party, to prevent succour being afforded to the barber's clerks. At a given signal, four buckets of water, provided for the occasion, were emptied on the Tritons; and they were sent up with our compliments to Neptune and his party, and a message to the effect, that we had set up a new shaving establishment, on our own account, below; and if any one wished to descend, we would give them a shave, "free, gratis, and for nothing."

Your amateurs of horseplay seldom like to have their jokes turned on themselves. Purcell and his companions, according to Sancho, went abroad for wool, and returned shorn. I never saw men so crest-fallen as they looked.

As soon as the hatchway was opened, Neptune himself staggered down, and endeavoured to seize the major. To overpower Jenkins was no difficult matter, far gone as he was in liquor. We forced him into a chair, but his head was even then too elevated to be operated on, by reason of his unnatural length of body: he was laid on the floor, his body supported, and we clipped his locks, not liking to shave him for fear of accidents, he being too drunk to keep his head steady. He struggled hard, and, at length, lay exhausted on the floor, and I ordered his cravat to be loosened. He was completely helpless.

Those on deck called on the crew of the vessel to assist them; but the latter refused, finding that we were too numerous for them, and not wishing to get their heads shorn. The rest of Neptune's party desisted from their abortive attempt; and thus ended the shaving on board the Saucy Jack.

I took advantage of this event, and organised a society for the suppression of practical jokes, called, *"Tar and Feathers."* We kept a bucket of tar ready *in terrorem*,[†] telling the admirers of sky-larking that the first person who should practise any improper jest should be tarred and feathered. This kept them in awe for three days; the fourth; Purcell stole some cowhage[†] out of the medicine-chest, and attempted to place it in the berth of one of the Germans, which would have tortured the foreigner at night. He was caught in the act, and told he would be tarred and feathered. To avoid this, he carried a loaded pistol about him. In the evening, as he was descending the companion-ladder, three buckets of water were thrown on him. He drew his pistol; but, being wet, it would not go off. We now overcame him, stripped him naked, painted his body with tar, and emptied a whole pillow of feathers on him; at the same time informing the rest of the naval passengers, that we would serve all in the same way who should attempt any improper joke.

This act had the desired effect: it put a complete stop to "taking lunars."

A culinary proverb says, "Too many cooks spoil the broth:" in our case, too many sailors spoiled the voyage. At the beginning of the passage, the naval gentlemen formed themselves into watches, to assist in navigating the schooner; hence the crew had little to do — that little they neglected. The mate was as careless a young man as ever skulked from his duty; the captain was generally locked up in his state-room with his wife: hence, the schooner was managed; or mismanaged, by the passengers. How we arrived safely is wonderful, considering the way the Saucy Jack was navigated. Often, in the Western Ocean, have I gone on deck in the night when not a sailor was to be seen, — the *gentlemen* kept watch by caulking the deck (sleeping on the deck), — save the steersman, who, being drunk, was keeping the schooner's head due north, at the time when our course lay south-west; in other words, going to North America, when we wished to go to the West Indies. The mate came to me one morning, and asked if I had been on deck in the night? I said I had.

"At what rate," inquired he, "was the schooner going?"

I replied, I had no opportunity of knowing, having had a bucket of water thrown on me, which immediately obliged me to go below to change my dress. He asked another, who said, when he was on deck, he thought she was going at the rate of six knots.

"I'll give her six all night," said the careful mate.

The fact was, he had slept during his watch, and, of course, never hove the log.

To those who live at home at ease, it may be well that I inform them that the log is a small piece of wood, by means of which, a knotted line, and a minute or half-minute glass, the rate of a ship's sailing is ascertained. At the beginning of the voyage, the mate reported the schooner to be going eight knots, or miles, an hour. Trevallion looked at the sea with an experienced eye, and declared his doubts of the vessel's going so fast. He hove the log himself, and found eight knots run out. Notwithstanding this, he persisted that she was not going so fast, but said the line must be too short, or the glass too long, or both. He was right in the last surmise — both the line and the glass were defective.

A vessel navigated with such shameful negligence as was the Saucy Jack could not be where the dead reckoning made her, unless by wonderful chance. Her latitude was easily to be found, by means of a solar observation with the quadrant; but, as we were without a chronometer, her longitude was attempted to be taken by lunar observations.† Now, whether those who took the lunars really understood observing the angular distance between the moon and a fixed star, or not — for it is a nice operation; or, whether they did not make the voluminous calculations necessary, I cannot say. Perhaps they possessed the requisite skill, but thought more of skylarking than observing the planets, and of rum-drinking than of consulting the

Nautical Almanack. Certain I am, that their lunar observations gave the same longitude to the vessel as the captain's dead reckoning. He praised their skill, because it coincided with his calculations; they complimented his accuracy, because he agreed with their lunar observations; and all parties were two hundred and eighty-seven leagues from the mark, owing to bad steering, short log-lines, and long minute-glasses.

Were these memoirs to be read by nautical men as mere fiction, the above statements would be pronounced too improbable for romance. All I need say on the subject is, that there are alive, at present, three persons in Trinidad who can vouch for the accuracy of my statement. I should have paused before I related these facts; but, lately, I was told that a vessel crossed the Atlantic, with the intention of going to the West Indies. She ran, passed the whole of the Islands, and never stopped until she crossed the Gulf of Mexico, and went to Louisiana; but I suppose she had not any of the Saucy Jack's lunar observers on board.

On the seventy-seventh day of our voyage, the dead-reckoning was up, and our longitude was run down, according to the naval passengers; but — alas for the credit of their skill! — no land appeared. We had certainly run more than the distance between England and the West Indies; but we had not run the right way. All day we sailed on, and in the evening land was announced a-head. Trevallion, who happened to be only half-tipsy, said, "That is such land as you may shove your thumb through. It's 'Cape Fly-away.' " The others remarked, that it must be land, because it agreed with the dead-reckoning and lunar observations. Night set in, and the cautious captain hove the vessel to for fear of running past the island in the night; hence, we lay to 800 miles to the eastward of land. Morning came, and the land of the preceding night melted into thin air.

The schooner was again sped on her way. We ran all day, and at night another cloud acted the part of 'Cape Fly-away.' Again we lay to for land, which vanished as morning dawned. A third time was this most ridiculous farce repeated. In the morning the land was not to be seen. The lunar observers, and the skipper, looked crestfallen; and the military passengers asked them if the moon was within observing distance.

In the evening, that marine Will-o'the-wisp, 'Cape Fly-away,' played his pranks again: a cloud was declared "land a-head." We did not heave to, because there was not a breath of air stirring, — "A sure sign," said the skipper, "that we were close to one of the islands, because it was the land-calm." I said I never heard of the land-calm before. The skipper employed thorough English logic to convince me he was right — he offered to lay a wager. So confident were the naval passengers that they were but a few miles from land, that they let down a boat. Eight of them got in, taking a compass and, of course, a quantity of grog; but when they had pulled about eight miles from the vessel, what Captain Canter called the land-calm ceased, and a violent succession of squalls blew. They were glad to hurry on board the schooner, where they arrived at midnight, worn out with fatigue.

The next day, we wished to speak several vessels we saw; but, conceiving, I suppose, the Saucy Jack was a suspicious-looking craft, they ran from us, and our schooner was too dull a sailor to come up with them. The following day, however, we spoke an American brig, who gave us the right longitude; although, I dare swear, the ignorant Yankees had not one on board capable of taking a lunar like the passengers of the Saucy Jack. Finally, on the eighty-fourth day of our eventful voyage, we passed the Angeda passage.[†]

That night, with the Virgin Islands full in view, the candidates for commissions in the Columbian navy took several most beautiful lunar observations; and fairly demonstrated that the rock of Sombrero was precisely in the same longitude that it was at the time every chart on board was engraved. At the end of our voyage to St. Thomas's, the captain measured the log-line, and, as Trevallion surmised, found it too short. He compared the minute-glasses with his watch, and found a great deal too little sand in them. This precaution of measuring the line and ascertaining the inaccuracy of the glasses, after we were in sight of land, will be applauded by nautical men.

The next day we entered the port of St. Thomas, where old Mendez told us we should meet with a Columbian agent.

CHAPTER 30.

"Repelled from port to port, they sue in vain,
And track, with slow unsteady sail, the main."
Leyden.[†]

Scarcely had we entered the harbour of St. Thomas's before the harbour-master came on board. He was a Dane; but, like most well-educated men of his nation, spoke English. He informed us that the Columbia agent had left the island, and that the cause of the Republicans was desperate; insomuch that it would be madness for us to join them. This was heavy news for us: most on board were destitute of the means of returning to England.

The harbour-master, however, told us that there was a resident of the island, although at that moment absent, who was a Jew merchant: he had lent considerable sums to the Columbians; he was momentarily expected to return; and, doubtless, would assist us, and give us counsel how to proceed.

The Dane further informed us, that a brig, with volunteers for South America, had arrived a few weeks before us; and the passengers, having landed, behaved so badly, — boxing, duelling, rioting, drinking, and getting in debt, — that the governor would not allow us to land. In vain we pleaded that St. Thomas's was a free port, and that the Saucy Jack was under British colours, from a British port, with British papers: the harbour-master said, such were the imperative orders of the governor. He further told the captain to anchor between Blackbeard's Fort and a large Danish frigate, the Minerva. He told us our motions would be watched by the frigate, and cautioned us against going ashore, unless we wished to be fired at by the man-of-war.

The captain said that, in consequence of the length of the voyage, we were short of water. The harbour-master wrote a note, and sent it by his own boat on board the Minerva. In half-an-hour, two boats, rowed by a set of stout, red-haired Danes, came alongside, with six puncheons of good water, which the captain caused to be pumped into our own casks.

The captain of the frigate came on board, and we, in vain, remonstrated with him about the injustice of not allowing us to land. Our skipper said we were all well-behaved gentlemen, and would act differently from our predecessors — (God forgive him for the assertion!)

Canter's anxiety to land us proceeded from a desire to get rid of us, in order that he might carry the schooner away and sell her, before she had performed her engagement of landing us in South America. This I afterwards learned. But his lie was thrown away — the Danes would not allow us to go ashore.

The fact was, the authorities at St. Thomas's, finding the cause of the Republicans desperate, wished to propitiate the Royalists, by whom they were, not without reason, suspected of favouring the opposite party.

The harbour-master, having heard several persons give me the title of doctor, inquired of me if I was in the medical profession? I answered in the affirmative. He told me that the yellow fever was raging ashore, and amongst the neighbouring islands; therefore, if I applied to land, my application would be granted, as the want of sufficient medical men was sorely felt ashore,[†] and that I should meet with great encouragement in St. Thomas's. All I had to do, was to submit to a few questions from the medical society; and, if my answers were approved, they would grant me a license to practise.

I desired a few moments to think about his proposition, and walked aside.

Purcell now stepped up to me, and said, — "You cannot go ashore, doctor."

"What is to hinder me?"

"Honour, sir; that is, if you have any. You have beaten me — you have caused my head to be shaved — you got me tarred and feathered. Go ashore on this island; you know I cannot follow you: go, and thus skulk from giving me the satisfaction my injuries demand."

"Enough, sir," said I; "I will continue with the schooner until the end of the voyage, although she should sail to the regions of the damned." I immediately went to the harbour-master, and told him I declined leaving the vessel.

Many will blame me for my conduct; I now blame myself. I owed Purcell no satisfaction; he had behaved like a blackguard, and I merely treated him as he deserved: but, to be accused of skulking from a duel through fear, was not to be borne by a man of my age, spirit, and education. From my infancy I had been taught to believe that none but poltroons feared duelling, and that cowardice was more disgraceful even than murder. The inculcation of such maxims on my young mind was not to be wondered at; for, according to a tradition preserved in our family, an Arundell was the first who brought into fashion duelling with pistols. The tradition alluded to ran thus.

Early in the seventeenth century, André de Rossey,[†] a French freebooter of dauntless courage, used to associate with Dutch and English rovers, for the purpose of plundering their mutual enemies, the Spaniards; but he seldom sailed long in company with any of their vessels before he contrived to quarrel with, and kill, some of his associates. His practice was to challenge the parties to meet him at the first place of landing, leaving the choice of arms to the challenged; but, such was his dexterity in the use of all sorts of steel weapons employed by the bucaniers, from the long boarding-pike, to the short poniard; from the light rapier, to the common matcheti; from the French épée, to the Spanish espadron, — that, choose what arms his opponents would, De Rossey always killed them. He slew, in single combat, more than thirty men. My ancestor, Christopher Arundell, having incurred the anger of André, the latter challenged him to go on shore at Tortuga, and decide their difference by mortal combat, leaving the choice of weapons to the Englishman. Arundell went on shore, and brought a pair of pistols, as the arms with which he chose to decide the combat. The Frenchman demurred at this innovation of the ordinary rules of duelling; for, up to that period, fire-arms had never been used on such occasions. Christopher threatened De Rossey to put the greatest indignity on him if he refused to fight with pistols. Finally, pistols were employed. At the first discharge, Arundell shot the terrible Frenchman through the heart; hence, in most private combats amongst the freebooters, pistols were the arms afterwards resorted to, as being less unfair than any other weapons. Finally, this mode of settling affairs of honour was adopted in most *civilised* and *Christian* countries. I mention this family tradition, because it influenced my determination of meeting Purcell.

The harbour-master left us. As evening set in, the moon rose, and shed her placid light on the beautiful bay, crowded town, and sterile hills, of St. Thomas's. How different was the scenery, compared to the broad and monotonous face of the ocean, which I had viewed for the last three months! I enjoyed the change, as I walked the deck.

I went to bed late; and, notwithstanding my bad prospects, slept soundly. In the morning I was awoke by a gun, fired from the Danish frigate. Scarcely were my eyes opened, before I heard the cocks crowing on shore. I instantly recollected where I was, and felt the bad tidings of the previous day more deeply than before: this sensation I have often experienced. When calamity first comes on us, it stuns us like a heavy blow; it is after a night's sleep that we feel the effects of evil news.

Early in the morning a boat left the shore, and made towards our vessel; she was intercepted by one from the Danish frigate, and ordered alongside, so narrowly were we watched. After being detained by the Minerva, the boat approached us. A passenger was seen in her, who was rightly conjectured to be the Jew merchant spoken of by the harbour-master. Half-a-dozen spy-glasses were levelled at him to catch what they called the cut of his jib. He was pronounced a handsome, dark-eyed little man. As he came within pistol-shot of the schooner, I thought I knew the person. I was right: he was my old fellow-passenger, Moses Fernandez. Our astonishment and joy at this unexpected meeting were mutual.

Fernandez gave us information that old Don Mendez was not the recognised agent of the Columbians, but, as he (Fernandez) suspected, a mere adventurer, leagued with the owners of the Saucy Jack and other vessels. But, he added, if we went to the Main, our services would be acceptable to the republicans; and, although Mendez had no right to grant commissions, yet, in consequence of our shewing a willingness to serve them, the insurgent chiefs would, doubtless, give the appointments which Mendez had promised.

Fernandez seemed to think the cause of South America by no means so bad as the harbour-master described. The domination of Spain over her colonies might linger on for a few months, perhaps for a year or two; but the great South American continent must and would be free. At the same time he candidly admitted, that hope might somewhat influence his opinion, as he had embarked his fortune in the cause. He counselled our beating up to Trinidad, and obtaining the best advice and assistance we could from an agent of the Columbians we should meet with there; and whence we might easily get up the Orinoco, the Garapichie, or down to the island of Margarita, which were *pointes d'appui* of the insurgents.

After having given this information to the passengers in general, he took me aside and asked me in what capacity I came. When I told him, he seemed quite pleased; because he said the South Americans were more in want of surgeons than naval and military adventurers, who came out to avoid a prison. He said this in a low voice, for he seemed somehow to guess the characters of my fellow-passengers. He gave me, in detail, much the same account of the progress of the revolution which he had given to the rest. He added, —

"I feel confident that the Lord of Hosts[†] has ordained that the sun of America shall rise, while the blood-red star of persecuting Spain is setting. Yea, the proud Castilians, once so haughty that they would suffer none but themselves to navigate these seas, will, in a few years, be here destitute of a harbour to shelter their vessel from a storm. Brion, who, like me, is a Jew of Curaçoa,[†] has already driven their fleet out of the Caribbean Sea. Spain, I say, will sink: the curse of the Twelve Tribes weighs her down. Arundell!" said the Israelite, in an impassioned tone, "I bear a Spanish name,[†] and my fathers possessed rich and broad lands in Grenada,[†] which bore the blessings of the earth, — corn, wine, and oil, — until, instigated by the rancorous priests, those preachers of humility, yet children of pride; those tongues of mercy, yet hands of blood — instigated by these bigots, she seized our lands and drove my ancestors from her soil, in the vain hopes of ending Judaism. Vain, vain hopes! What, though in all her idolatrous temples a list of martyred Jews is exhibited? yet, even in the days when the flames of the *Auto da Fe*[†] gleamed like the element of hell, could a Jew travel from the south of Spain to its northern extremity; and in every town, village, university, and even monastery, could he meet with his persecuted brethren, who held fast in the faith in which his fathers, for four thousand years, lived and died. Spain end the religion of Abraham, Isaac, Jacob, and the prophets! No! the children of Israel shall be gathered by the Messiah into the land which Elohim[†] gave to their sires, and will give again to them; and they shall worship Him in the third temple, the splendour of which shall surpass that of the first, although built by the wisdom of Solomon. At a time when the bears shall descend from the Pyrenees, and prowl in the deserted cities of Iberia, and when wolves shall howl in the ruins of the Escurial,[†] Spain shall be what Tyre and Sidon[†] are; when the Holy City shall rise into glory from mournful ruins, and when the curse of barrenness is removed from Judea!

"Yes," continued Fernandez, in an impassioned tone — his speech partook more of soliloquy than dialogue, insomuch that he seemed scarcely conscious that any one was listening to him, so far had his feelings abstracted his reason — "yes," continued he, "thanks to the Lord of justice, Spain is falling! Already she is like a seeming goodly tree, whose heart is rotten. She persecuted the children of the covenant; she drove the learned Moors from her soil; she exterminated a whole race of God's creatures in this western world.[†] But she prospered not. She brought gold into Europe, like as an ass carries precious metal: the richer were her galleons, the poorer became her children. She depopulated her mountains and alleys, to send her offspring to the New World; and she imported disease in return: and now her colonies turn against her, like as the children of the wicked rise against their parents; while a bigot — an embroiderer of petticoats — sits on her throne, to misdirect her energies during his life, and bequeath to her the curse of civil war at his death."

After saying this, Fernandez walked the deck hastily for some minutes, ere his emotion subsided. At length, he said, —

"Pardon me this abstraction, Mr. Arundell; but, since my youth, hatred of Spain has been my ruling passion. I have long plotted her downfall in this hemisphere, and I now see a prospect of my darling hopes being realised."

After this explanation he became calm. He promised to send me, in the course of the day, letters of introduction to all the insurgent chiefs; with the whole of whom he was in correspondence. He then inquired into the state of my finances. I told him these were low enough; all I had was about nine dollars, which I got exchanged for a trifle at a shop of one of his tribe, at Common Hard, Portsmouth.

"Well," replied Fernandez, "when I send you off the letters, I will also remit you one hundred dollars, by way of a loan. No words of refusal or thanks; you will be able to pay me shortly, as I intend visiting the republican army. Remember, it will be a loan; although I will not take a Shylock-like mortgage, or a pound of your Christian flesh.[†] One day or another you will be able to pay me; but, should I die before that day arrive, give the sum to the first poor despised Jew you meet, and tell him to place it in one of the boxes kept in all synagogues,[†] to relieve the wretched Israelites who still, like ghosts, haunt the ruins of Jerusalem. Is there any thing else I can serve you in?"

I suggested that, from the length of our voyage, a little fruit would be acceptable. He made a note of it, and then took a formal leave of my fellow-passengers, and a friendly one of me, saying, — "The Lord bless and preserve thee; the Lord make his face shine on thee, and give thee peace!"†

Three hours after this, his clerk arrived on board with the promised letters, one hundred dollars, a large box of oranges, limes, shaddocks, and other kinds of citron, and a smaller box of pine-apples and other West Indian fruit. As this acceptable present was sufficient to last the whole of the passengers until we should arrive at Trinidad, I made a general distribution of the fruit. After having lived for three months on salt provisions, fruit is most luxurious: hence, my sharing the two boxes among the passengers got me into more favour with them than if I had given them a thousand dollars. Even the lunar observers said I was not a bad fellow after all; and I am told that Britton declared, "that the first man who said I was not a gentleman, he would give him one blow," &c.

After obtaining two more puncheons of water from the frigate, we, that afternoon, left the, to us, inhospitable island of St. Thomas's. We came alongside of a small uninhabited island, on which, we were told, the governor of St. Thomas's kept hogs. Several passengers volunteered to go ashore and shoot some. The schooner was hove to, a boat lowered, and pulled to the island. In about an hour it returned, loaded with swine. I was not concerned in this robbery, but I partook of the pork; soothing my conscience with the reflection that my not eating the stolen meat would not benefit the owner of the pigs. I was a bad casuist; but I had a good appetite.

We had a long dead beat† from St. Thomas's to Trinidad; but the behaviour of the passengers, in general, was comparatively orderly — for three reasons: first, the doubtful tidings we heard at St. Thomas's threw a damp on their animal spirits; secondly, the existence of the tar-and-feather club overawed the lunarians; and lastly, but not the least cause of tranquillity, the large quantity of bad rum we had was finished; so that, of necessity, we had what is now called a temperance society on board.

We were thirteen days beating up to Trinidad, so contrary was the wind, and so badly the schooner sailed. This length of passage did not displease those whose heads had been shaved, as it allowed their hair to grow; it being now more than five weeks since this operation was performed.

As we came to anchor off Port of Spain, a person named Hervey came on board. He had come out on a similar errand to the one which brought us across the Atlantic, but had settled in the island. He gave us far more gloomy accounts than we heard at St. Thomas's. The agent we expected to meet had left the island, a ruined man. Angostura, up the Orinoco, had fallen into the hands of the royalists, and Margarita was now the only rallying point of the insurgents. The governor of Trinidad (Sir R. Woodford) sent us word that the cause of the rebels, as he called the patriots, was so desperate, that he thought it his duty to dissuade us from going to join them. And, if we promised not to do this, all those of the passengers who chose to remain in Trinidad, and were capable of exercising any trade or profession by which they might gain their living, should have all his interest to get employment. Such as chose to turn planters, he could easily obtain situations for; and for those who wished to return, he would endeavour to get them cheap or free passages to England. In the mean time, the government possessed a large unoccupied building, called Cumberland House, which Sir Ralph Woodford offered as a temporary dwelling. The governor only kept his word so far as related to Cumberland House. As soon as the mass of the passengers came ashore to reside, the governor took no further notice of them. But, in justice to his memory, I must here observe, that the conduct of my fellow-passengers was sufficient apology for the neglect of Woodford. A daily repetition of such scenes as took place on board the Saucy Jack occurred at Cumberland House; with this addition, the unfortunate inmates were often without food: hence, they commenced a system of marauding on the neighbours for provisions. So many *fowl* robberies were committed, that poultry became scarce in that end of Port of Spain; until yellow fever and new rum thinned, most awfully, the passengers of the Saucy Jack.

But I anticipate. The passengers, before they would accept of the governor's proffered aid, desired to consult on the subject. We held a council of war on board the Saucy Jack. Gloom presided over our consultation; adversity seemed to weigh down the spirits of the whole, but particularly those who, during the passage, had been most turbulent: all looked and spoke with gravity. This was not the gravity of wisdom, but of disappointment and despair. Much was said, but nothing resolved on, until Trevallion spoke thus:—

"As we have been duped by the owners of the Saucy Jack, let us start with her to Margarita, and there get a privateer's commission, and trade on our own account. There are plenty of arms and ammunition on board: these were intended as a speculation, but let us profit by them. We have six bull-dogs[†] (pieces of ordnance) in the hold: these will be sufficient to rig out this schooner as a rover; and all the spare small arms we'll sell to the people of Margarita for provisions. We are enough of us to navigate and fight the sloop; and we are, thanks to old Mendez, men of desperate fortunes. There are enough of prizes to be found in this part of the world: if not, away we start to the South Seas, where we shall find plenty of Spanish ships, or vessels which look like them. True, the Saucy Jack is but a tub of a sailer; but the first better ship we take we'll sink the schooner. There is booty enough in the Pacific to make our fortunes in six months. True, we run a small chance of being taken; but who would not rather risk being shot, or strung up at a yard-arm, in obtaining a fortune, to remaining here as an object of charity? The yellow fever, or the yellow boys, for me! Hurra for a hundred-weight of gold, or an ounce of lead! Who say a rover's life, hold up their hands."

The address of Trevallion was suitable to the desperate fortunes of most on board. All, even the mate and regular crew of the vessel, held up their hands, except myself. I begged to decline going with them, not wishing to introduce a gibbet into the escutcheon of the Arundells, by way of bend sinister. True, the first of my race that came into these seas was a rover; but he was so in different times, and with different means; for I foresaw that on board the Saucy Jack there would be too many officers, who, with the exception of courage, possessed not one quality necessary for an enterprise such as Trevallion proposed.

Having expressed my dissent, several persons asked me if I wished to discover their enterprise to the governor of Trinidad.

Before I could reply, Trevallion said, "That the doctor does not, or he wouldn't openly and fairly express his determination not to join us; however, I am sure he is too honourable a man to betray our secrets."

I pledged my word not to do this, and went on deck, leaving them to settle the minor arrangements of their wild undertaking. It was agreed that Trevallion was to command, and Canter was to be the first-lieutenant, if he chose to accept of the post. A deputation went to his state-room to consult with him, but he was not to be found. In a few minutes after this, the collector of his majesty's customs came on board with a picquet of soldiers,[†] and informed us that the schooner was seized for having arms on board contrary to law. Her anchor was taken up, and she was moored right under the guns of the old Spanish fort, whence escape was hopeless. This, in a moment, put an end to the notable scheme of Trevallion, took away the enthusiasm from the passengers, and restored their despondency.

The history of the seizure of the vessel was this:— Canter, as soon as he heard the proposal of Trevallion to carry off the schooner, went ashore unseen by us, and offered a custom-house officer a small bribe to allow him to land certain arms and ammunition he had on board the Saucy Jack, confessing, in pretended confidence, that he had no legal title to have them.

Sir Robert Walpole said every man had his price.[†] The truth of this axiom was known to Canter, for he knew all the weak points of human nature; he, therefore, was aware, that if you offer a man much less than his price, he feels it as an attack on his honour and dignity. Thus, one who, for ten thousand pounds, would betray his friend, would resent, as a deep insult, an offer of one hundred pounds as the price of his honour: hence, the commander of the Saucy Jack promised a bribe to the custom-house officer much less in amount than the said officer could obtain as his share of the booty, were the vessel seized. The result was, that the officer promised Canter to wink at his landing the contraband arms; but, a few minutes after, he caused the schooner to be seized. He did his duty — because it coincided with his interest.

By the humanity of the collector, the passengers of the vessel were allowed to go ashore with their luggage. No sooner were we out of the Saucy Jack, than, as if a sudden recollection had occurred to Canter, he went into his cabin, and produced the copy of an order in council, which fully authorised the schooner to carry arms and ammunition. The custom-house gentlemen scrutinised this paper, and were obliged to confess that they had no right to put the broad arrow[†] on her. That mark was taken off, and the disappointed collector missed his prey. The fact was, the whole seizure was a manoeuvre of the captain to get quit of the passengers, and prevent their committing the villainy of carrying her off, by performing the meditated robbery himself.

He started with the vessel that evening, sold her, together with her cargo, to the patriots, pocketed the money, let the crew shift for themselves, and went to the United States —

"To add one freeman more, America, to thee."[†]

Thus the owner took in the passengers, the passengers wished to retaliate, but Captain Canter was too keen for both parties. What became of this respectable character in America I never heard. Brother Jonathan[†] is no advocate for capital punishment, or I'd wager, that before Captain

Canter dies, he will be an *exalted* character. Should he ever return to England, he will not die in a horizontal position.

CHAPTER 31.

"Read thou this challenge; mark but the penning of it."
KING LEAR.[†]

"Ducunt ad seria nugae."
HORACE.[†]

On going ashore, I found that my old friend Dr. Lopez had left the colony.

Not wishing to join the assembly at Cumberland House, I took up my residence at a tavern kept by Fanny Nibbs, in Port of Spain. The first morning of my residence there, I had a visit from Beadle. His request astonished me: it was, that I should stand his friend in a duel between himself and Lieutenant Jenkins, whom, it appeared, little Beadle discovered to be the person who was the principal in the disgraceful transaction of dragging him out of his bed, and suspending him by the heel, on board the schooner. I thought this delicate youth, with his girlish face, the last person who would have recourse to fighting. Often, when practising with a pistol during our passage, he used to quit the deck, declaring himself too nervous to hear fire-arms go off without starting; and, I believe, up to this moment he had never exploded an ounce of gunpowder in his life. But, notwithstanding his feminine appearance and weak nerves, he was not a coward; as the result proved. I informed him that I would have been his second, but that, from some expressions which fell from Purcell, I myself momentarily expected a hostile message from him. Beadle left me, to seek old Major Glenlyon.

About two hours after this, as I expected, I was waited on by Lieutenant Jack, who handed me a written challenge from Purcell; a postscript of the letter containing the challenge, stated that the lieutenant was to attend as his (Purcell's) friend.

I asked Jack about the time and place of meeting. He told me that the laws of Trinidad were most severe against duelling; but that, in the Gulf of Paria, and about thirty miles from the Port of Spain, lay an islet, called Lospatos,[†] which, being neither in this jurisdiction nor owned by the Spaniards, was commonly made a place of hostile meeting by persons living on both sides of the Gulf.[60] He proposed that the next morning we should go thither in a sailing-boat: further, that Jenkins and Beadle, who also were about to "turn out," should accompany us. Thus we should form a hostile *parti quarré*.[†] To this I agreed; and, having appointed the place where the boat was to start before daybreak next morning, the lieutenant left me.

I called on Trevallion, who consented to act as my second. I had an excellent pair of Mortimer's pistols in my trunk, which we agreed should be used on the occasion. Trevallion dined with me; and, after dinner, we walked out together.

Gloomy as were my prospects, I could not but admire the noble scenery by which we were surrounded, and the marked improvements which had been effected in the appearance of the country by the present governor. We walked into the country until we came to the plantation that, a few years since, was the property of Don Thomaso and my uncle George. We were kindly received by the present proprietor, who shewed us all over the estate, telling us what a bad planter his predecessor was, and what improvements he had made; above all, he tried to impress us with a magnificent idea of what an extraordinary crop he was going to make next year. He did not know me, for, since the death of my uncle, the plantation had passed through a dozen hands; but every proprietor was ruined by purchasing it, although every merchant that negociated its affairs got rich.

At a late hour in the evening we arrived at Mrs. Nibbs's tavern. I persuaded Trevallion to sleep in the same chamber with me, lest he should be visited by an evil spirit, which often haunts Europeans in the West Indies, called *tafia*. As the name of this spirit is not to be found in King James's book on demonology, I must acquaint the English reader that it is better known by the denomination of new rum.

A little before daylight next morning, we were at the place appointed for embarking to Lospatos. Early as we were, I found the companions of my voyage waiting for me. These were, Purcell and his second; Beadle and his

---

60. It is now considered as part of the colony of Trinidad.

friend, the major; Jenkins was attended by Britton: finally there were Trevallion and myself. We got into the boat hired for the occasion, hoisted sail, and, with a light breeze, steered towards Lospatos. We were a mile or two from shore ere day opened.

During the first part of our little voyage Purcell slept; but sudden starts and mutterings rendered it evident that he enjoyed not tranquil slumber. From the relation in which I stood to him, I could not appear to notice him minutely; yet, now and then, as I cast a glance at him, I could not but observe that his ruddy features appeared flushed, and were quivering, as though he suffered extreme mental or bodily pain; and now and then a deep sigh escaped the sleeper.

Lieutenant Jack once shook him: he opened his bloodshot eyes, and, with a bewildered stare, looked around him.

"What is the matter with you?" said his friend; "have you been drinking?"

"Did you not see him?" said Purcell.

"Him! who?"

"Why, my father! How he shook those gray locks at me, which I brought with sorrow to the grave!"

"Lie down, my good fellow, and, if possible, sleep off this ill-timed intoxication."

Again Purcell lay down on his back in the bottom of the boat, and soon commenced snoring, as though he were stifling. I whispered Trevallion that it was necessary to untie his black cravat, turn him over on his side, and raise his head, as he lay in an uncomfortable position. My advice was followed; he ceased snoring, but commenced muttering in his perturbed sleep. His murmurings were, at first, inarticulate; he paused for about half a minute, and said plainly, —

"That curse again! Is it not enough the old man died cursing me, but he must come over the great ocean, after he is dead, to repeat his curse, now he knows I am about to die?"

He started violently and opened his eyes. After looking wildly around, he said, "Is it not strange the old man won't let me rest? But both he and I never forgave ———"

Lieutenant Jack shook his head; he appeared under an impression that Purcell was the worse for liquor. I perceived that he was under the influence of fever; which caused a determination of blood to the head, and consequently he was delirious: in fact, he was attacked with that disease which, for want of a better name, is called yellow fever. He was just such a subject as this demon would mark for his victim; he being plethoric,[†] sanguine,[†] and of intemperate habits. Such were my speculations; but I was obliged to keep them to myself.

While I was looking intently at him, Lieutenant Jack observed me; but misconstrued my thoughts.

"I fear;" said he, "that my friend will not be in a fit state to meet you; and therefore, to prevent disappointing you, I shall be obliged to take his place — that is, if you have no objection to me as his substitute."

I bowed courteously low. Gentlemen should be extremely polite to each other when arranging their amiable plans to blow each other's brains out.

The sun had risen high in the heavens; and was intensely hot, as we neared Lospatos. Purcell slept, muttering continually: now and then we caught a word or two of what he articulated. His sleep seemed to be disturbed with the recollections of his father's having cursed him. As we were entering the little harbour of the islet, he woke and called for drink.

"You seem to have had too much drink already," said his friend,

"Give me water!" cried Purcell. "I don't want your cursed grog, which tastes like a river of hell! Give me clear, cool, blessed water. Oh, would to God my gullet were the channel of the Thames!"

A large calabash of water was given to him, which he could not be said to drink: he swallowed it with such avidity, that the glucking noise caused by his throat sounded louder than that of a thirsty horse. The boat was run aground and secured: we went ashore. Purcell asked what we came here for, but immediately replied to his own question, "Yes, yes, I now recollect; I came here to be shot by that fellow, Arundell. I see now the cause that made the old man appear three times to me in the boat. However, you will allow me to say my prayers before you shoot me, doctor: no one killed a man without allowing him to pray. Those who are run up at the yardarms are allowed to see the chaplain before they die."

Saying this, he walked, with an unsteady step, until he got under a sand box-tree,[†] where he kneeled and repeated various snatches of supplication; running one part of the Book of Common Prayer into another. His friend watched him intently. It was evident that he was not drunk; but the lieutenant believed his principal insane.

While he was at his wild devotion, the seconds proposed that the duel between Beadle and Jenkins should be decided. Ten paces were the distance agreed on. While this was being measured, Jenkins commenced to draw the outlines of a ship on the sand, with a cane he held in his hand. The pistols were loaded and placed in the hands of the parties. Just before the word "fire" was to be given, Beadle, as if suddenly recollecting himself, cried out, "Hold, for one minute!"

He then took out of his pocket a letter.

"Send this," said the young man; "it is addressed to my poor mother. Inclose it in a letter of your own; and I beg of you to say that I am no more. But don't, for God's sake, tell her the disgraceful death I am to die. Poor old soul! she will not long survive the news of my death! But don't break her heart suddenly, letting her know that I died in a drunken broil. I am her only, her darling son: she sold all her trinkets to provide me with a passage; and I came on this accursed expedition because I hoped to make a fortune, in order to render her old age and widowhood comfortable. But God's will be done — or rather the devil's! for we are here on an unblessed business. But no matter."

Tears were stealing down the poor little fellow's cheeks, when I interfered, and said, "For the sake of Heaven, gentlemen, proceed no further in this business! Lieutenant Jenkins, I am sure, will make an apology for his bad joke, which Mr. Beadle, for the sake of his widowed mother, will accept; and" —

Here Jenkins interrupted me. He was still employed drawing his ship on the sand. He looked up, and said, "None of your slack-jaw, doctor; I did not come here to make apologies."

"Nor I to receive them," firmly replied Beadle.

It was agreed that Britton should give the word to fire. I stood aside, to observe the appearance of the parties. The ludicrous features of Jenkins had a trait of doggedness, otherwise they were of the same comic cast. I saw that those of Beadle seemed pale, and I could even observe a slight blue tinge on his lips; but he seemed firm and collected. He appeared conscious that he stood on the brink of eternity; but he still stood firmly. He exhibited a strong instance of constitutional timidity conquered by moral courage. Britton gave the word "fire!" Both pistols were discharged the same instant; both pistols fell to the ground together; and, at one and the same moment, Beadle fell forward on his face, and Jenkins sprang up high, and came down on the sand: his ball had passed through the temple of the apothecary, while the ball of Beadle had passed through the aorta of the lieutenant. A brief pang of agony, and Beadle was no more: after a violent, but short tremor, the heart of Jenkins ceased to beat. Scarcely an ounce of blood stained the sand of Lospatos, on which lay the corpses of the late enemies, who were both sent, at the same moment, to answer to their Creator for their enmity.

Thus fatally ended a dispute originating in a cruel joke. We all stood astounded at the awful, unprecedented, and unexpected result of this affair. It was known to us all that Jenkins was one of the worst shots on board the Saucy Jack; and, for the little apothecary, I believe the shot which sent his adversary into eternity was the only one he ever fired.

Lieutenant Jack, the major, Trevallion, and Britton, stood paralysed at the dreadful result of the duel. I staggered, and should have fallen, if I had not caught hold of a mangrove-branch. All visible objects — the sun, the Gulf, the clouds, the sands on which I stood, and the trees, seemed to whirl rapidly round with me; until I shut my eyes, and felt a cold perspiration oozing out of every pore of my frame, a deadly sickness of stomach, a difficulty of breathing, and a dimness of vision.

Gradually my senses returned, but I was confused: a vain hope arose in my mind, viz. that all I had witnessed for the last five minutes was a horrible dream. I let go the branches of the mangrove-tree, and passed my hand across my eyes to wipe the big sweat drops that had fallen on them from my brow. This done, the accursed objects, — the bodies of the slain men, who, but a few moments before, were in life and health, — came on my vision. Oh, how I wished that I had been drowned ere I reached the hated shores of Lospatos!

Long minutes fled, and we scarcely changed our position. Now and then we gazed on the two corpses, and then looked at each other and shuddered. Suddenly we were aroused from our lethargy by Purcell, who, with the looks of a demoniac, rushed amongst us.

"Ha, ha!," said he, "both fallen! both at the same time have finished their voyage, and know in what latitude hell lies! The old man told me this would happen, the last time he appeared in the boat. And look aloft, there! Do you not see that?"

He pointed above, and we cast our eyes upwards to the clouds to which his finger was directed.

"Do you not see," said the delirious man, — do you not see my old father's frowning features, and his hand pointing upwards — don't you see it?"

We all remarked that one of the noon-tide clouds of the tropics, which hung over Lospatos, had assumed the form of a gigantic profile of a human face; and, just above it, another fantastic roll of vapour had curled itself into the delineation of a hand, with a finger pointing upwards. Of course, imagination aided this vaporous formation; yet so remarkable was this cloudy portraiture, that it struck us all, at the same moment, as bearing a striking resemblance to a human visage and hand.

"See! see how the old boy frowns on us all! and see, where his finger points aloft, to where, in fiery letters, is written his curse! I never knew that a vindictive old father's curse would be logged in the sky. Oh, that my poor mother had not died before him! Would she not, think you, have dissuaded the old man from having his malediction against her favourite child written in heaven? An enraged father knows not pity; but a poor mother will plead at the throne of heaven, like an angel, for an erring child. Oh, my poor mother! would that I could lay my head on your bosom: a tear from your eye would quench the hell-flames burning on my brow!"

He pressed his hands to his burning temples, as a flash of lightning rent the clouds which had acted upon his imagination, and glared on the dismal, ill-omened island. At the same instant a long peal of thunder roared over Lospatos, and was echoed from the Gulf.

"Hark!" said the delirious man, "how the old fellow howls at me! I'll hide myself in the sea!"

He made two or three hurried steps towards the water; but, his strength failing him, he fell on the sand. We carried him into the boat, and covered him with a sail, by way of awning. I moistened his lips with a little water, and he became less turbulent. He yet muttered about his father's curse; so terribly had it taken possession of his imagination. I felt his pulse, and found he had so violent a fever that its beating could not be counted.

The appearance of several vultures, winging their gloomy way from Trinidad, and approaching to where the bodies were lying, called our attention to them. Silently we drew near, drove off the carrion birds, and turned the face of the dead upwards. Both the countenances of the slain men bore the marks of extreme agony: their cadaverous looks were sickening to behold. We cut a few mangrove sticks, with which we made a deep hole in the sand, above high-water mark, in which we placed the bodies of Jenkins and Beadle, and covered them with the sand we dug from out the grave. Now and then, a short ejaculation, or brief supplication for mercy, broke as it were involuntarily from us. Our prayers were not for the dead: our devotion was selfish.

None of us had that day tasted food. Our little store of provisions, laid in for this inauspicious voyage, was now produced. Some of us ate a little, but complained that the viands had no taste; they, however, drank less sparingly. I could swallow nothing but water. Few words were spoken, none wasted. We seemed, to use the expression of Wordsworth,

"All silent, and all damned."[†]

We rose to depart. Lieutenant Jack addressed me thus: "From the unhappy state of my principal, Mr. Arundell, custom might require that I should stand in his place as his second; but I hope the awful termination of one duel —" He paused.

I replied, "Enough, sir; there is sufficient blood on our hands already."

"I hope," said the lieutenant, "that our courage will not suffer in the opinion of the world."

"Curses on the opinion of the world!" I replied; "behold the result of the influence of that opinion!" pointing to the mound of sand that lay over the grave of the duellists.

We launched the boat with some difficulty, in consequence of Purcell being in it. The afternoon breeze wafted us soon from the hated shores of Lospatos; and, from that time to the present, I have never been able to look on its gloomy, unpeopled shores, without shuddering. We arrived in Port of Spain that night at nine o'clock: we landed secretly. No one saw us depart for, and none saw us return from, our unblessed voyage: we quitted the island with the caution of fugitives from justice; we came to it as stealthily as murders.

Medical assistance was that night procured for Purcell. We informed the physician of what was the fact, that he was attacked with fever while sailing on the Gulf. The doctor's look at once bespoke despair: the disease had already got beyond the management of science; for that mysterious forerunner of death, black vomit,[†] had made its appearance. Through the night, and the next day, he raved about his father's curse; and the third morning after the attack commenced, he was borne to a hasty grave.

CHAPTER 32.

"Sent in this foul clime to languish,
   Think what thousands fall in vain;
Wasted with disease and anguish,
   Not in glorious battle slain."
             GLOVER.[†]

About this time, *i.e.* in 1817, the demon of civil war was distracting South America; and, as if this curse were not a sufficient visitation, yellow fever[†] infected the air of the whole continent. Soon the pestilence reached the West Indies. Whence this disease came, or whether it be importable are questions that need not be mooted in this work: sufficient it is to observe, that the same kind of fever circulated round the entire tropical parts of the globe. In most of the southern, and some of the northern states of America; in many parts of India lying without the tropics; and even in Europe, — an epidemic prevailed, which, if not what is here called the yellow fever; was a malady very like it in its general character, but rendered less violent by a more temperate climate.

Nothing could look more gloomy than the capital of Trinidad, during the prevalence of this malady. Business seemed to stagnate: many fled into the country, vainly hoping to escape the disease: nothing was heard but the tolling of funeral-bells, and little seen but the long processions of the showily arrayed Catholic priests, and their red-habited choristers, acolytes, and crucifers,[†] going to administer extreme unction, or singing funeral dirges, and carrying the scarcely cold, yet already putrid, victim of the epidemic to the house appointed for all.

The tolling of the funeral-bells became so incessant and disheartening, that Sir R. Woodford ordered their discontinuance.

A great misfortune in the colonies was the supply of Peruvian bark ran out; insomuch, that it was sold as high as forty or fifty dollars the pound.

This is disgraceful to the West Indies, which possesses a soil and climate well adapted for the culture of the tree which produces this bark: nor does it speak much in favour of the botanical knowledge of the Trinidadian; as in that magnificent island are to be found, growing wild, substitutes for that valuable drug, little, if at all, inferior to the best cinchona.[†]

Several persons were attacked with the disease in question at the tavern at which I put up. On one or two occasions I ventured to give my opinion to the medical man in attendance: he thought something of my skill, because my views of the case coincided with his own. Most men think highly of the judgment of those who judge as they do. He inquired if I were a regular member of the profession: I told him under what circumstances I left England without a license: he advised me to call on the governor, and explain this matter; and he would, doubtless, give me a note of introduction to the medical board, who would examine my qualifications, and if these were found respectable, that body would give me a license to practise. Pursuant to this counsel, I waited on his excellency.

I went to Government House, and announced myself: I was instantly admitted into the presence of Sir R. Woodford, who, unlike most governors, was neither absent from his post during hours of business, and at all times and places accessible. I was struck with the majestic appearance of the governor. He wore the Windsor uniform;[†] his eye was penetrating, his brow capacious, and all his features regular, handsome, and even noble, but indicative of a haughty disposition. He was most unlike the portrait which, some years subsequently, Sir Thomas Lawrence[†] painted for his excellency. The cause of this was, his countenance had two distinct kinds of expression, the most unlike each other that any set of features ever could assume. The one might properly be called his official face, which had, in an extraordinary degree, an air of hauteur, mistrust, and penetration: but his non-official countenance was affable and amiable; insomuch that, if Sir Thomas wished to paint the *beau-idéal* of a finished gentleman, he could scarcely have chosen a better study than Sir Ralph Woodford while entertaining his guests at St. Ann's.[†] The painter copied the features of the private gentleman; and the portrait, therefore, bore no resemblance to the governor of Trinidad.

His excellency received me with a haughty politeness; but, in one sense, his manner was not *distant* — for he came so close to me that, at one time, I thought he wished to salute me in the New Zealand fashion, by joining noses. The cause of this was, Sir Ralph possessed the sense of smelling most acutely, and had a mortal detestation to the odour of strong drink. No priest ever hated toleration more intensely than Woodford hated drunkenness. Hence it was his custom, on receiving a visit from any one who came to pay his respects to the governor, to approach him sufficiently close to catch the scent of the breath of the party. If the visitor had drank the smallest quantity of spirits within many hours of the visit, Sir Ralph would detect it, and write him down in his powerful memory as one accustomed to indulge in ardent spirits. Few of those ever obtained favour from his excellency.

Having been submitted to this singular scrutiny, he retired a foot or two, and then deliberately viewed me from head to foot, when his haughty features relaxed into a smile of condescension and approval. He asked my name. I told it. He at once said, "Ah! Mr. Warner Arundell — I recollect now. You came out as surgeon to the Saucy Jack?"

I bowed assent.

"I regret," continued his excellency, "that a gentleman of your appearance should have come hither on so fruitless an enterprise, and am more sorry that your fellow-passengers should have been persons so wild in their conduct. I am told," said the governor, looking into my eyes as though he were fencing with me, — "I am told that, not satisfied with the ravages created by the present insalubrity of the climate, your fellow-passengers are committing rapid suicide on their reasons, and slow suicide on their health, by continued intoxication. And I am further informed, that already two of the inmates of Cumberland House have disappeared in a mysterious manner. Now, sir, I have strong reason to suspect —"

Here the governor was interrupted, fortunately for me, or he would have observed my confusion. The interruption proceeded from a Portuguese servant, who had followed Sir Ralph from Madeira. The man spoke to the governor in Portuguese, and announced that Dr. Chicano waited on his excellency.

"Admit him," said the governor.

I was now about to retire, when Sir Ralph motioned me to remain.

"He is only a Spanish lawyer that waits on me. Our conference will be very brief," said his excellency.

Dr. Chicano was admitted. He was a middle-aged South American, with a form inclined to corpulency, a bright twinkling eye, and a humorous Cervantic cast of countenance.[†] The governor addressed him in Castilian, which, in common with almost all European languages, Sir

Ralph spoke fluently. It was evident the governor, supposing me a stranger, conceived I knew not the language he spoke; consequently, he addressed the lawyer as though he were holding a private conversation with him. I, of course, did not seem to notice what he said.

"I have sent for you," said Woodford, "Doctor Chicano, to consult you as a lawyer: the question I shall put to you will be brief, and I know you too well to suppose you will give me a complicated answer to a simple query. You are aware that the illustrious board of cabildo[61†] has of late been shewing some signs of contumacy to my will: in fact, it is trying to imitate those petty but turbulent bodies in the old English colonies, called houses of assembly. Now, my question is this: what power does the Spanish law allow me as governor and president of the cabildo; and what are the duties of the rest of the members of this illustrious body?"

"Sir Ralph," replied Chicano, "I will define your legal powers, and their duty, in a few words. You have the power, by Spanish law, of ordering the illustrious board to do whatever you please; and it is the duty of the rest of the members to say, 'Si, señor.' "

Saying this, the doctor of laws bowed politely low; and the governor bowed still lower, in approval of this short but significant advice.

I had resolved not to seem to understand what took place; but the laconic, yet complete definition of the authority which the Spanish law gave to a governor took me by surprise, and I smiled involuntarily. Sir Ralph's eye caught my countenance, and his penetration instantly informed him that he had erred in addressing Chicano before me, under the presumption that I did not understand the language spoken.

"You understand Spanish?" said he to me, in that language.

"Si, señor," was my reply, bowing lower than either.

A flash of displeasure passed over the brow of the governor; his lips curled, until, with his fine teeth, he bit the under one. He drew up his form, and addressed me with greater hauteur than he had yet used.

"Pray, Mr. Arundell, to what cause am I to attribute the honour of your visit?"

With as few words as I could condense my sentiments into, I informed him of my motive for waiting on him; which was, to solicit a letter of introduction from him to the medical board, in order that I might be examined, and, if found competent, licensed to practise as a medical man: politely

---

61. The cabildo is a kind of town-council.

reminding him of his promise to aid any one of the passengers of the Saucy Jack who chose to remain in Trinidad, instead of joining the insurgents on the Spanish Main.

"Have you, sir, any diploma or surgical license?" said the governor.

I replied in the negative; explained how I hastily left England when on the point of being examined; at the same time shewed him certificates of having attended lectures, walked hospitals, and studied under eminent men, who all wrote handsomely about my assiduity. In fact, I possessed more vouchers of having received a tolerable medical education, than did most of those who practised the healing art in the West Indies.

The governor looked over my papers carefully, but coolly.

"Humph!" said he, "as newspapers observe, *very important if true.*"

He said this in a tone which made me understand that he doubted the authenticity of my papers.

He added, "I never knew any one who came out to join the rebels on the Main, but could produce unexceptionable testimonials as to character, as advertisements state."

I felt displeased at his remarks. From my infancy I abhorred falsehood, and never could tolerate any one's throwing a slur on my veracity.

The governor continued, "I fear, sir, I can be of little use to you in recommending you to the medical board. It meets to-morrow. You may apply to be examined, and it is in their power to license you; but, so far from recommending you, I will caution them to examine you with the greatest rigour, and, if you are not found to possess knowledge which shall bear out these fine certificates, I will advise them to reject you."

"And I presume," said I, "according to that gentleman," pointing to Chicano, "you have the power of ordering them to do just what you choose, and it is their duty to say, 'Si, señor.'"

This ill-timed retort brought a frown on the brow of his excellency: it made Dr. Chicano smile; which, when Sir Ralph observed, his face grew red, insomuch that, passing his hand down one of his cheeks for a moment, the white marks of his fingers were visible.

"I have a duty to perform, sir," said the governor, "guarding his majesty's subjects from trusting their health to the care of ignorant persons. If you have received the education you pretend to, you need fear no scrutiny of the medical board; but, if it shall be found that, like many who come to this part of the world to turn doctor, you are merely from the counter of an apothecary —"

"To prevent such a discovery," interrupted I; "to prevent the medical board's licensing a mean, ignorant apothecary, I decline being examined."

I took my papers, bowed, and was taking my leave, when he said, in a milder tone, "Pardon me, young man — I meant not to offend you: you seem susceptible, and rather proud."

"My pride, Sir Ralph, is defensive pride."

"All pride is sinful," said his excellency.

"Then what a sinner you must be!" thought I. But I replied, "I cannot help my pride; I am of a proud race, who, until the last five minutes, never suffered any one with impunity to question their veracity." Saying this, I bowed again, and left Government House.

During this interview I was much to blame, nor was the governor's conduct very commendable; he roused my anger, by more than hinting his doubts of my veracity. I know I have a reasonable stock of vices; but mendacity, I believe, is not of their number. I hope I am not destitute of virtues; but in the brief catalogue of them humility is not to be found.

Sir Ralph, as I was subsequently informed, regretted his harsh treatment of me; more especially when Dr. Chicano, who, it appeared, knew me, informed him that I was nephew to an old and respectable colonist of this island. He made inquiries about my character: these satisfied him, and added to his regret of having offended me. He proposed reconciling me at his supper-table the following night; and no man knew better to gain the good-will of his guests than Sir Ralph Woodford. But, just as his invitation arrived the next day, I was on the wing for the island of Margarita.

An independent schooner that afternoon arrived from the Main, bringing news that Angostura was recaptured by the independents; that Bolivar, assisted by M'Gregor, had given the royalists a defeat; and, finally, the independent cause was flourishing. The schooner was despatched by Brion to Trinidad, where, it was supposed, many persons were waiting to join the patriots.

I did not hesitate to embark on board the schooner, which was going to Margarita. Glenlyon, the two Germans, Trevallion, Britton, Jack, and several passengers of the Saucy Jack, went with me. The rest were discouraged from proceeding, and found employment in the island, or were provided for by — new rum and yellow fever.

Just as I was embarking, the governor's Portuguese servant put a note of invitation to supper into my hands. I returned a pencilled answer, politely declining the intended honour, as I, at that moment, was embarking to pay a visit to General Arismendi, the commandant of Margarita, and the enemy of Sir Ralph Woodford. The governor of Trinidad hated all the insurgent chiefs, and their cause.

Our voyage was pleasant: the next day I was in the populous, but arid island of Margarita.

CHAPTER 33.

"Avansar, avansar, companeros!
Con los armas al numbro avansar;
Libertad pora sempre clamenos;
Libertad, libertad, libertad!"
PATRIOT SONG.[†]

The island of Margarita, considering its size and want of fertility, possesses a dense population, which is, perhaps, the most industrious and energetic of any people that speak the Spanish language. The Margaritans were more devoted to the cause of freedom than the inhabitants of any part of the adjacent continent: hence, this island was repeatedly the last stronghold of South American freedom, wherein the defeated, but undaunted, patriots retreated, and whence they sallied forth to liberate the New World.

There being as yet no history of the South American revolution, the following brief sketch of it may not be unacceptable to the reader of these memoirs. It may serve to give him such an idea of this strangely neglected, but most important event, as a rough map, drawn by a pen, without scale or compass, may give a man of the general outlines of a country.

In the present advanced state of knowledge, it is, perhaps, superfluous to remind the reader, that whenever a colony gets too strong for the parent state, she will shake off her dependence: for, let a colony be however well governed, it will still contain some discontented spirits — some disappointed men, who are ready to magnify every trifling, real, or imaginary grievance, into tyranny on the part of the parent state. But, so extraordinarily misruled were the Spanish dependencies, that, had not the bulk of the colonists been the most loyal people that ever breathed, they would have revolted a century ago. Every article imported into the New World was made a monopoly. In short, the whole Spanish colonial system was one of monopoly, and of that sort of tyranny which is founded on the ignorance of those whom it oppresses; and is, consequently, opposed to permitting any political knowledge to the people. In English colonies, lying about the same distance from the metropolis as those of Spain from the Peninsula, the produce and manufacture of the parent state may, in general, be bought in the wholesale at the rate of from 25 to 60 per cent above their first cost; but in the Spanish Main, from this practice of monopoly, few goods, unless smuggled, could be bought for less than 500 per cent above their European price, and often 5000 per cent profit on certain articles was exacted by the purchaser of the monopoly. This state of things caused discontent, and, as a matter of course, a wish for independence.

Again, Spain, by a degree of infatuation to which history can scarcely find a parallel, encouraged the North Americans to throw off their dependence on England, on account of a dispute about a trifling duty on tea and stamps, while she herself was exercising the most cruel system of taxation on her colonies ever recorded. Had Washington not succeeded, Bolivar had remained a mere amiable, but indolent creole; and Paez, a wild tamer of scarcely more wild cattle.[†] Whatever were the grievances of the insurgents of North America, the conduct of the Bourbons of France and Spain,[†] in assisting the rebellious subjects of England, was as foolish as it was wicked; and their folly and wickedness recoiled on their own heads. The spark which set France in a state of conflagration, wherein Louis XVI[†] lost his crown and life, was brought by his subjects from America. The King of Spain sent partisans to liberate North America; and, amongst these, Miranda, the father of South American liberty,[†] learned the art of war, which he used to free his oppressed land.

But the greatest cause of the South American revolution was the shameful partiality shewn by Spain to her native population, in preference to her transatlantic subjects. A Spaniard quitted his country with a barren title of nobility, and in some provinces of the Peninsula all are noble: he came to the New World, made a large fortune, which his descendant, born in America, might inherit; yet was the latter considered as an inferior to the *parvenu*[†] who came out yesterday a penniless and illiterate adventurer. The Spaniard was considered noble because he was a *Cachupin*.[62†] South America had her native aristocracy; but Spain looked on them as a race

---

62. This word was taken from the Mexicans, who called white men *Cachopines*. The Spaniards applied the term to any one of their countrymen who settled in the New World during the war of independence. The word *Cachupin* was used to designate a Royalist.

inferior to her native plebeians: hence, the Marquis del Toro, the Marquis de Berroteran, Count Xavier, and the Marquis de Casa Leon, were refused offices which were trusted to clerks of Cadiz.

Although Spain attempted to keep her colonists in utter ignorance, yet occasionally knowledge would find its way into South America. She could not prevent them from paying occasional visits to North America, where they beheld a people, who had thrown off their dependence on the mother country, without having a millionth part of the complaint against England which the southern division of America had against Spain.

These, although not all, were the principal causes which rendered South America the soil of independence; but England has the honour or disgrace of sowing the seeds of revolt in this soil. Spain, at the end of the last century, found herself unwillingly obliged to join France in a war against England. Great Britain cast her eyes on the colonies of Spain; these she could not spare an army to conquer, but she supposed she could easily revolutionise. To do this, Spain had set her the example. The year after war was declared, Trinidad was taken — an island, from its situation, of great importance to further the plan of aiding a revolt in South America: hence, Dundas sent to Governor Picton orders to promote an insurrection on the Main.[63]† These orders the governor executed with such zeal, that Don José Antolin del Campo, notary-public to the government of Margarita, offered, by proclamation, a reward of 20,000 dollars for the head of Don Thomaso Picton. To this proclamation the governor humorously replied, by offering a reward of 20 dollars for the head of Don José Antolin del Campo. Truly the head of the hero of Badajos† was worth a thousand times as much as that of a Spanish escribano.

The result of these efforts to revolutionise South America was a conspiracy by Gual, and two other state prisoners, who were shut up in La Guayra.† This conspiracy was detected and suppressed by the Spaniards.

All the time England was at war with Spain, she encouraged the insurgents; but, when the latter was overrun by the French, the relation of Great Britain towards South America became changed; she could not aid her to throw off the yoke of the mother country, and at the same time preserve her faith with the imprisoned Ferdinand, whose cause she had espoused. She could not, in policy, assist the royalists in Columbia, because it seemed more than probable that Napoleon might eventually

---

63. See Picton's Proclamation, June 26, 1797.

succeed in establishing his brother Joseph[†] on the throne of Spain: hence England preserved a kind of wavering neutrality. This was hard on the insurgents, who continually looked to Great Britain for assistance.

All was now confusion in South America: the enlightened part of the creole population wished for independence; the Cachupins wished to remain loyal, but knew not to whom to be loyal. Joseph Buonaparte commanded them to obey him as king; the junta of Seville, the regency of Madrid, and the junta of the Asturias,[†] sent their respective commands to America; and each ordered the colonies to submit to and acknowledge their authorities, and deny the authorities of the others: while each important city in South America set up a little junta of its own. All this time, Miranda was making progress in rendering his native land independent.

This patriot was a native of Caraccas. He had served in North America, where he formed the plan of liberating his country. In furtherance of this design, he entered into the French army during the early part of the revolution. Disgusted with the atrocities of the Reign of Terror, from which he narrowly escaped, he for years wandered about Europe, soliciting by turns each power to aid his design. In 1806, he sailed from North America with a small private expedition, and came to Trinidad, where he got many recruits; for, since the conquest of that island by the British, it always afforded an asylum to the discontented on the Main: hence Miranda found there many men of desperate fortune, not altogether unacquainted with the smell of powder, because in Trinidad almost every man is obliged to be in the militia; and, since the government of Picton, Trinidad has possessed the most respectable militia in the West Indies.

There can be little doubt that Miranda would have finally succeeded in his many and persevering attempts to give liberty to his country, but for the occurrence of the earthquake in 1812, which I witnessed. This event happening on Holy Thursday, and on the anniversary of the declaration of independence, the priests, who by the new constitution were deprived of many privileges, persuaded the mass of the people to believe that the awful convulsion of nature was a Divine visitation for their having thrown off their allegiance to Ferdinand. Miranda suffered now considerable reverses; and, after labouring for thirty years for the deliverance of his natal soil, he surrendered to the Spaniards, under a promise of amnesty. This was violated, and he died in prison at Cadiz.

Yet was not all lost to the patriots: still they made head, and fought for years. Santiago Mariño[†] brought an expedition from Trinidad, and joined the great Simon Bolivar, who liberated and armed his slaves for the deliverance of his country.

In 1815, Morillo[†] arrived in Columbia, with a well-appointed army of ten thousand men. He was joined by all the Cachupins, by the Islaños (Canary Island men), and by many of the loyal creoles. The cause of the patriots now looked desperate: they possessed many a bold partisan chief but no soldier whose knowledge of tactics could compete with the new Spanish commander. He, however, committed one error, or, more properly speaking, crime, which ruined his cause. After his arrival in America he informed his king that the only way to conquer Venezuela was to exterminate two-thirds of its inhabitants. His acts corresponded with his atrocious advice, or rather exceeded it in atrocity. It soon became evident that his aim was to exterminate or reduce to ruin every man, woman, and child, born in Columbia.

When weak insurrections arise in a state, the government may, in policy, treat all the insurgents as rebels: when a rebellion is dangerous from its strength, the first object of the government should be its suppression, and, when that is accomplished, the punishment of its chiefs: but when the insurrection is so general that it is doubtful if the state can conquer it, policy dictates that the horrors of civil war should be alleviated by treating prisoners captured from the insurgents in the same way as ordinary prisoners of war are treated by civilised nations. Every execution of an insurgent, while the insurrection is unsuppressed, calls for retaliation; each act of inhumanity engenders another sanguinary measure, and lessens the chances of conquest on the part of the government, by making the rebels desperate — as most men would prefer dying in the excitement of battle, wherein they can sell their lives dear, to perishing by the hands of the executioner. An army, like that of Morillo, which attempts the conquest of a country by the indiscriminate massacre of its inhabitants, places itself in an awful dilemma: if it be defeated in its object, the vengeance of the country will annihilate it; if it succeed, it gains a dear triumph over a land of desolation.

Until repeated disasters had endangered the existence of his army, Morillo wished to be a second Pizarro,[†] but he had not a set of naked Peruvians to slaughter. The atrocities of the Spanish general disgusted the Americans, and called forth retaliations; until acts of inhumanity, at the recital of which nature shudders, became common in both camps. Soldiers in war are, in general, pitiless beings, despite the severest discipline; but the discipline of Morillo, Boves, and Morales,[†] commanded the indiscriminate slaughter of the aged, the infirm, the mother, and infant at her breast. This naturally caused abhorrence to the Spanish name. Spain warred on old men and women; the aged and females of Columbia warred on the Spanish murderer in self-defence. While the creoles were partly Royalists, the war was doubtful: when the whole of the South Americans joined against Morillo, his army melted away like ice, imported from Europe, exposed to a tropical sun; and the remains of the people of Columbia, reduced to a sixth of their number, became independent. Such is the brief outlines of the South American war of independence.

The Spaniards never possessed any party in Margarita. On their landing they sacked Assumpcion, the capital of the island: the men fought while they could, and then retired to the mountains. The aged, infirm, the women and children, took refuge in the churches and convents: here they were slaughtered by the Royalists. I saw the blood of the murdered near the altar of one of their churches; Arismendi, the patriot commander of Margarita, would not allow it to be washed out.

"Behold," said he, "men of Margarita, the church of your God stained by the murderous Spaniards with the blood of your fathers, wives, sisters, and infants! Swear on the altar of the eternal God, which the slaves of Ferdinand have strewn with the gray hairs of age, and the tresses of the maidens of this island — swear on it to avenge this outrage!"

And the Margaritans swore vengeance against the Royalists: well, too well, were their oaths fulfilled.

Repeatedly the Spaniards landed at Margarita to exterminate the inhabitants of this last fortress of independence; but as often they retreated, baffled, from this island, leaving one half of their numbers to feed the vultures. These attempts were so often repeated, and so uniformly defeated, that the inhabitants used to hail, with stern joy, the arrival of the Royalists in the Bay of Pampatar.[†] Men, women, and children, would exclaim, "Hurra! the Cachupin dogs come!" Uttering an untranslatable oath, they would retreat to the mountain of Macanon;[†] which being covered with prickly pears,[†] they could not be pursued with success. From this height they continually rushed down on the invaders, who were allowed no rest night nor day; until, from the incessant attacks of the Margaritans, the Spaniards retreated from the island, baffled and disgraced. A people resolved to be free cannot be conquered. Morillo, and his ten thousand men, were insufficient to subdue an island which contained a surface of but thirty square leagues, although the islanders were obliged to oppose stones and clubs to his muskets and artillery.

When I landed, I was introduced, by the captain of the vessel I sailed in, to Colonel Arismendi, a man of middle age, whose straight and glossy hair indicted that he was a *mestezo*, i.e. of mingled Spanish and Indian blood.[†] He received my fellow-passengers and myself cordially, and advised Trevallion, Britton, and two others, to join Brion's fleet,[†] at that time in the Oronoco. This they agreed to, and that evening we took leave, and they went on board a sloop. Glenlyon, the two Germans, three other passengers, and myself, he proposed to send in a launch to Cumana,[†] in order to join a small party that were going to cross the Sierra de Bergantia[†] to join Bolivar, who was about to make an attempt for the relief of Maturin,[†] which was closely invested by the Royalists. We consented to this arrangement, and Arismendi invited us to dine with him.

We went with the commandant to his dwelling. Passing a sentinel at his own door, Arismendi asked the soldier for his cigar: the latter thought he wished it to light his own, and gave it to the colonel; but, perceiving the commandant coolly put it in his mouth, smoke it, and enter at the door, the sentinel followed his officer, exclaiming, "*Caramba!*[64] commandant, you are not going to steal my cigar!"

He spoke in anger; the commandant swore at him; and he returned the compliment with compound interest. Arismendi told him he would send him four other cigars, and walked into the house. This was the first scene of republicanism I beheld: it gave me a poor opinion of the discipline of the army I was about to join.

Trifles often indicate great political changes. For three centuries the parrots of South America were taught to speak a rough couplet, indicative of the hatred between the Spaniards and Portuguese. It ran thus:

> "Lorita real
> Por l'España, no por la Portugal."[†]

The parrots of Margarita were now taught to say, "*Lorita patriota por l'America, no por l'Espana.*"[†] The heads of all the poor birds that persisted in uttering the old cry were mercilessly wrung off.

I slept that night at the quarters of Arismendi. The next morning, an Independent privateer, commanded by one Captain Griffiths, entered the

---

64. An exclamation equivalent to 'indeed!'

Bay of Pampatar. She brought a Spanish brig, which she had captured; and a lady, whose arrival excited universal joy.

Some months previous to this, the commandant's second wife, a most beautiful woman, while bathing at night, was captured by a party of Morillo's army. About the same time her husband attacked an advanced post of the Spaniards, which he cut to pieces, save one Colonel Monter, and about one hundred and fifty men, whom he made prisoners. This colonel was one of the most merciless of those concerned in the massacre in the church. Morilllo knew his worth, and sent a messenger to Arismendi to say that, if Colonel Monter was spared, he would restore the lady; if not, she should be slain. This threat would have placed an ordinary patriot in a trying situation, for the commandant was tenderly attached to his wife; yet, the blood of his slaughtered countrymen called out for vengeance on the infamous Monter. But Arismendi possessed the stern feelings of a Spartan: on receiving the message, he caused his own son to sever the head from the body of the blood-thirsty colonel before the messenger of Morillo, and sent him back with a threat that, if his wife were slain, he would hang up the hundred and fifty prisoners he had captured. Nothing could exceed the rage of Morillo at this: he ordered Arismendi's wife to be killed; but several officers, fearing the vengeance of the patriot, interceded for her. A solitary act of humanity was now performed by Morillo: he sent the lady prisoner to Cadiz, whence she escaped a few days after in man's attire, and got on board a Spanish ship bound for the Havaña: this was captured by a privateer off the Azores, and the lady was brought safely, by Captain Griffiths, to the arms of her husband.

A general joy pervaded the island of Margarita on the debarking of the lady. Nothing was heard but *"Vivâ la patria!"* "long live our noble commandant and his lady!" She landed under a salute of artillery. All the inhabitants were mustered on the beach to receive her. A car was procured, in which she was placed — the men dragging and the women strewing flowers in her way; while the aged and children invoked blessings on the beautiful wife of the patriotic Arismendi. The car was dragged to the house of the commandant, more than a league up the country; after which she walked, in solemn procession, to the church, the floor of which was stained with the blood of the Margaritans. She knelt, and returned thanks to the Supreme Disposer of events, for her happy deliverance, while the solemn edifice was filled with people, who joined in her devotion.

CHAPTER 34.

"Along the banks of Oronoc,
⠀⠀The voice of freedom's heard at length;
Thy Sambos, Maturin, are woke
⠀⠀With dauntless hearts, and arms of strength."
⠀⠀⠀⠀⠀⠀CASADIAN SONG OF LIBERTY.[†]

T HE next morning I took leave of Arismendi, and went on board a Patriot launch, with the two Germans, Major Glenlyon, and three other of my fellow-passengers of the Saucy Jack.

The commandant told us to be sure and keep our fire-arms loaded, as the coast between Margarita and Cumana was infested with Royalist launches.

This advice we, fortunately, did not neglect. We (that is, the late passengers of the Saucy Jack on board the launch) elected the major as our commander; and the patron of the launch, a gigantic Sambo[65†] — a sullen man, but brave and cool — took charge of the rowers, and eight volunteers, of mixed Indian and European race, who were going with us to join the Republican army. We were half the day pulling over to the Main; we then wound round the various points of land, in a westward direction, towards Cumana, until evening, and then anchored all night.

The next morning we took up our wooden anchor, and proceeded on our voyage; the Sambo patron cautioning us to keep our arms loaded. This caution was not needless. As we approached a point of land, we heard, on the other side, a voice exclaim, in Spanish, — "Pull away, my boys!" and a great number of men replied, *"Viva el Rey Fernando!"*

"To arms!" exclaimed our patron, in a low voice. Instantly every musket we had was cocked, and all our loaded pistols were in our belts. We had fourteen muskets and two blunderbusses[†] in the boat, besides a

---

65. A man of mixed Indian and negro race.

number of pistols: we also had a swivel[†] in the bows of the launch, which was loaded with musket-balls. The exclamation of the Royalists gave us warning of their approach, ere we could see each other, being on different sides of a projecting tongue of land. This circumstance allowed us a precious minute for preparation, which we failed not to improve. We rowed to the point, and ran into the mangrove-branches, which skirted the shore and hung over into the sea. The rowers took in their oars and seized their arms. This was not done a moment before it was necessary, for a large launch, having twice our numbers, shot round the point; and the first notice they received from us was a discharge of great and small arms. One of the Germans levelled and fired the swivel with murderous precision, using a spark from his *meerschaum*[†] for the latter purpose.

The great arms being discharged, we did not remain to load again; the Sambo ran us on board ere they had time to recover from their surprise or fire a single gun at us. Our pistols completed the confusion: a shot from one of mine laid low one of their rowers. Major Glenlyon reserved the fire of one of the blunderbusses, which he now discharged at the Royalist patron, a white man. He killed him, and wounded another. Several of the Cachupins jumped into the sea. We boarded — a brief struggle took place — and the launch was ours. I regret to say, that one of the Germans and Major Glenlyon were killed in boarding.

Besides these, we had two rowers and three Margaritans badly wounded.

I am sorry to say, that, after the capture of the launch, our patron made his people fire on the wretches whom we had driven overboard. Few of these escaped.

The prize was valuable on account of its freight, being loaded with arms and salt. She had belonged to the patron, a European, who had a plantation of indigo, near Barcelona; and the crew were his own negro slaves. This capture was mainly owing to their exclamation of *"Ramos muchachos! Viva el Rey Fernando!"*[†] which caused us to surprise them.

Four of the poor negroes were allowed quarter, by the intercession of the passengers, on condition that they would volunteer to join the Patriots; and help to row the prize. All the Margaritans lent their aid to do this; and in the evening we arrived, without accident, at Cumana. Poor Major Glenlyon, after escaping twenty glorious campaigns, was killed capturing a miserable launch; and Müller, the German, who expected to die a Columbian general, was slain before he reached the Patriot army.

As we entered the Gulf of Cariaco,[†] we admired the magnificent scenery, the noble harbour, the beach, on which vegetated gigantic specimens of cocoa-trees.[†] Date, and other palm-trees, raised their elegant forms, and mingled their graceful fronds amid the dark and thick foliage of the tamarind. The tall flamingo flew about the coast, while the winged jackals of the south, the galinazo, vulture, or turkey-buzzard,[†] hovered above for prey. War, horrid war, had too well fed these gloomy birds.

We landed, and were hailed with joy, in consequence of our capture. Colonel Rocio was the commandant *ad interim*, and he made us as welcome as his confined means would admit. Arismendi had given me a note of introduction to him, and this procured me tolerable quarters. The town of Cumana, before the revolution, had 20,000 inhabitants; but scarcely 500 were now in it. I slept in a cotton hammock; and the next day, after partaking of an early breakfast, we set out on our journey across the country, to the Guaripichi. We were eighteen in number, including two guides: I had three mules, one to carry myself, and two others for my baggage. It was night before we reached the foot of the Brigenteen mountains, which is a spur of the great range of the Andes. Here we encamped under an ajoupa, or hut of palm-leaves, erected by ourselves. We all slept in hammocks carried for the occasion.

The next day we commenced scaling the Sierras Brigantia — a task attended with both difficulty and danger, owing to the abrupt and stupendous rocks, dried channels of torrents, and chasms rent by earthquakes. I never could have supposed that laden animals could achieve the passage across such gaps as our mules passed; but we arrived, without accident, on the banks of the Guaripichi, five days after we set out, although the actual distance, in a direct line, is scarcely thirty leagues — so laborious is the passage of the Brigenteen mountains.

I arrived, in good health and spirits, at the quarters of General Bolivar, who had joined the division of the army intended for the relief or recapture of Maturin. I sent to that celebrated man the letter of introduction which Fernandez gave me, and was immediately conducted by his nephew, who was his secretary, into his presence. He received me with great joy, telling me that his army was much in want of gentlemen of my profession. He inquired if I had a tolerable set of instruments; I satisfied him in this respect. He sent for them to inspect them, and expressed himself well pleased; insomuch that he kept me in conversation half the night, making me sling my hammock in his ajoupa — which, however, differed in no respect from that of the poorest soldier — until, worn out with fatigue, I ceased to answer his questions, being hindered from continuing the conversation by sleep.

I must now describe this great *libratador*. He was a middle-sized spare man, with a fine aquiline set of features, and a capacious forehead. This, much mental and corporeal labour had already marked with furrows, and had commenced to turn his raven locks gray, although, at this period, he was scarcely thirty-two years of age. His eye was at once mild and penetrating; his voice was remarkably mellow; he spoke English fluently, although with a foreign accent; but his pronunciation of Castilian was perfect music. He generally expressed himself in good language; but his discourse was rather too figurative for ordinary conversation, save when he confined himself to asking questions, which he would do for hours together.

From what I heard and saw of this great man, I believe his military genius was not of the highest order. All the good he did as a warrior was caused by his undaunted perseverance, his indefatigable activity, and the confidence he inspired by his disinterested patriotism. By freeing and arming his immense number of slaves, he performed an act of real devotion to the cause of freedom — a parallel to which we may look for in vain in the history of the North American war of independence. Before the revolution he had a princely fortune. He, during years, commanded the armies, established the liberty, and swayed the destiny, of his country; and he died poor, although he neither was extravagant nor luxurious. These are facts which will be told of him by History, which can shew no greater patriot in her records than Simon Bolivar.

I next was introduced to the redoubtable Sir Gregor M'Gregor. In England he is principally known as the author of the Poyais scheme;[†] here, he was spoken of as the hero of twenty battles. He was a dark-haired powerful man; and, with the exception of Paez, one of the most terrible men for acts of personal bravery in the Republican service. He had two faults, which were the cause of all his misery and degradation: the first was, an immoderate thirst; and the second was, an aversion to water.

Having mentioned Paez, I must say a word or two of him. He is stated to be a mulatto, but, judging from his appearance, I should pronounce him of that mixed race of Spanish, Indian, and negro blood, which resembles the class in South America called Peons. At the beginning of the long war of independence, he was a mere *Llanaro* (*Anglice*, man of the plains), a keeper or hunter of wild cattle on the great savannas. He is a man not of extraordinary stature, but yet one of matchless strength and activity. By a dexterity peculiar to South Americans, he could throw down the fiercest bull that ever bellowed on the plains; his feats of horsemanship would astonish an Arab; he soon became distinguished above his comrades for acts of daring, insomuch that he was the terror of the Spaniards. No man, since the days of Samson, ever slew so many as Paez (always excepting those who kill by patent medicine). Yet, with all, this Paez was a mere savage; he knew nothing of the theory of war; all he could do was to slaughter, and excite others to slay by mere personal example. He would fight until he fell from his horse in a state of exhaustion, and go into a kind of hysteric, which was peculiar to him; when, his friends conceiving it dangerous to touch him, he was left to foam and struggle during the paroxysm. His accomplishments consisted in being able to speak Spanish, with the slight corruption which that language has suffered in South America; he could say, by rote, the Paternoster,[†] and utter a few oaths in broken English.

Behold the effects of education! An English officer, on whom Paez doted, with that real friendship which fears not to tell unpleasant truths, informed Paez that he was, with all his bravery, a mere barbarian, and that he would remain one until civilised by letters, when he would become a truly great man. Amid the privations, toils, and alarms, of a terrible war of extermination, did Paez, under the direction of his English friend, learn his alphabet. Middle-aged as he was, he acquired knowledge with extraordinary rapidity; and he is now a man of respectable attainments. He has been president of Columbia; which situation he has filled with honour to himself, and advantage to his country. He writes his own despatches, but his secretary corrects a word or two here and there; he speaks to the congress fluently, sensibly, and, at times, eloquently. In short, José Antonio Paez, who, but a few years ago, was a mere ferocious partisan, is now a politician and an accomplished statesman. Twice has his moderation and patriotism saved Columbia from the horrors of a civil war.

I also became acquainted with Santiago Mariño, who was, perhaps, the best strategist in the Columbian service. His capture of Gueria with a handful of men from Trinidad — his destroying a whole division of the Spanish army, by manoeuvring to get to windward of them, and then setting fire to the savanna — might do honour to a better soldier than was supposed to have been engaged in this war. But he was haunted by a demon, which often besets the South American creole: that fiend is — gaming.

We marched up the Guaripichi, along the magnificent savanna which spreads from the Oronoco to the Brigenteen mountains. Far as the eye could reach, one immense and apparently boundless plain extended until it was lost in the horizon: all around, the verdure of pasture melted into the circling ether, presenting to the eye the vastness of the ocean, without its monotony. Here and there a river wound through this vast savanna, whose meanders might be traced by the forests which flanked its banks; while in other places arose groves of the gigantic trees of the tropics, which, in the distance, shewed like green islands elevated out of the ocean like pasture. Flocks of wild horses, although thinned by the war, were yet visible, each troop under the command of two or three noble stallions. But the mares outnumbered the males, by one hundred to one; for the latter are so vicious as to destroy all the rivals they can master. Most of the females were followed by a beautiful foal or two. All the flocks were of one colour, a brown bay: they approached our outposts, gazed wildly at us, sniffed the air; and, at the neigh of one of their commanders, they set off at full gallop, occasionally flinging their hind heels in the air, as if in defiance of us. We also met several immense herds of wild deer, sporting over the glorious plains. Here was a beautiful country! Providence intended it as a paradise — man made it a hell!

We approached Maturin. The siege was abandoned, and the garrison made an unsuccessful *sortie* on the retreating Royalists. But, although the people of Maturin were beaten back into the town and half-dismantled fort, they aided Bolivar; and, but for this sally, the Spaniards would have effected their retreat in good order, without coming to an engagement. Finding they could not do this, they formed in line as the patriots advanced, and a distant cannonading commenced as the two divisions approached.

I was on horseback on a little eminence, so that I was enabled to command a view of the affair. Both parties were formed in one line, without having any reserve. We had eight small pieces, the enemy seven; but theirs were of larger calibre. In this affair, as well as most of the engagements that happened, until the last year or two of the war, ammunition was scarce. We had the numerical advantage in cavalry; but the Spanish troops were rather better armed. Both cavalries were mounted on native horses. In general the Spanish troops used the sabre, and the creole the lance.

I saw the two lines flanked by their respective cavalry, slowly advancing, cannonading each other. Three of our pieces were well served by English gunners, and they produced a visible effect on the enemy's line; the other four were worked by creoles, and their fire was a waste of ammunition. The Spanish guns produced little better effect on our line. As they advanced within musket-shot of us, I could perceive a body of Maturinians sally forth cautiously in their rear, to take advantage of any disaster that might happen to the Royalists. This obliged the latter to despatch a part of their cavalry to keep them in check, or they would have been attacked in the rear. Both parties halted within about one hundred and thirty yards of each other, as if by mutual consent, and each line fired a volley of musketry. I saw the flash, and clouds of smoke of both lines, and perceived men fall on either side. Before I heard the reports, they again loaded, and, at double-quick time, advanced, halted within twenty yards, and again each party discharged an irregular, but well-directed volley. Before the smoke blew off, both lines rushed together, both were broken and mingled, and all were fighting with the naked steel; the Spaniards using the awkward bayonet,[66] the creoles, the less warlike, but more dexterous macheti, having flung away their muskets. The cavalry, on both sides, engaged with mutual slaughter, but without producing any decided effect. The infantry displayed little discipline; but no soldiers could fight with more fury, or rather animosity. The general *melée* of infantry lasted about ten minutes. The Royalists gave way; but, their cavalry coming to their relief, the insurgents could not pursue them, although they remained masters of the field. Again, our troop charged the Spanish horse with little success: however, this charge enabled our line to re-form and re-arm itself with the muskets which they had discarded while the enemy retreated behind its cavalry; and, by a rather confused attempt at an *echellon* movement,[†] gained a wood a little to the left. The insurgents had captured two guns.

Again the Patriots advanced, apparently to dislodge the Royalists from the wood; but, on receiving and returning an irregular fire, they seemed to be thrown into confusion, and formed behind their cavalry. The Royalist horse now charged ours, and were repulsed; when a cry of *"Viva la patria!"* was heard in the woods, which made the Spanish dragoons retreat in great disorder, followed by the insurgent cavalry. The fact was,

---

66. In the line the bayonet is a tremendous weapon; but it is an awkward instrument in a single combat, being purely offensive, and very unwieldy.

on the appearance of the partisans from Maturin, the brave Paez, at the head of his mounted guerillas, made a long detour, in order to join them, unperceived by the enemy. This junction he could not effect; but he got into the small wood, where he dismounted his troops, until he perceived the Spaniards take up a position at its entrance. He now mounted, and made one of his furious charges on the enemy. The Spaniards were taken by surprise; and, before their own cavalry could come to their relief, they had fled in all directions. They were followed by Paez, who cut down great numbers of them. Some attempted to seek refuge in the town, but the Maturinians formed beyond the suburbs, and cut them to pieces. Five of the Spanish guns were captured, and the greatest part of the baggage fell into our hands. The Patriots, headed by Paez, pursued the enemy until night.

This affair decided the fate of Maturin. We entered it as victors, or rather as deliverers. It had long been defended by its inhabitants, but was on the point of yielding when Bolivar arrived with relief. A body of women had fought in one of the forts, hence called "*El fortizulo de las doncellas —* the little fort of the maidens." Amongst these Amazons there were many young and beautiful, who fought to defend their virtue and their lives; for no mercy could be expected by women from the Spaniards, had they taken this patriotic town.

A circumstance occurred during this engagement which made a strong impression on my mind. I have already stated that I was on a little eminence which commanded a view of the engagement. Several women, whose homes had been destroyed, and whose only resource was to follow the camp, stood beside me. When the first discharge of musketry took place, I heard a woman, of mixed European and Indian race, called Mestija,[67][†] exclaim, "He has fallen! José, my son, my first-born, is down!"

At the second discharge she shrieked again, "Oh, God! I am childless! My poor boy, Francisco, is slain! The curses of the widow on the Cachupins! My house is destroyed; my husband was murdered in the hammock; and now, my two boys, whom I blessed, and bade go forth and revenge their father's death, have both fallen! Holiest mother of Heaven, I am now a friendless outcast!"

She wiped her eyes with her black and dishevelled locks. When she again looked up, and beheld the Spanish and creole lines mixed, she

---

67. Feminine of Mestijo.

shouted as loud as though she wished to be heard by her countrymen, "Fight on, brave patriots! fight for vengeance! fight to revenge Maria Gonzales, whom the Spaniards have robbed of house, home, husband, and children! The execration of the houseless wretch, — the malediction of the widow of a murdered man, — the curse of the childless mother, on the dastard who turns his back on the bloodhounds slaves of Ferdinand!"

How this woman could perceive her sons fall (for all they both did) is to me astonishing, considering the distance she was from the lines, and the confusion and smoke which existed. I cannot suppose she merely guessed these events; and yet it seems all but impossible that the human vision, quickened as it was by the love of a mother for her sons, could have discerned the fall of two particular men, at such a distance, and under such circumstances.

At night, I was going over the field to render what professional assistance I could to the groaning wounded.[†] The full moon had risen over the little wood near the field of battle, on the branches of which perched a thousand vultures, in order to be ready for their horrid breakfast the next day. Again I perceived the wretched Maria Gonzales, crouching, in a manner peculiar to people of the New World, her thighs doubled, as it were, on the calves of her legs, and the whole weight of her frame supported on her heels. She held up the body of one of her sons who was slain, while her head drooped over the shoulder of the corpse.

Touched with this pitiable sight, I held a lantern that I carried to see if there was yet hopes of recovering him; but he was dead. The poor mother looked up, with utter despair, and said, "He is dead! My brave boys, my poor children, must feed the vultures!"

A groan near us startled the Mestija: she shot a glance around, and, perceiving it came from a wounded Spaniard, she started on her feet, exclaiming, "The curse of the widow on you and your country!"

She caught up a part of a broken musket, and, with one vengeful blow, put the Spaniard beyond his misery.

CHAPTER 35.

"We are but warriors for a working-day:
  Our gayness and our guilt are all besmerched
  With rainy marching in the painful field...
  And time hath worn us into slovenry."
      SHAKESPEARE.[†]

I was now fairly embarked in the cause of South America. I led a wandering life, generally seven or eight hours a-day on horseback; and the rest of my time was chiefly employed in the arduous duties of my profession. My quarters were in the forests which border the Oronoco, in the great plains of Guiana,[†] the mountains which branch off the main chain of the Andes, and terminate on the shores of the Caribbean Sea, or on the rich savannas of Varennes; watered by the Apuré,[†] the Arauca, the Meta, and a hundred other rivers, which, although noble streams, are mere tributaries to the monarch-flood — the Oronoco.

Often, in the unrecorded skirmishes and battles which took place in 1817 and 1818, in Columbia, was I obliged to join in the fight in self-defence: sometimes when the party to which I was attached was attempted to be surprised; and often have I acted as a volunteer.

These affairs were too numerous, and had too much sameness, — and, I regret being obliged to add, were marked by too many deeds of horrors, — for me to relate. I cannot reflect on the scenes through which I passed at this period of my life with pleasure, nor can I describe them without pain. I shall, therefore, spare the reader, as well as myself, the misery of the recital; but will merely give a slight sketch of the insurgent army.

Nothing could be more picturesque than the appearance of the Columbian troops; and, in one sense, nothing less military. The men were dressed in all the various habiliments of the English, French, and Spanish armies; and many had the undress of the aboriginal Indians. One would have a British artilleryman's coat, ornamented with French worsted epaulettes; a Spanish sash, a cavalry helmet, and blue Pennistown trousers, such as are worn by the negroes in the West Indies. Another would wear a blue surtout,[†] *minus* collar and skirts; an old staff cocked-hat, which bore the marks of former splendour — the tarnished gilt lace seemed

"The poor remains of beauty once admired;"[†]

while his lower man bore no other habiliment than the Indian *guiacou*.[68]

Their arms were as various as their *uniforms*, if uniforms they could be called that uniform were not. We had muskets of all European nations, — musketoons, rifles, fowling-pieces, carabines,[†] and blunderbusses; Indian bows and arrows of all sizes, from the six-feet bow of the Caraibe to the two-feet bow of the Choca Indian.[†] The latter generally was used to shoot poisoned arrows, matchetis, and even hard wood. Indian clubs were often resorted to; and I have seen men, armed with these sharp and heavy clubs, do terrible execution in close encounters. The colour of our soldiers included all complexions and intermixture of European, Indian, and African races. The most effective troops of the patriots were their cavalry, mounted on the hardy horses of the Savanna. They were generally furnished with matchetis, and sometimes with sabres. Pistols were often given to the troops, but seldom carried, and seldomer used. Their favourite weapon was a lance of about eight feet in length: this was handled in various ways; sometimes with one hand, but often with both. It was but rarely thrown.[69] Some had carabines, but the South American cavalry preferred the blunderbuss to all kinds of fire-arms. This they used to load with slugs.

The dresses of the savanna cavalry were truly of primitive cut, consisting in general of what they called a poncho; *i.e.* a blanket, with a hole in the middle through which the head was admitted: this was tied round the middle with a lazolian, or wild vine. Some of these ponchos were more elegant, being made of coarse blue cloth, and lined with red or yellow flannel, while some of the chiefs indulged in the luxury of drawers and check shirts. During the heat of the day, these ponchos were taken off, and placed between the saddle and the rider, and at night they did duty for

---

68. A piece of cloth or leather, of about four inches by seven in extent, ornamented with beads, &c. The guiacou is the full dress of the South American Indian.

69. Morillo was dangerously wounded with a lance, thrown at him while he was in the centre of a hollow square. So dexterous were the Patriots in the use of the lance, that the Spaniards used to say, "Por una lanza una bàla" (a lance can only be opposed by a ball.)

blankets. Their saddles were of wood, made in the Spanish fashion, high behind and before, such as we see in the old Castilian editions of 'Don Quixote;' they were, however, covered with the undressed hides of the savanna cattle. Their reins were of the same materials; but they had bits of such power, that, with ease, they could stop their half broke-in horses amid their most furious career, and throw the animals back on their haunches. A chinchorin, or net-work hammock, made of the bark of certain trees, and a parcel of tasajo (smoked beef),[†] were generally fastened behind the saddle. Such was the appearance of these Tartars of the savanna. As regular troops, they could not have stood against European cavalry; but as partisans, the Spaniards, to their cost, found them truly terrific.

Of the British auxiliaries of this period, I regret that, in general, I cannot speak favourably. They were too much like the passengers of the Saucy Jack, and were perpetually complaining of the inconveniences of their stations. Most were professed gamblers; and in no situation could that interesting class of English (the gamblers) be placed, in which they had greater scope to indulge their amiable peculiarities, than in the insurgent army.

Most of them had come to Columbia in full expectation of finding it a land, not of milk and honey, but of gold and silver; where there would be little fighting, much pay, and immense plunder. They found hard fare, hard fighting, no pay, and but little plunder. They seemed not displeased at the continued recurrence of hard blows; on the contrary, as if the enemy did not afford them enough, they were perpetually exercising their pugnacious propensities upon each other.

Exceptions must be made to the above sweeping censure. When, at a later period, so many British joined the Patriots that they were enabled to act in a body, they shewed the Spaniards the mettle of their pasture. When the British legion was acting, not as mere partisans, but in pitched battles, it was the terror of the Spaniards. The division of Colonel Farrier, in 1821, at Caribobo,[†] retrieved the day, and fully proved that they were of the same materials which formed the squares of infantry at Waterloo, against which the cavalry of France spent their fury in vain.

But in 1817, many of the Patriots were so annoyed by the reiterated complaints, and perpetual duels of the British, that they used to say, all the English were good for, was to fight amongst themselves. However, Paez, no bad judge of the qualities of warriors, was of an opposite opinion. He became so attached to the British, that, for months together, the English language was the only one which he would condescend to curse and swear in. He would shout, while leading on his Llanaros, "Avancar, muchacos! God dim my eye! Muéron los Cachupinos;[†] the bloody devils!" &c. &c.

When he uttered these and similar expressions in battle, Heaven might have mercy on the souls of the Spaniards which came within reach of his lance or sabre, for José Antonio Paez had none on their bodies.

The want of a commissariat was severely felt by the insurgents. Owing to unnecessary waste at one period, for weeks together we were constrained to live on smoked and fresh beef, without a particle of salt, bread, or vegetable food. I remember once, on the Upper Oronoco, a muleteer arrived in our camp with two animals loaded with bags of salt: every handful of this was literally sold for an ounce of gold, or a pound weight of silver. A doubloon, or sixteen dollars, was actually paid for the privilege of dipping the hand into one of the bags of salt and taking out as much as the hand could contain. After the rapid and advantageous sale of his condiment, the muleteer commenced drinking gurapo,[70†] and gambling with some Sambos and negroes; until, heated with drink and gaming, the party fell to quarrelling, and he was killed that night with a poniard. There was no coroner's inquest held on his body, nor any judicial inquiry made as to what became of his doubloons and dollars.

After a time, we became somewhat reconciled to our carnivorous mode of living; but the privations of our army were often extreme. I recollect once making a long march, in the height of the dry season, across the savanna, near Tabasco. We were dreadfully in want of water, until we approached a clear spring of this necessary element. Impelled by thirst, we hurried towards the water, when, to our vexation, we perceived a party of the enemy making towards the spring in an opposite direction. We had with us a number of women and children; but the passion for drink (for appetite it was not) overcame the fear of death. The women and children rushed before us, while the men prepared for battle. The former approached the spring, while the Spaniards fired on those famishing and defenceless creatures. We returned their compliment. After a few random shots, by which several poor females and two children fell, the ammunition of both parties were expended: we mutually rushed forward, and met at the spring. Here a deadly struggle took place, in which I mixed, and was fortunate enough to cut down the commanding officer of the Spanish party: yet, while the men fought, the children ran between their legs, and took hasty draughts of

---

70. A fermented liquor, often made of cane-juice and pineapples.

water with their little hands. I even observed that some of the Patriots stooped, and, while with their right hands they warded off the blows of the enemy, they employed their left in dipping them in the stream, and moistening their parched lips. At length the enemy, fewer in numbers than we, and, perhaps, less under the influence of unsupportable thirst, were beaten and driven from this *Esek*, or spring of contention.[†] I was now about to drink, but turned from the water with loathing, on account of its bearing the guilty colour of the late affray; but the women drank, exclaiming, *"Esta dulce con la sangré del enemigo."*[71] I related this anecdote not through a love of the horrible, but because it may give those who love to sit quietly, surrounded by the comforts of happy peaceable England, and read of battles, some idea of the war of independence. The rancorous feelings of the belligerents made it truly a *guerra à muerta* — war to the death.

Our stock of medicines was soon exhausted. This was of less consequence in South America than, perhaps, it would have been in any other country, on account of the abundance of vegetable medicines which that country produces. But little of my attention was taken up as a physician: most of my professional labour was required for the cure of the wounded. Contrary to the practice of most military surgeons, I found the number of gun-shot wounds bore no proportion to those inflicted by steel. This could be accounted for by the scarcity of ammunition to which I before alluded, and which gave this war of extermination a peculiar character.

On one occasion, while I was dressing the wounded at the house of a desolated cocoa estate at Curupano, I remarked that the few gun-shot wounds I was treating turned out much worse than I had reason, from their nature, to anticipate; hence, I began to suspect that the bullets with which those wounds were inflicted, were poisoned. I told my suspicion to a Sambo colonel, who was standing near me. He asked me if I thought the poison used on this occasion was the Indian bane. I replied, I supposed not, because that poison caused death a few minutes after it mingled with the blood; while the poison that I suspected was used, only aggravated the wound, and rendered it more dangerous, although I could not say how much the effects of the Indian poison might be modified by the heat which the lead acquired in being discharged. On the whole, judging from the appearance of some bullets I had extracted, and wounds I dressed, I judged that it was mineral poison which the enemy used.

---

71. 'It is sweet with the blood of the enemy.'

"Can you not poison our bullets, señor doctor?" said the Sambo.

I replied, that it was my duty to heal, and not to poison.

"And yet," replied the colonel, "I have seen that you can kill as well as cure. You possess the character of a troublesome fellow to the Cachupins with your pistols. I myself saw you bring down two in one day on the Apuré."

"But, señor," I rejoined, "I acted, in the excitement of battle, as a volunteer and a soldier. I cannot abuse my art as a surgeon — which is one of humanity — by turning poisoner."

The Sambo could not understand my reasoning. He said, that he thought it no worse to destroy an enemy by poison than by steel or gunpowder, after the enemy had set us so bad an example as to have recourse to so dastardly a method. He declared his determination to steep all the balls used by the regiment in curari, or Indian poison.[†] I believe he kept his word.

This Sambo was the famous, and, subsequently, the infamous Castillo,[†] who, many years posterior to this, attempted a counter-revolution in Columbia.

The hatred evinced by the South Americans to priests was surprising, considering they are so superstitious that they lately, in one province, anathematised and excommunicated the mosquitoes; but it was easily accounted for, by recollecting that the priests were all determined and, most of them, sanguinary Royalists. Many of them, not satisfied with preaching against the revolution, took up arms and furiously fought for Ferdinand. Seldom were they known to shew or entreat for mercy to a prisoner; and, on the other hand, when any of those warrior priests fell into the hands of the insurgents, they were butchered without mercy.

An Andalusian[†] Capuchin, called Padre Andres, but better known by the *nom de guerre* of Barba Negro, or Black Beard, used to boast that he was invulnerable to the balls of the insurgents. He, perhaps, believed this himself, and his many and wonderful escapes from battle, and the way he used to expose himself with impunity, impressed many of the insurgents with a belief that he wore a charmed life. He used to wrap his cloak round his arm by way of shield, rush forward into the lines of the republicans, and, with his heavy *toledo espadin,*[72][†] deal death and terror around him. Some thought him the devil; the Royalists thought him a saint. At length,

---

72. Spanish sword.

Barba Negro's career was cut short by Schmeder, my German fellow-passenger. Having heard that the priest was invulnerable, he resolved to try the effects of his carbine on him. He sought him long; and, at length, discovered his black beard streaming like a meteor on the troubled air. He took a good aim, and shot the priest through the head.

"The Capuchin," said Schmeder, "could not resist a ball fired from the carabine of a heretic."

Those of the South Americans who heard this, doubted not that he would be damned; but, at the same time, they admitted he was a good shot.

CHAPTER 36.

"Je crus que c'étois *la vièrge de dernières amours*, cette vièrge
qu'on envoie au prisonnier de guerre pour enchanter sa tombe;
dans cette persuasion je lui dis, en balbutiant, et avec un trouble
qui, partant, ne venoit pas de la crainte du bûcher, 'Vièrge, vous
êtes digne des premières amours, et vous n'êtes pas faite pour les
dernières.'"

Atala, par CHATEAUBRIAND.[†]

Fortune now set in full tide against the republicans. Morillo carried
every thing before him. Victory after victory crowned his efforts. He
had in Columbia alone nine thousand Spaniards, and four thousand native
troops, and a vast number of Canary Island men, whose devotion to
Ferdinand was boundless. Morillo's rage for extermination was without
limit; it increased with his power to do mischief: while the insurgents were
disputing and disagreeing amongst themselves, dispirited by repeated disasters, unpaid, badly armed, worse clad, and depending entirely on the
wild cattle of the savannas for food. They had lost all the strong fortresses
on the Caribbean Sea, and held possession of nothing but the natural fast-
nesses of the Oronoco, and the unconquerable island of Margarita, which
should be as sacred in the eyes of the South American patriot as
Thermopylae was to the Greeks.[†] Despair alone held the bulk of the army
together; but it was the despair of bravery, which preferred death on the
battlefield to death on the scaffold. The chiefs were undaunted. The brave
Libratador, the indefatigable Paez, the Spartan Arismendi, the skilful
Mariño, the daring Sublett, and the furious Monagos, now broke up their
regular army, and commenced a system of guerilla warfare, which allowed
the Royalists no rest, and which, after many months of hard fighting,
ruined their army.

My situation during this guerilla war was any thing but agreeable. As a
volunteer, and as a surgeon, I had gained much approbation, but little or

no pay. My well-provided chests were at first plundered, and then lost, together with a part of my instruments: the dress I wore was the only one I possessed, save one which I had stripped from the body of a Spanish officer, whom I killed in a skirmish at Rio Carribes. One of these dresses I used occasionally to get washed by some of the unhappy females who followed the camp, for the poor protection it afforded. Many of these had been educated as ladies, reared in the lap of luxury, and had been the *belles* of Venezuela; for no fault of theirs they were now doomed to be the wretched dependants on our wild army. These poor women willingly performed the most menial offices for any one who would share with them such miserable rations as we obtained. Such was the consequence of the crimes of Spain — crimes, in this respect, unlike those of the first ravagers of the New World, for they were committed in vain.

One night, after a hard day's ride, I arrived at a post far up the Oronoco, which was commanded by one Colonel Penango. Here was a party destined to attack the enemy, who were encamped at the mission of Alta Gracia; but, unfortunately, we had that day captured from the enemy a quantity of fiery Spanish wine, which the colonel injudiciously allowed his troops to drink. The effects of this imprudence soon became visible: several quarrels took place; the colonel interfered, and an Indian, of the tribe called Yaruros,† struck him. Had he slain the man on the spot, or had him tried by such courts-martial as were used in the insurgent camp, the matter would have blown over; but, unfortunately, Penango had seen the way in which the British auxiliaries treated men guilty of insubordination, by appealing to their feelings with the aid of a cat-o'-nine-tails, and was determined to introduce the practice of flogging amongst his partisans; without recollecting that, the naked Indian being two thousand years in civilisation behind the modern English, the former could not appreciate the beneficial effects of the said cat, with its unnatural number of tails. We all know that in the British army flogging is absolutely necessary for the maintenance of its morality and discipline; or, if we know it not, it is not for want of being told; but savages conceive that flogging is fit only for dogs and slaves:[73] hence the whole of the Yaruros in our camp vowed revenge for the insult offered to one of their tribe. Penango had marched to surprise Boves; but, encamping during his march, Poré, the chief of the

---

73. The last Maroon war in Jamaica, in 1795–6, which kept, for eighteen months, that island in a state of alarm, and cost one million sterling, arose from flogging two Maroons. Had they been shot, their comrades would not have noticed it.†

Yaruros, sent a message to the Spaniards, informing them of the expedition under Penango, and advising them to attack the insurgents in the night, when the Yaruros would rise on the Patriots, and assist the Spaniards. In pursuance of this advise, Boves despatched one Colonel Borero, and one hundred and fifty men, to surprise Penango. The Spaniards did not arrive until half-past four in the morning, by which time the Indian traitors had given over all hopes of an attack that night, and were asleep, when the Spaniards shot the sentinel and attacked the Patriots. The Indians rose from their sleep; but, in the confusion and darkness, knew not one person from another: they rushed on the Royalists and insurgents, each fighting the first he met. All was confusion; and it so happened that most of the Patriots effected their escape. More of the Spaniards fell; but of the treacherous Yaruros scarcely one survived the night attack; for the Royalists, observing several of the Indians fight against them, conceived they were betrayed, and turned on the Yaruros, who obtained the reward of their treason. The whole affair was badly conducted by all parties.

But I must relate my share in this transaction. I had, the previous night, arrived in Penango's camp, much fatigued, having that day fairly knocked up two hardy horses, having been three times attacked by skirmishers, and having swam five wide streams, before I tasted any other food than tasajo and some water. I found in the camp plenty of provision, which had been taken from the Spaniards. I supped very heartily, and drank much more strong wine than I was accustomed to take; but I stopped short of intoxication. I tethered my weary horse under a tree, and, with my hammock, ascended its trunk. Having tied this to two branches, I got in, but in vain essayed to sleep; being hindered therefrom either by excessive fatigue, or by having taken too intemperate a meal, or by both circumstances combined. I passed rather a feverish night. At length I recollected having about my person a small well-secured phial of laudanum, which I was in the habit of carrying with me, in order to drop a very small quantity into the very bad water I was sometimes necessitated to drink in the savannas. I applied to this somniferic, and soon felt its effects: I fell first into a heavy sleep; hence, when the camp below was attacked, I knew nothing of the circumstance, although I recollect dreaming of having been in a battle.

The Patriots having at length been driven from the camp, day opened, and the Spaniards were masters of the dear-bought field. One perceived my suspended bed, and pointed me out to his comrades. Instantly a volley of musket-balls came rattling about my leafy chamber. None hit me, but one cut the cord of my hammock. Down I fell, fortunately feet foremost. I plunged from branch to branch in a state of insensibility, until I alighted on a bearded Spaniard — one of those who had sworn never to shave until Ferdinand was restored to his dominions in Venezuela. This man's neck broke my fall, but my fall broke his neck.

I was stunned with the tumble; and, when I came to my senses, I found myself tightly bound, and in custody of two Catalonian soldiers.[†] They told me not to stir, for my life, until their colonel came. This personage soon approached me: he was a little dark Andalusian. He ordered me to rise; I did so. He looked sternly at me, and asked what rank I held in the insurgent army. I told him.

"I asked," said the Andalusian, "because, ammunition being scarce, his excellency has ordered us to sabre every man below the rank of captain. To those of or above that rank, we give a musket-ball."

"A pretty dilemma I am in!" thought I.

"But," continued the colonel, "General Morillo said nothing about barber-surgeons; and I know not what rank they hold. However, I suppose I must compound matters with you, and give you a pistol-ball. What would you advise us to do, señor doctor?"

"My advice to you," replied I, "is, that you treat me as all civilised nations treat prisoners of war."

"Modest and disinterested advice this, *camarade*; but what good should we get by following it?"

"Why, colonel, General Bolivar might be induced to treat one of your party, whom the fortune of war may place in his power, after a similar humane manner. Besides this good, you might avoid some evil. I am a British subject; and, should you kill me in cold blood, it might get to the ears of my nation, and induce them to look with little favour on your cause."

"Ferdinand the Beloved[†] cares not for your nation, nor all the nations of the earth united. God gave the New World to Spain, and we will subdue its rebellious sons. Wo betide the king who interferes to aid the rebels! we will hurl him from his throne, as we hurled Napoleon from his usurped seat. But, I must say, I respect the English: they rendered the victorious Spaniards some service in one battle that I saw. This took place at Salamanca."[†]

All this was very modest, considering that at Salamanca the loss of the Spaniards, in killed, wounded, and missing, was four men, thought I. The little colonel continued, "But what right have you to claim consideration as an Englishman, after being taken in the camp of the rebels?"

"Where," added I, "I was exercising my humane profession as a surgeon."

"He who assists insurgents with his skill in medicine equally deserves death with him who aids them in battle. What right had you to join South American rebels, who wish to rob King Ferdinand of his colonies?"

"About the same right that your countrymen had to assist North American rebels, who wished to rob King George of *his* colonies. Your nation, señor, aided the people of the United States to throw off their dependence on Great Britain. During the war in North America many Spaniards were taken by the English, but no one was slaughtered in cold blood."

"Ay," said the Spaniard; "but our king declared open war against yours, and, as always was and ever will be the case, Spain triumphed in war. We liberated the North Americans, and now the ungrateful villains are selling arms and ammunition to the rebels of Venezuela. The North Americans were rebels, until our king pleased to proclaim them a nation. When that was the case they were no longer insurgents, but became a people, at war with England, and Spain became their allies; so that it was necessary to treat all persons taken on both sides as prisoners of war. But you do not join one people at war with another; you join a parcel of creole banditti, and must pay the forfeit of your own act. I am sure you can have nothing reasonable to urge against my arguments, because I know that I am right, and that you are in the wrong; so there need no more be said about the matter. Here, Francisco, load your pistol. Kneel, Englishman: take this handkerchief as a bandage."

"I can look death in the face, señor, therefore want no bandage. Here are three doubloons I have about me; you may as well have them as another. Will you be pleased to grant me but five minutes for prayer, before I quit this world?"

"The English heretics are always generous," said the Andalusian, looking at the coins: "but I never knew that they prayed before. However, ten minutes shall be yours."

I knelt to pray, and a cold perspiration ran from my forehead. In a moment, all I ever did of good or evil crowded on my memory. My thoughts, despite myself, wandered from devotion. At one time I looked at the noble scenery by which I was surrounded, and recollected that in a few minutes my mortal eyes would shut on it for ever. I glanced at my own person, and remembered that, in a few hours, it would be festering in the equinoctial sun, the prey of tigers and vultures. At length I ceased altogether to pray, on hearing the following dialogue: "Colonel, for the love of the Holy Mother of God, save that Englishman!"

"Why so, Captain Raymond?"

"He saved my life."

"How did that happen?"

Captain Raymond, a creole Royalist, now told the Andalusian that, after a skirmish at Barancos, I found him on the field, wounded and faint from loss of blood; that I dressed his wound, carried him to a copse which lies beside the village of Barancos and the Oronoco, and there supplied him with a small quantity of provision. After many days' hiding about, he at length rejoined the Royalist army.

"You know," said Borero, "that it is our general's orders to give no quarter; and, according to the Priest Diego, it is a soldier's duty to obey, should his general order him to commit the seven deadly sins; because, in that case, the soul of the general, and not that of his officer, would have to pay for it in purgatory. Nevertheless, it is a pity to shoot so fine a young man, especially after having saved your life. He is as generous as his countrymen usually are: do you know, the poor devil gave me three doubloons immediately after I ordered him to be shot! and what renders this act the more meritorious is this, I never should have thought of having him searched for money. He is not altogether destitute of religion, because he just now asked to be allowed to pray; although he must know that, being a heretic, die when he will he is sure to go to perdition. However, all I can venture to do is to conduct him to the headquarters of Boves, and leave him for that general's consideration. He may be saved in this world, although he is certain of being damned in the next. You had better interest Padré Salomon and Señoritta Ximines in his behalf, as they are always for saving prisoners. Captain Raymond, I leave this prisoner in your charge, while I go to give orders to Sergeant Perez to search the dead rebels; perhaps they may have doubloons about them as well as this Englishman, and it is necessary for the king's service that I take possession of them.

Saying this, the Andalusian went to speak to his sergeant.

I now rose and grasped the hand of the grateful Raymond, for I fully felt the obligation I owed him for his rescuing me from immediate destruction. When maddened by the excitement of battle, I feared death no more than one might who was conscious he possessed a hundred lives, but no soul; yet, when I was no longer dazzled by the false glory of war, but had calmly to look on the king of terrors, I felt the awful truth, — namely, that I was unfit to die. Through life, I had thought more of conducting myself as a gentleman than as a Christian; I meditated much on the laws of honour, but little on the laws of God.

Several of the Spaniards being wounded, I volunteered to dress them. Both the colonel and Raymond were pleased with my proposition; to aid which, my instruments were found and brought me. Some refused to be dressed by an insurgent, lest I should purposely treat them unskilfully; but, when informed I was an Englishman, they all gladly submitted to my operations, saying, the English were not assassins.

I was nearly two hours professionally employed, and the wounded were carried into three canoes, to be rowed up the Oronoco.

After partaking of a breakfast of aripa (Indian corn bread) and smoked beef, we set out on our march to Alta Gracia. A sergeant was about to tie my hands, when Raymond again interfered, and forbade this, saying he would be responsible for my custody. The colonel said, if I would give my honour not to escape, he would allow me to ride a mule. I acceded to this, but said, that if any attempt was made by the insurgents during our march to rescue me, I would be merely passive; and, if they succeeded in the attempt, and I got back safely to the army of Bolivar, I would procure the liberation of some Royalist prisoner of my own rank.

"I admire your candour," said the colonel; "but, should any attempt be made on us during our march, I will order two of my men to blow out your brains."

With this amicable understanding, we commenced our march. This was conducted in so irregular a manner, that I half regretted giving my honour not to escape; for, even had I been bound, it would have taken less talent than Vidocq[†] possessed to have given my conductors the slip; but when I recollected that, by so doing, I should compromise the grateful Raymond, I thought it infamous to attempt to escape, even had I not given my honour not to do this.

I observed that the Royalist troops were less ragged than the Patriots; but those by which I was surrounded might have served George

Cruikshank as studies for Falstaff's regiment,[†] save that they looked rather too *outré*.

After a hot march of three leagues, we came to a halt. All the party, sentinels included, took a regular siesta; in a few minutes they were 'all nodding,' and some snoring. Oh, how I wished for a party to rescue me! but, I suppose, the Patriots, about this hour, were also taking their nap.

About five o'clock we again set out; and, after marching about half-a-mile, we came to a post of the Royalists. Here we crossed to the right bank of the Oronoco in several large canoes; and, after a short march, we arrived at the head-quarters of General Boves, at a mission called Alta Gracia. I was instantly lodged in a large thatched building, which was dignified with the title of Casa del Rey (the king's house.)

I was well secured, by having my right leg and hand chained: these chains were fastened to a thick iron bar, within a foot of the unfloored ground; I, however, was able to stand, sit, or lie down. Scarcely was I fastened before I heard a gruff voice exclaim, "In with you, dog of a Hollander!" and two men dragged in a well-dressed little man, who, by the twilight, I discovered to be my friend, Moses Fernandez. I was about to utter an exclamation of surprise, when he checked me, by placing his finger on his mouth. I instantly comprehended his sign, and suppressed all appearance of recognition. His looks bespoke deep regret at our respective situations. They placed the Curaçoa man in a pair of stocks at the other end of the hall: they then left us to our meditations or conversation. Moses spoke to me in English, lest we should be overheard.

"Our days," said he, "I fear, are numbered; but do not seem to know me."

He asked me how I came to be taken? I briefly told him my late adventure. He, on his part, informed me that he was captured in a patriot launch going up the Oronoco.

Our conversation was interrupted by another companion in misfortune being put into the stocks. He was a middle-sized, well-built Frenchman, with a military mien. He had been despatched by Paez with a flag of truce: his mission was to ascertain if I was taken; and, if that were the case, to offer a Spanish major and subaltern[†] in exchange for me; and, at the same time, to threaten that, if any injury were done to me after my capture, the said major and subaltern should lose their heads the next morning, although neither of theirs might exactly fit my shoulders. The white rag which did duty for the flag of truce had been purposely destroyed by some

Indians who waylaid the Frenchman; and the poor officer, instead of being received as an envoy, was treated as a prisoner by an army which gave no quarter. The Spaniards would have butchered him on the spot, but several creole Royalists protested against it, and the Frenchman's fate was referred to General Boves, who was momentarily expected. The fact was, the unfortunate bearer of the flag of truce was a freemason, and he met with several of his craft amongst the Royalists: these were doing what they could in order to get him released.

"Bonjour, camarades," said the Frenchman to us.

We returned his salute.

"We are, I surmise, pretty near our last gasp. I know not how you feel, gentlemen; but, for me, if they give me the death of a soldier, I care not how soon it takes place: life I have not found so happy as to make me dread falling into annihilation. Yes! let bigots, who believe in childish stories of heaven and hell, fear death; we philosophers know it to be a cessation of life, and nothing more. What priests call the soul, my friends, is but the mechanical action of the brain: this thinking part of the human frame is born with the body, is imbecile with the body during infancy, strengthens with it, decays with it, and, doubtless, perishes with it. Life after death! a pretty story for knavish priests to tell, and credulous fools to believe; I would as lief give credence to one who tells me of the soul of a steam-engine, which, after being broken to pieces, will animate another and more perfect steam-engine!"

Little religion as I possessed, I was shocked with this ill-timed, uncalled-for, and senseless blasphemy. Fernandez seemed to feel as I did; but the present was no time for religious argument, and the Frenchman seemed neither to expect nor desire controversy. He added, "I forget, *camarades,* you may be of a different way of thinking: if so, I beg pardon; and, lest my opinion may disturb your devotion, I will bid you good night for the present."

Saying this, he lay down, and in a few minutes was asleep.

Before I could make any remarks on the language of this atheist, we heard the guard turn out to receive the general. He did not enter the Casa del Rey, but stood at the door, in conversation with Padré Salomon, a priest, who had been humanely interceding to save us. The stern Boves was not to be moved from his sanguinary resolves. We could not see the speakers, although we heard them. Every third word the Spanish general uttered was an obscene oath, with which I need not stain my paper.

"A pretty affair this!" said Boves: "Borero takes the English barber-surgeon, a heretic, forsooth; and yet you, a priest, beg mercy for him! Gomez captures a rascally Curaçoa merchant, who was going to supply the rebels with arms, and brings him all the way here, instead of allowing the alligators of the Oronoco to make food of him; and José Maria catches a Frenchman, a pretended bearer of a flag oftruce. Instead of settling these fellows at once, I must be plagued to give orders to have them shot or sabred: but their execution shall takeplace this night, by the ———"

"Swear not!" interrupted the priest. "Would you destroy their souls? Will you allow me no time to prepare them for a future state? Be it so; their sins be at your door; and on your own immortal soul be the offence of sending three men before their Creator unconfessed!"

"Do you not know that two out of the three are heretics, being a Dutchman and an Englishman?" responded Boves. "However, I will not incur the censure of the church by cutting them off too suddenly: I'll defer their execution until to-morrow noon. Are you satisfied? Well, satisfied or not, it shall be so. I will go and give orders to Colonel Ximenes about this matter."

We heard the general depart, and the priest tell the sentinel that he was going to confess a dying man, but that, in half-an-hour, he would return to attend to us.

Fernandez and myself exchanged a few melancholy words, and then each commenced praying — Fernandez using the Hebrew language.

"Do, good sentry, let me in," said a silvery voice.

"It is against the general's orders, señoritta," responded the sentinel; "but he is never long angry at any thing you do, for who could be displeased with *la angela de la misericordia* (the angel of mercy)? Go in, *con dios*."

The door now opened, and I discovered a female form, carrying a small silver lamp fed with cocoa-nut oil: this threw a doubtful light into the hall. She went to the stocks, and there perceived the Frenchman asleep. She exclaimed, "Holy Virgin! to sleep at such a time!"

She then held the lamp so that it threw its small but clear light on the Jew; but he, absorbed by his devotion,[†] paid no attention to her, and continued his prayer in a language to her unknown.

"The saints aid you!" she said; "but where is the tall and handsome Englishman they told me of?"

She held up the lamp; and, perceiving where I sat on the floor, crossed over to me, and lowered the lamp in order to see me. By this means I had a full view of her person; and, heavens! what a divine vision I beheld! She seemed

"In form a woman, but in years a child,"[†]

not being more than seventeen: and yet she was taller than the generality of women; while her stature seemed increased in height by a part of her long raven tresses being rolled into a mass, and confined on her head by means of a very large tortoise-shell comb, ornamented with gold and Margarita pearls. These shewed like a coronet, while a part of her glossy tresses hung beside her small ears, and played on her deep bosom. From her comb depended a rich black veil; her dress was of black velvet. She wore a profusion of rich jewels; these could scarcely be said to set off her queenly form and noble features, in which seemed to be united the Castilian traits of romance with the indications of creole benevolence. And I must here observe, that the feminine beauty of Spain, when transplanted into the New World, seems to flourish with greater loveliness than that of any European nation. Her large black eyebrows surmounted a pair of eyes quicker in their expression than any I ever beheld. Their darkness contrasted strongly with the alabaster whiteness of her pellucid skin; and, when she spoke, she displayed a set of pearly teeth, beautiful beyond any I had ever seen. Her voice was rich and silvery, while a natural and commanding grace accompanied all her movements.

Such was the apparition which stood before me, and which I contemplated by means of the small lamp she held. On any occasion I should have beheld with pleasure this Columbian flower of feminine beauty; but, after having for months seen no other woman but such wo-begone females as followed the insurgent camp to prevent their being massacred, and partook of all the privations and sufferings of a civil war; for me to be visited, in my present situation, by aught so lovely, was unlooked-for happiness. I for some moments believed she was a being from the region of the blessed, who had descended to console my approaching death. Long I gazed at her before I recollected that I was in a sitting posture. I rose; and, as my chains clanked, I gained my feet. This divine creature still regarded me, at first with deep curiosity, and then I perceived a smile of pleasure steal over her features; at length she uttered the words, "Poor fellow! and you, too, must be butchered, to add to the crimes of the sanguinary Boves!"

Instantly her eyes became suffused with tears.

I must now inform the reader that, although I had never before beheld this lovely female, yet I had often heard of Maria Josefa Ximenes, by her well-known appellation of *la angela de la misericordia*. Her cousin, Colonel Ximenes, having been captured by one of Bolivar's parties, he was about to be put to death, in retaliation for an insurgent colonel slain by Morales; when Maria Josefa, with a degree of praiseworthy enthusiasm, clad in all her rich habiliments and jewellery, left the Royalist army, and arrived at the out-posts of the Republicans without accident — for her beauty protected her from insult. At her request, she was conducted to Bolivar, before whom she pleaded so eloquently for the life of her cousin, that the Liberator, who was not stern by nature, but rendered so by circumstances, granted her prayer, on condition that she would endeavour to obtain the liberation of one Colonel Borroteran, a nephew of Bolivar, and his secretary, who was at that moment a prisoner in the Royalist camp. This she promised to do, and well kept her word. The ferocious Morales was not to be moved by her elo-quence, and the nephew of Bolivar was ordered to be shot; when a great number of creoles in the Royalist camp, thinking themselves slighted, by having their favourite's prayer rejected, began to murmur aloud, and a dan-gerous mutiny was likely to result from the sternness of Morales. He then found he had better yield with a good grace than risk a disturbance in his camp; for at this period the cause of Ferdinand looked doubtful.

The colonel was sent to his uncle; and, from that time forth, Maria Josefa, being aware of her influence amongst her compatriots, used it for benevolent purposes. She fearlessly passed between the belligerent camps, and was respected by both parties as a sacred person, even when a priest of eighty years of age would have been molested. Many an unfortunate Royalist and Patriot owed their lives to her intercession, which some of the less sanguinary chiefs of both armies chose to encourage; while, in the Royalist camp, the more cruel officers feared the influence she possessed. She often alleviated the miseries of the wretched women and children who were compelled to follow both camps.

Her endeavours to soften the rigours of this savage war were so incessant and successful, that both parties called her the angel of mercy. She even made a feminine weakness which she possessed (viz. a love for splendid dress) subservient to her benevolent exertion. As her jewellery threw a dazzle around her person by which she was recognised from afar, the wildest guerilla of Paez knew Maria Josefa, and would as soon think of plundering the gems of his patron saint, as of taking one pearl from the necklace of Señoritta Ximenes; the roughest Llanaro, whose dress was but an old blanket, and whose looks were more savage than those of a naked Indian, would crouch his lance and bow his head with the courtesy of a knight-errant, when he saw the well-designated angel of mercy approach; while the most clownish Biscayan or Catalonian of the Royalist camp would hail her return from the insurgent lines with *"Viva la angela de la misericordia!"*

"Poor fellow! and you, too, must be butchered, although you saved the life of my compadre,[74†] Raymond!" said Maria Josefa.

"So says your general, beautiful senoritta."

"Are you a good Christian?"[75]

"I hope I am a Christian; but fear I cannot apply to myself the epithet, good. I resemble you, fair lady, too little for that."

"Would you wish a priest to administer to you the last consolation of religion?"

"I am a Lutheran Christian," replied I (for by that designation the less intolerant creoles call Protestants, instead of the more obnoxious word, heretic). I added, "Yet, I believe that the prayers of a worthy priest will do no harm to a doomed man, even should we differ in our modes of worship."

"That is well. We say the English are heretics; yet we know them to be generous, honourable, and humane. If they are not, they ought to be Christians. Padré Salomon will shortly be here. He will attend you and your two companions there; although the one is asleep, and the other seems to pray in a language I never before heard. But would you wish to write, before you die, to your father or your poor mother?"

Here her eyes became again filled with tears. She continued, "Ah, little did that mother think, when she pillowed your head on her bosom, that the fair locks[76] of that head would be stained with your life's gore ere the days of your youth were passed! But I wander. I can procure you pen, ink, and paper, if you desire to write to your parents."

"I have none, sweet señora. My father died in my infancy, and my poor mother left this troublesome world the day I entered it."

"But you have brothers and sisters, caballero Inglese?"

---

74. Gossip. This kind of relationship is more sacred amongst the Spaniards than amongst us.†

75. *Bueno Christiano*, amongst Spaniards, means a Catholic.

76. Light hair is, in South America, considered most beautiful.

"I have, fair creole; but I would not wish them to know the death that your stern general has doomed me to die to-morrow."

"But have you not," said my interrogatress, lowering her voice, "some lady that loves you, or whom you love? Yes, surely you have, for I see you pause. Send her some love-token, before you quit this world. You know not what to send. Be advised: send her a lock of your fair hair; and, if she be worthy of your love, she will never part with this simple, but natural, dying gift. Here are my scissors. Tell me where the lady of your love lives, and I will endeavour to despatch it to her by the first safe opportunity that I meet with; and, in the mean time, I promise, on the honour of a descendant of a Castilian, to wear the lock in my bosom for security."

"Cut the lock yourself, fair damsel," said I.

She did so; and then said, "To whom am I to send it, señor?"

"You promised to wear it in your bosom, señora. Keep your word, and I shall die happy."

"But to whom am I to send it? Who is the lady of your heart?"

"Had I been asked the question but ten minutes ago, I should have replied that I had no lady of my heart; but now I have one, the print of whose feet on the earth I am not worthy to kiss."

"What say you? Is it possible? — I mean, who is this person that, within a few minutes, has conquered your affection?"

"She is called — and rightly denominated — the angel of mercy."

A sudden blush overspread the beautiful features of Maria Josefa. She looked at me with a smile. This soon vanished; and she said, "I knew not, señor, you were a Frenchman."

"I am an English creole, lovely demoiselle. What made you suppose I was French?"

"Because we have been in each other's company but ten minutes, and yet you employ your wit in trying to flatter me."

"Flattery, fair one, is the meanest species of falsehood. I am English — therefore, of a nation not remarkable for flattery. I am a gentleman,[77] and therefore disdain falsehood. I am a Christian, and, consequently, would shudder at a lie, standing as I do on the brink of eternity. But I declare to you, as an Englishman, a gentleman, and a Christian, that until I beheld you I knew not love; but, since my eyes were blessed with your

---

77. The word *caballero*, in Spanish America, is understood in a sense exactly as we understand the word gentleman in its noblest signification.

appearance, I am your unworthy but most passionate lover. I have no object to gain by my avowal, well knowing that the marine Morales[78] has doomed me to death to-morrow noon. But keep your sweet promise: wear but the lock of hair you have severed from my head in that lovely bosom, and I will die contented; while my last breath shall be employed in invoking blessings on you."

She again blushed, and smiled through her tears. After a pause, she said, "I am wrong to listen to an amorous declaration. No, no; Maria Josefa has a more sacred duty to perform than to listen to tales of love. The soft passion accords with happy times. Heaven has made me the instrument of good to others, and I will faithfully fulfil my destiny."

She again paused; and, pressing her hands to her temples, said, in a tone of soliloquy, "Is there no way to save him?"

Her cogitation was disturbed by the noise occasioned by the sentinel of the door presenting arms; and suddenly entered a handsome creole, in the dress of a Spanish colonel. He bore a torch of resinous wood; his face was ornamented and disfigured by black whiskers and mustachios. Yet, notwithstanding these, and a stern military air which he had, his features ware so strikingly like those of the lovely Maria Josefa, that they might have been taken for twins. He shot a look of suspicion at me, and a glance of displeasure at his cousin, for such she was.

How keen-sighted is passion! Colonel Ximenes loved Maria Josefa. One would have thought there was nothing in our respective situations to excite his jealousy; yet his features told me that I caused it. At the same moment, I felt a sudden degree of abhorrence for the handsome Colonel Ximenes. I thought — would I had my good steed and trusty matcheti, and that you were equally well armed and mounted, and we had a clear stage and no favour; I think I could give these fine features of yours a slash, which should injure their beauty. I believe we were not in each other's company above two seconds, before we hated each other as cordially as though we had been *friends* for twenty years.

A conversation now took place between the cousins, which I shall relate, omitting the says he and says she; to which I have an aversion.

"Maria Josefa here! How is this?"

"Does Colonel Ximenes ask why I am here, when I have victims to snatch from cold-blooded slaughter?"

---

78. Morales was a marine sergeant at the battle of Trafalgar.

"True, señoritta, you are called the angel of mercy. To your active humanity I owe my life."

"And to my exertion shall this young gentleman — I mean, these three people, owe their lives."

"Impossible! Our general has sworn ———"

"To continue a butcher. I have heard of his amiable vow. He calculates on exterminating the race of creoles; but let Morillo, Boves, and Morales, not be too elated with their success. Bolivar is beaten, but not subdued; Arismendi has sworn vengeance, and he ever keeps his oaths; while Paez hovers about their army like a fiend of destruction. Sick of this war of death, I have long entreated that it might be conducted with some slight degree of mercy. But I will cease to entreat: I command that the lives of these men be saved!"

"Are you mad, Maria?"

"No, I am sensible — sensible of my power. Let me but utter one word, and every creole in the Royalist camp, who now raises his traitorous arms against his country, will join the Patriots, strike for liberty, and Columbia will be free!"

Here her sweet countenance assumed an air of majesty, and she spoke with the boldness of an inspired prophetess.

"Rash girl! are you weary of life? Speak low, for the love of God!"

"No; I will speak out! It is long since I ceased to fear death. Call in the sentinels, and I will tell them that Spain is tyrannical. Spaniards are blood-hounds; and creoles who aid them are traitors and fools!"

Every limb of Ximenes shook with emotion. He caught his cousin's hands, fell upon his knees, and then said, in a whisper, "For the sake of Heaven, for the love of your friends, for the sake of your country, be pacified, Maria. You know not what you do. You will involve us all in ruin. Be patient, and South America shall be free. Your rashness will betray the land of your birth."

Maria replied in a low voice, but which I distinctly heard, being too interested in the conversation to lose a syllable, "Be it so. I have long suspected this. May your plot succeed! But, at all events, that Englishman must be saved. Rather than he should be sacrificed, I will, ere morning dawns, raise three thousand creoles to his rescue. Nay, nay, frown not on that youth. Antonio Ximenes, is this a time, when war is desolating your native land, to think of love or jealousy? Shame! shame!"

"Maria, retire a minute or two. I will think how to rescue this Englishman."

She now passed over to where Fernandez and the Frenchman were confined, and entered into conversation with the former. Meanwhile, the colonel was lost in meditation. The torch he held threw a red glare on his fine features, and enabled me to observe their appearance. They seemed to be strongly agitated; and once or twice he put his hand on his forehead. At length he said, "No, no; she saved my life, and I will rescue him, even if he be born to blast my happiness."

He now advanced towards me, and held his torch near my face. Suddenly, his stern look relaxed into wonder: he exclaimed, "Is it possible? My old friend! Do you not recollect me?"

I answered in the negative.

He said, "Do you not remember giving me an orange when I was a prisoner?"

I now recollected that, when Ximenes was taken, he was marched many miles, exposed to the rays of a burning sun, until he was nearly perishing with thirst. I happened to have an orange, with which I moistened his parched lips, his own hands being at that time bound. Little did I think, at the moment I performed this act of common humanity, that it would have conduced so much to my advantage. Instantly the colonel's behaviour totally changed.

"Give me your hand!" he cried; "I tender mine in friendship."

"And I accept yours with the same feeling."

Maria Josefa beheld our salute with tears of pleasure; which, when Ximenes observed, his features again became stern. He motioned her to retire. She withdrew a few steps.

"I will," said the colonel, "endeavour to effect your escape. Major Peña wishes to save yonder Frenchman, who, careless of his fate, sleeps soundly. Peña and he belong to some foolish secret society. I will consult with him; but, if I aid your flight, you must promise me, on the well-known faith of your countrymen, to quit South America, and not appear here for four years."

I looked at Maria, and saw, by her countenance, that she wished me to accede to her cousin's proposition. I, therefore, agreed to the proposal, provided that my friend Fernandez, and the Frenchman, should be also allowed to escape. To this stipulation he promised to conform, and said, "Now let me seek Peña and Padré Salomon. Maria Josefa, we have not a minute to lose. Is this a time for you to coquette with a man whose life is at stake? Away! call hither to me the Indian, Guiocolo: he can be trusted; he shall guide these three men to English Guiana. At the same time, tell Pedro to procure something for these people to eat and drink — they have need of it: away!"

Maria Josefa did not move off so quickly as her cousin wished. She read in my countenance expressions of doubt, and said to me, "Fear not, caballero: Colonel Ximenes is passionate, but not dishonourable; he acts from sudden emotions, but those are never treacherous."

"I believe you," replied I; "no one can be dishonourable whose features resemble yours, fair señora."

"Away!" said the colonel, and handed her to the door. She went: he then said, "I have much to prepare, and little time; let me get you four swift horses, and provisions for your arduous journey."

Saying this, he quitted me.

The latter part of our conference was spoken in suppressed voices; but at one time the passion of Maria Josefa so far got the better of her discretion, that I wonder she was not overheard by the sentinels who were ordered to watch the Casa del Rey. But these people were busily employed, twenty yards from the building, drinking guarapa, smoking rank Virginia cigars, and playing at *monte*[79]† for rials, with a small and dirty pack of cards.

I was about to congratulate Fernandez on our prospect of escape, when I heard the gambling sentinels without shout, "Welcome, Padré Salomon; give us your benediction, and we are all of us sure to win."

Shortly after, the priest entered, and a remarkable scene took place. I, at that time, was not aware what was going on, because I knew not the language used on the occasion; but, subsequently, Fernandez recounted it to me.

As the priest (an old and venerable-looking man) entered, Fernandez was repeating, in Hebrew, from Deuteronomy, chapter iv. verse 4, what the modern Jews conceive to be the foundation-stone of their faith.

"Hear, O Israel! Jehovah is our Lord; Jehovah is One."†

When he saw the priest enter, he suddenly stopped in his devotion, lest the padré should discover his religion; for, although he knew that the learning of Spanish priests, in general, is confined to being able to say mass by rote in Latin, which they scarcely understand, yet some few of them are

---

79. A game of chance.†

very learned. This was the case with Salomon; he instantly perceived of what religion Fernandez was, and a conversation took place, in that mixed and corrupt Hebrew[†] which is spoken by Jews of the present day.

"What," said the priest, "does a child of Israel do in the camp of Christians?"

Fernandez made no answer, not wishing to confess, although he well knew the priest had discovered it. The latter continued, "Proceed with your prayers: fear me not; I will not betray you to the bigoted soldiers, or they will tear you in pieces. I come to you with tidings of mercy."

"When did not a priest of that religion which pretends to believe in the Pentateuch, and yet dares to alter Jehovah's commandments, by suppressing the second[80†] — when did not such a one talk of mercy; yet when did he ever practise it towards the suffering race of Israel? You know my language; you know my creed. Go to your savage general, tell him that I am the Curaçoa merchant whom Christians name Fernandez, but who is called Masha Ben Simon when summoned to the desk of the synagogue[†] to hear that Law read which Jehovah gave to his chosen people."

"No," replied the priest, "I will not betray you. I pity the errors of the children of Israel, but I will never harm any of them. I am, myself, a descendant of one of the Twelve Tribes."

"Why wearest thou the dress of the Christian priest?"

"Because I am one."

"I hate a Spaniard; I doubly detest a Spanish priest: but, for thee, I at once loathe and despise thee, because thou art an apostate. Be thou cut off, and thy name erased from the book of life!"

As Fernandez said this, he spat on the ground, to shew his contempt.

"I was prepared for all this, when I told thee I was a servant of the Christian altar. I have chosen my creed; remain, if God wills it, by thine. But we lose time. Leagued with Peña, I come to aid your escape, and that of your companions."

"I will not be indebted for my life to an apostate."

"Then remain to be slaughtered, and have thy body devoured by wild beasts and obscene birds, instead of being interred in ground consecrated by an Israelitish rabbi. Hast thou no sons nor daughters, whose descendants, thou vainly hopest, will be the Messiah that thou expectest?"

"I have, like Jephthah, an only daughter,[†] for whose dear sake will I

---

80. Catholics omit the second commandment, and divide the tenth into two parts.

even thankfully accept of life at the hands of one who has forsaken the religion of his fathers."

"Be it so: I forgive your reproaches, and go to aid your escape. Awake your sleeping companion, if you wish to save him. I go to assist Peña and Ximenes in preparing for your flight."

At this instant Maria Josefa entered, followed by an Indian of the Chyma tribe,[†] together with a negro, who bore a small basket of provisions for our repast, and a heavy bunch of keys, the same which confined my chains.

I must inform the reader, that Ximenes had sent to the sentinels a quantity of rum, which was part of the cargo taken in the launch with Fernandez. What with the spirits and the pack of cards, they neither knew nor cared for what took place in the Casa del Rey.

Maria Josefa saw the priest, but doubted if he was fully acquainted with the plot for effecting our escape. She threw herself on her knees, clasped his, and exclaimed, "Father, for the love of all the saints, betray me not; but suffer me to deliver this dear, dear English youth! Oh, do not refuse my prayer; or you will break my heart!"

"Blessings on thee, dearest child!" said the priest, laying his hands on her head; "truly hast thou been called the angel of mercy. Hitherto thou hast saved men for the love of Heaven; but now, poor child, thou urgest thy humane prayer for the love of your handsome Englishman! Nay, blush not, nor droop thy beautiful head: Heaven, in its own good time, will reward thy virtue, and, perhaps, bless thee with thy lover. I go to aid your cousin in his preparations for the flight of these three men. God be with thee!"

The priest now left us: and, while Fernandez awoke the Frenchman, whose name was D'Aubert, and acquainted him with our prospect of escape, Maria hastily informed me of the means of our flight.

We ate a hurried, but hearty supper, which consisted of Indian corn bread, South American cheese, and turtles' eggs. We drank, between us, a bottle of tolerable sack.[†] All this time, Guiocolo was busy unlocking my chains, and loosing the stocks; while he placed in the middle of the hall a large quantity of palm-leaves, which had been brought into the Casa del Rey to new thatch it. This it was designed to set fire to, in order to cover our retreat, and account for our disappearance. While this preparation was going forward, a more serious task devolved on Peña, Ximenes, and Raymond, who willingly joined in the plot, in order to requite my having saved him at Barancos.

Supper being finished, Guiocolo, after carefully reconnoitring, told us that, by passing a back-door which he opened, we might evade an encounter with the sentinels. We cautiously stole out, accompanied by Maria, and led by the Indian; but we left the faithful negro, named Pedro, to kindle the fire amongst the palm-leaves, about an hour after our flight: this he was punctual in doing.

When we got about six hundred yards from the Casa del Rey, we were challenged by a drowsy sentinel. We gave the pass-word, of which we were informed, and were allowed to proceed. Twice, after this, were we challenged by sentinels, and with the same result.

Maria Josefa, enveloped in a cloak, leaned on my arm, and accompanied us. As soon as we passed the out-posts of the camp I conversed with my fair preserver.

I will not repeat all that took place between us: let it suffice that, encouraged by her admission that I was not so indifferent as others she had rescued from the Spaniards, I had the cruelty to propose that she should fly with me.

"No," she said; "that would be disgraceful in a daughter of the house of Ximenes, and dishonourable to my cousin Antonio, to whom I have not plighted my faith, but yet I promised never to give my hand to another, until the conclusion of this unhappy war. Here I remain, to fulfil a sacred duty, to which I am vowed; that is, fearlessly to use all my best endeavours in order to soften the rigour of this cruel civil war. My cousin has stipulated that you return not in less than four years. If Heaven at the end of that time should preserve us, and if you really love Maria Josefa Ximenes, you will, doubtless, find her somewhere in Venezuela: if, however, at the end of five years I hear nothing of you, I go to Cuba, and become the bride of Heaven. Take this ring, dear Englishman: it is of value; but part not with it, unless you should be pressed by necessity."

"Much sooner will I part with my life!"

I kissed her long, slender hand, as she gave me the ring; when, with the rankness of pure and holy innocence, she offered me her cheek. I pressed the trembling girl to my bosom: she wept, prayed for my deliverance, and asked my name. I told it, but regretted that I had no writing-materials whereon to inscribe it.

"Warner Arundell!" said she. "I shall ever remember it — for it is written here. I am wrong, perhaps, so far to encourage an utter stranger; but the Virgin will not, I am sure, suffer poor Maria Josefa to love one unworthy of her affection! No, no dear heart! your honest features tell me that the Mother of Heaven has not suffered such an affliction to fall on me. But, hold! I had nearly forgotten. Here is a belt in which are sewn twenty-two doubloons: these may serve you, dearest Warner Arundell! But see, Guiocolo and your companions are impatient, and wait; therefore let us part. God bless and restore you to me in happier times!"

We again embraced; and then, by a violent effort, we separated. I felt as though my heart was torn from my bosom, as she left me and hastily walked towards the camp: and if my companions had not returned and hurried me on, I should have remained for some time rooted to the spot.

We walked forward, at a round pace, for about a mile, when we joined a party of five, consisting of the Padré Salomon, Colonel Ximenes, Captain Raymond, Major Peña, and my old friend Colonel Borero, who had captured me that morning; but who, for a small douceur[†] given by Raymond, under pretence of a loan, assisted our escape. Four noble horses, well caparisoned, and partly loaded, but without their bridles, were feeding on a quantity of Indian corn meal.

"Let the horses feed," said Ximenes; "we have still half-an-hour before us ere the Casa Real will be fired by Pedro."

He addressed me apart, while the Frenchman entered into conversation with Peña, and Fernandez talked to the priest, to whom he seemed reconciled.

Ximenes informed me that Guiocolo would, by a circuitous route known to few, conduct me across the immense plains, rivers, forests, and mountains, which lay between us and the River Essequibo;[†] and that he had made every preparation for the occasion which time and circumstances would admit of. He enumerated all the articles he had supplied us with: these consisted of three horse-pistols;[†] an English fowling-piece; four pounds of powder; a proportionate quantity of shot; a small bladder full of salt; a quantity of tasajo; and four hammocks. In a portmanteau, attached to my saddle, he placed three shirts; he gave us two long knives and an axe; while Guiocolo was furnished with two Indian bows, and a quantity of poisoned arrows. Each horse carried a small bag of Indian corn. After enumerating these, the colonel said, "Depart, in God's name, señor Inglese; but I fear you carry away the heart of one who is dearer to me than my own soul. Would that Maria Josefa had never seen you! however, I have promised to aid your escape, and I have kept my word. Have I acted the part of a generous rival?"

I expressed my satisfaction at his honourable conduct.

"Remember," said he, "your promise not to return during four years."

I told him I would not break my word.

We shook each other cordially by the hand; and, the horses having made an end of their provender, the Indian bridled them. While he was doing this, Colonel Borero stepped up to me, and apologised for not having the three doubloons which I gave him in the morning to return to me, because, he said, he had lost them at monte. He produced a dirty pack of cards, and offered to cut double or quits for the money. How he was to pay if he lost, he did not say; I, however, humoured him, and lost, which I was glad of.

We all took a cordial leave of our deliverers. Even Fernandez said to the priest, "The God of Israel bless you! We have chosen different roads; but I hope we shall meet in Paradise."

By this time the Casa Real was fired. Pedro had managed affairs so well, that the house was in full blaze before the fire was discovered. Its combustible materials burned so readily, that we were, as I afterwards learned, supposed to have perished in the flames. The fire illuminated the night-clouds, and the sparks flew in all directions. The church-bell at Alta Gracia rang an alarm, and the drums, fifes, and bugles, called in vain for the soldiers to extinguish the flames.

We heard these notes of alarm; it was our signal to mount our well-laden and noble horses, and commence our arduous journey — Guiocolo, the Indian, leading the way. Our animals carried us at a tremendous rate. In a few minutes we were out of hearing of the drums, bells, and bugles, of the Royalist camp, and were on our way to Essequibo.

CHAPTER 37.

———— "To traverse o'er
Plain, forest, river, — man nor brute,
By dint of hoof, nor print of foot,
Lay in that wild luxuriant soil;
No signs of travel, none of toil."
                    BYRON.[†]

All night our guide rode before us, at the full speed of our horses, shaping his way by the stars, for road or track over the country there was none. Neither D'Aubert nor Fernandez were first-rate horsemen; but the fear of death is an excellent riding-master. It was about midnight when we started, and, as day opened, we were, as I calculate, about fifty miles from Alta Gracia, when Guiocolo drew up his horse: we did the same. He advised us to dismount, as the animals were completely blown. Down we got, leading the horses, to cool them, but walking as fast as we could on our journey. We walked about four miles, when we came to a broad but not deep stream. I saw the propriety of the Indian's advice. The animals were now cooled, and could cross the river without injury. Guiocolo told us to allow them to drink: we did so. The stream was not out of the horses' depth. On the other side of the river the Indian gave them a greater quantity of corn than I conceived was prudent; but he said the horses were heavily laden, and could better carry corn in their bellies than on their backs. I do not think the admirers of the English turf will agree to this mode of feeding; but it occasioned no apparent inconvenience. We drank some water while the horses fed, and each ate a small piece of aripa.

Again we mounted. At first we walked; we then gradually increased our pace to a quick gallop, which we continued till about noon, when we came to a thick forest, the branches of which hung too low to allow us to ride. We dismounted, and walked for about half-an-hour, when we came to a pool of not the clearest water. Here we bathed, and fed ourselves and our horses. About three p.m. we again set out, riding across a steep range of hills, until about eight at night, when we came to the borders of savanna land, through which ran a stream. Our careful Indian now tethered our horses with lazoes;[†] and we suspended our hammocks to low savanna trees, and slept in open air. We took the precaution of making a good fire to frighten away tigers and pumas, as well as to keep the horses near us, in case any of them got loose; for those animals will keep instinctively near the fire. So fatigued were we, that we all slept soundly; but, every subsequent night of our journey, one always watched while the others slept.

We enjoyed undisturbed repose for about eight hours; and, as day opened, we were awoke by the notes of the pouie, or South American turkey.[†] Again were our horses fed with grain, and watered. While the animals were eating, Guiocolo brought down with his bow a large pouie: off this we made a hasty breakfast; and, notwithstanding that it was killed with a poisoned arrow, it tasted deliciously. We perceived a very fine tiger; but, on our shouting, he decamped, running with surprising grace. The symmetry and beauty of these animals are astonishing. Those who only behold them pent up in cages can form no conception of their elegance of form and colour. However, as they are apt to give travellers rather ugly scratches in the great savannas, they, after all, are better seen in the Zoological Gardens than met with in the plains of South America.

The Columbians say the jaguar, or tiger, mixes with the puma (South American lion), and produces an extremely ferocious mongrel.[†] I doubt this, but record it as a mere report, which, however, is currently believed.

We rode until about noon, when some cocoanut trees, planted in rows, informed us that we were approaching a *hato*, or breeding farm. The Indian threw off all his light clothing, save a *guiacou*, in order to look like one of the unreclaimed savages. This he did to approach the hato and reconnoitre, lest we might meet with enemies at the farm. He returned in a few minutes, telling us we might safely approach, as there were not people enough to attack us. The war had left but three boys and one woman in the place.

We walked our horses to the large unfinished house of the hato. The poor woman who possessed it was much alarmed at our appearance. We soon found means of quieting her fears: this done, her joy and hospitality seemed to know no bounds. She gave us an excellent meal, replenished our supply of aripa, Indian corn, and tasajo; she gave our horses, what is very common on hatoes, a pail of milk each with aripa broken up in it. This is an excellent mode of feeding cattle intended for a long journey; but I do not expect it will be practised in England.

The old woman pressed us to stay that day. To this we consented, it being the last house we expected to enter, save two days' journey on, where was a mission under Padré Rodrigo, an Andalusian Capuchin.

What a beautiful place is a South American hato! with its flocks of wild dark-bay horses, each squadron led by its captain; its immense droves of horned cattle; its general appearance of plenty, content, and, I had almost said, happiness; but happiness is not merely the absence of misery; it is a positive, not a negative enjoyment. Man was not made to live in the wild seclusion of a South American hato; the inhabitant of which, having little to think of, seemed to think of nothing. The poor woman who owned the place appeared scarcely able to command sufficient words, in her native language, to express her limited ideas. She, however, was most kind to us. We offered her money, some of which I possessed, thanks to the generosity of my angel of mercy; but the woman would accept of none. She, however, was most thankful for five or six charges of powder, which we gave her. She thought herself overpaid.

The next day we set out rather overloaded with presents, from the hato; but, conceiving ourselves beyond danger, we went on at leisure. We journied a great part of the day across a savanna, without coming to a drop of water for the horses, and had nothing to drink ourselves but guarapa, which we took from the hato. Towards evening we came to a wood, which, like most of those in South America, abounded in the wild pines which adhere to branches of trees. Each of these contain, in the driest season, a quantity of pure and cool water. With some labour, we collected a sufficient quantity for our horses, and crossed the wood. At the edge of this, we erected an ajupa, lit a fire, and slept in our hammocks during the night; each watching about two hours in his turn, while the rest slept. D'Aubert had a pinchbeck† watch, which served us to divide the night. This kept pretty regular time, as it *only* lost about a quarter of an hour out of every twenty-four; but we easily regulated it. The Indian guessed the time, pretty accurately, by the stars.

We started at daylight the next morning, for our abundance of provisions obviated the necessity of our looking out for game. After a somewhat fatiguing ride, we, in the evening, came to a mission of the Paraigotote Indians, under the direction of the Capuchin before mentioned. On stating what was truth, in one sense, that we came from the camp of the Royalists, we were kindly treated. The Indian alcalde,[†] or chief officer, received us in great state, and turned out a whole regiment of naked Indians to escort us to the Casa del Rey, a kind of caravansary. They provided a tolerable repast for us and our horses. The Indian magistrate behaved with great state and munificence, because D'Aubert gave him the brass seal which was attached to his watch. Our horses were well fed, and we slept soundly, after having paid our respects to the padré.

The next morning we viewed the mission, which seemed an earthly Paradise. It was situated on the banks of a beautiful stream, which was flung from a rock about six hundred feet in height. This cascade looked like a falling stream of molten silver. The land about the mission was extremely fertile; the houses, although formed of slight materials, were built with regularity; all the necessaries of life, and many of its luxuries, were abundant. The old padré was in his eighty-seventh year. Poor man, his extraordinarily long sojourn amongst the Indians had nearly extinguished his mental faculties. Although he was still able to attend to the old routine of his clerical duties, he was absolutely ignorant of the war which was desolating a part of the very province in which he lived. Some of the Indians told him of this; but he would not believe that the people of South America could ever be so impious as to talk seriously of warring on the King of Spain. We, of course, did not broach the subject: it was quite enough for him to know that we were on our journey across Spanish Guiana to Essequibo. He seemed not to like to talk of the news of the day, but asked us if it was true that the French had decapitated Louis the Sixteenth?[†] On our answering in the affirmative, he said, "Holy Virgin! what will they do next?"

It being one of the numerous *fêtes* of the Spanish calendar, the naked alcalde requested that we would stop and spend the day at the mission. We hesitated at this; but, at the particular request of Fernandez, we remained. I thought I observed that he seemed more devout that day than any other.

We exchanged a few charges of powder and shot for as many turtle-eggs, prepared in a mass, smoked deer, dried fish, and cassada bread, as we could conveniently take with us; and the alcalde ordered four Indians to carry a part of our luggage over a mountain which we had to cross, but which could not be ridden over. The second morning after our arrival, we mounted our horses and set forward at a walk, with four Indians on foot.

We did not halt until we reached the foot of a steep and rocky mountain, which the Pariagotoe Indians† called Guiago. After partaking of a temperate meal, and watering our horses, we commenced climbing this steep ascent on foot, the Indians leading our horses. We were soon out of breath, and were forced to pause and hold on by branches of dwarf trees, which sent their roots into the crevices of the rocks, and appeared to vegetate with very little assistance from the earth. All the rest of the day, and long after the sun had set, we continued our toilsome ascent. About nine at night we arrived at a place where the horses could stand at ease, and where we found the remains of an Indian hut. Here we slung our hammocks, and, worn with fatigue, we slept soundly; but, towards morning, we found the weather so cold, owing to our elevated situation, that we were constrained to warm ourselves at the fire which, as usual, was lighted to keep off tigers, as they abounded in these mountains.

At daylight we commenced our descent. This was less fatiguing, but far more dangerous, than our ascent. Repeatedly we slung ourselves, by branches of dwarf trees, down rocks and across chasms. How the animals passed these obstacles is astonishing, but they had the agility and security of foot of goats. We crossed a small stream of water, in which we bathed the horses; and which, we were told, became one of the many mighty tributary rivers of the Oronoco. We rested on the borders of this stream during the night, and the next day came to a most magnificent savanna, but one that was only inhabited by pumas, tigers, serpents, and wandering Indians, equally wild. Here our pedestrian felllow-travellers proposed to leave us, but Guiocolo entreated them to proceed as far as a grove and stream which lay about three leagues and a half further, where we intended to encamp, as he much feared being attacked by Caraibes. The Pariagotoes demurred at this, until I offered them ten charges of powder to come with us. This munificent offer they could not resist. We mounted our horses, and the Indians bounded forward with such activity that they kept our animals in a smart trot. Of course, we soon arrived at this grove, but the horses would not enter it: they all smelt the air, laid their ears back, bounded in all directions, but no efforts of ours could make them advance.

"There must be a tiger there," said Guiocolo.

Instantly the Indians threw off their *guias*, and each fitted an arrow to his bow and advanced. I left my horse in charge of D'Aubert; and, having loaded my fowling-piece, proceeded with them. As we entered the grove, a deep growl told us we were near our quarry. A large and lank tigress appeared, with a cub in her mouth. One of the Indians shot his arrow and wounded her; two others missed; and Guiocolo struck her in the back with a poisoned arrow: but still she was making off. I took aim, and sent a bullet right into her brain: this finished her career. On looking round, we found the cub she carried, as a cat carries her kittens, and another: these appeared scarcely two days old. The fear of losing her young hindered her flight, and cost her her life. The Indians said they would endeavour to keep the little creatures alive, and bring them to the mission as a present to the padré. The tigress must have lately struck down a deer, for the greater part of its carcass we found near her. It had been killed within an hour or two, so that we dressed and ate it. The Indians preferred the tigress, which, they said, was better food. Strange to say, they preferred the flesh of the jaguar to beef or venison. It grieved Fernandez to partake of food not slaughtered after his own manner; however, he had but the choice of eating it or starving.

We made our ajupa that night in the grove: the next morning we parted with the Pariagotoe Indians.

We fed our horses well; for a clear ride of one hundred miles lay before us, through a country inhabited by wild tribes. We started about seven o'clock, according to D'Aubert's pinchbeck chronometer. We rode all that day, and half the night, ere we came to a place where we could conveniently bait[†] our horses. When we did arrive, we had difficulty in keeping the animals from drinking too much.

Unfortunately, we had no kind of instruments with us, so as to enable our taking any kind of observation: we had not even a compass. This I regret the more, because the most fertile and noble country lying between the Upper Orinoco and the Essequibo is entirely a *terra incognito*. Pretended maps of it exist, but, to my own knowledge, they are most inaccurate — placing mountains, rivers, and lakes, where plains only exist; and *vice versá*.

Our route was circuitous and wandering in the extreme; sometimes we went for two days without advancing as many miles. This was occasioned by some inaccessible mountain or other obstacle lying across our path: hence, the actual distance we went was very disproportionate to the progress we made in a direct line. Often we took immense circuits in order to avoid hostile and savage Indians, of whom Guiocolo stood in great dread; for this man, although faithful to his undertaking in an extraordinary degree, and courageous when opposed to animals, was, I suspect, cowardly when encountering men. His timidity, I surmise, cost us many a day's journey.

The sixth day after we left the mission, our Indian guide advised a halt, as our horses wanted rest — telling us, that about five leagues onward lay a river, which he called the Matagatoe.[81] Fernandez dissented from the opinion of Guiocolo; and said that, although our animals were weary, we were not, and advised us to dismount and lead our horses. I was astonished at this, because Fernandez was the oldest of the party; in fact, he had long passed the prime of life. We, however, agreed to follow his advice; and, after a long and tedious walk, we came to the banks of a noble river. Here we rested, previous to our crossing it. Scarcely had we time to repose, ere the Indian regarded the stream with some alarm, and said we must cross instantly, or we should be detained for several days. The fact was, he noticed, by the visible rising of the river, that a flood of rain must have fallen in the mountains, and that the banks would be soon overflowed; in which case, we might be detained for weeks before we could cross it — for we now might daily expect the rainy season. It was fortunate that we had followed the advice of Fernandez in not halting, as the Indian proposed, although he did not foresee the result of his good counsel. We crossed the river, swimming our horses, and holding on by their manes. So strong was the current setting in, that we were carried down the stream nearly half-a-league before we were able to cross it; and then, with great difficulty, we mounted the steep bank. Almost all the rivers of South America have a shallow bank on one side, and an abrupt one on the other.

We erected our leafy tent on the banks of the Matagatoe before sunset; and the next day, men, as well as horses, were so completely fatigued, that we were constrained to halt. We could not do this in a better situation. We had wood, water, forage, fish, and venison, at our command; and such abundance of the terekay, or small river turtle,[†] and its delicious eggs, at our very feet, that it would be worth while for a London alderman to take a journey to the river Matagatoe for the purpose of enjoying it: but (shocking to relate!) we were obliged to broil all we ate, having no cooking utensils.

The first evening after we passed the Matagatoe, I observed that Fernandez became more than usually devout. This I at first attributed to his being thankful for having safely crossed the river, as he could not swim; but, although I could not understand the language in which he prayed, for

---

81. Every Indian tribe calls rivers, mountains, &c. by a different name.

this he always did audibly, yet I thought I could distinguish the word Sabbath in Hebrew. It now struck me that it was the eve of the Jewish Sabbath. This at once accounted for his anxiety to rest the last week at the mission, and to push on this day, in order that he might rest on the morrow. When he had finished his devotion, I questioned him on this subject, and I found my conjecture correct.

When I recollected that for months I had never known one day from another since I joined the insurgents, nor the days of the week, I stood rebuked in the presence of the pious Jew. I told him so, and praised him for recollecting, amid all his toil and wanderings, the ordinances of his religion.

"Why," said he, "Warner, should we forget the service of God? Has He forgotten us, when, in six days, He created this globe; the sun, that animates all nature; the moon, whose silvery light now glitters on the swelling river; the stars, which gem yon blue vault? When He had breathed the breath of life into the nostrils of our first parents, whom he created after his own image, He rested the seventh day, and consecrated it. The river *Sabathjon*, therefore, flows during six days, and on the seventh, its waters are stationary;[†] the very damned in hell have rest on the Sabbath. Why, amid this desert, the dwelling-place of the tiger and the cannibal, should we forget our Creator, seeing He abandons us not? When I repose beneath our wretched ajupa, I close my eyes in sleep[†] with the full assurance that the archangel Michael stands at my right hand; at my left watches Gabriel; Raphael and Uriel are stationed at my feet; while, above me, hovers the spirit of the living God. This yon poor atheist would call the dream of enthusiasm; but it is a dream I would not like to be awoke from. Kneel, young man; praise the God you worship, for His having delivered you. Kneel, Warner, and supplicate a blessing on the head of one whose name I often hear you murmur in your sleep; implore a benediction on Maria Josefa, the angel of mercy. I like not the appellation of angel to be given to a mortal; but, if ever daughter of Eve deserves it, she does. Doubt not, you will meet again in happy times, when the maiden shall be as a crown unto you."

For the first time for some years I shed a devout tear: I knelt, and prayed fervently. D'Aubert knew not what Fernandez said to me; for he understood scarce a syllable of English, in which language we conversed. It is singular, that of four persons thus brought by chance together, one was a Jew; the other, although baptised, was a mere heathen; another was, or pretended to be, an atheist; and, finally, I was an unworthy Christian.

"Warner," said Fernandez to me the next evening, "I think I shall convert you to Christianity, although a Jew myself. Be advised: let us not proceed to-morrow, but keep *your* Sabbath. We are here surrounded by rude abundance, and the horses will be better for another day's rest. Remain here to-morrow, and I will collect tortoises and eggs, and stand cook for the party."[†]

I mentioned this to D'Aubert, and he consented to remain. He cared not for religion, but was too polite to ridicule it before Fernandez and myself. He amused himself in shooting, and singing little French songs.

Previous to this remarkable journey across Guiana, Fernandez was a martyr to gout and rheumatism: but the exertion he was obliged to use, and to which he cheerfully submitted; the rude fare he was necessitated to partake of; the frequent immersions he underwent; and his sleeping continually with no other shelter than an ajupa, — which is merely a few leaves to keep off the dew, — all combined to cure him completely of his chronic diseases.

Twenty-five days after we left Alta Gracia, we came to an encampment of comparatively civilised Caraibes, called Buck Indians: they spoke no Spanish, but a little broken English.[†] These conducted us to a muddy-looking, partly natural and partly artificial, canal, which leads to the Essequibo. We agreed to give our pistols and the remains of our powder to them, if they would convey us to the British settlements. This they consented to do; and we embarked in a large canoe, having given our horses and fowling-piece to the faithful guide, Guiocolo, who, I afterwards learnt, disposed of the fine animals for a trifle, and returned by himself to Alta Gracia.

During the journey I was by far the most active of the party, not excepting the Indian; but the confinement in a canoe for several days in a cramped posture, together with the miasma from the swamps of old Dutch (now British) Guiana,[†] conjoined to give me a very bad intermittent fever.[†] This increased in violence until we arrived at Essequibo. I hailed with joy the appearance of the British flag.

A boat, with several officers, came alongside of our canoe. These gentlemen were astonished at our wild appearance. This was scarcely to be wondered at. Our clothes hung together in tatters; our toes were peeping through our shoes as though they were looking out for fresh lodgings; our hair had not had the benefit of a comb for some weeks; and we had each a month's beard on our faces. On Fernandez informing the officers that we had escaped from the Royalists, and had journeyed from Alta Gracia, they behaved most humanely to us. These gentlemen had come in a brig, on what is called a maroon party, *i.e.* a party of pleasure.[†] They sent for a boat, and had us removed on board the brig. Each underwent shaving from the hands of a military barber. After this the kind officers had a meeting, and each agreed to furnish us with some articles of clothing; hence, we were enabled to enjoy the luxury of clean linen, and appear on deck in decent attire.

A military surgeon being of the party, I requested his advice as to my malady; he immediately ordered me into a berth, and gave me a glass of hot sangaree. In short, we were most kindly entertained by these gentlemen; and, the next day, we safely landed in the town of St. George's, Demerara.[†]

★　★　★　★　★

END OF THE SECOND VOLUME.

Volume III

CHAPTER 38.

"Farewell the grave pacific air,
  Where never mountain zephyr blew,
  The marshy levels, lank and bare,
  Which Pan with Ceres never knew:
  The Naïads, with obscene attire,
  While round them chaunts the croaking choir."
           AKENSIDE.[†]

I lodged in a pretty good tavern in St. George's, and was attended by the military surgeon. When it became known that I was of their profession, several medical men came to see me; but, in spite of all their care and skill, my fever increased in violence.

I lent D'Aubert three doubloons from out of the belt which the generous Maria Josefa gave me: with these he purchased necessary articles of dress, applied to several of his countrymen, and got employment as a teacher of the French language, and of dancing and fencing. A Frenchman never wants the means of gaining a livelihood in the West Indies, because he can turn his hands or feet to any thing: when all other trades fail, he is sure to find employment in the kitchen — for all Frenchmen are born cooks.

Fernandez called on me during my sickness. I asked him if he wished I should return the whole or a part of the money lent me at St. Thomas's? He replied in the negative; telling me that he had his wants supplied by a Dutch Jew from Surinam.[†] He added, that he wished me to go with him to the Virgin Islands, to which he intended proceeding immediately; but, having consulted my medical attendants, they declared that a voyage in my present state of health would be dangerous.

"Therefore," said Fernandez, "we must separate; as I have just heard news from Bolivar that renders it absolutely necessary I should go instantly to St. Thomas's. You, Arundell, are bound in honour not to return to Columbia in less than four years: long ere that time the Spaniards will be driven from Costa Firmia."[†]

Considering the desperate state in which we had left the Independent forces, I could not help expressing my wonder at Fernandez's confident prediction.

"You do not seem to be aware," replied he, "of the influence of commerce. Spain is fighting for the re-establishment of her old anti-commercial and monopolising system; while the patriots contend, amongst other things, for the freedom of commerce. Hence, the merchants of all the world favour the cause of independence; and the sovereign who is insane enough to oppose them will find their influence more potent than his mercenary million of bayonets and sabres. The time has arrived when battles are to be decided on the Exchange. Believe me, the small bunch of keys in the hands of Rothschild[†] is more potent than the legions of the despot. While Napoleon warred against the bigoted sovereigns of continental Europe, his military genius prevailed; but when, maddened by revenge against England, he attempted to war on commerce, civilisation rose against him, and he fell. His ruin was more owing to his frantic Berlin decree than to the swords of Russia, his reverses at Leipzig, or his defeat at Waterloo."[†]

Fernandez took a friendly leave of me, requesting that, as soon as I should be able, I would join him at St. Thomas's.

My disease, from an intermittent, became a continued fever;[†] from which, after two months' confinement, I recovered sufficiently to walk out.

During my malady, I received the greatest kindness from the good inhabitants of St. George's. I was an utter stranger to them; but, apparently for that very reason, they paid me all the attention in their power. The visits of these kind strangers became so frequent, that my medical friends were obliged to interfere. During my sickness and subsequent convalescence, I wanted for nothing which could be obtained in Demerara. At length I was sufficiently recovered to visit in my turn these kind Anglo-Dutch Samaritans.

The Dutch had originally settled in the upper and more healthy country, but removed down, near to the mouths of the rivers, for no other reason that I could ever find out, but because they discovered Demerara to be as complete a South American Holland as heart could well desire; where swamps, dams, dykes, canals, frogs, and agues, are to be enjoyed in the greatest abundance and perfection.

St. George's is a fine-looking town, but is nearly all built of wood; hence it has been burned down twice every three years, more or less, on an average. The inhabitants are a fine-looking race of people. Their customs are a mixture of those of Holland and England; but I must protest against the general habit they have of drinking *schnaps* (small glasses of Schiedam)[†] early in the morning. In this respect, the people of Dutch Guiana differ from the inhabitants of the British West Indies: the latter, in general, are so abstemious that they seldom get inebriated before dinner, and scarcely ever drink any thing before noon stronger than sangaree, punch, and grog.

The lower orders here speak a jargon, called Poplomento, which is a mixture of Dutch and Spanish.[†]

Until I dined with a Dutch family, I never sufficiently appreciated the humour of Falstaff's comparing himself, when confined in the buck-basket, to a Dutch dish stewed in grease.[†] The cookery of Demerara is far too unctuous for my palate. One dish I must except from this sweeping censure: it is called "pepper-pot."[†] The relish for this, like the taste for olives and Avoceda pears,[†] is only to be acquired by practice — it being by no means a tempting-looking mess; as the reader may judge, when I inform him, it is composed of the refuse of all the edibles from the table, saved from day to day. Like Sir John Cutler's stockings,[†] it (the pepper-pot) is continually changing, but never allowed to wear out. Fish, flesh, fowl, and amphibious viands, are continually added to this everlasting mess, boiled up each day with strong American peppers and casaripe.[82][†] The older the pepper-pot, the more it is relished by the true gourmands of Demerara; insomuch, that I was told Mynheer von ———, when he went to Europe, took with him his ancient iron boiler of pepper-pot, and a sufficient supply of casseum[†] and casaripe to last him during his voyage home and out again. Notwithstanding the want of elegance in this *omnium gatherum*,[†] I can assure the reader that, when the taste for it is once acquired, the thing is exquisite.

My convalescence advancing slowly, I gained strength enough to look about me; when I began thinking of ways and means, and calculating what I had better do before all my money was spent. One morning early, while I was deeply engaged in these ruminations, D'Aubert came to me, and said, that a French sloop of war had come up to St. George's, on board of

---

82. A rich sauce, made from the juice of the poisonous casara root.

which was a distant relation of his, who had informed him, that his (D'Aubert's) elder brother was settled in the colony of Cayenne, and was part proprietor of a fine estate there. He said he was going to see his brother, and persuaded me to accompany him; adding, that he thought I could do better at Cayenne than amongst the low swamps of Demerara.

"At all events," said he, "a voyage thither would do you good, in your present weak state of health.

I consented to this arrangement; with the proviso, that D'Aubert should interest himself with the officers of the French sloop of war, so as to procure me a passage. This he readily did. He paid me the three doubloons I had lent him: with these I augmented my travelling ward-robe, and, having first taken leave of my new-made, but hospitable, friends in Demerara, I embarked on board of Le Moustique sloop of war, bound for Cayenne.

The French officers were gentlemanly men, and behaved in a very friendly manner both towards D'Aubert and myself. We were repeatedly called on to recount the particulars of our escape from Alta Gracia. One of them lent me Duxion Lavayesse's entertaining book on Trinidad and Venezuela.[†] I read it with much interest: firstly, because it was a well-written work; secondly, because I had lately passed through the countries described; and, lastly, because, in the course of my travels, I had met with the author.

When we read a good work, we are generally disposed to think highly of the author; but the perusal of Lavayesse's work would by no means give the reader a true insight to his character; the production being a very laudable one, whilst its author is as infamous as political intrigue, *espi-onage*, and bigamy, or, rather, polygamy, can make him. Picton having detected this man in some nefarious transaction, whilst the latter resided in Trinidad, Lavayesse was obliged to fly to a French colony. Picton declared that, if he ever caught him, he would hang him. Lavayesse heard of this; and, knowing Sir Thomas to be a man of his word, he sailed at once for France, lest the fortune of war should place the island in which he had taken refuge in the hands of the British: he settled in the south of France.

When the English invaded France (in 1814), Lavayesse was snugly located with one of his three wives in a village near Bourdeaux. One fine morning he awoke, and found that, during the night, the British forces had taken possession of the village. A sentry was promenading before his door, of whom he asked, in English, to what division of Wellington's army he (the sentinel) belonged? "General Picton's," replied the soldier.

"*Sacré bleu!*" exclaimed the startled Lavayesse, well remembering the threat of his old enemy, whom, by the by, he had likewise abused in his book. "*Sacré bleu!* has he crossed the Atlantic, Portugal, Spain, and the Pyrenees, to find me out here!"

He mounted his horse, and never stopped till he reached the gates of Paris.

Although the distance between Demerara and Cayenne is trifling; yet, it being a "dead beat," with many adverse currents, we were ten days getting there: however, I did not regret the length of the passage, as the sea air renovated my health, and gave me the appetite of four English ploughmen.

At length we landed in the well-fortified city of Cayenne. The meeting between my companion D'Aubert and his brother was affecting; and, when the former introduced me as a partner of his escape, the elder D'Aubert received me with great cordiality.

I now found myself, for the first time in my life, in a French colony. The slaves of Cayenne are humanely treated; but the laws against free blacks and people of colour are a disgrace to France. Would it be believed that, in a French colony, in 1819, coloured people were forbidden the use of shoes, and that the women of the mixed race were not allowed to wear either bonnets or gowns. Hence the beautiful Mulattesses and Mustezes of Cayenne, out of sheer opposition to these stupid ordinances, used to parade the streets without shoes, according to law, but, at the same, time, with most elegant silk stockings.

Owing to these laws, the French women of colour invented the dress which, in their colonies, is called *à la Capresse*.[†] This consists of a rich and valuable Madras kerchief, tastefully tied round their heads, in lieu of the forbidden cap or bonnet. The strongly contrasted colours of the Madras well harmonise with their dark complexion and brilliant eyes. Instead of the forbidden gown, they wear a *jupe*, of a colour to match with their Madras; over this they wear an apron of *linon*, furnished with little pockets, embroidered and fringed. An elegantly plaited and fringed chemisette, with sleeves reaching but half way to the elbow, confined with massive gold buttons; a heavy necklace, and ear-rings of the same metal, complete their costume; while the bosom is covered with an Indian kerchief. I have often seen beautiful European women dress *à la Capresse* at a masked ball; the costume sets off their persons to admiration.

My health being fully re-established, I spoke to the elder D'Aubert about commencing my medical practice. He immediately introduced me to Doctor de Beau, the principal physician of the colony, as an English physician and surgeon who had escaped from the Spaniards, but who had the misfortune to lose all his papers; amongst which, said D'Aubert, with great seriousness, were at least half-a-dozen medical diplomas from *l'université d'Angleterre*. Having some scruple about telling downright lies myself, I felt most grateful to Guillaume d'Aubert for saving me that trouble, by telling them for me.

Doctor Le Beau expressed his willingness to obtain for me a license to practise in Cayenne; for which purpose, he stated, it was necessary I should pass examination before the medical committee.

"I presume, sir," inquired I, "the examination will be conducted in Latin?"

"No, sir," replied the doctor, "in French: you seem sufficiently to understand our language for that purpose."

I answered in the affirmative; but I perceived that my proposal of being examined in Latin caused the doctor to regard me with a good deal of respect.

Two days after, I waited by appointment on the committee,[†] four in number. Their examination was lengthy, but by no means difficult. It consisted principally of anatomical questions. When they asked me any thing relative to physiology, or the practice of physic, it came in the form of queries as to what was the practice in England; inquiring, in each case, *"Comment fait-on chez vous?"*[†] &c. Yet, on the whole, the examination impressed me with rather a favourable opinion of the medical knowledge of the committee; and, what was more important, I succeeded in creating a similar impression on the committee, who granted me a license to practise medicine and surgery in Cayenne.

After the examination was over, one of the committee informed me that a surgeon of the colony, who had lately died, had left all his books and instruments to his *ménagère*; (this word has, in the French colonies, the same signification with 'housekeeper' in the English islands); and he suggested to me that I might obtain the books and instruments at a reasonable rate from her. I waited on her, and found her a very handsome Musteze woman. She seemed to mourn for her late paramour as sincerely as any widow could. When I entered her humble apartment, she was seated beside a cotton hammock, in which slept her sweet babe; whilst she watched her young orphan, and brushed the flies off with a small tamarind branch.

On informing her of the purport of my visit, she shewed me the books and instruments. The former consisted principally of odd volumes of medical works, and three or four divorced tomes of Voltaire. Their companions had been lent out; and in the colonies no one ever thinks of returning borrowed books. The instruments, although inferior to those I had lost on the Main, were yet positively good, and in complete order. I asked her what she expected for them. She said she would leave the price to me. I offered her one hundred and twenty dollars. This she at once accepted, and with so much gratitude, that I easily perceived she considered that she was overpaid. She exclaimed, as I gave her the money, *"Vous autres Anglais êtes si genereux!"*[†] The poor woman with this sum stocked a little shop, and did very well.

I took up my quarters on D'Aubert's plantation, which was near the city; and, there being few medical men, and much sickness, I soon got into extensive practice.

CHAPTER 39.

—— "But, chief of all,
Oh, loss of sight! of thee I must complain;
Blind amongst enemies. Oh, worse than chains,
Dungeon, or beggary, or decrepid age!"
                    SAMSON AGONISTES.†

"Three civil brawls, bred of an airy word."
                    ROMEO AND JULIET.†

Walking along the city one day, I perceived a negro boy leading a blind old man, with long white locks hanging on his cape and over his shoulders. The old man stopped to take a pinch of snuff, when, the careless lad's attention being attracted by two dunghill cocks, who were fighting for their own amusement on the opposite side of the way, he crossed over to see the battle. The blind man missed his guide, and called out, "Jean Louis, where are you?"

The boy's attention being engaged, he did not reply. The old man again called the lad, when the boy answered, in Creole-French, *"Mi moi ici, monsieur"* (I am here, sir); but still stood looking at the cocks. The blind man got into a furious passion, and attempted to cross the street.

At that moment, a cart, loaded with coffee, and dragged by three mules, was trotting down the street. The negro carter was (no unusual event) asleep on the shaft. Perceiving the old creature's danger, I sprang forward, and caught him up in my arms just in time to prevent his being run over. I then carried him under a kind of piazza.

When informed of the situation from which I had rescued him, the old man thanked me, and offered me a pinch of snuff. I was surprised at observing on the lid of his box a portrait of Robespierre.

"But," said the old man, "where is that *polisson*,† Jean Louis?"

"I am here," said the careless lad; but, at the same time, keeping out of the reach of his master's gold-headed cane.

"Where are you?" again exclaimed the sightless man.

"I am here," said the little blackguard, crouching beside a large bale of cotton.

The old man stepped forward, and groped about where the voice appeared to come from, till he caught hold of a corner of the bale, which he mistook for a part of the dress of his careless guide. Uttering a countless number of *"Sacré tonneres!"* &c., he commenced beating the cotton-pack. Between each blow, the young rascal called out, "Pardonne, Monsieur Victor!"

Had the boy really received the blows which the blind man intended for him, every bone in his body must have been broken: the old gentleman seemed in a most vindictive mood. At length, he ceased beating from sheer want of breath, when the lad seized him by the sleeve, and began leading him away.

"Where," inquired the blind man, "is the person who saved my life?"

On stepping to him, he said, "I thank you, citizen — I mean, monsieur; and I shall ever be grateful."

I replied, that I had done no more than the most common act of humanity; to have neglected to have acted so would have been to have stamped me as a monster.

"Monsieur," said he, "vous êtes veritable Français."

"Je suis Anglais, monsieur," I replied.[†]

"Monsieur," rejoined he, "I honour your country." He took off his little old-fashioned cocked hat, and said, "Give me your hand."

I did so.

"Come," said he, "you must go with me to my *château*.[†] I respect the English: although, as a patriot, it was for years my duty to act against them, yet I honour them, because they were the first who shewed modern Europe the example of bringing a royal tyrant to justice. You behold in me a poor, blind, and despised old man; but, in my day, I have made some noise in the world, and history will do me justice. Like your great Milton, I have fallen on evil days.[†] Still am I the hater of kings, kingcraft, and priestcraft."

Wishing to know who this old man was, who modestly compared himself to Milton, I inquired whom I had the honour of addressing?

"Victor Hugues," said he, drawing himself up with much pride.

Gracious God! I had rescued and shaken hands with the Robespierre of the Antilles[†] — the infamous, the sanguinary Victor Hugues! — to whose machinations I owed the death of one, perhaps both, of my parents.

"How are the mighty fallen!"†

I had lived to see the butcher of thousands of prisoners of war — the man who, when governor-general of the French West Indies, struck terror through the Caribbean Islands. I had lived to behold him a helpless object of compassion — the sport, the mockery, of a wretched negro boy.

So great had this man's power been in the West Indies, that he was able to set the French Convention at defiance; and he kept possession of the government of Guadaloupe in their despite, until he was displaced by stratagem, and sent to rule Cayenne. With a part of his ill-gotten wealth he purchased a valuable estate here; and when, in 1809, that colony surrendered to the British, Captain Yoe, with that spirit of criminal lenity for which the English are laughed at by foreigners, allowed Victor terms of honourable capitulation, and sent him to France.† There, even Napoleon, who subsequently sanctioned the atrocity of Davoust at Hamburgh, was, or pretended to be, shocked at the murders and robberies of Hugues; but, in conformity with his usual policy, he judged it better to make him disgorge the greater part of his plunder than to bring him to a public trial. For some years he lived despised in his native country. At the first restoration of the Bourbons he returned to Cayenne, where he still possessed his estate. Afflicted by unhonoured age and blindness, his house was still the rallying point of all the discontented Jacobins who voluntarily went, or for their crimes were sent, to French Guiana. Here he lingered until 1826. Few men's lives were better formed

"To point a moral, and adorn a tale."†

But I anticipate. On his announcing himself as Victor Hugues, I felt a shudder as though I had been handling an old fangless rattlesnake. With a sudden effort I disengaged myself from the bloody hound, and involuntarily uttered the word "Villain!" in a suppressed voice. I articulated the expression by surprise; for who, in calmness, could have used harsh language to one so fallen? but the old revolutionist caught the word, and understood my sudden action. He turned his face towards me — his sightless orbs glared around — all his features were writhed into a most savage expression; and the last disciple of Robespierre stood revealed. He muttered something in the Marseilles patois, the meaning of which I could not catch, and then whispered something to the boy. I left him, but perceived that the little negro followed me, while his old master waited under the piazza.

The next afternoon, going on board an American schooner, to attend two seamen who were ill of the intermittent fever, the captain — a tall, slender Kentuckian, called Ezekiel Coffin — said he was going on shore to play a match at billiards with a French officer. As he knew not a word of French, he begged me to meet him at the billiard-room, to act as interpreter. This I promised to do; and at the appointed hour (six o'clock) I was there.

Coffin's opponent belonging to a regiment of the garrison, the room was rather crowded with French officers: amongst these were several disappointed soldiers out of commission. Many of these were existing at Cayenne, and were called by the liberal inhabitants, 'vieux moustaches;' but by the royalists they were denominated, 'Napoleon's last-stake ruffians.' I observed, after I entered the room, that Victor Hugues' boy was there. He whispered to one of these 'old moustaches,' and, pointing to me, quitted the room.

Coffin was an over-match for his opponent, and was eleven points a-head, when a disputed stroke occurred, which created some discussion. I was appealed to by Coffin as interpreter, and by the other party as a judge; but I declined interference in the latter capacity, stating that I had no knowledge of the game. The officer to whom the negro lad had whispered stepped up to me, and said, in a rude manner, "Sir, you know the game well enough, but do not wish to give your opinion, because it is against your friend."

I pledged my honour that such was not the case.

"Your honour!" said he, with an insulting look, "the honour of a Monsieur *Ros-boeuf et pomme de terre!*"[†]

It was evident that this man wished to pick a quarrel with me. I resolved to do all I consistently could to baulk his amiable intention; so I pretended not to hear his insult. Meanwhile, the majority of the company decided (very unjustly, I have been told) that the game should be recommenced. It was so; and my friend Ezekiel beat his opponent with ease, and afterwards challenged any one in the room to play for one hundred dollars a game. But no one would take up the gauntlet; so we adjourned to another room, and, calling for a bottle of claret and cigars, we commenced drinking, conversing, and smoking.

Scarcely were we comfortably seated at our wine and cigars, when the rude officer entered the room. He advanced towards me, and said, "I hate the smell of tobacco."

"Many persons," replied I, coolly, "have the same antipathy;" and I continued my conversation with the American captain. This provoked the Frenchman, who added, "I have said I hate the smell of tobacco: I must add, sir, I also detest those who use cigars."

It was evident I could not escape a quarrel with this man, without the appearance of cowardice. So I replied, "Perhaps, sir, you have not an equal hatred to the smell of powder, nor a similar detestation against those who use pistols."

"There, sir," rejoined the Frenchman, "you have divined aright. I delight in the smell of powder, and in those who have courage to draw a trigger. Are you of the number, Monsieur *Goddem?*"

"I am an Englishman — I hope I have answered your polite interrogation; if not, I must add, that I am an early riser."

"Will you rise early enough to meet me at the pasture of St. Louis's plantation to-morrow morning at seven o'clock, with pistols, Monsieur *Pomme de terre?*"

"I will not fail to be there, Monsieur *Soup-maigre.*"

"Enough, sir," said the Frenchman, and he left us.

Coffin's ignorance of the French language prevented his understanding what had taken place; so I explained it to him. He volunteered to stand my second, and to lend me a pair of good American pistols.

It was now past eight o'clock, and the gates of the city were closed: we were, therefore, constrained to remain at the tavern. I slept little that night; for thoughts of religion, and of Maria Josefa, would intrude on my mind. I felt I acted wrong in acceding to the wish of a ruffian, who, it was evident, had endeavoured to insult and irritate me into a duel. But when I recollected that the high-spirited señora would doubtless despise me were I to conduct myself like a poltroon, I became somewhat reconciled to my conduct.

Just as the gun fired, at five the next morning, Ezekiel left me, went on board his vessel, and brought me a plain, but very good, case of pistols. They were not hair-triggers, but went off very easily; and their barrels were remarkably true: this I found on firing at a mark.

A few minutes before seven we were at the place of appointment, when we perceived a concourse of persons approaching us. I was about to retire, but perceived the mob was headed by St. Foix, the officer whom I came to meet. He advanced towards me, and, presenting to me a slender, genteel-looking French officer, said, "Permit me to introduce to you Major Dumoulin, who will act as my friend on this occasion."

I wondered at St. Foix bringing with him so many persons to witness that which, amongst the English, is generally conducted in secrecy. I, however, announced to Coffin the office of Dumoulin. Unfortunately, it happened that the seconds could not understand each other's language; so I was obliged to perform the part of interpreter between them.

"The captain proposes," said Dumoulin, "that you fight a *volunteer*."

Neither Coffin nor myself knew what the Frenchman meant by fighting a volunteer. The major explained that, in the French colonies, what is called a volunteer, is, placing the combatants at the distance of twelve paces, arming each with a loaded pistol, and a quantity of ammunition. At a given signal the fight commences; each discharging his pistol as soon as he chooses, and loading and firing as fast as he is able, until one of the parties fall. This method of fighting, with some variations, has now become common in Martinique, Guadaloupe, Cayenne, and St. Lucie.

Coffin expressed his surprise at the proposed method: "But," said he, "I guess it's the custom of the place; and so, doctor, 'when we're in Turkey, we must do as the Turks do.'

We were soon prepared with loaded pistols, and stood at twelve paces.

"Commence," said Dumoulin.

This was the signal agreed on. St. Foix, fearing, perhaps, that I should get the first shot at him, discharged his pistol too quickly — a common fault with young duellists: the ball passed several inches in front of me. He then commenced to reload. I had reserved my fire; feeling confident I should have no occasion to load a second time. I aimed at giving him a flesh-wound in the upper part of the thigh. Well knowing that I could hit the centre of a card at ten paces, I doubted not that I could send a ball through any given inch of the body of a man at twelve yards; without recollecting that a card is easier hit than a man — because, the former not being able to return your fire, your nerves are much steadier. I levelled, and pulled the trigger. My ball struck my antagonist, but hit him more than a foot above the place I aimed at: it entered into the hip-bone, and inflicted a wound of a very serious nature. As the smoke cleared off, I saw the late insolent St. Foix groaning, kicking, and writhing on the ground.

I joined the surgeon of the garrison in examining the wound. We noted the direction of the ball, and both shook our heads. A hammock had been provided, in which St. Foix was placed, and he was immediately borne off the ground by two negroes.

Coffin and myself were about moving off, when Dumoulin accosted me thus: "Monsieur, you seem to be an excellent shot: will you allow me the pleasure of trying my skill against yours in using the pistol?"

"I am not," replied I, "in the habit of firing on those with whom I have no quarrel."

"But, sir," rejoined the major, "if you knew how it would gratify me, I am sure a gentleman of your politeness would not refuse me the felicity of exchanging a shot or two."

"Well, sir, to gratify you, let us load."

Load we did. The major stood on the same spot where his principal, but a few minutes previously, was placed I took up my old position as near as I could guess, for we did not measure the ground. I wished to give Dumoulin the precedence in firing, but he desired me to take the first shot. We paused. At length I said, "Will you please to fire?"

"*Après vous*, monsieur," replied the major, with the greatest politeness.

In fact, had we been brothers, and our pistols charged with corks instead of balls, we could not have conducted the matter with greater *bien-séance*.[†]

Finding neither of us was willing to fire first, I proposed to toss up a franc-piece for the first shot. I did so, and lost. We resumed our distance. The major elevated his pistol too much. I perceived this, and, before he fired, called out, "Too high — lower your aim, sir."

He fired as he aimed, and the ball passed through my Leghorn hat, near enough my head to touch my hair.

"I told you you were too high, major."

"Your shot," said he, "will be a better one, I presume."

"Let me try," I rejoined. At the same time I discharged my pistol, and struck him six inches below where I shot St. Foix. The ball entered the muscles, but, being turned off by the bone, made one of those extraordinary routes which pistol-balls will sometimes take. It made a semi-circle of one-half of the major's body, tearing its way between the muscles and the bones. The wounded man staggered — drew his breath through his closed teeth with a hissing sound, but uttered neither complaint nor groan. He soon steadied himself, and recommenced loading; but, before he had well got the powder into the barrel, he again staggered, fell, and fainted.

I was now in hopes that the day's work was over; but, as I was again moving off with Coffin, a grenadier officer, of ferocious aspect, exclaimed,

"*Restez f——!*[†] You shall also shoot me, or I will avenge the death of my comrades."

He added much abuse, which I need not repeat. I, for the third time, loaded my pistol most unwillingly, to fight another "volunteer." Again was the word, "*Commencez,*" repeated. I again wished to give my opponent precedence. He deliberately took aim — I fairly saw into the barrel of his pistol. He wished to be sure of his mark, therefore delayed too long to pull the trigger. This is a defect in duelling, almost as bad as firing too quickly: keeping the arm extended for some seconds renders it nervous and unsteady, so that, when the trigger is pulled, the hand is jerked. I observed that the more the grenadier officer attempted to steady his hand, the stronger its tremor became. He paused for several seconds. The torture of standing in such a situation, with a mortal enemy deliberately aiming at my life, became most insupportable. My anxiety grew into rage: a sudden Cain-like thought flashed on my mind. To conceive and to execute vengeance, with my proficiency at aiming, and with a loaded pistol in my hand, was the work of one and the same instant. I fired, and struck my opponent right over the region of the liver. This jerked his arm — his ball went several feet above my head — he gazed wildly around, uttered a deep groan, and fell on the earth. The looks of the bystanders indicated that he was mortally wounded.

"I calculate," said Coffin, "they'll let you alone now."

His calculation was fallacious: several voices called out for satisfaction and for vengeance; but all proposed to fight with the small sword.

"Be it so," said I; "I can only fight one at a time. Choose your weapons." I added, in English, to Coffin, "They want my life, and I'll sell it dearly."

"That's right," answered the American; "make hard bargains to the last. Just our way in old Kentuck."

My readiness in acceding to fight with the small sword made several hang back; but, under pretence of sending to the garrison for a pair of swords, some delay took place, during which, as I afterwards learned, the following manoeuvre was put in practice. There was in the fort a corporal, who was considered the best swordsman in the colony. A friend of the man I had last wounded ran to him hastily, and briefly told the corporal what had taken place; offering him two louis,[†] and his interest to obtain him promotion to a halbert,[†] if he would fight me. The corporal readily consented, but remarked that I, being an Englishman, might object to fight with a *sous-officier*.[†] To obviate this, an officer's coat, far too tight for him, was procured; and he came thus dressed on the field, with a pair of small swords: of these he offered me the choice.

From my boyhood I was an excellent fencer, and at this period was in good practice, as I used to take a bout at the foils every day with the younger D'Aubert; so that I felt as confident of success with the sword as the pistol — and in mortal combat, confidence, to use a homely phrase, is "half the battle."

I cast a glance at my opponent. He seemed a well-made young man, but his appearance was injured by his epauletted coat, which, I have before said, was far too small for him. Having on only a light nankeen jacket, I did not strip for the encounter, but merely turned up my sleeves.

"Pull off your coat, François," said several officers to the corporal. He took it half off; but, by this act, the French soldier discovered a very ragged shirt. He hastily put it on again.

"Take off your coat," again exclaimed several friendly voices.

"Never," said the man, in an under-tone, which, however, I overheard; "never will I allow the English *coquin*[†] to laugh at the ragged shirt of a French soldier."

The poor fellow's honest, yet ridiculous national pride, was at once ludicrous and pathetic.

The encounter commenced. My opponent handled his weapon well, but I had several advantages over him. Firstly, his unfortunate tight coat acted considerably against him, by restraining the free use of his arm. Secondly, he expected that I was a novice in the use of the sword, and treated me with contempt, until a prick on the upper part of his right arm convinced him that I understood the use of my weapon. Lastly, I had the advantage in length of arm. I acted almost wholly on the defence, till he longed out too far. I parried his thrust, returned it with a feint, and pricked him in the breast with a *coup de seconde*.[†] This was merely a flesh wound, but it made the corporal lose his temper. He tilted at me with such fury that I could have repeatedly taken his life, but contented myself with giving him a third scratch, as I now felt confident I could master him at pleasure. He had lost much blood — he became furious as he grew weak — he leaped forward at me so quickly, that he nearly plunged his sword through me. But my life was saved by a mere accident. In springing forward he alighted on a mushroom, which made him slip and fall. I lowered my sword as he fell.

"Bravo!" exclaimed twenty voices.

Again the corporal came to the scratch; but he acted with more caution, as several voices called out to him to keep his temper. I now became the assailant; and, after a feint or two, I put in practice a trick which my uncle George had taught me when I was a boy, and which was peculiar to him. It was a manoeuvre by which you get your opponent's sword-point into your own guard; and, with a sudden jerk, not easily learned or described, you disarm your antagonist. The trick succeeded. My opponent's sword flew out of his hands, and he stood at my mercy. He gnashed his teeth, stamped, tore his hair; until, overcome with the violence of his feelings, and the loss of blood, he fainted.

It was evident to the spectators that I could repeatedly have killed him. They looked on me with awe, for I had defeated their best swordsman; yet did they eye me sullenly — afraid to attack me, but most unwilling that I should leave the field with a whole skin.

Suddenly, the two D'Auberts, with a party of Royalists, appeared: for hitherto all the spectators present were of the Jacobin faction; and party-spirit, at this period, in Cayenne, was at a pitch of frenzy.

"Where are the assassins," said the younger D'Aubert, "who have plotted to take the life of my brave comrade, to gratify that rancorous old blind adder, Victor Hugues?"

In an instant the whole cause of the duels stood explained. I now understood why Hugues's negro boy followed me; why he pointed me out to St. Foix, and whispered to him in the billiard-room; and wherefore the latter had fastened a quarrel on me. The fact was, I had mortally offended the old wretch, by uttering the word "villain!" as I left him. He vowed vengeance, and had endeavoured to keep his vow.

In a French colony it is difficult to find an assassin; but duellists have ever abounded in them. All the men I had wounded (save the corporal) were the direct agents of Victor Hugues; the soldier was indirectly in his employ.

On the arrival of the D'Auberts and their party, all was confusion. The most violent language was used on both sides; at least every third word was an oath, and every oath comprised three or four r's, which rattled in the throats of the swearers so roughly, that one would have supposed each of them had swallowed a curry-comb, which was yet sticking in their throats. Each man wished to speak, and none appeared to care about being heard. From nasal speaking, cursing, swearing, struggling, and stamping, they came to boxing, *à la Française;*[†] in which scientific combat the nails were more used than the knuckles.

At length, this furious uproar was put an end to by the intervention of the *gens d'armes,*[†] who had been concealed spectators of the whole affair behind a hedge. They now thought proper to shew themselves, and disperse the combatants.

During the *fracas*, a Frenchman, who had been a prisoner of war in England sufficiently long to learn a little of our language, gave a challenge to Coffin. The American replied that he would fight him; but, as the challenged party, he was entitled to the choice of weapons. He, therefore, proposed to meet the challenger with either rifles or harpoons. The Frenchman called him *un sacre barbare,*[†] and left him.

After this concourse of noisy persons was dispersed by the police, I went to my own apartment, where I was met, and congratulated on my escape, by the poor Mustese woman from whom I had bought the instruments. She it was who had overheard the conspiracy on the part of Victor Hugues, St. Foix, and their associates. She informed the police of what she had overheard, who sent their lazy *gens d'armes* to prevent mischief. They never interfered, as I have shewn, till at the end of the fray. The poor woman also related to D'Aubert the same circumstance; and by his interference, in all probability, my life was saved. The Mustese thought I had acted liberally towards her, and she was grateful.

After she quitted me, I attempted an act of devotion for my signal deliverance; but I found my mind too much weighed down by a sense of guilt for me to pray. I then went on board the American schooner to visit my patients. Here I met Coffin, who advised me to quit Cayenne instantly, as I should always be looked on with hatred by the Jacobin party in that colony. He said that, having met with but a dull sale for his "notions" at Cayenne, he was about to proceed to Trinidad, to which island he would give me a passage. I promised to think of his kind offer, and returned ashore; and, on my arrival, inquired concerning the men I had wounded. I may as well inform the reader at once what became of them.

St. Foix, although lamed for life, lived long after. Dumoulin had the ball extracted, and was well in six weeks. The wounds of the poor corporal were very slight. But the most astonishing casualty was in the case of the furious grenadier officer, whom I had supposed mortally wounded: he had received but a slight hurt. The fact appeared, either I had overloaded or underloaded my pistol. The ball struck him on one of the false ribs: this, yielding to the blow without breaking, saved him from a wound in the liver. The ball, which had scarcely penetrated the skin, was easily removed; the false rib was restored to its former position, and in a week the patient was well. All this I heard at a later period than the one I now write of; at which time I merely learned that the wounded men generally were doing well.

I was hesitating about taking the advice of the American skipper, when the French government saved me the trouble of deciding. The day after my duel, an ordinance was duly published in the colony of Cayenne, and throughout all other French colonies, which prohibited any Englishman from holding real property in any French colony, or from exercising any trade or calling therein, the profits of which amounted to six hundred dollars per annum.

I must beg the reader's permission to say a few words on the subject of this just and liberal law.

At the end of the last war,[†] the standard of England and her allies floated triumphant over the gates of Paris. Every French colony was in possession of the English; and they had been dearly purchased with the blood of thousands of the children of Great Britain, slain in their conquest, and tens of thousands who had perished in keeping them. Yet, at the peace, in the exercise of that spirit of generosity which the English consider magnanimity, but which foreigners deride as sheer folly, our ministers gave back to France, Martinique, Guadaloupe, Cayenne, and the Isle of Bourbon, without any reservation in favour of such British subjects as had embarked large capitals in these colonies, while in possession of England. A few years after this wisely negotiated peace, the French government expelled every Englishman from those islands, and from Cayenne, like convicts, at a few weeks' warning, obliging them to sell their properties for any thing the French colonists chose to give them. Yet, at this same time, Frenchmen were, and still are, in possession of the most valuable properties in Canada, the Isle of France, St. Lucia, and Trinidad; where they contrived, and still contrive, to make fortunes much quicker than Englishmen, and where, in fact, they acted, and still act, as though they were the rightful proprietors of the soil — heading every contemptible faction against the government, and insolently treating the English as mere interlopers. In the colonies last mentioned, the language is more French than English: they will not condescend to learn our barbarous tongue; they always send their children to France, to be educated as Frenchmen, in detestation of Englishmen. *Cochon Anglais*† is the common designation applied to us; and French priests[83] in these colonies are continually preaching damnation to all heretics. Verily, John Bull,† thy designation is only a *nomme de guerre* — in peace thou shouldest be called John Calf.

I gathered in as many of my debts as I conveniently could, took leave of the D'Auberts and one or two of my acquaintances, and embarked, with my books, trunks, instruments, and about four hundred dollars in money, on board the Ark, Captain Coffin, for Trinidad.

---

83. This remark applies, not to Catholic priests in general, but only to the French priests in those colonies.

CHAPTER 40.

"The wild deer and wolf to a covert can flee;
But I have no refuge from sorrow and danger —
A home or a country remains not for me."
CAMPBELL.[†]

I t was afternoon when I went in a canoe on board the Ark. Going towards the vessel, I met the skipper in his gig, pulling ashore. He told me that he could not sail before evening, as his people had to take off some molasses: he had to wait, besides, for five passengers and their servants. Unwilling to return ashore, after being well prepared for my departure, I went on board the schooner.

The only men on board were my two late patients, who were now con-valescent, yet scarcely able for active duty. I went below, and, with the assistance of these men, got my small travelling mattrass into the best berth — using thus the tact and selfishness of an old traveller. Experience may often improve our wisdom, but it seldom amends our morals.

Being somewhat wearied with the exertion of getting ready for my little voyage, I lay down in my berth, took a volume of La Fontaine,[†] and enjoyed that pleasing state a man gets into when reposing from corporeal labour, and tasting the sweets of mental leisure.

About an hour after I came on board, I heard a canoe approach the vessel. I perceived, from the berth I occupied, that a man and a woman came on board. The man spoke in Creole French to the people of the canoe about the price of bringing him on board, when he suddenly said, "Great God, Julia! I have forgotten the rosary that my poor mother gave me: it hangs over the chamber-door; for Heaven's sake return and get it."

After some grumbling, the female consented to return, and she went ashore in the canoe.

The male passenger now addressed the two Americans in French, and asked when the captain would be on board?

"I guess I can't understand your gibberish," said one of the people.

The man now walked aft, and commenced talking to himself; for he seemed one of those who have the infirmity of being obliged to think aloud.

"They speak not French: I must not seem to understand English, or that circumstance might betray me one day or other."

He paused: then said, "Would that we were fairly at sea! I shall never deem myself out of old Victor Hugues' power until I am far from this nest of pestilence; then will the blind wretch who, for twenty-five years, has been my evil genius, be balked of his victim. But should I be discovered at Trinidad! 'Tis scarcely possible; and, at worst, I can but finish this hunted, persecuted being, by taking the dose old Julia has prepared for me. Let the priest say what he will, I will not die the death of a felon, although I may perish like a dog: the gibbet shall never claim my body as a traitor, although Satan may get my soul through my suicide."

I heard the above soliloquy involuntarily: it was evident he who uttered this strange monologue intended it not for other ears, as it was enough to cause him to be looked on as an object of suspicion where he was going. Not wishing to overhear more of his discourse with himself, I left my berth; passed forward between the decks, crawling over the remains of the Ark's cargo of 'notions.' By these means I got before the mast, and came up by the fore hatchway. I then entered into conversation with the two American seaman, while the unknown passenger walked backward and forward on the after part of the deck, muttering to himself. At length, on perceiving me, he desisted from his walk, and sat down on a hen-coop.

I walked aft to salute him, and perceived that I had seen him before ashore; for, once seen, he was too remarkable to be forgotten. He replied to my salute, and seemed to wish to avoid me. I will, however, describe him. He was a man much above the middle stature, very large-boned, or, to use a more appropriate term, raw-boned. Never in my life saw I any one who better deserved the appellation of a 'living skeleton' than my fellow-passenger; he would have been an excellent *subject* for Brookes to give a lecture on osteology. His hair was crisped, but gray: he was, I suppose, a mulatto; but his skin had such a pallid hue, and his visage seemed so cadaverous, that it was not easy to decide from what race or races he was descended. His eyes were vivid, shooting their restless glances around, as if in suspicion; they had that appearance of wildness which I should judge symptomatic of latent insanity; they were protruded, yet surrounded by a deep hollow, as if the bony orbits were too big for his organs of vision. He had a large and remarkably fine set of teeth; these (as his mouth was rather wide) looked conspicuous, and contrasted with his pale lips and lank cheeks, which seemed little more than parchment-like skin. His fine teeth would have ornamented an ordinary set of features, but they added to the ghastliness of his spectral lineaments. His inclination to soliloquy I have already noticed; but when he was listening to another, and thinking of what he should reply, his lips moved as though he practised inaudible speech, if I may be allowed the expression. This reminded me of the action of some people, who, if suddenly asked which is their right hand, cannot reply until they go through the motion of handling a pen.

The female companion of this singular looking being now came on board, and gave him the missing rosary, together with a small bag of relics which many of the old creoles carefully wear round their necks: she called him by the name of Saint Jago.

This woman seemed rather under the middle size; her attitude was erect, her teeth perfect, her skin of glossy blackness, and her eye clear enough to belong to a person who had only attained middle age: yet, on looking closely at her shining bald head, and a hundred minute wrinkles on her forehead and cheeks, any one accustomed to behold those remarkable specimens of longevity which are often met with amongst negroes (especially of Jamaica and Martinique), would pronounce that the old woman was near a hundred years of age. Such, indeed, was the fact; although she seemed as active and healthy as most persons of half her patriarchal years.

Presently, Captain Coffin came off with the molasses he had long been waiting for. Another boat came, with three more passengers and their servants: these consisted of an English gentleman who had settled in Cayenne, but who was obliged to quit the country on account of the late laws; a very beautiful young lady, who was his daughter; and his son. The latter had been sent, at the age of ten, to France, for his education: there he forgot his native tongue, without properly acquiring the French vernacular; hence he now spoke English with a French accent, and pronounced French like an English traveller, who, posting through Europe, obtains enough of French to make himself understood.

The anchor was weighed; we set sail with a fine breeze, and, two days after this, the Ark was making her way amongst the Grenadines.

The sun was setting, as the light schooner careered merrily amongst the islets. As we approached my native land, Grenada, Saint Jago, my mysterious fellow-passenger, who, until this part of the voyage, was always below deck, now came up. Leaning over the bulwarks, he looked intently at the outlines of the island, which now appeared on the edge of the horizon, as it were, mingled with the clouds of the evening. He did not speak; but his lips moved, and he repeatedly sighed. A tear now and then gathered in his wild eye, and rolled down his pallid cheek. Night came on: still this singular man remained fixed in the same position, and as immovable as the figure-head of a ship.

Leaving Saint Jago still on deck, I descended the companion-ladder, and at a late hour went to my berth and slept. I awoke the next morning very early: the moon being full, I mistook its light for twilight, until I came on deck, when I perceived my error; but, being now abreast my native isle, which the vessel was slowly passing, I resolved not to return to my dormitory, but to remain on deck, and get a good view of Grenada as the sun rose. By the light of the moon I again perceived this spectral mulatto, apparently in the very position I left him the previous night. Still were his eyes fixed on the land of my birth. I climbed into the main-top, in order to get a good view of Grenada.

Soon the brief twilight of the tropics mingled with the lunar rays, until, through a congregation of black clouds, fringed with fire, the beams of the sun penetrated. Soon the day-god was fully revealed, and shed his cheerful light on the countless islands. The light breeze freshened, but it was scarcely stronger than was necessary to give the blue waters a ripping motion. The dolphin sported around the shining copper bottom of the schooner; the flying fish skimmed on the surface of the waters, every minute sinking to wet their wings; while the skipjack leaped out of his element, and bathed in air as animals bathe in water.

Beautiful looked Grenada, as we passed it, while the sun and the clouds of the morning gave it all the hues of the humming-bird. I heard Saint Jago again break into a soliloquy, as he still gazed on the land.

"Dearest Grenada!" said this man, "land of my birth, do I once more behold thee! but, alas! I may not again tread thy shores — a felon's death awaits me there. Yet it is something to have my old eyes blessed with the sight of thee. Precious is to thy poor exile the very breeze that blows from off thy healthy mountains and from thy fertile valleys."

Saying this, he opened his arms in ecstasy, as if to embrace the wind that now blew from off the land.

Much of this man's history was now explained to me. It was evident that he was one of those who were obliged to quit Grenada in 1796, on account of the part they took in the civil war amid which I was born. I felt an interest in this singular-looking being, because he was my countryman, and because he loved the island whence he was exiled on account of his errors, or perhaps of his crimes.

The evening of that day the Ark entered the Gulf of Paria, and the next morning we anchored off Port of Spain. A medical officer came off to us, to see if we had any infectious disease on board, according to the laws in such cases. Having heard the skipper address me as doctor, he asked if I was in the medical profession? On my replying in the affirmative, we entered into conversation. He asked me about the state of the faculty,[t] and the prevalent diseases in Cayenne. I went ashore with this new-made acquaintance, and he introduced me to his venerable father, who, being told I was from Cayenne, inquired if Victor Hugues was alive? This naturally led me to give old Dr. A. an account of my encounter with the miserable creature, and of my duels. The doctor listened to my recital with deep interest.

At the beginning of the war which followed the French Revolution, he had been captured and kept on board a prison-ship at Guadaloupe, where he suffered and witnessed incredible cruelty from this now fallen man. In short, in this conversation I gained the friendship of Dr. A.

I now consulted my new-made friend about obtaining a license. I related under what circumstances I left England, under whom I had studied in London, and informed him of my active practice in Columbia and at Cayenne.

"I believe," said Dr. A., "you will not find it difficult to pass the medical board, of which I have the honour of being president, and to which I can introduce you. We meet to-morrow week: in the meantime, if you wish to brush up your medical studies, my library is at your service."

I took the hint, and for a week devoted most of my time to the library of Dr. A.; and on the appointed day presented myself as a candidate for examination before the medical board, which consisted of a president and three members.

The first inquiries of this body were directed to ascertain my knowledge of Latin.[t] This they did not do by putting questions to me in that language; but they placed in my hands Gregory's 'Conspectus,'[†] and asked me to translate a page or two. As it wanted neither a Parr nor a Porson[†] to construe this, I easily made the extempore translation required.

The first question asked of me was by a Dr. Burke, a gentleman of respectable medical attainments, but one who wished to pass himself off for a wit.

"Suppose," said the would-be facetious doctor, "you were called in to attend a patient who was attacked with *typhus icteroides*,[†] and he were to die the second day of your attendance, what would you do?"

"The same as most West Indian medical practitioners would do," was my reply.

"And what is that?"

"Try to make the executors of the deceased pay me for killing him."

This retort on the ill-timed joke of the doctor turned the laugh against him.

I will not repeat the rest of the examination: it consisted of a jumble of questions from the members, on the subjects of surgery, anatomy, physiology, chemistry, the *materia medica*, the practice of physic,[†] and one or two questions about botany. When the members had exhausted their inquiries, the president took me in hand.

I found that Dr. A. possessed the art of sounding the depths and shallows of my medical knowledge in a superior degree to the other three. He had been at one time an examiner in the University of Edinburgh:[†] he had received his education there during the days of its glory; besides this, he boasted thirty years of medical experience in the West Indies. The doctor seemed determined to draw me out: he, however, ceased questioning me, and declared himself satisfied with my proficiency: in this opinion the rest of the board concurred.

The worthy president waited on the governor, and announced that I had been found competent to practise physic and surgery in Trinidad. Sir R. Woodford granted me a license, which was announced in the gazette of the colony.

The town was at this time overstocked with medical men; but one part of the island was much in want of them. From the Great Pitch lake,[†] all the way to the southern extremity of the island, not one physician was to be found to attend the thinly scattered population.

I hired a small, wooden, cottage-looking house, about three miles from the village of La Brea;[†] purchased a horse, and very soon obtained an extensive, but not very lucrative, practice. The fact was, the population in this part of the island only live in detached spots on the sea-border; hence I was often obliged to ride thirty miles to visit a patient. My exertions and labour were severe; but I cared little for this. I had still three years to spend away from Columbia, wherein all my hopes were centred. I counted the days that I was to pass before I could cross over to the Main in search of Maria Josefa, who occupied all my dreams and much of my waking thoughts. Little news from the Main ever reached me, on account of the furious way the war was carried on in Columbia, and the unaccountable hatred of Sir R. Woodford to the cause of South American independence.[†] We in Trinidad, although living in sight of the Main, knew no more of what went on there than we did of the politics of China.

CHAPTER 41.

"The chiefest action of a man of great spirit
is never to be out of action. We should think
the soul was never put into the
body ⋆ ⋆ ⋆ to stand still."
JOHN WEBSTER.[†]

There was one advantage in my present situation. I was kept in continual and in laborious employ by my practice. This supported my animal spirits. He whose body and mind are active seldom becomes melancholy. Had it not been for this circumstance, my four years of hopeless banishment from her who was mistress of my heart would have been intolerable.

My practice was not very lucrative, for the greatest number of my patients were poor people of colour, who had little or no money to pay me. They generally, however, sent me so many presents of fish, poultry, vegetables, and eggs, that I lived well at very little cost. I attended a few plantations by the year, as is the custom in this country; and the profits which I derived from them more than supplied my wants; for, although, as I before said, I never was a good manager in pecuniary matters, yet, on the other hand, I never was extravagant.

I must now relate a circumstance that had considerable influence on my fortunes. The negroes in Trinidad were, generally, well treated. This I attributed to the prevalence of the Spanish law, beyond comparison the most humane for the government of slaves of any ever devised; but I need scarcely add, that, in spite of the most humane laws, from the nature of slavery the bondsman's situation must depend on the disposition of his master or manager. Many have asserted, that all who govern negro slaves in the colonies are monsters. This absurdity is believed by the mass of the people of England; while those who attempted to defend the abominable system of West India slavery, pretend that instances of cruelty never occur. Those who manage slaves have immense power over their happiness; and human power never did, never can, exist without being abused. Great violence has been shewn by the condemners and approvers of colonial slavery: I think, however, it will be found that the crimes of slave-owners, in general, have been exaggerated; but that the system itself was not, in fact could not, be too loudly condemned. Such are my opinions of slavery;† which are necessary here to be stated, in order that the following circumstances may be understood.

There was a plantation near my dwelling, owned and managed by a foreigner, of the name of Jacopo. One day, as I was riding by the beach between my house and his plantation, I perceived a wretched negro lying on the sand and moaning. I dismounted to learn what was the matter with the poor creature. I found him suffering under the disease called *mal d'estomac*, and from the effects of a most unmerciful flogging, which appeared to have been recently inflicted. I never saw a man's skin so terribly torn. Perceiving, from the symptoms of the man, that he was in an alarming state, I called to two fishermen, who, for a small sum of money, conducted the miserable slave to my dwelling. Here I dressed his lacerated back, and gave him a little wine and other restoratives; for medicine the patient could not take. I asked him who was his master? He told me it was Jacopo. The slave then related to me occurrences of atrocity perpetrated by this man, which horrified me. I should scarcely have believed all this, but for three corroborative circumstances. Firstly, Jacopo never suffered either myself or any other medical man to visit his estate; secondly, the frequent deaths which occurred on his plantation were suspicious; and, thirdly, the appearance of the miserable object relating these acts of atrocity, who was evidently in the last stage of *mal d'estomac*, and yet had received that day a flogging sufficient to endanger the life of a healthy man.

"What shall I do with this poor creature? It would be inhuman to send him to his master," apostrophised I aloud.

The negro heard this, and rose from the pallet on which I had placed him. He looked at me, and said, "No, no, good massa doctor; no send me to cruel massa; let me die here, and I will pray God Almighty to bless you with my dying word."

To have returned the man to his remorseless master would have been an act of the greatest inhumanity. I immediately wrote a note, explaining the situation of the slave, to the commandant (for so the magistrates of Trinidad were called), and ordered my servant to mount my horse and ride there: but on his way I told him to call on two of my neighbours, and urge their immediate attendance at my residence; for I felt assured that the poor creature had not long to live. When my servant left me, the African's fatal symptoms increased rapidly; his dark skin turned to a livid paleness, his eyes rolled wildly, his pulse became weak and irregular, his hands and feet were as cold as marble, and he closed his eyes. Hopeless, I poured a little burnt brandy into his mouth: he rejected it, but opened his eyes, looked wildly at me, and said, "Is that you, good doctor? God bless — bless you!"

After this, the fatal symptoms increased, and the death-rattle sounded in his throat.

My servant had now been gone sufficiently long to return from his errand: but it appeared the commandant was on a visit to town; and, to the disgrace of the local government be it spoken, this island possesses no coroner. At length I perceived my servant riding along the coast, followed by three persons mounted: these I soon made out to be the two friends I had sent for, and Jacopo. The latter walked into my hall in a furious passion, followed by my two neighbours. He was a remarkably dark man for an European, and wore ear-rings. He addressed me with great wrath in French, which he spoke badly, and with a singing Italian accent. The following dialogue took place.

"How dare you encourage my runaway negroes in your house?"

"I am not in the habit of being addressed so abruptly; and when *gentlemen* come into my house, they take off their hats. But to your questions: your slave was not a runaway. I found him on the beach in a state of exhaustion, and had him carried into this house."

"And how dared you to interfere between me and my slaves? Surely I may do what I like with my own slaves. I *will* do so, in spite of every Englishman in the island, and of the rascally English government, who wish to plunder me of my property."

"If I am rightly informed, Mr. Jacopo, you came sixteen years ago to this island, with a pedlar's pack, from Martinique: you, I have been told, now possess a barrel of dollars and doubloons. I do not mention your former poor state to hurt your feelings, but only to remind you that, in common prudence, you ought not to abuse the government in whose territory you have raised yourself, in a few years, from beggary to wealth."

"You shall answer for this abuse, doctor. But I have come for my slave Quashé; he is in this house, and I will have him — he is my property."

"He will scarcely be worth the trouble of being carried home, sir, as a piece of property."

"Being carried home! the villain shall walk home, and I'll horsewhip him every step of the way. I insist on seeing my negro."

"Behold him!" exclaimed I: at the same time I threw open the inner door of my apartment, and pointed to the corpse of the murdered wretch, as it lay on the pallet, with the visible marks of having died from ill treatment upon him. "Behold your property!"

The two spectators of this scene recoiled with horror. Jacopo turned blue in the face as he beheld the remains of the victim of his cruelty. I pointed to my door, and motioned him to quit my house, as I regretted I had not the means of arresting him. He did not obey my directions, but, after a pause, commenced abusing me in the most outrageous manner in Italian; a language which, although I could read and understand, I could not speak.

"Quit my house, sir!" exclaimed I. He used his scurrilous language with redoubled violence, employing every oath in his native tongue; and few languages have such a variety of imprecations as that of Italy. Hitherto my indignation was so intense, that it restrained my ire; but his persisting in refusing to leave my apartment, together with his scurrility, made me break out into open rage. I seized the scoundrel by the shoulder, and exclaiming, "Quit my house, murderer!" I flung him from me with such fury that he went through my door, and fell against a kind of wooden railing. This gave way to the velocity with which I threw him, and he rolled down a hill on which the house stood. Recovering himself, he recommenced his abuse; until, perceiving I was again advancing on him, he mounted his horse, and galloped along the beach towards his own plantation.

I now opened and made a *post-mortem* examination of the body before my two friends; and, it being impossible to keep it much longer, I caused it to be as decently interred as circumstances would admit of.

I then hired a fishing-boat, in which I went to town, and distinctly related all that had occurred to the governor. His excellency thanked me for the promptitude and zeal I displayed in the matter; sent me to the attorney-general, who took down my deposition, to which I swore; and a warrant was despatched by the alguazil mayor to apprehend Jacobo.

Unfortunately, the movements of the alguazil mayor were conducted with too little secrecy. He embarked on his duty in a sloop; but the friends of Jacopo, having got information of what was going on, despatched a shore-boat with information to him. The alguazil mayor's vessel was becalmed, and therefore the boat got down eight hours before him. Jacopo hired a French smuggling vessel from Martinique, to carry him off the colony. He passed through the Serpent's Mouth, taking with him his barrel of money and the execration of his slaves.

As this affair was never allowed to appear in the newspaper of the island, how the account of it got to England I never could discover; but this I know, that, four months after, I received a franked letter[†] from the secretary of the Anti-slavery Society,[†] thanking me for having brought to light the cruelty of Jacopo, and requesting me to give him information on a number of subjects respecting slavery in Trinidad. He begged me to answer a whole list of queries; and, by way of a postscript, the secretary added, that the society would gladly reimburse me for any expenses I might be at in obtaining the information required.

I saw through the real purport of this letter: it was merely offering me a bribe to become a spy on the community amongst which I lived. I wrote to the secretary in reply, that I did not like to become a member of either the anti-slavery or pro-slavery party; that, with regard to the affair of Jacopo, I had only done my duty, and hoped I should always act the same way, should I be placed in similar circumstances; further, that, although I knew a spy to be a *necessary* evil, yet it was an *evil*, and that, as a gentleman, I abhorred taking on myself so mean an office: finally, I begged to decline further correspondence.

After writing this letter, I sealed, directed it; and sent it to town by a drogher, requesting the master of the vessel to put it in the post-office. Here I did wrong: I should have taken the letter to town myself; for the captain, an illiterate man, instead of putting my letter in the post-office, sent it, with twenty other letters for town, into the news-room (there is no internal post-office in Trinidad): it lay there for two weeks, exposed on the table to the gaze and speculation of all the violent pro-slavery gentlemen that visit it. Inquiry was set afoot: the letter was found to have come from me, and instantly I became a man suspected of corresponding with the enemy. No one would touch the letter. Had it come from a land of pestilence, it could not have been more avoided; until a half-pay officer, who was settled in the island, took it to the post-office. This gentleman was a violent anti-slavery partisan; but he was a man of so uncontrollable a temper, was so imprudent, and had such a total disregard for truth, that he would have hurt the most righteous cause that ever existed. When attacks were made on my character, he inflicted an injury on me by attempting my defence. He said he was my friend; that I was right to expose the horrors of the present system; that I was a man of first-rate courage and talent; and that, in a short time, I would make the 'slavers' tremble at my name. This person's defence of me injured me much. Although I never spoke to the man in my life, I knew not these circumstances for a month after this event, but then I found them out to my cost.

All this suspicion and misrepresentation might have been avoided, had I myself placed the letter in the post-office. Our duty to our neighbours forbids our doing wrong; our duty to ourselves bids us avoid the *appearance* of doing wrong.

CHAPTER 42.

"Were the seconds as averse to shedding blood as the principals,
duels would be less fatal than they generally are."

LACON.†

A few days after sending this letter, I was called one morning to endeavour to restore animation to a boy that was apparently drowned. After
nearly exhausting all the methods used on such occasions, I had the happiness of succeeding in resuscitating the youth. I ordered him to bed; told
the people in attendance what to do, and returned to my house. I found
there, waiting for me, a gentleman named Powel. He asked to speak with
me in private. I took him into my chamber, and he opened his commission. It appears a Mr. Naysmith, a friend of his, had got into a quarrel with
a Mr. Smith, after having dined together at Powel's house. The cause of
this important dispute was this: as the wine circulated, the parties indulged
in that ill-natured kind of raillery called quizzing.† Naysmith said to Smith,
that "he would not have such a name as Smith had, for it indicated that his
ancestor who gave name to the family must have been a blacksmith."

"Very true," replied Smith, "he was so; and your great-grandfather was
his apprentice. But my ancestor found yours such a dunderheaded fellow,
that, after serving six years with him, the master kicked the apprentice out
of his shop, telling him that he was so stupid that, do what he could, he
would be *nae smith*. This is the cause of your family's name of Naysmith."

Would it be believed, that this most ridiculous pun on a man's name
brought on a quarrel — a challenge — and was likely to terminate in a
duel? I being the only medical man in the quarter, Powel called on me, by
consent of both parties, to offer me one hundred dollars if I would attend
on the ground as surgeon.

"You, Mr. Powel, are the friend of Mr. Naysmith: who is the friend of
Smith?"

"Mr. *Smithson*," replied Powel.

"Enough smiths on this occasion," rejoined I, "to stand a hammering: no doubt they will not flinch from *fire*. Where is to be the place, and what the hour of meeting?"

"The parties are to meet," said Powel, "at the back of the old boiling-house[†] on Sheddock-grove estate, at five this evening."

"Enough, sir; I will be there."

With this assurance the second quitted me.

Left to myself, I began to consider on the affair seriously. Here were two young men about to try to take each other's lives, on account of a quarrel too ridiculous even for laughter. I put both parties and their seconds down as fools, but I often found that fools could fire good shots. On the whole, I conceived it to be my duty to apply secretly to a magistrate of the quarter, Mr. Pennyfeather, and get the parties bound to keep the peace. I rode to the estate of that gentleman, who lived about a mile from my residence. His mansion stood off the ground, elevated on hard wood posts, so that a carriage might be driven under the floor of his dwelling. As I approached this Trinidad Temple of Themis,[†] a paper was blown out of the window, and into my face. As it was not sealed, I had the curiosity to look at this document. It commenced thus: "Personally appeared before me, Richard Pennyfeather, magistrate, myself, Richard Pennyfeather, esquire, planter, who, being duly sworn," &c. &c. The fact is, the worthy Mr. Pennyfeather swore to an affidavit before himself, taking the oath as a planter, swearing himself, and duly authenticating the paper as a magistrate.[†] This stray paper gave me no idea of the wisdom of Mr. Pennyfeather.

I walked up the steps of his wooden house, and entered the hall. Here the magistrate was seated at a large cedar table, dressed in his *robe de chambre*.[†] On his head was tied a madras kerchief, and he wore slippers; one ear was uncovered, in order to allow it to support a pen. He had a round contented face, which he did all he could to compose into magisterial solemnity. He appeared —

"As who should say, I am Sir Oracle,
And when I ope my lips let no dog bark."[†]

His table was covered with papers. On it were placed, 'Johnston on the Law of Spain,'[†] and a prayer-book, with two stripes of blue paper, in the form of a cross, pasted on one side of it, for the benefit of such Catholics as wished to be sworn. He sat in an arm-chair, with one leg thrown over the side, dispensing justice; or, rather, dispensing with justice, in true West Indian style. I gave him the affidavit which the wind had blown out of the window. He thanked me, placed a lead on it, and proceeded in listening to a charge of assault. The particulars of this I will relate.

An assistant to the alguazil mayor having a writ of execution against an inhabitant of the quarter, he went to meet him, after the latter had dined and wined. The defendant refused to pay the debt, give up a levy,[84] or to go with the officer. The latter, after vainly remonstrating, proceeded to enforce his writ by tapping the defendant on the shoulder, when the debtor knocked the marshal's-man down. Two or three friends, being present, now interfered, and paid the amount of the writ; but the officer sought justice before the magistrate on account of that assault. The facts were fully proved, and not denied by the defendant, who only alleged that the officer came at an improper hour; as he should not disturb people after dinner.

"Very improper conduct on the part of the marshal's-man: besides, Mr. What's-your-name, you began the assault," said the magistrate.

"I began the assault?" replied the officer, — "how so?"

"Why, you tapped him on the shoulder."

"But, sir, this was not an assault; I did this in virtue of my writ: it authorises me to arrest the defendant, unless he pays the money, or gives up some property to be levied on. Here is the writ of the Complaint Court."

At this the magistrate did what no magistrate should do — he got into a passion.

"D——n the Complaint court and its proceedings! let it take care of its own officers. I have nothing to do with it or its writs. Why, it was only last May that the judge of the Complaint Court gave forty dollars damages to a free black woman, who brought an action of false imprisonment against me, for having sent her to gaol for a month on a charge of *high treason*. Judge Warner not only released the woman the first day she was imprisoned, but gave her forty dollars damages — for all she was proved to have been guilty of *treason*, having said that she hoped to see the day when the negroes would be white, and the white people black! I hate the very name of the Complaint Court. No, no, no! Mr. Thingumy; you began the assault, by tapping the defendant on the shoulder; and, if he knocked you down, he was justified, in self-defence. That's my decision."

---

84. In Trinidad, the marshal is entitled, by writs of execution, to take body or goods.

The poor assistant alguazil mayor was feign to submit. As he was leaving the hall, he said to himself, —

"A time there was, that, when the brains were out, the man would die."

"What's that you say?" asked the magistrate, — "you'll knock my brains out?"

"No," replied the officer; "that's utterly *impossible*." And he left the room.

The magistrate being now disengaged, I asked and obtained a private interview. I informed him that Messrs. Smith and Naysmith were about to fight a duel, and requested that he, as a magistrate, would put the parties under an arrest, and bind them over to keep the peace.

"To tell you the truth, doctor," said the justice, "I do not like to put any body under arrest, since Judge Warner made me pay forty dollars and all costs for imprisoning a woman for *high treason*. I only committed her for one month; but the judge said I committed myself. However, can you swear they are going to fight?"

"No, sir," said I; "but I will swear that I believe, if not prevented, they will fight."

"But," said this Solomon, "I can't arrest people on belief."

"Well, then," said I, "I will swear that *I suspect* that they intend a breach of the peace."

"Intend a breach of the peace! Don't you know, doctor, that the laws never nourish *intentions*? If you will swear positively that the fight will take place, I will send a warrant to arrest them; but not else."

"But consider," rejoined I, "no mortal, ungifted with prophecy, can swear that an event will take place. Beside, Mr. Pennyfeather, if I could positively swear that they were predestined to fight, I could also swear that you could not prevent the battle, and my applying to you would be folly."

"I care not for your argument about predestination, for I am no predestinarian: all I can say is, if you won't swear positively that the parties will fight, I will have nothing to do in the matter until after the duel has taken place; and then I will be sure to be right."

"Their blood be upon your hands!" said I, and left him. Verily, the breed of Dogberries and Verges will never be extinct: they are as common now as in the days of Shakespeare, and are as rife in the colonies as they were at Messina.†

As there was no other magistrate within twenty miles of me, I despaired of putting a stop to the duel by the interposition of the law. I might prevent some injury by going to the ground, but could do no good by remaining away. Hence I had my instrument left at a house near where the duel was to take place, and took with me a pocket-case and two tourniquets. I arrived on the spot about a minute after the time appointed, and found the parties ready, and waiting for me. Naysmith and Smith seemed two good-looking men, of not more than twenty-six years of age. They, within a few years of this time, had been taken from the plough-tail in their own country; but, having got to be managers of estates, they were resolved to settle their difference like gentlemen, in this land of powder and ball, instead of fighting it out with the fist or stick, as they would have done in their native country. Powel was an easy-tempered man, who seemed out of his element as second; while Smithson was by far the oldest of the party: judging by his gray hairs and weather-beaten features, he could scarcely have been less than fifty-four. He was middle-sized, very stout made, and had a dogged and forbidden countenance. He looked as though he were on ill terms with himself and all about him.

Powel commenced measuring the distance (ten paces were agreed on): when he got to the third step, Smithson said, —

"Stop, sir, — you are making strides, not paces."

Powel, too yielding for a second, stepped shorter. The men were placed in a position different from the general way that duellists stand. They stood face to face, instead of the common station of persons who fight with pistols, which is this: the principals are placed in a line with each other; if the one faces to the east, the other faces to the west, so that each presents his right side to his opponent; the right foot is turned to the adversary, and the head is inclined a little to the right shoulder. In this position a man can aim well, and yet the chances of a mortal wound are much less than if the parties faced each other fairly. I went out of my way as surgeon to rectify the position of the duellists. Smithson, who did not approve of the interference on my part, gave the word, "Fire!" The parties discharged their pistols as soon as the word was given — for neither wanted courage; but two more complete Yahoos[†] at handling pistols I never saw. The balls of the principals went nearer to the seconds than to each other. One passed so close to Smithson, that he turned deadly pale. Powel (who was little fit for a second,) gave me a look which solicited advice from me. I beckoned him, and, when he came near enough, I whispered, —

"For God's sake propose an accommodation; the quarrel was foolish, and enough has been done to satisfy the parties."

In accordance with this counsel, Powel proposed that each party should advance five paces, and shake hands.

"If the gentlemen came here," said Smithson, "to shake hands, they need not have brought pistols with them, nor fee'd the doctor there with a hundred dollars."

There was something insolent in the manner of this man towards me. Again were the pistols loaded, and again were they discharged. What became of Naysmith's ball I never discovered; but Smith's ball struck a stone near the foot of his antagonist, and turned past him.

I now openly interfered, saying, —

"For the sake of Heaven, gentlemen, fire no more; this most ridiculous affair has gone far enough: two shots a-piece are surely sufficient."

Again the sullen Smithson put a negative on my proposal of accommodation; and added, —

"The doctor wishes to earn his fee easily, but he shall have at least one man's wound to dress, unless one should be beyond his relief."

Two things were evident to me: first, Smithson wished to see mischief done; and, secondly, he wanted to shew ill-will towards me. He had a reason of his own for this, which, long after, I learned.

For a third time were pistols loaded and fired. But on this occasion the ball of Naysmith cut the knot of the cravat of Smith; while the ball of the latter carried away the waistcoat button of Naysmith. It was evident they were improving by practice.

The looks of the combatants, and of Powel, indicated that they thought an accommodation should be now agreed on. Smithson, however, deliberately employed himself loading the pistol of Smith, in a cool business-like manner.

"For the sake of humanity let us desist," said Powel. "It is downright murder; each has fired three shots."

"Yet neither has even hit," added Smithson. "Murder or manslaughter, I care not. If they fire every particle of powder and shot we have, I do not stir until claret is *drawn*."[†]

I now interfered. There was but one pair of pistols on the ground, which belonged to Powel. I asked him to allow me to load the pistol of his principal. He gave it me. I brushed out the pan, cleaned the barrel, and poised the arm; it was of Mortimer's make, and, judging of it without trial, I believed it excellent. I carefully loaded it, addressed Smithson, and asked him if he thought a fourth shot necessary.

"Ay, Doctor *Bolus*,[†] I care not how many times they fire; I will not stir from here until a man is on the ground, by G—— !"

"Then, by G—— ! sir, one of these men shall be either you or I. You hold one pistol, I the other; choose your distance, and let Powel give the word."

Smithson's looks were suddenly changed. Until this moment they were those of a bully; but, on perceiving the turn which the affair was likely to take, his mouth was thrown open — he drew a deep inspiration, but his respiration seemed suspended. Big sweat-drops appeared on his forehead, while his weather-beaten countenance turned into a sort of dark blue. He exhibited such miserable tokens of fear, so immediately after having expressed a resolution to bring others into that danger which he himself had not courage to meet, that scorn and contempt for him were plainly depicted in the countenances of the spectators.

A long pause ensued; during which, the wretched Smithson attempted to speak, but could not plainly articulate a word.

"Away, sir!" said I; "never meddle more with affairs of honour. These gentlemen and myself will keep the secret of your miserable fear, and your sanguinary disposition. Your gray hairs and cowardice protect you from merited chastisement. Return to your house, look into a mirror, and say whether your face, on which time has inscribed many a furrow, should belong to one who stirs young men to deeds of blood, from which you yourself recoil with terror. Come, gentlemen," added I, "shake hands."

The late duellists did so willingly.

By this time, Smithson became sufficiently collected to speak. He tried hard mechanically to screw his courage to the sticking point: he closed his teeth and inflated his cheek. At length, after a considerable effort, he said, —

"Doctor Arundell, you shall answer for this another time."

"No time like the present," said I.

Again I cocked my pistol; as I drew back the trigger, his jaw fell; and Smith, Naysmith, and Powel, burst into a horse laugh at the almost ludicrous fright which his visage betrayed.

I let down the hammer of the pistol I held. Powell went up to Smithson, and took the weapon he held from him, then wiped it, as though the touch of a coward had been infectious. He then put his hand on the poltroon's shoulder, and said, —

"Go away, miserable! go! We will not betray your secret; but never speak of one of us more. Away with you!"

Smithson now mounted his horse slowly; but, as soon as he was well seated, he buried the rowels of his spurs in the flanks of his heavy Canadian steed, which bounded forward with all the swiftness it possessed. However, ere he started, he darted at me the blackest look of malevolence I ever witnessed.

We now agreed to keep secret the whole affair, unless Smithson should be incautious enough to mention it himself. This man possessed a small breeding farm near the savanna, at Chaguanas; to which place he hurried. He had the prudence to keep his own secret.

Smith and Naysmith became friends after this — never making puns on each other's names. It was known they had been out and fired several shots without effect; the particulars of the duel, however, did not transpire. We all adjourned to the dwelling of Powel, who provided an excellent supper. The next morning the cautious magistrate sent his alguazils for them, and had them bound over to keep the peace after their war was over.

CHAPTER 43.

———— "Why shoot to the blast
Those embers, like stars from the firmament cast?
'Tis the fire shower of ruin all dreadfully driven."
CAMPBELL.[†]

"The baser mind itself displays
By cankered malice and revengeful spite."
SPENSER'S *Fairy Queen*.[†]

Trinidad, although beyond comparison the most fertile of the West India Islands, is, in proportion to its size, the least populous; in fact, in general the only cultivated lands lie along a part of its coasts. The interior of this noble island is covered with virgin forests, rendered impassable on account of underbrush; and one quarter is separated from another by undrained but most fertile lagoons: hence the common way of going from Port of Spain to distant quarters is by boats, or small vessels. When, however, the dry seasons are longer than usual, persons who, like myself, are fond of solitary rides, may pass over the lagoons, and through old Indian tracts of the forests, to the capital of the island. This was the case about a week after the late duel. I mounted a half-blood creole galloway[†] I owned, rode over the Pitch Lake, and passed the woods to Oropouche, where I obtained a guide, who conducted me to the comparatively populous district called Naparima.[85][†] Here I visited a medical friend, with whom I dined, and at whose house I slept.

My business in town was to learn, if I could, how the wars were going on in the neighbouring continent; but, as I had to call on several acquaintances in my route, I preferred going by land rather than sea. The next morning I set forward; proceeding about two miles of actual distance before I advanced one in a direct line. I called upon several persons in my

---

85. Corrupted from the Indian word *annaparuma*, 'single mountain.'

way, and about noon I arrived at Chaguanas. This quarter is separated from town by a savanna of about six square miles in extent; but, to the reproach of the colony be it known, that, for want of a few drains, this fertile piece of land is inundated and rendered swampy, for eight or nine months in the year, by the River Carony.[86]† Finding no boat by which I could get to town from this quarter, I wished to go across the savanna, but could get no guide: however, I met with a Mr. Brumlow, a surveyor, who had just come from town. Over this plain it was an effort of some difficulty to pass, because the river, having during the whole of the rainy season inundated the fertile land, had covered it with immense tall grass and rushes. The Spaniards had not as yet set fire to the savanna, which they do, during most dry seasons, to render the plain passable, as well as to burn the deer and other animals which harbour in the rushes. A savage method this of taking game, as fifty animals are reduced to cinders for one which is discovered fit to eat.

Mr. Brumlow saluted me, and I replied to him. I never liked him: he possessed a set of features which indicated shrewdness and ill-natured irony. He was a man of undoubted courage, and possessed a remarkably bold and full voice. He had a little wit, which he ever employed in quizzing. A professed quiz I always regard as either a misanthrope or a fool: if he has wit enough to succeed in his ill-natured banter, he is the former; if he has not, he is a blockhead.

Brumlow seldom smiled, except when he uttered an ill-natured jest; his smile was indicative of any thing rather than benevolence: in short, this unamiable man was a living sneer. Having been disappointed in obtaining a situation from the local government, he was always at the head of every contemptible little faction in this community. On one occasion, he took advantage of violent discontent which was prevalent in the island, and proposed, at a public meeting, that the inhabitants of Trinidad should throw off the *yoke* of England! Had they been insane enough to follow his advice, and a few frigates had entered the Gulf of Paria and battered the capital of the colony about the ears of his *independent* inhabitants, Mr. Brumlow would have stood on his hilly residence, three miles from the scene of action, smiling at the folly of his dupes, and coolly calculating the effects that each broadside produced on the devoted town. Yet this man was considered the Caesar of a little place — the patriot of Trinidad!

---

86. There is a fine river in Columbia bearing the same name.

"A fine horse that, doctor," said Brumlow; "a North American, I presume?"

"No, sir; he is a creole, of part English blood," answered I.

"We have few of that breed here," said Mr. Brumlow; "although creole asses, of English blood, abound in these colonies."

Brumlow smiled, after his manner, at his own witticism.

"There was a laughing devil in his sneer."[†]

I added, "Judging from the appearance of your dress, covered with 'burrs,' I suppose you have ridden from town across the savanna."

"I have," said the surveyor.

"Can you please direct me the road across?" inquired I.

"Certainly," said Brumlow. "Pass through yonder canuco (small plantation),[†] and then keep in a northward direction until you come to four remarkable palmiste-trees, which grow in a row; here cast your eyes across the savanna, and you will perceive a bluff point of land — a spur of the northern mountains, which terminates in the plains. Here, the difficulty of the route commences. You will have to force your way through the fox-tail grass and the tusk-rushes,[†] which will cover yourself and horse; but steer by the mountain, in a direct line, for about three miles and a half, and you will come out at the Carony, which you may easily swim, and get to St. Joseph. I would, however, advise you to borrow or buy a cutlass, as you may meet with snakes in the way. I would lend you mine, but I want it myself, having to survey in the woods to-morrow. You can buy a cutlass of any of the free people about here."

I thanked him for his minute direction and advice. We separated. I had not ridden a hundred yards before I came to a cottage, belonging to an old discharged soldier of a condemned regiment, which, some years since, was disbanded here.[†] This man was trimming some coffee-trees in front of his house, before which sat a lame negro. I asked the soldier if he could sell me a cutlass: he offered me the one with which he was working for a dollar. I paid him the money, took the tool, or weapon (for it is here used as both), and asked him for a drink of water.

"That you shall have, strengthened, if you wish, with a dash of the finest new rum in the island. I keep none of your old stinking stuff at my quarters."

"I would rather take the water unmixed," said I.

"Just as you like," said the old soldier; "but please to unlight,[87] and come into my barracks, at all events."

---

87. A creolism for "alight."

I did so. The cottage was dark. I saw some one lying in a hammock, but could not distinctly see his features, until the soldier opened the window and light streamed into the house. By this I perceived that it was Smithson who was lounging in the hammock. There was a mixture of shame and sullen anger in his iron features, which gave him a peculiarly gloomy look. I turned from him, drank water from a large calabash, took my cutlass, mounted my horse, and proceeded on my journey.

My animal being somewhat jaded, I walked him. We soon got into grass of about five or six feet in height, when I perceived that I was followed by some one, I could not see whom. I stopped my horse; the person who followed me stopped also. I called to him, he retreated and disappeared.

I now came to the four palmiste-trees, well described by Mr. Brumlow, and perceived the point of land towards which I was to make. Hitherto I had found his directions correct, and therefore doubted not the rest was equally so; but, when he said that to strike across from the palm-trees to the bluff point of land was the most direct way, he told truth only in one sense of the word; it was the direct way, but not the route I ought to have taken, nor that which he himself took. I should have made a detour to the eastward, to avoid the very fox-tail grass and tusk-rushes through which his mischievous love of hoaxing sent me.

I now entered a dense mass of vegetation, the like of which I never beheld. The inundations of the Carony, the immense fertility of the land, and the inter-tropical sun, produced a growth of rushes each thicker than a man's arm, and from fifteen to eighteen feet in height. These grew so close that it was with great labour my horse could force his way through them. The difficulty of our progress became so great, that, recollecting Brumlow's love for quizzing, I was about to return: however, I still proceeded, at the rate of a mile an hour, hoping every minute to come to where the vegetation was less gigantic and dense. Having crossed from Alta Gracia to Essequibo, I felt ashamed of turning back from a journey of four or five miles; for I knew by the form of the hills, of which I sometimes got a glimpse, that every laborious step the horse made brought me nearer to St. Joseph.

The poor beast fairly groaned under his exertion amid the tough tusk-rushes, which seemed to grow taller and taller. I now perceived with astonishment a great number of fallow-deer rush past me, for these animals never herd together in Trinidad.[88†] Presently, a quantity of

---

88. Before Mrs. Carmichael said she saw a deer in Trinidad put its *antlers* in at the windows of a house, I never heard of a deer in this island that had antlers.

agoutees (Indian conies)[†] leaped past me, running as though for their lives in the same direction; yet I heard no dog bark, nor any sound of a chase. An alco (wild dog) or two, and several racoons,[†] bounded past, but seemed not in pursuit of the agoutees. Again, as my horse proceeded, he put his hoof on a land-tortoise;[†] the slow animal drew his short legs and small head into his tough shell, over which a waggon might have passed without cracking it; and no sooner was the horse's hoof off the tortoise, than he took his tardy way in the same direction that the number of animals were going.

A flock of quank, or musk-hogs,[†] and several lapes,[†] now rushed by, grunting and squeaking. Presently a large tiger-cat,[†] followed by six or eight kittens, ran past me; and now I perceived a large boa-constrictor gliding among the rushes. I grasped my cutlass, and dismounted to defend myself from the enormous reptile; but it passed on, followed by several other snakes: it neither wished to attack nor to avoid me.

What could all this mean? Was I in my proper senses, or were all the animals in the island at peace with each other, and about to meet in grand congress? I remounted my horse, who, to my amazement, followed in the track of the large boa; and, although the poor beast was jaded, it plunged forward, using exertion which astonished me, until the animal was covered with foam.

A breeze shook the heads of the gigantic rushes. What could those roaring and crackling sounds mean; and that smoke, too? Gracious Heavens! the truth now flashed on my mind: the savanna had been set on fire! My suspicion at once pointed to Smithson; and I was right in my conjecture, as I afterwards found. The flight of the various animals was at once explained: they were rushing from the devouring element.

Hopes of escape amid this immense mass of inflammable vegetable matter I had not: yet I spurred my horse. It was needless: the poor animal seemed instinctively to know our danger before I did, and plunged through the rushes with all the strength he was master of, taking the same route as the rest of the animals. "On, on, good steed! if the conflagration, which roars and cracks with a deafening sound in our rear, catches us before we get from amongst these accursed rushes, we shall be reduced to cinders in a few seconds!"

I closed my eyes, on account of the smoke which rolled onwards, and which nearly choked me. The flames pursue us on the wings of the wind; but, merciful Providence, I see a chance of deliverance before me! the rushes decrease in size, and the ground becomes humid: yet the devouring element pursues us. We were saved! a few desperate plunges of the horse brought us into a muddy perennial lake, to where all the animals of the savanna had sped, or were speeding. Had we been five seconds later, the roaring and cracking flames would have caught us; and, as my horse plunged into the middle of the pool, which teemed with animals and serpents, the fire absolutely passed over our heads from the sides of the lake. I dismounted, stood up to my breast in muddy water, which steamed from the heat; the animals groaned from the effects of the insupportable calorie: none attacked, none seemed to fear another.

I saw several poisonous snakes, that were overtaken by the flames on the banks of the pool, turn round, and, with stupid rage, attempt to fight with the fire. As they felt it burn their extremities, they erected their slender forms, opened their wide jaws, elevated their baneful fangs, and darted at the flames: in a few moments they were reduced to black cinders.

As the conflagration spread its pyramidical arms above the streaming and muddy waters, my situation was almost insupportable: yet I thanked Providence for my deliverance. It was true I was in purgatory; but, for miles round me raged a hell.

At length the wind, which was blowing with violence, remitted, and shortly after died away; the flames shot up in a vertical direction, and my aching eyes were blessed with the appearance of the clouded sky. The fire now burned with a steady roar for about five minutes, when another breeze sent the flames over the yellow lake. I stooped until my chin touched the thick water to avoid the heat: finally, I ducked my head underneath for a second to cool it, when the wind again lulled; and I, with my hand, sluiced water over the head of my groaning horse. The breeze now finally died away, and the clouds above me indicated that a heavy shower of rain was near falling.

The fire slackened; and, in about half an hour after I had taken refuge in the perennial lake, it had burned out, but the surface of the earth was calcined like a brick, and too hot to be passed over by the foot of any animal. If the rain did not fall, I had the uncomfortable prospect of spending many hours in my present situation, and with my present company of reptiles, who, although now at peace with their neighbours, might soon recommence hostilities. I made my horse wade its way to where stood the branchless trunk of an old crooked savanna tree, which, being in the middle of the water, had escaped burning. I buckled the bridle to this tree while I went to reconnoitre, in order to ascertain where I could most conveniently throw water on the calcined earth, to get room for myself and my horse to stand on *terra firma* until the rain, or dews of evening, should sufficiently cool the ground to allow our passing over.

I had not left the horse a minute before it uttered a neigh of distress. I grasped my cutlass and ran to its aid. I found that an enormous mackawel, or boa-constrictor,[†] of about twenty-five feet in length, had caught the poor beast in its fold: a part of the reptile was knotted round the old tree; two coils were about the beast. The serpent had passed his body between the fore legs of the horse, and was in the act of seizing it by the throat, when a thrust from my cutlass pierced its eye, and entered right into its head.

The ire of the mackawel was now turned on me: it elongated its body so that six or seven feet of its neck was clear of the horse, which, however, it shewed no disposition to relinquish. It rose its head over me; its double tongue quivered in its mouth; its jaws opened until they seemed to be dislocated; and it breathed on me with its infernal breath, the odour[89†] of which is unlike aught else I ever smelt. It hesitated to lower its head for the attack; I stooped into the water; it also stooped; until judging it within reach of my arm, I rose and made a cut at it, which divided its lower jaw. The boa now turned from me: I made a blow at the part which was coiled round the tree, and divided its tail from the rest of its body. This seemed to be a *coup de grace*: it appeared to lose all power; its bleeding head fell into the water, and the poor horse uttered a note, something between a snort and a groan, at being relieved from the strangling convolutions of the serpent, although they were still about it, until, with my cutlass, I divided one of the coils, near the saddle, and the reptile's severed body fell, bleeding and writhing, into the water.

A most welcome shower of rain, such as occurs occasionally in Trinidad during the dry season, now fell; the burning earth absorbed it, while it hissed and sent up clouds of steam.

I got my horse out of the river, but he was too much exhausted to carry me; I therefore led him to the Carony river, where I bathed him and myself, going into the water with my muddied clothes. Crossing the Carony, I came to the plantation of the worthy Baron de ———, a gentleman born in Grenada, of noble French blood,[†] whose father took the right

---

89. I have reason to believe that snakes can emit this odour to frighten their prey; in fact, this is what is called their fascination.

side of the civil war of that island — that is to say, the side that was eventually successful. When he, that evening, found I was a countryman of his, his hospitality was warm in the extreme. This was fortunate; for my savanna adventure, and the broiling and stewing which I got in the muddy lake, brought on a slight inflammatory fever, which confined me to the house of the worthy baron for twelve days.

My fine creole galloway took a cold, and died two days after our escape from the fire.

CHAPTER 44.

"The world is full of strange vicissitudes,
And here was one exceedingly unpleasant."
            BYRON.†

"The very butt of slander, and the blot
For every dart their malice ever shot;
The man that mentioned him at once dismissed
All mercy from his lips, and sneered and hissed."
            COWPER.†

I rode to Port of Spain on a borrowed animal, belonging to the worthy
baron. On my arrival I wrote a letter to Fernandez, in which I
recounted to him what had taken place since we parted. I requested to
know from him how affairs were going on in Columbia: above all, I
inquired if he had heard any news from my dearest Maria Josefa. Finally, I
told him I had written three times since I came to Trinidad, but received
no answer. The cause of this was, I had sent my letters to town, forgetting
to have them paid, and being directed to a foreign colony, they remained
in the post-office.

While I was in the humour of scribbling long letters, I wrote one to my
brother Rodney, entreating him to acquaint me what was the cause that
neither he nor any of the family had ever answered my letters. The writing
of those lengthy despatches employed me until evening. The next
morning, early, I went to place them in the post-office. It was not yet
opened, so I took a stroll down to the king's wharf. Here, against the
harbour-master's office, I saw a paper pasted, running thus:

"To sail on the 20th for Antigua, St. Kitt's, and St. Thomas's,
the fast-sailing cutter 'Pickled Timber.' For freight or passage
apply to the captain, on board."

It struck me that, by giving the letters to this captain, I might stand a better chance of their reaching their destination than by sending them through the post-office. I called a shore-boat, and ordered the men to put me on board the Pickled Timber.

"Could I see the captain?" said I, as I got on board.

"I *is* the captain," said a very good-looking, middle-aged black man. "I *is* the captain, at service."

"Do you go to St. Kitt's and St. Thomas's?"

"I *does*, please the Lârd. Do you want a passage, sir?"

"No, my friend: but I wish to know if you are acquainted with a man of colour in St. Christopher's called Rodney Arundell?"

"To be sure I *does*, and all his fam'ly, brothers and sisters, and all: good people they *is*, too. I knowed the father from whom they *is* degenerated (he meant descended). They *is* as well to do as any brown people in the West Indies."

"Thank God! thank God!" said I.

"Why, Lârd bless me, sir, sit down on the hen-coop, until the boy brings a chair. Is you relations to the Arundells?"

"I am their brother."

"You their brother! Are you the young gentleman that went away against their consent for to learn to be a doctor, but of who they could never find out what had become? For the Lârd's sake, Mr. Arundell, come with me to St. Kitt's; they'll all be *too*[90] glad to see you. Your poor sister Jane is my oldest boy's godmother. Many a day has she come to my house, and cried until her heart was ready to break, because she did not know what had become of you. Why did you not write to them?"

"I did, my good fellow; I wrote twenty times, but never got an answer."

"Strange they never heard a word from you; and when they used to ax at Keen and Leech, they never got no satisfaction. Once your brother Clarence met old Leech, and axed what had become of you, and Leech told him he believed you had taken to bad courses."

"The villain!"

"That's just what your brother Clarence called him: he said he was a villain; and, being a good *hand* at *butting*, he fired his head into old Leech's stomach, that upset him, for which he was sent to gaol for two months."

---

90. Too glad, *i.e.* very glad.

"My poor brother! it must be those villains who intercepted my letters."

"Well, sir, I knows well they often wrote to you, but, not knowing where to find you, they put in the letters to 'Mr. Warner Arundell, Esquire, England.' All the letters came back, and they had to pay the postage twice over."

"My worthy fellow, will you take charge of this letter; and further tell them, I will depart from this island to see them in less than six weeks?"

"I will," said the man, "please the Lârd;" and he put the letter in his Bible, which he locked away. "Lârd, Mr. Arundell, I knowed your father before you was born; many a black dog (copper coin)[†] has he given me. As to your poor brothers and sisters, they'll cry for joy at hearing you *is* safe; and I declare you *is* as tall as any of your brothers, but a great deal more handsome. Lârd! they is more uglier than you by a great deal."

"Do you know a merchant of St. Thomas's, or Curaçoa, called Fernandez?"

"Oh, for the matter of that, every body knows the rich Jew merchant, Fernandez."

"Will you carry a letter from me to him?"

"To be sure I will. But where do you stop (reside)?"

"When I am in town, at Patty Chalotte's tavern; but my general residence is down the coast, beyond the Pitch Lake."

"I axes, sir, because I wishes to send you a case of liquors and a bundle of German sausages, which I brought with me from St. Thomas's, if you will take them for a present."

"I would rather buy them of you. What is their price?"

"I'd rather give them to you, for they don't cost me much; because why? I *has* a bad memory."

"How can your having a bad memory have any thing to do with the cost of your merchandise?"

"Why, sir," said he, in a whisper, *"I forgets to pay duty."*

This good man, for such he was, told me a number of anecdotes of my family, which, however important to myself, can little interest the reader. I took breakfast on board the Pickled Timber, and at about ten o'clock went ashore in good spirits. The cutter sailed five days after this.

On landing on the king's wharf, I went into the news-room, a small airy building, erected on posts over the sea. I was a subscriber to this establishment. On entering, I nodded to several persons with whom I had formed a slight acquaintance, and was astonished that my nods were only repaid with frowns. All I looked at turned their backs on me. What, in the name of all that's odd, can this mean? thought I. Several persons quitted their chairs as I seated myself, and all commenced whispering to each other, and pointing with their chins at me. They then called an old gentleman, who was keeper of the establishment, and whispered to him. The old man advanced towards me, and commenced humming and hawing, as if to clear his throat, in order that he might deliver a disagreeable message. At length he opened his gold snuffbox, and addressed me at the same moment.

"Dr. Arundell, I hope you will not be offended with *me*; but I am desired by the committee to announce to you, that your last quarter's subscription will this day be returned to you, and that, in future, your presence in the news-room is not expected."

"And pray, Mr. ——, what may be the cause of all this?"

"I am not charged with giving any explanation, and do not like to proceed further with a disagreeable commission than I can help; but I suppose that the gentlemen of the committee will explain when they send you your subscription."

The old man bowed, and I quitted the room, puzzled beyond bearing at all this mystery.

Two hours afterward, I received a letter, enclosing the amount of my last quarter's subscription, and the letter which Pringle, the secretary of the Anti-slavery Society, had sent me; together with an epistle, which ran thus:

"To WARNER ARUNDELL, ESQ., Surgeon, &c. &c.
　"SIR,

"Suspicion was thrown on your conduct by our seeing a letter, which was traced to have come from your address, to the secretary of the Anti-slavery Society. This suspicion was strengthened by a declaration of Ensign ——,[†] the notorious emancipationist, who said you are his friend, and that you are a *saint*,[†] who will play the *devil* in this island. But some unknown friend of the colony has fully proved that you are a spy in the camp, a traitor to the community which gives you bread; in fact, one who *wishes to cut all our throats behind our backs*. We have most *circumspectively* investigated your conduct; and when we *look to the right and to the left we see straight before us*.

"We enclose you the letter of the Anti-slavery Society, which, having the post-mark on it, cannot be a forgery, and must have been received by you.

"Not wanting to have any thing further to say to one who wishes to instigate our *happy* [slaves] to murder us, we beg you will not again enter the news-room. We return you the last quarter's subscription.

"Mr. Wilthrope having told us you were a great duellist in Cayenne, we inform you that, in order to save you the trouble of calling on any of us for an explanation, we have consulted the officers of the first division of the militia forces, and they agree that no gentleman ought to meet a person of your character.

"We are your obedient Servants,

"ROBERT BLADDER,

JOHN ROUGHHEAD,

FREDERICK BRUMLOW,

GEORGE LANCASTER,

JAMES LUMBER,

THOMAS JEWEL, M.D."

Vexatious as this affair was, I could not help laughing at its extreme absurdity.

In my unlucky correspondence with the Anti-slavery party there was nothing, if fairly considered, that the most bigoted colonist could blame; yet circumstances were against me. My incaution in sending my letter by an illiterate man, who left it on the table of the news-room, instead of putting it into the post-office; the downright lies of the violent ensign, who injured me by his abominable attempt at defending me; and, above all, the anti-slavery secretary's letter being placed in the news-room, — all these, taken together, certainly justified suspicion — suspicion which I could not remove, and which, if I could, I would not be allowed to remove.

But I began to consider how this letter could have been obtained. Two weeks ago I left it locked up in my desk, down the coast. In this desk there were forty-four doubloons and some dollars — all I possessed in the world. I felt alarmed; for I knew that, when party-spirit once sets in against a devoted man in a little community, almost every species of villainy against him is considered justifiable.

Some years ago, in this colony, a set of libels appeared in the gazette against the character of one of the most enlightened judges that ever presided over any tribunal in the West Indies. An action was entered against the libellers. The night previous to the day fixed on for the trial, a ruffianly set of men, headed by the notorious Crawford,[91†] broke into the court-house, and stole therefrom an iron chest, in which was the original declaration, without which they could not conveniently go to trial. The next morning the chest was found in a neighbouring field, broken to pieces; the declaration, and a considerable sum of money, having been taken from it. The greater part of the money was subsequently returned by an Irish priest, who said he received it under the seal of confession, but the declaration was destroyed. Would it be believed, that the well-known perpetrators of this outrage were not only received in society as gentlemen, but applauded as having done a meritorious act? I relate this anecdote to shew how far party feeling is carried, at times, in this island.

It was clear to me that my desk must have been broken open or stolen to obtain this letter; and those who took the letter would not leave the money behind.

To recount all the ingenious ways I was tormented would be tedious. Almost all the free population of the island rose against me; every species of crime was ascribed to me, or rather was included in one monosyllable, *i.e.* 'saint.' I was called a *saint*, and threatened to be made a *martyr*.

The packet, which should arrive twice every month, was long over-due; so that for four weeks no news was heard from Europe: hence the gallery whisperers† in Port of Spain, who form what has been called 'The Trinidad Society for the Diffusion of Useless Knowledge,' wanted a subject to talk about, when, fortunately, the popular clamour set in against me. These worthy gentlemen attacked me, as the chameleons of the island attack flies, with their tongues. The gazette had long been in want of a leading, or a misleading, article; it now teemed with violent paragraphs on the subject of my turpitude. Besides these heavy columns of prose, three sharpshooters fired at me in verse.

The first of these was one George Lancaster, who used to spend one half of his time in getting drunk, and the other half in getting sober.

The second of this triumvirate was James Lumber, an Irishman, who ran away from America to get quit of his wife. This man was continually

---

91. A wretch who, on his death-bed, confessed to his having poisoned five men.

learning scraps of poetry, in order that he might 'spout' them in company and appear very learned.

The third was a young man, who was not the worst of me; but, unfortunately, some fools or knaves of his acquaintance had flattered him into a belief that, when scribbling wretched rhymes, he was composing original poetry. His verses used to remind me of a certain reptile, which, from the obtusity of its extremities, is called the double-headed snake. Look at it as you will, you never know its head from its tail.[†]

The joint productions of these three luminaries blazed conspicuously in the paper of the colony.

CHAPTER 45.

"— Unnatural deeds
Will breed unnatural troubles: infected minds
To their deaf pillows will discharge their secrets."
Shakespeare.[†]

Being more alarmed about my money, which I feared had been stolen, than at the fanatic persecution which I was suffering, I took a passage on board a drogher which was going down to the Pitch Lake. I arrived, long after it was dark, at the singular village called La Brea, built on the sea-shore, near this lagoon of bitumen, on a stratum of pitch. This stratum is continually subject to a slow action: hence, one who visits the village will perceive every house in it to have a slant or inclination towards the sea. Let him return in a month, and every house, perhaps, will have gained its perpendicular. Perchance, in another month, he will find all the houses slued from the sea. Sometimes they are at 'right incline,' and sometimes they 'oblique to the left.' All the houses are built, of course, of slight materials.

I did not like to remain at this village, being anxious to get to my dwelling, which lay beyond the dark lake of asphaltum. This can easily be traversed on one side, near a range of bushes which vegetate on a slight stratum of earth, lying on the pitch; but, if you go far from the bushes, you meet with a quantity of shelving chasms of from three to five feet in depth, filled with water, rendered sulphurous and tepid by some subterraneous, or rather sub-bituminous action. The night was the darkest I ever beheld; not a star was to be seen; the heavens were black as a closed vault; the Pitch Lake, and the water in the crevices, were so black that I could not tell the one from the other. I strayed from the bushes, got into the middle of the black lagoon, and, every third step, fell into the apertures already described, and involuntarily partook of one tepid bath after another. I felt my way with my feet, until I came to what I thought to be a

347

crevice. I prepared to leap across, made a strong effort, but, instead of jumping over, I floundered in the centre, although the chasm was only four feet in width, and I must have jumped nearly twice that distance. This blunder I repeated twenty times. I now lost all idea of the points of the compass. I looked up, but no stars appeared to direct me. I knew that at a certain part of the lake the pitch is fluid, and, in my wanderings in the dark, I might get into this spot, from which there could be no hope of escape. This danger now appeared so pressing, that, at one time, I thought of remaining on the hard pitch until the moon, which would soon arise, should lend her friendly light to get me out of my present difficult situation. But, although the water in which I had been immersed was tepid when I fell into it, yet, when I came out, it soon got cold: hence, I began to feel chilled.

Hoping to arouse some of those who have cottages on the borders of the lake, I raised my voice, and called for succour. After hailing three times, I perceived a light about two hundred yards from me. I redoubled my calls for aid, and some one, from whence the light gleamed, called out in Creole French, —

"*Qui moune ça* — (who is that)?"

I replied, in the same dialect, that I had lost my way in the lake, and asked if any part of the pitch between me and the light was soft.

"Some part," replied the voice, "is too soft to bear the impression of a foot, but you will not get ancle-deep into it. Advance in a direct line on the light."

I did so, slipping into the water at every twentieth step. At length I got to the beacon: a tall man held it; a woman stood by his side. They were near two houses. At length, on approaching the parties, to thank them for their aid, I perceived that the man was no other than the breathing spectre with whom I came from Cayenne; and the woman beside him I recognised as the ancient negress who also came with us.

I thanked this singular-looking being for the service he had rendered me, and asked him if he had any servant whom I could pay to guide me over the lake.

"I have no servant but this ancient dame, and she is old enough to be my grandmother, although I am not a young man."

"Have you a flambeau, or some splinters of hard wood to make one of, by the light of which I may traverse this lagoon?"

"I have not, sir; but — "

He paused, and looked at the beldam: her appearance was most inhospitable. The man added, "You can wait here until the moon rises, when you can pass the lake with ease."

He again looked at the female; she shook her head at him, as if blaming him.

"Come in," added this living skeleton.

I entered one of the two small wooden houses; he put down the lamp he held, and, for the first time since our present meeting, looked me full in the face. He very seldom looked directly at any one, even when speaking to him.

"I think," said he, "we have met before, sir?"

"We came together from Cayenne," replied I.

His lips made an involuntary motion, and he looked down again.

"True, true; we came from Cayenne together, as you say. Nay, old Julie, do not beckon me so much; we cannot be so inhospitable as to refuse shelter to a benighted traveller. You must stop here to-night. Go, old dame, to the other house; heap more fuel on the fire to dry the gentleman's clothes — they are all wet."

The negress departed.

"Here," said this singular man, — "here is a dry shirt, and a warm *robe-de-chambre*: take off your wet clothes, and put on these; they will serve you for the night, and, by the morning, your own suit will be dry."

I changed my dress, and Julie returned, took my clothes, and hung them to dry in the other house, about forty yards from the one in which I was. The disposition of Saint Jago (such was the name by which he went) seemed to warm; and he, by persuading the old woman, and his own assistance, got me a tolerable supper, composed of an *original* omelette and a part of an agoutee, being its second appearance on the board, together with a remnant of a bottle of *vin de côte*.† Of these I ate heartily, but drank sparingly.

"You are," said the man, "so temperate in your draughts, I should scarce take you for an Englishman."

"I am an English creole."

"Of what island?"

"Grenada."

At hearing this island named, his face elongated, and he changed significant glances with Julie. After a pause, he said, looking any way but at me, "You are a young man, I take it; therefore cannot remember — I mean, have no recollection ———"

He seemed confused, and the old negress gave him a dark, reproachful look. He said, more collectedly, "You are, as I was saying, a young man; may I ask what year you were born in?"

"1795," replied I.

It was now evident that I had touched one of the cords of his heart. The appearance of this man, at all times cadaverous, now became peculiarly ghastly. As his jaw fell at my naming the year of the rebellion of Grenada, it was evident I had recalled an unpleasant train of recollections.

We again attempted to enter into conversation, but there was something constrained about our discourse. The negress, whose eyes, notwithstanding her extreme age, gleamed like those of a rat, never ceased watching the mysterious Saint Jago.

After apologising for want of accommodation, and saying, what I believe was the truth, "that, since his arrival in Trinidad, he had never entertained a guest," he lighted me to the place where I was to sleep. This was a kind of rude first-floor, or garret; for it united both, as it was the highest part of the house. I went up to it by seven or eight steps of a ladder, and, when there, the palm-thatch by which the cottage was covered scarcely afforded me room to stand upright. A hammock was suspended for my accommodation, and my host bade me good-night, telling me that he was about to sleep in the other room.

I lay down to rest, but not to sleep. The manner of St. Jago was extraordinary, he seeming always afraid of the old woman, who continually watched him: their conduct was remarkable, if not suspicious. True, he had fulfilled the rites of hospitality; but this he did hesitatingly, and with a bad grace — while in the countenance of the old woman I read vexation at my intrusion, and strong hatred against me. My situation was one of constraint. I could not quit the house without a violent breach of good manners; yet, by remaining where I was, I felt that my presence was a restraint on my host, and knew that I was incurring the malediction of his ancient domestic.

I lay down in the hammock, but could not sleep. The night was sultry: I opened the window to admit air, and beheld a singular scene.

The clouds, which had overspread the vault of heaven, had been driven by the night wind to the southward and westward, where they were piled on each other in black and heavy masses; while, ever and anon, they were rent in all directions by the successive coruscations of lightning, although no sound of thunder disturbed the profound stillness which reigned over this extraordinary lake of pitch.

The waning, yet still almost full, moon had risen high in the heavens, and shed her placid light over the broad lagoon of solid and fluid pitch, which was of intense blackness; while the crevices crossed each other, and broke the dark plain into ten thousand sections. These cracks were filled with water, on which the moon's rays falling, they seemed like an immense net of silver spread over this lake of bitumen. The effect of the lunar beams on this square league of asphaltum, intersected all over its surface by apertures filled with water, is indescribable, and unlike any thing else in nature. I almost regretted my resolution of passing the night in a house where I felt I was not welcome; for, by the light of the moon, I now could plainly see the way I ought to have crossed — and, like most enlightened persons, I wondered how I could blunder in the dark. But to leave the house now, after, as I supposed, my host had gone to his repose, would have looked suspicious. Feeling, however, no inclination to sleep, I descended the ladder, passed through the lower room of this slightly-built house, and quitted the cottage, in order to walk about the lake until I should feel inclined to sleep; as to lie awake under the warm thatch was intolerable.

In order to avoid some bushes, I was obliged to pass the other small house, about forty yards from the one I had left, to which St. Jago and the old woman had retired. This was built as lightly as the other: both were formed of palmiste boards, so badly jointed, that one standing outside might see, through the crevices, what was going on within, without any effort at peeping. Hence I was enabled to see my skeleton host and his African servant had not yet retired to rest, but were in conversation. I was about to make a detour, in order to avoid eaves-dropping, when an expression that fell from Saint Jago arrested me. His words were as follow: "What, murder that fine young man! I have enough blood-stains on my soul already, thanks to your counsel and the orders of Victor Hugues."

Having heard, by chance, these suspicious words distinctly, on account of the stillness of the night, although they were spoken in a tone little above a whisper, I felt that I should be justified in listening to more. The force of a robber may be repelled by force; with greater reason may the plots of the cunning assassin be counteracted by the cunning of the intended victim. Taking off my slippers, I passed with a noiseless step to the side of the house nearest where this singular pair sat, and overheard the rest of their confabulation. The negress replied thus to Saint Jago: "Well, let him go; and to-morrow he will inform the commandant, that the secluded man who lives near the Pitch Lake is Julien Fedon, the brigand chief. Remember, I, Julie Sanois, who never was a false prophetess, tell you that yonder white cockroach[92] at this moment knows who you are."

"So," thought I, "here is a discovery! My old fellow passenger is the infamous Fedon, whose escape from Grenada was connived at by my father, and to whose act of gratitude I owe my life."

This man was supposed to have been drowned, because his canoe, with a compass nailed to the bottom of it, was picked up at sea; although there prevailed an obscure rumour that he had been taken on board a French vessel and landed in this island. The dialogue continued. Fedon said, "I cannot believe that a man who possesses so frank and open a countenance can betray one who has relieved him and hospitably sheltered him."

"Believe it not, although I, the sibyl of St. Domingo, say it! Believe it not, although I never predicted falsely!"

"You have made some remarkable guesses."

"Guesses! call you my prophecies guesses? When I told my *compère*, Joupaint l'Ouverture,[†] that, if he entered into any treaty with the faithless French, he would end his days in a miserable prison, far from his native land, — was this a guess? When, years after this, I heard that he had perished, amidst cold and wretchedness, in a dungeon, by order of one who hated the race of Apica,[93†] and who trod on the necks of kings, I cursed the minion of fortune, and foretold his downfall. Fall he did, like a ball of fire which is spit from the jaws of a volcano, and which shoots up to heaven, but sinks to its native hell! Was it by guessing that I predicted the singular fate of Marie Joseph Tascher?[†] More than two score years since she came to me, a smiling creole girl, who wished for nothing but to dress and coquet. 'Julie Sanois,' asked she, 'can you tell me my fortune?' 'I can,' said I; 'it will be a remarkable one. Twice you will marry, but neither of your marriages will be happy; once you will be a widow, but you will die neither wife nor widow.' 'Terrible predictions these,' said Marie Joseph; 'but tell me more.' 'Ask me no more, Mademoiselle Tascher.' She urged to know all. I said, 'You will be greater than the Queen of France, but will die, broken-hearted, in an hospital.' She affected to laugh at all this; but twenty-five years after, when she was hailed as the Empress Josephine, she must have remembered the prophecy of the sibyl of St. Domingo, and shuddered at that portion of it

---

92. A term of reproach applied by negroes to white people.
93. Napoleon's dislike to negroes was remarkable.

which was to be fulfilled. Some dozen years passed again, and the smiling creole died at the old hospital of Malmaison, neither wife nor widow, but a divorced and broken-hearted woman."

Here was another discovery. The singular old woman was no other than the celebrated sibyl of St. Domingo, as she was called, Julie Sanois, whose remarkable prediction respecting the Empress Josephine I had heard years before it was fulfilled; it having been currently talked of in the colonies. But to continue with what I overheard. Fedon replied to her, "Prophetess or impostor, whichever you be, I will not allow this young man to be injured with my consent, and wash my hands of his blood."

"His blood shall not be spilt ere he departs hence. He shall take from my hands some of my poison, which, although it has no taste, colour, nor odour; yet a single particle, placed beneath the nail, kills as surely as a cannon-ball."

"Julie, I know it is impossible to move you from your purpose; therefore, good night," said Fedon.

"Where go you? to sleep in the house with the Englishman; to awake him with talking to yourself (your old trick), and cause him to quit the cottage, and betray you? Remain here, if you wish not to die the death of a felon."

I now heard Fedon repeat the Lord's Prayer in Latin; for, although he was far from a well-educated man, he like most Catholics, knew his *Paternoster*. With a noiseless step I regained the house I had quitted, and, by the light of the moon, perceived in the lower room a cutlass. This I took into the upper apartment, and laid it under my hammock, lest any attack should be made on me. After thanking Heaven for my new deliverance, I again threw off the *robe-de-chambre* I wore, and lay down, but felt neither the disposition nor wish to sleep.

I lay for two hours in the hammock, listening to the occasional hooting of the owl and the continued ticking of my watch. The time seemed to move with a leaden pace; when, about two in the morning, I heard the door below open, and could see, through the kind of trap-door in the floor, that Fedon entered, bearing a lamp in his hand. He muttered to himself, "I cannot sleep in yonder smoky hut." He set down the lamp, and partly mounted the ladder. I pretended sleep. Judging from his voice, he only raised his head high enough to look at me, and then said, "Sleep in peace, poor youth! Please Heaven, in the morning I will caution him against taking aught from the hands of old Julie."

He descended the ladder a few seconds after this. I opened my eyes, and saw that he was undressed, all but a hair shirt, which he wore for penance.[†] "Let me," said this man, "again say my prayers. Perhaps Heaven will bless me with sleep." He knelt before a wooden crucifix, and repeated the evening prayers of the Catholic church; he then took a Prayer-book, and read aloud the seven penitential psalms. He trimmed his lamp, added some castor-oil to it, and then lay down on a small mattrass placed on a kind of rough wooden settee.

I watched this man for nearly an hour. He turned from side to side, as if in the vain attempt to obtain sleep. As he fell into a kind of slumber, he would start, or rather shudder, and open his eyes. At length, lying on his back, he slept with comparative tranquillity for about half an hour. I had taken my eyes off him for some short time, and begun to feel drowsy, when my attention was aroused by the sleeping Fedon's saying aloud, — "Who calls?" I cast my eyes downwards, and saw that the restless wretch had in his sleep started from his couch: his eyes were wide open, and their pupils awfully dilated and fixed. This I could plainly perceive by the light of the lamp which he had caught up, and held in his left hand, near his frightful visage, which had now assumed traits of terror that made me shudder to look at. Was he insane, or under the influence of somnambulism?

"Who calls?" again said the conscience-struck wretch. His voice was sepulchral, his lips scarcely moved as he spoke, and the words sounded, as they proceeded from his breast, like the tones of the voice of a ventriloquist. He spoke with long pauses between every sentence.

"Who calls? Ah! is it you, Captain Deserée? What! have they dared to attack Belvedere? — Order the negroes and mulattoes to fight for liberty and equality! — What! they threaten to dislodge us? — then down with the governor and the rest of the prisoners! — Why hesitate? I tell you it is Citizen Victor's orders, and he must be obeyed! — Tell Captain Joseph to shoot and cut down the prisoners, I say! — Right, Coteau! pass your cutlass through the bodies of the English swains! — Remove the filthy corses![†] the flies are settling on them — see what a vapour arises from them, as the sun warms their stiff wounds!"

The tortured wretch now paused for a few seconds; his countenance, which had taken the traits of stern command, gradually changed their appearance, until they assumed the looks of acute agony and utter despair; while his sepulchral voice sunk almost to a low moan. He said, "Behold, father! behold the acts for which I beg for absolution. No, no! neither hair shirt, flagellation, prayers, nor fasting, though I have continued them twenty-five years, can plead at the throne of mercy for pardon; after these murders it cannot be. Were I forgiven, there would be none damned, and hell would be tenantless. It cannot be — you flatter me. Were I forgiven, they would not visit me as they do. I tell you that often, amid the darkness of night, and sometimes in the glare of the sun, the forty-eight murdered men[†] glide before me in middle air — they come even now — do you not see them? — there they are, marked with blood and soil, closely grouped together, like a bunch of crushed red grapes! See, see!" — he continued, in a voice much louder than he had yet used — "see, see! how they jabber; and each gory spectre grins, and points his right hand at me!"

The somnambulist held the lamp close to his protruded eyes, and pointed with his right hand to the group which his foul imagination had conjured up. The big sweat-drops poured from his forehead, and his large temporal artery beat as violently as though it were bursting.

I was rather fearless by nature, and I had been for some time accustomed to look real danger in the face as coolly as other men who are used to war; but beholding the horrors of the ghastly somnambulist made me shake like a coward.

I was soon aroused to act in self-defence. The old sibyl had heard the last sleep-ravings of Fedon, and came from the other house hastily to awaken the wretched man. She shook him rudely.

"Ah!" he exclaimed, "has Satan seized me, despite of all my penitence? I thought it would be thus."

She seized a calabash of water, and dashed it in his face, on which he fell; but not like one who falls from the effects of a wound. It seemed as though all the muscles which support a man's frame while he stands, had suddenly given way.

"Awake, *malheureux!*"[†] exclaimed the old negress.

She shook him rudely, and raised his face from the ground, for the room was unfloored.

"What! has all the bloody group vanished? Ah! thank God it was all a dream!" said he.

"Arouse yourself — you are betrayed!" shrieked the African.

"Betrayed! by whom? ha?"

He rushed to the corner in search of his cutlass, but, of course, did not find it.

"You have betrayed yourself! The Englishman above knows your secret: he overheard your ravings in your sleep. I heard them myself. He must be destroyed!"

"Where is my cutlass?" said Fedon.

"Safe with me," I replied: "so is your secret. Do not attempt aught against me: if you try to mount this ladder, you are a dead man. I am armed, younger, stronger, and more active than yourself; but fear me not — I am not your enemy."

"Fire the house, and burn him!" shrieked the beldam.

"Fools, forbear! I can leap the window long before the flames can reach me; but I will not betray you — by the heavens above me, I will not! Listen, Julien Fedon. I owe my life to you: I was born in your camp. In short, I am the son of Bearwell Arundell, *le Bagué Tigre!*"

"Merciful Heavens! you the son of Bearwell Arundell!"

He clasped his hands and fell on his knees; while I descended the ladder — taking care, however, to keep possession of the cutlass. The caution was needless; he rose from his genuflection, fixed his eyes on me, and, after minutely inspecting every feature in my face, said, "It is he! it is the son of the good white man, who vindicated the cause of the poor despised mulatto, and whose mother died in my camp. Ah, I am sick at heart — lead me to my seat!"

We did so; when, overcome with his feelings, he fainted. It was some time before I recovered him. He then addressed the old negress: "See!" said he; "behold the infant that you aided to bring into the world. Do you not recollect being his mother's midwife — that mother whom he resembles? and you, this eventful night, wished me to destroy him! Where is your prophetic power?"

"Said I not, Julien Fedon," replied the sibyl, "that he knew who you were?"

"Away, sorceress! you would have murdered the son of my dearest friend; but God pardon you, and me also! I need not entreat you not to betray me; I believe no traitor's blood flows in your father's race."

I had no wish to give this unhappy man up to justice. True, he had committed one act which is scarcely to be paralleled in the annals of the crimes of civil war; but, with his 'thousand crimes,' he possessed one virtue: he was grateful, and to his gratitude I owed my life. His death on the gibbet at this time could have answered no good purpose; and the local government would not have thanked any one who should have forced them to punish a man for crimes committed a quarter of century ago.

He related his adventures to me. After he took leave of my father, a violent storm arose; when he and his fellow fugitives saw a French privateer, towards which they made. A part got on board,[94] the rest were drowned, having perished in the attempt to board the privateer: his boat being picked up, caused the report of his having been lost to be credited. The privateer landed Fedon in Trinidad; here he remained until the next year, when his old enemy, Abercrombie, took the island. He then went into the woods in the centre of the island; and, for two years, lived the life of a recluse. He then visited the uninhabited northern shore, where a French vessel having put in for water, he got on board and escaped to Martinique.

Soon after this the British made an attack on that island, when the timid and hunted Fedon concealed himself on board of an American vessel, and went to the United States; in which *land of liberty*† free coloured persons are so ill-treated and degraded, that they may be truly said to be slaves without owners. He was glad to escape from this republic on board of a vessel bound to St. Domingo. Here, in 1803, he was taken by Rochambeau, and sent prisoner to France: after a time he was permitted to go at large.

Under the directions of a priest that he met in France, he commenced the series of austere penance, which he still practised. The climate of Europe being too cold for him, he came out to Cayenne in 1808, where he met with Julie Sanois, whom he had left in Grenada twelve years since. The following year his old enemies, the English, captured the colony. Although he had taken the Spanish name of Saint Jago, he feared his old foe might still discover him; he, therefore, left the colony, and joined a wandering horde of Indians, with whom he remained five years. At the peace of 1814, Cayenne was restored to France, and he returned amongst civilised men.

The blind Victor Hugues, having heard that Fedon had buried a considerable treasure in Grenada, advised him to go to recover it. Fedon refused to venture to the land of his birth. Some words took place between the parties, and the blind ruffian threatened to get Fedon assassinated. The timidity of the old brigand chief having increased with his years, he so feared the threat of the old revolutionist that the restless exile came in the same vessel with me to Trinidad.

---

94. I have reason to believe that there lives at this moment (1836) in Trinidad, a man who escaped with Fedon.

A more wretched being than this, perhaps, existed not. Exiled from the land he loved, hunted like a flying-fish, fearing human and Divine vengeance, practising the most severe acts of mortification and penance, and yet despairing of Heaven's mercy.

At daylight I took leave of this unhappy man, and never saw him more; for the very next day he quitted the island in a smuggling cutter bound for Martinique.

CHAPTER 46.

— "His poor self,
With his disease of all-shunned poverty,
Walks like contempt alone."
                              SHAKESPEARE.[†]

O n my arrival at my house, I found my servant (a free lad of colour)
wearing a countenance so pale and wo-begone, that I might have
been alarmed, but that I long since anticipated the worst that could
happen. Old Croaker says if I recollect right, that there is this advantage in
fretting away our misfortunes before they come, for that, when they do
arrive, we do not feel them. This I now verified, when I heard of my letters
being stolen. I judged that he who was scoundrel enough to break open
my desk to get at a letter, would not be honest enough to leave my money.
My conjecture was correct. Two nights after my departure, my servant
went to a *belair* (a negro dance), and did not return until daylight the next
morning, when he found the house had been broken open, my desk
forced, and a small cedar box, containing almost all my money, and some
of my papers, stolen. The young man went immediately to the magistrate,
Mr. Pennyfeather, who came, inspected the premises and the desk, shook
his head, said it was a clear burglary, both according to English and
Spanish law, and went away.

I made a few inquiries, and, after a little investigation, found out the
following facts. The afternoon preceding the robbery, a strange white
man, with a lame negro, came in a boat from up the coast. They landed
in the evening, and the white man, leaving the cripple in charge of the
boat, took the road to my house: he stopped at a cottage, and inquired his
way. The occupiers described him as a middle-sized spare man, with red
hair, and an erect military carriage. This description answered exactly
with that of the disbanded soldier; and I now recollected having seen a

lame negro, making *mahoo*[95]† ropes before his door. One of my neighbours, who saw this boat during the evening, noticed written on her stern, 'J. Smithson, Chaguanas.'† The lame negro slept in a kind of shed, wherein sugars are placed, at La Brea, and, in the night, the white man called him hastily, and hurried him down to the boat, when they set off, rowing together towards town. An old watchman, situated in the shed, saw all this, and remarked that the white man, when he arrived and called the negro, had under his arm a small box, exactly answering the description of the one stolen from me.

All these circumstances taken together, although they did not amount to legal proof, left no doubt on my mind that the robbery was committed by the old soldier; and I had nearly as little doubt but it must have been abetted or connived at by Smithson, who, being the only man in the colony with whom I had a dispute, probably himself placed the letter of the anti-slavery secretary in the news-room, or induced the soldier to place it there.

I wrote all this to the chief of the police establishment, but never heard that any thing was done in consequence of my letter.

Having lost my horse, I wrote to a neighbour, one Monsieur Le Jeune, for the loan of one of his for a week or two. Some months previous to this I had attended him while he was attacked with a desperate fever, from which I was fortunate enough to recover him, and his gratitude knew no bounds; at least he said so. He proffered to give me, I know not what; but the promises of a convalescent to his physician are seldom remembered after the patient is entirely well. This was verified by Monsieur Le Jeune: he now wrote me a most insulting note, refusing to lend me a horse, "unless he were sure," said the letter, "that it would break my neck." He added, by way of postscript, "that he should dispense with my future attendance as medical man on his estate."

"Oh, oh!" said I; "my fame has travelled before me; I have been canonised for a *saint* already in this quarter."

There was something like retribution for this ungrateful affront. After writing and sending the letter spoken of, he worked himself up into such a furious passion at what he termed my villainy, that he called for his horse, saying he would go to me, and personally tell me what he had written. The horse was brought. In order to overtake the boy whom he had

---

95. Ropes made from the inner bark of the mahoo-tree.

despatched with the note, he spurred the animal violently: the horse was spirited, and Le Jeune a bad rider; away went the steed, and off went Monsieur Le Jeune. He came to the ground, dislocating his left shoulder in the fall.

I walked as far as Powel's house, hoping I might borrow a steed from him. I found with him Smith and his late antagonist, Naysmith. I addressed them; they replied coolly, and seemed under some restraint. After a few words Powel whispered to Smith, Naysmith joined them, and I was left standing by myself. I was about to quit the room with indignation, when Powel said, "Stop, doctor; these gentlemen wish to pay you one hundred dollars, which they owe you for attending them in the late *affaire d'honneur*. They have not the money, but I can lend it to them: here are six doubloons and four dollars.

"Mr. Powel," said I, "had I merely attended these young men as a surgeon, I would have accepted the amount you offer; but, as I mixed myself up in their quarrel, and, in fact, was near becoming a combatant myself, I cannot think of taking money for my services: it looks too much like selling honour for gold."

Powel looked astonished at this, and said, "Is this possible? and you have been robbed, too!"

"Of nearly all I possess in the world," said I; "but that has nothing to do with the present question."

"It cannot be true what we have heard," said Powel.

"What have you heard?" demanded I.

He then told the story of my being found to be a *saint*. The tale had undergone considerable alterations, and had received many additions in its passage to La Brea; for, in the West Indies, scandal, like Madeira wine, always improves by transportation.

When he had done, I explained the real state of the case, observing, that it was true I had received the unlucky letter from the anti-slavery secretary, and I had replied to it; but I told them the purport of my reply. I also related to them my adventures in the savanna, and the grounds that I had for believing that Smithson attempted to destroy me by setting fire to the rushes. I also acquainted them with all I had found out respecting the robbery of my money and papers; and put it to them to judge, whether the whole was not a plot to effect my ruin on the part of the sanguinary coward, Smithson, whose hatred I had incurred by entering into their dispute?

"By Heavens, doctor, I believe every word you say! you are a noble fellow, and we were fools and ungrateful to believe a word said against you. It is all a villainous plot of the poltroon, Smithson," said Naysmith.

Both Powel and Smith agreed with him.

Powel said that he had finished crop, and would visit Chaguanas, and find out the whole affair. "You will hear of me in less than a week," said he.

We parted good friends, although Smith and Naysmith candidly told me that they had positive orders from the merchants, charged with the agency of the estates of which they were managers, not to allow of my visiting the said plantations as medical attendant.

On my arrival at my house I found a negro boy, with a note and a horse. The note was in a lady's hand-writing. I opened and read it. It was written in French, by Mademoiselle Celeste, the sister-in-law of Monsieur Le Jeune, apologising, in the most humble strain, for the rude and insulting note of her brother-in-law; informing me of the accident which had befallen him; and praying me, for charity's sake, as a Christian, to come and reduce his dislocated shoulder,[†] as there was no surgeon within twenty miles of him: his torture was insupportable, and the lamentation of Madame Le Jeune was distressing.

I never could bear resentment against a fallen foe, although of thriving malice I am as sincere a hater as Dr. Johnson could desire.[†] Taking the necessary implements with me, I mounted the horse, and in a few minutes was at the mansion of Monsieur Le Jeune, a creole of St. Domingo.

"This is kind, doctor," said Mlle. Celeste; and she ushered me into the patient's room. I found him in great pain; but I soon reduced the dislocation, prepared the necessary medicines out of the domestic medicine-chest, and ordered the servants and his wife to keep him quiet.

As I came out, Mlle. Celeste paid me a number of compliments on what she called my magnanimous conduct to her *beau-frère*.[†] As she really was a very pretty sprightly creole, there was no impropriety in calling her a *belle-soeur*;[†] but to denominate such an ugly caricature of a baboon as was Le Jeune, *beau-frère*, it was preposterous; there was nothing *beau* about the little wretch.

The young lady was rather inclined to coquet. She said it was a pity so good a young man as I should have the misfortune of being a *philantrope*;[†] for, by a common perversion of terms, *philantrope* has the same sinister signification amongst the French colonies, as *saint* has amongst the English.

I replied, it was fortunate for her brother-in-law that I happened to be a *philantrope*, or I never would have reduced his dislocation after receiving so gross an insult from him.

"But I mean, it is to be regretted," said she, "that you are *ce que les Anglais appellent enceinte*."[†] A *saint*, she meant to have said, but the blunder made me smile.

A few weeks after this, Mlle. Celeste made Mr. Naysmith the happiest of men; and, according to Sheridan, he has been a miserable dog ever since.[†]

I continued my visits for two days, when I found Mons. Le Jeune could do without my further attendance. He now thought proper to apologise for his conduct. He offered me a small purse of gold, and said that he hoped in future to serve me with his friendship and patronage.

"You are now, Monsieur Le Jeune," said I, "out of danger, and can do without my further attendance; but I take this opportunity of telling you, that I have the most sovereign contempt for your money, enmity, friendship, and patronage."

Saying this, I left his house, and never again entered it.

Having received notice from all the managers of the plantations I attended, that my services would be dispensed with, I got in as many debts as I could. These were few; as, in general, when I sent for the money due to me, I received for answer, that I was a *saint*, and might sue for what was due, and be ———.

"Adieu to this colony," said I. "I have no family here, nor am I rooted to this soil like one of its many-trunked fig-trees."

I packed up my clothes, instruments, and books, paid off a few little debts, and went on board a vessel going to Port of Spain, in which town I landed with four dollars in my pocket.

I was resolved to quit the country, but lacked the means of procuring a passage. I possessed a gold watch and appendages, which I bought at Cayenne; I now sold it to a goldsmith for two doubloons — less, by the by, than the cases were worth. He asked me if I wished to part with the diamond ring I wore? "Rather," was my reply, "would I part with my life!" It was the ring that my dearest Maria Josefa gave me.

The story of my being obliged to sell my watch got wind, and, would it be credited, afforded a source of triumph to the party which was persecuting me? In the next gazette a gentlemanly article appeared, from the pens of the three worthies already described, on the subject of my poverty. The only part of this theme which I recollect, is a line stolen from Pope —

"Foe to his pride, but friend to his distress."[†]

During this frantic persecution, I once or twice was half-tempted to take summary vengeance on some persons who insulted me; but restrained myself by recollecting, that he who has the misfortune of being falsely accused does not rebut the charge by knocking down his accuser.

I walked towards the wharf, to look out for a passage to St. Christopher's. I saw before me a dapper little man, reciting, after a manner, the 'Death of General Moore.'[†] There was no mistaking the voice, although one might mistake the man: it was my old fellow passenger, Lieutenant Jack.

Although I was never intimate with him, yet I was glad to see him, as an old acquaintance. Our pleasure at meeting was mutual. He invited me to go on board a cutter which he owned. I did so. He informed me that, having made a little money on board a Columbia privateer, he left the trade of war, and became a reformed man. Having purchased the cutter we were on board, he commenced trading amongst the islands, but did not improve his fortune until, like my friend of the Pickled Timber, his memory became defective; that is to say, he commenced forgetting to pay the duties. He was now carrying on a most lucrative trade, by supplying the inhabitants of Trinidad with certain articles from Martinique and St. Thomas's.

I informed him how I was situated, and of my intention of going off the island.

"Do nothing of the sort," said he. "It is not a month since I saw at St. Thomas's your friend Fernandez. He has heard you are here, and you may expect to see him or hear from him every day. I apprehend he has good news for you. Do not quit the island for some weeks, at all events. I go to Martinique in a day or two, whence I return in a fortnight: if, by the time I come here, you heard nothing of Fernandez, I'll give you a passage to St. Thomas's. In the meantime, I can supply you with whatever you may want in regard to money matters."

I thanked him, but declined his offer of pecuniary aid.

He told me that he was going on the morrow down to the quarter called the Carenage, and begged me to join him, as he intended to take on board a quantity of provisions, which, in consequence of a late hurricane, sold well in Martinique, but which he intended to take off without troubling the custom-house about invoices or clearance. He also said he would shew me some curious caverns in the now uninhabited islet called Gasper Grande; especially one that he himself discovered. I stopped with him until the evening, and then went to my lodgings, in the suburbs of the town. Here I found a letter from Powel: it ran thus:

> "DEAR ARUNDELL, — I told you that I would bring something to light respecting your papers; I believe I shall be able to keep my word. The soldier, whom you suspected as the robber who carried off your money, has been found murdered; and there is more than suspicion entertained that Smithson has slain him. He has just been brought up as a prisoner, and a quantity of papers have been found in his possession; amongst the rest, those you miss. Have patience: all will come to light.
> "Yours faithfully,
> "E. POWEL."

The next day I went, on board Jack's cutter, to Gasper Grande, an islet about a mile and a half off Trinidad; and, while the mate shipped a quantity of farine (the flour of manioc),† and other provisions, we inspected the caves. These are extraordinary productions of nature: they favour the contraband trade admirably.

"Do you see that ruinous boiling-house on the main-land side?" said Jack.

"What, that building so thickly covered with leaves and parasites?"

"The same."

"Well, what of it?"

"It is said to be haunted."

"Pshaw! what of that? I have seèn thousands of places *said* to be haunted."

"But," added Jack, "that place is said to have been the scene of a murder, when this island was taken by the English. It is supposed that the ghost of the murdered man hovers about these ruins; and the story favours me. No one will approach them at night; and I can land what part of my cargo I like there, without fear of interruption. I never met the ghost of the rich old Spaniard, whose murdered body was found on the beach, but whose money is said to have been buried somewhere thereabouts. I wish he would shew me where it lies, for I am almost weary of the life of a sailor, and wish to settle ashore. I have not shewn you my grand magazine. I see the mate is busy getting in the provisions, so we have time to visit this cave, which I by chance discovered. I am the only one who knows of its existence."

Saying this, he led me up the interior of the little island, until we came to a decayed and hollow tree. This he entered, and bade me follow. We descended about twenty feet. I was in darkness, amid rocks, and surrounded by thousands of bats. Jack procured fire by means of a bottle of phosphorus: he then lighted a wax taper. Our passage was now wide enough for two persons; but I felt it oppressively hot. Suddenly we came to an apparent termination of the passage; but, by removing a stone, an opening appeared. We passed this on our hands and knees. Another long gallery was to be traversed, and then we came to a magnificent cave, illuminated by masses of natural crystal from above, and ventilated through the immense rocks which formed the roof of this singular subterraneous apartment. Through these crevices the water dripped from above, and petrified in its descent, hanging, like dark coloured icicles, on the stone roof.

After inspecting this cavern we returned to day, and heard a whistle; it was a signal from the mate of Jack. He informed his chief that the vessel was loaded, all to a few barrels of Indian corn.

"Sail the vessel towards the Bocases, and be ready for a start. If the corn does not come by eight o'clock, bring the boat to this island, and send us a good supper, with a jar or two of olives, and some brandy fruit, as a present for the doctor here."

Away went the mate; and we entered into conversation, each recounting the adventures he had met with since we parted.

At the hour appointed the mate sculled a small boat to the islet, and brought an excellent supper, together with the present for me. We sat at the entrance of one of the caves, near the sea, making a hearty repast, and drinking some fine wine of the vineyard of Château Margaux. All this time the cutter was standing on and off between Gaspar Grande and the Dragon's Mouth, ready to slip out of the Gulf of Paria at a few minutes' notice; Jack, mean while, cursing some one who had disappointed him in not supplying him with some Indian corn that he expected.

CHAPTER 47.

"That night a child might understand
The Deil had business on his hand."
BURNS.[†]

There was no moon visible, but it was one of those balmy nights which generally follow a heavy day's rain in Trinidad, and which are peculiarly pleasant. To the northward and eastward, however, there was a mass of inky clouds, that portended heavy rain before midnight.

We had finished our supper, and Jack remarked that a heavy fall of rain would soon take place.

"I believe," said he, "that of all parts of the globe, Trinidad has the most frequent and most tremendous falls of rain. However," said he, "you have not the curses of the other islands, which are droughts and hurricanes: in short, you have nothing to alarm you but, now and then, a few earthquakes, as I am told."

"These," said I, "come so frequently, that we are used to them: and, after all, they have never been known to do any damage."[96†]

"What is that?" said Jack, starting on his legs; "lend me your nightglass,[†] Crowther," addressing his mate. "By Heavens, 'tis the custom-house boat! What can bring it down here? Do they suspect what is going forward? No matter, we are prepared; the current and light wind favour us, and we'll be out of the Bocas before they can overtake us. Arundell, can you get ashore with the little canoe there?"

"I can," said I.

"Then I'll leave her in charge of you. She is as light as a cockle-shell; she is easily managed with a single paddle, and can be carried on a strong

---

96. Subsequent to this period (on the 2nd of September, 1825) an earthquake did a little damage to the tower of the Protestant church:[†] it was, however, built on an unsound foundation.

man's shoulder. If you go to town, leave her in charge of St. Vincent, a free black man, who lives at L'Ance Metan.† Find out, if you can, what brings the custom-house boat down here. I have no time, but must away.— Come, Crowther."

They jumped into their boat, and in an instant she rushed through the sparkling waters. I now observed that the long custom-house boat approached the island; but she pulled heavily, while the skiff† of Jack shot along the waters with the velocity of a steam-carriage on a railroad. Soon was Jack on board his cutter. I observed she stood immediately towards the Bocas, and was going rapidly through the water. I again looked at the custom-house boat: there was but one pair of oars in her, although a boat of her size required at least two pair. Even this single pair were badly managed, as the boat was yawing about in all directions; either because the men in her pulled unequally, or because there was no one to steer her, or from both these causes combined. She came opposite the cave, and the parties in her seemed to hesitate whether they should make for the islet or pull ashore. At length they did the former. I never saw two worse rowers in my life than were in this boat. At length they approached the very cave at the entrance of which I stood. I believe the people in the boat did not perceive Jack's departure, on account of a projecting point of land between them.

Resolved, if possible, to discover the cause of the custom-house boat coming down here, I caught up the cutlass which Jack had left me, and concealed myself amongst the lime-rocks at the entrance of the cavern. I had no particular wish to turn smuggler, but I wanted to render a service to an old acquaintance, who had not abandoned me while under general persecution. The boat was run alongside the cave; in doing this, the two men mismanaged her so that they dashed her bow against a projecting rock. A negro, dressed like one of the lower orders of Columbia, got out of her, swearing in Spanish. He was followed by a man, whom, from his features, rather than from his complexion, I made out to be a white man. He exclaimed in English, "D——n the boat! she's too heavy." "Is it possible," thought I, "this can be Smithson?" It was his voice, his form, and his stooping gait; but of his features, there was scarce enough light for me to be assured of them. Powel had written me that Smithson was imprisoned on suspicion of having committed murder. But how came he here? — Let me listen.

I did so — taking care not to be seen. The medium of conversation between these men was the dialect called Creole French, which, however, neither spoke fluently. When the black man was at a loss for an expression, he used one in Spanish; and when the white man hesitated for a word, he used English. Having the advantage of knowing all three of these vernaculars, I generally caught the meaning of the parties before they understood each other. The first part of their dialogue consisted of mutual accusations of not rowing well. The Englishman said that he was not used to rowing; the black said he was better acquainted with the paddle than the oar. The Englishman was now seized with a violent cough.

"What is the matter?" said the negro.

"I am again attacked with this vomiting of blood. I shall never recover the shock I got leaping the accursed prison-wall."

"So," thought I, "I was right: this is Smithson, who has broken gaol."

The Spanish negro replied, — "Never mind a little blood; better die of its loss than by a sore throat caught while under a gibbet."

"No fear of that," replied Smithson; "they never could hang a white man on suspicion; for no one saw me throttle the old soldier, and dead men tell no tales — unless, as some think, their ghosts arise, which I scarcely believe; for I never saw one, unless in my dreams, although I have done for three, including a girl whose throat I cut: she was with child by me in my own country. That affair brought me out to this part of the world, and made me take my present name."

"But let us away," said the negro; "we have little time to lose."

"Let us rest for a few minutes, or I never shall be able to pull over to the main-land. Have you brought the mason's hammer from the gaol?" said Smithson.

"No," replied the black, "I left it in the prison-yard; but I have in the boat what will do us more service — the spade."

"The hammer," said Smithson, "did some execution in prison; without it we never could have escaped."

"We!" replied the negro, "speak of yourself. Do you think that the gaol in Port of Spain could have held me, Juan Pedrosa? I, who have broke out of every prison in Ferdinand's Indies? I should have escaped last night, but that they put you in the same cell with me. What is that?" he added, and made a few paces towards the water. "Here is good fortune! a capital light canoe; with this we can easily get across to the main-land. Let us sink this heavy boat, to avoid suspicion. This canoe will do well to get to the other side; it is too light to cross to Columbia; but, on the opposite side, there are enough fishing-boats. It must now be bout two hours to midnight; by one o'clock we can dig up the treasure, and before daylight we will be off the Island of Checachacara,[†] whence to the Main we may pass in about two hours. We have no time to lose."

Saying this, he took out the plug from the custom-house boat, which they had stolen, and left her to sink near the cavern. The parties designed to steal the canoe left in my charge.

"Are you ready yet?" said the Spanish negro.

"Yes," replied Smithson. "But one moment: you say the boiling-house is said to be haunted; do you believe the current report?"

"No," replied Pedrosa; "the report, I think, arises thus. When your countrymen took this island, my old master, Don Juan Baptista, took it into his head that his money would be safer under ground than exposed to the chances of war. He put it into a heavy trunk, and had it conveyed to an old estate of his, but which had been abandoned, because he found better land to the southward. I was a young man at that time, and his favourite slave; in fact, my mother dying when I was born, his wife suckled me at her own breast, and so I became his confidential slave. Well, he employed me to dig a hole behind the boiling-house. We let down the trunk, placed a parcel of leathern bags, full of gold and silver, and covered it with mogass[97][†] ashes, so that no one would suspect what was below it. Now you must know that it is an old trick to cause a slave to help to bury money, and then kill him, in order to have the secret well kept. I believe this was the intention of old Don Baptista. Now, in order to be beforehand with him, as he came out of the boiling-house, I made a cut at him from behind with my matcheti, which half took his head off. I then bundled him into a canoe, paddled out to sea, tied two or three stones to him, and pitched him into the water, hoping the sharks would take care of him, and resolving at my leisure to take up the money. Well, as the devil would have it, the ravenous fish, although no one can breathe here for them, would not touch the carcass of Don Juan, and the tide threw him ashore, right opposite where his darling treasure was buried. Well," continued this villain, "a report was set on foot, I know not how true it was, that his ghost hovered about that spot. As soon as things got a little settled, after Gudoy[†] sold this island to the English,[98] I was taken on suspicion of murdering my master, and put in gaol. I easily made my escape, and got over to Cumana. I

---

97. The refuse of the sugar-cane, when the juice is expressed, is called mogass. This is used for fuel.

98. The Spaniards believe that Gudoy sold Trinidad to the English.

returned here a few nights since, after many years' absence, to dig up the treasure, bringing an old comrade with me to assist; but we quarrelled on landing, and I gave him eight inches of my poniard, which stopped his wind. I was lodged in the prison, and here I am with you — although you, as I suspect, have but a faint heart; but I am ready to do a job which will make both our fortunes. Are you disposed now to move?"

"Yes," said Smithson.

They both got into the canoe, and paddled over towards the main-land.

"Shall I allow this pair of villains to carry off a treasure, and escape justice. True, they are two to one; but, armed in a good cause, I am equal to that Spaniard and his cowardly associate."

This thought passed through my mind the instant they got into the canoe.

"God, I throw myself on thy righteous protection!" said I, and threw off my jacket, shoes, and hat, caught my cutlass between my teeth, passed round a rock, and plunged into the water, swimming in the wake of the canoe, which sparkled with phosphoric light. I kept sufficiently distant not to attract their notice, when one of those tremendous showers of rain which are almost peculiar to Trinidad commenced falling. The big drops descended so heavily as to render it difficult for me to breathe, with my cutlass in my mouth; but I struck out manfully. I, however, lost sight of the canoe. The rain fell like a mighty cataract, and the thunder bellowed on the Gulf, and was re-echoed amid the world of mountains on shore. I scarcely knew the way I was swimming, until a flash of lightning again shewed me on which side the main-land lay. I struck out, and made for the nearest point, which was two hundred yards below where the old ruins stood, and to where the canoe was making. I landed almost exhausted; but there was not time to be lost, as the canoe must have got ashore a quarter of an hour before me. I walked cautiously towards the boiling-house: it was covered with such a mass of lianes, parasite plants, wild vines, tendrils, and mosses, that no part of the building materials was visible.

The confederates had forced their way towards the furnace-mouth outside of the ruins. This had been covered with a wooden shed, which had stood the wreck of time better than the rest of the building; for, while the rain poured through the vegetable-covered roof in torrents, scarcely a drop fell through the shed, which had been made of the incorruptible hard wood of the country. They had kindled a fire here, doubtless to give them light. The glare of this was visible from the sea-shore, and informed me where they were. I crouched, and made my way through the mass of vegetable matter on my hands and knees. The rain poured on the ruins in such torrents as to make the sound deafening. This circumstance prevented their hearing my motions, as, amid a thousand breaking sticks and bending lianes, I approached them, at times gliding forward like a serpent. I drew near, and cautiously rose on my legs. A large vat, that had formerly belonged to the distillery which joined the buildings, was between the treasure-seekers and myself. Like all about this abandoned sugar manufactory, it was covered with vegetable matter; but this allowed me to conceal myself from the view of Smithson and Pedrosa, although I could watch all their motions.

As the red fire gleamed on the countenance of Smithson, I noted him well. Notwithstanding his weather-beaten face, which appeared to have stood the tear and wear of a rough existence for more than half a century — notwithstanding that his features were exaggerated, — yet any one, looking at him attentively, would have judged that, in youth, he must have possessed a handsome physiognomy. Pedrosa had a fine muscular body, but, like most males of African descent, his lower limbs were not stout in proportion. He seemed a man of about forty-five years: his countenance was bold, and he possessed what is uncommon in negroes, viz. a fine pair of whiskers. In forming both these men's countenances nature had not acted unfavourably; but long courses of vice and crime had thrown such traits of dogged surliness and sullen misanthropy into the looks of Smithson, and such an appearance of ferocity over the lineaments of Pedrosa, that two worse specimens of the human face divine never were covered with a white nightcap.

"Do you think the money is still here?" asked Smithson.

"We shall see," replied the negro.

He took the spade which they had brought, and, after making the sign of the cross, commenced working most vigorously, until the perspiration flowed copiously from him. Meanwhile, the rain had ceased, and every shovelful of ashes he threw from him was echoed in the deserted building. Had I stirred, the noise of my motion would have discovered me.

The negro soon became weary of his exertion.

"Here, take the spade," said he to his associate.

Smithson took it, to aid him.

"Heretic Jew!" exclaimed Pedrosa, "do you commence working without making the sign of the cross?"

"I think the practice of signing the cross," replied Smithson, "a piece of papistical idolatry."

The black called him, in Spanish, a "God-forsaking Englishman."

Merciful Heavens! here stood two sanguinary ruffians, — one of them had commenced his career of murder by cutting the throat of the woman he had seduced; the other, in his youth, had assassinated the man whose wife's bosom suckled his infancy: yet those two monsters were disputing about the ceremonies of religion!

Smithson worked as hard as his companion, until, suddenly, his cough seized him, and he again vomited blood. The negro took the spade, and soon announced that it struck against the lid of the coffer. The loose ashes were soon cleared from it, and they tried to open it, but in vain. They had not the key, and the lock resisted all their efforts. They tried to break the lid with the spade: that tool bent, but made no impression on the iron-bound coffer.

"It shall yield!" exclaimed Smithson.

And the old planter crept under the furnace-mouth: here he detached a grating-bar, a heavy piece of cast-iron, weighing about fifty or sixty pounds.

"Batter in the lid!" said he.

Pedrosa seized it, and, in a few seconds, smashed the lid to pieces.

The ruffians looked at each other: I saw by their countenances that the treasure was there. Smithson, who was pale with the loss of blood, jumped down and seized a small leathern bag, which, judging from its size, might have contained, as I suppose, one hundred ounces of metal.

"There!" said Pedrosa, in Spanish, "there is the soul of old Don Juan Baptista: no wonder his apparition haunts about this old ruin!"

"What!" thought I, "shall I allow those villains to carry off a treasure to the Main? Yet, what can I do? I cannot capture two men, but believe myself capable of slaying them, with the aid of Heaven. They deserve death: summary justice is still justice; but I'll not attack even murderers unprepared."

All this passed through my mind, as the Spanish negro said, "No wonder the apparition of Don Juan Baptista haunts about this ruin!"

I grasped my cutlass, and, with a voice of long-suppressed wrath, shouted, "Villains!" The word was echoed in the ruins. I attempted to rush on them, but was restrained by the lianes and tendrils by which I was surrounded. Slashing with my cutlass, I at length made my way through them.

My motions were stimulated by wrath, those of Smithson by a more violent passion; viz. terror. His shrieks re-echoed in the ruins, sounding more like the cries of a deer caught in the convolutions of a boa-constrictor, than any other wounds I ever heard: in an instant he made towards the sea. The negro stood half a second longer than the poltroon. I caught a glimpse of his countenance: every crisped hair of his head stood up like a bristle: he thought the interruption supernatural. I would not attack the assassin unprepared, but shouted in Spanish at the top of my voice, "Villain, defend yourself!" I made a blow at him with my cutlass: had it reached him, it would have cleaved his skull; but he was not destined to fall by my hand. My cutlass was caught, in its descent, by one of those tough withes called supple-jacks:[†] this balked the blow, although I severed the liane. The negro waited for no second stroke, but ran for his life. I followed; but, missing my step, I fell: my head came against a stone, and I was nearly stunned. I, however, rose again; but, before I got to the clear beach, both the men had disappeared. I saw, by the marks of their footsteps in the sand, that they had taken a northerly direction; but pursuit was hopeless.

I returned to the treasure, and heaped on the fire more fuel, which I found about. "Shall I," said I, "give all this up to the local government? That will be carrying honesty too far. Who will be the better for it? it will lie for years in the treasury, under pretence of finding the rightful heir of the murdered man who buried it. Beside, the villains may return and plunder it before I can get it removed, if I stand on ceremony. By taking this gold, I rob no one; by leaving it, I serve no real good purpose; and, if ever I can find the rightful heir of Don Juan Baptista, I will restore the whole, or a part of it. I am no Timon, to spurn a discovered treasure."[†]

I caught a blazing brand, and examined the old trunk. It was made in Trinidad cedar;[†] and, by the broken parts of the lid, I found it as fresh as the day the boards were sawed. Its contents were a quantity of bags, made of half-dressed goats'-skins, with the hair on. These contained gold and silver coins, and a quantity of pieces of uncoined precious metal, with rude crosses stamped on them, called *macaquina*, or weighed money, because it passes current in Spanish colonies by weight. Partly owing to the shed under which the coffer was buried being dry, and partly owing to its being covered with about five feet of mogass-ashes, all the bags were in an excellent state of preservation.

My soliloquy and scrutiny took not above a minute. I lifted out a bag of silver, but it was so heavy I could scarcely raise it to the surface. In the attempt, a quantity of ashes fell into the trunk, and nearly choked me. I would have given a thousand dollars at this moment for a drink of water, could I have obtained it without being discovered. I untied the bag, and fastened its strong twine to another: this I got up with less difficulty than the first, as I raised the second by dragging it up the side where no ashes were thrown. Again I descended into the trunk, and got up another precious bag by means of the string. This mode I repeated until the coffer was empty, save a small box, which I afterwards found to contain a valuable quantity of jewels, and some papers. I got this also out, and went to see if all was quiet on the beach. All was as still as death, save that at L'Ance Metan, about two miles from me, some men were employed fishing by torch-light. I returned, and passed an old dismounted sugar-pan,† which the late rains had filled with water: I refreshed my burning mouth with the sweetest draught I ever remember to have taken. I now brought to the beach one load of precious metal, and then another. I carried my cutlass constantly with me, lest the murderers should return. I had little fear of losing any of this in my absence, as I listened, but heard no one approach. In a still night, the human foot on the strand, or the sound of an oar or a paddle, is heard from afar. I soon got the whole of the treasure near the canoe, which I shoved off until it floated, for the receding tide had left it high and dry.

I was obliged to throw out of the canoe several stones which had been used as ballast, or the light vessel would not have floated with its heavy cargo. I then took a burning stick of dry rotten wood, in order to kindle fire at pleasure on the Island of Gaspar Grande. This done, I extinguished the remainder of the fire, lest it should attract notice.

I got into the canoe, and commenced propelling it across the channel to the islet. It was so deep that its sides were within five inches of the water; but, fortunately, not a breath of air stirred after the rain, and the surface of the Gulf was as smooth as a mirror. The clouds looked menacing, as though another torrent of rain was about to fall. This, had it happened, would have soon filled the canoe, and, consequently, sunk it. I paddled as though I worked for life, and got over safely to the mouth of the cave where I had supped. Here I found a part of a bottle of wine. I drank deeper than I was accustomed to do, but I was nearly exhausted by excitement and exertion.

I felt renovated, and got out of my canoe two bags of gold, which I placed at the entrance of the cave, and returned for more. I found the canoe adrift. Regardless of sharks, which abound hereabout, but which, I believe, seldom attack during the night, — at all events, they did not attack me this night, — I swam after the canoe, and nearly upset it getting into it. The paddle was ashore: I tore out a thwart by main force, and with it propelled the canoe again to the mouth of the cave. Here I lashed her fast to a limestone rock. She was soon emptied.

Another arduous task now devolved on me: this was to bring the metal up the island to the entrance of the hollow tree; for in the cave discovered by my friend Jack I resolved to place my treasure, well knowing that it was most improbable that any one would find it there before I could get the means of removing it safely to town. This I resolved to effect myself, without any assistance.

The last bag I removed contained pieces of uncoined silver. It was heavy; and, to my vexation, the seams of the goat-skin bag broke. I, however, gathered most of the silver up safely, although some pieces escaped me. These I resolved to collect as soon as day opened, lest they might be found, and cause suspicion.

I now conveyed the treasure into the hollow tree, and got some dry wood out of the cave near the sea. This, with the fire I got from the mainland, I kindled into a blaze, but in a low spot, which could not be seen from off the island. I, with a fire-stick,[†] entered the hollow tree, and with much difficulty got, bag by bag, the whole of my wealth brought into the cave. I concealed it behind a rock, in such a situation that it would have taken even Lieutenant Jack much searching to find it.

This done, I gladly returned to the surface of the earth, took another sip of grateful wine, made a good fire at the entrance of the cave, to dry my clothes, and lay down more fatigued than ever I was in my life, before or since. I had used more exertion that night than most men could have undergone.

"Yesterday," thought I, "I was poor, insulted, despised; this morning I am powerful, for I have the power of wealth. Hitherto I have despised money, and was thought despicable myself; tomorrow, men will accost me as one, in the cant of the world, 'who is respectably off.' Yesterday I was 'a poor devil,' whose indigence was made a theme of triumph for newspaper scribblers. Such is the opinion of mankind; but, alas! what says conscience? Why, that yesterday I was a man who had never done a dishonourable act, nor entertained a dishonourable thought; and now I am one who has been scheming and eaves-dropping to circumvent a pair of villains, in order to get possession of wealth that belongs not to me.

But, conscience avaunt! I will seek out Maria Josefa Ximenes, my angel of mercy, and lay this wealth at her feet."

My cogitation was broken here by the screaming of a hundred parrots, which were taking their flight from Trinidad to the Spanish Main. I raised my head, and found it was daylight. I had not slept, yet the night's strange adventures seemed like a dream.

CHAPTER 48.

"And how felt he, the wretched man
  Reclining there — while memory ran
  O'er many a year of guilt and strife;
  Flew o'er the dark flood of his life,
  Nor found one sunny resting-place,
  Nor brought him back one branch of grace?"
        Moore.[†]

"So bad a death argues a monstrous life."
        Shakespeare.[†]

As day opened I arose, put on my clothes, including those I had taken off the preceding night, before I swam over to Trinidad, gathered up all the remainder of the pieces of silver which had fallen when the bag broke, and crossed to Trinidad in the canoe. Several fishermen of colour, whom I passed, stared at me. Seeing a white man paddling a canoe excited their astonishment, until one called out, in the general language of the humble order, — I mean Creole French, — "Poor devil! let him pass; he is obliged to work for his living like one of us. All his own class have turned against him, because he wishes to do good to the slaves."

"God bless him for it!" responded another dark tall man; "he shall never want a fish or a plantain to eat while I, Jerome, have it to give. I'll speak to him."

This conversation I overheard between two people in different boats, who were, like me, rowing towards shore. I was astonished at the celerity with which news flies, and could not imagine how those fishermen had heard of my persecution; but, in a little community, scandal has swift wings. For obvious reasons, I avoided the friendly Jerome, and put ashore at the scene of my last night's adventure. I found the shovel which the two villains had brought, and hastily pitched in the ashes thrown out by

Smithson and his associate; after which, I watched until the coast was clear, and then I again got into my canoe, paddled a little way out, and threw the shovel into the water.

I anchored my canoe, and came ashore, for I felt a slight headache, and therefore wished to procure what all here take early in the morning — I mean a cup of coffee. I entered a decent-looking *tapia* house.[99] Scarcely had I done this, before a coloured lad ran to me, and said, "How do you do, doctor? Don't you know me?"

It was a boy whose suspended animation I had restored some weeks since at La Brea. The boy's father was much moved at being told that it was I who had saved his son's life. He was the same Jerome who had spoken so friendly of me a few minutes before. His expressions of gratitude, and those of the mother of the boy (who was, however, not Jerome's wife), were almost distressing to me! How strongly contrasted was his conduct to that of Monsieur Le Jeune! He brought out a quantity of money in a little red cotton bag, and offered it to me, saying, I should find there twenty-seven dollars: he regretted he had no more money, but said he hoped to make it up to fifty in the course of a month or two. I would not accept of any part of it, but asked him for a cup of coffee: my want was supplied as soon as it was named. I begged for the loan of shaving materials: these were also brought. The little boy whom I had saved attended me.

"Excuse me, doctor," said Jerome, "but your dress appears a little in disorder — Lucy, my woman, would be glad to wash them; at the same time, would you please to wear a suit of mine." I gladly accepted of this friendly offer. I bathed in the sea, and, after, that, put on a very decent suit of clothes belonging to my host. He begged me to stop and breakfast with him; he caused Lucy to prepare an excellent repast of fish, which he had that morning caught, and new-laid eggs.

Thinking I might confide in this man, whose countenance and manner indicated extreme good-nature, I asked him, if I had any thing to carry to town which I wished to land at night, whether he would assist me?

"Listen to me, doctor," said Jerome; "I do not like to smuggle, because it defrauds the King of England, God bless him! and the King of England gives to the poor man of colour what no prince ever gave us — that is, he has made men of us by protecting us. I have visited Spanish colonies, and

---

99. Tapia is a wall composed of reeds, clay, and grass.

seen the mulatto nominally free, but, in fact, degraded. The French treat us worse. But, in this island, which does not belong to the people of it, like Barbadoes and other English colonies, but is ruled immediately by our good king, the man of colour has justice;† therefore, I dislike defrauding George the Fourth of his fair duties. Nevertheless, doctor, my boy owes his life to you, and I'll lend you a hand to run your cargo ashore in Port of Spain, despite of all the custom-house officers in the island."

I was pleased with the man's loyalty, and assured him, on my honour, that what I wanted to land was not contraband articles. He promised to aid me. It was agreed between us that I was, that night, to bring what I wanted ashore; he was to lend me a large trunk, in which to put what I brought, help me to get it to town, and ask no further questions.

Scarcely had we entered into this arrangement, when some one called from the outside of the house, "Hallo! Jerome, are you within?"

We both went out, and found a gentlemanly-looking man, mounted on a very fine, but restive English horse, which stood kicking and biting in all directions, in consequence of being plagued with mosquitoes and sand-flies. The rider had a military air, although dressed in plain clothes; in fact, he was a retired officer, turned planter.

"*Bon jour*, commandant,"† said Jerome.

The commandant did not dismount, but said, "Jerome, you must start for town as quick as a shell jumps from a mortar. Prepare a good pair of oars, and a paddle to steer. It is a matter of life and death. Charge what you will, in reason, the quarter session will pay you. There has been a murder committed; and I want you to go with a letter to the chief of police, and another to the attorney-general."

In less than a minute, Jerome took the letters, was in the boat, with a companion, rowing, and his own son steering with a paddle.

"Adieu, doctor!" said the active Jerome, as he went off.

"Doctor!" exclaimed the commandant, looking at me. "I presume, sir, I have the honour of addressing a gentleman of the medical profession?"

I coolly nodded assent; for persecution had made me feel shy of every white man in the island.

"If you are a surgeon or physician, as magistrate of this quarter I call upon you to assist me in investigating a case of murder, in the name of the king."

"And I, sir, refuse to go, in the name of the people."

"Really, I do not comprehend, doctor."

"I will explain, commandant. My evidence would not be believed by any respectable (that is to say, white) man in the community; for I am called a *saint*, thought a spy, and persecuted as a scoundrel."

"May I — stand still, Vixen — (this was addressed to his mare) — may I ask your name, without giving offence, sir?"

"I believe I cannot tell it, without giving offence — It is Warner Arundell. You must have heard and read of me; if not, look to the newspapers of this island. Good day, sir."

I was making off, when the commandant, still on horseback, replied, "I have both heard and read of you: but I have, Dr. Arundell, been long enough in these islands to know how much I can depend upon public rumour and newspaper paragraphs, when they speak of one who commits the crime of differing in opinion from our colonial many-headed monster. I, however, put it to yourself, as a gentleman (and this humble dress you have does not disguise you sufficiently for me to take you for any other but a gentleman), — I put it to yourself, whether the braying of a set of frantic asses justifies your neglecting your duty as a subject of his majesty, in refusing to aid me in this case? Besides, sir, common humanity should induce you to assist the wounded man."

"A wounded man! I thought the party was dead. Nay, that alters the case. Where is he? I will go instantly to see him."

"You will find him at the third house of the little village on the shore: there it is, about two miles distant. I fear it is beyond your skill to aid him. Nevertheless, I will procure you a boat to take you to the spot. I would offer you this quadruped devil, but she will keep you dancing for half an hour, with one leg in the stirrup, before you will be able to mount her, and then, most likely, throw you."

"Please to dismount and lend me your whip. I have a way of my own in mounting and managing vicious horses."

The commandant did as I requested, and narrowly escaped being kicked. I never saw so wicked a brute: she was an English blood-mare, transported to this island for having killed a groom.

I had not spent years in South America without learning to daunt a restive horse. I got behind her, made a short run, vaulted into the saddle over her crupper, and seized the reins. Perceiving herself so unceremoniously mounted, she reared and plunged desperately, before I got my feet in the stirrups. I got her head towards where I wanted her to go, then gave her the whip. Away she went, with the fury of a flying demon; but she soon wished to slacken her pace — firstly, because she perceived she had a rider on her back; and secondly, the tide having risen, she had to take her furious course through two feet of water, which rendered her career laborious. I now pushed her as hard as I could; and, by the time I got to the house wherein the wounded man was lying, she was most completely tamed.

The commandant followed in a boat. I am told he said, "If that proud, but daring young fellow is a spy, then I have no judgment in human nature."

I entered the house, or rather large hut, where the wounded man lay: he was no other than Smithson. He lay stretched out on a board supported by stools, partially covered with an old boat-sail. He was bathed in blood; had five wounds about him; while by his side lay the cuchilla, or Spanish knife, with which his late associate had stabbed him.

I afterwards learned the particulars of this murder. Spurred by fright, because he thought he heard and saw a supernatural object in the ruins the preceding night, he ran, with his associate, for more than two miles along the coast, until he got near the village in which I saw him. Here he fell from exhaustion. He had ruptured a small blood-vessel in leaping the prison-wall, and his violent fright and exertion brought on again a vomiting of blood. His comrade raised him from the ground: in doing this, he felt that Smithson held the small bag of gold which he had taken from the coffer before I interfered. Pedrosa attempted to take this; but Smithson, although weakened with the loss of blood, was still a powerful man. He held the gold fast; the other drew his cuchilla, and, the instant that was out, the savage glutted his love for blood. In a second five desperate wounds were inflicted on the body of Smithson: he fell, still retaining the gold, and shrieked for succour. Several men, who were going to fish by torch-light, ran to his rescue, and the ferocious Pedrosa was driven from his prey, while Smithson was carried into a hut. Pedrosa, in the meanwhile, ran along the coast, and was about breaking a chain by which a canoe was fastened, in order to endeavour to escape with it to the Main; but he did not see, in the dark night, that the owner of the boat was sleeping in it. The noise of the breaking the chain awoke the man: he asked who was there? The reply of the savage was an attempted thrust with his ever-ready cuchilla — for he had still a second knife about him. This the boatman evaded by jumping into the sea. He had his cutlass with him: indeed, few of the labouring people of Trinidad ever stir without it. Again Pedrosa rushed towards him; but he found a man as active as, and better armed than himself. With a cut of his weapon he nearly took off the right hand of the murderer; and, following up his advantage, transfixed his body with a thrust. Thus expired the sanguinary Pedrosa. No one thought of burying him, even in the sand: his body was carried out to sea by the tide, and, doubtless, devoured by the sharks. But, to return to the wounded man.

As I entered the hut, Smithson started, and exclaimed, "Ah! What, have you come to enjoy my downfall? Away! my curses on you!"

"Wretched man, I came not to triumph over your misery. When I entered this hut to render assistance to a wounded man, I knew not it was you."

"You now know me. Away, I say! I hate you! I detested you since the first moment I beheld you, when you interrupted the duel between a pair of fools. To one of them I owe a hundred dollars: I was in hopes a bullet would have balanced our accounts, but you must pick a quarrel with me. I have been revenged. Away, I say! I abhor you! I detested your villainous father before you were born."

"Villain, your pestilential breath cannot taint the fair fame of my parent! Were it not, crushed scorpion, unmanly to assault you, miserable coward, you dared not say what you have. My father never injured you."

"Was it no injury, on the public parade in Grenada, to collar and shake me as though I were a slave: and wherefore? because I chastised the mulatto dog Fedon — Fedon, who played some fine tricks, even the same month. I struck him. Forty-eight of his murders are recorded in the church of Grenada. Never injured me, said you! when I wished to serve in the third rank instead of the first, your father called out to my sergeant, 'take away that poltroon, lest his fear infect the rest of the line.' Your father and yourself appear to have been born to expose my constitutional defect of timidity; but I have been revenged. I was sentinel on board the Hostess Quickly when she was surprised. I saw the canoes come to the attack. I would have given the alarm, but your pale-faced mother was on board. She I disliked not for herself, but because she was the wife of your accursed father. Instead of giving the alarm, I jumped overboard, leaving the drunken captain, sleeping crew, and the puny creole, your mother, to the tender mercies of your father's *protegé*, Fedon. You, too, exposed my natural fear. I am revenged on you: the island abhors and despises you."

"And this," thought I, "is the wretched Smithson, whose coward blow made Fedon the dupe of Victor Hugues."

I paused, to look on the miserable man. He was pale as death, yet were his mental faculties as unclouded as ever I remembered them; his voice was weak, but his speeches were any thing but brief. The most astonishing part of his behaviour was this: hacked most cruelly with the dagger-knife of Pedrosa, his countenance was often contorted with agony, and yet he uttered no complaint, made no moan; he did not even heave a sigh. Still I knew this man to be a coward, mentally and physically — a miserable poltroon. I have seen brave men who groaned with the pain which a slight wound gave; and yet, here lay one, whom the fear of fighting turned almost frantic, bearing the agony of five of the worst wounds which I ever saw upon a living man, with the constancy of a martyr.

After a pause, I said, "Smithson, I came not here to talk of old enmity with you, but to dress your wounds. Shall I examine them, or do you wish me to retire?"

The wounded man said, after a pause, "Were I without offspring I should say, retire; but I am the father of four wretched children, whom I leave to poverty."

He here paused. A tear glistened in his stern eye. I knew not that he had the fountain of sympathy in his frame; but love for his offspring appeared the only trait which seemed to humanise his bosom. He continued, "I weep not for myself; 'tis for my poor children. But each tear I shed will turn to a flame of hell, to burn the soul of Pedrosa."

"Wretched man, curse not a fellow-criminal, but supplicate mercy for your own acts of murder."

"I never killed one who was the father of children: nay, I never killed any one. Can you call setting fire to a savanna murder? True, the old soldier who robbed you was found drowned in a stream of three feet of water, and his throat bore black marks of some strong hand; but who can prove that hand was mine?"

"Smithson, we lose precious time, and you exhaust yourself with talking. Unless your wounds are quickly looked to, you will soon be before a tribunal over which presides an awful Judge, who requires neither witnesses nor proofs."

I threw off the old sail which covered him, to look at his wounds. Two of these were in the abdomen, and three in the thorax. The slightest of these five stabs was dangerous, but three out of the five were mortal wounds. How this man survived for several hours after receiving the whole of these wounds, appeared to me most wonderful. It brought to my mind the case of a soldier, who lived for three weeks after he had received a musket-ball in the left ventricle of his heart, at the battle of Curña.

Smithson watched my countenance, and, seeing me pause from inspecting his wounds, said, "Can you save me? — save me, for the sake of my poor children, who shall bless you, although I never can. But, oh! save me."

"Call on your Creator to save your soul; human aid or skill is useless to your body. Call on that Being by whose miraculous mercy you are permitted to live, and be of sane mind, although you have wounds enough to destroy four men."

"My poor wretched children! Ah, their curses light on Pedrosa!"

"Imprecate not. Think on your own past life."

"Ah, of what part should I think? Of my boyhood — I robbed my poor widowed mother; or, should I recollect my youth, I murdered the woman who adored me, because she would not destroy the fruit of our guilty love. Can I reflect on my thirty years' living in the West Indies? Alas! every year has been stained with a crime. Within one week I attempted your life, caused you to be robbed, and throttled the robber when he was in a fit of intoxication. I joined an assassin to dig up a treasure, until frightened from our purpose by the most hideous spectre that ever left hell to terrify the damned on earth."

"It was your guilty fear, and no spectre, that tormented you last night."

"As sure as the name I bear in the West Indies is Smithson, as sure as the name I got at the baptismal font was Henry Rigby, so surely did I hear and see, last night, the foulest ghost that ever hovered about a treasure."

"Unhappy man, will you not utter one supplication for mercy ere you die?"

"He that may hope for mercy beholds not such apparitions as I saw, nor hears such sounds as I heard, within a few hours of his death."

"Let not the thoughts of what you saw and heard last night in the abandoned boiling-house cause you to despair. The sound and the apparition were both mortal. Listen to me, Smithson, or Rigby: what your fear caused you to mistake for a spectre was myself. I saw you and Pedrosa put into Gaspar Grande, heard your conversation, swam amid the rain-storm after your canoe, dogged you into the ruins, saw you take the gold, for which Pedrosa stabbed you, and rushed upon you."

Every word I said seemed to act like a poisoned dart forced into his bosom. He now groaned, gnashed his teeth, and eyed me with such a look of demoniac hatred, that he was fearful to behold. The look which a dying tiger gives to the huntsman, who has mortally wounded him, is gentle, compared to the gestures of Smithson. He, at length, burst into a fearful laugh, exclaiming, "Fool! fool! fool! and coward!"

He struck his forehead again, laughed, and fainted.

I thought his final struggle had passed, but his blood resumed its circulation, and the miserable dying man again opened his eyes. By this time the commandant had arrived. Smithson beckoned him to approach: it was to give him the small bag of gold, to keep which had cost him his life, and which he had placed under his head, making the magistrate promise, on his honour, to give it to the mother of his children. He motioned the commandant to withdraw: the latter did so.

"Arundell, where are you?" said he, in a faint voice.

"I am at your side," replied I.

"Come hither: I have something to communicate. Approach me: why fear you a dying man? Nearer — I cannot raise my voice. Said you not, or was it all a dream, that it was you who frightened us from the treasure last night?"

"It was: but think of other things ere you die."

"And said you not my wounds are mortal?"

"I did."

"Stoop your ear down to my mouth," said the dying man, in a scarcely audible voice; "I have something I wish you to listen to before I expire."

"What is that?" said I, bending my ear to his mouth.

"It is — die, wretch!" shouted he, with demoniac energy; at the same instant mustering his failing strength for a final murderous effort. He grasped me by the throat with his left hand, while with his right he caught up the knife which was lying at his side. Before I recovered from the surprise of this event, the treacherous weapon was at my side. My danger was but momentary; a quantity of uncoined silver I had in my waistcoat pocket, which I had picked up at break of day, turned off the point of the knife. The infernal effort of Smithson brought on a sudden internal haemorrhage. He fell back, shuddered, and expired, in that most awful and malevolent state of mind — dying as he lived. I wrung my hands with horror, as I watched the pallor of death steal over his features, which were rendered diabolical by revenge. My heart sickened as I gazed at the dead ruffian.

CHAPTER 49.

"Vengeance and justice on the villain's head!
Ye magistrates, who sacred law dispense,
On you I call to punish this offence."
DRYDEN.†

The commandant hurried me from the spot, and induced me to visit him. I gave my evidence on oath respecting the death of Smithson, but, for obvious motives, I gave no account of what took place the preceding night. I confined my statement to a description of his wounds, and the dying effort the wretch made to stab me. This part of my evidence the commandant himself confirmed.

Scarcely was my deposition taken, before the commandant put down the declaration Smithson made respecting his murder before I saw him. It is remarkable that this man said nothing about having dug for the treasure, but merely stated that he and Pedrosa saw and heard a spectre in the old boiling-house. I suppose he entertained hopes of recovering, and wished to make another attempt to get possession of the treasure. Jerome returned with a letter from the chief of police, which stated that he would be down that evening.

Jerome told me that the custom-house boat had been stolen in the night, and that a reward of fifty dollars was offered for its recovery. I left the commandant's house with him, and when we were alone I told him I could shew him where it was. He thanked me, called two companions, and, taking the necessary implements to raise her, I again crossed to the islet, and shewed him, under the clear water off the cave, where the boat was sunk. He threw off his dress, dived down, while his companions agitated the water with oars to frighten the sharks. He fastened a rope to two of her thwarts, came to the surface, and, with the help of his comrades, raised her. The hole was soon found, and plugged. He then baled her out, and easily earned fifty dollars.

While this was going forward, I walked into the cave to bring out the olives and other trifling presents which Jack had given me the preceding night. Suddenly I heard several persons laugh within the cave. Their laughter produced a singular effect, as its echoes were repeated several times. What could it mean? In a moment it was explained. No less a personage than the governor, Sir Ralph Woodford, followed by several ladies and gentlemen, came out. The fact was, Sir Ralph, and a party of strangers on a visit from a neighbouring colony, had come down in the steam-boat called the Woodford, to visit these caves. I could have shewn them one more curious than any they had seen, but did not think myself called on to do this.

I bowed to the governor; he courteously returned my salute. I was about to withdraw, but he beckoned me to stay, and continued a story which had made the party laugh in the cave. It related to this same steam-boat, which was anchored off the island, when, in 1818, it first came to Trinidad.

Sir Ralph Woodford made a voyage with her down towards the Dragon's Mouth. The first appearance of a steam-boat in this part of the world truly 'astonished the natives.' The Spaniards called out 'Santa Maria!' and, almost at the same time, made an exclamation which cannot be written. The creoles uttered a hundred interjections, which defy orthography; and the negroes called out, in creole French, '*Hé, hé! begué sorcier oui* — truly, white men are sorcerers.'

But on this little voyage of the governor, lower down than the Island of Gaspar, the steamer met a South American vessel. Not one on board of this had ever before seen or heard of a steam-boat; all were, therefore, seized with consternation at bcholding a vessel, without a sail or oar, going against wind and tide, raising the echoes amongst the mountain-forests on shore by its roaring, and sending into its rear a long stream of smoke. An European or American Spaniard, when he meets with any thing which he cannot comprehend, very philosophically ascribes its operation to the devil: hence, the crew of the South-American craft concluded that the nondescript was propelled by demons; and immediately, with oaths and prayers, put about. Sir Ralph divined what was going on, and ordered the steamer in pursuit. The alarmed Spaniards ran their vessel as close in shore as they could: every man, with one exception, jumped overboard, and sought refuge amongst the woods from the infernal 'spectre ship.'

The governor and his party boarded the South American, and found but one poor creature in her, who was too sick to quit the vessel. He lay in his berth shivering with the ague, calling on his saints to help him, and holding in his trembling hand a pistol *minus* a lock. It was a long while ere Woodford could convince this poor man that he (the governor) was not his Satanic majesty. Only think of the handsome baronet, in his Windsor uniform, being taken for the prince of darkness!

This anecdote, which Sir Ralph related with considerable humour, created much mirth. Before this subsided, he walked towards where I stood, and entered into conversation with me apart from the company.

"Your name, sir, if I mistake not, is Arundell?"

"It is, your excellency."

"I believe I saw you, some years since, at Government House?"

"Even so, Sir Ralph; I had the honour of an interview with your excellency before."

"During which interview, I recollect treating you somewhat harshly. But I now wish to make you an *amende honorable*;† for I hear you are of good family, a skilful, attentive, and successful medical practitioner, and, what is more to your credit, a humane, honourable, and high-spirited young man."

I bowed to the fine compliments of the governor, at the same time wishing him — no matter where — because I wanted to visit my secret cave. However, it was necessary that I should reply; and I said, "What your excellency has heard respecting my character by no means tallies with public report, which, at this moment, accuses me of being every thing base and infamous."

"Pshaw!" replied the governor, "you allude to the scandal of the day, of which you are the subject, because the newspapers from home have brought no intelligence of interest lately. Learn, young man, to despise popular clamour. You, I fear, act too much from impulse: for instance, I gave you a cool reception when you arrived in this island, but, instantly repenting of my conduct towards you, I sought a reconciliation. This you avoided, left the island in dudgeon, and spent two or three of your best years in the service of the insurgents." — N.B. He used to call them rebels.
— "A set of newsmongers now call you a *saint*, because they think you differ in opinion with them; at this you again take umbrage, and give up a respectable practice. Surely the accident of Le Jeune should have taught you how soon the outcry against you would have subsided. The fact is, you were too necessary a personage in and about La Brea for the inhabitants to be long at variance with you there. Any sprain in the ancle, or pain in the

head, with which any member of any particular family should have been afflicted, would have reconciled you to the head of that family.

I wondered at the correctness of the governor's information. The fact was, he used to keep open house to all the magistrates and principal inhabitants of the colony, when they visited town. He would contrive to draw from them every thing that happened in the district from whence they came; and what Sir Ralph Woodford once heard, he never forgot.

I replied to the governor by saying, that I was told by almost all the inhabitants of the quarter which I had left, that my services were no longer required; and added, that I never would force my attendance on any one as a medical man while I could get my bread by quarrying stone.

"Or by being concerned with smugglers," added the governor, at the same time darting significant looks, first at me, and then at the cave, at the entrance of which he met me.

He added, after a pause, "I see you change colour, but say nothing. Well, I have hopes of you; you do not like to confess the truth of my observation, and yet have too much honour to tell a falsehood. Come hither," said Sir Ralph. "As you left the cave, I saw, although no other did, that you were standing near a small Martinique basket. I will not ask what that contained, nor take further notice of it, as it would be unbecoming the governor of this colony to turn custom-house informer: but I would advise you to leave smuggling to outcasts and desperadoes; it does not become a person of your appearance, character, and education."

"I thank your excellency for your good advice; but it is needless. I pledge my word that the articles which your quick eye detected near me, are a few presents, received last night from a friend. I further declare, that I never had, until yesterday, any connexion with smugglers, nor ever intend having any again. Permit me to display to your excellency the extent of my possession of Martinique *bagatelle.*"†

Saying this, I brought the basket near him for his inspection.

"Who was it made you these presents, Dr. Arundell?"

"Your excellency has truly said that it would be unbecoming of the governor of this island to turn informer: would it be well in a gentleman to take on himself that mean office, in order to betray a friend?"

"These seem the finest olives I ever saw," said the governor.

"Will you, Sir Ralph, please to accept them?"

In an instant the governor's countenance looked haughty and dignified: its expression changed quicker than a scene is darkened, in a theatre, by the sinking of the stage-lights. He said, "When a French merchant, of Port of Spain, once sent to my great predecessor, Sir Thomas Picton, a present of a cask of excellent wine, Picton returned it, with a laconic note, running thus:— 'When my king cannot afford to allow me to drink wine, I will drink water.'"[100]

I apologised for having offended him by offering him a present, and he gave me an invitation to dine with him in the steam-boat, on board of which he was going in about an hour. I begged to be excused, on account of my unsuitable dress: this apology he would not accept. He said, "You are aware, doctor, of our colonial etiquette. Nothing but actual sickness can excuse any one for refusing the invitation of a governor: you are not allowed even to plead a previous engagement, as a governor's invitation supersedes all others."

Finding I could not escape dining with the representative of his majesty, I despatched the ever active Jerome, who had now got up the custom-house boat, with the trifling present of Jack, to his house. He returned in about half an hour with my suit of clothes; and, while the governor and his party were inspecting one cave, I went into another, made a rough sort of toilet amid the rocks, and got into decent attire.

The governor rejoined me, and smiled at the improvement in my dress. A few minutes after this, Jerome was again employed in putting all the party on board, for the boat belonging to the steamer had been injured. Sir Ralph gave him four dollars for his trouble.

The party was pleasant, the dinner excellent, the wines exquisite, and the governor one of the most polished and entertaining men I ever met with at table. It was late ere the cloth was removed, and I could not hail a boat from the shore: the steamer's boat had been nearly shattered to pieces against one of the rocks. Sir Ralph proposed that I should go up to town, and that he would send me down in his own boat. I consented to this arrangement, for I felt assured no one would discover my treasure.

Away went the steamer, her piston plunging down and rising up, her paddles roaring, and her funnel smoking. We soon came opposite the village of Courite; when the Woodford (so called after the governor), one of the worst steam-vessels that ever came from the Clyde, suddenly struck work. The engine was taken with that disorder which, medically speaking, I should have called asthma; but, not being a mechanist, I know not the right name of this *vaporous* disease.

---

100. A fact.

The captain and *un*civil engineer now mutually accused each other of bad management; but neither their efforts nor their curses could make the engine work. We had no boat to go ashore, and could call none, as it was late. The only thing to be done was to hoist a lug-sail,[†] in the hope of a breeze springing up in the night.

We were obliged to remain all night on board. The accommodations for passing the night here were not very numerous. The cabin was given to the ladies; the governor slept on a mattrass on deck, under an awning; the rest, to use a man-of-war phrase, 'caulked it;' that is, slept on the bare deck. I took my station without the awning, and reposed on a bench. Habit had rendered me hardy: hence I could, without inconvenience, pass a night in indifferent quarters, and, when I could get it, enjoy a comfortable chamber. The spoiled children of luxury can do neither of these.

On this occasion, however, although I had spent the preceding night without sleep, I enjoyed (as some people say of ill health,) a bad night. This was, perhaps, occasioned by the great fatigue and over-excitement that, during the last twenty-four hours, I had undergone. I turned, restless, from side to side; and, ever and anon, as I was getting into that half-conscious state between sleeping and waking, a sudden nervous jerk of the whole body awoke me. Again I tried to sleep, and, as I thought, felt a heaviness stealing over my senses. I was so much pleased at the prospect of getting a little slumber, that the joyful anticipation completely awoke me. Again I turned, and this time slept for, I suppose, a few seconds; when I dreamed that I stood on one of the stupendous rocks of the cavern of Gaspar, and that an impending rock was falling. Methought that I leaped from the rock on which I stood to save myself: again I awoke with a start. Once more I fell into a state of drowsy mania: all sorts of fantastic visions flitted athwart my over-wrought imagination in the utmost confusion. At length my dream became somewhat less unconnected. Methought I was in the secret cave, and the bags of precious metal were lying at my feet; when, suddenly turning round, I perceived the figure of my father, bearing the resemblance of the image of him preserved in my memory.

"How came you possessed of so much money?" said he.

"By snatching it from a murderer, who was himself murdered," replied I.

Methought my father frowned on me. I said, "Surely you do not think that *I* murdered the man? His blood is not on my hands, although I have the money; and, as he said himself, the dead reveal no tales."

"Warner, you have done wrong!" said my sire.

"But, consider the temptation," I replied. "Yesterday I was despised; my indigence made the theme of public joy to my enemies: to-day, by snatching the wealth of yon miscreant, I am respected, feared, and courted. But I know that yesterday I was innocent; this day my conscience tells me I am a villain!"

Methought now the governor joined in the conversation, and said, "Ha, you confess it! But was it you who assassinated the man?"

I felt considerable indignation at this question, and could not reply, for I was tongue-tied with passion; while I thought I saw flitting before me the apparitions of Fedon, Pedrosa, and Smithson. All three grinned horribly at me, until I shrieked, and, with another start, awoke; and I thought I perceived the figure of Sir R. Woodford making from my side, and seeking his mattrass.

I easily attributed all this incongruous train of imagery to the effects produced on my mental and corporeal faculties by the singular events of the two preceding days. Had I looked closer into the matter, I should, perhaps, have concluded that those dreams were occasioned by a conscience which, for the first time, found itself surcharged. I relate the above dreams, because they were fated to have an influence on the events of the following day. All men are insane in their dreams; but it is only weak minds that brood over the mad vagaries of the imagination during sleep.

I did not attempt to slumber again, but walked the deck. A very light breeze had arisen, the lug-sail was filled, and the vessel had just way enough to feel her helm. The shipping of Port of Spain began to appear, when I felt very drowsy. Midnight had passed. I lay down, and enjoyed a sound sleep for five hours. I was awoke by the morning gun, fired from the Spanish fort, which was within a very short distance.

Sir Ralph was stirring. I walked aft to salute him, and was astonished at his giving me an angry look, and turning his back on me.

"What's in the wind now?" thought I.

Several boats came off to us, and all the company went ashore. I wished to land also, but was told by the governor's servant, John, that I must not. This man was a German. I knew him, for he had served in the Columbia war with me. He had been taken by the Spaniards, and had made his escape from the Oronoco, in a canoe, with two others, all the way along the Coroni and Rio Negro, until they got to the Amazons, and finally made their way to Portuguese Guiana.†

"What is the cause of my being detained here, John?" said I, to this man.

"*Ich wissen nicht*, Mr. Arundell, *aber*† — The governor did say you muss not go, by Got!"

While the German was giving me this satisfactory answer, two *alguacils* (police-men) came off in a boat; and one tapped me on the shoulder.

"You are our prisoner, in the name of the king," said he.

I became alarmed, lest the treasure adventure, which was ever uppermost in my mind, should have been discovered, and said to the men, "On what charge do you apprehend me?"

"On a charge of murder," said the alguacil.

"Oh! is that all?" said I; and instantly my mind became calm.

"That all!" said the policeman. "I think it quite enough to hang a man; and that in this country, where it requires much interest to get hanged."

The alguacil now took out a pair of handcuffs, and was proceeding to put them on, when I said, "Fair and softly, my friends; I can go without manacles."

"But," replied the policeman, "you shall be handcuffed."

"Never," I exclaimed, "while I have the power of resisting such an indignity, will I submit, being innocent of the charge against me. I will go quietly: hold me, if you wish; unbutton, if you please, my braces, so as to prevent my running away; if your force be not sufficient, send for more; but do not attempt to degrade a gentleman with handcuffs, or I'll pitch the first man that approaches me overboard.

One of the alguacils now got into a boat, which made for the sea-fort; while the other drew a pistol, and, presenting it at me, said, "If you run away, you are a dead man."

I replied, "If I don't die until that pistol kills me, I shall have a brevet commission for immortality. My friend, whenever you draw a pistol to frighten a man of weak nerves unless his eyesight is also weak, don't forget to prime it, and shut the pan."

The alguacil stamped with rage, while I laughed at him. A serious thought came across my mind.

"The poor fellow is only doing his duty. But what could induce any one to charge me with murder? It is absurd; yet, I know that so dilatory is the Spanish law, that I may lie for months in prison before any charge is brought against me. Meanwhile, the smuggler will return, visit the cave, and, perchance, find the treasure. As soon as he arrives I must send and let him know of the matter, and we will share the gold and silver. But what," thought I, "if he visit the cave before I send to him. Ah, here comes off a boat of soldiers, with the alguacil. I, however, see there is an officer in it. To his feelings will I appeal against being shackled."

It is necessary that I relate what brought an officer with the men. The alguacil went to the fort in a ludicrous fright, and stated that he and his fellow-policeman had arrested a murderer, who refused to go with them — that he was a desperate fellow; he therefore, he said, left him in charge of the other alguacil, and came to call on the soldiers, in the name of the king, to assist them.

The colonel in command of the island garrison happened to be inspecting the fort: he said, "You seem to be terribly alarmed. Two of you could not take one man, and yet you leave him in charge of only one. I do not like to let the men of my regiment go to aid the civil authorities, unless an officer be with them: as there is no other present, I will go with you myself."

Go he did. When he arrived on board, he said, "Where is the murderer?"

"I am," said I, "not a murderer, but the man who is charged with murder."

"Is it possible?" said the colonel. "Warner Arundell!"

"Rivers!" exclaimed I, in an instant.

We embraced like brothers. He was the officer with whom I went to England. How changed was he from the poor man, borne down by disease and poverty, that I relieved in the miserable garret in London!

Fortune had been kind to Rivers since I saw him. Being too poor to live on half-pay during the peace, on his return from the Continent he exchanged with an officer whose regiment was going to Ceylon. Here he met with his wife's father, who, when informed of the honourable way in which he had behaved to his daughter, used all his interest for his promotion. He, after three years' services, got a majority,[†] and then returned to England. Meanwhile, his father, although he made several wills, which cut off his son, according to a proverbial expression, with a shilling, neglected to sign any of these testaments before he died. The consequence was, that Rivers succeeded to a valuable estate; but, loving the army, he purchased a step,[†] and now appeared in Trinidad, as lieutenant-colonel and commander of the forces.

"But what is this, Arundell? how are you accused of murder?"

"I am, it seems, so accused; but wherefore, I know not; unless attending a wounded man, who died in the act of making a desperate attempt on my own life, be considered murder. But tell me, Rivers, how is your lady?"

"She is well, and in Port of Spain, the mother of five children. But what, Arundell, caused you to threaten resistance to these men?"

I explained, that I merely offered to resist their attempt to handcuff me. The colonel asked the alguacils why they offered such an indignity to me? when one said, that, having been told by the governor to apprehend me, several *gentlemen* on the wharf who heard the order given, told the alguacils to take care of me, as I was a desperate fellow, and would not hesitate to kill one or both of them, if I could thereby make my escape: they, in fact, advised the policemen to manacle me. I had no hesitation in fixing on the generous gentlemen who gave the alguacils this information; but, as I went ashore, walking arm-in-arm with the colonel, I disappointed their amiable anticipations.

By direction of the governor, I was lodged in the police-office.

"With what am I charged?" said I to the clerk of the office.

"With the murder of one Smithson."

"And who is my accuser?"

"His excellency the governor."

Here I was puzzled beyond measure to know what put it into Sir Ralph's head to accuse me of so extraordinary a crime.

While expressing my astonishment at the charge to Rivers, an elderly dark gentleman entered the office, looked hard at me, and said, "Is it possible, Mr. Arundell, you can have committed such a crime as murder?" The querist shook with emotion as he spoke. No wonder; he was the friend of my orphan boyhood — the benevolent Dr. Lopez, who had just arrived in the island. After some moments spent in endeavouring to regain my calmness, I related to Dr. Lopez and Rivers the whole of the history of the murder of Smithson, commencing at the time of the commandant's calling in my aid to inspect the wounded man, and omitting all about the treasure; not because I feared to trust either of my worthy friends, but because I thought a police-office an unfit place to make such disclosures.

"Warner," said the friend of my youth, "I believe you incapable of telling a direct falsehood. I have lived long enough to know that some vices of youth may be left off in riper years, and that some possess in youth virtues which leave them as they become contaminated by intercourse with that selfish mass of mankind called the world; but there is one virtue, which, if a youth possess, he never loses through life: I allude to the love of veracity. As a boy I believe you never told a falsehood. I do not think you would practise that despicable vice now that you are a man. You have told us, I believe, the truth, and nothing but the truth; but have you told us the whole truth?"

I paused to recollect, and replied, that I had not stated one part of my connexion with the unhappy Smithson. I then related to him all the particulars of the duel, and the robbery of my desk. After this, I stated that there was one more anecdote connected with this affair, which I declined relating at present. The worthy doctor was satisfied, immediately sent for his clerk, and wrote a note to the chief of police. As that officer had not returned from the carenage, where he went to take depositions respecting the murder with which the governor charged me, the clerk of Dr. Lopez was ordered to take a boat and go after him, and to hurry him up to town.

Notwithstanding the vexation of my present situation, I made a hearty breakfast; which meal the colonel sent me. We entered into conversation. He told me that he should not let his amiable wife know that I was in the island, lest she might find out my present situation. This might disagreeably affect her, as she was in an interesting situation.

About noon the attorney-general and the governor arrived at the police-office. The former commenced taking what, in Spanish, is called *summaria:* that is, he began the voluminous and almost interminable body of evidence, hearsay and direct, which the Spanish criminal code requires to prove and to mystify the clearest case. He commenced, as usual in such cases, to examine me on *poscionës*, that is to say, putting questions which must be answered categorically, although the accused is allowed to give any explanation he likes. At the same time, the attorney-general protests against any thing you may say in your favour; taking all the admissions which the prisoner makes against himself. I will give a specimen of this mode of examining a prisoner on *poscionës*.

"Is it true you had a serious quarrel with the deceased?"

"Yes, it is." Taken against me.

"Is it not true that, in consequence of your suspecting him of having placed a letter in the news-room, you entertained strong indignation against him?"

"Yes, it is true; but my indignation was mixed with contempt."

The first part of my answer taken, the latter part protested against.

"Is it not true that, when the officers of the police were about apprehending you, on board of the steam-boat, you threatened to pitch them overboard?"

Answer. — "I did not do this until they wished to degrade me by putting handcuffs on me."

Attorney-general. — "I must have a categorical answer; any explanation you choose to give must follow your affirmation or denial."

He repeated the question. I answered in the affirmative, but explained that my resistance did not proceed from a wish to oppose their authority, but that I thought they were using me badly, by offering to put manacles on me. My admission was taken; but my explanation was protested against, as being in my favour.

I will not weary the reader with giving an account of the whole of the absurd questions put to me; but merely state that, at the end of these, I addressed the attorney-general, and told him he was taking a great deal of trouble to no purpose. If he would wait for the return of the chief of police, he would find that Smithson had been murdered by the man with whom, two nights since, he had escaped from prison.

My advice was not followed, and the proceedings were continued. I was sent into another room, and the attorney-general commenced examining the housekeeper of Smithson; for, by the Spanish law, the witnesses and prisoner are never confronted, nor are the former ever subjected to that searching examination which, in an English court, often draws truth from the most reluctant witnesses, and confounds the artful fabrication of the most perjured. No: any thing the witness chooses to say is written down: and, at any time during the trial, while the *summaria* is open, the party may alter, add, diminish, or correct his deposition. All the prisoner can do is to get the court to put to the witnesses a certain number of written questions.

In my case, the only witness examined was one Mary Anne St. Martin, the woman who lived with the deceased; and she knew nothing of the matter, save from conversation with him a week before his death. All this hearsay evidence was, however, taken, until the whole proceeding was stopped by the arrival of the chief of police and the commandant of the quarter. These gentlemen laughed outright at the blunder in accusing me of the murder of Smithson. They produced the whole of the testimony taken on the spot, including Smithson's own account of the murder. Sir Ralph looked carefully, and, at first, incredulously, over the depositions. He put a few questions to the commandant; and that gentleman gave an account of meeting me, and of the desperate attempt the dying wretch made on my life. The governor then said, "Is it possible that I could be so mistaken? I seem doomed continually to wrong this Warner Arundell. What think you, Mr. Attorney-general, after this evidence of the prisoner's case?"

"That he is," said the attorney-general, "innocent, beyond a doubt. Here is the commandant's testimony, the evidence of a dozen disinterested spectators, and the man's own declaration that he was wounded by Pedrosa, a villain that had escaped gaol with him. This ruffian, it seems, subsequently made an attempt on the life of a fisherman named Briggs, who, in self-defence, slew him; thus saving the colony the trouble and expense of hanging him. But let us go into the next room and dismiss Dr. Arundell, who seems to have acted on this occasion in a praiseworthy manner."

The whole of the parties now came into the hall in which I was; and the crown-lawyer said to me, "Mr. Arundell, the proceedings against you are quashed; for you are found not only totally innocent of the charge brought against you, but it appears, by the testimony of the commandant, that your conduct in this transaction was highly laudable. Alguacils, Mr. Arundell is acquitted."

I cast a glance at his excellency, who looked rather ashamed of himself; and said, "Permit me to ask Sir Ralph Woodford, who, as governor, thinks it degrading to become a spy, how he came to induce me to go on board a steam-boat, under pretence of inviting me to dine with him, and on his arrival in town to send two policemen on board to put a degradation upon me, by endeavouring to bring me handcuffed through the streets, like a petty-larceny knave?"

"I never authorised any one so to degrade you," said Sir Ralph Woodford, with much warmth, well pleased to be enabled to shift some part of the blame of my late unworthy treatment on others. His excellency, being displeased with himself, wished to give others the benefit of his displeasure.

"When I invited you on board the steamboat," he continued, "it was not with an intention of inveigling you to town to bring a false accusation against you. How could you think me guilty of such dishonourable conduct?"

"If I have wrongly accused Sir Ralph Woodford, I beg his pardon. But we are all liable to err — for even the governor of Trinidad sometimes is mistaken in his suspicions; although how I became the object of those suspicions, is to me a mystery."

"My suspicions arose from your murmurings in your sleep. I never saw one so restless, nor have I ever heard of an innocent man who muttered such things in his slumber as you did. You talked of murder, of great temptation, of blood being on your hands, and of dead men telling no tales. You said yesterday you were innocent, but that your conscience told you that this day you were a villain. When I heard you say this, I thought you had some deep crime on your conscience; and, by speaking to you, I was in hopes of taking advantage of your restless sleep, in order to draw from you the truth. You uttered nothing distinctly, but the name of Smithson. Now, having heard the preceding day that one of that name had been murdered, I concluded you were connected with this assassination, but am happy to find I was mistaken."

"Oh!" thinks I, "the murder is at length out. So it was in reality your voice I heard amid my dream, and your form that I saw as I awoke. Strange that sleep should play me nearly the same pranks that it did Fedon last week!"

I was about to reply to the governor, when I heard some one outside the hall, saying, "I wish to see Mr. Warner Arundell. I am told he is here."

"You cannot see him now," said a policeman, "for he is with the governor."

"But I must and will see him!" exclaimed the unknown voice, rising an octave higher.

The alguacil rejoined: "You can't and shan't see him now: he is being examined about a murder that he has committed."

"You lie in your throat — you lie!" roared the other, in furious altissimo. "You lie in your throat, to say my poor brother has committed murder. The blood of a murderer never flowed in the veins of one of my father's children. Oh, poor Warner! why did you leave your family, to be accused of murder in the unchristian country?"

Scarcely was this uttered, when in rushed my brother Rodney, pursued by the policeman. He perceived me, and exclaimed, "Warner, my dear Warner! do I meet you accused of murder? Say it is not true; for I know you would not lie to save your life!"

"No, Rodney," I replied; "as you said, the blood of a murderer never flowed in the veins of a son of our father. I was accused, but am acquitted."

The poor fellow now rushed forward, embraced me, and, although old enough to be my father, he wept like a child.

Colonel Rivers had just arrived, and was affected by this scene; and even the governor, under pretence of having occasion to use his handkerchief, wiped his eyes. Rivers hurried me out of the police-office; he placed me in his handsome curricle,[†] bidding his servant shew my brother his residence, and begging the latter to come there. He drove me to his house.

It was my letter which brought my brother to Trinidad. He came in a fine schooner he now owned, and brought with him three of his tall sons, and a packet of news for me, by which I was informed by a young, briefless, but clever lawyer, that, if I would return to St. Christopher's, he (the lawyer) would make Keen and Leech disgorge all the property of which, he said, he could easily prove that they had plundered me.

I was conducted into a splendid apartment, and left with my brother Rodney, while Rivers went to prepare his wife for an interview. How different were the fine apartments, open in all directions to let in the air, and surrounded with palms, laurels, and bamboos, compared to the wretched garret in which I found Rivers, some eight years since, in London!

I learnt from my brothers that all my letters had been intercepted. I never found out how this happened, but have been led to believe it came to pass thus:— When a packet arrives in the West Indies, there is always great bustle in the post-office of the colony. Merchants, having the greatest number of despatches to receive, always send in their clerks first; and these are, of course, soonest attended to. Some are in the habit of taking up letters for various persons living in the country; hence it often happens that, besides asking for any letters for their house, the clerks hand through the little pigeon-hole a list of other letters required, and pay the postage of all together. I believe the worthy firm of Keen and Leech, by this method, saved my brothers the expense of the postage — and the trouble of reading my letters.

I enjoyed the conversation with my brother for about a quarter of an hour, when the lovely Mrs. Rivers entered, leading in her hand a fine lad of about eleven years, the same whom I had rescued from the baboon Jumbie. She wept with joy at our meeting. I kissed her hand.

"Nay, Warner, and you salute so coldly! You are not a true creole," said her husband.

I snatched a kiss from her lips: by accident her comb fell out, and her fine hair broke loose like a mill-dam, and flowed down to her heels.

"You see, Mr. Arundell, my hair is restored; but do not think I shall sell it again to your old friend in Warwick Street."

She said this with a grateful tear in her eye.

When I told her of my recent suffering, persecution, and accusation, she again wept. They had been in the island during the last month, but the colonel did not mix himself up in the trifling politics of the place; and, as to the newspaper which had attacked me, it never mentioned my name — and, of course, Rivers made no inquiry about who was the object of their scurrility.

Speaking of the paper reminds me of the following anecdote. As we were talking, the newspaper arrived, wet from the press. It contained, by way of a leading article, these words: "*We* stop the press to announce to our subscribers, that the infamous W.A., of saintly-spying notoriety, has just been brought to town guarded, and lodged in the police-office, on a charge of having murdered the poor man who, a week or two since, exposed, in the public news-room, the proofs of this miscreant being a tool of the anti-slavery faction. *We* understand the proofs of the villain's guilt are conclusive. *We* caution our judge that *our* eyes are upon him, and that *we* will look sharp that he does his duty in punishing this villainous saint, without any fear of the influence of the Aldermanbury faction.

"With that spirit of impartiality which has ever characterised our columns, *we* abstain from further observation on this man's case, lest *we* should *prejudice* him, and prejudice his case."

Having enjoyed a hearty laugh at the above, I absolutely wished its author less contemptible, that I might have had the pleasure of taking little 'we' by the nose.

As soon as the lady retired, I related to Rivers and my brother the whole account of the adventure in the ruins, and stated where I had deposited the treasure. My brother and the colonel were overjoyed at my good fortune, and we agreed on the following plan.

Rivers was to send on board my brother's schooner a military chest, large and strong enough to contain the whole of the bags of gold and silver. We, under pretence of going marooning, should anchor off the island; when the colonel, my brother, his three sons, and myself, should get into the cave, bring out the treasure, put it in the chest in a boat, and bring it to town. Our plan succeeded admirably. We sailed by daylight, and went into the secret cave. I found the treasure where I had left it. We got it safely to town, and lodged it in the colonel's quarters before evening, without suspicion. I found myself in possession of coins, gold, and silver, to the amount of eighteen thousand pounds sterling, besides some valuable jewels.

CHAPTER 50.

"La fortune tourne tout à l'avantage de ceux qu'elle favorise."
ROCHEFOUCAULD.[†]

Fortune now set in full tide in my favour. Two days after the events recorded above, as I was reading in the apartment of Rivers, some one sent in his address to me. I looked at the card, on which was written, "Abbé Sablé." This abbé was rather an original. He was a Vendean during the long civil wars of his native land:[†] he fought bravely in defence of his king. His intrepidity procured him the rank of a chief. His fame spread so much, that the Convention doomed his death over and over again; but there is not taking off the head of any man until he is caught, and Jean Jacques Sablé was not to be caught. In vain the Republic offered large sums for his body, dead or alive; in neither state could it be taken. At length La Vendée was over-run, and the brave Chuans were obliged to yield; yet Sablé disdained to submit to the Republic, although a general pardon was offered to all concerned in the war. He wandered about the Bocage for some months, concealing himself like a hunted fox. He then passed over into Brittany; and, after many months' concealment, contrived to get on board a British frigate, which brought him to England. He lived, Heaven knows how, in London, until he got the situation of servant to an emigrant bishop — one of those unfortunate wanderers to whom the British nation (much to its honour) allowed a small pittance. The bishop, finding Sablé apt, instructed him in Latin, and finally ordained him. A more benevolent man scarcely existed; at the same time few men possessed a temper less suited to the priesthood. He was hasty, violent, choleric; and, withal, mixed so much of the soldier with the priest, that, but for his well-known integrity, he scarcely would have been tolerated. His sermons were full of military phrases and allusions. He would get into such furious passions while preaching against sin and immorality, that his homilies seemed like downright scolding. He seldom mentioned the names of the party against whom his invectives were levelled; yet, his allusions were so pointed, that few in a small community but knew who had excited the abbé's indignation.

I believe Addison told a story about a country clergyman,[†] who threatened that, if a certain squire of his parish did not amend his morals, he (the clergyman) would pray for him before all the congregation. In like manner, Abbé Sablé would threaten to put certain immoral characters into his sermons. When he kept this threat, he would make the besetting sin of the party the subject of his discourse. In the middle of this he would fix his eyes on the offender, and break into a violent apostrophe.

"Methinks," he would say, "I behold before me a hoary-headed man, a veteran in sin, almost on the superannuated list, who possesses a whole regiment of grand-children: instead of setting a good and virtuous example to these, he is continually parading whole troops of vices," &c.

Thus he would proceed, describing the incorrigible old man in his warlike terms. Sometimes, when his preaching failed to produce the desired effect, he would threaten to cuff his refractory parishioners — a menace he frequently carried into effect. If the husband of any woman of the humbler order of society was getting intoxicated in an alehouse, or embroiled in a mob, the wife would immediately run to the Abbé Sablé. If not otherwise engaged, the latter would rush into the crowd, or alehouse, catch the brawler or drunkard by the back of the neck, exclaiming, "Go home! *Sacré canaille!*[†] am I to preach for ever in vain? Home to your wife!"

It is remarkable that, although *canaille* was his general appellation for the populace, yet the lower orders all esteemed him; for, after all, they knew the old, warm-hearted, but peppery-tempered Vendean chief to be their friend. He had a number of rich legacies left him, the whole of which he disposed of in benevolent acts. Such was the Abbé Sablé, who came to wait on me.

The business which the abbé wanted with me was of an extraordinary nature. I need not relate the entire particulars of our interview, but tell the result in general terms. After Fedon — the restless Fedon — had fled from this island, on board a smuggling schooner, the vessel was wrecked off the island of Grenada. Several persons were drowned. Amongst the rest, the old sibyl, Julie Sanois. Fedon swam ashore, and, after twenty-six years of wandering, found himself, by chance, thrown amid the scene of his crimes. No one recognised in the worn skeleton, St. Jago, the portly Republican general, Fedon. At length he found an old associate, who had made his peace with the government, although deeply implicated in the guilt of rebellion. This man protected his old chief; and they went together to dig up a treasure which Fedon, previous to his flight, had buried. But, unlike the gold and silver of Don Juan Baptista, it had been discovered and removed years previous to their search: all they found was a small iron chest, which had a little money, and a great number of papers belonging principally to my late father.

A few days after this, Fedon was taken mortally sick. He sent for a priest, revealed who he was, under the mask of confession, and desired the papers in question to be sent to me, who, he truly said, would be found in Trinidad. The priest could not come over himself, but sent them to me through the Abbé Sablé. This was the cause of his visit to me.

These papers, which, during the wars of 1795, had fallen into the hands of the rebels, were of the greatest importance to me, in furthering the recovery of my property. They consisted of copies of correspondence between my father and Messrs. Keen and Leech; receipts for sums with which, subsequently, his estates were charged; copies of bills of exchange, drawn in favour of this house, with acknowledgments for the same; the will of my maternal grandfather; a deed of mortgage, executed by my father, in favour of the father of his wife; and a great number of papers which, little as I knew of law, plainly shewed me that I had been kept for years out of my rightful property.

Scarcely was the priest gone, ere my friend Powel entered.

"I told you," said he, "that I would fathom all the plot of Smithson against you, and I have kept my word."

Powel, although not a man of brilliant endowments, was possessed of much perseverance and honesty; he had, without consulting with me, taken much trouble to undeceive the public — a task I would advise no man to undertake, unless he is prepared to undergo persecution, for pretending to be wise by proving his neighbours fools. However, Powel got up a plain statement of what took place at the duel between Smith and Naysmith, and the shameful and cowardly behaviour of Smithson on the occasion. This explained the cause of the malice of the latter. He then took the evidence of several persons respecting the robbery of my desk. This, he fairly made appear, was committed by the old soldier, with the connivance and by the assistance of Smithson. This man, he fairly proved, had left the letter of the anti-slavery secretary at the news-room.

But the most important discovery Powel brought to light, was in finding the copy of my reply to the Anti-slavery Society, taken not with a pen, but by means of a machine which I possessed for copying letters. This document was found amongst the rest of my papers, in the house of Smithson, when it was searched by the police. Powel made all present certify to the paper being discovered there. The reading of this copy of my letter completely exposed the absurdity of the clamour lately raised against me.

The entire evidence obtained and given by Powel made it appear to all men of calm minds, in the island, that I had been injured. But I never, myself, stirred in the affair; I was completely passive: I had seen enough of the public opinion of a small community to despise it; and, what was better, I was rich enough to defy it. Calumny can only wound the indigent; the opulent, whether guilty or innocent, she cannot reach.

"Thrice is he armed that hath his quarrel just;"†

but he who can afford a suit of golden mail is invulnerable.

In general, the popular voice changed in my favour; but several of those who were loudest in the cry against me now hated me more than ever, because they found they had wronged me.

One of those persons was a medical man. The cause of this individual's dislike to me was singular. Some months previous to this, I had written a few remarks on the treatment of *mal d'estomac*, which I sent to an English medical journal, without any signature, but merely dated it from Trinidad. The author of this piece, Doctor ——— in vain attempted to discover, and took it into his head to father the foundling himself. He so often said he was the author, that perhaps he himself believed it, although others might not. Doctor ———, one day, met me in Port of Spain, and asked me what I thought of the remarks on *mal d'estomac* alluded to. I gave an evasive answer; and he added, "I ask your opinion, Arundell, because I want your judgment of my production."

Not wanting to contradict him, nor to make him repeat his lie, I endeavoured to change the conversation; but he would not permit it.

"I see," said he, "you doubt that I wrote the article alluded to; but, come this way — I will convince you."

Saying this, he took me by the arm, and hurried me into his library, to convince me that he was the author of my own production.

"Sit down there," said he, "and I'll shew you the original MS. before I corrected it to send home."

I seated myself, and he pretended to look for a paper which was not in existence. I felt such a mixture of pity for this person's vanity, contempt for his mendacity, and mirth at my own awkward situation, that I underwent almost torture to keep from laughing, while he with a grave countenance looked amongst his papers, exclaiming, "Where can it have got to?" At length, taking up an edition of Joe Miller, which happened to be at hand, I fixed my eyes on some good old joke, and, making this an excuse, laughed until the tears ran down my cheeks.

Whether the doctor saw through my dissimulation, and suspected what a fool he had been making of himself, I cannot tell: certain am I that, from that day forth, he hated me cordially, and was the first to commence, and the last to leave off, traducing me. Such is human nature.

About this time I received a letter from Fernandez; its contents were both pleasing and painful to me. The writer expressed his joy at hearing that I was well, and learning where I was; he having in vain inquired what had become of me. He stated that, in consequence of the burning of the Casa del Rey at Alta Gracia, on the night of our flight, General Paez, conjecturing that their camp was attacked, made a furious onslaught in its rear. This completely succeeded, and the Royalists were routed with great slaughter. Paez, having supposed that Fernandez, D'Aubert, and myself, were slain, retaliated on six of his prisoners, whom he cut down with his own hand. Morales now prepared to put to death a number of prisoners which he possessed, when 'the angel of mercy' attempted to interfere; but Morales, fired with anger at his late defeat, not only refused her humane request, but treated her with some indignity, saying, that he would exterminate the whole race of creoles in South America. Her cousin, Colonel Ximenes, interfered, when Morales raised his hand to strike him. He drew his sword. Morales called his guard, and ordered Ximenes to be shot; on which a general affray took place. A revolt of three thousand creoles, which had been long getting strength in secrecy, now burst forth, and gave a death-blow to the cause of Ferdinand.

Post by post was lost by the Royalists; every creole capable of bearing arms now joined the patriotic standard, and each day brought new disasters to the army of Morillo. In the whole of the immense continent of South America, the Spaniards possessed but one fortress of importance, viz. Porto Cabello, which was daily expected to fall.

Fernandez further informed me, that when Bolivar was made acquainted with my escape, he expressed great joy. He was pleased to say, I had done the state some service;[†] he ordered me to be paid all my arrears, and up to the date of his letter: the amount of this he sent to Fernandez immediately after his capturing a million of dollars from the Royalists. He also sent me an invitation to rejoin his army as soon as my parole expired.

Fernandez told me I might draw on him for my money at pleasure, and requested that, if I did not prosper in Trinidad, I would run down to St. Thomas's, where he possessed the means of aiding me.

Thus much of Fernandez's letter was pleasing; but, like a scorpion, it bore a sting in its tail. The last paragraph informed me that Colonel Ximenes had been killed, and no one knew what had become of Maria Josefa or her family, further than this, — that they had left the Main, and had gone to Curaçoa, where, after they had disposed of a quantity of jewels, they embarked in an American brig, bound on a trading voyage: it was uncertain whither this vessel went.

This news threw a damp on my spirits. I joyed in my good fortune, because I hoped my dearest Maria Josefa would have shared in it. Without her, riches were to me as dross. I was happier while pursuing my laborious occupation at La Brea, than amid the idleness they induced me to indulge in.

My kind brother Rodney perceived the dejection which this letter produced, and, to stimulate me to that exertion which is the best remedy against grief, he told me I had a duty to perform to others, in rescuing my late father's slaves from the tyrannical grasp of Keen and Leech. This advice had the desired effect. I packed up the documents sent me by Fedon, took an affectionate leave of Rivers and his amiable lady, bid farewell to honest Powel, and seized the hand of one of my old fellow passengers in the Saucy Jack,[101] who now filled an humble situation in the island. The circumstance that endeared him to me was, that he was one of the few who, amid my persecution, dared to combat fame in my behalf. This, without doing me any service, got him into the bad graces of the community.

I embarked on board my brother's schooner, which, four days after, anchored in St. John's, Antigua. All my affectionate coloured sisters and brothers came on board to visit me. Our meeting was painfully affectionate: I was hailed with triumph, and looked on with pride. That scoundrel,

---

101. The Editor of these papers.

Leech, who had intercepted my letters, told them that I had 'taken to bad courses:' my appearance satisfied them this was a calumny. I came rich to them, and they rejoiced in my prosperity. Had I come to them in indigence, they would have shared their last meal with me.

On going ashore, my gawky cousins came in clusters to see cousin Wâârner, as they called me. None inquired where I had been, save the youngest; who said, "I'm told, buddy, you've been 'home;' what sort of a place is England?"

Before I could reply to his comprehensive question, he answered it himself, by saying, "I'm told it's rather hot in summer, but rââlly cold in winter."

This satisfactory account of 'home' I confirmed.

CHAPTER 51.

"Me, wrangling courts and stubborn law,
    To toil, and crowds and cities, draw;
    There selfish faction rules the day,
    And pride and avarice throng the way."
        SIR WILLIAM BLACKSTONE.[102]

I MUST now give an account of my legal campaign with Messrs. Keen and Leech. The senior of this 'highly respectable firm' had died, leaving his property to his junior partner, who had married the daughter of Keen. Leech was in the enjoyment of good health, and a large ill-gotten fortune.

On my arrival in Antigua, I immediately sent for the young enterprising lawyer who had told my brothers that he could recover the whole of my property, which had been put into the possession of the above-named firm by a decree of chancery,† over which presided a man-of-war chancellor: for it is a fact, even at this day, captains and lieutenants of the navy preside over chancery courts in the West Indies.

The lawyer's physiognomy pleased me. He was tall, rather slender; gray, but penetrating eyes; spoke little, but what he did say seemed much to the purpose. Altogether, his features indicated patience, shrewdness, and coolness. After relating by what extraordinary accident I had become possessed of the papers which I received from Fedon, I submitted them to his perusal. In a moment he was profoundly engaged in their inspection.

During his long scrutiny of the mass of documents before him, I anxiously watched his countenance as he carefully inspected paper by paper, docketing some, putting others aside, and folding up others most carefully in paper. Repeatedly he uttered interjections of surprise and joy; now and then exclaiming, "So, Messrs. Keen and Leech, is this the way you conduct business? charge principal and interest on an account paid twenty

---

102. From a little poem called 'The Lawyer's Farewell to his Muse.'†

years since? What's this? by all that is lucky, a prior mortgage on your St. Kitt's estate in favour of old Stewart Warner! And here, too, is the old gentleman's will, made in favour of his daughter. Had she any other children than you, Mr. Arundell?"

"No other. I am her first and only child, Mr. Gayton" — (that was the lawyer's name).

"All is right: you are the natural heir of Stewart Warner. And what is here?"

He read over the copy of a letter carefully, and then observed: "Here is something that may lead to a discovery of a most important secret. Although I have enough here to ruin those villains, I must follow up a clue which this letter gives me. Rodney, is old Codrington in St. Kitt's?"

"He is," replied Rodney.

"Then," rejoined Gayton, "you must get your schooner under way *instanter*, to carry me down directly. I must see this old man."

My brother went to get the vessel ready, and the lawyer said to me, "Take the greatest care of these documents. All is right. I will make this Leech disgorge the blood he has been sucking, but must go down to St. Kitt's without delay. Do you think this old man, Codrington, well-inclined to your interest?"

"I believe so. He treated me kindly when I visited St. Christopher's in 1812, despite the threats of Keen and Leech, whom he set at defiance."

"Well he might. I believe he was in possession of a secret that would have ruined them, and may yet do so."

"Mr Gayton, you seem both enthusiastic and sanguine in my cause: permit me to give you a retainer."

Gayton looked well pleased at the heavy fee I put into his hand: it was the first he had received.

My brother Rodney returned to tell Gayton that the schooner was ready, when two strange men entered the room. One of them addressed me, and asked me if my name was Warner Arundell. I replied in the affirmative. He tapped me on the shoulder, and said, "I arrest you in the name of the king, for one thousand pounds, at the suit of Keen and Leech."

I was puzzled at this event, until my lawyer explained. The fact was, old Leech having got alarmed at my unexpected arrival in Antigua, anticipated a legal war between us: he, therefore, resolved to commence operations offensively by capturing me; and so, oaths being very cheap, he swore to a debt, and got a writ against me.

412

"We must," said Gayton, "go to the marshal's office. Call your brother Clarence. You two will bail Mr. Arundell?"

"Willingly," said Rodney, who had returned. "Clarence is close at hand, and we'll be at the marshal's office before you."

He kept his word, and we all met at the marshal's office. I saw Arnold there. This person had formerly been head clerk to the house, but now was a partner. Gayton offered as my bail my two brothers: these the marshal seemed willing to accept, until a nod from Arnold made him reject them.

"I offer you good and sufficient bail: you are well aware that either of these gentlemen possesses twice the amount of property which is named in this writ. At your peril refuse it!"

The marshal paused, when Arnold whispered, "I'll bear you harmless."

"Do you reject the bail tendered?" asked Gayton.

"I do," said the provost-marshal.

"Then, sir, we must try the question of false imprisonment."

I now interfered, and said, — "Run, Rodney, home. Here are my keys; you will find in my desk more than that sum in doubloons. Bring it to me." Away went my brother.

An old gentleman, who wore military boots, powdered hair, and a queue, who was present at this scene, said, "Are you, sir, the son of Bearwell Arundell?"

"I am."

"Indeed! Welcome, the son of my old patron! Your father purchased my first commission. Mr. Marshal, will you take my security for this young man for a thousand pounds?"

"I will, willingly, colonel," said the marshal.

He immediately signed the bond, and I was free. I thanked the worthy colonel for his kindness; and the other, in true West India style, gave me an invitation to spend a year or two on his estate.

Thus ended the affair of my arrest; but Leech became more alarmed than ever. It was now evident that I possessed the sinews of justice — money. Yes; although gold is said to be the root of all evil, very little good can be done without it.

The next manoeuvre of the enemy was to send a clerk to me. He found me at the house of my brother George, whose birth-day it happened to be, and the whole of the numerous family were assembled. The young man opened his commission to me before all the assembled descendants of Bearwell Arundell. It was this. Old Leech sent me a proposal by their clerk to quash all proceedings against me, and allow me two hundred and fifty pounds sterling per annum, provided I would make a conveyance in their favour of all my property, and quit the West Indies.

Scarcely had the knight of the quill finished delivering this modest proposal, ere the whole family of sisters, brothers, nephews, and nieces, gave tongue together, in all tones, keys, and pitches of voice — bass, tenor, treble, and soprano. The young man looked alarmed, and was in absolute danger of suffering from the nails of the female part of the assembly; but I exerted my influence, rescued him, and got him out by a back entrance, telling him to inform his employer to send me no more messengers or messages. My affair, I said, would shortly be in the hands of competent judges, who would not allow old Leech to escape into his grave without obliging him to disgorge his ill-gotten wealth.

The following day, as I was seated in my own apartment, looking at a portrait of my father, which had been given to me by one of my cousins — as a picture it was an indifferent performance, but the likeness to the old gentleman was remarkably well preserved — while my eyes were fixed on this portrait, old Leech entered.

This man, although as great a knave as ever disgraced commerce, was, in appearance, a portly old gentleman. Through life he had been active and temperate, and he now enjoyed a healthy age.

"Good morning to you, Mr. Warner," said he; "what are you looking at? the portrait of your father? Well, you are really like him, but that you are taller; and I may say, without flattery, better looking."

"Have you any thing more to say, with or without flattery?"

"I called on you, Mr. Arundell, to give you the best advice, and to make you aware that you are in the hands of a great knave — I allude to Gayton, the young lawyer."

"I have long, I believe, been in the hands of two great knaves — I allude to Keen and Leech."

"Nay, young man, some respect I hope you will have for the friend of your father; or, if you do not respect me, respect my gray hairs. I do not come to bandy words with you, but to give you some of the best of advice. Take care, I seech you, of this young lawyer, Gayton. He will recommend you to spend all your savings (and they cannot be of great amount) in litigation: your estates will be thrown into chancery; and the child is not yet born who will see the end of the process. Now listen to me. Why should old friends quarrel, when we can decide our disputes in an amicable manner? True, I possess the Arundell and Clarence estates by as good a title as the law can give me; but then I am getting old, and do not wish to be annoyed with lawyers. You were at church last Sunday: do you not recollect, in the next pew sat a fine young lady, with auburn hair?" (red should have been the word): "Well, Mr. Arundell, she is my daughter. Buck up to her, win her, and have her. I will give you, as a dowry, half the estates which your father forfeited to me by a foreclosure of mortgage, and a great deal more when I die; besides which, you will be near me, and I shall always be able to give you the best advice."

After saying this, he paused for a reply. I rose and said, pointing to the portrait of my parent, "Please to look on this picture. I direct your attention to it for this reason: it was taken many years since, about the time you came to this country a poor friendless boy, who had run away from his cruel guardian of the workhouse, and worked his passage out to Antigua on board a merchantman. All this I have heard from good authority. I have further been informed that, after you landed, you wandered friendless in the streets of St. John's; you knew not the name of one person in the island — no one knew you. At length, pressed with hunger, you entered my father's store, and begged for something to eat. Shocked and surprised at a good-looking white lad being in your destitute state, he brought you into his house, caused your hunger to be relieved, and clothed you. His goodness did not stop here: he made you lumber-clerk.[103] He wished to advance you; but he found your education had been too much neglected to introduce you into his counting-house; he, therefore, sent you to school. You learned rapidly; he gradually advanced you to be his head-clerk, and, finally, his partner. He retired from mercantile business, and left you at the head of a commercial establishment. You then became the partner of the house of Keen and Leech. My father's fortunes began to decline; you became his creditor. He died; you seized on the property of the man who had relieved your hunger and clothed your nakedness; you plundered the orphan child of the man who educated you, and advanced your fortune; you left him to want in the inhospitable streets of London; you intercepted his letters to his affectionate brothers and sisters; you calumniated him to those brothers; while wallowing in wealth which belonged to the son of your patron, you obliged him to become an adventurer in South America.

---

103. One whose business is to receive boards, shingles, and staves, from American vessels.

On his arrival in the land wherein his father had relieved you from want, you commit perjury, to cause him to be arrested; and, after all this, you come to this plundered son of your kind patron, and, before the portrait of his injured father, say to him, 'Marry my daughter!' "

After this long speech I rose, and motioned him to the door. He did not go, but made two or three attempts to reply, all of which failed. He at length said, "My young friend, you are not sufficiently a man of the world; let me give you a piece of the best of advice."

"I am sufficiently old, and man of the world enough to know, that there is nothing essentially good that does so little good as good advice. Away! sir. Quit my sight! lest, by looking on this portrait, and then on you, I should remember my father's wrongs, and mine, until I forget the respect due to your gray hairs. Away! sir, you have had your answer."

Crest-fallen, he quitted my presence. Gayton came in after this; to whom I recounted what had taken place.

"So," said he, "he wishes to terminate this war, by negociating a marriage between his red-haired daughter and yourself. Well done, old best-advice! But, enter into no arrangement yet; we have five points of the law in our favour, any one of which is enough to ruin him. But I suspect he will try another plan. However, you surely will not fight with the bully of the house?"

"Explain, sir," said I.

"Why," replied Gayton, "when Keen retired, and Leech got old, he admitted into the concern this Arnold, because he could bully, carry a heavy hammer-headed horsewhip in his hand, and a pistol in his pocket, quarrel, and box over a molasses-cask, and occasionally fight a duel. He has been several times out; but his duels are affairs, not of honour, but of dishonour. He always fights about money matters, concerning some dishonoured bill, some protested order, or some one who duns him too hard; in short, he undertakes all the fighting department of the house."

"A fine character, truly!" said I.

"But you would not go out with such a man?" said Gayton.

"Not I: I had enough of fighting in my day. At Cayenne, I fought four men one morning; and, when in Columbia, I had, according to O'Flaherty, a bellyful of fighting, and a plentiful scarcity of every thing else.[†] And as to the affair with old Leech, I'd rather it should be decided by your tongue than with my pistol."

With this assurance, the lawyer left me.

The next morning, I went into the news-room for amusement. There was no one there but a tall man, reading a paper. As I entered, he looked up, when I discovered it to be my old friend, Ezekiel Coffin, of the Ark. We saluted each other warmly; and I gave him an invitation to spend a few days at my house. As I was talking to this Kentucky man, Arnold entered the news-room, with a large hammer-headed horsewhip in his hand. He addressed me, and said, "Mr. Arundell, I want a few words with you."

"Say them, and I'll listen," said I.

"I mean, I wish some private conversation."

"You can have no conversation I wish to conceal from this gentleman."

"Ha! What, he is your friend, I presume? I have called for an explanation of your conduct to the senior of our house. He is too old, himself, to bring you to an account; but, as his junior partner, it is my duty to see that he is not insulted with impunity."

"I have, sir, no explanation to give. I thought my long speech to Mr. Leech sufficiently explanatory."

"Do I understand you rightly, Mr. Arundell?"

"I guess," said Coffin, "the squire speaks plain enough."

"Then, sir, I must send a friend to you for an explanation."

"Your friend can save himself that trouble."

"Then, sir, I'll call you out."

"There, again, you can save labour in vain: according to the Irish boy — 'the more you call me out, the more I won't go.'"†

"Then, sir, I'll post you as a coward."

"If that will be any gratification to you, I would advise you to do it."

"Or, perhaps, I may horsewhip you."

"That I would scarcely advise you to attempt."

By this time, several persons had arrived in the news-room. Arnold looked at me, as though he meditated putting his threat in force, but seemed irresolute. He was a well-made man, of middle stature; but I was considerably taller, although I was scarcely muscular in proportion to my height: yet, most persons would pronounce me, from appearance, capable of performing feats of great strength and activity. We looked, for some seconds, at each other; and, thinking he declined assaulting me, I turned to Coffin, and asked him to come and spend the day with me. This invitation the latter refused, because, he said, he was to meet a merchant in the news-room. I was about to leave, when Arnold rushed towards me from behind. I anticipated this manoeuvre, and jumped aside. He struck a blow, which never reached me. To close with him, and wrench the horsewhip out of his hand, was but the work of a second. I caught him by the pole of his neck, and flogged him with his own ruffian whip, until his jacket was cut to ribands. He turned, and I found he had drawn a pistol — an awkward weapon to use in a scuffle; you cannot carry it about you without its being stopped, and before you can draw back the stop-lock, and cock it, your brains may be beaten out. I have generally found that those who, in towns, carry pistols in their pockets, are bullies, who calculate on frightening cowards. But, to return to my narrative: before Arnold could cock his pistol, I closed and disarmed him. With one blow on his head, given with his own pistol, I prostrated him. He lay on the floor, bleeding and groaning. I flung the pistol at his side, and quitted the news-room, saying, "I advised you not to attempt horse-whipping me."

Several persons removed the almost stunned Arnold. One old gentleman in the place observed, that I was not a man to be assaulted with impunity. "Nevertheless," said he, "his father would have acted differently on such an occasion."

"If," said Ezekiel Coffin, "you make this remark against the courage of Mr. Arundell, then I guess you are tarnation mistaken. He who buys Arundell for a coward, will lay a long time out of his money. Why, when I was in Cayenne, I was his second: I saw him slick off four Frenchmen, one after another, as smart as a streak of greased lightning through a gooseberry bush."

Coffin then related, with some little exaggeration, the whole of my duels at Cayenne. The story gathered as it travelled, like Paez's guerilla corps, which always gained recruits as it passed onward. At length, the four men I had wounded increased and multiplied faster than Falstaff's two men in buckram,[†] until I was said to have killed two dozen men (more or less) before breakfast.

It is now time that I related what were the principal points my lawyer intended to proceed on. Firstly; the foreclosure of the mortgages, when I came of age, was an illegal act; as they made it appear, by charging for accounts of which I held the receipts, that the estate was in their debt, when, on the contrary, they were overpaid. Secondly; the whole of the proceedings were liable to be set aside, on the score of usury; they having taken illegal interest on sums never advanced. Thirdly; my Antigua estate being an entailed property, it could only be mortgaged during the lifetime of my father. This Keen and Leech knew well at the time they accepted the mortgage. Fourthly; the estate in St. Christopher's had a mortgage of a date anterior to the one held by Keen and Leach. This mortgage was made in favour of my maternal grandfather, Stewart Warner, who, dying, bequeathed it to my mother. I was, of course, her natural heir: the will was amongst the papers restored by Fedon. But the fifth point was the most extraordinary: this requires some explanation.

During the last war, Guadaloupe remained a long time in possession of the French; but our cruisers so crowded the Caribbean Sea, that little of that island's produce ever reached France. Hence, when sugars in our islands were worth ten dollars the hundred-weight, they could have been bought in Guadaloupe for two dollars. Now, although the latter island was a refuge for privateers, which cut up our commerce, yet there were merchants base enough to assist the enemies of their country by smuggling sugars from Guadaloupe to our islands. This had been done during the American war, and my father anticipated it would be practised in the war following the French Revolution; he therefore wrote repeatedly to Keen and Leech, forbidding this disgraceful commerce being practised on his estates. The copies of these letters, found amongst my father's papers, attracted the attention of my lawyer, who inquired relative to this matter. He discovered that, my estate being well situated for this nefarious kind of smuggling, so many hogsheads of sugar were clandestinely brought from Guadaloupe, that, as old Codrington, the manager, expressed it, "what with carting up to the estate, and carting down from it, he never could tell what was made on it." But the custom-house and treasury books cleared up the point. By these it appeared that for years immense crops had been shipped, as the growth, produce, and manufacture of the Clarence estate, in amount ten times as extensive as was ever credited to the estate in their accounts.

This placed the defendants in a terrible dilemma. Either they were obliged to acknowledge that their demands against my father were ten times overpaid, or to confess that they had committed a most extensive fraud on the revenue.

They could not escape both horns of this dilemma, and either was ruinous. They were caught in their own trap.

No sooner did old Leech find that we were in possession of these facts, than despair seized him. His lawyer offered to give up my properties, with ten thousand pounds sterling, to say no more about the matter. I refused to come to terms. Leech met me by chance, and entreated, with tears in his eyes, that I would not ruin him. I was inexorable. At length, one morning, my servant announced that a lady waited below. "Who is she?" asked I. My man could not tell me; she was closely veiled. "Bid her send up her name." This she refused to do. "Bid her walk up." Up she came. She threw off her veil, and, behold! she was the daughter of old Leech. Notwithstanding her red hair, she was a fine young woman, and really worthy of a better father.

After apologising for the liberty she took in waiting on me, and assuring me — which was the fact — that she came without the knowledge of her parent, she burst into tears, and begged me, for the sake of charity, to have mercy on his old age, and not drive him to extremities, as that would bring his gray hairs with sorrow to the grave. The poor creature's feelings so far overcame her, that she fainted, and it was a long time before I could recover her.

The sincere tears of a virtuous woman would make an impression on a harder heart than mine. I had her conveyed home, promising to consider her intercession. The result of this was, that I proposed the following arrangement. I was to receive the two plantations free of debt. Leech was to give up the last year's crops of both estates, pay all the law charges, including a gratuity of one thousand pounds sterling to my lawyer, and give me, over and above, twenty thousand pounds. These terms old Leech readily acceded to; but he never more held up his head. His daughter, after his death, married one of my cousins.

It was a glorious day on both my plantations when I took charge of them. Oxen were roasted, and the poor slaves wept with joy. Under the direction of Keen and Leech, they were overworked and ill-treated: under my father they were well off. I promised to follow up my parent's system, and I hope I have kept my word. I believe my people are as happy and contented as any labourers on earth. To have emancipated them before the glorious measure of general freedom was taken by the English nation, would not have served them so well as treating them humanely as bondsmen. I believe, had I offered freedom to any of my people, prior to the general emancipation, the boon would not have been considered a favour.[†]

On the Antigua estate I found two mulatto children: they were the illegitimate offspring of old Leech, who, notwithstanding, kept them in slavery, and gave up the plantation without stipulating any thing in their favour. I freed them. They were very ignorant: I got them instructed by one of those worthy men, the Moravian brothers.[†] They chose to remain on the estate, or, as they expressed it, on their "born land."

CHAPTER 52.

"Un mauvais arrangement vaut mieux qu'un bon procès."
FRENCH PROVERB.[†]

THESE transactions necessarily took up some months, during which time I did not neglect my interest in Grenada. Application was made at the Colonial Office for a proportion of the compensation which, at the end of last century, had been conceded to a number of planters who had suffered by the wars of Grenada in 1795 and 1796. A sum had been awarded to my father amounting to 7000*l*. This, in consequence of his indolence and infirmity, had never been paid, and, in fact, was never thought of.[104] I sent home to the colonial secretary an account of my claim. This was backed by the interest of Colonel Rivers, who had returned to Europe; and the money was paid.

I recovered all my negroes and their progeny from the successors of Messrs. Sharp and Flint. Both of the latter were dead. The sale of these people was declared illegal; and their pretended owners were obliged, by the decree of court, to pay over a large sum as damages.

The estate of my father, which had been desolated by the wars, had long lain fallow. By a deed of occupancy, as it is called, it was granted, by the local government, to a merchant of St. George's conditionally, until claimed by the rightful owner, who, on paying an equitable sum for the improvements, could regain it. The latter part of the grant was liable to a legal contest. It had passed through several hands, and was now held by a house in St. George's, on account of some one at home, who had taken it for a doubtful debt.

---

104. During the month of May 1836, a worthy old creole gentleman died in Trinidad, in straitened circumstances, who, it was well known, had claims on government for a much larger amount than the above-named sum, for losses sustained by his father in the Grenada wars; yet, out of sheer negligence, he never could be induced to claim it.

I was about to enter proceedings against these people — for I had acquired a taste for litigation — when I received a message from one of the parties, offering to submit our difference to arbitration. As I conceived those who wish to settle disputes by allowing them to be decided by persons unconnected with courts of law, are generally honest men, I agreed to this reasonable proposition, and chose two old gentlemen, who were relics of the war of Grenada: they had served through the whole of the insurrection with my father. The merchants, on their part, appointed two inhabitants of St. George's.

The matter to be submitted to their consideration lay in a small compass. The lands of the plantation I had a clear right to: the question was, whether I ought to pay for the various improvements in building, &c. as well as for the slaves that were placed on it; or, whether the large crops which had been reaped from it (and it was a productive estate), should be considered a set-off for those improvements? As to the grant of occupancy made by the local government, it was an act of a very doubtful nature, and would not have stood in a court of law; but the arbitrators had to decide on the broad principles of equity.

On the first meeting, these gentlemen sent to inquire of me, whether I would prefer taking a sum for my right to the property, or paying a sum to obtain it, with all its improvements? I preferred the latter; for I wanted a place wherein to put the slaves I had recovered from the succession of Sharp and Flint.

They then decided that I was to have the estate, with all its improvements and slaves, on the payment of 6000*l.* sterling. This decision gave satisfaction to all parties.

On asking the merchant if he would accept bills of exchange for the amount on a certain house in London, he said that his constituent would have no objection to them: he told me that the party whom he and his partner represented in this affair, had arrived a few days previously to me in the island, and was an old friend of mine.

"Who can he be?" I inquired.

The merchant would not let me know; but said, the next evening all the papers would be ready, and that we should meet at my residence to conclude the business.

I wondered who this old friend could be, but could not conjecture. The next morning the papers were all ready for our respective signatures, and my bills ready drawn. The merchants and arbitrators were present, and we all waited for the principal, who was to receive the bills of exchange.

"Who the devil can he be?" said I to myself; when I heard a voice from below stairs singing the following elegant stanza:

"Moll's flash man was a Chick Lane cove,
With his garters below his knee;
He twice was lagged,[105] and once nigh scragged,
But escaped by going to sea."

Wondering who could be chaunting this sublime and beautiful verse, I looked below, and beheld, mounting the stairs, the Herculean figure of my old friend, Hollywell, looking as stout and rosy as ever I saw him. He was the man who was to receive the bills of exchange.

"How are you, Arundell, my covey? Tip us your bunch of fives: it's long since we squeezed each other's maulies," said he.

I expressed myself, as I felt, delighted at unexpectedly meeting this good fellow. He put a number of questions to me; some of which I answered. Others I could not understand, owing to want of knowledge of the polite language he used.

I asked him why he did not call on me sooner?

"Why, Master Arundell, I knew you were a little softish about the blunt, so I did not like to let you twig that I was the man you had to deal with, lest our old *pallship* should make you act like a spooney."

I understood him to say, that he did not wish to make himself known to me, lest recollecting how kindly he had behaved to me while I was in adversity, I might sacrifice my interest to my gratitude. Poor Hollywell, although he used the language of the outcasts of society, was possessed of the strictest integrity, and the nicest sense of honour.

The papers were ready for signature, — the business was formally transacted, and I gave Hollywell the bills of exchange. He took them, and, after proper examination, deposited them in his pocket-book, exclaiming, "Two-pence is money, when there's no coal in the house! Is it all right, my boys? Is all the business concluded?"

The lawyer declared it was. Hollywell deliberately opened his ample waistcoat, saying, "I've something to tip you, my ball of wax."

He loosed a watch-guard, and pulled out the very watch and appendages of my father, which I sent to him previous to my leaving London.

---

105. Transported.

"There," said he, "there is your tattler — your box of minutes. I've kept it about me ever since you sent it to me."

The good feeling evinced in keeping this watch out of view until all the business was transacted, did not escape me; it brought fully to my mind, that when I was in distress in London he offered to supply me with money to a considerable amount, and sent me a fine set of surgical instruments. I now wished to pay for these, but he peremptorily refused to receive the money.

As he was about to return to Europe immediately, I offered to make him my London agent. This proposition he gladly acceded to. As my consignments from the West Indies were extensive, my agency was very profitable to Hollywell. On the other side, a more diligent, intelligent, and honourable correspondent than this worthy fellow, no one ever possessed.

My fortune was now ample, beyond my wishes. I had two objects to accomplish, which completely occupied my mind. The first was the discovery of my dearest Maria Josefa. In this, I was doomed to continued disappointments. I, however, consoled myself with the reflection that, in one month more, my four years of banishment from the Main would expire, and that then I could, myself, go and seek her all over the world, until I found her, or knew what had become of her.

My second object was the discovery of the rightful heir of Don Juan Baptista Ojeda, whose treasure I had discovered in Trinidad. When I found it, I was poor; and although my act of concealing this fortune was scarcely legal, it could hardly be said to be dishonourable; at all events, it was a venial offence against the rigid laws of morality.

From the hour I got possession of this treasure, fortune seemed to shower her favours on me; and, whatever excuse I might have had for snatching her first gifts, I conceived it would be criminal to withhold this treasure from its rightful proprietor. I, who had suffered much by bad men, who defrauded my orphan minority of my rightful wealth, was shocked at the idea of being possessed of gold, silver, and jewels, of another — perhaps of an orphan or widow, who might be struggling against indigence and its concomitant evils, scorn and contempt; for it has been truly said, that the world ever says, "poverty is no sin," yet ever acts as though it were the greatest of sins.

I carefully examined some old papers found in the box of jewels. These were of no further consequence than to indicate that the treasure belonged to Don Juan Baptista Ojeda. I left the jewels in the possession of my worthy old friend, Doctor Manuel Lopez, and requested him to inquire about the murdered man. He informed me he had found out that, at his death, he had left a family of three sons and one daughter. All the sons had died childless, within a few years of their father, but the daughter had left the island twenty-four years ago, for the Main, but had never been heard of since.

By the advice of Dr. Lopez, I introduced an advertisement into the papers, to this effect: that if the next of kin to Don Juan Baptista Ojeda would apply to Dr. Lopez, of Trinidad, or Moses Fernandez, of St. Thomas's, he or she would hear of something much to his or her advantage. The advertisement set forth that the don had been murdered in Trinidad the day the British took that island. It also offered a reward to any one who would give satisfactory information concerning the party.

This advertisement I translated into Spanish and French, and caused it to be inserted in all the newspapers in the West Indies, and in the few published in Columbia. I even sent it to the gazette of Madrid; but, for some months, I heard of no results from my exertions to discover the heir of the murdered Spaniard. On my arrival at Grenada I wrote to Dr. Lopez, to inquire if he had heard any thing of the party we had been so long in quest of; and, four days after, had the pleasure of receiving a reply, stating that all was satisfactorily discovered: the daughter, who had left Trinidad some years since, had seen my advertisement in the island of Cuba, and come to Trinidad, having taken Porto Rico in her way. He stated that the lady had been twice married, and had a daughter by her first marriage, that she now bore the title and name of Doña Maria Doloricita de Ojeda y Azaza. Lest any one should start at the length of these appellations, I must explain, that most Spanish ladies are called Maria, which seems a general name of a female amongst them; Doloricita is a diminutive of *dolor* (*Anglice*, pain) — this was her familiar and domestic name; Ojeda was her family name, which Spanish ladies always bear; and Azaza was the name of her last husband. So much for long Spanish names.

As I knew the worthy doctor to be too much a man of business to admit the claim of the lady to the treasure without sufficient scrutiny, I hired a small vessel, sailed for Trinidad, and, in twenty-four hours after I left St. George's, landed in Port of Spain. This was my fifth time of landing on the shores of the island. My first voyage here, I came a poor, friendless, defrauded orphan. The second time I came, was after having witnessed that awful visitation, the earthquake at Caraccas in 1812. Some years after this I disembarked in the character of an adventurer, going to seek his fortune in the wars of Columbia. Again, I came here to pass a year or two in the useful employment of a medical man. I now landed in the full possession of health, prosperity, and fortune, for the honourable purpose of restoring, to its rightful owner, a treasure which I had rescued from the clutches of a pair of murderers.

CHAPTER 53.

"It is happily and kindly provided, that in every life
there are certain pauses and interruptions, which force
considerations upon the careless, and seriousness on the
light points of time, when one course of action ends and
another begins, and, by vicissitudes of fortune, or alteration
of employment, or by change of place, we are forced to say
of something — *this is the last.*"

DR. JOHNSON.[†]

I landed early in the morning, went up to the house of my worthy friend,
Dr. Lopez, and put on a West India morning dress. This consisted of a
Panama straw hat, lined with green silk, a black cravat, tied loosely, white
jean trousers, a light blue jacket, frogged and braided, and yellow boots,
made of Madeira leather. I had on no waistcoat, but wore silk braces, fastened with gold buckles.

Dr. Lopez complimented me on my looks, and on the appearance of
my undress; observing that, he noticed, I, in general, paid too little attention to toilet.

"The fact is," said he, "men of sense often observe, with contempt, that
people of weak minds bestow too much attention on dress; hence they
commit the fault of paying too little. Reversing folly is not always wisdom.
Nothing is unimportant that is apt to influence a person's fortune. That
dress often does this, we every day may see. The fact is, in the eyes of all
who do not think profoundly, — that is, nineteen out of twenty, — the
dress is confounded with the wearer."

After this brief lecture on habiliments, the doctor and myself set out
to the residence of Doña Maria Doloricita. A negro boy went with us, to
carry the case of jewels. We stopped at one of those numerous ornamented cottages in Port of Spain, which are sweetly nestled amongst
clusters of cocoa-nut and other palm trees. This small habitation consisted

of a hall, a sitting-room, opening to a view of the gentle gulf of Paria, and two side chambers.

The doctor entered the hall, and asked a pretty half Indian, half Spanish girl, if her mistress was within?

"Not my young mistress; she has gone to mass."

"I wish to see your old mistress. Announce to her that Dr. Lopez, and the English gentleman I told her of last night, wait on her."

The girl went, and returned in a few seconds, saying, "Enter, gentlemen."

We walked into the back apartment. Here reclined, in a beautiful hammock, Doña Maria. This hammock was of net-work, made by Indians from the fibres of various trees. The small cords of this net were of all the colours of the rainbow, and all the shades and dies which these colours could combine to form. The whole was fringed with the splendid plumage of a thousand humming-birds. Scarcely less than this number would have been sufficient to ornament this magnificent hammock.

The lady was reposing, and amusing herself by playing with a Tabasco parrot, of green and red plumage. She put by her pet, rose from the hammock, and courtesied gracefully. She appeared about forty-five years of age, and bore marks of having been very beautiful in her youth. She wore the weeds of widowhood.

Dr. Lopez introduced me as his friend, who came to restore her property.

"He is welcome, because he is the bearer of good news; he is more welcome for his own sake; he is most welcome, because he is the friend of Dr. Lopez," said the señora; and she again courtesied.

In a moment we were all seated. The lady commenced the conversation, by saying to me, "When I asked the worthy doctor how you became possessed of the long-lost treasure of my father, he refused to tell me, always referring me to his friend: will you now please to explain this?"

I had a long story to tell: this I got through pretty well, save that I, now and then, was interrupted with *'Santa Maria, valgame Dios! Animas bendita!'*† and other pious interjections, on the part of the lady, at my astonishing recital. When I came to the part of my story which related to the conversation which I overheard take place between the villain Pedrosa and his worthy companion, and stated that Pedrosa said he suspected his master had an intention of murdering him, which suspicion induced him to anticipate old Don Juan, his daughter's indignation broke forth. She rose, exclaiming, "Oh, the monster! he lied most falsely. Although, unhappily, my poor father took alarm lest your countrymen should plunder his wealth, and, in common with fifty other inhabitants of the island, buried it, yet a more honourable and noble descendant of a Castilian than Don Juan Baptista Ojeda never was born in the New World. Yet, why should I feel for calumnies uttered by a wretch who murdered my father, after he had been nursed at the breast of my mother?"

I calmed her indignation, and proceeded. When I told her that I swam after the canoe,

"*Valgame San José!*"† exclaimed the doña. "Had you no fear of sharks, señor?"

"None whatever," I replied. "These fish have never been known to bite at night, unless it happens to be moonlight."

When I told her how I rushed on the villains, she exclaimed, "*Virgin Santa!*† and you ventured your dear person against two such ruffians!"

"There was no great risk," said I. "The one I knew to be a coward, and I was better armed than the other: but they took me for a supernatural being, and both flew like demons from an exorcist."

During the rest of the narrative, she repeatedly crossed herself, and exclaimed, — "Brave Englishman!"

At length I came to the end of my story, and gave her the jewels, worth many thousand dollars. The coins and precious metal I had exchanged, so that I was in her debt about eighty-three thousand dollars, in round numbers. This I proposed paying her as soon as I could sell bills of exchange for that amount. In the meantime, I possessed, in cash, about five hundred doubloons, which, if she wished, I would advance her.

She had already been made acquainted with the extent of her good fortune; hence, the latter information produced a less violent effect than it otherwise would have done. She, however, examined the rich jewels with great delight; and, after a pause, said, "These jewels will I accept, because they have been in the family of Ojeda from the time when the first Spaniards settled in this island. At that period it bore the name of Iëre, and was possessed by the Aroage and Chyma Indians.[106] These gems have

106. When Columbus first discovered Trinidad, the Indians called it Iëre; *i.e.*, island of humming-birds, a beautiful and (considering the immense number, variety, and splendour of the humming-birds found here) an appropriate appellation. It was held by a tribe called the Aroages, or Arrowhawks, and another race called the Chymas. One district is, at this day,

been preserved to us by a miracle: I will gratefully accept of them. For the money, I would reject that, but I possess a dear daughter, whom I would willingly behold as rich as becomes the last scion of an exotic tree, which was transplanted from old Spain more than three centuries since into this island. Yet, must we not be unjust. You bravely recovered our treasure, you generously tender it; but we must reward your bravery, and not impose too much on your generosity. Let us accept of half the amount of the money, and keep the rest as your own inadequate reward."

"Señora," replied I, "I will not accept a real[107] of your fortune. When I drove the ruffians from the old ruins, I did it to baulk them of their prey. I secured the treasure through feelings of selfishness, from which none are exempt. A few days after I possessed your riches, fortune, which had long persecuted me, began to smile. I used your money to bring to justice a set of bad men, who had long defrauded me of my patrimony. I am now rich — rich even beyond my wishes — and shall I take from the widow and orphan a part of that treasure which Heaven made me the humble means of discovering, and which enabled me to recover my own fortune? No, not one real of it will I keep. In a few days you shall be in possession of all I owe you."

"Brave, generous Englishman! Ah, my poor child, thy prospects brighten. God, I thank thee!"

She now became devout, with tears in her eyes. She ejaculated blessings and mixed supplications, with intercessions, until her feelings became too powerful for her to support. The worthy old Dr. Lopez led her to an adjoining chamber, and then returned to me.

"I am sure, Warner," said the doctor, "you must feel the truth of the observation, that 'virtue is its own reward.' "

"I do on this occasion, sir; but seldom are men placed in circumstances like me, to feel the reward of virtue."

"Oftener than the vicious and selfish imagine: for example, now eighteen years since, a humane surgeon brought to me a poor, friendless orphan boy: I liked the child's appearance, and took him into my house: even in your boyhood I found you veracious, brave, and generous: I endeavoured to cultivate the seeds of virtue which I perceived in you. You

---

called Carapichaima, *i.e.* island of the Chymas. A few of the pure descendants of the Aroages, and, if I am rightly informed, a single family of Chymas, consisting of thirteen persons, are all that remain of two once numerous races.[†]

107. A Spanish coin, about five-pence English.

were an apt scholar: I sent you to the University of Caraccas. Fortune, after this, divided us; but, after many years separation, you have well repaid my care. I, at this moment, taste the luxury of having done a good action. I behold the poor orphan child whom I cherished, grown into a noble-minded man. Do you think," said the worthy old lawyer, "that which I have this day heard and seen is not a triumph for me in my old age, Warner Arundell?"

I embraced the amiable and venerable doctor, until a slight noise roused our attention: I heard someone enter the little hall, and Anacletta, the Mustya girl, exclaimed, "Do not go in, señoritta, until I have told you all the news which I listened to. The Englishman has arrived who found all the money of your grandfather, which had been buried twenty-five years in a haunted ruin; it was dug up by the two men who murdered Don Juan. The Englishman killed both of them, and the spirit of your grandfather helped him; and so, señoritta, the Englishman swam over to Gaspar, carrying on his head one hundred thousand dollars, and none of the sharks would touch him — San Antonio forbade them. And so, you know, señoritta, after this, the brave English *caballero* brought your mother a whole boxful of jewels, and as much money as would make a viceroy rich, and he offered them all to your mother; and so she wanted to give him half, but the English caballero would not take a dollar, but said, 'It is all for you, señoritta;' and he is such a tall, handsome young man! But, Santa Maria, señoritta, what makes you weep? I never knew good fortune made young ladies cry before unless when they were going to be married."

The house, or rather cottage, was so small, that very little could be spoken in it without being heard all over it: hence, Doña Maria, who had recovered her self-possession, heard a part of the rambling and marvellous tale of Anacletta. She came into the room in which we were, and, saying, "My daughter has returned from mass; excuse me, señors," she hastened to the anteroom, where was her daughter. They whispered. At length I heard the old lady say, "Nay, child, come in; he will not eat you. Surely you will express your gratitude to the brave and generous English caballero."

The old lady now entered, leading in her daughter. She was plainly clad in white, closely veiled; a costume common to ladies going to mass in Trinidad. The veiled figure courtesied low: her mother removed her veil; and, gracious Heaven, there stood before me, revealed to my astonished eyes, Maria Josefa Ximenes, the angel of mercy!

Amazement made me stagger backward, and I exclaimed, "Oh, God! what do I behold?"

I could say no more: excessive joy and surprise made my tongue cleave to the roof of my mouth. Her eyes were fixed on me; but she could not recognise, in the well-dressed stranger, the ragged and haggard insurgent officer, whom her humanity had snatched from death. Memory at length came to her aid, and she looked at me as though her soul was concentrated in her eyes. I, at length, exclaimed, "Does not Maria Josefa know Warner Arundell?"

She shrieked, and fainted: I caught her in my arms, or she would have fallen. Her dark hair escaped from its combs, and hung on the floor, as I supported her beautiful head on my shoulder, while Dr. Lopez and her mother gazed on us with astonishment. Her swoon lasted scarcely a minute; but, in that short minute, I suffered an age of agony.

"Why does she faint?" thought I; "perhaps, she has given her heart to another; or, perchance, my sudden appearance will for ever overturn her reason. If that be the case, my own intellects will never stand the shock!"

I cursed my ill stars, and want of presence of mind.

If her fainting fit had not been brief, I could not have supported my terrible state of suspense. Gradually her pulsation returned, and her reddening cheeks confessed that her blood was sent into them from her heart. She opened her large dark eyes, looked for a second or two wildly around, until, perceiving her mother, who was chafing her hand, she exclaimed, "Dearest mother, was it all a dream?"

Her glance now rested on me; and she said, "Ah, no! Santa Maria be praised, it is he himself! it is my dearest Englishman!"

She, sobbing, buried her face in my bosom: I felt her heart beat; its motion thrilled through my frame like electric pleasure. All the misery I had ever suffered was overpaid by that moment of ecstasy.

Again she raised her head, and minutely examined every feature of my face.

"Speak, speak to me," she said, as if wishing to assure herself of my presence by more than one sense; "speak to me; say it is thee, dearest heart."

"It is, Maria Josefa."

"'Tis he; 'tis he himself!" she cried, and a flood of tears again relieved her overloaded heart.

She now caught my right hand to examine it: I understood the cause of this.

"It is there, sweetest," I said; "I would have parted with my life before I would suffer the ring you placed there to be removed from my finger."

She kissed my hand: I raised her beautiful head, and, with mild violence, saluted the lips of the blushing girl.

> "So sweet a kiss the golden sun gives not
> To the fresh morning drops upon the rose"†

as the protracted kiss I took from Maria Josefa. She now drew from her bosom a small silken bag which she wore; it contained the lock of hair which she had cut from my head. She said, *"Mira mi corazon!"†* I have worn your hair as near my heart as it would lie."

"Bless you both!" exclaimed the worthy doctor.

Her mother said, "Amen! amen!"

Maria Josefa stared; for, until this moment, she knew not that she was in the presence of the doctor. Her mother now led her into her chamber.

"Warner!" said Lopez, "I said virtue was its own reward; but Heaven has been pleased to reward your virtue with something more substantial. You came to restore one treasure that you found, and have discovered another, the value of which is beyond estimation."

After a short delay, Maria Josefa appeared, and I was condemned to relate the twice-told tale of the discovery of the buried money. She seemed to devour every word I said, and, at times, was so agitated, that I became alarmed. At length, when I concluded, she said, with triumph, "Mother! dearest mother! when you reproved me for giving my heart to a stranger, said I not that Heaven would never so far afflict poor Maria Josefa, as to allow her to bestow her love on one unworthy of her affection?"

"You often did so, dearest child; and he who possessed your heart is worthy of the love of a queen. Kneel, dearest children, and receive my blessing; the blessings of an affectionate mother on her pious daughter — the benediction of the widow on him who is the friend of the widow!"

"Let me add my blessing," exclaimed Dr. Lopez; "the benediction of an old man never harmed mortal."

The day passed, I know not how. I ate some food; yet knew not, nor cared what it was. We thought not of time, for the world was naught to us; we were all to each other. With my dearest Maria Josefa I could have been happy in an ajupa, amid the trackless and unbounded woods, or on the immeasurable savanna of South America. I now possessed her, together with a fortune ample beyond my desire.

Her history was soon told. After I left Alta Gracia, a disgraceful insult, which Morales offered to *la angela de la misericordia* and her cousin, aroused the indignation of all the Royalist creoles in the camp. This was the spark that ignited a train which had long been laid: its explosion was fatal to the Spaniards. Three thousand creoles, who had long been disgusted with the cruelties of the Spanish officers, and indignant at the continual threats of Morillo, of not leaving a man, woman, nor child, nor a domestic animal, in Columbia, broke into open revolt. This insurrection was headed by Colonel Ximenes, and Spain was chased from the forests, mountains, plains, and cities of the New World.

Ximenes having been dangerously wounded, he was attended for nearly a year by his fair cousin. He died; but, before his death, he entreated Maria Josefa to give her hand to the Englishman to whom she had given her heart at Alta Gracia.

After this, the contest for South American liberty assumed a less ferocious character. During the plenitude of his power, Morrillo openly asserted that he would exterminate two thirds of the people of the New World: when the fortune of war rendered it doubtful if he could be able to save the remnant of his army, he solicited that the war might be carried on in accordance with the manner of civilised nations. This proposal the patriots humanely acceded to; although, a few years previously, Morillo had refused to receive a flag of truce from those whom he denominated rebels.

The result of this was, that Maria Josefa no longer found it necessary to use her exertions and influence in rescuing the unfortunate prisoners from cold-blooded slaughter. Conceiving she had fulfilled her duty, she and her mother went to the island of Curaçoa, where, after disposing of her jewels, she took her passage on board of an American vessel bound for the Havanna. Here she remained until her native land was in a state of tranquillity. She was about going to Jamaica, to return, by way of St. Thomas's, to Columbia, when a priest called upon her mother, and shewed her my advertisement. This induced her to return to Trinidad, where our happy meeting took place.

The day after this, our old friend, Moses Fernandez, arrived, and was overjoyed at my good fortune. He solicited, and obtained, a private interview with Señoritta Ximenes. The evening of this day, the town of Port of Spain seemed possessed with the demon of mirth. It was carnival, and in no part of the New World is the mummery of carnival kept up with such spirit and buffoonery as in Trinidad. Every one appeared in some kind of masquerade, from the man of wealth, who rode through the town richly clad in the dress of a Turk or grandee, to the ragged negro-boy, who covered his black face with a sheet of brown paper. I turned from the harmless but noisy mirth, and made for the quiet residence of Maria Josefa. I entered. There sat her mother, in conversation with Fernandez.

"Where is Maria?" said I.

"She is dressing," said the doña, with a smile.

"What! is *she*, too, preparing to masquerade?"

"Yes, she is."

"And what, dearest madam, is the character in which she will appear?"

"You will see."

As the old lady said this, Maria Josefa entered the hall, dressed precisely in the same manner as she appeared to Fernandez, D'Aubert, and myself, at the Casa del Rey of Alta Gracia. She bore the identical silver lamp, and wore the same jewels which decorated her noble form when she visited us as *la angela de la misericordia*. The fact was, old Fernandez had seen her jewels offered for sale at Curaçoa; and, grateful for her having saved his life, he bought them, and presented them to her during his private interview.

I attempted to embrace her. She retreated into the back apartment, set down the lamp, and then placed herself by my side.

"Sweet love," said I, "do you not wish to ride or walk about the town with me to see the maskers?"

"No, dearest heart; I wish to remain here, and see and listen to you alone."

A few weeks after this, on the feast of Saint Joseph,[108†] Maria Josefa Ximenes added Arundell to her name; but the appellation I ever delighted to give her was, *la angela de la misericordia*. The difference of our religious creeds has (thank Heaven!) never given each other pain. Since that day, the current of my life has been too smooth, and my happiness has been too uniform, for a description of it to be interesting. Hence the creole, Warner Arundell, has no more adventures to recount.

★ ★ ★ ★ ★

THE END.

---

108. In Trinidad, Catholics do not marry during Lent, except on St. Joseph's day; San José being the patron saint of the island.

Annotations

p. iv

† **Maqueripe Bay**: A bay close to the end of the north-western "corner" of Trinidad. This scene is a view looking westward, with the islands of the Bocas in the background.

† **Cazabon**: Michel Jean Cazabon (1813–88), painter and lithographer, is especially known for his portraits and his paintings of Trinidad scenery. He was the son of François Cazabon, a "free coloured" man who came to Trinidad from Martinique, and Rose Debonne Cazabon. At the age of thirteen, Michel was sent to be educated in England. After his return to Trinidad, he practised painting. In 1837, he went to Paris to study art and exhibited his work. He married a French woman, Louise Rosalie Trolard, with whom he had two daughters and a son. In 1848 Cazabon returned to Trinidad, where he set up a studio in Port of Spain to paint landscapes and sites, as well as illustrations for local and London newspapers, and taught pupils. He published several series of works, including *Views of Trinidad, 1851*; *Album of Trinidad, 1857*; and *Album of Demerara* (1860). In 1862, the Cazabon family moved to Martinique, but returned to Trinidad in 1870, where he taught at Queen's Royal College and St Mary's College. He lived out his last days in relative poverty and died in 1888. See Geoffrey MacLean's reprint of *Views of Trinidad* (Port of Spain: Aquarela Galleries, 1984); *Cazabon: An Illustrated Biography of Trinidad's Nineteenth Century Painter* (Port of Spain: Aquarela Galleries, 1986) and *Cazabon: The Harris Collection* (Port of Spain: Maclean Publishing, 1999).

Introduction

p. 2

† **The Life, Adventures and Opinions of Warner Arundell, Esquire**: Likely an echo of *The Life and Opinions of Tristram Shandy, Gentleman* (1759–67) by Laurence Sterne. *Tristram Shandy* is a rambling work, written over a period of several years. Sterne raises digression to an art form, and eventually abandons the main plot in favour of commentaries, arguments, and embedded narratives. (See discussion in the introduction to this edition.)

† **a history of the war of the independence of Columbia, Mexico, Peru, Chili, and Buenos Ayres**: The wars for national independence from Spain, 1810–24, fought by Columbia (modern Venezuela, Ecuador and Colombia), Mexico, Peru, Chili (Chile) and Buenos Ayres (Argentina).

† **Main**: The mainland of Central and South America, as opposed to the islands of the Caribbean.

p. 3

† **Spanish creole**: A person of (primarily) Spanish descent – and therefore "white" – born in the New World.

† **phlegm**: In the old scheme of physiology, regarded as one of the four "bodily humours". "Phlegm" was considered cold and moist, and when predominant was thought to cause constitutional indolence or apathy (but, in some interpretations, the ability to persist).

† **Abbé Raynal's historical romance**: Abbé Guillaume-Thomas Raynal, a French historian and *philosophe*, wrote *L'histoire philosophique et politique des établissements et du commerce des Européens dans les deux Indes* (1770), a radical history which condemned colonial trade and settlement. Warner Arundell's reference to the book as a "historical romance" which strains credulity may reflect his disagreement with Raynal's critical stance.

p. 4

† *foolscap*: A long size of paper, often for legal use.

† **Bucaniers**: Buccaneers, that is, pirates or freebooters.

† **Sir Thomas Warner**: The pioneer of English settlement in the Caribbean islands in the early 1620s; governor of St Christopher's (St Kitts). Descendants of his were important in the history of nineteenth century Trinidad, especially Charles Warner, Attorney-General 1844–70.

† **Maroon wars in Jamaica**: The wars between the Maroons and the English in the 1730s which resulted in the Jamaican Maroon communities, descended from runaway enslaved Africans, receiving quasi-independence and freedom by 1739; and the Maroon uprising of 1795.

p. 5

† **creolisms**: Linguistic features characteristic of the local varieties of English, influenced by English Creole and French Creole, themselves influenced by various European and African languages.

p. 6

† **Lospatos**: Known today as "Patos" (officially "Isla de los Patos"), a dependency of Trinidad until ceded by Britain to Venezuela in 1942. It is the most westerly of the small islets in the area of the sea known as the "Dragon's Mouth", between the northwest peninsula of Trinidad and the Paria Peninsula of Venezuela.

Volume I

p. 7

† **"Days o' lang syne." Burns**: "Lang syne" or "langsyne" is a Scottish dialect term meaning "long ago" or "long since". Joseph may be confusing "Auld Lang Syne" by Robert Burns with the lesser-known "In the Days o' Langsyne" by the later Scots poet Robert Gilfillan (1798–1850). Gilfillan's poem, with its emphasis on the glories of the past – "In the days of langsyne we were happy and free, / Proud lords on the land, and kings on the sea" – seems more appropriate to the context than Burns's tribute to "auld acquaintance".

† **Normans and Dutch . . . settlement in the island of St. Christopher**: French and Dutch settlers, mostly Protestants.

† **nom de guerre**: Literally "name of war"; a pseudonym assumed or given to someone involved in an enterprise or action.

p. 8

† **French creoles**: Persons of French descent – and therefore "white" – born in the New World.

† **Governor Park**: Daniel Park, governor of Antigua, was killed in 1710 by members of the island assembly and their supporters, the climax of a long-simmering dispute.

† **Prince William Henry**: The future William IV (1830–37) of Britain, who served as a young naval officer in the Caribbean in the late eighteenth century.

† **Dundas's eighteen manoeuvres* *the Prussian manoeuvres**: General David Dundas's *Principles of Military Movements* (1788) became the basis of the British army's *Regulations* (1792), and established eighteen basic manoeuvres (movements that soldiers are supposed to perform as a company, with perfect precision and uniformity) as the

standard military drill. It took some time, however, for this new drill system to be enforced throughout the army.

† **drill pantaloons**: *Drill* refers both to military exercise or training and to a coarse twilled linen or cotton fabric.

† **black regiment . . . West India militias**: During the Revolutionary and Napoleonic Wars (1793–1815), the British raised regiments of black troops to defend the colonies. Most were former slaves and many were African-born men imported into the Caribbean before 1807.

p. 9

† **in his escutcheon a bend sinister**: An "escutcheon" is a heraldic shield bearing a coat of arms; the "bend sinister" in heraldry indicates illegitimate birth.

† **Coke, Holt, Forster, and Blackstone**: **Sir Edward Coke** (1552–1634) held the offices of solicitor-general, Speaker of the House of Commons and attorney-general. "As such he championed the crown and its prerogative powers . . . As a prosecutor he was frequently savage and tyrannical . . . [However, in] 1606 he became Chief Justice of the Common Pleas and . . . [became] the embodiment of the common law and an opponent of royal power." Coke's earlier publications "form a corpus of the common law, civil and criminal, as it stood in the sixteenth and early seventeenth centuries . . . Above all, in his Institutes he wrote the first textbook on the modern common law. Of the four books, the first, known as *Coke on Littleton*, contains Littleton's *Tenures* with an elaborate commentary . . . it is virtually a legal encyclopaedia." The last three parts, dealing with the Magna Carta and other medieval statutes, the criminal law, and various courts, became the basis of much of modern British constitutional law (Walker 1980, 240). **Sir John Holt** (1642–1710), chief justice of the King's Bench, was "a learned common lawyer . . . able to develop legal rules to the needs of changing conditions . . . He revolutionized criminal proceedings by his fairness to the accused, developed the doctrine of employer's liability, . . . and gave judgments in many important cases involving the liberties of the subject, and the rights of the citizen in relation to Parliamentary privilege" (Walker 1980, 577). **John Forster** (1667–1720) was solicitor-general, attorney-general, and eventually chief justice of the Common Pleas in Ireland. **Sir William Blackstone** (1723–80) was solicitor-general, a judge of the King's Bench, and finally a judge of the Common Pleas. He gave the first lectures on English law in a university (Oxford); his lectures became the basis of his major work, the *Commentaries on the Laws of English* (1765–79), which dealt in four volumes with the Rights of Persons, the Rights of Things, Private Wrongs, and Public Wrongs. The *Commentaries* went through many editions, but "was at once recognized as a classic by reason of the breadth and depth of learning displayed, the systematic and logical structure of the book, the accuracy of statement, and the literary grace with which the matter is presented. The book was also the best historical account of English law which had yet appeared, and the first exposition of that law as a system, in a connected narrative, and it had considerable influence on the subsequent development of the law" (Walker 1980, 136).

† **unprofessional West India gentlemen of the old school**: Lay justices or magistrates with no legal training.

p. 10

† **chance-medley**: Accident or casualty not purely accidental, but of a mixed character; an action into which chance largely enters.

† *felo-de-se*: One who deliberately puts an end to his own existence or commits any unlawful or malicious act, the consequence of which is his own death.

† *sangaree*: A drink made of diluted, spiced wine.

† **Antigua House of Assembly**: The British Caribbean colonies had elected assemblies, with the franchise limited to propertied white males; they claimed the privileges of the British House of Commons.

p. 11

† **"Nursing their wrath to keep it warm"**: From Robert Burns's "Tam o' Shanter: A Tale" (1791) where Tam, in defiance of his wife Kate's warnings, rides home late and inebriated one market day and encounters a witches and warlocks' dance. The angry Kate is evoked in the opening lines as the typical "sulky sullen dame", waiting up for the straggler, "Gathering her brows like gathering storm, / Nursing her wrath to keep it warm."

† **"Hampden, who, with dauntless pride, The little tyrant of his isle withstood"**: A somewhat loose quotation from stanza 15 of Thomas Gray's "Elegy Written in a Country Churchyard" (1751): "Some village Hampden, that with dauntless breast / The little tyrant of his fields withstood." Like much of "Elegy", these lines speculate about the seeds of greatness (here the courage to oppose tyranny) that may have been present among the obscure village dead. Though the elder Arundell has enjoyed some fame, the comparison to Gray's "village Hampden" remains apt, since his resistance to governors' various encroachments has been forgotten by the time his son comes to write about it. John Hampden (1594–1643) was a parliamentary leader during the English Civil War under his cousin Oliver Cromwell; he first came to fame by resisting payment of "ship money", a tax levied by Charles I to raise money for his navy.

† **bought a borough**: Before the Reform Act (1832), many boroughs or cities in England sent members of Parliament to the House of Commons on the votes of very few electors. These were the "rotten boroughs" which could be "bought" by a wealthy West Indian planter.

† **Lord Shelburne**: Prime Minister of Britain, 1782–83.

† **negro-driver**: An overseer on a slave-worked plantation.

† **Chiltern Hundreds**: The Crown held the manorial rights to these eight sections of land in Buckinghamshire and Oxfordshire, and appointed nominal stewards and bailiffs over them. Since members of Parliament were normally prohibited by law from resigning – but were also required to resign if they accepted profitable offices under the Crown – one who wished to resign needed only become a steward or bailiff of the Chiltern Hundreds; his resignation would then be automatic.

p. 13

† **"Oh, bloody times! / Whilst lions war and battle for their dens, / Poor harmless lambs abide their enmity." Shakespeare**: From *3 Henry VI* (II.v), a scene emblematizing the horrors of civil war, which introduces a son who has killed his father, and a father who has killed his son. This reflection by King Henry comes between the first and second of these examples of the "bloody times"; the allusion has obvious relevance to the war here recounted. The play has "Whiles", not "Whilst".

† **St. Domingo**: The French colony of Sainte Domingue, scene of the great slave uprising which began in 1791 and resulted in the independence of Haiti (1804).

† **Victor Hugues**: French Jacobin leader (1762–1826), who governed Guadeloupe 1794–95, using his control of the island to make it a base for spreading revolutionary, republican ideas and fomenting anti-British uprisings in the Eastern Caribbean including Grenada.

† **the scanty population of Trinidad, which, both in manners and language, were more French than Spanish**: With heavy immigration by French- and French Creole–speaking white and mixed-race settlers – along with their slaves, most of whom spoke French Creole as at least a second language – since the late 1770s, Trinidad, though a Spanish colony up to 1797, was dominated by French culture and language.

† **black Caraibes**: The mixed African-Amerindian Carib people who rebelled against British rule in St Vincent in 1795. Usually spelled "Black Caribs".

p. 14

† **Julian Fedon**: A mixed-race ("free coloured") planter who was the leader of the Grenadian uprising against British rule in 1795. Usually, and sometimes here, spelled "Julien Fédon".

† **Lavallée**: Probably refers to Jean-Pierre La Vallette, a "free coloured" leader of the Fédon Rebellion.

† **Louis La Grenade**: A mixed-race Grenadian who served as a captain with the British forces deployed against Fédon.

† *point d'appui*: Support place; base.

† **Abercrombie**: Sir Ralph Abercromby (1738–1801), a British general who commanded British forces in the Caribbean expeditions of 1795–97 and the conquest of Trinidad in 1797.

† **Governor Home**: Lieutenant-Governor Ninian Home, who was killed by Fédon as a prisoner in 1795.

p. 15

† **sansculottes**: Literally "without trousers", the term used during the French Revolution to describe the masses.

† **General Lyndsay**: British General Lindsay commanded a failed attempt to defeat Fédon's forces in March 1795 and subsequently committed suicide.

p. 16

† **schooner**: A small sea-going vessel, fore- and aft-rigged, that is, with triangular sails set parallel to the length of the vessel.

† **Hostess Quickly**: No doubt named after Shakespeare's Mistress Quickly (*1 and 2 Henry IV*; *Henry V*; *The Merry Wives of Windsor*), the hostess of the Boar's Head Tavern. There may be an allusion to Mistress Quickly's questionable reputation as an acquaintance of the wild Prince Hal and his riotous companions.

† **gyars, a sort of rude basket, attached to the shoulders, back, and forehead, to carry loads. The name and invention are Indian**: A type of wickerwork knapsack, hung upon the back by straps around the arms, used for carrying heavy loads. Also spelled "guayare", "guiyal", "wires" and "wyares", from Arawak "waiari".

† **Cadjo**: A generic name for an ordinary black man, sometimes negative. From the West African Ewe day-name for a boy born on Monday. Usually spelled "Cudjo" or "Cudjoe".

† **Coromantee**: "Coromantee" or "Coromanti", now usually "Mina", was used in English for Akan peoples generally. Akan (Western Kwa) is considered either a language or a cluster of languages, the primary components being Fante, Asante, and Akuapem. It is widely spoken in Ghana.

p. 17

† **"me want for pay him, because he curse my mama in Guinea, and call me black nigger-dog; Goromighty make black man first, white man after; but debil put it in a buckra man and nigger woman head to make (beget) mulatta bastard"**: "I want to pay him back, because he cursed my mother in Guinea and called me 'black nigger-boy'; God Almighty made the black man first, the white man after; but the devil put it into the heads of a white man and a nigger woman to have mulatto bastards."

† **carronades**: Short, large-calibre cannons used primarily on ships.

† **grape and canister**: "Grape", or "grapeshot", is shot made of small iron balls firmly connected together, usually in a canvas bag. "Canister-shot" or "cannister-shot" is similar, except that the iron balls are packed into a tin case. "Grape and canister" was a common term for firing with this sort of ammunition, which was used to sweep men from the rigging and decks of the enemy ship.

p. 18

† **darkies**: A generally derogatory term for Africans or blacks.

† **Johnny Crapaus**: A contemptuous term frequently used by the English to describe Frenchmen, especially soldiers and sailors, from the Napoleonic Wars to the early twentieth century; from French "crapaud", that is, "toad"; also spelled "Crappo", "Crapo", "Crapeau".

† **carenage**: A place of anchorage and especially a place where ships are cleaned, caulked, or repaired. Also spelled "careenage".

† **curaçoa**: A liqueur consisting of spirits flavoured with bitter orange peel. Usually spelled "curaçao".

† **conchs**: *Strombus gigas* (English marine conch), a large edible mollusc. The outside of the shell is whitish, with several large prominent points; the inside is smooth, shiny pink. Usually known locally as "lambi".

† **chip-chips . . . A sort of shell-fish**: *Donax denticulatus*, or *D. striatus*, an edible small triangular bivalve mollusc, shell white with variably coloured bands, found in the sand especially on the eastern beaches of Trinidad.

p. 19

† **beque**: A white man. Usually "bakra", "backra" or "buckra" in English and "beke" in French; probably from Igbo "beké", that is, "white man; European".

† **ajupa (a temporary hut)**: A small, thatched lean-to or hut, sometimes without walls, usually used as a temporary shelter for hunting or working in the fields. Usually spelled "ajoupa" or "joupa".

p. 20

† **Shakespeare . . . "a timely parted ghost."**: As Joseph's note indicates, this line comes from *2 Henry VI* (III.ii), the scene in which the Duke of Gloucester's death is announced. Warwick here argues that the blood-suffused face of Gloucester's corpse – unlike that of a "timely parted ghost" – proves that he has been murdered.

† **What Ossian, or Macpherson, called "The joy of grief"**: In the late eighteenth century, James Macpherson brought out several "translations" of poetry supposedly written by "Ossian", son of the legendary Irish hero Fingal (whom Macpherson transformed into a Scot). In fact, though some of the poems are loosely based on Gaelic originals, the rest are purely Macpherson's invention. The "Ossian" poems were much read and admired, even after the hoax was definitively exposed in 1805. "The joy of grief" appears several times in the poems; the phrase reflects their dominant emotions and their elegiac stance: the bard Ossian mourns a lost past and yet also revels in the memory of loss.

p. 21

† **"Rest thee, my darling, the time it shall come, / When thy sleep shall be broken by trumpet and drum"**: From an apparently anonymous lullaby, "O Slumber my Darling"; it may be found in anthologies such as John Hullah's *The Song Book: Words and Tunes from the Best Poets and Musicians* (1866). As a knight's son, the baby in the lullaby will inevitably take up arms in the future: "For war comes with manhood, as light comes with day."

† **creole French**: French Creole, an Afro-creole language; the majority of its vocabulary is derived from French. Varieties of this language have been or are spoken in numerous Caribbean territories (as well as elsewhere). Also known as "broken French", "Negro French" and "patois".

† **Fire in a mountain! . . . A rebellious negro song**: Cited as an "insurrectionary song" in Mrs Carmichael's *Domestic Manners and Social Condition of the White, Coloured, and Negro Population of the West Indies*, vol. II (London: Whittaker, Treacher and Co., 1833; reprint New York: Negro Universities Press/Greenwood Publishing, 1969), pp. 301–2:

Fire in da mountain,
Nobody for out him,
Take me daddy's bo tick (dandy stick),
And make a monkey out him.
Chorus.
Poor John! nobody for out him,&c.
Go to de king's goal, You'll find a doubloon dey;
Go to de king's goal, You'll find a doubloon dey.

Mrs Carmichael writes: "The explanation of this song is, that when the bad negroes wanted to do evil, they made for a sign a fire on the hill-sides, to burn down the canes. There is nobody up there, to put out the fire; but as a sort of satire, the song goes on to say, 'take me daddy's bo tick,' (daddy is a mere term of civility), take some one's dandy stick, and tell the monkeys to help to put out the fire among the canes for John; (meaning John Bull). The chorus means, the poor John has nobody to put out the fire in the canes for him. Then when the canes are burning, go to the goal, and seize the money. The tune to which this is sung, is said to be negro music; it is on a minor key, and singularly resembles an incorrect edition of an old Scotch tune, the name of which I do not recollect."

p. 22

† **Grand Etang**: A large lake in the centre of the island of Grenada in the caldera of an "extinct" volcano.

† **negropennistoun**: A type of coarse woollen cloth used for slaves' or workers' garments. Usually spelled "penistone"; here also "Pennistown" (p. 252).

† **cartouch-box**: A "cartouch" or "cartouche" is a cartridge – a roll or case of paper, parchment, and the like, containing the charge of powder and shot for a gun or pistol. A "cartouch-box" holds such cartridges.

† **Indian corncobb**: A cob – the long, thick, somewhat woody stalk to which are attached the grains of "Indian maize" or "Indian corn", *Zea mays*. It can be used to make doll bodies, pipe bowls, and so on.

† **compère**: A term used between the father and godfather of a child or between close friends.

† **Quashy**: A generic name for an ordinary black man, sometimes negative. From West African Twi *Kwàsi*, day-name for a boy born on Sunday.

p. 23

† **buckra**: See note to p. 19, "beque".

† **a brute named Smithson**: This unpleasant character, Henry Rigby Smithson, was probably based on a combination of Thomas Smith and James Rigby. (See Pocock 1993, 156–68.)

p. 25

† **"What have I gained by this adventure? / A child." Beaumont**: An inexact quotation from *The Chances* (*c.*1617), probably a play by John Fletcher (1579–1625), but by con-vention included in the collected works of Beaumont and Fletcher, as Francis Beaumont (1584–1616) wrote many plays with Fletcher. Don John, a hot-headed Spanish gentleman, assumes that the infant recently thrust into his arms in a dark street is someone's illegitimate child, and exclaims, "What have I got by this now? What's the purchase? / A piece of evening Arras worke, a childe" (I.v.8–9). The associations may not seem apt for Warner, but the "piece of evening Arras worke" does turn out to be the legitimate son of a duke. (*The Dramatic Works in the Beaumont and Fletcher Canon*, vol. 4, ed. Fredson Bowers [Cambridge: Cambridge University Press, 1979].)

p. 29

† **"Oh! that I were once more a careless child." Coleridge:** The last line of Samuel Taylor Coleridge's sonnet "To the River Otter" (1796). The river in the poem evokes youthful memories which ease "lone manhood's cares" but also arouse the vain desire to return to "careless" childhood.

† **"the sere and yellow leaf":** From Shakespeare's *Macbeth* (V.iii). Macbeth, hearing reports of more Scots who have fled to join the forces advancing on his castle, reflects on his hollow position as king over an ever-shrinking number of subjects, facing age ("the sere, the yellow leaf") without the "honour, love, obedience" that should come with it.

p. 30

† **ramier:** A large wood-pigeon, probably *Columba speciosa* in Trinidad, and *Columba squamosa* in Grenada.

† **nankeen spenser:** "Nankeen" is a type of yellow or pale buff cotton cloth. A "spenser", usually spelled "spencer", is a short double-breasted overcoat, without tails, worn by men in the latter part of the eighteenth century and the beginning of the nineteenth century.

† **Chatoyer:** The best known Black Carib chief in St Vincent in the 1790s.

† **Sir William Young:** He had estates in several islands in the late eighteenth century and wrote a book about the Black Caribs.

† **yams:** Edible starchy tubers of the genus *Dioscorea*, forming a major part of the African and West Indian diet; most varieties are believed to have originated in Africa.

p. 31

† **Tom Pipes in "Peregrine Pickle":** Tom Pipes is the servant of Peregrine Pickle in *The Adventures of Peregrine Pickle* (1751) by Tobias Smollett. Having ruined a love letter from Peregrine by carrying it in his shoe, Tom pays an accomplice to write another in its place; the expressions of love in the new one are so ludicrous that the young lady thinks Peregrine is making fun of her, and turns very cold towards him.

† **wo:** "Woe"; this spelling has long been prevalent in exclamatory and poetic use.

p. 32

† **white cockroach:** A derogatory term for a white person, from the sickly white colour of an immature cockroach.

† **Sligo:** A city in Ireland.

p. 33

† **yellow fever:** A highly infectious mild or severe viral disease, characterized by fever, vomiting, jaundice, liver degeneration, and so on. (See discussion in the introduction to this volume.)

† **chicken-turtle:** *Chelonia mydas*, the marine green turtle, a large edible sea turtle.

† **grouper:** Any of a number of large, edible marine fish, usually *Epinephelus* sp.

† **rock-hynd:** An edible marine fish, *Serranus* sp.; also spelled "rock-hind".

† **sappotillas:** *Manilkara zapota*, a tree and its small round fruit, having brown slightly fuzzy thin skin, and light brown sweet mealy flesh, with a cinnamon-like flavour. Usually spelled "sapodilla".

† **shaddocks:** *Citrus maxima*, a large, brownish-yellow bumpy and thick-skinned citrus fruit with somewhat bitter flesh.

p. 34

† **"Last scene of all, / That ends this strange eventful history, / Is second childishness, and mere oblivion." Shakespeare:** From Jacques's famous "Seven Ages of Man" speech in *As You Like It* (II.vii). Beginning with the idea that "All the world's a stage", Jacques goes on to enumerate the traditional seven "acts" or "ages" of life.

p. 35

† **learned Theban**: An allusion to Shakespeare's *King Lear* (III.iv). Lear calls Edgar, disguised as Poor Tom, a "philosopher" and a "learned Theban", or scholar. "Theban" is a generic term for one learned in ancient philosophy and natural sciences.

† **Cayenne**: French Guiana, where the famous penal colony was later established.

† **Warwick Lane**: A London street identified with doctors' offices and medicine; the Royal College of Physicians was located in Warwick Lane. The reference to the sixth commandment ("Thou shalt do no murder") suggests Arundell's low opinion of the medical profession.

† **"Having three times shook his head, / To stir his wit up, thus he said"**: From Samuel Butler's satirical poem *Hudibras* (1633–80). Hudibras has accused the charlatan conjuror Sidrophel of trickery (II.iii), and Sidrophel, an apt counterpart to D'Alentour, prefaces his blustering reply by shaking his head as here described.

† **The doctor ordered my father**: Medical treatment at this time was typically oriented to treating the individual person in a particular situation, not the disease per se.

† **leaves of the Palma Christi**: *Ricinus communis*, the castor oil plant. Joseph's reports of medical practice generally appear similar to European practice. This use of leaves is one of the few references in the novel to local/indigenous medical treatments, often utilized by doctors on the assumption that local remedies might be appropriate for local disorders. After the mid-nineteenth century, this view diminished, and European ideas and materials took over, though of course the general population continued to use various kinds of folk medicines.

p. 36

† **if his prescriptions did no good, they did no harm**: "To do the sick no harm" was a common slogan for hospitals, based on one of the tenets of the Hippocratic oath sworn by physicians: "I will prescribe regimen for the good of my patients according to my ability and my judgment and never do harm to anyone."

† **a mind diseased**: An allusion to Shakespeare's *Macbeth* (V.iii). Macbeth asks the doctor if he cannot cure Lady Macbeth, and "minister to a mind diseased"; the doctor's reply is "Therein the patient / Must minister to himself."

† **gill**: A liquid measure, one quarter of a standard pint.

† **flint in the soup as recorded by Joe Miller**: The well-known joke book *Joe Miller's Jests or Wit's Vade Mecum* (1739) was mostly not written by the celebrated clown Joe Miller but rather put together after his death by John Mottley. This enormously successful book had many comic stories and jokes added to it in subsequent editions, until "Joe Miller" came to be associated with any well-worn comic tale. "Flint in the Soup" no doubt refers to the old tale, now better known as "Stone Soup", in which a hungry traveller tells his stingy hosts he can make soup for them all with only a stone and water, but slowly persuades them to give him a variety of other ingredients to add to it.

† **surgeon**: One who heals by manual or operative means, treating wounds, fractures, deformities or disorders by surgery. Also, a senior medical officer of a military unit.

† **physician**: An authorized practitioner of medicine, graduated from a college of medicine and licensed by an appropriate board; a physician uses both medicine and surgery. The division between physicians and surgeons existed, but was broken down with mixed practices.

† **Mais . . . nous autres Français prononçons la langue Latine avec le veritable accent du pays Latin!**: "But we French pronounce the Latin language with the true accent of the Latin country!"

† **bilious fever**: A fever considered to be caused by an excess production of bile.

p. 37

† **eau de magnésie**: "Magnesia-water", hydrated magnesium carbonate, used medicinally as an antacid and a cathartic.

† **crême-de-tartre**: "Cream of tartar", crystallized bitartrate of potassium, used medicinally as a diuretic, etc.

† **calomel**: Mercurous chloride, or "protochloride" of mercury ($Hg_2 Cl_2$); used as a medicine in the form of a white powder tinged yellow, becoming grey on exposure to light. It is still, though rarely, used today as a cathartic.

† **joe**: A Portuguese gold coin, once widely used as currency in the West Indies.

† **poisonous fish**: Ciguatera disease, marked by gastrointestinal and neurological symptoms, is due to the ingestion of ciguatoxin, secreted by the dinoflagellate *Gambierdiscus toxicus*, concentrated in the tissues of certain marine fish, especially in larger specimens.

† **mamanilla-apples**: The small round green fruits of *Hippomane mancinella*, a tree, all parts of which contain a copious white latex which has a blistering effect on the skin. Usually spelled "manzanilla"; also known as "manchineel".

p. 38

† **"Do all we can, / Death is a man, / Who never spareth none." P.P. the parish clerk**: From "Epitaph on P.P. Clerk of the Parish, said to have been written by himself": "Look down upon this Stone; / Do all we can, Death is a Man / That never spareth none." "P.P. Clerk of the Parish" was a pseudonym adopted by Alexander Pope, John Arbuthnot, and other members of the satirical Scriblerus Club in "Memoirs of P.P. Clerk of this Parish" (1727), their skit on Bishop Gilbert Burnet's *History of His Own Time*. The epitaph was attached to the skit and is probably – at least in this version – the work of Pope.

p. 39

† **sloop of war**: Originally, a "sloop of war" was any small ship-of-war that did not fit into any other category, but by the early nineteenth century, "sloop of war" had come to mean a smaller two- or three-masted square-rigged naval ship, that is, one with square sails set into the wind, at right angles to the length of the ship.

† **standard of St. George**: The English flag.

† **reduction of Trinidad**: The British conquest of the island from Spain in 1797; also known as the Capitulation.

p. 41

† **to teach the young idea how to shoot**: From the "Spring" part of *The Seasons* (1726–30) by James Thomson. This line is virtually a cliché extolling the pleasures of child-rearing: "Delightful task! to rear the tender thought, / To teach the young idea how to shoot" (lines 1152–53). Joseph gives a humorous twist to the phrase's conventional meaning by using it literally, to refer to pistol practice.

† **calabashes and cocoa-nut shells**: The dried, hard shells of the fruits of the calabash tree, *Crescentia cujete*, and the coconut tree, *Cocos nucifera*, often used as containers for food and water, especially by the poor.

p. 42

† **privateers**: "Privateers" were privately owned vessels of war, which operated as irregular adjuncts to regular naval forces, usually with letters of commission from the country they served.

† **Guave**: A village on the western (leeward) side of Grenada, about a third of the way south from the top of the island. Usually spelled "Gouyave".

p. 43

† **"O'er the glad waters of the dark blue sea, / Our thoughts as boundless and our souls as free." Byron**: These opening lines of Byron's poem *The Corsair* (1814), which follows the adventures of the pirate chief, Conrad, form part of the pirates' song, a celebration of the freedoms and risks of their wild life.

† **junk**: A chunk or small piece.
† **"who live at home at ease"**: From "Song" by Martyn Parker (d. 1656), in which the "gentlemen of England / That live at home at ease" are said to take no thought for "the dangers of the seas".

p. 44
† **Cariacou**: One of the larger islands of the Grenada Grenadines, between St Vincent to the north, and Grenada to the south. Usually spelled "Carriacou".
† **Union Island**: The largest of the small islands of the St Vincent Grenadines, between St Vincent to the north, and Grenada to the south.
† **Mayaro**: Mayreau, one of the St Vincent Grenadines, between Canouan to the north and Union Island to the south. ("Mayaro" is a village on the lower part of the eastern coast of Trinidad.)
† **Canaan**: Canouan, one of the small islands of the St Vincent Grenadines, between St Vincent to the north, and Grenada to the south.
† **Governor Bentinck**: Henry William Bentinck, governor of St Vincent 1802–4, who divided up the lands of the defeated Black Caribs.
† **lugger**: A small, swift, usually two-masted, vessel with four-cornered cut sails, set fore and aft, used for coastal trading and fishing. Privateer luggers often had three masts.
† **Caraibe war**: The suppression of the Black Carib rising in St Vincent, 1795–96; usually "Carib war".

p. 45
† **long Tom**: A common name for a large ship's gun with a long range.
† **warp**: Turn aside from a current course; deflect direction.
† **kedge**: A small anchor, usually used in addition to the large ship's anchors, to keep a ship steady while riding at anchor.
† **galdings**: Herons; any long-legged wading birds.

p. 46
† **flying-gib**: A light sail set before the "gib" or "jib" – a supplementary triangular sail set in front of a boat's primary sail(s) – to catch more of the wind and thereby increase speed.
† **patois**: See note to p. 13, "creole French".

p. 48
† **"Near fair St. Vincent, quite unknown to fame, / An island stands, and Bequia is its name." Lines in the *St. Vincent Gazette***: The source of this quotation has not been traced.
† **Sayeb was a Mandingo of the tribe called Foulahs**: "Mandingo" is a term referring to various ethnolinguistic groups who speak a Northern Mande language. "Fula/Peulh/Fulfulde" refers to speakers of (West) Atlantic languages. Early in the transatlantic slave trade, most of the Africans taken from Senegal were Fula and Wolof (both Atlantic ethnolinguistic groups); soon, however, most of the captives were taken from further inland. They were more likely to be speakers of Northern Mande languages. The phrasing of this sentence suggests that Sayeb was Fula, an ethnic group that extends from Senegal across to Cameroun. However, the linking of the Fula to the Mandingo suggests that Sayeb came from Senegal.
† **Caffres (heathens)**: "Kaffir" is a derogatory Muslim term for a non-believer.

p. 49
† **Petty Nevis**: Petit Nevis, one of the small islands of the St Vincent Grenadines, between St Vincent to the north, and Grenada to the south.

p. 50

† **Bequia**: One of the small islands of the St Vincent Grenadines, between St Vincent to the north, and Grenada to the south. Bequia is the northernmost, closest to St Vincent.

p. 51

† **drogher**: A slow, clumsy, West Indian coasting vessel.

p. 52

† **"Ac velut ingenti Silâ, summove Taburno, / Cum duo conversis inimica inpraelia tauri, / Frontibus incurrant." Virgil**: "As in great Sila or the top of Taburnus, when two rival bulls charge together in combat, head to head." These lines, from Virgil's *Aeneid* (12:715–17), come at the beginning of the climactic battle between the hero Aeneas and the Latin prince Turnus; applied to this context, however, the passage takes on something of a burlesque air. The quotation is inaccurate: "inpraelia" needs to be "in proelia" (as it is in all editions of the *Aeneid* now) to make sense, and "incurrant" should be "incurrunt".

† **where Gall places them**: Though Franz Joseph Gall (1758–1828) was in many respects a good scientist whose findings were borne out by later research, he also founded the pseudo-science of phrenology. Gall's phrenological system relates human attributes to the shape of the skull, seeing the bumps on the skull as "organs" of benevolence, conscience, and so on.

† *siege of Badajos*: A battle of the Peninsular War (1808–13) fought in Spain in 1812.

p. 53

† **Mollineux**: In 1811 Tom Molyneux, a freed American slave, fought a famous boxing match with the British Tom Cribb, and nearly won. In the end, Molyneux had to give up the match because he developed a cramp from waiting through a long time-out called by Cribb.

p. 54

† **Ihn sagt . . . derselben unterliegen**: Joseph's German spelling is not standard; he may have written the words down as he pronounced them. In standard German, "Ihn" would be "ihr"; "Dotch" would be "Doch"; "glluck" would be "glück" (dialect forms "gluck" or "glick"); and the nouns would be capitalized. The awkward translation is largely accurate, though the German is better rendered "be defeated" rather than "to retreat".

† **lobster-backs**: British troops, from their red coats.

† **brownies**: Mixed-race men.

p. 55

† **Kingston**: Kingstown, the capital of St Vincent, on the south coast of the island.

† **Fort Charlotte**: Located on Johnson Point, the northern part of Kingstown Bay.

† **grampus**: A dolphin or porpoise.

p. 56

† **Portsmouth Point**: Probably the port town of northwestern Dominica.

† **Spanish galleon**: A kind of ship, shorter but higher than the "galley"; a ship of war, especially Spanish; also the large vessels used by the Spanish for trading.

† **three sheets in the wind**: Very drunk. A "sheet" is the line, or rope, which secures the bottom corners of the sails; a ship with her sheets in the wind, or loose, is unsteady and rolls.

† **"Me no da stand, me no da run, but me da come for bring you a lille (little) taffia"**: "I'm not standing still, I'm not running, but I'm coming to bring you a little taffia."

p. 57

† **screwjack**: A machine, usually portable, for lifting heavy weights by force acting from below; in the commonest form, having a rack and a pinion wheel or screw and a handle turned by hand; usually "jack-screw".

p. 58

† **Stanzas on the Grenadines**: Possibly by James Grainger (1721–66), who emigrated to the West Indies in 1759.

† **marine eggs**: Spiny sea urchins; usually "sea eggs". Some species are edible; many have poisonous spines.

p. 59

† **Soufriere**: The volcanic crater on St Vincent; it erupted in 1812. Although "soufrière" refers in French to a sulphur deposit, the word in the French Caribbean refers to volcanic craters on several islands.

† **"I sell the story for the same price I bought it"**: Also, "I sell it as I buy it", that is, I'm simply repeating what I heard, without vouching for its veracity.

† **round jacket**: A jacket cut and made in such a way as to envelope the body in a circular manner, and cut with a circular hem.

† **inexpressibles**: Men's breeches or trousers.

p. 60

† **look through nature up to nature's God**: A quotation from Alexander Pope's "An Essay on Man" (1733–34). In context, this line praises non-sectarian breadth of mind: "Slave to no sect, who takes no private road, / But looks through Nature up to Nature's God" (IV 331–32). Dickson, however, hardly seems the sort of person Pope had in mind.

† **Albion**: "Albion" is a poetic term for England, from the Latin word "albus", that is, "white", a reference to the white cliffs on the southern Dover coast.

† **"The poet's eye, in a fine frenzy rolling, often glances at a lucky thought." From Shakespeare's *A Midsummer Night's Dream***: Duke Theseus here discounts the lovers' overnight experience in the woods, attributing it to their overactive imaginations. Though parts of this speech (V.i) are often used in praise of poets, Theseus is hardly complimentary: he is comparing the poet's "fine frenzy" to madness, and begins by asserting that "The lunatic, the lover and the poet / Are of imagination all compact."

p. 61

† **"But who, to dumb forgetfulness a prey . . . Nor left one poem, verse or rhyme behind?"**: Dickson is here "judiciously altering" lines from Gray's "Elegy": "For who, to dumb forgetfulness a prey, / This pleasing anxious being e'er resigned, / Left the warm precincts of the cheerful day, / Nor cast one longing ling'ring look behind" (stanza 22). (See note to p. 11.)

† **peri-wigs**: An artificial imitation of a head of hair, or part of one, first worn as a fashionable headdress, retained by judges, barristers, etc. as part of their professional costume.

† **Sir Cloudesley Shovel**: Admiral Sir Cloudesley Shovel commanded the English fleet from 1704 to 1707, during an era when large periwigs were in vogue.

† **"for, e'en though vanquished, he can argue still"**: Slightly altered from Oliver Goldsmith's "The Deserted Village" (1770; line 212), these words describe the village schoolmaster's argumentative skill. The schoolmaster, not unlike Dickson, combines solid worth with a naive delight in his power over "words of learned length and thundering sound" (line 213).

p. 62

† **the proverb which makes tailors ninth-parts of humanity**: A reference to the derogatory proverb, "Nine tailors make a man"; a tailor's occupation was supposed to

make him feebler than other men. Some interpreters see the joke as on customers rather than tailors, that is, it takes nine tailors to make a gentleman's attire, but the long tradition of derogatory tailor jokes makes that unlikely. By the time *Warner Arundell* was written, the proverb also contained an implied pun on "teller" (a stroke on a bell): the funeral bell tolled three times for a child, six times for a woman, and nine times for a man.

† **non est inventus**: "Not to be found", a proverbial reference to truants and shirkers, originating in the words a sheriff writes on a writ when the defendant has absconded.

† **gentlemen of the long robe in Westminster Hall**: "Gentlemen of the long robe" is a conventional phrase for lawyers; Westminster Hall was England's chief law court until 1870.

p. 63

† **"Tidd's Practice of Pleading", "Coke on Littleton", "Wood's Institutes", "Blackstone's Commentaries"**: William Tidd (1760–1847) had a great reputation in special pleadings. His fame rests on his book *The Practice of the Court of King's Bench in Personal Actions* (1790–98), which was for fifty years nearly the only authority in matters of common law practice and the rules of procedure. **Sir Thomas Littleton** (1402–81) was a judge of assizes and a justice of the Common Pleas. He is best known for a short treatise on *Tenures* published about 1481, giving a scientific account of the tenure of land. "It is the first great book on English law not in Latin . . . and wholly un-influenced by Roman law, and sums up the development of what was then the most important branch of the common law" (Walker 1980, 772). **Coke on Littleton** (see note to p. 9). **Thomas Wood** (1661–1722), a barrister and cleric, published *New Institute of the Imperial or Civil Law* (1704) dealing with the influence of Roman law, and differences between English and Roman and canon law. In 1720, he published *An Institute of the Laws of England, or Laws of England in their Natural Order According to Common Use*, to supply a methodical book on English law for the use of students; it was eventually superseded by **Blackstone's Commentaries** (see note to p. 9).

† **Mortimer's hairtriggers**: "Hair triggers" or "set triggers", are devices enabling a light-pull trigger release of the firing mechanism; they are characteristically found on sporting guns (used for hunting and target practice) and on duelling pistols. H.W. Mortimer was a famous sporting gunsmith of the late eighteenth century.

† **in propriâ personâ**: Latin "in propria persona", that is, "in person".

† **This event was what Scotch lawyers would call *charge of horning***: "Horning" generally refers to cuckoldry, that is, "giving horns" to a spouse, usually a husband, by the partner, usually the wife, committing adultery. The pun here is on the non-metaphoric nature of the actual incident.

† **shambles**: A slaughterhouse, a place where animals are killed for meat; a place where meat is sold.

† **cattle . . . neat kind**: "Cattle" may refer to all domestic livestock; "neat cattle" are bovine – oxen, bulls, cows and calves.

p. 66

† **"With haste, / To their known station cheerfully they go; / And, all at once disdaining to be last, / Solicit every gale to meet the foe." Dryden**: From John Dryden's 1666 poem, *Annus Mirabilis: The Year of Wonders, MDCLXVI*. Dryden's poem celebrates the heroic behaviour of the English during several events of 1667, including war with Holland, and the Great Fire of London. This stanza (77) describes the preparations for the second day of a naval battle between the Dutch and the battered and outnumbered English.

† **the insalubrious island of St. Lucia**: Considered unhealthy perhaps because its heavily forested mountains encouraged yellow fever and malaria.

† **brig of war**: A "brig" or "brigantine" is a two-masted, square-rigged ship, but carrying

on her mainmast a lower fore-and-aft sail. A "brig of war" is such a ship fitted with guns for naval battles.

† **the Saints**: Small islands off the southern coast of Guadeloupe, between Guadeloupe and Dominica.

† **merchantman**: A large ship intended for long ocean voyages, built for trade rather than battle, and so carrying few if any guns.

† **keep the weather-gage of**: Of a ship, to be windward of another vessel.

p. 67

† **square-dirk**: A kind of dagger or small sword.

† **raise tacks and sheets; mainsail haul; let go, and haul**: These are commands for making sail, that is, spreading sails to the wind. For "sheets", see note to p. 56; "tacks" are lines used respectively to brace the yards. To "raise" them usually means to get them in hand in preparation for adjusting sail. To "haul" a line is to pull on it; "let go and haul" orders one party of sailors to release their line while the others haul. (A "line" in nautical terms is a rope in use; "rope" is used only for detached, spare rope lying in storage.)

† **backed her main-topsail**: To "back" a sail is to place it so that the wind will blow directly on its front, and thereby slow the ship's movement. Backing a mainsail can be used to stop a ship, as seems to be the case here. The main topsail is the second sail on the mainmast, one above the course, or lowest sail; the mainmast is the chief mast of a ship, usually the second mast from the bow.

† **stern chasers**: Guns mounted in the stern of a ship.

p. 68

† **lee scuppers**: "Scuppers" are gutters that run all around the deck of a ship, intended to catch any shipped water and return it to the sea through a series of holes. The "lee scuppers" are those on the leeward side of the ship, away from the wind.

† **yard-arms**: The "yard" is the lateral spar to which a ship's square sails are attached; the "yard-arm" is the end of the yard which projects beyond the edge of a sail.

† **bowsprit**: A large spar or boom running out from the (front) stem of a vessel, to which the foremast stays are fastened, as well as the jib-boom and flying jib-boom, which extend beyond it.

† **companion**: Companion-ladder, a ladder leading from the deck to a cabin.

p. 70

† **"A man severe he was, and stern to view; / I knew him well, and every truant knew. / Full well they laughed, with counterfeited glee, / At all his jokes – for many a joke had he." Goldsmith**: From Goldsmith's "The Deserted Village" (lines 197–98, 201–2). Like the earlier quotation from the poem (see note to p. 61), this describes the village schoolmaster, an appropriate counterpart to Tom Harris.

† **dog is a small copper coin**: A low-value coin of French origin, made of copper and silver and widely used in the seventeenth and eighteenth centuries. Also known as "black dog" from its tendency to tarnish darkly.

p. 71

† **tamarind-rods**: Whips made from the strong, thin, flexible branches of *Tamarindus indica*, the tamarind tree.

† **"neither crab nor creole, but a true-born Barbadian"**: "Crab" here is a contraction of "Carib". The proverb expressed pride in Barbadian birth.

† **brother Jonathan**: An American or "Yankee"; gradually superseded by "Uncle Sam" during the nineteenth century.

p. 72

† **Five Islands**: Applied today to the peninsula immediately southwest of St Johns, on which is Five Islands Village. The name may originally have designated a group of islets north of this peninsula.

† **Sam Matthews**: Samuel Augustus Mathews was a skilled carpenter and craftsman who was born and lived most of his life in St Kitts. "At the end of a day's work, Samuel Augustus could find relaxation from his work on the estates . . . He could allow "the lazy fit" to overcome him and he could engage in talking, writing poetry and singing to his heart's content . . . [but] he was also allowing himself to run into debt" (p. 53) and spent time in (debtors') prison. His mastery of "slave language" or "negro language" was demonstrated in his apparently well-received public performances of songs such as "Buddy Quow" and "Sabina". He published these along with other songs in his book *The Lying Hero* (1793), in which he attacks Moreton's *Manners and Customs of the West India Islands*: "The general tenure of Mathews' book lay in portraying the Methodists as swindlers, Moreton as an ungrateful liar, the planters as perfect gentlemen, and slavery as an acceptable means of managing society in the Caribbean" (p. 55). See Philip Baker and Adrienne Bruyn (eds.), *St Kitts and the Atlantic Creoles: The Texts of Samuel Augustus Mathews in Perspective* (London: University of Westminster Press, 1998), including Victoria Borg O'Flaherty's article "Samuel Augustus Mathews: His Life and Times", pp. 49–58.

† **madeira Portuguese**: A person from Madeira, the Atlantic island settled by Portugal in the fifteenth century.

p. 73

† **Dominique**: Dominica, one of the Windward Islands.

† **hooker**: Usually, a two-masted Dutch coasting or fishing vessel.

p. 74

† **lignum vitae**: Several trees and shrubs native to the West Indies, especially *Guiacum officinale* and *G. sanctum*; the wood is very hard and very heavy.

† **Point-Petre**: Pointe-à-Pitre, a town on the central west coast of the island of Grande Terre, across a narrow strait from the more westerly island of Basseterre, which together make up the bulk of Guadeloupe.

† **'peached**: Accused; informed against.

† **calls for *quarters***: That is, ask for mercy in sparing the life of one who surrenders.

† **I nail my colours to the mast**: "Colours" are the flag or standard of a regiment or ship; to "nail one's colours to the mast" is to adopt an unyielding attitude.

† **strike**: To lower the "colours", that is, to surrender.

† **chain-shot**: A kind of shot formed of two balls, or half-balls, connected by a chain, chiefly used in naval warfare to destroy masts, rigging and sails.

† **starboard pin**: That is, his right leg.

† **Basseterre**: In Guadeloupe, a town on the west side of the island of Basse Terre, near the southern tip; usually "Basse Terre".

p. 75

† ***leg*-bail**: That is, to run away.

† **Qui va là?**: "Who goes there?"

p. 76

† **flambeaux**: Singular "flambeau", a torch; originally a flare made of rushes, later a torch made of wood wrapped in kerosene-soaked cloth, or a wick in a bottle of oil.

† **sacréing**: Blaspheming; swearing.

† **battery**: A platform or fortified work, on or within which artillery is mounted.

† **Cudjoe* *A general name for a negro**: See note to p. 16.

† **frigate**: A swift three-masted ship, with 20–50 guns, used for scouting and cruising.

† *jury* **paddle**: An improvised paddle. "Jury" is a nautical term used to describe any temporary or improvised part of a ship or ship's equipment.

† **stand towards**: To sail or steer a course in a specified direction.

† **sculls**: A kind of short, light oar, used in a pair by one person.

† **St. Martin**: The northernmost of the Leeward Islands, between Anguilla and St Barts; divided between St Maarten (The Netherlands) and St Martin (France).

p. 77

† **main-topmast**: The second part of the main mast, one above the lowest part of the mast.

† **the shipwreck of Paul**: See the Acts of the Apostles 27, where St Paul, on his way to Rome as a prisoner, is wrecked on the shore of Malta in a ship from Adramyttium.

† **"Laid him low on the deck, and he never spoke more"**: The source of this quotation has not been traced.

p. 79

† **"Nothing like your real Trinidada." Ben Jonson**: "Trinidada" or "Trinidado" is a type of Trinidadian tobacco, considered the best available in the seventeenth century, when tobacco was a new and fashionable delicacy in England. This is probably an inexact quotation from Jonson's *Every Man in His Humour* (first performed 1598; published 1601 and again with extensive revisions and character name changes in 1616, the edition followed here). The cowardly braggart Captain Bobadill, having praised some tobacco as "your right *Trinidado*", touts tobacco's nutritional and medicinal value (III.v).

† **gig**: A light, open, two-wheeled carriage, pulled by one horse.

† **creole Spaniard**: A person of Spanish descent born in the New World.

† **yacht**: A light, fast-sailing ship, usually one used primarily for pleasure excursions or for conveying important people.

p. 80

† **sport a main**: Engage in a match between fighting cocks.

† **wild pines**: Wild bromeliads, resembling pineapple leaves, that grow along tree branches.

† **the giant** *Bombex cieba*: *Ceiba pentandra*, the silk cotton or kapok tree, an extremely large native tree, one hundred feet tall or more; the trunk often has huge buttresses.

† **fig-tree, with its hundred trunks, twisted its *ungrateful* leaves,* *The Spaniards call these leaves, which at first get support from surrounding trees, and then destroy them, *los ingratos*. The English negroes give them the less poetical, but more humorous name of *Kotchman* (hugging creole)**: Several species of strangling trees, including *Ficus* sp. and *Clusia palmacida*. These eventually kill the trees on which they began growing.

p. 81

† *bocas,*— **passages formed by several small but beautiful islands, which rise abruptly from the flood, and stand, like bold sentinels, between Trinidad and the opposing point of South America**: The "Bocas" (from Spanish "boca", that is, "mouth") are sea channels between the island of Trinidad and the Paria peninsula of Venezuela. The northern entrance to the Gulf of Paria off the northwest peninsula of Trinidad is the Dragon's Mouth, or Boca del Drago, with four channels: the First Boca (also Monos Boca or Boca Monos, and Apes' or Monkeys' Passage), between the island of Monos and the Trinidad mainland; the Second Boca (or Boca Huevos) between Monos and Huevos, and the Third Boca (also Boca de Navios or Ships' Passage), between Huevos and Chacachacare. Beyond Chacachacare is the main passage, the Boca Grande. The channel between the southern shore of Trinidad and the South American mainland (Venezuela) is the Boca del Serpiente, or Serpent's Mouth.

† **one called Tamana, the other Montserrat**: Mount Tamana is the highest mountain in the northeastern section of the central range of mountains in Trinidad. The Montserrat hills are in the southwestern part.

† **Captain Columbine has made a good survey**: The *Survey of Trinidad in 1803, to Commodore Hood*, by Captain Columbine; excerpts were published in the *Port of Spain Gazette*, 3–14 August 1849.

p. 82

† **Mallet's map**: This map was "made by the order of His Excellency Ralph Abercrombie, Lieutenant-Governor and Commander-in-Chief of the British forces in the West Indies by F. Mallet, Captain of the surveying engineers, 1797, published in 1802 in London by W. Faden, Geographer to His Majesty and HRH the Prince of Wales".

† **a mere blundering transcript and translation of the Spanish map**: Joseph is objecting to Mallet's plagiarizing, and not even bothering to have his cartographers check the Spanish translation. That is, on the Mallet map, the word "breakers" is printed all over the Gulf of Paria, though there are normally no breakers there to trouble a mariner except when a storm is brewing. The original Spanish cartographers, whom Joseph is claiming that Mallet plagiarized, had "brazos" – actually "gravel" – in the gulf-locations; this is a legitimate piece of information for mariners slinging lead weights over the side of the ship to find water depth, as this means that the sea-bottom there is gravelly.

† **Coleridge**: Henry Nelson Coleridge, author of *Six Months in the West Indies in 1825* (London: John Murray, 1826).

† **"Zuñiga's History of the Philippines"**: This work has not been identified.

† **flamingoes**: *Eudocimus ruber,* the scarlet ibis, a large scarlet-red bird with a large down-curved bill.

† **seven-coloured parroquet**: *Touit batavica,* the lilac-tailed parrotlet or seven-coloured parrakeet, a common bird in forested areas of Trinidad. Overall appearance black and green, with yellowish green, lilac, bluish green, red and yellowish gray.

† **the large and gaudy macaw**: More commonly the blue and yellow macaw, *Ara ararauna,* but at this time there were possibly numbers of the scarlet macaw, *Ara maracao,* which would definitely be considered more colourful.

† **red, or Alouto monkeys**: *Alouatta seniculus insularis,* the red howler monkey, native to Trinidad; it makes a very loud howling call in the forests at dusk and dawn.

p. 83

† **Gaspar-Grandé**: The larger of two small islands to the west of the Five Islands, in the waters off Chaguaramas in northwestern Trinidad. The larger of these two islands was called by the Spanish Gaspar Grandé "Big Gaspar", and the smaller one Gasparillo "Little Gaspar" after Don Gaspar de Percin, to whom these islands were granted at the time of the Cédula de Población. Later, Gaspar Grandé became better known as Gasparee, and Gasparillo as Centipede Island.

† **Spanish admiral, Apodaca**: In February 1797, with the British expeditionary force approaching Trinidad, Apodaca (various spellings) scuttled his fleet in the Gulf of Paria. Harvey commanded the British naval squadron in February 1797.

† **beautiful valleys of Cuesa, and Diego Martin**: The Cuesa River flows through what is now usually called Tucker Valley, formerly mainly cocoa estates. To the east is the Diego Martin Valley, formerly a major agricultural estate area for cocoa and sugar cane.

† **pouij**: *Tabebuia serratifolia,* a tree with bright yellow flowers, visible on hillsides from great distances; also *T. rosea,* a pink-flowered variety. The wood is hard and supple, and sticks of it are used for kalinda "stick-fighting". Usually spelled "poui".

† **"bois-immortels"**: *Erythrina poeppigiana,* the (mountain) immortelle, a tall slender tree with brilliant orange-red flowers, used to provide shade to crops, especially young cocoa trees.

† **the chocolate-nut . . . the cocoanut**: *Theobroma cacao*, the cacao or cocoa tree; the seeds are used to make chocolate. *Cocos nucifera*, the cocoanut or coconut tree; the large nut-fruits yield white flesh used for cooking, oil, and copra.

† **palmiste**: *Roystonea oleracea*, an extremely tall, straight-growing palm often used for avenue planting.

p. 84

† **"Oh! villainy, villainy, villainy! / I think upon't; I think I smell it; oh, villainy!" Shakespeare**: From *Othello* (V.ii): Emilia has just realized that Othello's jealousy and his murder of Desdemona have been engineered by her husband, Iago, and is denouncing him. (Joseph's original text has both villan[y] – now an obsolete spelling – and villain[y]; it has been regularized to the latter throughout.)

† **officer of the line**: An (infantry) officer of the regular army who will likely see actual combat, unlike an officer in the guards or the auxiliary forces, for example, who tended to be assigned to domestic or defensive duties. Line regiments were often considered less fashionable, since richer and more influential men tended to avoid active service, but on the other hand, their participation in battle did give them a kind of heroic glamour.

† **cue**: A long roll or plait of hair worn hanging down the back, from the head or a wig. Usually spelled "queue".

† **Chinese**: A small group of Chinese labourers had been imported into Trinidad in 1806–7.

† **sambo* *The mixed race between the Indian and negro**: "Sambo" was applied to persons of mixed Amerindian and African descent, especially in the Hispanic Caribbean.

† *Péons*: In Trinidad, working-class immigrants from Venezuela of mixed Amerindian, African and Spanish descent.

† *cuchillo* **(knife, or poniard)**: A "cuchillo" is any instrument with a steely blade and a handle, such as a knife. A "poniard" is the Spanish "puñal", an offensive weapon 8–12 inches (20–30 cm) long that can only hurt with the point. But "cuchillo" is familiarly used for knives, poniards, surgeons' scalpels, etc.

p. 85

† **mulattoes, mestees, and quadroons**: Terms used to describe various degrees of African-European mixtures.

† **Guinea**: The European name for a portion of the west coast of Africa, extending from Sierra Leone to Benin.

† **creole drawl**: The French and English spoken by white creoles, people of European descent born in the Caribbean, were often considered by Europeans to be spoken in a slow, lazy, careless manner.

† *escribano*, **or notary**: Spanish term for a court clerk or registrar.

† **The Spanish law, in force in the island**: Although Trinidad became a British colony in 1797, Spanish laws and judicial practices were continued (with some modifications) until the 1840s. Of course British settlers generally disapproved of them. (See the introduction to this volume.)

p. 86

† **noyeau**: A liqueur made of brandy flavoured with the kernels of certain fruits.

p. 87

† **the fleet of Nelson did appear off the northern coast of Trinidad**: In 1805, Admiral Lord Nelson's ships entered Trinidad waters in pursuit of the combined French-Spanish fleet. He finally met and defeated this fleet at Trafalgar, off the coast of Spain, in October 1805, thus thwarting Napoleon's projected invasion of Britain.

† **an old Spanish fort on an eminence, at the place called Las Cuevas**: Las Cuevas is

at about the mid-point of the north coast of Trinidad, the next large bay eastward from Maracas; the small fort is on a northeastern promontory guarding the bay.

† **spiked his two guns**: To "spike" is to render a cannon or large gun unserviceable by driving a pointed piece of steel into the touch-hole.

p. 88

† **Oronoke**: A major river in Venezuela, flowing about 1,500 miles from its source in the Parima plateau near the Brazilian border, northwestward to the modern Colombian border, then north and east across Venezuela into the Atlantic Ocean. With its principal tributaries – the Guavire, Meta, Apure, Caura, and Caroni – it constitutes one of the three major river systems of South America. The mouth of the Orinoco is a vast swampy delta, across the Serpent's Mouth from the south side of the island of Trinidad. Though usually spelled "Oronoco" by Joseph, it is "Orinoco" on modern maps.

† **General Heslop**: Sir Thomas Hislop, governor of Trinidad 1803–10.

† **Fort George**: This was constructed by Hislop to be a fall-back point for defending against invasion from the northern seacoast. It was eventually finished but never used.

p. 89

† *cocorite*: *Attalea maripa,* a large palm tree; leaves were once widely used for thatching.

p. 90

† **vinegar**: See next note.

† **had fainted, and some were attacked with *coups de soleil***: "Heat syncope" results when the body senses insufficient blood flow to the skin to cool the body and responds by dilating all blood vessels, resulting in a rapid drop in blood pressure and subsequent fainting; typically, vigorous physical activity precedes such an episode. More serious is heatstroke, here literally "blows of the sun". This life-threatening emergency is caused by thermoregulatory failure and is characterized by rapid onset, brain dysfunction, impaired consciousness, high fever and absence of sweating. Treatment of heat-related disorders is generally aimed at rapidly reducing body temperature – hence the external use of vinegar – then controlling the secondary effect of the exposure.

† **conflagration of Port of Spain**: In 1808 much of Port of Spain was destroyed by fire.

p. 91

† **respectable in the sense of the word as used by the witness in Thurtell's trial – "because he drove his gig"**: During the 1824 murder trial of John Thurtell, a witness was supposed to have asserted that he thought the suspect respectable because "he drove his gig". The reports of the trial contain no such assertion, but the incident was passed on as fact, notably in the works of Thomas Carlyle, for whom the idea of gig-driving respectability became a shorthand reference to what he saw as his era's grossly materialistic outlook.

p. 92

† **"With stern, resolved, despairing eye, / I see each aimed dart; / For one has cut my dearest tie, / And quivers in my heart." Burns**: From "Ruin" (1786), where the speaker's loss makes him not only endure but even invite ruin to come and "close this scene of care".

† **Dr. Manuel Lopez**: This character is, thinly disguised, Dr Ramon Garcia, LLD (1778–1869), Father-General of Minors. Dr Garcia had fled from the revolution in Venezuela to Trinidad and was immediately appointed to high office by Sir Ralph Woodford. (See Pocock 1993, 141–42, 184–85, 227, 461–62.)

† *rarae aves in terris*: "Rare birds in the lands". The singular *rara avis* or "rare bird" is proverbial for anything especially unusual. The original phrase, from Juvenal VI.165, is *rara avis in terris nigroque similima cygna,* "a rare bird in the lands, and very like a black swan".

p. 93

† **Benedico te in nomine Patris, et Filii, et Spiritús Sancti! Amen**: "I bless you in the name of the Father, the Son and the Holy Spirit." Usually accompanied by the sign of the cross, this standard blessing is used in baptism, to dismiss departing congregations after mass, etc.

p. 94

† **seven penitential Psalms**: Seven psalms (6, 32, 38, 51, 102, 130 and 143) are designated for penitential use in Christian – especially Roman Catholic and Anglican – liturgies.

† **Angostura**: A city on the River Orinoco in Venezuela, now called Ciudad Bolívar.

p. 95

† *alguacils*: Spanish term for policemen, police constables, used in Trinidad up to the 1840s.

† **Cumana**: A city in Venezuela, on the coast, fairly close to southern Trinidad. Venezuela was a common place of sanctuary for criminals or the persecuted in Trinidad.

† **oydores, assessors, escribanos, depositaries, sequestrators, advocates, alguacils, alguacil-mayors**: Various kinds of legal and law enforcement officials under the Spanish system. The **alguazil mayor** was a senior policeman, the chief constable.

† **"Coke's Institutes"**: (See note to p. 9.)

p. 97

† **"O'er the wild mountains, and luxuriant plains, / Nature, in all the pomp of beauty, reigns." Montgomery**: From Part 1 of James Montgomery's *The West Indies* (1810), a poem written to commemorate the British abolition of the slave trade in 1807. This section describes an idyllic, pre-colonial Caribbean, before the "fell legions of invading Spain" arrive to decimate the population and create the demand for an imported slave-labour force.

† **"March the heavy mules securely slow, / O'er hills, o'er dales, o'er crags, o'er rocks they go." Pope's *Iliad***: From Alexander Pope's translation of Homer's *Iliad* (1715–20) (XXIII.140–41). The mules are being driven up to "Ida's spreading Woods" by wood-cutters, to collect the wood to be used for Patroclus's funeral pyre.

† **La Guayra**: A city on the north coast of Venezuela, directly across the Serpent's Mouth in the Gulf of Paria. Now usually spelled "Güiria".

p. 98

† ***Matcheti* is a kind of cutlass**: A "machete" or "cutlass" is a long, broad-bladed, metal cutting implement, larger than a knife, shorter and wider than a sword, usually with one edge slightly curved. In one form or another, it is the ubiquitous agricultural work tool of the Caribbean.

† **Humboldt**: Baron Alexander von Humboldt (1769–1859) was a German naturalist who travelled widely to make comparative studies in geography, botany, geology, ethnology and other areas of natural science. After his first trip, five years in South America and Mexico, he published many widely read and influential works, beginning with *The Equinoctial Plants* (1805) and *Ideas for a Geography of Plants and a Nature Picture of the Tropics* (1805).

† **Mr. Lockhart of Trinidad**: David Lockhart (d. 1846) was an English botanist engaged by Governor Sir Ralph Woodford. In 1818 he established and was the first curator of the Botanical Gardens on the grounds of the governor's residence, St Ann's Cottage, Port of Spain. He collected rare and ornamental trees and plants from neighbouring countries and farther afield; many of the trees he planted are still standing.

p. 99

† **the happy valley of Rasselas**: In the didactic romance *The History of Rasselas, Prince of Abyssinia* (1759), by Samuel Johnson, Rasselas and his companions leave the idyllic Happy Valley in search of a greater range of experience.

† **Like Lord Monboddor he conceived that man originally had a tail**: James Burnett, Lord Monboddo, anticipated Darwinian theories of evolution in his *Of the Origin and Progress of Language* (1773–92). Monboddo believed that children are born with tails.

p. 100

† ***Pons Asinorum***: Literally, "The Bridge of Asses". Euclid's fifth proposition (Book I) is known as the Pons Asinorum from the difficulty the complex theorem (demonstration) poses for the neophyte. The geometric proposition itself – that the angles opposite the two equal sides of an isosceles triangle are equal – is relatively straightforward.

p. 101

† **"I plunged beneath the ocean wave, / And viewed the monsters of the deep."** *Old Song*: This "Old Song" has not been traced.

† **savannas**: A "savanna" is a naturally flat open space, covered mainly with very low vegetation.

† ***un medio real***: A Spanish coin, a half real. The real was worth one-eighth of a peso, or five English pennies, and was used in Trinidad until the 1840s.

p. 102

† **Leander**: In the Greek myth of Hero and Leander, Leander swims every night across the Hellespont (the strait dividing Europe from Asia, now known as the Dardanelles) to see his beloved Hero. This allusion is rather ominous, since Leander eventually drowns one stormy night, whereupon Hero throws herself into the sea in despair.

† **pearl-seekers of the island of Margarita**: Margarita, off the Venezuelan coast near the Paria Peninsula, was famous for its pearl divers.

† **laidly**: Hideous; repulsive.

p. 106

† **torture**: Spanish law permitted the use of certain kinds of torture to extract confessions from suspects.

† **oydor* *Judge; literally, a hearer**: Spanish term for a judge or magistrate. Usually spelled "oidor".

† ***Partidas* *Spanish code of laws***: A "partida" is a registry of baptism, confirmation, marriage or death written in the parish books or the civil registry. "Las Siete Partidas" are the set of laws, constituting the core of the Spanish legal code; they were compiled by the thirteenth-century King Alfonso X "El Sabio" (the wise one), king of Castille and León, who divided them up into seven parts.

p. 107

† **bells, books, and candles**: This refers to a form of excommunication which closed with the words, "Doe to the book, quench the candle, ring the bell!"; it is also used as summarizing the resources of the hierarchy against heretics.

p. 108

† **"Earth felt the wound, and nature from her seat, / Sighing through all her works, gave signs of wo." Milton**: From *Paradise Lost* (1667, IX.782–83). At this point, Eve has just eaten the forbidden fruit, and the transgression sets off a tremor through the earth. Like the earthquake in this chapter, Eve's action brings death to humankind.

† **Voltaire**: Voltaire was perhaps the best known of the French Enlightenment

"philosophes" and advocated free thought and democracy.

† **Tom Paine**: Thomas Paine, a British radical writer, was a major inspiration for the leaders of the American Revolution.

p. 109

† **Passion-week**: The week between Palm Sunday and Easter is Passion week, leading up to Good Friday. The Gospel accounts of the Passion (the events from Christ's entry into Jerusalem up to Good Friday) formed the set readings for those days in Catholic and many other churches.

† **Holy Thursday**: Holy Thursday, or Maundy Thursday, is the day before Good Friday; it commemorates the Last Supper and hence the institution of the mass. The mass said on the evening of that day is usually the last said until Easter.

p. 110

† **"terror" which had taken "devotion's mien"**: Possibly an echo of Shakespeare's *Hamlet* (III.i), where Polonius fussily remarks that often "with devotion's visage / And pious action we do sugar o'er / The devil himself."

p. 112

† **The earthquake of Caraccas prolonged the domination of Spain over Columbia**: Francisco de Miranda led an abortive rising against Spain in 1806, but it failed to win wide support. He and Simón Bolívar proclaimed independence in 1811, but a disastrous defeat by Spanish troops, coupled with the earthquake in 1812, put an end to hopes for liberation until 1814. Eventually Bolívar secured Venezuelan independence (1821) as part of a larger state, Gran Colombia.

p. 113

† **"*Pistol. — Si fortuna me tormenta, / Sperato me contenta.*" *Henry IV*:** "If fortune torments me, hope contents me" (Shakespeare, *2 Henry IV*, II.iv). Ancient (Ensign) Pistol, calming down after an extravagant battle of words with Mistress Quickly, here subsides into quoting this proverb, in a rough mixture of Spanish and Italian. The "fustian rascal" Pistol is an odd person for Warner Arundell to identify himself with, even though the slightly misspelled quotation itself suits his mood at the time. (The original is "si fortune me tormente, / Sperato me contento".)

† **latine sails**: Triangular sails, suspended by a long yard (lateral spar to which a ship's sails are attached) at an angle of forty-five degrees to the mast. The yards for lateen sails were often longer than the boat itself. Usually spelled "lateen".

† **tasso* *Smoked beef**: Salted dried beef, a major trade item at the time; also "tassajo", or "tassa salé".

† **cassada bread, flour, starch**: Made from the tubers of *Manihot esculenta*, cassava, an important food source native to South America.

† **inferior kinds of sugar-loaves, called papilones**: "Papelón" is a kind of solid molasses-sugar in a conical form; the molasses is not extracted from the cane juice, so its colour is dark yellowish-brown.

† **pompions**: Pumpkins; in the West Indies this is a variety of *Cucurbita pepo*, a ground vine bearing large round fruit with a hard mottled green and yellow skin, and orange flesh.

† **ant-bear, or sloth**: *Cyclopes didactylus didactylus*, a slow-moving mammal that spends the day rolled in a ball on tree branches. About fifteen inches long (including tail), with tapered snout and prehensile tail; the fur is soft, silky, and pale yellowish brown, darker above. Also known in Trinidad as "ai paresseux", "ants-bear", "poor-me-one", and "silky anteater", and more generally as the "two-toed anteater".

† **tiger**: The South American jaguar, *Felis onca*, a large wild cat; the fur is yellowish-brown with darker spots.

p. 114

† **Sir Ralph Woodford**: The first civilian British governor of Trinidad (1813–28). He was responsible for rebuilding Port of Spain after the devastating fire of 1808, and for the construction of both Marine Square and Brunswick (now Woodford) Square, the purchase of the Paradise Estate (now the Queen's Park Savannah), and the establishment of the Botanical Gardens.

p. 115

† **an expression of Junius, "he was a good lawyer, but no prophet"**: The reference is probably to "Junius", the pseudonymous author of a series of letters in the *Publick Advertiser* (1769–72); these attacked George III and a number of political figures of the day. Though no exact match for this saying has been found, Joseph may have had Letter LXI vaguely in mind; there Junius argues against an opponent's use of Biblical history to support an argument about a court case: "But Sir, the Bible is the code of our religious faith, not of our municipal jurisprudence . . . an English jury have nothing to do either with David or the prophet."

† *corpus juris civilis*: A nation's body of civil laws.

† **laws of the Indies* *So the Spanish colonial code is called**: In 1836 Spanish laws were still in force in Trinidad, thirty-nine years after it became a British colony. There had, however, been many modifications, effected by Orders in Council from the British Crown, and by the application of English common-law principles. (See discussion in the introduction to this volume.)

† **Sir Francis Freeling**: A book collector and civil servant, Freeling (1764–1836) was made a baronet in recognition of the many improvements he brought about in the British postal service.

† **according to Tony Lumpkin, "a man may rob himself at any time."**: Tony Lumpkin is a boorish but good-natured character in Oliver Goldsmith's play, *She Stoops to Conquer* (1773). He steals money from his mother, but sees his thefts as merely taking the fortune that will be his when he comes of age, for "an honest man may rob himself of his own at any time" (III.i).

p. 116

† **The busy hum of man had ceased**: A slightly altered quotation from Milton's "L'Allegro" (*c.*1645), a poem that celebrates refined joy and mirth: "Towered cities please us then / And the busy hum of men" (lines 117–18). The quotation is taken somewhat out of context here, since this part of the poem celebrates the pleasures of the imagination, poetry and drama; the cities are dreamt or imagined rather than seen.

† **Bryan Edwards**: A well known writer at the time whose book *The History, Civil and Commercial, of the British Colonies in the West Indies*, first published in 1793, was a standard text.

† **murder sleep**: A quotation from Shakespeare's *Macbeth* (II.ii), rather a facetious one in this context. The words form part of Macbeth's guilt-stricken conversation with Lady Macbeth after his murder of Duncan: "Methought I heard a voice cry, 'Sleep no more! / Macbeth does murther sleep'." (Note the reference to "the ominous voice which the Scotch usurper heard" in Joseph's next paragraph.)

† **curses, not *deep* but *loud***: Another reference to *Macbeth* (V.iii), from the same speech as the "sere and yellow leaf" noted above for p. 29. This phrase is almost burlesqued here by the context and the reversal of two key words: in the play it reads "curses not loud but deep", and refers to the "mouth honour" that Macbeth's subjects give him out of fear even as they turn against him.

† **mosquito doses**: According to Joseph's note for "The Maroon Party" (appendix to this volume), "grog [that is, rum] taken at bed-time".

p. 117

† *rudis indigestaque moles*: "A rough mass without shape"; from Ovid's *Metamorphoses* (I.vii), where it refers to Chaos.

† **thrasher**: *Alopias vulpes,* a shark with a long upper division of the tail. Also "thresher-shark/fish".

† **as Polonius has it, was "very like a whale"**: In his famous and fatuous attempt to humour Hamlet, Polonius agrees to even patently contradictory statements about cloud shapes (*Hamlet* III.ii). "Very like a whale" has become almost a proverbial phrase for referring to automatic, mindless agreement, though here the point seems to be rather that the large whale-like shape actually is a whale.

† **"The fishermen forsook the strand, The swarthy smith took dirk in hand"**: The source of this quotation has not been traced.

† *ore rotundo*: With rounded lips.

p. 118

† **"'T was *grease*, but living *grease* no more"**: A pun on a famous quotation from Byron's "Oriental" poem *The Giaour* (1813): "'Tis Greece – but living Greece no more!" (line 91). In this opening section of the popular poem, the poet reflects on the captivity of Greece, then part of the Ottoman Empire; in Byron's view, the contemporary Greeks had become "craven crouching slave[s]" (line 108).

† **lubbers**: A sailor's term for clumsy persons, unseamanlike fellows.

† **Greenland trade**: Commercial whale hunting.

† **"you are not *hacting* according to *Oil!*" (he was a cockney.)**: To "act according to Hoyle" is a proverbial expression meaning to play by the rules; it refers to Edmond Hoyle's *The Polite Gamester* (1745, with numerous later editions into the present day), a compendium of the rules for various games. The "addition" and "omission" of initial "h" is perhaps the best-known characteristic of the accent of a London Cockney; here it also allows a pun on whale "oil".

† **"Rose from sea to sky the wild farewell— / Then shrunk the timid, and stood still the brave"**: A slightly altered quotation from Byron's *Don Juan* (1819–24) (II.52): "Then rose from sea to sky the wild farewell, / Then shrieked the timid, and stood still the brave." In Canto II Juan is shipwrecked; this stanza recounts the sinking of the vessel from which he has just escaped.

† **depicted by Cruikshank. Johnny Gilpin flying by the Bell at Edmonton**: In 1827 the caricaturist George Cruikshank produced a series of six illustrations for a re-issue of William Cowper's comic poem *The Diverting History of John Gilpin* (1782). Cruikshank revelled in the comic opportunities provided by this tale of a middle-aged linen-draper whose horse runs away with him as he rides towards an inn to celebrate his twentieth wedding anniversary.

† **"flat, stale, and unprofitable"**: An altered quotation from Hamlet's first soliloquy, where to his alienated perception, "all the uses of this world" seem "weary, stale, flat and unprofitable" (*Hamlet* I.ii).

† **barocoutas (creole cod-fish)**: *Sphyraena barracuda,* a large marine fish, with large jaws and teeth, prized as a gamefish; large specimens sometimes cause ciguatera poisoning. Usually spelled "barracouta" locally, and "barracuda" in general English.

† *black* act: A severe law against poaching, trespassing, etc.

p. 120

† **"A conflagration labouring in her womb . . . / Dark and voluminous the vapours rise, / And hang their horrors in the neighbouring skies; / While though the Stygian gloom that blots the day, / In dazzling streaks the vivid lightnings play."** Cowper: A slightly altered quotation from William Cowper's poem "Heroism" (1782), in which the 1780 eruption of Mount Aetna is used as an allegory for monarchs who

invade neighbouring countries and lay waste to them, as does the volcano to the lands below it. The heroism is ironic: the speaker sees "laurel'd heroes" as "But Aetnas of the suffering world."

† **cutter**: A type of small, single-masted vessel.

p. 121

† **the Bermuda negro fears exile more than slavery – at least, the mitigated slavery of Bermuda**: Bermuda was not a plantation colony and its few slaves enjoyed relative freedom employed on small farms or in maritime activities.

† **free paper**: Certificate of manumission from slavery.

† **three points free**: That is, the course they want to steer is three cardinal points of the compass to leeward from the closest point of sailing on the wind for that tack; they can therefore sail a straight course for their destination, with a small margin for maintaining that course should the wind turn against them.

† **bow-chasers**: Guns mounted in the bow of a ship.

† **went about**: Changed direction.

† *monsieur soupe-maigre*: "Mister Thin-Soup".

† **dig cane-holes**: The digging of holes in the fields to plant new pieces of cane; one of the primary tasks in the cultivation of sugar cane.

p. 122

† **Mustique**: One of the small islands of the St Vincent Grenadines, between St Vincent to the north, and Grenada to the south.

† **ran his cutter under her counter**: That is, steered his cutter near the stern of the brig of war. The "counter" is the curved part of a ship's stern.

† **drums beat to quarters**: The crew of a man-of-war were summoned to their respective stations by a drum.

† **galba**: *Calophyllum antillanum*, a large tree with strong hard durable wood.

† **Souffriere, or volcanic mountain**: This refers to the major eruption of the Soufrière volcano of St Vincent, in 1812.

p. 125

† **"What strange event, what aggravated sin? / They stand convicted of a darker sin." Hannah More**: From "The Black Slave Trade" (1788), also known as "Slavery", a poem written for the Abolitionist cause, to assist the passage of William Wilberforce's resolution (May 1788) binding Parliament to consider the slave trade in its next session. This part of the poem identifies the motive of the trade as "sordid lust of gold", without any offences on the part of the enslaved to provide even a specious excuse for their bondage.

p. 126

† **dry-nurse**: A woman who takes care of and attends to a child, but does not suckle it, as does a wet-nurse.

† **gang**: A group of workers – slave, indentured or free – usually with a specific task.

† **scouted**: Mocked; derided; rejected with scorn.

p. 127

† **Colonial Office**: The Colonial Office was located on Downing Street, London; after 1812 it was engaged in a project of "ameliorating" the condition of West Indian slaves.

† **Lundy-foot coloured soil**: Blackish earth, from "Lundy-foot snuff". "Lundy Foot's Irish Blackguard" is a pungent black snuff, made by charring tobacco and then pulverizing it into snuff.

p. 128

† **"frisked beneath the burden of threescore"**: A quotation from Goldsmith's "The Traveller, or a Prospect of Society" (1764), a poem which chronicles a meandering European journey. This line, from the section on France, celebrates the country's "mirth and social ease", and the pleasures enjoyed by all ages, including the "gay grandsire" who, like Codrington, frisks "beneath the burden of threescore", that is, is at least sixty years old.

† **to the tune of "Go to the devil and shake yourself"**: Apparently a folk-song or dance tune, though the precise source has not been traced. Charles Dickens refers to the expression in chapter 26 of *Great Expectations* (1860–61): "he added in a lower growl, that we might both go to the devil and shake ourselves".

† **purchasing a commission for me in a West Indian regiment**: An officer's commission was normally a matter of purchase at this time; the cost depended on the status of the regiment, but commissions in the (distinctly unfashionable) colonial regiments were much cheaper.

† **"bloody wars and sickly seasons"**: The source of this quotation has not been traced.

p. 131

† **ballahoo schooner**: A sharp-floored fast-sailing schooner, with taut fore-and-aft sails, and no topsails, common in the West Indies; the foremast rakes forward, the mainmast aft. Also used as a term of derision for an ill-conditioned, slovenly ship. Sometimes spelled "ballahou".

p. 132

† **plantains, sweet potatoes, edoes, arrowroot**: "Plantains" are varieties of *Musa paradisica* with large, banana-like, somewhat angular, horn-shaped fruits, containing less sugar than bananas, cooked before being eaten. "Sweet potatoes" are the edible tubers of *Ipomoea batatas*, usually having thin reddish skin and white flesh. "Edoes" or "eddos" are also edible tubers, *Colocasia esculenta* var., slightly elongated and covered with small brown scales. "Queensland arrowroot", *Canna indica*, is a plant with rhizomes rich in starch, used for clothing and cooking.

† **Guinea and Indian corn**: "Guinea corn", *Sorghum indica*, refers to durra or Indian millet; "Indian corn" refers to *Zea mays*, a cob corn originating in South America.

† **tamarinds**: The long pod fruit of *Tamarindus indica*; contains edible dark brown pulpy flesh.

p. 133

† **"And now I'm in the world alone, / Upon the wide, wide sea." Byron**: From *Childe Harold's Pilgrimage* (1812–18, I:182–83). These lines are from Harold's farewell song as he departs from home on his travels, leaving behind him the detritus of a dissipated life, and "No thing that claims a tear".

p. 134

† **quadrant**: An instrument which allows a navigator to determine a ship's longitudinal position by taking the altitude of the stars. See discussion in Dava Sobel's *Longitude* (1995).

† **"John Hamilton's Moon Tables"**: John Hamilton Moore's *The Practical Navigator and Seaman's New Daily Assistant* (1772) includes "A Table for Finding the Moon's Age", though the most important contribution of the book was "The New Solar Table for Finding the Latitude by Two Observations".

† **chronometer**: A time-piece, more accurate and finely balanced than an ordinary watch or clock. Accurate timekeeping was crucial to navigation by longitude.

† **"Dead reckoning" means the situation of the ship, calculated according to the distance run, without regard to observations made by quadrant or sextant**: The explanation Joseph gives is fairly clear, but dead reckoning also involves the use of a com-

pass, and corrections for currents, and so on. It is a dangerous way to navigate in or near inshore waters for any length of time, since a mistake could mean running aground.

† **corvette**: A type of relatively small warship with one tier of guns.

† **caught a Tartar**: That is, caught hold of someone who unexpectedly proved impossible to beat or to shake off; usually a nautical phrase.

† **yard-arm and yard-arm**: The "yard-arm" is the end of the yard which projects beyond the edge of a sail. Ships standing "yard-arm and yard-arm", so that their yard arms touch or come close to touching, are as close as they can get to one another.

p. 135

† **waist**: The middle part of a ship.

† **supercargo**: An officer on a merchant ship whose role is to supervise the cargo.

† *ci-devant* **mate**: "Former mate"; "ci-devant" was frequently used to refer to aristocrats and others displaced by the French Revolution.

† **"bang-up," "how are you with your eye out?" and other phrases equally Attic**: "Bang-up" is British slang, first recorded in the early nineteenth century, for "first-rate". "How are you with your eye out?" is more obscure, though clearly meant for a facetious greeting. "Attic" – Athenian, thus characterized by refined simplicity – is here obviously ironic. Most of Holywell's language, here and later in the novel, is authentic early-nineteenth-century slang. Joseph may occasionally have been inventing, though it is also possible that some of the terms had too short a life to be recorded.

† **the ring, not of Hyde Park**: The "Ring path" in Hyde Park was a fashionable place for walking, driving and riding.

† **Molsey Hurst**: A well known venue for boxing in London.

† **the court at St. James's**: To be presented to the reigning monarch at St James's Palace was a sign of having attained high social standing.

† **the "fives-court"**: "Fives", a game of handball played in a three-sided court, was popular in the early nineteenth century; the courts were often also used for boxing matches.

p. 136

† *science* . . . **the knowledge of boxing**: "The noble science of defence" referred originally to boxing or fencing; by this time it was a well established jocular slang term for pugilism.

† **felon side of Newgate**: That is, inside the walls of Newgate, a famous London prison demolished in 1902.

† **double-headed shot**: Shot consisting of two balls joined together.

† **"inverted blessings"**: The source of this quotation has not been traced.

† **mess**: Take one's meals; usually military or nautical usage.

† **laws of the Pentateuch**: The basis for the Jewish dietary laws appears in the Pentateuch – the Five Books of Moses – the first five books of the Hebrew Bible. Biblical dietary laws proscribe the consuming of blood (hence the need for ritual slaughter and bleeding of the animal) or the cooking of a kid in its mother's milk (hence the subsequent separation of milk and meat). They also distinguish between clean, that is, edible, and unclean animals of all kinds. These laws were fully developed in the Oral Law of the rabbis, or teachers, as set down in the Mishna and the Talmud between the third and sixth centuries CE.

† **traditions of the rabinim.* *Commonly written rabbins, – as the plural of seraph is commonly written seraphs**: Rabbis, or teachers. The correct Hebrew plural is "rabbanim"; however, the French is "rabbin", plural "rabbins", so perhaps Arundell (or Joseph) was influenced by that.

† **phylacteries**: At the beginning of the weekday morning prayer service, Jews (traditionally men) bind phylacteries – "tefillin" in Hebrew – to their forehead and upper arm while reciting special blessings, in keeping with a commandment which appears four times in the Pentateuch to keep the words of the law as "a sign upon your hand and as

frontlets between your eyes". Tefillin are leather boxes, attached to leather straps, which contain small pieces of parchment on which a scribe has copied the four biblical passages mentioning this commandment. The practice of "laying tefillin" goes back at least two millennia, and is one of the most basic observances of Judaism.

p. 137

† **mulatess**: A female "mulatto", of half white European and half black African descent. Usually spelled "mulatress".

† **Jumbee* *An African word, denoting an evil spirit**: A ghost, spirit of a dead person. Usually spelled "jumbie" or "jumby".

† **Anguilla passage**: Probably the Anegada Passage, between the Leeward Islands to eastward, and the Virgin Islands to westward.

† **sprung her mainmast**: Cracked or split the mainmast.

† **St. Thomas's – a Danish island, at that time in our possession**: St Thomas was a Danish colony, under British military occupation during part of the Napoleonic War. Denmark was the first European nation to abolish its Atlantic slave trade (1804).

p. 139

† **"For England when with favouring gales." Dibdin**: Joseph may have been thinking of *Sea Songs and Ballads* by Charles Dibdin (1745–1814), but this inexact quotation is actually from a popular song by William Pearce, which begins "For England when with favouring gale / Our gallant ship up channel steered". The song, usually called "Heaving the Lead" or "The Heaving of the Lead", was widely anthologized, and is originally from an opera called *The Hartford Bridge, or the Skirts of a Camp* (1792) by William Shield, for which Pearce wrote the libretto. The song celebrates sailors' joy and renewed energy as they approach the home port.

† **accidence**: That part of grammar which deals with the "accidents" or inflections of words; the rudiments of grammar.

† **"A votre santé, monsieur" . . . "Vous sentez, monsieur" . . . "Vous mentez, monsieur"**: "To your health, sir" . . . "You stink, sir" . . . "You lie, sir."

p. 140

† **"a succession of light airs, languishing to calms," as midshipmen's log-books have it**: Midshipmen were required to keep logs and write descriptions of daily events. Arundell seems to be quoting or imagining a flowery example of the genre by a young man not yet "salty" enough to drop poetic expressions.

† **mizen-chains**: The "mizenmast" or "mizzenmast" is the third mast from the bow on a vessel with three or more masts. "Chains" is the collective term for the contrivances used to extend the shrouds of a mast (that is, the lines used to steady the mast) outside the ship's side: doing so increases the mast's stability. The term also refers to the method of attaching the yards to the masts, and since Jumbee is heading up the mizenmast, it may be these chains that are meant here.

† **mizen royal yard**: The yard to which the mizen royal sail is attached; the highest yard on the mizenmast.

p. 141

† **"grinned horribly a ghastly smile"**: The source of this quotation has not been traced.

† **royal halyards**: A "halyard" is a line (rope) for hoisting a sail up a mast; the "royal halyards" are the lines attached to the royals, the highest set of sails on a square-rigged ship.

† **"The cords slipt lightly through his glowing hands, And, quick as lightning, on the deck he stands"**: A loose quotation from John Gay's popular ballad "Sweet William's Farewell to Black-Ey'd Susan" (1720). William is up on the yard when Susan comes on board to see him off, but as soon as he sees her "The cord slides swiftly through his glowing hands, / And, (quick as lightning,) on the deck he stands."

† **like William in the song, to receive kisses sweet**: Like the previous quotation, this is from "Sweet William's Farewell": William receives "kisses sweet" from Susan as soon as he drops into the "nest" of her arms.

p. 142

† **"As lifeless as a painted ship, / Upon a painted ocean"**: From Samuel Taylor Coleridge's *The Rime of the Ancient Mariner* (1798) (lines 117–18). In this section of the poem, not long after the Mariner's shooting of the albatross, the ship is becalmed. The actual line is "As idle as a painted ship, / Upon a painted ocean".

† **quarter-deck**: That part of the upper or spar-deck which extends between the stern and after-mast, and is used as a promenade by superior officers and cabin passengers.

p. 143

† **long-boat**: The largest boat kept on board ship, and normally used for going ashore. It was also used as a life-boat, and as an improvised jail cell.

† **taffrail**: The centre part of the poop-rail (the rail on top of the ship's stern).

p. 144

† **main-top-gallant-mast**: The third highest and sometimes topmost part of the main-mast, where the third set of sails (the top-gallants) are set, after the courses and the top-sails. Some ships had a royal section on top of the top-gallants.

† **shrouds**: Lines used to steady a mast.

† **main-top**: In this context, the platform just above the lowest section of the mainmast.

† **mizen-stay . . . mizen-top . . . mizen-shrouds**: On the mizenmast, the "stay" and "shrouds" are lines used to brace the mast; the "mizen-top" is the second part of the mizenmast, counting from the deck.

† **pap**: Soft or semi-liquid food for infants or invalids, made of bread, meal, and the like, moistened with water or milk.

p. 145

† **jib, storm-staysail, and fore-topsail closely reefed**: To "reef" a sail is to reduce its area by rolling and securing it; in preparation for the storm, only these small sails – and with their area greatly reduced – are "showing". The "fore-topsail" is the topsail on the foremast (the one closest to the bow), and the "storm-staysail" is an auxiliary sail designed for running before a storm. The general idea is to save sails from storm damage and to keep some manoeuverability during the storm. The foremast sails are used because that keeps the bow downwind and counters the tendency of the wind to push the stern around; they are also "lifting sails", which lift the bow out of the water, as opposed to sails set further aft, which would tend to drive the bow under – clearly an undesirable effect in a storm.

p. 147

† **"the chops of the Channel"**: The entrance into the English Channel from the Atlantic Ocean.

Volume II

p. 149

† **"England, with all thy faults, I love thee still." Cowper**: From Cowper's *The Task* (1785, II.206), a long rambling poem, nominally about a sofa (in response to a challenge from "a lady, fond of blank verse"). This part of the poem reflects on recent political and military events within Europe and the British Empire.

† **post-chaises**: A travelling carriage, either hired from stage to stage or drawn by horses so hired, usually having a closed body for two to four passengers.

† **the sheep, clad in thick woolly coats, so different from the light hairy jackets in which Nature has arrayed the sheep of the Caribbean Islands**: The "hair sheep" common in the Caribbean have thin short hair rather than wool.

p. 150

† **Cowper has said, that "God made the country, but man made the town."**: Another slightly altered quotation from *The Task* (I.749). This line, from a part of the poem which contrasts London with English country life, has become a proverbial saying. The original has "and", not "but".

p. 151

† **Covent Garden**: The site of London's major produce market from 1670 to 1973.

† **preceptor**: Teacher; instructor.

† **Bedford Square**: A square in the Bloomsbury area of London. By the early nineteenth century Bloomsbury was becoming less than fashionable, though certainly cheaper than the West End where Molesworth has his practice. Artists and lawyers predominated in this quarter, and the proximity to hospitals would have made it convenient for doctors; Bedford Square itself did have some aristocratic inhabitants.

† **West India Docks**: The London docks where West Indian shipping came in.

p. 152

† **all the medical springs and baths in England**: The use of spas was common in England, as they were considered important in restoring "balance" in the body's home environment.

† **at Cheltenham . . . one of the water-nymphs of the place**: Cheltenham was a fashionable watering place, and as such notorious for husband-hunters (presumably the "water-nymphs").

† **the old proverb about the "gray mare"**: "The grey mare is the better horse" (that is, the wife dominates the husband).

† **marching regiment**: A regiment with no permanent quarters; one which could be sent to any part of England or the Empire at a moment's notice. By the mid-nineteenth century, the term had also come to denote a regiment of the line (see note to p. 54).

† **"The Domestic Manners of the English"**: Mrs A.C. Carmichael published in 1833 her book about St Vincent and Trinidad, *Domestic Manners and Social Condition of the White, Coloured and Negro Population of the West Indies*.

† **haut-ton**: People of high fashion.

† **Bond Street**: Then as now, a fashionable shopping street, running from Picadilly to Oxford Street.

† **Almack's**: A suite of famous London assembly rooms founded by William Almack in 1765 and surviving until 1863. "Assembly" in this context means any social gathering (especially dances) whose primary purpose is pleasure or entertainment.

† **breve**: A long note in music, equivalent to two semi-breves (or a double whole note in North American musical notation).

p. 153

† **mal' d'estomac**: Probably a disorder resulting from malnutrition: "Dry beriberi's symptoms are remarkably similar to those of a mysterious illness of the slaves called the *mal d'estomac* in some islands and *hatiweri* or *cachexia Africana* in others. Physicians first thought that the lack of energy, breathlessness, and nerve problems including an unsteady, high-stepping gait . . . were caused by dirt eating; later investigators have suspected that the cause was hookworm disease. But . . . dry beriberi remains the best explanation for this particular ailment" (Kiple 1993, 501).

† **Cornhill**: A hill and street, associated with booksellers and publishers, in the heart of London's financial district or "City".

† **Mr. Muscovadoe**: See note to p. 174.

† **Dry River**: A river whose waters run mostly during the rainy season; sometimes lined with stone or cement. The most well known is the St Ann's River that runs through parts of Port of Spain.

p. 154

† **Hummums**: A hotel on the south-east side of Covent Garden. "Hummum", or Turkish bath, is a version of the Arabic word for hot bath, "hammām"; the hotel was named for the Turkish baths which once stood on the spot.

† **Bloomsbury Square**: Like Bedford Square, located in Bloomsbury. By the early nine-teenth century, this once fashionable square was inhabited primarily by professionals, intellectuals and artists.

p. 155

† **Sloane Street**: A street in the Knightsbridge area of London, developed in the late eigh-teenth century for affluent occupants.

† **list**: Probably a variant of "lisse", a kind of silk gauze fabric.

p. 156

† **"cook-room"**: The kitchen in many traditional West Indian houses was a one-room building separate from the main house, to decrease both risks from fire and cooking smells in the house.

p. 158

† *argumentum a posteriori*: An argument which reasons from effects to causes (for example, if there is smoke, there is fire). Joseph is of course using the phrase as an ironic pun, to refer to "persuading" the slave by whipping his "posterior".

† **"province covered with houses"**: A translation of a comment by Jean-Baptiste Say, a French political economist. "Londres n'est plus une ville: c'est une province couverte de maisons!" comes from Say's *De l'Angleterre et des Anglais* (1816).

† **those magnificent receptacles for the maimed and worn-out defenders of their country at Greenwich and Chelsea**: Greenwich Hospital and the Royal Hospital at Chelsea were residences for retired seamen and soldiers respectively. "Hospital" in this sense does not mean a place for the sick, but rather a charitable institution designed to house the needy. Christopher Wren designed the Chelsea Hospital and parts of the Greenwich Hospital; both buildings are architecturally distinguished.

† **palace at St. James's**: In Pall Mall, St James's Palace, built by Henry VIII, actually ceased to be the monarch's principal London residence in 1762, when George III moved his family to Buckingham House (later rebuilt into Buckingham Palace). It was, however, still the primary royal court for purposes of state, and the state apartments were refur-bished after a fire in 1809. To the eyes of a visitor in the early nineteenth century it might well have seemed cramped and decrepit.

† **tight-lacing . . . *tournure* . . . consumptions**: For much of the nineteenth century women wore stays to compress their waists; the laces of stays could be drawn more or less tightly as the wearer chose or as fashion dictated. "Tournure" (graceful manner or bear-ing), a French word, was often used by upper class English people in the eighteenth and nineteenth centuries. "Consumption" as used in the nineteenth century covered a number of wasting illnesses, but referred most specifically to tuberculosis. Tightly laced stays would hardly cause consumption in themselves, though by making it difficult for the wearer to eat, they might contribute to malnutrition over time, and hence susceptibility to disease.

† **Caraibs**: An indigenous people, widespread over areas of the Eastern Caribbean and South American mainland prior to European contact. Usually spelled "Caribs".

p. 159

† **flock**: A material consisting of the coarse tufts and refuse of wool or cotton, or of cloth torn to pieces by machinery, used for stuffing quilts, cushions, beds, mattresses, etc.

† **"Sternhold's creeping lays"**: In 1549, Thomas Sternhold and John Hopkins published one of the earliest collections of metrical psalms in English. These were republished and augmented several times, and came to be known as "Sternhold and Hopkins"; many new psalm versions were added by revisers. Metrical psalms, following a specific syllabic meter, were the only hymns officially sanctioned by the Church of England until 1821, but they were on the wane by the time of *Warner Arundell,* and Joseph was not alone among his contemporaries in disliking them. "Sternhold's creeping lays" is a quotation from John Langhorne's "The Country Justice" (1774), a poem that urges justice for the poor and the powerless. Langhorne here castigates the "grave church-warden" who drives out an unwed mother, leaving her to die of exposure, and then goes to church and "pours . . . / His creeping soul in Sternhold's creeping lays".

† **Psalms done into English by Tait and Brady**: Nahum Tate and Nicholas Brady published *A New Version of the Psalms of David* (1696); it gradually supplanted Sternhold and Hopkins, or the "Old Version".

† **parish-clerks call – "singing to the praise and glory of God"**: Parish clerks, whose office was to lead the congregation, might introduce a psalm or hymn by exhorting the congregation to sing it to the praise and glory of God. However, Joseph may also be referring to the practice of "lining out" psalms: that is, singing one line and then having the congregation repeat it to be sure they could follow the music.

p. 160

† **send to Antigua for negro Methodists**: Antigua was the centre of Wesleyan Methodism in the Caribbean, a denomination well known for its hymn-singing.

† **Somerset House**: This public building, designed by Sir William Chambers in 1776, was occupied at this time by the Navy and the Royal Academy, among others.

† **Wren, Inigo Jones, Gibbs**: Sir Christopher Wren (1632–1723), Inigo Jones (1573–1652) and James Gibbs (1682–1754) were all architects. Wren is known for his leading role in the rebuilding of London after the Great Fire of 1666, and especially for building St Paul's Cathedral. Jones is best known for introducing the Palladian (neoclassical) style of architecture to England. Gibbs, a Wren disciple, built several London churches, including St Martin-in-the-Fields.

† **Lady Randolph**: Lady Randolph is the leading female character in John Home's *Douglas* (1756), a verse tragedy based on an old Scots ballad.

† **"I found myself, / As women wish to be who love their lords"**: A line from *Douglas* (I.i), in which Lady Randolph relates finding herself pregnant by her father's enemy Douglas, whom she has secretly married.

† **Otway's "Orphan"**: *The Orphan* (1680), a verse tragedy by Thomas Otway.

† **"Why was I born with all my sex's softness?"**: A slightly altered quotation from *The Orphan* (I). Monimia, the heroine, having heard that her beloved Castalio has offered to give her up to his brother, and (falsely) declared himself uninterested in marriage, here begins to think that she has committed herself too rashly. The original has "made" rather than "born".

† **Kemble and his still more illustrious sister**: John Philip Kemble (1757–1823) and his sister Sarah Siddons (1755–1831) acted to general acclaim in the late-eighteenth- and early-nineteenth-century London theatre. They were both most popular in Shakespeare's *Macbeth*.

p. 161

† **after-piece appeared to please "the million"**: Typically an evening of theatre in the eighteenth and early nineteenth century consisted of two plays; the after-piece was usually

a short comedy, sometimes containing an equestrian act. Afterpieces were in fact usually aimed not at "the million" (that is, the lower classes; see Shakespeare's *Hamlet* II.ii), but at a middle-class and professional audience who found the theatre's usual 6 p.m. curtain too early.

† **Siddons**: See note on Kemble above.

† **croakers**: Persons who talk dismally or despondently, foreboding or predicting evil.

p. 162

† **Tower**: The Tower of London, a famous London landmark, palace, repository of the Crown Jewels, armoury, and prison. Like the Bank of England, the Tower is a national symbol and hence a likely target for revolutionary attack.

† **long wars**: The Revolutionary and Napoleonic Wars (1793–1815).

† **national schools**: Schools run by the National Society for Promoting the Education of the Poor in the Principles of the Established Church, founded under Church of England auspices in 1811. Despite gloomy predictions such as those Arundell hears, the aim was largely conservative, to prevent revolution rather than to instigate it, and to compete with rival non-sectarian schools largely supported by Dissenters.

† **the cultivators of the soil, the hewers of wood and drawers of water**: A biblical phrase, from Joshua 9. The people of Gibeon escape destruction at the hands of Joshua and the Israelites by pretending to come from far away. When Joshua discovers the truth he does not break the covenant he made with them as apparent strangers, but the Gibeonites are cursed, so that they will always be "bondsmen, and hewers of wood and drawers of water" (9:23). This verse has often been used to justify racial discrimination and slavery.

† *Jacqueries*: The term used in France to describe peasant rebellions, from "Jacques" as a common name for a peasant.

† **Wat Tyler and Jack Cade**: Leaders of medieval English peasant revolts.

† **Reign of Terror**: The phase of the French Revolution when thousands were executed for alleged crimes against the Republic, especially 1792–94.

† **"the great unwashed"**: The lower classes; the masses; the mob. The phrase became proverbial in the nineteenth century, though it is usually the political writer Edmund Burke (1729–97) who is credited with its coinage.

† **George III**: British monarch who reigned 1760–1820.

p. 163

† **Some years since, a book was published, purporting to be a description of the West Indies**: This particular book has not been identified, though it is not the one by Dauxion Lavaysse.

† **"the Island of Demerara"**: Demerara, later part of British Guiana, is located on the South American continent.

p. 164

† **"Oh! woman, in our hours of ease, / Uncertain, coy, and hard to please . . . / When pain and anguish wring the brow, / A ministering angel thou." Scott**: From Sir Walter Scott's poem *Marmion* (1808, VI.xxx). The narrator comments here on the heroine's "feminine" compassion; despite having been persecuted by Lord Marmion, when she encounters him at death's door she quickly decides to tend his wounds and slake his thirst.

† **"I at last their miseries viewed, / In that vile garret, which I cannot paint." Crabbe**: A slightly altered quotation from George Crabbe's "Sir Owen Dale" (*Tales of the Hall*, 1819, XII.754–55). Ellis, Sir Owen's tenant, recounts his discovery of his wife, her lover and their child. The story is a cautionary tale about the hollowness of vengeance; having come to revenge himself upon the couple, Ellis is moved by their

470

abject poverty to help them instead. As with the *Marmion* quotation, the point is presumably that the elder Rivers, with much less to pardon, has shown much less pity. The original has "misery", not "miseries".

† **packet**: A "packet" or "packet-boat" plies at regular intervals between two ports for the conveyance of mails, goods and passengers.

† **pupil**: Medical training in England at this time typically included apprenticeship, attendance at lectures, walking hospital wards, and being an assistant.

† *materia medica*: The remedial substances used in the practice of medicine; that branch of medical study which deals with drugs, their sources, preparations and uses.

† **Brooks's, Carpue's, and Bell's lectures**: (**Brooks** has not been identified.) **Joseph Constantine Carpue** (1764–1846), an English surgeon and lecturer, was the first to introduce the Indian method of nose reconstruction by grafting skin from the forehead. **Sir Charles Bell** (1774–1842), a Scottish surgeon, anatomist and physiologist, was a pioneer in clinical neurology. A brilliant lecturer, he left the University of Edinburgh for London, where he was instrumental in founding the Middlesex Hospital and Medical School. Bell was the first to recognize that lesions of the seventh nerve could give rise to facial palsy.

† **Middlesex Hospital**: A London hospital and medical school.

† **dresser**: A surgeon's assistant, in a hospital, whose job is to dress wounds, and so on.

p. 165

† **the gentlemen of Warwick Lane refuse to grant a diploma to any one who has not washed his hands in the Cam or Isis**: In other words, the Royal College of Physicians (in Warwick Lane) refused to permit anyone to become a physician who had not attended Cambridge (on the river Cam) or Oxford (on the river Thames or "Isis").

† **the West Indies, where the obsolete distinction between physician and surgeon is little attended to**: In the colonies, there were many military surgeons, who often undertook general practice with civilians. In provinces in England, general practice – physic (medicine) and surgery – was common; the maintenance of the division between physician and surgeon required a wealthy clientele to pay fees.

† **Warwick Street, Golden Square**: Warwick Street, near Regent Street, was not especially fashionable, though the adjacent Golden Square had been until the mid-eighteenth century. During the early nineteenth century, the area was primarily occupied by artists and foreign legations.

† **crumpet-looking features**: "Crumpet-face" was a slang term for a face marked with smallpox scars; presumably this is what "crumpet-looking" means here. It may also refer to a very pale complexion, like a crumpet before toasting.

p. 167

† **blackamoor woman**: Contemporary term for African or black.

p. 168

† **pawnbrokers' duplicates**: When an article was pawned, a pawnbroker made two copies of the receipt; the duplicate enabled the customer to redeem the article by paying back (with interest) what the pawnbroker had given for it.

p. 169

† **like P.P. the parish clerk, to bleed adventures he not, except on the poor**: In "The Memoirs of P.P. Clerk of this Parish" (see note to p. 23), the conceited narrator speaks of his skill at various things, including medicine: "Chirurgery also I practised in the worming of dogs; but to bleed ventured I not, except the poor". (See note to p. 54.)

† **selling her teeth to a dentist**: Just as hairdressers sought human hair for wigmaking, so dentists in the early nineteenth century bought teeth from the poor to make dentures.

† **inveterate tertian fever**: A chronic fever characterized by a pattern of a rise in temperature and sometimes chills every three (that is, alternate) days; it is usually associated with *Plasmodium vivax* or *P. ovale* malarial infections.

p. 170

† **Fleet Market**: A meat and vegetable market between Fleet Street and Holborn, where Farringdon Street now runs.

† **the rock of Sombrero**: A small island northwest of Anguilla.

† **Cayenne**: French Guiana, later the site of a notorious penal colony.

† **Ceylon**: Now Sri Lanka, it was ceded by the Dutch to Britain in 1802.

p. 171

† **Dr. Baillie**: Matthew Ballie (1763–1823) was a famous anatomist and the author of *Morbid Anatomy*; he favoured structural rather than humoral (fluid/functional) explanations of disease.

† **Chorea Sancti Viti**: St Vitus's Dance, a disorder characterized by involuntary contortions and convulsions, having several possible causes. This may refer here to Sydenham's chorea, an acute, usually self-limited, disorder of early life or pregnancy, and closely linked to rheumatic fever.

† **antimony**: A crystalline metallic element forming various medicinal and poisonous salts. It was formerly used in the treatment of *Schistosoma* infections, and as a nauseant emetic, but is very toxic.

† **submuriate of mercury**: A chloride of mercury, a metallic element liquid at ordinary temperatures and dissolved in acid. Mercury and its salts were employed therapeutically as purgatives, in chronic inflammations, and as antisyphilitics, intestinal antiseptics, disinfectants and astringents. However, it was later found that these are absorbed by skin and mucous membranes, causing chronic mercury poisoning.

† **arsenic**: A nonmetallic element, a grayish solid, toxic by inhalation and ingestion, and carcinogenic. It was at one time widely used medicinally, now rarely used but still important in the treatment of certain tropical parasitic diseases.

† **Peruvian bark**: Quinine, a bitter alkaloid derived from the bark of *Cinchona* trees, first discovered by Europeans in Peru; it is still used against some forms of malaria to control high temperature.

p. 172

† **"The doctor tease, / To name the nameless, ever new disease"**: A slightly altered quotation from George Crabbe's *The Village* (1783), a poem which counters the idealized pastoral vision with accounts of actual rural life. In this section, Crabbe contrasts the "real pain" of the poor with the "fantastic woes" of the idle rich, who "with sad prayers the weary doctor tease, / To name the nameless ever-new disease" (I.254–55).

p. 173

† **Buonaparte, having escaped from Elba, set Europe once more in a ferment**: Napoleon Buonaparte, emperor of the French, was exiled to Elba in the Mediterranean following his defeat by the allied powers in 1814. In 1815 he escaped, re-entered France and rallied the French Army to him, until his final defeat at the Battle of Waterloo and exile to St Helena in the South Atlantic.

p. 174

† **"Ah! I am but a ball for Fortune's foot, / To spurn where'er she lists." *The Two Citizens***: *The Two Citizens* has not been identified.

† **muscovadoes**: Raw or unrefined sugar obtained from the juice of the sugar cane by evaporation and draining off the molasses. See also p. 153.

p. 175

† **cool as Cooper**: Sir Astley Paston Cooper (1768–1841), who was attached to Guy's Hospital, London, was a celebrated surgeon as well as a pioneer in vascular and experimental surgery. He was one of the early proponents of total immoblization for treating compound fractures.

p. 176

† **the ridiculous prejudices of creoles against shopkeepers**: Apothecaries were associated with trade, rather than a learned profession.

† **a nation of shopkeepers**: Adam Smith, in *The Wealth of Nations* (1776) refers to the English as "a nation of shopkeepers"; the phrase became proverbial, particularly after Napoleon took it up to express contempt for his enemies across the Channel. In turn, France, in many British eyes, was the nation of "cooks and dancingmasters".

† **surgeon on board a South Sea Whaler**: The post of ship's surgeon could be a good one, depending on the ship, though a South Sea whaler would be unlikely to pay as much as one carrying passengers and cargo, and living conditions would be rough.

† **vessel bound to Sidney with convicts**: Until 1867, British criminals were often given the sentence of transportation to Australia, for a term of years or for life; once there they either lived in penal colonies or worked for farmers.

† **Recorder of London**: Arundell is sarcastically suggesting that he may as well go as a convict. The Recorder of London was the magistrate or judge with legal jurisdiction over the city; he delivered court sentences and judgements.

† **Old Bailey**: London's chief criminal court.

p. 177

† **Haymarket**: A street and (until 1830) hay and straw market near Pall Mall.

p. 178

† **South America; the whole continent is in a state of war**: The Wars of Independence against Spain, 1810–24.

† **Bolivar**: Simón Bolívar, the Liberator, leader of the independence struggle in Venezuela, Colombia and Ecuador.

† **You are a surgeon – not licensed; but no matter, you are able to set a broken limb, or, if necessary, to dock one: that's all that is required**: That is, qualifications were not well regulated nor even considered essential: experience and endorsement counted as much as paper qualifications.

p. 179

† **the Company's service**: The East India Company, through which Britain governed parts of India up to 1858.

† **sepoys**: Indian troops under British control.

† **the grand army of *Raja Roul Jowler Rum Un***: This appears to be a joking reference to a stereotypical Indian raja, or local king. "Roul Jowler" is probably a rendition of a name; "Rum Un" (rum one) appears similarly Indian but means an odd or strange individual.

p. 180

† **Farnese Hercules**: A large and famous marble statue of Hercules, the mythological hero renowned for his strength; it shows Hercules as heavily muscled and weary. Signed "Glykon", the statue is a copy (of uncertain date, between the first century BCE and the third century CE) of a smaller, now lost bronze by the ancient Greek sculptor Lysippus (fourth century BCE), and takes its name from the Farnese Palace in Rome, where it was from 1546 to 1787.

p. 181

† **Day and Martin-looking composition which, I believe, is a mixture of sloe-juice and gin, but which the inhabitants of London swallow for port, *"neat as imported!"***: Arundell describes sloe gin, a potent mixture of gin and the juice of sloes (blackthorn fruit). "Day and Martin" is a slang term for black people, after a shoe-black-ing firm; presumably the idea here is that the sloe gin is very dark. "Neat as imported" is evidently an advertising slogan, indicating that it is undiluted and unadulterated.

p. 182

† **Teague**: That is, Ireland.

p. 183

† **the boxer Crib, after his defeating an American negro**: See note to p. 32.

p. 185

† **"While I have time and space, / Before I further in my tale do pass, / It seemeth me accordant unto reason, / To tell unto you all the condition, / Of each of them – so it seemed to me; / And who they were, and of what degree." Chaucer**: From the "General Prologue" to Chaucer's *Canterbury Tales* (late fourteenth century). The nar-rator is about to introduce his fellow-pilgrims, who will tell the stories that make up the *Tales*. This is a modernization of Chaucer's Middle English.

† **"On, on the vessel flies – the land is gone, / And winds are rude in Biscay's sleep-less bay." Byron**: In *Childe Harold's Pilgrimage* (I.198), these lines come immediately after the end of Harold's farewell song (see note to p. 80). The Bay of Biscay lies between western France and northern Spain; Harold's ship is on its way from England to Portugal.

† **Baltimore clipper**: The ship from which the later "clipper ship" evolved. It was a small, swift coastal packet developed by shipbuilders in Chesapeake Bay, Maryland, during the eighteenth century. Often used by privateers, for conveying perishables, and in the slave trade, they were rigged with various combinations of fore-and-aft and square sails.

p. 186

† **such a mouth as used to be painted on a signboard, ere John Bull learned French, when the Boulogne Mouth was represented by a bull, and a human, or rather inhuman mouth**: Presumably the inn signboard represents the corruption of "Boulogne Mouth" into "The Bull and Mouth".

† **the countenance of Liston**: John Liston (1776–1846), was a famous London comedian, comic actor and impersonator.

p. 187

† **"The Elephant and Castle"**: A traffic junction and coaching terminus in South London.

† **Astley's**: An amphitheatre built in 1794 by Philip Astley, replacing the circus ring he had until then used for his equestrian dramas.

p. 188

† **"Tally high O the grinder"**: A line from one of Charles Dibdin's songs, "The Grinders" (see note to p. 139).

† **the "Dead March" in Saul**: The "Dead March" in Handel's oratorio *Saul* (1739) is a famous piece of sombre music, often used for funeral processions.

† **Wolfe (the "Death of Moore" was his favourite), Byron, Moore, Scott, Campbell and Coleridge . . . Milton's "L'Allegro," and "Il Penseroso"**: The Reverend Charles Wolfe's poem, "The Burial of Sir John Moore" (1817), commemorating the

death of Sir John Moore at the (victorious) battle of Corunna (1809), was very popular in the first half of the nineteenth century, and was referred to by a variety of titles. Milton's "L'Allegro" and "Il Penseroso" (*c*.1645; see also note to p. 115) are companion pieces which celebrate joy and melancholy respectively; they were also well known, though Milton was a little less popular than the other poets listed (Byron, Thomas Moore, Walter Scott, Thomas Campbell and Coleridge).

† **a native of Shields, and what is called in the navy a north-country Jock**: "Jock" is nautical slang for a North Country seaman; North Shields and South Shields are towns in the county of Northumberland.

† **Like Hamilton, Britton was "single-speeched": he seldom said more than two or three words at a time**: William Gerald Hamilton was known as "Single-Speech Hamilton", not because he spoke little but because his first speech in Parliament (1755) was supposed to have been his last. The story is not true, but the name stuck.

† **Front du Boeuf**: Sir Reginald Front du Boeuf, one of the villains in Sir Walter Scott's *Ivanhoe* (1819; dated 1820). A Norman knight, he is noted for his large size as well as for his cruelty; his name literally means "bull-face".

† **"smell hell"**: That is, to be knocked down, so that one's nose is in the dirt.

p. 190

† **cobbed**: Spanked with a flat instrument.

p. 191

† **pipeclay aristocracy**: "Pipeclay" is a fine white clay used for making pipes and also – especially by soldiers – for cleaning white trousers; "aristocracy" here is clearly ironic.

† **loblolly-boy**: An attendant who assists a ship's surgeon and his mates in their duties. "Loblolly-doctor" is a sailor's name for a ship's doctor; "loblolly" is a ship-doctor's simple medicines.

† **"index of his mind"**: That is, the middle of his face, following the idea that the face expresses a person's mind. The phrase itself is proverbial.

† **arnotto-coloured**: An orange-red dye produced from the seeds of the shrub *Bixa orellana*, used in cooking. Usually spelled "anatto", and known in Trinidad as "roucou".

† **"human face divine"**: From Milton's *Paradise Lost* (1667–74, III.44). This rather incongruous quotation forms part of Milton's moving reflection on his blindness. The "human face divine" is one of the things he is now cut off from by "ever-during dark".

† **"the arms of Murphy" (Morpheus)**: Morpheus is the god of dreams; hence the proverbial expression "to be in the arms of Morpheus" (that is, to be in "dreamland").

† **the infant Achilles being dipped by Thetis into the Styx**: While still an infant, the mythological Greek hero Achilles was dipped by his mother in the river Styx (chief river of Hades, the realm of the dead) in order to make him invulnerable. Since she held on to him by his heel, the water did not touch him in that part, which remained vulnerable. Achilles was eventually killed by a poisoned arrow shot into his heel.

p. 195

† ***skean dhu*, or Highland dirk**: A "skean" is a kind of short dagger.

† **companion-ladder**: See note to p. 68.

† **bowse**: To haul with tackle.

p. 196

† **locked-jaw**: "Locked-jaw" or "lockjaw", a common name for tetanus, so called because the principal symptom is a continuous muscular spasm which makes the jaw go rigid. Even minor wounds and punctures can easily become infected.

† **'peach the major**: "'Peach" is short for "impeach"; in this context, it might mean to charge with assault.

p. 197

† **Alexandria . . . Maida**: The battles of Alexandria (or Aboukir; 1801), in Egypt, and Maida (1806), in southern Italy, were both British victories over the French during the Napoleonic Wars. The "invincibles" have not been precisely identified, but the bayonet charge of the 42nd Highlanders under Major General Sir John Moore (see note to p. 188) was a turning point in the battle of Alexandria. Unfortunately, however, the Highlanders were overenthusiastic in pursuing the enemy, allowing the French cavalry to renew their attack, and so contributing to the wounding of General Moore, and the death of General Sir Ralph Abercromby, who had won Trinidad from Spain in 1797.

p. 198

† **play Guy Fawkes, and send us up into the air**: Guy Fawkes, one of the conspirators in the Gunpowder Plot, was caught on 5 November 1605 before he and his colleagues could blow up Parliament. The day has traditionally been celebrated with bonfires, fireworks, and the burning of a stuffed-clothing "guy".

p. 200

† **Fué por luna y volvio trasquilado. Cervantes**: This quotation, correctly "Fue por lana y volvió trasquilado", that is, "He went to get some wool and came back sheared", occurs several times in *Don Quixote* (1605–15), by Miguel de Cervantes. Most instances come from Sancho Panza, an inveterate proverb-spouter, and one comes from Don Quixote's niece, both down-to-earth types and foils to the impractical knight. Though he is more admirable than the unruly sailors in *Warner Arundell*, Don Quixote's chivalric ritual does somewhat resemble their "crossing the line" rituals.

† **"No peace beyond the line"**: A proverbial saying. The *Oxford Dictionary of English Proverbs* (1948) cites Sir Walter Scott's *The Pirate* (chapter 21) as an example: "There is never peace with Spaniards beyond the Line."

p. 201

† **Amphitrite**: In Greek mythology, goddess of the sea, and consort of Poseidon.

p. 202

† **Who left their country, for their country's good**: A quotation from Henry Carter's "Prologue written for the Opening of the Play-house at New South Wales" (written in 1801, several years after the actual opening): "True patriots all; for be it understood / We left our country for our country's good." This work was for many years attributed to George Barrington, a notorious transported convict who was supposed to have spoken it at the playhouse opening in 1796. Most of the actors in the opening performance were transported convicts, as the prologue suggests.

† **Dibdin's songs, commencing "Daddy Neptune one day", and . . . trying to sing "The tight little island"**: "The Tight Little Island" (1797), a patriotic song and probably the best known song written by Thomas Dibdin (son of Charles Dibdin, see note to p. 83), begins "Daddy Neptune one day to Freedom did say . . ." The island of the title is Britain, which Freedom identifies as his "own island".

p. 204

† *in terrorem*: As a threat (a legal term).

† **cowhage**: The stinging hairs of the seed pod of *Mucuna pruriens,* used against intestinal worms. Also spelled "cowage", and "cow-itch".

p. 205

† **as we were without a chronometer . . . lunar observations**: A very unreliable method; see Sobel's *Longitude.*

p. 207

† **Angeda passage**: The Anegada Passage, between the Leeward Islands to eastward, and the Virgin Islands to westward.

p. 208

† **"Repelled from port to port they sue in vain, / And track, with slow unsteady sail, the main." Leyden**: From John Leyden, *Scenes of Infancy* (1803; III.175–76), a poem which tracks Leyden's youthful memories, but also covers many other subjects, such as the slave trade. This part tells a legend of the first slave ship, cursed with "speck-led plague", "repell'd from port to port", left to drift as the crew sickens and dies, and finally struck by lightning and burned, only to reappear in ghostly form during storms.

p. 209

† **if I applied to land, my application would be granted, as the want of sufficient medical men was sorely felt**: Trust in any "professional", and problems of supply and demand, assured that regulations were often overlooked.

p. 210

† **André de Rossey, a French freebooter**: A notorious French buccaneer in the heyday of the pirates and buccaneers in the Caribbean.

p. 212

† **Lord of Hosts**: "YHWH tsevaot", one of the biblical epithets for God. (See note to p. 158.)

† **a Jew of Curaçoa**: The island of Curaçao was captured by the Dutch from the Spanish in 1634. By 1651, there was a settlement of Jews, mostly from Holland. They were origi-nally allowed to settle for agricultural development, but the rocky soil and arid climate encouraged them to take up trade and shipping. By the mid-seventeenth century, Jews were prominent in local commerce, philanthropy, and civic affairs.

† **I bear a Spanish name**: Here Fernandez expresses his fury at the fate of Jews in Christian Spain, when even those who agreed to convert were subjected to the persecu-tion of the Inquisition, and those who did not convert were finally expelled in 1492. For centuries after the expulsion, a small group of "Conversos" (formerly known as "Marranos") lived a clandestine Jewish existence in Spain. There were also Jews who sin-cerely adopted Christianity at the time of the Inquisition, and even rose high in the ranks of the Church; hence, the priest who appears later on fits a certain model. The personal-ized passion of this character may be connected to a Sephardic (Spanish-Jewish) origin for Joseph's family.

† **Grenada**: Granada, in southern Spain.

† ***Auto da Fe***: The Spanish Inquisition burned at the stake "New Christians" – converted Jews – suspected of relapsing to Judaism.

† **Elohim**: A Hebrew word meaning "God"; one of the most common divine names in the Bible. Spain shall be what Tyre and Sidon are: The ancient Phoenician cities of Tyre (now Sur) and Sidon (now Saida) on the coast of Lebanon were famous trading centres for centuries. Both were destroyed and rebuilt several times, but Tyre never recovered its former importance after its destruction by the Mamluks in 1291. Sidon's trade dried up after the governor of Lebanon, then under the Ottoman Empire, drove French merchants away from the city gates in 1791.

† **Escurial**: El Escorial (built 1563–84), is a palace, monastery and royal mausoleum in central Spain.

p. 213

† **persecuted . . . world**: Spain persecuted the Jews and the New Christians, expelled the Muslims (Moors) from Andalusía in the south, and wiped out the aboriginal inhabitants of the Caribbean.

† **Shylock-like mortgage, or a pound of your Christian flesh**: A reference to Shakespeare's *Merchant of Venice*. At the beginning of the play, the Jewish merchant Shylock lends Antonio money, taking as surety a bond promising a pound of Antonio's flesh. When Antonio cannot pay, Shylock attempts to have the actual pound of flesh.

† **boxes kept in all synagogues**: The synagogue, as the centre of communal life, was the appropriate place to keep alms-boxes for a variety of charities and services maintained by the community. These included charity for the poor, for widows and orphans, for destitute brides, for the burial society, and so on. Funds were also collected to send to the Jewish community in the land of Israel, which had been growing slowly in the eighteenth and early nineteenth century. This comprised city-dwelling religious Jews, usually in poor financial circumstances, and it was considered part of the duty of Jews in the diaspora to enable Jews to live in the Holy Land and pursue religious studies there.

p. 214

† **"The Lord bless and preserve thee; the Lord make his face shine on thee, and give thee peace!"**: Here is condensed the slightly longer passage from Numbers 6:24–26, which reads (in the King James translation): "The Lord bless thee, and keep thee: The Lord make his face shine upon thee, and be gracious unto thee: The Lord lift up his countenance upon thee, and give thee peace." This passage, which quotes the words of Aaron the High Priest, is known as the "Priestly Blessing", bestowed on special occasions, for example on children by their parents at the start of the Sabbath.

† **dead beat**: To sail directly (or as close as possible) into the wind, therefore to take a difficult and slow route.

p. 215

† **bull-dogs (pieces of ordnance)**: Cannons or other firearms.

p. 216

† **picquet of soldiers**: A small detached body of troops, sent out to watch for the approach of an enemy.

p. 217

† **Sir Robert Walpole said every man had his price**: Although it is virtually proverbial, this saying is commonly attributed to Walpole (1676–1745), a British statesman and prime minister under George I and George II.

† **broad arrow**: The arrow-head-shaped mark used by the British Board of Ordnance and placed upon government stores.

† **"To add one freeman more, America, to thee"**: An altered quotation from the last line of Byron's "Venice: An Ode" (1819). After contemplating Venice's subjection to Austrian rule and other examples of what he sees as European tyranny, Byron ends with a paean to the United States, and the thought that it is better to "Fly, and one current to the ocean add / . . . One freeman more, America, to thee".

† **Brother Jonathan**: A personification of the United States of America; gradually superseded by "Uncle Sam" during the nineteenth century.

p. 219

† **"Read thou this challenge; mark but the penning of it." King Lear**: In a poignantly ironic moment from Shakespeare's *King Lear* (IV.vi), the mad Lear shows an imaginary challenge to Gloucester, who has been blinded.

† **"Ducunt ad seria nugae." Horace**: Probably intended for "hae nugae seria ducent / in mala" ("These trifles will lead him into serious difficulties"). The comment, from Horace's *Ars Poetica* (451–52), emphasizes the need for careful proofreading and editing of one's poetry. Like the *Lear* quotation, this one seems rather incongruous for the duelling episode.

478

p. 220
† **Lospatos**: (See note to p. 4.)
† *parti quarré*: Literally, "a party of four".

p. 222
† **plethoric**: Of a morbid condition, characterized by over-fullness or excess of blood or other humour.
† **sanguine**: Characterized by a predominance of blood over the other humours; indicated by a ruddy complexion, and a courageous, hopeful and amorous disposition.
† **sand box-tree**: *Hura crepitans*, a very large, spiny-trunked tree. Usually spelled "sandbox tree".

p. 226
† **Wordsworth, "All silent, and all damned"**: From William Wordsworth's poem, *Peter Bell*. Near the end of Part First, Peter has a sudden, alarming vision, which the narrator does not describe, but speculates about; in this stanza he asks whether Peter sees an infernal group in a crowded parlour, "Cramm'd just as they on earth were cramm'd" but "All silent and all damned!" Wordsworth deleted the stanza after the first (1819) edition, where it follows line 515. The wild and hard protagonist Peter resembles Purcell and his friends: he is about to toss an ass into a river, but his vision (like the "cloudy portraiture" that unnerves Purcell) throws him into a swoon.
† **black vomit**: Vomit discoloured black; sometimes occurring during serious cases of yellow fever and other conditions in which blood collects in the stomach.

p. 227
† **"Sent in this foul clime to languish, / Think what thousands fall in vain; / Wasted with disease and anguish, / Not in glorious battle slain." Glover**: A slightly altered quotation from "Admiral Hosier's Ghost" (1740?), a poem by Richard Glover which contrasts the 1739 victory of Admiral Vernon over the Spanish fleet near Porto Bello with the fate of Admiral Hosier and his fleet, sent to the West Indies in 1726 but forbidden to engage the Spanish; they ended up dying of fever in large numbers, and Hosier is said to have died of a broken heart. These lines appear in the version of the poem collected in *Percy's Reliques* (1765 and later editions); most other printed versions of the poem omit them. The *Reliques* text has "fell", not "fall".
† **choristers, acolytes, and crucifers**: Members of an ecclesiastical procession. "Acolytes" are altar-boys (likely carrying candles or censers); "crucifers" carry large crosses in front of processions.

p. 228
† **substitutes for that valuable drug, little, if at all, inferior to the best cinchona**: Probably *Enicostema verticillatum*, an annual plant (known locally as "zeb kinin" or "quinine bush"), and *Quassia amara*, a very small tree (locally known as "quassia" or "bitter ash"). See discussion in the introduction to this volume.
† **Windsor uniform**: A blue coat with red collar and cuffs, and a blue or white waistcoat. Designed by George III as a royal household livery, it was worn by him and by members of the royal household at Windsor Castle, his favourite residence. Sir Ralph may have been admitted to the privilege of wearing it at some point; more likely, though, he is imitating the royal custom.
† **Sir Thomas Lawrence**: Famous British portrait painter of the early 1800s.
† **St. Ann's**: The governor's residence outside Port of Spain, now the site of the Trinidad Hilton Hotel.

p. 229
† **humorous Cervantic cast of countenance**: That is, a face recalling the ironic narrative tone of Cervantes in *Don Quixote*.

p. 230

† **the illustrious board of cabildo* *The cabildo is a kind of town-council**: In Spanish colonies, cities were governed by councils called "cabildos". Their members, however, possessed certain powers wider than those usually exercised by municipal bodies. In Trinidad, the cabildo was located in Port of Spain and continued to exist despite the British conquest until 1840. Woodford accuses it of asserting claims similar to those made by the elected assemblies in other British colonies (Trinidad had no elected assembly).

p. 234

† **"Avansar, avansar, companeros! / Con los armas al numbro avansar; / Libertad pora sempre clamenos; / Libertad, libertad, libertad!" Patriot Song**: "[¡]Avanzar, avanzar, compañeros! / Con los armas al hombro avanzar; / Libertad para siempre clamemos. / [¡]Libertad, libertad, libertad!", that is, "Forward, forward comrades! / With weapons/rifles on the shoulder, forward. / Freedom forever we shall demand. / Freedom, freedom, freedom!"

p. 235

† **Had Washington not succeeded, Bolivar had remained a mere amiable, but indolent creole; and Paez, a wild tamer of scarcely more wild cattle**: The success of the American Revolution inspired the struggles for Latin American independence, led by (among others) Simón Bolívar and José Antonio Paez.

† **Bourbons of France and Spain**: In the late eighteenth century, both France and Spain were ruled by monarchs of the French Bourbon dynasty.

† **Louis XVI**: A Bourbon ruler, he was executed in 1793 by the revolutionary regime in France.

† **Miranda, the father of South American liberty**: Francisco de Miranda, a Venezuelan, is known as the precursor of Latin American independence, for his tireless struggles on behalf of this cause from the 1780s. He led an abortive rising in 1806.

† *parvenu*: An upstart; a person of obscure origin who has obtained wealth or position beyond that of his class, especially when unfitted for the position.

† **Cachupin**: From "Cachupín", in turn from the Portuguese "cachopo", that is, "boy"; this was a nickname used for Spaniards settling in the Americas, particularly in Mexico.

p. 236

† **The year after war was declared, Trinidad was taken – an island, from its situation, of great importance to further the plan of aiding a revolt in South America: hence, Dundas sent to Governor Picton orders to promote an insurrection on the Main.* *See Picton's Proclamation, June 26, 1797**: Trinidad was captured by Britain in February 1797. To damage the enemy, Spain, the secretary of state for war and the colonies, Lord Dundas, instructed Sir Thomas Picton, the first governor of British Trinidad, to foment unrest among the Spanish colonists of Venezuela, which his Proclamation of June 1797 attempted to do.

† **hero of Badajos**: Picton was a hero of the Peninsular War (1808–13) and fought at the Battle of Badajoz in Spain (1812).

† **a conspiracy by Gual, and two other state prisoners, who were shut up in La Guayra**: Manuel Gual led an abortive rising against Spanish rule in Venezuela in 1797, centred in the port city of Güiria, close to Trinidad.

p. 237

† **brother Joseph**: Napoleon imposed his brother Joseph Buonaparte on the Spanish throne, which eventually led to the British defeat of French forces in Spain in the Peninsular War (1808–13).

† **junta of Seville, the regency of Madrid, and the junta of the Asturias**: Councils formed in different cities or regions of Spain during the crisis caused by Napoleon's imposition of his brother Joseph as king of Spain.

† **Santiago Mariño**: A Venezuelan who held property in Trinidad on Chacachacare Island; he organized an expedition from there in 1813 and fought with Bolívar in the War of Independence.

p. 238

† **Morillo**: General Pablo Morillo, the leader of Spanish forces fighting against the "patriots" in Venezuela and Colombia, was notorious for his harshness against civilians. He led a large Spanish army which re-conquered Venezuela and Colombia in 1815.

† **Pizarro**: Francisco Pizarro, the leader of the sixteenth-century Spanish conquest of Inca Peru.

p. 239

† **Boves, and Morales**: José Tomés Boves and Francisco Tomés Morales, Spanish generals fighting against the "patriots".

† **Bay of Pampatar**: A bay on the eastern side of Margarita Island.

† **Macanon**: A hill on the Macanan peninsula of Margarita.

† **prickly pears**: *Nopalea cochenillifera*, a tall spiny cactus, with many ascending or spreading oblong, flat, fleshy sections and red ovoid fruits. Known locally as "rachette".

p. 240

† *mestezo*, **i.e. of mingled Spanish and Indian blood**: A person of mixed European and Amerindian descent. Usually spelled "mestizo".

† **Brion's fleet**: Luis Brión was in command of the "patriot" naval forces in 1816.

† **Cumana**: A coastal city in Venezuela, across the Bay of Cariaco from the island of Margarita.

† **Sierra de Bergantia**: A mountain range beginning near the Gulf of Paria, lying on a northeast-to-southwest angle, between the coast and the Orinoco River.

† **Maturin**: A Venezuelan town about a hundred miles southeast of Cumana.

† *"Lorita real, Por l'España, no por la Portugal." . . . Lorita patriota por l'America, no por l'Espana*: "Lorita real, por España, no por Portugal . . . Lorita patriota, por América, no por España", that is, "The little parrot for Spain, not for Portugal . . . The patriotic little parrot, for America, not for Spain." (A "lorita" is a little parrot; "lorito real" may be a local phrase.) The play on words here is that "real, realista" was applied to people loyal to the crown during the independence wars, as opposed then to "patriot".

p. 242

† **"Along the banks of Oronoc, / The voice of freedom's heard at length; / Thy Sambos, Maturin, are woke, / With dauntless hearts, and arms of strength." Columbian Song of Liberty**: This song has not been identified further.

† **Sambo**: Although identified by Joseph as a man of mixed Indian and African descent, usually this term referred to a person of mixed African and "mulatto" descent, that is, considered three quarters black.

† **blunderbusses**: A short gun with a large bore, firing many balls or slugs, and capable of killing within a limited range without exact aim.

p. 243

† **swivel**: A "swivel-gun" or "swivel" is a gun or small cannon mounted on a swivel, a pivoted rest for a gun especially on the gunwale of a boat, enabling it to turn horizontally, or to be elevated, in any direction.

† *meerschaum*: A tobacco pipe, the bowl of which is made of meerschaum, a clay-like substance.
† *"Ramos muchachos! Viva el Rey Fernando!"*: "[¡]Vamos, muchachos! [¡]Viva el Rey Fernando!", that is, "Let's go, men! Long live King Ferdinand!" (Ferdinand VII).

p. 244
† **Gulf of Cariaco**: A large gulf or basin on the coast of Venezuela, between Cariaco and Cumana to the east, and Caracas to the west.
† **cocoa-trees**: That is, coconut palms.
† **the galinazo, vulture, or turkey-buzzard**: Probably *Cathartes aura*, the turkey vulture, being dark-brown with a bare-skin reddish head; the most common vulture in the area after *Coragyps atratus*, the "black vulture", which is dark all over.

p. 245
† **Sir Gregor M'Gregor . . . the author of the Poyais scheme**: "Latin-American countries began borrowing and defaulting as soon as they gained independence in the 1820s. The first wave of bonds issued in London were the subject of a speculative mania . . . a Scottish adventurer who had fought under Simón Bolívar succeeded in floating a 200,000 bond for 'the ridiculous and largely mythical Kingdom of Poyais,' ostensibly a new country in Central America. Gregor MacGregor, the 'prince of Poyais,' made off with the proceeds of the issue and was never heard of again" (Darrell Delamaide, *Debt Shock: The Full Story of the World Credit Crisis* [Garden City, NY: Doubleday, 1984], 96).

p. 246
† **Paternoster**: The Latin version of the Lord's Prayer.

p. 248
† *echellon* **movement**: An "echelon" or "echellon" is a formation of troops in which the successive divisions are placed parallel to one another, but with no two on the same alignment, each division having its front clear of that in advance.

p. 249
† **of mixed European and Indian race, called Mestija,* *Feminine of Mestijo**: A woman of mixed European and Amerindian descent, feminine of "mestizo". Usually spelled "mestiza".

p. 250
† **At night, I was going over the field to render what professional assistance I could to the groaning wounded**: Until World War I, disease caused more deaths in war than did combat. Wounds were the key factor affecting healing, when they were not clean and if damage to the tissues was widespread. Infection varied with terrain and weapons used.

p. 251
† **"We are but warriors for a working-day: / Our gayness and our guilt are all besmerched, / With rainy marching in the painful field. / And time hath worn us into slovenry." Shakespeare**: Lines from a famous speech in *Henry V* (IV.iii): "We are but warriors for the working day: / Our gayness and our gilt are all besmirch'd, / With rainy marching in the painful field . . . / And time hath worn us into slovenry." King Henry, leading a weary and sick English army, here delivers a message of defiance to the French herald Mountjoy, who has brought a demand from the French that the English surrender and pay a ransom. The English win the battle in the end.
† **Guiana**: The region south and east of the Orinoco River, around Ciudad Guayana.
† **the Apuré**: The Apure River flows into the Orinoco from the west, more or less parallel to the northern coast.

p. 252

† **a blue surtout**: A kind of man's greatcoat or overcoat.

† **"The poor remains of beauty once admired"**: A quotation from *Douglas* (IV; see note to p. 94). Here Lady Randolph, having just told the young shepherd Norval that she is his mother, and that he is the late Douglas's son, deflects his compliment on her beauty: "In me thou dost behold / The poor remains of beauty once admired".

† **musketoons, rifles, fowling-pieces, carabines**: A "musketoon" is a kind of short, large-bore musket. A "rifle" is a firearm, especially a musket or a carbine, having a spirally grooved bore. A "fowling piece" is a light gun used for shooting wild fowl. A "carabine" or "carbine" is a kind of firearm longer than a pistol and shorter than a musket, used by cavalry and other troops.

† **Choca Indian**: One of the numerous Amerindian groups in Venezuela.

p. 253

† **tasajo (smoked beef)**: ~ tasso (see note to p. 68).

† **Colonel Farrier, in 1821, at Caribobo**: A British division which fought at the Battle of Carabobo (June 1821), at which Bolívar decisively defeated the Spanish.

p. 254

† **"Avancar, muchacos! . . . Muéron los Cachupinos"**: "¡Avanzar, muchachos! Mueran los Gachupines"; that is, "Forward, men! Death to the Cachupins."

† **gurapo* *A fermented liquor, often made of cane-juice and pineapples**: Also spelled "warap" and "guarapo", from Quechua "huarapu".

p. 255

† **this *Esek*, or spring of contention**: This refers to a biblical confrontation: "And Isaac's servants dug in the valley and found there a well of living water. And the herdsmen of Gerar strove with Isaac's herdsmen, saying, 'The water is ours.' And he called the name of the well Esek, because they contended with him" (Genesis 26:19–20). The Hebrew word "esek" means contention or strife.

p. 256

† **curari, or Indian poison**: A blackish-brown resinous bitter substance, obtained as an extract from *Strychnos toxifera* and other plants of tropical South America, used by Amerindians to poison their arrows.

† **Castillo**: Manuel del Castillo was a Colombian rival to Bolívar for the "patriot" leadership.

† **Andalusian**: A large region of southern Spain.

† **toledo espadin* *Spanish sword**: Toledo, a city south of Madrid, was famous for its steel; an "espadin" is a small narrow sword, sometimes triangular, mounted on an ornamented handle.

p. 258

† **"Je crus que c'étois *la vièrge de dernières amours*, cette vièrge qu'on envoie au prisonnier de guerre pour enchanter sa tombe; dans cette persuasion je lui dis, en balbutiant, et avec un trouble qui, partant, ne venoit pas de la crainte du bûcher, 'Vièrge, vous êtes digne des premières amours, et vous n'êtes pas faite pour les dernières.' " *Atala, par* Chateaubriand**: "I believed that she was 'the virgin of the last loves', the one sent to the prisoner of war to grace his last hours; so thinking I said to her, stammeringly, and with a confusion that did not come from the fear of the stake, 'Maiden, you are worthy of a first love, and are not made for the last ones.' " François-René de Chateaubriand's *Atala* (1801) is a Romantic novella. Here, Chactas, a hero in the "noble savage" tradition, meets the heroine Atala for the first time. He is

imprisoned and soon to be tortured and killed by her people; she comes to comfort him, but draws back when she discovers that he is not a Christian, as she is. Later she frees him and they flee together. There are two mistakes, possibly compositor's errors, in the quotation: "que c'étois" should be "que c'étoit", and "partant" should be "pourtant".

† **as sacred . . . as Thermopylae was to the Greeks**: At the battle of Thermopylae (480 BCE), the Persians annihilated a force of three hundred Greeks who were attempting to defend the pass of Thermopylae. The battle became an emblem of heroic resistance in the face of overwhelming odds.

p. 259

† **Yaruros**: An Amerindian group mainly resident in the Orinoco delta; in the past, they occasionally traded or resided in Trinidad. Also spelled "Guarahoon", "Guaraoon", "Guarauno", "Wallahoon", "Warahoon", and "Warao"; the group usually meant locally by the name "Wild Indian".

† **The last Maroon war in Jamaica, in 1795–6, which kept, for eighteen months, that island in a state of alarm, and cost one million sterling, arose from flogging two Maroons. Had they been shot, their comrades would not have noticed it**: The Maroon uprising in Jamaica in 1795 was triggered by the imposition of corporal punishment on two members of the Maroon community; this was felt to be unacceptable treatment of people guaranteed quasi-independence and freedom by treaty with the British.

p. 261

† **Catalonian soldiers**: From Catalonia, a region of southern Spain.
† **Ferdinand the Beloved**: King Ferdinand VII of Spain.

p. 262

† **Salamanca**: The Battle of Salamanca, a British victory in the Peninsular War (1812).

p. 264

† **Vidocq**: Eugène François Vidocq (1775–1857) was a fugitive from French justice who became a police spy and eventually the first head of the Sûreté in 1811, and is considered the father of modern criminal investigation. He was the basis for both Jean Valjean and Inspector Javert in Victor Hugo's *Les Miserables,* and Balzac's character Vautran, in *Père Goriot.* The fugitive Magwitch in Dickens's *Great Expectations* was also inspired by Vidocq's exploits.

p. 265

† **might have served George Cruikshank as studies for Falstaff's regiment**: Arundell here imagines the caricaturist and illustrator Cruikshank (1792–1878) depicting the soldiers commanded by Shakespeare's Sir John Falstaff in *1 Henry IV.* Falstaff first drafts men with money who are reluctant to go to war; they then bribe him to release them from service, and he fills up the company with thin, ragged and desperate "scarecrows" (IV.ii). Though Cruikshank does not appear to have actually done such a drawing before 1838, Shakespeare was an important influence on him, and he did later illustrate a *Life of Sir John Falstaff* (1858; text by Robert Brough).

† **major and subaltern**: That is, an officer of senior rank (usually the second officer of a regiment) and a junior officer (below the rank of captain).

p. 267

† **absorbed by his devotion**: The portrayal of the noble Jew, a man of gentility and strong principle steadfastly devoted to the ancient faith of his forefathers, gets some play in nineteenth-century English literature, from the novels of Disraeli in the 1820s and 1830s to George Eliot's *Daniel Deronda* (1876).

p. 268

† **"In form a woman, but in years a child"**: From Byron's *The Island* (1823), a poem loosely based on the story of the mutiny on HMS *Bounty*. Here the idealized heroine, Neuha, "gentle savage of the wild / In growth a woman, though in years a child", is introduced (II.vii). She later saves the life of Torquil, who, thanks to her foresight and courage, becomes, in Byron's account, the only survivor of the mutineers.

p. 270

† **compadre**: Literally, "godfather of one's child", or "father of one's godchild"; also used to indicate a very close friendship.

† **Gossip. This kind of relationship is more sacred amongst the Spaniards than amongst us**: A now-archaic word for godparent.

p. 275

† *monte*: A gambling game in which three cards are displayed and one chosen; then all are turned face down and moved around. People then bet on which is the one originally designated.

† **in Hebrew, from Deuteronomy, chapter iv. verse 4, what the modern Jews conceive to be the foundation-stone of their faith. "Hear, O Israel! Jehovah is our Lord; Jehovah is One."**: Known as the "Shema" (the first word of the Hebrew verse), this is indeed the foundation-stone of Jewish faith, a credo which is recited during the morning and evening prayer services, before going to sleep at night, and – perhaps with particular application to the story here – on one's deathbed. This declaration is followed by a declaration of fundamental duties: to love God with heart, soul and might; to remember all the commandments and instruct children in them; to recite the words of God when retiring or rising; to bind those words on the arm and head (that is, tefillin or phylacteries); and to inscribe them on the door-posts of the house and on the city gates. The divine name "Jehovah" is rendered as "Lord" in most English translations, reflecting the fact that this Ineffable Name of God, the Tetragrammaton, is not pronounced; although its consonants could be transliterated as "jhvh" or "yhwh", the vowels that accompany the name in the biblical text reflect the accepted pronunciation of "adonai" (Lord). According to tradition, only the High Priest knew how to pronounce the Tetragrammaton, and he would do so only once a year, on the Day of Atonement, in the Holy of Holies in the Temple in Jerusalem. When the Bible was translated into European languages such as German and English, translators sometimes combined the original consonants with the vowels of "adonai" (hence "Jehovah") or attempted to reconstruct the original pronunciation ("Yahweh" was a popular transliteration for many years).

p. 276

† **mixed and corrupt Hebrew**: Presumably a reference to Ladino, the language of Sephardi Jews, which combines the Hebrew alphabet and some Hebrew words with spoken Spanish.

† **alter Jehovah's commandments, by suppressing the second* *Catholics omit the second commandment, and divide the tenth into two parts**: The Catholic (and the Lutheran) church regards the prohibitions on false worship in the Ten Commandments, "Thou shalt have no other Gods before me" and "Thou shalt not make unto thee any graven image" (Exodus 20:3–4; Deuteronomy 5:7–8), as one commandment, with the second subsumed under the first. Under this system, the tenth commandment is divided into two, a division most readily made in the Deuteronomy version: "Neither shalt thou desire thy neighbour's wife" (5:21) thus becomes the ninth Commandment, and the second part of the same verse ("neither shalt thou covet thy neighbour's house, his field . . . ") becomes the tenth. According to Fernandez's perspective, Christians seem to be ignoring the second commandment in their worship of Jesus.

† **who is called Masha Ben Simon when summoned to the desk of the synagogue**: At three morning services a week (on Monday, Thursday and the Sabbath), Jews read from the Torah (Pentateuch) scroll at the desk or podium of the synagogue. Members of the congregation (traditionally only men) are called up to recite a blessing before each section of the Torah portion is read; they are called by their Jewish/Hebrew name, the name they were given at their circumcision. That name is a combination of their own name and their father's, connected by the word "ben", that is, "son of". Thus, here, Masha (probably a variation on Moshe or "Moses"), son of Simon.

† **like Jephthah, an only daughter**: The biblical story of Jephthah and his daughter is found in Judges 11.

p. 277

† **Chyma tribe**: An Amerindian people of Venezuela. Usually spelled "Chaima".

† **sack**: A dry, rough Spanish wine often sweetened with sugar. The word was eventually applied to most strong white wines from southern Spain and the Canaries, including sherry.

p. 279

† **douceur**: A conciliatory present or gift; a gratuity; a bribe.

† **River Essequibo**: The major river in modern Guyana (formerly British Guiana); Essiquibo is also the name of a large county in that nation.

† **horse-pistols**: A large pistol carried at the pommel of a saddle when on horseback.

p. 281

† **"To traverse o'er, / Plain, forest, river, – man nor brute, / By dint of hoof, nor print of foot, / Lay in that wild luxuriant soil; / No signs of travel, none of toil."** **Byron**: From *Mazeppa* (1819, xvii), a poem in which the titular hero recounts his wild ride as a youth, bound naked to the back of a wild horse (in punishment for being discovered having an affair with a married woman). Half dead on the horse the next morning, he sees the sun rise in an apparently uninhabited place where it seems he can expect no rescue; hence the comment "What booted it to traverse o'er / Plain, forest, river . . .". Byron has "Nor dint" for "By dint", and "in the wild" for "in that wild".

p. 282

† **lazoes**: A long rope of untanned hide, from ten to thirty yards in length, having at the end a loop or noose to catch cattle and wild horses; Spanish "lazo", in English usually spelled "lasso".

† **the pouie, or South American turkey**: *Aburria pipile*, a large turkey-like bird. Usually spelled "pawi", also "pauji".

† **The Columbians say the jaguar, or tiger, mixes with the puma (South American lion), and produces an extremely ferocious mongrel**: This is scientifically highly unlikely; this folk belief probably results from a confusion of the melanistic (black) phases of the jaguar, *Felis onca*, and the puma, *Felis concolor*.

p. 283

† **pinchbeck**: An alloy of about five parts copper with one of zinc, resembling gold, used in cheap jewellery, clock making, and the like.

p. 284

† **Indian alcalde**: Native official or magistrate of an Amerindian mission community.

† **Louis the Sixteenth**: The French king was executed in 1793 by the revolutionary regime.

p. 285

† **Pariagotoes**: One of the Amerindian peoples in Venezuela.

p. 286

† **bait**: To give food and drink to a horse or other animal, especially during a journey.

p. 287

† **terekay, or small river turtle**: There are several small freshwater turtles to which this might refer.

p. 288

† **The river *Sabathjon*, therefore, flows during six days, and on the seventh, its waters are stationary**: The legendary river Sambatyon (also "Sabbatyon" and "Sanbatyon") is mentioned by the rabbis of the Talmud and also in historical sources from the first century CE such as Pliny and Josephus. According to tradition, part of the ten tribes exiled from the land of Israel by Assyrian king Shalmaneser in the eighth century BCE were sent across the Sambatyon and were unable to return. This was because the river raged mightily six days a week; on the Sabbath, when the Israelites were unable to undertake a journey, it rested.

† **I close my eyes in sleep**: This passage reflects, somewhat altered, the prayer that is recited by Jews before going to sleep. The prayer, which one says three times, reads: "In the name of the Lord, the God of Israel, on my right is Michael, on my left is Gabriel, before me is Uriel, behind me is Refael [Raphael], and above my head is the shekhinah [spirit/presence] of God."

p. 289

† **I will collect tortoises and eggs, and stand cook for the party**: Neither tortoises nor their eggs are considered edible according to Jewish dietary laws, so presumably Fernandez did not intend to partake of these himself.

† **Caraibes, called Buck Indians: they spoke no Spanish, but a little broken English**: "Caribs" (see note to p. 93), one of the Amerindian peoples in Venezuela and elsewhere in the region. "Buck" was a derogatory term for Amerindians in British Guiana. The Caribs living close to British settlements along the Essequibo River spoke some English.

† **old Dutch (now British) Guiana**: The Dutch colonies of Demerara/Essequibo and Berbice, were captured by the British in 1796, and formally ceded by treaty to Britain in 1814. In 1831 the two colonies were united as British Guiana.

† **intermittent fever**: Recurring paroxysms of elevated temperature, separated by intervals during which temperature is normal.

p. 290

† **a maroon party, *i.e.* a party of pleasure**: Maroons were runaway slaves, and expeditions were organized to hunt for them. From this practice, the term "maroon party" came to be used for a pleasure trip. (See Joseph's "The Maroon Party: A West Indian Sketch" in the appendix to this volume.)

† **St. George's, Demerara**: The capital of Demerara, the main county of British Guiana. Usually rendered as "Georgetown", the present capital city of Guyana.

Volume III

p. 291

† **"Farewell the grave pacific air, / Where never mountain zephyr blew, / The marshy levels, lank and bare, / Which Pan with Ceres never knew: / The Naïads, with obscene attire, / While round them chaunts the croaking choir." Akenside**: From Mark Akenside's "Ode VIII: On Leaving Holland" (1745), which compares Holland unfavourably to England. Arundell's idea of Demerara's coasts as regions of swamps and agues echoes Akenside's sarcastic view of Holland's "marshy levels", antipathetic to both Pan (Greek god of woods and pastures) and Ceres (Greek goddess

of harvest), and suitable only for the Naïads, or water-nymphs. Joseph omits a line after "attire" – "Urging in vain their urns to flow" – and changes "Which Pan, which Ceres" to "Which Pan with Ceres".

† **a Dutch Jew from Surinam**: Surinam was explored early on by the Spanish, Portuguese and English, and had European settlements by the first half of the seventeenth century. Jews first arrived in Surinam, by then a Dutch colony, in 1636 from Brazil and Holland, having fled the Spanish Inquisition. Experienced traders and agriculturalists, they set up sugar cane plantations, and enjoyed considerable religious freedom and prosperity. However, by the end of the eighteenth century, their fortunes were declining.

p. 292

† **Costa Firmia**: Mainland South America, more usually referred to as "Tierra Firma", the Mainland.

† **Rothschild**: The Jewish banking family of Rothschild was popularly thought to have determined the outcome of many political events in nineteenth-century Europe. The role of Nathan Mayer Rothschild, who settled in England, was considered particularly instrumental in the victory over Napoleon.

† **His ruin was more owing to his frantic Berlin decree than to the swords of Russia, his reverses at Leipzig, or his defeat at Waterloo**: The Berlin Decree (1806) attempted to prohibit continental Europe from trading with Britain. Napoleon's invasion of Russia (1812) was a disaster for France, and his troops were decisively defeated at the Battles of Leipzig (1813) and Waterloo (1815).

† **continued fever**: A fever which does not vary more than 1.0 to 1.5 degrees Farenheit in twenty-four hours.

p. 293

† *schnaps* **(small glasses of Schiedam)**: A strong spirit resembling Hollands gin; "Scheidam" is a variety of gin, so called from the town in Holland where it is distilled

† **a jargon, called Poplomento, which is a mixture of Dutch and Spanish**: "Papiemento" or "Papiementu" is an Afro-Creole language mostly spoken in Aruba, Bonaire and Curaçao. The majority of its vocabulary is derived from Spanish and Dutch.

† **Falstaff's comparing himself, when confined in the buck-basket, to a Dutch dish stewed in grease**: In Shakespeare's *The Merry Wives of Windsor*, Falstaff is tricked into supposing that Mistress Ford loves him. When her husband arrives to search for her supposed lover, she hides Falstaff in a "buck-basket" (washing basket) and arranges for him to be taken out and thrown into a muddy ditch. Falstaff later describes his state under the dirty washing as one of near-suffocation: "I was more than half stewed in grease, like a Dutch dish" (III.v).

† **"pepper-pot"**: A dish most famous in Guyana, but known throughout the Caribbean, in which cassareep (see below) and spices are added to salted or fresh meat, or both, and boiled at length. A pepperpot is traditionally kept going by adding new ingredients to whatever is left over after meals.

† **Avoceda pears**: The oily, non-sweet, pear-shaped fruit of *Persea americana*. Usually spelled "avocado".

† **Like Sir John Cutler's stockings**: According to one of many stories told about this seventeenth-century miser, his maid mended his cheap worsted wool stockings with darning silk so often that at last they became silk stockings.

† **casaripe.* *A rich sauce, made from the juice of the poisonous casara root**: Made by boiling the poisonous juice expressed from grated cassava, this thick, black, sticky substance has preservative qualities and is used in pepperpot. Usually spelled "cassareep".

† **casseum**: This item has not been identified, but may refer to cheese, the Latin for which is "caseus".

† *omnium gatherum*: A mixture of all sorts of things.

p. 294

† **Duxion Lavayesse's entertaining book on Trinidad and Venezuela**: J.J. Dauxion Lavaysse, a Frenchman, published in 1813 *Voyage aux Iles de Trinidad, de Tabago, de la Marguerite et Dans Diverses Parties de Vénezuela dans l'Amerique Méridionale*. An English translation appeared in 1820.

p. 295

† *à la Capresse* . . . **Madras kerchief** . . . *jupe* . . . **apron of** *linon* . . . **chemisette**: That is, in the style of costume of a "capresse" (also "cabresse"), a woman of mixed descent, usually Amerindian and Spanish, with or without some African heritage. The style results from a combination of preference and laws (especially in the French colonies) forbidding such women certain items of dress. In Joseph's *History of Trinidad* (1838b, 3: 10), he describes the style thus: "Owing to these laws, the French women of colour invented the dress which, in their colonies, is called *à la Capresse*. This consists of a rich and valuable Madras kerchief, tastefully tied round their heads, in lieu of the forbidden cap or bonnet. The strongly contrasted colours of the Madras well harmonise with their dark complexion and brilliant eyes. Instead of the forbidden gown, they wear a *jupe* [skirt], of a colour to match with their Madras; over this they wear an apron of [linen], furnished with little pockets, embroidered and fringed." "Madras" is a name applied to large brightly coloured plaid handkerchiefs or yard goods, originally of silk and cotton and later of cotton only, exported from Madras, India.

p. 296

† **I waited by appointment on the committee**: Oral examinations of this type were common practice.

† *"Comment fait-on chez vous?"*: "How is it done in your country?"

p. 297

† *"Vous autres Anglais êtes si genereux!"*: "You English are so generous!"

p. 298

† **"But, chief of all, / Oh, loss of sight! of thee I must complain; / Blind amongst enemies. Oh, worse than chains, / Dungeon, or beggary, or decrepid age!"** *Samson Agonistes*: John Milton's *Samson Agonistes* (1671), a dramatic poem, is based on the biblical story of Samson. These lines come from Samson's opening speech, where he laments his state as a blind captive. Though the villainous Victor Hugues makes an odd Samson, the quotation suggests that, like Samson, even apparently impotent old enemies may still be dangerous. The poem ends with Samson's destruction of the Philistines and himself. In Milton's original, "must complain" is "most complain", and "amongst" is "among".

† **"Three civil brawls, bred of an airy word."** *Romeo and Juliet*: Prince Escalus, in the opening scene of *Romeo and Juliet*, here chastises the feuding houses of Montague and Capulet for disturbing the peace with street fighting. The *Romeo and Juliet* feud provides an apt parallel for the duelling culture Arundell is involved in.

† *polisson*: Rascal; mischievous child.

p. 299

† **"Monsieur," said he, "vous êtes veritable Français." "Je suis Anglais, monsieur," I replied**: "Sir . . . you are a true Frenchman." "I am English, sir."

† *château*: A royal house; an impressive residence; here used ironically for his humble abode.

† **Like your great Milton, I have fallen on evil days**: In the invocation to Book VII of *Paradise Lost* (1667) Milton uses the poetic speaker to reflect on his own condition: "I

sing with mortal voice, unchanged / To hoarse or mute, though fall'n on evil days." A polemicist for the Commonwealth government under Oliver Cromwell, Milton lived to see that régime replaced, shortly after Cromwell's death. The 1660 Restoration of the Stuart monarchy left Milton disappointed, and relatively poor; he had already been blind for some years.

† **Robespierre of the Antilles**: This term refers to the famous leader of the Jacobin period of the French Revolution during which the Reign of Terror occurred.

p. 300

† **"How are the mighty fallen!"**: From David's lament for Saul and Jonathan (2 Samuel 1:19–27). Arundell clearly uses the phrase with some irony, since Hugues is much less admirable than Jonathan or even Saul.

† **Cayenne . . . when, in 1809, that colony surrendered to the British, Captain Yoe . . . allowed Victor terms of honourable capitulation, and sent him to France**: Hugues was governor of French Guiana or Cayenne 1799–1809. In 1809, it was captured by a joint British-Portuguese force and Hugues was sent to France, where he was tried on Napoleon's orders but acquitted. After the end of the war in 1815 he returned to Cayenne to manage an estate there.

† **"To point a moral, and adorn a tale"**: From Samuel Johnson's poem, "The Vanity of Human Wishes" (1749): "He left the name at which the world grew pale, / To point a moral, or adorn a tale" (lines 221–22). The reference is to Charles XII of Sweden, who after many victories was defeated by the Russians at Pultowa (1709) and finally died in an obscure battle; Johnson uses his story to demonstrate the transience of military glory.

p. 301

† **Monsieur *Ros-boeuf et pomme de terre!***: "Mister Roast Beef and Potatoes!" A typical French insult targeting the stereotypical preferred British diet. Usually spelled "Monsieur Rosbif et pommes de terre".

p. 304

† ***bien-séance***: Respect for the rules of politeness; good manners.

p. 305

† ***Restez f——!***: "Restez foutu", roughly equivalent to "Be damned!"
† **louis**: "Louis d'or simple", a French gold coin.
† **halbert**: A rank of sergeant.

p. 306

† ***sous-officier***: A non-commissioned officer.
† ***coquin***: Rogue; knave.
† ***coup de seconde***: In fencing, a low parry (defensive movement) at the right and outside.

p. 308

† ***à la Française***: In the French style.
† ***gens d'armes***: Armed members of a militia charged with keeping public order.
† ***un sacre barbare***: "A damned barbarian".

p. 309

† **At the end of the last war**: In the 1814–15 peace settlements which ended the Napoleonic War, Britain returned to France most of her conquered colonies, including the Isle de Bourbon, now known as Réunion, but retained the Isle de France (Mauritius) and St Lucia. French families, however, continued to be the main property-holders in

Lower Canada (that is, Québec), Mauritius, St Lucia, and Trinidad (never an actual French colony).

p. 310

† *Cochon Anglais*: "English pig".

† **John Bull**: A personification of the English nation; Englishmen collectively, or the typical Englishman.

p. 311

† **"The wild deer and wolf to a covert can flee; / But I have no refuge from sorrow and danger –, / A home or a country remains not for me." Campbell**: Slightly altered from Thomas Campbell's "Exile of Erin" (1801): "The wild deer and wolf to a covert can flee, / But I have no refuge from famine and danger; / A home and a country remain not to me." Exiled from Ireland, the speaker of this elegiac poem laments the impossibility of returning. The poem popularized the phrase "Erin go bragh" ("Ireland for ever").

† **La Fontaine**: Jean de La Fontaine, a French poet best known for his verse *Contes* (1665–82) and *Fables* (1668).

p. 315

† **the faculty**: That is, the medical profession.

† **knowledge of Latin**: Latin was used in medical terminology, but it was also a social qualification.

p. 316

† **Gregory's "Conspectus"**: James Gregory's *Conspectus Medicinae Theoreticae* (1788) was a widely used medical textbook.

† **a Parr nor a Porson**: Samuel Parr and Richard Porson were eighteenth-century classical scholars.

† *typhus icteroides*: Apparently a jaundice-like typhus. "Typhus" is a group of acute arthropod-borne infections caused by *Rickettsiae,* characterized by headache, chills, high fever, stupor and eye problems. "Typhoid fever" is an acute, generalized systemic febrile illness caused by *Salmonella* bacteria, usually spread by ingestion of contaminated food and water, characterized by fever, malaise, rash, abdominal pain, enlargement of the spleen, and slowing of the pulse. Typhoid became an increasingly serious health problem in the West Indies throughout the nineteenth century, although in part this trend doubtless reflects nothing more than better diagnosis as physicians learned to untangle typhus and typhoid from each other and both from the whole bundle of fevers that bedevilled the region (Kiple 1993, 501).

† **physic**: Knowledge of the human body, especially the theory of diseases and their treatments by the use of medicines and other non-surgical means.

† **University of Edinburgh**: Edinburgh was considered one of the top institutions of medical learning.

† **Great Pitch lake**: The largest natural deposit of "pitch" or "asphalt" in the world, several hundred acres in area. At present, it is estimated to be about 250 feet in depth, but was previously considerably deeper. The lake was first described in writing by Sir Walter Raleigh in 1595, who used the pitch to caulk his ships. The area began to be seriously exploited commercially only towards the end of the nineteenth century. The surface of the pitch is quite soft, and would have been softer and more liquid during Arundell's time; therefore, it would have been easy to get stuck in the pitch while walking across it.

† **La Brea**: The village next to the Pitch Lake, from Spanish "la brea", that is, "pitch; asphalt; tar".

p. 317

† **the unaccountable hatred of Sir R. Woodford to the cause of South American independence**: Sir Ralph Woodford (see note to p. 68), was strongly opposed to allowing Trinidad to become a base or recruiting ground for the "patriots" fighting for the independence of "Colombia" (that is, Venezuela and neighbouring provinces).

p. 318

† **"The chiefest action of a man of great spirit, is never to be out of action. We should think the soul was never put into the body to stand still." John Webster**: A slightly altered quotation from Webster's *The Devil's Law Case* (c.1620). Romelio, the play's villain, speaks these lines (I.i) to his sister's suitor Contarino, whom he wishes to be rid of; he therefore encourages Contarino not to be idle but to travel. Joseph omits a passage after "body" – "Which has so many rare and curious pieces / Of mathematical motion" – and changes "for a man" to "of a man".

† **Such are my opinions of slavery**: Arundell adopts a middle-ground position on the slavery issue, conceding abuses by the owners or managers of slaves but refuting "exaggerated" claims of extreme cruelty made by the antislavery lobby.

p. 322

† **franked letter**: A letter which was sent by a privileged person, for example, a member of Parliament, and therefore did not have to be paid for by the recipient on delivery. Before the 1840s, letters sent in Britain were paid for by the recipient, not the sender.

† **Anti-slavery Society**: The central (London) Anti-Slavery Society was established in 1823.

p. 324

† **"Were the seconds as averse to shedding blood as the principals, duels would be less fatal than they generally are." Lacon**: Paraphrased from Charles Caleb Colton's *Lacon: or, Many Things in Few Words; Addressed to Those Who Think* (1820–22), a two-volume collection of aphorisms. The Laconians (Spartans) were famous for their aphorisms; hence the title. Maxim 58 reads "If all seconds were as averse to duels as their principals, very little blood would be shed in that way."

† **quizzing**: Making sport or fun of; mocking; ridiculing.

† **boiling-house**: A building in which sugar cane juice is boiled down in the process of making sugar.

p. 325

† **Temple of Themis**: Themis, the Greek goddess of prophecy, the law and principles.

† **Mr. Pennyfeather swore to an affidavit before himself, taking the oath as a planter, swearing himself, and duly authenticating the paper as a magistrate**: At this period in the West Indies, most resident planters held commissions as unpaid justices of the peace, that is, magistrates.

† **robe-de-chambre**: Dressing gown.

† **"As who should say, I am Sir Oracle, / And when I ope my lips let no dog bark"**: From Shakespeare's *Merchant of Venice* (I.i). The gadfly Gratiano is here attempting to dissipate Antonio's melancholy, and half-seriously exhorts him not to affect "willful stillness" in order to be thought wise.

† **"Johnston on the Law of Spain"**: *The Institutes of the Civil Law of Spain*, by Ignatius Jordân de Asso y del Rio and Miguel de Manuel y Rodriguez, was translated from the Spanish, with notes, an appendix, and an index, by Lewis F.C. Johnston and published in London in 1825.

p. 327

† **the breed of Dogberries and Verges . . . as rife in the colonies as they were at Messina**: Dogberry (constable of Messina) and his partner Verges are bumbling comic

officers in Shakespeare's *Much Ado About Nothing*. Though they scarcely understand their own language and that of the malefactors they arrest, they do help to defeat villainy in the end (unlike Pennyfeather).

p. 328
† **Yahoos**: In "A Voyage to the Houyhnhnms", Part IV of Jonathan Swift's *Gulliver's Travels* (1726), Gulliver encounters the Houyhnhnms and the Yahoos: the former are wise, rational horses; and the latter are humanoid creatures of filthy and bestial habits. "Yahoo" has come to mean anyone whose behaviour seems coarse and stupid.

p. 329
† **until claret is *drawn***: That is, until blood flows. "Claret" (usually meaning a type of light red wine) was a slang term for blood.

p. 330
† **Doctor *Bolus***: A "bolus" is medicine in round shape, designed to be swallowed, but larger than an ordinary pill. The word is sometimes used to refer to medications for horses, or contemptuously.

p. 332
† **"Why shoot to the blast, / Those embers, like stars from the firmament cast? / 'Tis the fire shower of ruin all dreadfully driven." Campbell**: From Thomas Campbell's "Lochiel's Warning" (1801), a ballad based on the Jacobite Rebellion of 1745. In these lines, as throughout the poem, the Wizard warns the Highland chieftain Lochiel that the rebellion is doomed, and asserts that a recent meteor shower is a celestial sign of disaster. Lochiel refuses to take the warning.
† **"The baser mind itself displays, / By cankered malice and revengeful spite." Spenser's *Fairy Queen***: From Edmund Spenser's *The Faerie Queene* (1590–96). In the opening stanza of this canto (VI.vii), the speaker reflects on the different ways in which the "gentle heart" and the "baser mind" reveal themselves. The original has "In", not "by".
† **half-blood creole galloway**: A "Galloway" or "gallaway" is one of a small but strong breed of horses peculiar to Galloway, Scotland; hence a small-sized horse, especially for riding.
† **Naparima* *Corrupted from the Indian word *annaparuma*, "single mountain"**: "Naparima" or "the Naparimas" was the general name for the region around the Naparima Hill, a steep, once dome-shaped, almost flat-topped, six-hundred-foot high hill (now greatly diminished by quarrying) overlooking the town of San Fernando in southern Trinidad. Sir Walter Raleigh noted in 1595 that this hill was called "Annaparima" by the natives.

p. 333
† **River Carony* *There is a fine river in Columbia bearing the same name**: This river is south of the Gulf of Paria, flowing south to north, parallel to the coast.

p. 334
† **"There was a laughing devil in his sneer."**: From Byron's *The Corsair* (line 223) (see note to p. 26). This part of the description of Conrad emphasizes his demonic element: the "laughing devil" evokes fear and anger in others, and is linked to his "frown of hatred". Overall, however, Conrad's mixed character is not unattractive.
† **canuco (small plantation)**: An allotment of private land made by the Spanish to the Amerindians for agricultural purposes. Usually spelled "conuco", also found as "canook".

† **fox-tail grass and the tusk-rushes**: The former is probably one of various species of grass with soft brush-like spikes of flowers; the latter is probably one of several species of tall grass growing in clumps or tussocks.

† **an old discharged soldier of a condemned regiment . . . disbanded here**: Ex-soldiers of several of the West India Regiments, raised from former slaves during the Revolutionary and Napoleonic Wars (1793–1815), were settled in Trinidad in various places after the peace.

p. 335

† **fallow-deer . . . * *Before Mrs. Carmichael said she saw a deer in Trinidad put its *antlers* in at the windows of a house, I never heard of a deer in this island that had antlers**: *Mazama americana*, the red or small brocket deer, is a small deer, with small single horn-like antlers that are periodically shed. Usually referred to locally as "deer" or "biche".

p. 336

† **agoutees (Indian conies)**: *Dasyprocta leporina* is a large rodent, hunted extensively for food. Usually spelled "agouti".

† **an alco (wild dog) or two and several racoons**: Both of these are in fact the same animal, *Procyon cancrivorus cancrivorus*, the crab-eating raccoon. Also known locally as "mangrove dog".

† **land-tortoise**: *Geochelone denticulata*, the yellow-foot tortoise. Usually known locally as "morocoy".

† **quank, or musk-hogs**: *Tayassu tajacu*, the collared peccary, a kind of wild pig, hunted for its meat. Usually spelled "quenk".

† **lapes**: *Agouti paca*, the paca, is the largest rodent in Trinidad, and is hunted extensively for meat. Also spelled "lapa", "lappe" or "lap".

† **tiger-cat**: *Felis pardalis*, the ocelot, a small wild cat; fur yellowish with dark spots.

p. 338

† **enormous mackawel, or boa-constrictor, of about twenty-five feet in length**: Usually spelled "macajuel", this is *Boa constrictor constrictor*, a large, thick-bodied snake. A large individual can reach about twelve feet (four metres) in length, but such large specimens are now very rare; reports of much longer snakes attributed to boas are actually of pythons and anacondas; even a large adult macajuel would not be able to attack and subdue a horse (Boos 2001).

† **its infernal breath, the odour* of which is unlike aught else I ever smelt. *I have reason to believe that snakes can emit this odour to frighten their prey; in fact, this is what is called their fascination**: Gamble (1886) similarly noted that a "macaouel . . . whenever irritated inflates its body and then loudly emits a foetid and sickening breath which produces a sensation of faintness". Joseph also states, in his *History of Trinidad*, that when torpid after a large meal, "their odour is extremely unwholesome". Though an enraged or injured macajuel will hiss and "blow" very loudly, this belief is incorrect. Joseph more than likely based his assertion that the foetid breath or smell "given off" by snakes was known as their "fascination" on the information given in one of the major works of the time preceding his writing in 1838: *L'Histoire naturelle des quadrupèdes ovipares et des serpens*, by Count de Lacépède (1788–89). This work underwent several translations and contained the (incorrect) explanation that the fascination effect seemingly displayed by a snake towards its intended prey emanated from "the pestilential breath of the serpent, or noxious effluvia exhaling from his body" (Boos 2001).

† **Baron de ——, a gentleman born in Grenada, of noble French blood**: This may refer to the Baron de Gourville.

p. 340

† **"The world is full of strange vicissitudes, / And here was one exceedingly unpleasant." Byron**: From *Don Juan* (see note to p. 118). Juan and Haidee, his lover, have just been surprised by Haidee's father, the pirate chieftain and slaver. Wounded in his struggle with the pirates, Juan has been chained up on board the pirate ship (IV.51). The narrator's somewhat facetious tone here is characteristic of the poem.

† **"The very butt of slander, and the blot, / For every dart their malice ever shot / The man that mentioned him at once dismissed, / All mercy from his lips, and sneered and hissed." Cowper**: From Cowper's "Hope" (1782), a poem which celebrates the hope of salvation, and berates the worldliness of contemporary society. Here the speaker recalls the sufferings of "Leuconomus", a man of "blameless life" (line 577), but made "the very butt of slander" (558). "Leuconomus" is a (loose) Greek translation of "Whitefield"; George Whitefield, one of the founders of Methodism, was also one of the most criticized of the eighteenth-century Methodists, reviled in the press for his revivalist and confrontational tactics, and often regarded as something of a liability even by the Methodists. Cowper has "that malice", not "their malice", and italicizes "him".

p. 342

† **black dog (copper coin)**: See note to p. 43.

p. 343

† **Ensign ——**: This refers to Young Anderson, an officer in the Trinidad Militia who was associated with the *Colonial Observer*, Trinidad's only pro-emancipation newspaper in the 1830s.

† **saint**: An advocate of slave emancipation. The abolitionists led by William Wilberforce, who had strong Evangelical connections, were nicknamed the "Saints".

p. 345

† **the notorious Crawford**: This may refer to a celebrated court case in 1832, involving prosecutions of slave owners accused of purchasing slaves illegally, during which all the relevant court papers disappeared.

† **gallery whisperers**: Gossips; those people who sit on their galleries (front porches, verandahs), observing and commenting on people.

p. 346

† **a certain reptile, which, from the obtusity of its extremities, is called the double-headed snake . . . you never know its head from its tail**: Either of two non-venomous, snake-like, legless lizards, *Amphisbaena fuliginosa*, the spotted worm snake, and *A. alba*, the red worm lizard, whose bluntly rounded tail end resembles the head end.

p. 347

† **"Unnatural deeds, / Will breed unnatural troubles: infected minds, / To their deaf pillows will discharge their secrets." Shakespeare**: A doctor makes this comment in *Macbeth* (V.i), shortly after observing Lady Macbeth sleepwalking and talking about the murders she and her husband have perpetrated. In the play, "will breed" is "do breed".

p. 349

† ***vin de côte***: Here probably meaning wine imported from Europe.

p. 352

† **Joupaint l'Ouverture**: That is, Toussaint L'Overture, the main leader of the Haitian Revolution up to 1802, when he was betrayed by the French General Leclerc and sent

into exile in France on Napoleon's orders, dying in 1803 in a remote prison in the Jura mountains.

† **the race of Apica**: This reference has not been identified.

† **Marie Joseph Tascher**: The Empress Joséphine, Napoleon's first wife, was born Marie-Josèphe-Rose Tascher de la Pagerie, in Martinique (1779), daughter of a French Creole planter family of noble status.

p. 354

† **hair shirt, which he wore for penance**: The wearing of a shirt of woven hair, which by continually irritating the skin serves both to mortify the flesh and to remind the wearer of his sin, was common for penitents and ascetics, especially in the Catholic church.

† **corses**: "Corpses" (archaic or poetic usage).

p. 355

† **forty-eight murdered men**: The British prisoners, including Lieutenant-Governor Ninian Home, killed on Fédon's orders in 1795 during the Fédon rebellion in Grenada.

† *malheureux*: Unfortunate one; wretch.

p. 357

† **land of liberty**: A proverbial self-identification for the United States of America.

p. 359

† **"His poor self, / With his disease of all-shunned poverty, / Walks like contempt alone." Shakespeare**: From *Timon of Athens* (IV.ii). The servants of the once-generous Timon (the only people who remain faithful to him when he loses all his money) mourn his losses and the ingratitude of his friends. The original has another line after "poor self": "A dedicated beggar to the air."

p. 360

† *mahoo* **ropes* *Ropes made from the inner bark of the mahoo-tree**: *Sterculia pruriens*, a tall evergreen tree, whose inner bark yields strong fibre useful for cordage. Usually spelled "mahoe".

† **Chaguanas**: A town in west central Trinidad, about eleven miles southeast of Port of Spain.

p. 362

† **of thriving malice I am as sincere a hater as Dr. Johnson could desire**: This may be a double allusion, to a poem by Sir Charles Hanbury Williams, "On Benevolence: An Epistle to Eumenes" (1770), and to a remark Samuel Johnson made about Allen Bathurst (1st Earl Bathurst) as a "good hater". Williams's remarks about prosperous and distressed enemies are close to Arundell's: "An open candid foe I could not hate, / Nor even insult the base in humbled state; / But thriving malice tamely to forgive / "Tis somewhat late to be so primitive" (lines 136–39).

† **reduce his dislocated shoulder**: That is, heal by physical manipulation.

† *beau-frère*: Brother-in-law.

† *belle-soeur*: Sister-in-law.

† *philantrope*: Philanthropist; lover of humanity; but in an insulting sense here, roughly equivalent to "do-gooder".

p. 363

† *ce que les Anglais appellent enceinte*: The speaker means to say "what the English call a saint", but in saying "un saint", produces "enceinte", that is, "pregnant"; hence Arundell's smile.

† **according to Sheridan . . . a miserable dog**: The source of this quotation has not been found.

p. 364

† **"Foe to his pride, but friend to his distress"**: From Pope's 1735 poem, the "Epistle to Dr Arbuthnot" (371). This line refers to the critic and dramatist John Dennis, with whom Pope had a longstanding feud. However, towards the end of Dennis's life, when he was trying to raise money with an edition of his works, Pope helped him by promoting the edition.

† **"Death of General Moore"**: See note to p. 109.

p. 365

† **farine (the flour of manioc)**: Cassava meal or flour.

p. 367

† **"That night a child might understand, / The Deil had business on his hand."** **Burns**: Like the quotation on p. 3, this is from "Tam o' Shanter" (lines 77–78). Here Tam is just setting off for home, very drunk, and the narrator comments that on such a dark, stormy night, anyone should expect devilry.

† **earthquakes . . . have never been known to do any damage**: Though minor quakes are common in Trinidad, none (since European settlement) has done major damage.

† **the tower of the Protestant church**: This refers to the present Anglican Cathedral of the Holy Trinity in Port of Spain.

† **night-glass**: A short refracting telescope made for use at night.

p. 368

† **L'Ance Metan**: A small coastal area near Port Cumana, northwest of Port of Spain. Usually spelled "L'Anse Mitan".

† **skiff**: A small sea-going boat, adapted for rowing and sailing, especially one attached to a ship and used for purposes of communication, transport, towing, and so on.

p. 370

† **Island of Checachacara**: Chacachacare, an island about thirteen miles west of Port of Spain; the most westerly of the Bocas (see note to p. 49).

† **The refuse of the sugar-cane, when the juice is expressed, is called mogass**: Usually known in Trinidad as "bagasse".

† **Gudoy**: The Prince of Godoy was the most powerful figure in the Spanish Court in 1797 when the island capitulated without resistance to British forces.

p. 374

† **supple-jacks**: Thick but flexible whips made from tough vines.

† **no Timon, to spurn a discovered treasure**: Shakespeare's Timon (see note to p. 206), having become a misanthropist and retired to the woods to escape ingratitude, discovers buried gold coins as he digs for roots, but rejects the gold as an emblem of the corruption he has fled (IV.iii).

† **Trinidad cedar**: *Cedrela odorata*, a large deciduous tree; the wood is aromatic, used for cigar boxes, houses, and furniture.

p. 375

† **sugar-pan**: An enormous metal cauldron, originally copper and later iron, used for boiling off water from sugar cane juice in the making of sugar.

p. 376

† **fire-stick**: Usually, a stick or piece of wood, sometimes wrapped in oil-soaked cloth, on fire and burning slowly, used to transport fire from one place or household to another; here, a kind of "flambeau" or torch.

p. 318

† **"And how felt he, the wretched man, / Reclining there – while memory ran, / O'er many a year of guilt and strife; / Flew o'er the dark flood of his life, / Nor found one sunny resting-place, / Nor brought him back one branch of grace?"** **Moore**: From "Paradise and the Peri", in Thomas Moore's *Lalla Rookh* (1817), a series of "oriental" tales. In this tale, the Peri (a genie or sprite) is seeking the "gift that is most dear to Heaven" (line 41), and finally discovers it in the repentant tear of a violent criminal. These lines (459–64) comment on the criminal's thoughts as he observes a boy obeying the Islamic call to prayer. Shortly afterwards, moved by the child's innocent act, he kneels down beside him to pray himself. Moore italicizes "he" in the first line of this passage.

† **"So bad a death argues a monstrous life." Shakespeare**: Warwick's comment on Cardinal Beaufort's death in *2 Henry VI* (III.iii); the Cardinal, who has been hallucinating on his deathbed about his part in the murder of Gloucester, has just been asked by the king to hold up his hand to "make signal of [his] hope" in Heaven, but has died without doing so.

p. 380

† **in this island . . . the man of colour has justice**: Barbados and the other colonies had elected assemblies in which only white men could sit; Trinidad was ruled directly by the Crown (Crown Colony government). In 1829 the Crown ordered that all laws discriminating against free people of colour should be revoked. Hence Jerome's loyalty to George IV (ruled 1820–30).

† **commandant**: The judicial and executive official in charge of Trinidad's "Quarters" or administrative divisions, established before the British conquest in 1797.

p. 387

† **"Vengeance and justice on the villain's head! / Ye magistrates, who sacred law dispense, / On you I call to punish this offence." Dryden**: From "The Cock and the Fox" (1700), Dryden's translation of Geoffrey Chaucer's "Nun's Priest's Tale". Chanticleer, the rooster hero of this mock epic, tells his lady, Pertelot, about a dream that proved true, just as his own dream of the fox's attack on him will come true; these lines (273–75) are part of his story. A quotation from such a mock-serious source is apt, given the various legal travesties Arundell encounters in this chapter. Joseph changes "You" to "Ye", and "law" to "laws".

p. 389

† *amende honorable*: Public apology and reparation such as to re-establish the injured or offended honour of one who has been wronged.

p. 390

† *bagatelle*: A trifle; a thing of no value or importance.

p. 392

† **lug-sail**: A four-cornered sail, secured to a yard normally two-thirds the length of the foot of the sail, so that the sail hangs obliquely.

† **Portuguese Guiana**: A large region of Brazil close to modern Guyana.

p. 394

† *Ich wissen nicht . . . aber*: "I do not know . . . but". This appears to be the author's erroneous rendition of "Ich weiß nicht" or "ich weiß es nicht".

p. 395

† **majority**: The rank or office of a major.

† **purchased a step**: That is, bought a promotion. Just as officers' commissions were routinely purchased, so could a promotion or "step" be bought.

p. 401
† **curricle**: A light, two-wheeled carriage, usually pulled by two horses abreast.

p. 404
† **"La fortune tourne tout à l'avantage de ceux qu'elle favorise." Rochefoucauld**: "Fortune turns everything to the advantage of those She favours." Maxim 60 from the famous collection of maxims by François, duc de la Rochefoucauld, *Réflexions ou Sentences et Maximes Morales* (1664).
† **Vendean during the long civil wars of his native land**: The Revolt of La Vendée, in Brittany in western France, was a major counter-revolutionary popular rising in 1795. It was crushed by the republican regime (the "Convention"). (The inhabitants of Brittany are also called "Chuans".)

p. 405
† **Addison told a story about a country clergyman, who threatened that, if a certain squire of his parish did not amend his morals, he (the clergyman) would pray for him before all the congregation**: Addison tells this anecdote in one of his essays (*Spectator* 112, 9 July 1711), to illustrate how bad relations can get between clergyman and squire. The clergyman threatens to pray for the squire if he does not mend his "manners" (not his "morals" as Joseph has it, but "manners" as the eighteenth century defined them could extend even to morality).
† *Sacré canaille*: Damned, dishonest, worthless, good-for-nothing person.

p. 407
† **"Thrice is he armed that hath his quarrel just"**: From Shakespeare's *2 Henry VI* (III.ii). Suffolk, having been accused (rightly) by Warwick of arranging Gloucester's murder, has just quarrelled with Warwick and challenged him to a duel; the king makes this remark after they leave the stage.

p. 409
† **I had done the state some service**: Likely an echo of Shakespeare's *Othello* (V.ii). Othello briefly reminds the Venetians of his service to the state: "I have done the state some service, and they know't— / No more of that." After a few more lines, asking that they report recent events faithfully, he kills himself.

p. 411
† **"Me, wrangling courts and stubborn law, / To toil, and crowds and cities, draw; / There selfish faction rules the day, / And pride and avarice throng the way." Sir William Blackstone.* *From a little poem called "The Lawyer's Farewell to his Muse"**: In this poem (1744) Blackstone, chiefly known for his standard treatise on English law (see note to p. 6), mourns his need to leave poetry and the country behind for law and the city (lines 33–36). Towards the end of the poem, he concludes that the sacrifice is worth making as long as he remains committed to justice. In the original, "toil" is "smoak" (smoke).
† **decree of chancery**: "Chancery courts" administered the law of equity; they paralleled and in some cases superseded courts of common law, dealing with cases – especially with disputes over the settlement of estates – where justice might not be served by a strict application of common law. In England, the lord chancellor presided over this court, notorious for its drawn-out processes and runaway costs (see Dickens's novel *Bleak House*).

p. 416

† **according to O'Flaherty, a bellyful of fighting and a plentiful scarcity of everything else**: The source of this quotation has not been found, though "bellyful of fighting" is in Shakespeare's *Cymbeline* (II.I).

p. 417

† **According to the Irish boy — 'the more you call me out, the more I won't go.' "**: The source of this quotation has not been found.

p. 418

† **Falstaff's two men in buckram**: In Shakespeare's *1 Henry IV*, Prince Hal and Poins play a trick on Falstaff and his companions, who have just robbed some travellers. The prince and Poins attack the four thieves, who run away but later (II.iv) try to claim that they were attacked by a large body of men and fought bravely against them until overcome by sheer numbers. Falstaff claims to have killed two "rogues in buckram suits", then increases the number to four, then seven, and so on.

p. 420

† **To have emancipated them before the glorious measure of general freedom was taken by the English nation, would not have served them so well as treating them humanely as bondsmen. I believe, had I offered freedom to any of my people, prior to the general emancipation, the boon would not have been considered a favour**: General emancipation was enacted in 1833 and came into effect in 1834; the ex-slaves were, however, forced to serve an "apprenticeship" until 1838, when they were made completely free. Manumission before 1834 would, however, in fact have been considered a great "favour" by the slaves.

p. 421

† **Moravian brothers**: The Moravians, a German evangelical sect, had been active in working with enslaved people in the British and Danish West Indies since the mid-eighteenth century.

p. 422

† **"Un mauvais arrangement vaut mieux qu'un bon procès." French Proverb**: "A bad settlement is worth more than a good trial."

p. 428

† **"It is happily and kindly provided, that in every life there are certain pauses and interruptions, which force considerations upon the careless, and seriousness on the light points of time, when one course of action ends and another begins, and, by vicissitudes of fortune, or alteration of employment, or by change of place, we are forced to say of something – *this is the last*." Dr. Johnson**: In the last number of Samuel Johnson's series of periodical essays, in *The Idler* (1758–60), he comments that the endings of most "things not purely evil" cause uneasiness, because they remind us of the inevitability of death. Such a reminder seems "happy" and "kind" because endings force the thoughtless into a recognition of the mortal condition. (See also discussion in the introduction to this volume.) Joseph makes several changes to Johnson's text: omitting "very" before "Happily"; adding an *s* to "consideration"; deleting a semicolon after "light"; adding a comma after "time"; adding "or" after "employment"; deleting "or loss of friendship" after "place"; and italicizing "this is the last".

p. 429

† **"Santa Maria, valgame Dios! Animas bendita!"**: "Holy Mary, help me God. Blessed souls!"

p. 430

† *Valgame San José!*: "Help me, Saint Joseph!"

† *Virgin Santa!*: "Holy Virgin Mary!"

† **Aroage and Chyma Indians.* *. . . a tribe called the Aroages, or Arrowhawks, and another race called the Chymas . . . all that remain of the two once numerous races**: "Arrowhawks" is an eccentric spelling of "Arawaks", an Amerindian group originally from the Orinoco Delta who settled in Trinidad and elsewhere in the Caribbean. Certainly by the 1830s few "pure" Amerindians, of any ethnic group, remained in Trinidad.

p. 434

† **"So sweet a kiss the golden sun gives not, / To the fresh morning drops upon the rose"**: From Shakespeare's *Love's Labour's Lost* (IV.iii). In this scene, three of the play's four leading men are discovered reading sonnets they have written to their ladies, despite having sworn to give up the society of women for three years of study. These are the opening lines of the king of Navarre's sonnet, although "the fresh" should be "those fresh".

† *Mira mi corazon*: Literally, either "Look at my heart" or "Look here, darling", but given the context, a better translation might be "Behold, my love."

p. 436

† **In Trinidad, Catholics do not marry during Lent, except on St. Joseph's day; San José being the patron saint of the island**: The prohibition on marriage during Lent applies to other churches as well, including the Church of England, though it has not always been observed. The feast of St Joseph falls in the middle of Lent and was traditionally the only day during Lent that a wedding (or a party) could be held. As a major saint's day, St Joseph's would likely have provided an exemption in places other than Trinidad.

APPENDIX

"The Maroon Party; A West-Indian Sketch"

by

E.L. Joseph

Originally published in the *Monthly Magazine*,
new series., 1, no. 1, January 1835: 56–70.

The Maroon Party;[1]
A West-Indian Sketch.

T he morning gun, which in this, as well as in every West-India island, announces day-break, had just been discharged at the seaport of Port of Spain; as its echoes died away on the surface of the gulf of Paria, and amongst the circumjacent mountains, I started from my sleep, threw off my light covering, and dressed myself in jeans, the general morning dress in this island. The business of the toilet briefly dispatched, I hasted to the King's wharf, to meet a party who were going to make a sailing and maroon tour along the shores, and amid the mountains of the north of this island.

I met my associates on the wharf, and we embarked on board a beautiful Bermudian cutter, called "The Flying-fish." Our party consisted of five persons. The first was a Mr. Aikin, an amateur draughtsman, and a very talented fellow.

The second person of our party was a Monsieur Du Bois, a Creole of French extraction; he conceived Voltaire was a great philosopher, and that Shakespeare, or, as he pronounced it, Shack-es-pierre, was an inspired barbarian. Mr. Du Bois was in no way a remarkable specimen of his nation, save that he was passionately fond of hunting, shooting, and fishing.

Thirdly, there was with us a certain Javinia, F. Goodenough; he was a native of New England, and cared little for Old England. He believed that the Americans are the only free people on earth — that Dr. Franklin was the inventor of electric conductors, and a great swimmer, and that General Jackson is the most wonderful warrior that ever was seen since the days of Alexander the Great.

---

1. It was formerly the custom in Jamaica to make parties of pleasure, whose object was a ramble into the woods to visit the mountainous residence of the maroons. These parties took, during their stay, what in England is called *"gipsey-meals,"* and reposed a day or two amongst the maroon villages, subsequently the word "maroon-party" was used to designate any party of persons joining in making rough pedestrian excursions into the woods, or to other retired places for recreation.

The fourth person was Horace Rattoon. Natural history was his favourite pursuit, to study which he would plunge in the midst of the forest, armed with a gun, and furnished with a few instruments and drugs for the purpose of skinning and preserving birds, snakes, &c.; there a single wild cotton-tree, with its endless variety of mosses, wild pines, and parasites, would afford him study for a day. It was to him a living volume of botany; his food during these solitary excursions was a piece of sweetened chocolate, a roll or two of which, on these occasions, he always carried with him; his drink was of the forest stream, and, when that was not to be had, the water of *vitis indica*, or the wild pine, quenched his thirst — at night he would make a fire to keep off insects and reptiles; and under the shelter of an ajoupa, or even without any shelter save the thick foliage of the woods. He would sleep as soundly on a few palm-leaves as on the best mattress. In his wanderings he has collected a considerable quantity of objects of natural history. I made the fifth of the party.

The light morning-breeze springing up, we got under sail, and gently glided towards "the Five Islands." These are situated some two miles from the shore, and about eight from the Port of Spain. The scenery along the coast is beautiful, consisting of an intermixture of morass, covered with mangroves, pasture, and cane-fields, until the view is bounded by a range of mountains. We were soon off the plantation called Peru, the property of the Devenish family — the father of which, though an Irishman, resided here while the island belonged to the Spaniards. It was on this plantation that Abercrombie landed when he took the colony. When the Spanish governor Chacon, heard of this landing, and was advised to prepare for resistance, it is said he exclaimed; *"Por il amor de la santissima madre de Dios dexen los Ingeleses quietos ó nos hacien pedazos"* — For the love of the holy mother of God, let the English alone, or we shall be cut to pieces.

The following anecdote is likewise reported of this valiant gentleman; one day he was sitting in a gallery, in company with Admiral Apodaca, when a man was assassinated in the street before his face; shocked at the event, this august personage immediately fell on his knees, and, with tears in his eyes, began vigorously to pray for the soul of the deceased! Had it not been for the interference of the admiral, the assassin would have escaped.

When the British soldiers landed on the island, they broke open the boiling-house and distillery, and made grog in a most original manner, and on a very extensive scale. They rolled out three hogsheads of sugar, and seven puncheons of rum, which they emptied into a well of water, drew up the mixture in buckets-full, and drank it. This ingenious mode of making grog was introduced by the regiment under the command of Colonel Picton — the immortal Picton of Waterloo. During his government, he endeavoured to make the colonial department reimburse the proprietor of the plantation for the damage sustained on the landing of his regiment: this he was not able to accomplish. Sir Thomas Picton was one of the most able governors this island ever had. His way of treating debtors that had the means, but wanted the will to pay, was original; instead of undergoing the heavy delay of a Spanish law process, creditors were in the habit of going to Governor Picton; he would summon the debtor before him, and ask him if the plaintiff's claim was just; if the defendant answered in the affirmative, Picton rejoined, "Pay him, Sir, immediately;" perhaps the defendant would remark that he had not the money at the moment — "When will you have it, Sir?" — "This day week:" here the governor would say, addressing the plaintiff, "Here is your money" — at the same time paying him himself, and then turning to the defendant, he would add, "Take care, Sir, that you produce the money within ten days;" — this was enough; for few men would venture to trifle with the governor. He had the art of making himself loved and respected by the honest members of the community, and feared by the worthless.

The breeze which had been but light through the morning, now completely died away; and our sails flapped idly against the masts and yards. It was about ten o'clock — the period when the heat is most intolerable; after this, the ardent solar rays are rendered more supportable by the trade-winds, which generally vary from south-east to north-east; these are much less constant than is supposed. Our party assembled on the aft-part of the cutter, under an awning, where breakfast was provided, which consisted of chocolate, bread, some caribed snapper, or red fish, and avocado pears,[2] or, as they are commonly called, "vegetable marrow." During breakfast we were much amused by listening to a dialogue on the subject of religion between Cuffy and one of the negro sailors called Abdalla; the former was a creole and a Methodist, the latter a Mandingo, and, like all his country-men, a Mahometan. Cuffy was labouring hard for the conversion of the other, and, I am sorry to say, took an unjustifiable method to effect his purpose, considering his manoeuvres in the light of what are called *piqus*

---

2. The fruit of the Lauris Persea.

frauds. He did not scruple to abandon arguments in favour of Christianity by appealing to Abdalla's faith in the marvellous; and related several extra-ordinary miracles that he protested to have witnessed. Wishing to impress on the Mahometan's mind the necessity of keeping the fourth command-ment, he told him, that one Sunday he (Cuffy) visited a friend who was cutting down a tree in his grounds; he remonstrated in vain against this impiety; the other proceeded in his labour, but was converted by the fol-lowing incident:— Just as he gave the tree the *coup de grace*, much louder than the creaking noise which accompanies the falling of a tree, the friends heard the said tree call out the words, "Oh Lord, Oh!" The next marvel-lous anecdote of Cuffy's was of a more positive kind. He related that, some years since, he was attached to a plantation in Naparima. An acci-dent happening to a part of the frame of the sugar-mill in the middle of crop, the manager, not to lose time, ordered some of the negroes, and two yoke of oxen, to go into the woods the next morning, although Sunday, for the purpose of bringing home some timber; but the cattle well knowing they were included in the exemption from labour, "struck work." — In vain the negroes applied whip and goad to stimulate the animals; they would not move. — "D——n the oxen!" cried the manager; "why won't they draw?" — No sooner had he said this, than — according to Cuffy — one of them (a black Porto Rico oxen) spoke, and said in reply to the impious manager, "'Cause Gor-amighty make week wid seben days for work, and one for rest." — "Seben days for work, and one day for rest!" rejoined Abdallah, with an incredulous air — "I nebber ben sabby (I never knew) dat week hab eight days before!" — "You dam Willyforce nigger!" rejoined Cuffy, losing at once his temper and religious scruples at hearing his veracity impeached. — "You dam Willyforce nigger! — you tink cattle sabby reckon good as Cristin."

Of all people I ever met, West India negroes have the art of telling lies with the greatest gravity. Shortly after my first-taking up my residence in a distant part of the island, I observed that whenever I had poultry for dinner, the liver was missing; and asking the cook (an African) one day the reason of this, he gravely told me, that the poultry in this part of the country had no livers!

After we had finished breakfast a slight breeze sprung up, and under easy sail we glided along the coast. St. James's barracks had a beautiful appearance from where we then were; they are splendid buildings, but unfortunately placed in a most unhealthy situation. Many a brave fellow's valuable life has been sacrificed to the miasma of the Cocorite swamp situate in their neighbourhood. It is lamentable to reflect that a set of buildings, costing some hundred thousand dollars, should be erected on so insalubrious a site, when the medical gentlemen of this island, or even any of its intelligent inhabitants, could have pointed out a situation as healthy as any in the country, and one of much greater convenience for barracks than the present head-quarters of diseases, called St. James; but such was the reckless waste of public money in those days. A mile lower down the coast are other proofs of the inattention of the engineer department in placing military buildings in improper situations. The arsenal, and establishments connected with it, stand in one of the most pestilential spots in the island. As we sailed along the singular opening between two ridges of the mountain, the valley of Diego Martin presented itself to us in great beauty. This fine tract of country was formerly granted by the king of Spain to an Englishman called James Martin, whose name it still bears.

We came to anchor in the bay of the principal of the Five Islands. This contains about three acres of land, on which is situated a pleasant rural-looking house, belonging to Herbert Mackworth, Esq., the "alguazil mayor," of Trinidad (a situation resembling the high-sheriff of an English county). The Five Islands are his undisputed property — I say undisputed; for some years he applied to the governor for a grant of these islands. Sir R. Woodford referred him to the Colonial-office. On renewing the application in that quarter, Mr. Mackworth was informed that the Secretary for the Colonies knew nothing of the islands requested, as they were not noticed in the official map of the colony. Nothing further was said. Mr. M. conceiving silence gives consent, erected his present dwelling on one of the islands. A situation more beautiful, healthy, tranquil, and picturesque can scarcely be imagined. The house is built on an islet in a delightful part of the Gulf, about two miles from the shore, where the scenery is strikingly grand. A distant view of the Bocas and Spanish main finish the panorama.

Going on shore, we found that Mr. Mackworth and his family were in town; and after climbing about the islet, Mr. Du Bois proposed killing some birds, but it was intimated that the proprietor discouraged shooting any of the beautiful feathered tribe that visit his isolated domain with the exception of the pelicans, which commit sad ravages on the fish in the little bay. Du Bois, merely to gratify the cruel love of destroying, the characteristic of your *true sportsman*, killed three pelicans. These birds have too rank and fishey a taste to be good food. Two he threw away, the third Rattoon begged to be allowed to skin and stuff. Examine a dead pelican, or the drawing of one, and you will pronounce it a disproportionate and uncouth, if not a downright ugly-looking bird; and yet in his proper station, standing sentinel on a rock or mangrove branch, with his sullen look, his enormous pouch half filled with fish, and his keen grey eye watching his prey in the flood, his appearance harmonizes well with the surrounding scenery, and possesses an interest which he loses in any other situation.

Embarking, we set sail towards Gasparié — this is an island evidently of volcanic formation, as the naked eye may discover from the sea that its superficial soil is spread over a stratum of lava. The water is so clear that though deep enough to float the largest ship in the navy, we could plainly discern at the bottom the guns of the Santa Maria; for here it was that, when the English attacked this island, the brave Admiral Apodaca gallantly saved his four ships from falling into the hand of the British, by setting fire to them without discharging a gun,[3] and then boasted of having saved the image of San Jago of Campostella, his patron saint.

This is the chief station of the Trinidad whalers. I have been informed by several persons connected with this fishery that the leviathan may here be seen and even heard eating a kind of sea-weed that grows on the rocks[4] beneath the Gulf.

As we sailed along, a whale of about seventy feet in length made his appearance near us, and after blowing a mass of steam and water from his nostrils, with a deep roar sunk again. In about half a minute he re-appeared so near our vessel that we could discern his disproportionately small eyes. The enormous creature gambelled about our cutter as though it mistook it for one of its companions of the deep — now would it blow its cloud a-head of us with the force of a steam-engine discharging its vapour, and sink. Anon it appeared on our side — again under our stern it would shew its enormous form — its awkward evolutions, although harmless, and doubtless playful, were by no means agreeable to us. Du Bois having charged his gun with a ball, the next time he appeared, fired on him. I imagine he felt the shot on his blubber-defended back, as much

---

3. El San Vincent (a superb three decker), 84; El Gallardo, 74; El Arrogante, 74; El San Ceuslia, a frigate, 40 guns — these were burnt by the Spaniards, but El San Damasia, a 74, was captured without resistance — the English had four ships.

4. I have since heard this from a person of veracity of the whales of Bermuda as well as those of Trinidad.

as a tortoise feels a musquito sting. However, conceiving I suppose this to be a civil hint that his amiable visits were not desirable, he left us, much to our satisfaction. The great quantity of these fish found here, induced the Spaniards to call this *Golfo de Ballena,* or the Gulf of Whales. Whalers here find the sharks strong rivals in their trade — no sooner is a fish harpooned than a countless mass of these ravenous monsters attack it. In vain the people attempt to drive them off; so daring are those wolves of the deep that they will tear off large pieces of [blubber], while the men are belabouring them with their oars; nor is what they devour all the whaler loses — they will snatch large mouthfuls of blubber, swim a few paces, then with doglike-greediness, let them drop and return for more. It is supposed that the sharks eat and destroy as much as the whalers get. The flesh of the calf or young whale, is said to be excellent — it forms no inconsiderable part of the food of the poor of Bermuda, where however it is not sold — when a whale is cut up there, every one takes as much of the eatable part as he chooses. I once tried to eat it myself, but found or fancied it tasted of oil.

While on this subject I shall relate a circumstance which took place some twenty years since in Port of Spain:—

"The silver moon (according to the most approved novelist phraseology) had gained her zenith and the busy hum of man was hushed." Nothing was heard except the cicada's whizzing sound, which has gained him the appellation of razor-grinder; the buz of insects, which, as Bryan Edwards remarks, makes a "pleasing noise;" the chanting of about a thousand cocks, which here crow through the night; and the noise of about four hundred dogs, which kept up a continued chorus of barking, seemingly vying with each other which should yell loudest and longest. However, save these slight annoyances, "all was tranquil" in Port of Spain.

All at once was heard a booming, lowing, moaning — in short, an indescribable noise, which awoke all the inhabitants. The noise was of so remarkable a character as to defy conjecture. What was it? no one could explain the mystery. Some thought it the rumbling noise which precedes an earthquake; yet it had not a subterraneous sound. Others expected that it wa the bursting of the *soufriere,* or great volcano of St. Vincent; but the noise was not so distant. The Moco negroes declared that it was the great *Jombé.* The Coromantiens thought it their god *Accompong.* The Mandingoes said the sound was caused by their great king, Yoseph ben Mahomed, who always travelled with a band of one thousand musicians, playing on elephant's tusks; whilst all the politicians conceived it could be nothing less than the West India fleet engaging a French squadron. In fact, Port of Spain never was in such a state of alarm before, save in 1808, when it was destroyed by fire; and in 1805, when Nelson, entering the Gulf in pursuit of the combined fleets, was mistaken for the enemy, and the island placed under martial law.

The terrible noise continued, and many were the vows of repentance made in the fright of the moment; in vain, such as pretended not to care for the mysterious sounds, attempted to sleep. Sangarée and mosquito doses[5] were employed as composing draughts without effect. Some Chinese, inhabiting the island, swallowed and smoked opium, yet they could not sleep. The noise seemed to say, like the ominous voice in Macbeth, "SLEEP NO MORE!"

The marks of twilight at length became visible over the eastern hills; and from the sea-fort was heard a report, which, for a moment, drowned the unknown sound; namely, the morning gun was fired; and, as if in reply, the cracked bell of the old Catholic church announced that it was time to say mass.

The alarm created by the mysterious noise, which still continued, was so great, that terror, taking devotion's mien, induced an unusual concourse to flock to the sacred edifice. In the streets adjoining might be seen throngs of all colours rushing to church, most of them followed by little negroes bearing stools; many of them carrying prayer books upside down. As they approached the church, the noise grew louder; it sounded like the lowing that one might imagine an ox, as big as the Tamana mountain, would send forth.

But lo! on reaching the place of devotion the alarm was at once explained, for on the beach, within a few yards of the church, was found laying a large black substance, which, on examining, every body was of opinion was "very like a whale." It had perhaps been pursued by thrashers, until it got too near the shore, and the receding tide had left it "high and dry."

As the royal claim for whales found on the coast is unknown in this island, here was a prize for all who wanted blubber, oil, whalebone, or such of the flesh as is good to eat.

Many, laughing at their former alarm, now commenced the attack, all was bustle —

---

5. Grog taken at bed-time.

"The fisherman forsook the strand,
The swarthy smith took dirk and brand."

Axes, adzes, cutlasses, and large knives were put in requisition. In short, the whole of the lower order of the populace commenced hacking and hewing away at the fish.

The creature had ceased to bellow; and, from the large mass of blubber taken from him, they thought he was mere "dead stock." "Why don't you *hanchor* him?" said the mate of a London ship, who had been in the Greenland trade, "you don't *hact* according to *Oil*" (he was a Cockney).

This advice was lost on those to whom it was addressed. Each was too busy on his own account to think of doing anything for the public good. "Why don't you run a harpoon in him, and belay it with a lanyard to that house?" said the mate.

The only one who noticed this advice was a black man, who, like the whale, was *half seas over* (for the tide had risen), and he replied with a proverb, giving it a new reading, "every one for *myself.*"

Gradually the water came up, yet the dissection proceeded, when, unexpectedly, there

"Rose from sea to sky the wild farewell,
Then shriek'd the timid, and stood still the brave."

In fact, to the astonishment of all, the whale, with about twenty persons on his back, by a sudden effort launched itself into the middle of the Gulf. The involuntary passengers most lustily bawling and wailing, and the unfeeling spectators on shore giving them three cheers as they were going off.

After getting into sufficient depth of water, the fish sunk, leaving his *blubbering* tormentors to the care of the sharks and baracootas. Fortunately the crew, that performed this unprecedented voyage, were all picked up without serious accident.

The negroes made a song about it, of which the following is a specimen:—

"Who hearee tell such a tale afore,
    Of big fish left in a lurch,
No somebody sawy a whale afore,
    Take path for go in a church."

Although the current was against us, we had a breeze which quickly carried us to the Bocas or Dragon's Mouths. This is a scene of peculiar grandeur; the two points of land, one of Trinidad, the other of the Spanish Main, strongly resembling each other, being lofty mountains of similar forms, covered with forests, and distant from each other about fourteen miles. Between them are three small bold islands, looking, as some one had said, like sentinels to guard the peaceful gulph from the rude assaults of the Atlantic billows, or by a more poetical stretch of the imagination, we might suppose them to be three of the mountains pitched about by the Titans in their war with Jove. Between them run the long and narrow watery roads called Boca de Monos (monkey's mouth), Boca de Huevos (egg's mouth), Boca de Navios (ship's mouth), from the name of the respective islets; and outside, between the island Chacachacareo[6] and the Main is the noble passage called the Grand Boca (Boca Grande), beyond those singular passages the ocean sullenly roars — inside slumbers the "peaceful gulf" as it was well denominated in some old charts. Between those islands run strong, deep, but smooth and silent streams. There is something indescribably awful in sailing between those lofty mountains, whose height make the passage look narrow, and give to the noblest ship an appearance of insignificance. The first of these mouths is seldom attempted but by small vessels; the second used to be considered a safe entrance into the gulf by ships of any size, until the earthquake of 1825; it is an extraordinary fact, that immediately after that event, the first ship attempting to pass into the gulf this way, met with a counter-current, that nearly carried her on the rocks — she narrowly escaped destruction; — and, the very next ship, a fine new vessel, called the Naparima, was lost there. Many other wrecks have been subsequently made here, and many vessels have had narrow escapes. These circumstances have induced the underwriters at Lloyd's to forbid the ships entering the gulf, except at the passage called Navios, or between Chacachacareo and the Main. The fact of the second passage being safe previous to, and a perilous one after, the earthquake, I can vouch for; yet it is singular, that an earthquake that did no other damage than cracking a few walls, and injuring the tower of a church, built on infirm land, should have influenced the currents of the ocean.

---

6. So called by the Indians from a bird peculiar to this island, whose notes resemble the sound of this word.

5 o'clock, P.M. Through the day we had "light winds inclining to calms," as midshipmen's journals say; the breeze however now freshened. We attempted to pass through the small Boca, although the current was against us. The "Flying-fish" stemmed the stream beautifully, and in about fifteen minutes we were within a hundred yards of achieving the passage, and of the Gulf, when gradually the wind slackened. Of this we had intimation by perceiving that the cutter made little advance: in a minute or two she was only able to keep her way, the current sending her back as fast as the wind propelled her forward. "Out with the sweeps," cried the skipper; Goodenough took charge of the helm, and the captain and all the sailors went to the sweeps (long oars). All would not do — the light air subsided into a calm, and, in spite of the efforts of the sweeps we were entering into the Gulf stern foremost. Our voyage was one of pleasure — we therefore cared little for returning to the Gulf; but it vexed all the seamen on board to see the cutter "progress backward" (as Goodenough called it); however there was no danger in this, and in a few minutes we found ourselves on the inner-side of the Dragon's Mouth, in safe anchorage.

"Let go the throat-haulyards — down with the gaf-topsail — let go the anchor," sung the skipper; these orders were executed, and we went to dinner.

The principal dishes that composed our repast were a morocaye, a species of tortoise, equal, or superior to green turtle; a groper, a delicious fish, perhaps the finest in the West Indies, especially when stewed with claret; it is a fish, the growth of which is unlimited; some are taken that scarce weigh half a pound, and others of enormous size. In 1812, one was brought to the fish-market at Port of Spain, weighing nine hundred pounds! When very large they are called "Jew-fish."

We were scarcely seated at dinner, when our attention was rivetted by a new and most extraordinary phenomenon — it was no other than a concert; but the most original and singular of any that I ever heard. It was indeed one, that I should have scarcely venture to describe; but that an account of similar music occurs in White's "Voyage to Cochin China."

Immediately under our vessel we heard a commencement of wild and pleasing sounds, similar to those which we could imagine might proceed from a thousand Æolian harps, beginning in slow tones, but gradually swelling into an uninterrupted stream of harmony; to this might be added the booming of Chinese gongs, mellowed by distance — then again was heard to join sounds like the chorus of many human voices, chanting from the height of treble to a deep bass; indeed it is useless to attempt a description, for I am not able to find any satisfactory similitude to it, either in nature or art. During the time we heard this submarine concert, we felt, or thought we felt, a slight vibration of the vessel.

We paused at first from our meal, and each looked into the other's face with a vague inquiry. No one could afford information, until a seaman, who had formerly been a fisherman, informed us that it was caused by a shoal of trumpet-fish. Long after this little voyage was performed, I obtained a specimen of the vocal residents of the deep. Might not some similar vocal-fish have caused the fable of the syrens? The trumpet-fish is about thrice the thickness of a man's thumb, twenty-two inches long; including a singular kind of supplementary tail, or membrane growing out of its tail, about the thickness of strong twine, but tapering to a fine thread; this, I believe, to be the continuation of the vertebrae; it is about five inches in length. Its most remarkable peculiarity is its long bill, which justifies its appellation — this is about four inches long; but whether the sounds we heard were caused by the fishes fastening to the vessel, or, as some say, they possess the sonorous power independent of adhering to an object, and can utter sounds by elevating their trumpets above the surface of the water, I will leave naturalists to decide. In about fifteen minutes, the singular "sea song" died away.

The sun had sunk amidst splendid clouds beyond the mountains of Paria; the brief twilight of a climate within ten degrees of the equator succeeded; shortly after, the dark and tranquil waters of the Gulph glittered with the reflection of the full moon. Two small sloops entered the first Boca, and passed us as we were at anchor. As a brisk southern breeze had risen, round their bows and in their wakes were seen the phosphoric particles, which some nights render the waters here so luminous that vessels seem to sail amid a liquid fire. Several fishermen were employed at their avocation by torchlight. Altogether we had before us a delightful night-scene, which, by the light of a lantern, Aikin was sketching. Du Bois, meanwhile, was reading aloud, although for his own amusement, "Casimir Delavigne's Messiniennes," after the usual French fashion, in a chaunting tone, and making a long pause in every sixth and twelfth syllable:—

"A vous puissants du *monde* — à vous rois de la *terre*;
  Qui tenez dans vos *mains* — et la paix et la *guerre!*"

Goodenough spent the evening smoking cigars, and singing some two or three hundred sublimely-ridiculous stanzas, to the tune of "Yankee Doodle." More nonsense has been sung to this tune than to any other ever composed. Rattoon and myself walked the deck during the evening to enjoy the fine scenery. At an early hour we betook ourselves to our mattrasses under the awning; the heat prevented our sleeping in the cabin. Next morning we found that we had passed through the Bocas in the night, and were in the main ocean. *Tobago* loomed faintly through the mist of twilight, looking like a long tube[7] on the horizon; and, as the rays of the sun began to illumine the east, more faintly still might be seen the lofty eminences of Grenada, while, closer on our starboard, appeared the gloomy northern mountains of Trinidad, covered with a thick mass of vegetation, composed of giant forest-trees, each of which supports such countless numbers of tendrils, parasites, &c., that the gigantic tree itself is almost as hidden as a king in his coronation robes. Below, the earth is covered with a quantity of dense underwood, as if vegetation was determined to render it impracticable for man to pass over those mountains. When viewed at a distance, this superabundance of vegetation gives the northern shores a sombre aspect, but on approaching, they look grand, and even sublime.

The turbulence of the billows was so great, that the whole of our party, except the American, experienced that heaving sensation of the stomach and swimming of the head, which is caused by sea-sickness; a malady which, although laughed at by those who do not feel it, is by far more, for the time, insupportable than even the yellow fever. We felt no consolation when the captain said that the sea-sickness was extremely healthful; nor were we at all inclined to follow the prescription of Goodenough, who recommended as to take a certain remedy for the disorder — *videlicit*, a dish of salt-pork, seasoned with molasses!

At our desire, the skipper endeavoured to get closer in shore, where the sea is comparatively calm. To do this, we were obliged to make a stretch towards the Bocas.

"What is that triangular red streak in the sky, which slowly crosses over the Gulph towards the Spanish main?" asked Aikin. Rattoon informed us that it was a flight of flamingoes, crossing from Trinidad to the swampy lands, lying between the mouths of the Guarapechi and the Orinoco. They always fly in that manner, one leading the van, and occasionally falling in

---

7. Hence its name, *Tobago*, in the Indian language, signifies either *tobacco* or the tube used in smoking it.

the rear, while another takes precedence. We were too distant to discover this change of leaders.

The sun, which had now risen ten degrees above the horizon, shed its rays on their fiery plumage; and their appearance, as they seemed slowly to sail across the heavens, was inconceivably beautiful.

Having got close to the land, we passed the singular fishing village of "[Saut] d'Eaux," and came to anchor in a road about a mile below it. Here we left the butter in a boat, and rowed towards the shore, Rattoon promising to shew us a natural curiosity worth visiting. By his desire, the boat was pulled towards a mountain, covered, like all on this coast and most on the island, with a crowded forest. This mountain projected from the rest in bold relief. It was about 2,500 feet high, and rested on a natural arch of black rock.

Under this arch or cave, rolled the billows of the ocean with a sound like thunder. We approached this cavern, and surveyed it with admiration, not unmixed with terror. The pier that projected seaward, though necessarily strong to support the millions of tons of rock, earth, and vegetation, was so diminished in appearance by the immensity of the load it bore, that it looked to us like a small point. And what rendered this more fearful to contemplate, was the circumstance that for ages the sea had been wearing it away. It was visible that the continued action of the waves would so weaken this pier, as to render it unable to support its Atlas-like burden; and that the arch and mountain would be, at some future time, precipitated with a fearful effect into the waters.

I looked around, above, and beneath the cavern with wonder; so did Du Bois. Aikin took out his pencil and paper, but relinquished them in despair, being persuaded he could not delineate scenes of such awful sublimity. Rattoon, although he had visited this extraordinary spot before, gazed at it, rapt in admiration. Goodenough was the only person who betrayed no emotion. A long and almost breathless pause ensued. Silence was at length broken by the American, who, in a nasal tone, exclaimed, "I guess if that *there* mountain falls, it'll *'mash* up all the poor little fishes." Sundry shrugs of the shoulders were the only responses which this sally elicited, and which the Yankee doubtless did not interpret to his disadvantage.

Having inspected this mountain from several points, and rowed under its dark cavern, we made for the fishing hamlet of Saut d'Eaux, so called from two or three little cascades that fall here. This is an extraordinary site for a village; it is a sandy and rocky nook of nearly a triangular form, the base of which is the sea, and its remaining sides a mountain of about 2,000 feet high, so very steep that it is astonishing how trees force their roots[8] in the soil. The whole of the bight (to use a maritime phrase) is but twenty or thirty paces in extent, yet on this confined spot swell more than eighty souls, the constant inhabitants, and on an average one hundred transient persons using such shelter as about fourteen houses afford. These are huddled together with their respective mud-built walls touching each other. Some stand on the rocks, some in holes dug out of the mountains, but most of them on the sands, looking like large packages thrown promiscuously out of a ship when she discharges her cargo. There is no passage to it save the surfy bay on one side, and over the steep mountain on the other. How any one can climb it is astonishing; but this its inhabitants, and those who visit them for the purpose of bartering, do with heavy burdens on their heads. To achieve this, they make use of steps which they have dug in the mountains. Sometimes they pull themselves up by holding on the roots of the trees which project from the steep soil; and at others they climb large rocks which are loosely embedded in the surface of the soil. It seemed to us a strange place for one hundred and eighty human beings to fix their residence. The danger of an earthquake naturally suggested itself, or that some of those extended cataracts, called *Trinidadrains*, might loosen the rocks, which seemed but suspended over their crowded huts, ready at each moment to crush them, as the sword of the tyrant hung by a single hair over the bed of his guest! Our ideas at the time anticipated a catastrophe that took place some months after this visit, during one of those deluges which are almost peculiar to this island. A stream poured down the mountain with such violence, that some of the rocks above gave way; these, in their descent, brought down others; the lower this "ponderous ruin" descended the more terrific it became, until a mass of rocks, earth, and trees alighted on the wretched habitations of Saut d'Eaux, and in an instant they were buried in destruction! During the descent of this tremendous body, what must have been the feelings of the poor inhabitants? The chances of escape seemed few; hemmed in by the boisterous main, they could only take to their canoes, or plunge amid the surf. This they did; and, by the mercy of Heaven, all escaped, with the exception of seven, who were the next day dug from the ruins, literally crushed to atoms. It was marvellous that the greater part escaped this terrible visitation.

---

8. The *Croton gossytrifolium*, and twenty or thirty other varieties of the croton, are here found in great abundance.

It may be asked, what induces such a number of persons to choose so dreadful a spot for their residence, on an island capable of affording convenient room for one hundred times its population? There is no ocean so stormy, but that the prospect of gain will lure the navigator to traverse it — there is no mine so gloomy, but lucre will tempt man to labour in it — no spot so dangerous, inconvenient, and insalubrious, but that gain will stimulate some men to fix their dwellings on it. Saut d'Eaux is the only inlet for some miles on this mountainous shore, where are found the united advantages of fresh water, a good bay, and space for a village; besides, it is decidedly the best fishing station in the island. Of the abundance of the finny tribe that the sea here affords, the reader may judge, when he is informed that at certain times of the year it supplied the greater part of the fish consumed by the inhabitants of Port of Spain (nearly 12,000).

The villagers are generally peons, that is Spaniards from the main, of the mixed Indian and European race, some few mullattoes, and two or three negroes. I saw but one white resident. Their occupation is catching, selling, and carrying fish to town. Agriculture is here out of the question; and the only one of its inhabitants who enters into any other commerce, save the barter of their staple articles for the necessaries and conveniences of life, is a man of colour, the *soi-dissant* adjoint-commandant, their only magistrate; who, with that public spirit which becomes a justice of the peace, retails by license a (no very) slow poison, called *"taffia,"* better known to the English reader by the name of new rum.

We bought at this village a kingfish that weighed 15lb; this, excepting the groper, is the best fish which swims on our coast. It cost us a pistareen, about tenpence sterling; but from the relative value of money here and in England, it should not be considered above half the amount. Yet Cuffy quarrelled with the fisherman, telling him, "that he had taken us in, because we were *buckra*" (white men.)

Returning on board the Flying-fish, we took breakfast, and ran down a mile or two towards the Bocas; when, as it was agreed, we left the vessel, landed, and putting ourselves under the pilotage of Rattoon (who was well acquainted with the mountains) followed an Indian tract in order to pass southwards into the valley of Diego Martin, and then home.

The first things that took our attention were the mangroves,[9] a species of marine vegetable found in most countries lying between the tropics, the

---

9. The rhizophora mangle.

ocean washing the seeds from one shore to another, and this hardy vegetable takes root on every sea-coast of the torrid zone; but what renders
these mangroves most remarkable, is that a species of the oyster is found
to attach itself to its sea-washed roots, and even to those of its branches
which hang in the water. These oysters are very irregular in form, three or
four growing on each other in all manner of shapes. When Columbus discovered this island, misled by Pliny, he imagined that those oysters opened
their shells to receive the dews, which they converted into pearls. This,
though a more fanciful, was not a greater error than his taking the sea-side
or mangrove grapes[10] for the fruit of the genuine vine, which is not a native
of this island, nor the shore immediately opposite; nor can it be cultivated
here with any advantage.

Our way was up a hill, through thick woods of the bullet-tree, (*Achras
balata*), which bears a very sweet kind of fruit; a good idea may be formed
of the value of timber here, when I say that we saw two or three peons
felling some of these trees, merely for the sake of getting their fruit. "When
the savages of Louisiana," says the author of *L'Esprit des Loix*, "want fruit,
they cut down the trees;" he adds, in his forcible, but laconic style, "this
gives a good idea of a barbarous government."

As our ascent was laborious, we sat down on one of those trees which
had just been cut down, to rest ourselves.

"Do you know what this is?" said Rattoon, addressing Aikin, and presenting him with an insect of about an inch in length. Placing the insect in
his hat, and covering is so as to exclude the light, only leaving room for
Aikin to look in, the artist at once perceived it to be a *fulgora phosphorea*, or
great fire-fly; as the beautiful creature displayed in the dark his two green
lamps, which are placed above the eyes, and as he attempted to fly, a large
lambent sparkle of a deep ruby colour was visible in its abdomen.

"Some years since," said Rattoon, "a Spanish lady had a masquerade
dress trimmed and ornamented with these splendid insects, and *cicindelas*,
smaller, though not less brilliant, fire-flies, which emit scintillations while
in the act of respiring. The effect of this costume was magnificent beyond
description: the lady had them placed between plaits of very fine net; and
not as the author of 'Six Months in the West Indies,' insinuates, 'strung
through the middle, as children string cockchafers;' for, in fact, those
insects are so very beautiful that I scarcely think the most cruel naturalist

10. Coccoloba uvifera.

would have the heart to harm them. I, on one occasion, applied their lamps to some advantage. Being situated as an overseer on a plantation under the direction of a manager who considered all reading and writing, save that which was necessary to keep the estate's journal, as idleness, I was obliged either to relinquish my studies, or to prosecute them in secret. To accomplish the latter (not being allowed candles), I procured eight or ten fire-flies, which I secured in a tumbler, and fed them on small pieces of sugar-cane. I concealed them during the day; and at night while I was supposed to be in bed, I made use of my 'insect-lamp,' which afforded me sufficient light to read the smallest print."

"What insect is that?" inquired Aikin, "which but now fluttered with a humming noise across my face; and see, it is feeding on the fruit of the fallen bullet-tree, on the wing!"

"It is no insect; the diminutive creature is the crowned hummingbird; the smallest and most beautiful *Trochilus* or humming-bird known here; we are too far from it to note this wonder of the feathered tribe, it being less than some bees. But see, the daring little beauty approaches us; observe its graceful [form] — its plumage of variegated gold — its amethyst-like head — its ruff of light yellow, spangled with deep green, that looks like a second pair of wings; mark its long bill scarcely thicker than a needle, and above all its feathered crown!"

"It is a most beautiful creature," said Aikin.

"What an endless variety of birds is here," continued Rattoon, "I have myself collected twenty distinct specimens of the humming-bird alone; there are doubtless many more; this justifies the name that the Indians gave this country."

"What is that?" inquired Du Bois.

"The Island of Erie," replied Rattoon, "or Humming-bird; the few Indians we have call it so to this day. It is a beautiful appellation; but come, let us forward." We followed, Goodenough whistling "Morgan Rattler," until the steepness of our road made him stop his music in order to husband his breath.

At length we arrived at the North Signal Post, an establishment kept for the purpose of telegraphing vessels bearing towards this island, previous to their entering the Gulph. This is one of the most beautiful views in the island. It has been said with much truth that [Trinidad] scenery is more South American than West Indian, but this prospect unites both. The islands at the Dragon's Mouth look here magnificent, bearing the appearance of their having in former times connected the world of mountains that cross the northern part of the island with the almost endless chain of the Andes that cross the great South American continent. These mountainous islands and the Gulph form a complete South American view: while the lovely valley of Diego Martin beneath, presents as sweet a West Indian landscape as I ever beheld.

All stood gazing on this beauteous scene rapt in admiration; even Goodenough's countenance expressed astonishment and pleasure at the picture beneath and around him. Rattoon, who was marking the effect that his favourite view produced on his four companions, saw the American's countenance with delight, and seemed to forgive his former *gaucheries*, until the captain seeing Rattoon observing him, thought it incumbent to say something; he, therefore, thus expressed himself:— "I say, Mr. Rattoon, I guess you think this here prospect pretty considerably droll?"

Gentle reader, can you imagine a wild steed of the banks of Apura, going to slake his thirst in the stream, and while he inhales the cooling draught, an electric eel by way of giving him a friendly salute, rubs his benumbing form against the nose of the noble quadruped? Something of this sensation was endured by the poet, who very unceremoniously left the party and walked off home, evidently electrified by the unconscious Yankee. We were not slow in following, and after a short delay made our way down the mountains towards Diego Martin valley, and thence home, each delighted with his excursion.

References

Allen, Grant. 1888. *In All Shades*. Chicago: Rand, McNally.

Angrosino, Michael V. 1989. "Identity and Escape in Caribbean Literature." In *Literature and Anthropology*, edited by Philip A. Dennis and Wendell Aycock, 113–32. Lubbock: Texas Tech University Press.

Anthony, Michael. 1997. *A Historical Dictionary of Trinidad and Tobago*. Lanham, Md.: Scarecrow Press.

Antoni, Robert. 1992. *Divina Trace*. Woodstock: Overlook Press.

Archibald, Katherine. 1937. "Clipped Wings." In *From Trinidad: A Selection from the Fiction and Verse of the Island of Trinidad, BWI,* edited by Albert Gomes. Port of Spain: Frasers' Printerie.

Barash, Carol. 1990. "The Character of Difference: The Creole Woman as Cultural Mediator in Narratives About Jamaica." *Eighteenth-Century Studies* 23, no. 2: 406–24.

Baugh, Edward. 1983. "Friday in Crusoe's City: The Questions of Language in Two West Indian Novels of Exile." In *Language and Literature in Multicultural Contexts*, edited by Satendra Nandan, 44–53. Suva, Fiji: University of the South Pacific.

Bernhardt, Stephen. 1983. "Dialect and Style Shifting in the Fiction of Samuel Selvon." In *Studies in Caribbean Language*, edited by Lawrence D. Carrington, 266–76. St Augustine, Trinidad: Society for Caribbean Linguistics.

Berzon, Judith R. 1978. *Neither White nor Black: The Mulatto Character in American Fiction*. New York: New York University Press.

Bhabha, Homi K. 1984. "Representation and the Colonial Text: A Critical Exploration of Some Forms of Mimeticism." In *The Theory of Reading*, edited by Frank Gloversmith, 93–122. Totowa, NJ: Harvester, Barnes and Noble.

Boos, Hans E.A. 2001. *The Snakes of Trinidad and Tobago*. Austin: University of Texas Press.

Branscombe, Mrs Graham. 1876. *Edith Vavasour*. London: Hurst and Blackett.

Brantlinger, Patrick. 1986. "Victorians and Africans: The Geneology of the Myth of the Dark Continent." In *"Race", Writing, and Difference*, edited by Henry Louis Gates, Jr., 185–222. Chicago: University of Chicago Press.

Brereton, Bridget. 1979. *Race Relations in Colonial Trinidad, 1870–1900*. Cambridge: Cambridge University Press.

Brereton, Bridget. 1981. *A History of Modern Trinidad, 1783–1962*. London: Heinemann.

Brereton, Bridget. 1989. "Society and Culture in the Colonial Caribbean: The British and French West Indies, *c.*1870 to *c.*1980." In *The Modern Caribbean*, edited by Franklin W. Knight and Colin A. Palmer, 85–110. Chapel Hill, NC: University of North Carolina Press.

Brereton, Bridget. 1992. "Searching for the Invisible Woman." Review article. *Slavery and Abolition* 13, no. 2: 86–96.

Brereton, Bridget. 1993. "Social Organisation and Class, Racial and Cultural Conflict in

References

Nineteenth Century Trinidad." In *Trinidad Ethnicity,* edited by Kevin A. Yelvington, 33–55. Knoxville: University of Tennessee Press.

Brereton, Bridget. 1995. "The Nineteenth-Century Historians of Trinidad." *Bulletin de la societé d'histoire de la Guadeloupe,* no. 106, 4e trimestre: 37–48.

Brodber, Erna. 1980. *Jane and Louisa Will Soon Come Home.* London: New Beacon.

Bruner, Charlotte H. 1984. "A Caribbean Madness: Half Slave and Half Free." *Canadian Review of Comparative Literature* 11, no. 2: 236–48.

Cameron, J. Douglas. 1905. *Richard Malmort or Trinidad and Trinidadians.* Port of Spain.

Carmichael, Gertrude. 1961. *The History of the West Indian Islands of Trinidad and Tobago.* London: Alvin Redman.

Castello, Julio Martinez. 1937. *The Theory and Practice of Fencing.* New York: Charles Scribner's Sons.

Cobham, Rhonda. 2000. "Fictions of Gender, Fictions of Race: Retelling Morant Bay in Jamaican Literature." *Small Axe: A Journal of Criticism,* no. 8: 1–30.

Collens, James H. 1891. *Who Did It?* Port of Spain: Muir Marshall.

Cooper, Donald B., and Kenneth F. Kiple. 1993. "Yellow Fever." In *The Cambridge World History of Human Disease,* edited by Kenneth F. Kiple, 1100–1107. Cambridge: Cambridge University Press.

Cudjoe, Selwyn R. 1979. *Resistance and the Caribbean Novel.* Athens, Ohio: University of Ohio Press.

Cudjoe, Selwyn R. 1988. Introduction. In *Those That Be in Bondage,* by A.R.F. Webber. Georgetown, Guyana: Daily Chronicle, 1917. Reprint, Wellesley, Mass.: Calaloux Press.

Curtin, Philip. 1989. *Death by Migration: Europe's Encounter with the Tropical World in the Nineteenth Century.* Cambridge: Cambridge University Press.

D'Costa, Jean 1983. The West Indian Novelist and Language: A Search for a Literary Medium." In *Studies in Caribbean Language,* edited by Lawrence D. Carrington, 252–76. St Augustine, Trinidad: Society for Caribbean Linguistics.

D'Costa, Jean 1984. "Expression and Communication: Literary Challenges to the Caribbean Polydialectal Writers." *Journal of Commmonwealth Literature* 19, no. 1: 124–41.

De Lisser, H.G. 1919. *Revenge: A Tale of Old Jamaica.* Kingston: Gleaner Publishing Co.

de Verteuil, Anthony, ed. 1995. *The Urich Diary: Trinidad 1830–31,* translated from the German by Irene Urich. Port of Spain: A. de Verteuil.

Dorland's Illustrated Medical Dictionary. 1994. Douglas M. Anderson, ed. 26th edition. Philadelphia: W.B. Sanders.

Edmondson, Belinda. 1999. *Making Men: Gender, Literary Authority, and Women's Writing in Caribbean Narrative.* Durham, NC: Duke University Press.

Gaskell, Elizabeth C. 1853. *Ruth.* London: Chapman and Hall. Reprinted, A.W. Ward, ed., *The Works of Mrs. Gaskell in Eight Volumes.* London: Frowd, 1906. Knutsford edition, 1972.

Gilroy, Paul. 1993. *The Black Atlantic: Modernity and Double Consciousness.* Cambridge, Mass.: Harvard University Press.

Gonzalez, Anson. 1972. *Self-Discovery through Literature: Creative Writing in Trinidad and Tobago.* Trinidad: A. Gonzalez.

Harney, Steve. 1990. "Men Goh Respect All o' We: Valerie Belgrave's Ti Marie and the Invention of Trinidad." *World Literature Written in English* 30, no. 2: 110–19.

Hooker, J.R. 1975. *Henry Sylvester Williams: Imperial Pan-Africanist.* London: Rex Collings.

James, C.L.R. 1963. *The Black Jacobins: Toussaint L'Ouverture and the San Domingo Revolution.* New York: Vintage Books.

Johnson, Samuel. 1760. *The Idler* 103. *The Works of Samuel Johnson,* vol. 2, 314–16. New Haven: Yale University Press 1963.

Joseph, E.L. 1838a. *Warner Arundell, the Adventures of a Creole.* London: James Moyes.

524

Joseph, E.L. 1838b. *History of Trinidad.* London: A.K. Newman. Reprinted London: Frank Cass, 1970.

Khan, Aisha. 1993. "What Is 'A Spanish'?: Ambiguity and 'Mixed' Ethnicity in Trinidad." In *Trinidad Ethnicity,* edited by Kevin A. Yelvington, 180–207. Knoxville: University of Tennessee Press.

King, Dean. 1995. *A Sea of Words: A Lexicon and Companion for Patrick O'Brian's Seafaring Tales.* New York: Henry Holt.

Kiple, Kenneth F. 1993. "Disease Ecologies of the Caribbean." In *The Cambridge World History of Human Disease,* edited by Kenneth F. Kiple, 497–504. Cambridge: Cambridge University Press.

Lalla, Barbara. 1996. *Defining Jamaican Fiction: Marronage and the Discourse of Survival.* Tuscaloosa: University of Alabama Press.

Lalla, Barbara, and Jean D'Costa. 1990. *Language in Exile: Three Hundred Years of Jamaican Creole.* Tuscaloosa: University of Alabama Press.

Lamming, George. 1953. *In the Castle of My Skin.* London: Michael Joseph.

Lamming, George. 1954. *The Emigrants.* London: Michael Joseph.

Lamming, George. 1958. *Of Age and Innocence.* London: Michael Joseph.

Lamming, George. 1970. *Season of Adventure.* London: Michael Joseph.

Lewis, Vashti Crutcher. 1981. "The Mulatto Woman as Major Female Character in Novels by Black Women, 1892–1937." PhD dissertation, University of Iowa. University of Michigan Microfilms DA8210009.

Loudon, Irvine. 1986. *Medical Care and the General Practitioner, 1750–1850.* Oxford: Clarendon Press.

Masson, George. 1898. *Her Nurse's Vengeance.* New York: J.W. Lovell.

McDonald, Ian. 1969. *The Humming-Bird Tree.* London: Heinemann.

McWatt, M., ed. 1985. *West Indian Literature and Its Social Context.* Cave Hill, Barbados: Department of English, University of the West Indies.

Mendes, Alfred H. 1934. *Pitch Lake: A Story from Trinidad.* London: Duckworth.

Mittelholzer, Edgar. 1953. *The Life and Death of Sylvia.* London: Martin Secker and Warburg. Re-issued as *Sylvia,* London: Cox and Wyman, 1960.

Naipaul, V.S. 1961. *A House for Mr Biswas.* London: André Deutsch.

Naipaul, V.S. 1967. *The Mimic Men.* London: André Deutsch.

Nunez-Harrell, Elizabeth. 1985. "The Paradoxes of Belonging: The White West Indian Woman in Fiction." *Modern Fiction Studies,* 31, no. 2: 281–93.

O'Callaghan, E. 1984. "Selected Creole Sociolinguistic Patterns in the West Indian Novel." In *Critical Issues in West Indian Literature,* edited by E.S. Smilowitz and R.Q. Knowles, 125–36. Parkersburg, Iowa: Caribbean Books.

O'Callaghan, E. 1986. "The Outsider's Voice: White Creole Women Novelists in the Caribbean Literary Tradition." *Journal of West Indian Literature* 1, no. 1: 74–88.

Page, Norman. 1988. *Speech in the English Novel.* 2nd ed. Atlantic Highlands, NJ: Humanities Press.

Philip, Michel Maxwell. 1854. *Emmanuel Appodocca, Or, Blighted Life: A Tale of the Buccaneers.* London: C.J. Skeet. Reprinted, Port of Spain: Mole Bros, 1893; reprinted, Selwyn R. Cudjoe, ed., Amherst: University of Massachusetts Press, 1997.

Pocock, Michael Rogers. 1993. *Out of the Shadows of the Past.* Hastings, East Sussex: M.R. Pocock.

Ramchand, Kenneth. 1983 [1970] *The West Indian Novel and Its Background.* Revised edition. London: Faber and Faber.

Ramraj, Victor J. 1986. "The West Indies 1981–1984." *Journal of Commonwealth Literature* 21, no. 2: 134–59.

References

Ramraj, Victor J. 1987. "The West Indies: Bibliography." *Journal of Commonwealth Literature* 22, no. 2: 98–111.

Redcam, Tom [Thomas Henry MacDermot]. 1909. *One Brown Girl And—* All Jamaica Library Nos. 4 and 5. Kingston: Jamaica Times Printery.

Reid, V.S. 1934. *New Day.* New York: Knopf.

Rhys, Jean. 1934. *Voyage in the Dark.* London: Constable.

Rhys, Jean. 1966. *Wide Sargasso Sea.* London: André Deutsch.

Ross, Charlesworth. 1968. "The First West Indian Novelist." *Caribbean Quarterly* 14, no. 4: 56–60.

Samad, Daizal R. 1990. "In Quest of the Dialogue of Self: Racial Duality in John Hearne's *Voices under the Window.*" *Journal of Commonwealth Literature* 25, no. 1: 109–19.

Sander, Reinhard W., ed. 1978. *From Trinidad: An Anthology of Early West Indian Writing.* London: Hodder and Stoughton.

Sander, Reinhard W. 1988. *The Trinidad Awakening: West Indian Literature of the Nineteen-Thirties.* New York: Greenwood Press.

Sebastian, Anton. 1999. *A Dictionary of the History of Medicine.* New York: Parthenon.

Segal, Daniel A. 1993. " 'Race' and 'Colour' in Pre-Independence Trinidad and Tobago." In *Trinidad Ethnicity,* edited by Kevin A. Yelvington, 81–115. Knoxville: University of Tennessee Press.

Sharrad, Paul. 1989. "Exiles in Eden: The Popular Colonial Romance." In *A Sense of Exile: Essays in the Literature of the Asia-Pacific Region,* edited by Bruce Bennett, 89–99. Nedlands: Centre for Studies in Australian Literature, University of West Australia.

Sheridan, Richard. 1985. *Doctors and Slaves: A Medical and Demographic History of Slavery in the British West Indies, 1680–1834.* Cambridge: Cambridge University Press.

Sistren, with Honor Ford Smith. 1986. *Lionheart Gal.* London: The Women's Press.

Sobel, Dava. 1995. *Longitude: The True Story of a Lone Genius Who Solved the Greatest Scientific Problem of His Time.* New York: Walker.

Spivak, Gayatri Chakravorty. 1994. "Can the Subaltern Speak?" In *Colonial Discourse and Post-Colonial Theory: A Reader,* edited by Patrick Williams and Laura Chrisman, 66–111. New York: Columbia University Press.

Stepan, Nancy. 1982. *The Idea of Race in Science: Great Britain, 1800–1960.* Hamden, Conn.: Archon Books.

Stewart, John. 1989. "The Literary Work as Cultural Document: A Caribbean Case." In *Literature and Anthropology,* edited by P.A. Dennis and W. Aycock, 97–112. Lubbock: Texas Tech University Press.

Taylor, Patrick. 1993. "Ethnicity and Social Change in Trinidadian Literature." In *Trinidad Ethnicity,* edited by Kevin A. Yelvington, 254–74. Knoxville: University of Tennessee Press.

Walcott, Derek. 1970. *Dream on Monkey Mountain and Other Plays.* New York: Farrar, Straus and Giroux.

Walcott, Derek. 1977. *The Star-Apple Kingdom.* New York: Farrar, Straus and Giroux.

Walcott, Derek. 1990. *Omeros.* New York: Farrar, Straus and Giroux.

Walker, David M. 1980. *The Oxford Companion to Law.* Oxford: Clarendon Press.

Wallace, Karen Smyley. 1984. "Racial and Cultural Duality: A Mulatto Female Character in an African Novel." *Revue de l'Université d'Ottawa/University of Ottawa Quarterly* 54, no. 2 (April–June): 95–100.

Warner-Lewis, Maureen. 1982. "Samuel Selvon's Linguistic Extravaganza: *Moses Ascending.*" *Caribbean Quarterly* 28, no. 4: 60–69.

Watson, William N. Boog. 1970. "Four Monopolies and the Surgeons of London and Edinburgh." *Journal of the History of Medicine,* July: 311–22.

References

Watson, William N. Boog. 1973. "The Guinea Trade and Some of its Surgeons." *Medical History* 17: 203–13.

Weber, A.R.F. 1917. *Those That Be in Bondage*. Georgetown, Guyana: Daily Chronicle. Reprinted, Selwyn Cudjoe, ed., Wellesley, Mass.: Calaloux Press, 1988.

Winer, Lise. 1984. "Early Trinidadian English Creole: The *Spectator* Texts." *English World-Wide* 5, no. 2: 181–210.

Winer, Lise. 1993. *Trinidad and Tobago*. Varieties of English Around the World, Vol. 6. Amsterdam: John Benjamins.

Winer, Lise, and Mary Rimmer. 1994. "Language Varieties in Early Trinidadian Novels, 1838–1907." *English World-Wide* 15, no. 2: 225–48.

Wood, Donald. 1968. *Trinidad in Transition: The Years After Slavery*. London: Oxford University Press.

Wyke, Clement H. 1991. *Sam Selvon's Dialectal Style and Fictional Strategy*. Vancouver: University of British Columbia Press.

Yellin, Jean Fagan. 1972. *The Intricate Knot: Black Figures in American Literature, 1776–1863*. New York: New York University Press.